The Essenc

Emily Astillberry

First published in 2024 by Blossom Spring Publishing
The Essence of Bliss Copyright © 2024 Emily Astillberry
ISBN 978-1-0685693-5-7
E: admin@blossomspringpublishing.com
W: www.blossomspringpublishing.com

My first book is for my family. You are my inspiration. You are strong, passionate, somewhat chaotic and you are loved.

20 Years Ago

It began with mild agitation, a vague feeling of unease, which quickly shifted to anger, and within seconds, the placid, even temper of a six-year-old had been transformed into outright fury, a rage so intense that it had no business taking hold of a child. As the anger threatened to overwhelm me, a commotion approached from down the corridor, and I knew instinctively that the violence within me was somehow emanating from the approaching furore.

A truly wretched looking woman was being wheeled into the X-ray department on a mobile bed covered in hospital sheets that had been devastated by her struggles and lack of control. The sheets were smeared with a revolting murky brown and indefinable mixture of bodily fluids. The woman was accompanied by two uniformed police officers who were doing their best to keep her contained, but she was fighting them like a feral cat, all hissing and spitting and claws. She was handcuffed to the bed but still thrashing madly around, pulling the handcuffs tight against the metal rail and flailing her unrestricted arm and both legs ferociously.

She had dirty, greasy blonde hair and her unkempt fringe was falling into drawn, sunken eyes ringed with deep, dark purple bruises. Her skin was yellowing and the few teeth that remained had decayed to black. Her language was shocking. I had never heard such profanities in my life.

"When are you pigs going to give me something for the fucking pain, you cruel fucking bastards?" she demanded.

"You've had all the pain relief you can have. You're causing the pain with all the thrashing around you're doing. Just sit still and be quiet, Kathleen," one of the officers replied.

"Well, it wasn't enough, was it?" Kathleen spat back. "Because it still fucking hurts! And if you hadn't handcuffed me to this pissing bed, I wouldn't be fucking thrashing around now, would I?"

It was *her* anger. The pure, unadulterated rage inside me was emanating directly from Kathleen. I didn't understand it, but I knew that I needed to get away. I needed to put some distance between myself and the source of the emotions before they got the better of me and I started to shout and scream, breaking Mum's rules. I had to keep my temper under control. I had promised, but the all-consuming ferocity was coursing through my body, and I had the irrepressible urge to kick something or someone, to lash out, to cause pain or to shriek out my manic fury.

I had to get away from the emotions that were attacking me, corroding my control, my personality, so without thinking, I ran quickly down the wide, colourless, featureless hospital corridor in the vague hope that I could put enough distance between myself and Kathleen, to be free. I turned a few corners, a sharp left, a not so sharp right and through multiple sets of double doors. After a minute or two, I stopped and looked around. I had absolutely no idea where I was or how to get back.

I took some deep breaths, tried to ignore the ringing in my ears and reminded myself that the extreme emotions coursing through my body did not belong to me. I just needed to get my breathing under control and get back to Mum. She would panic if she came out of the X-ray room and realised that I was gone. She'd only left me for a few minutes to get Stephanie's arm looked at, and I wasn't supposed to move.

I just needed a minute. I leaned against a door, which gave way at my touch, opening into blessed darkness, and I slipped inside, closed the door behind me and sagged back against it in relief.

It was cool inside the room, cool and quiet, and I was finally able to take a breath. As my rapid breathing slowed and the rush of blood in my ears quietened, I became aware of another somebody in the room, their breath coming in uneven, ragged wheezes punctuated by a harsh gasping cough. An elderly woman's voice called out hoarsely with

2

great effort.

"Is someone there?" she croaked. "Nurse? Are you there?"

I froze.

"Please?" she begged. "If someone's there ..." She was wracked by a coughing fit. "Could you please help me with a sip of water? I have a cup but can't ... not on my own."

I couldn't ignore such a plea. I could feel her desolation and frustrated helplessness. Her loneliness called to me. It penetrated my mind, filling the gap that Kathleen's anger had left behind, and I instinctively moved closer so that neither of us were on our own. I wiped my eyes on the back of my hand and sniffed. I peered into the murky room and could make out the bed and the shape of a small human under the covers. I padded softly towards the bed and the old lady turned her head slowly to face me.

She was tiny, shrunken and almost skeletal. She gave the impression of being made out of a thin, almost transparent material, as if she wasn't quite solid, quite real. She was old beyond anything that I could have imagined, and her thin, wispy silver hair framed her fragile face in soft waves. There was such sadness in that face, such desperation, and yet her eyes still held the echoes of a life lived full of love and joy, laughter lines softening the suffering in her eyes.

I helped her take a couple of small sips from her cup and she nodded at me that that was all. She let her head fall back onto the pillow. Her eyes closed, exhausted by the effort.

"Thank you," she managed to croak, her eyes still closed.

"You're welcome," I replied.

There was a chair at the side of the bed, and I sat on it. I felt certain that my presence could be a comfort to this stranger and so sad that she was in a room in the semi-darkness all by herself. I wanted to be near her. I wanted to take away her pain. Her desire for company mirrored my own, or perhaps I was actually experiencing her emotions in my special way, but whatever the reason, I sat on that chair next to her bed and remained there. She lay in the bed next to me, her breath coming in long, ragged gasps, and neither of us spoke for a while.

After a few minutes, the old lady opened her eyes again. She looked at me, and there were tears shining on her lashes.

"I'm so scared," she whispered.

I was scared too, but I tried to be brave for her. She needed me to be brave.

"What are you scared of?" I asked.

"I've never been afraid of dying," she confided so quietly that I had to lean in to catch her words. "It's not really the dying ... even now," she went on, "It's being alone, you know ...? After ... forever. I've never doubted before, but now I'm scared. I'm scared he won't be there waiting for me. What if he's not there? What will I ...? What if he's not there?"

Tears began to spill down her cheeks, and her left hand moved unconsciously, searching for something. I instinctively grasped her trembling hand and held it gently in my own, soothing with human contact, skin on skin, resting them on the bed by her side and lightly squeezing in reassurance. I had never endured the pain of loss or the fear of dying myself — few children have — but I felt her pain. I absorbed her emotions and sensed the agony of grief and longing, the war between loss, hope and fear. It hurt my chest with a tightness, an ache, that a child should never even imagine.

Despite experiencing her emotions as if they were my own, they did not cripple me. They did not belong to me, and they were not violent emotions like the anger that I had felt only minutes before. This frightened old lady needed me to be strong, and so I said the only thing that I could say, the simplest of statements and exactly what she needed to hear.

"He'll be there."

I declared it with absolute conviction. I closed my eyes and willed her to believe. I gathered my inner strength and forced myself to believe in the miracle that I promised her. I found an inner peace and imagined that peace flowing from me into this frail, frightened creature.

Gradually, I felt the old lady's fear begin to ebb away. She absorbed the peace that I offered. Her hand stopped shaking and her breathing became more even, somehow easier. A stillness crept over her as she embraced the certainty that her soulmate was waiting for her beyond this mortal plane. I don't know how long I sat there for, holding the old lady's hand in mine, but after a time, her hand became slack and there was no more pain, no more fear, nothing.

I was utterly exhausted, drained of energy. I knew that I should get up and leave the room. I knew that Mum would be frantic, furious, but somehow I couldn't even seem to rouse myself to move. I needn't have worried because she found me. She always found me.

I felt her before I saw her. I always did. I felt them both. There was a fluttering deep within the recesses of my mind that bore their mark, their signature. She burst into the room with Stephanie in tow, a beautiful red cast on her arm, and Mum was crying and she was shouting, and she stumbled towards me and smothered me in hugs and kisses and remonstrations and declarations of love. After the panic of the last few minutes and the relief of finding me unscathed had passed, she took in the scene before her and she scooped me up out of my chair, took my place and held me on her lap. She held me so tightly that I thought that I might burst, but I held it together because I knew that she needed this.

A minute or two passed and Mum began to calm down. I gestured towards the old lady in the bed, thinking to explain my situation, thinking that she would be pleased with me because I had done something with my gift, something right.

"She needed me, Mummy. She needed me and I made it better for her. She was so frightened, and I made the pain go away."

Mum held my face away from hers so that she could look me straight in the eyes. She shook her head, brooking no

5

argument.

"I love you, Isabel. I love you so much. You're a special little girl with a special gift, and I am so proud of you, but this ..." She shot a glance at the figure in the bed, "No. Just ... no."

"But ..." I tried to explain.

"No, Isabel. No buts. The world isn't ready for you yet. The world isn't ready for this ... for you ... for what you can ... please, Isabel, trust me on this. Your life will be better without ... without this." She gestured between me and the body on the bed.

"You can be normal, live a normal life. You have to choose that life. Not this. Never this. No more, Isabel. I mean it. No more."

Chapter 1

"Alexa? Play Drops of Jupiter."
Playing Drops of Jupiter by Train.
I smiled at the familiar guitar chords, letting the vibrations from the base of my favourite song pulse through my body. I danced across the kitchen, flicked on Jack's jet-black kettle, and fetched two plain grey mugs. The shiny new things still felt slightly out of place in my grandmother's old quaint cottage, but they were concessions that I was willing to make for my new live-in boyfriend. I shimmied, wiggling my hips in time to the music as I took two teabags from my own cosy terracotta pot and rhythmically tossed them into the mugs. I felt buoyant and sang along tunefully, pulling the milk from the fridge with a dramatic flourish and spinning with it in what I imagined to be a perfect pirouette. I started on our packed lunches whilst waiting for the kettle to boil.
Tell me, did you sail across the sun? I sang into the teaspoon at the top of my voice, and then I danced joyfully around the kitchen in between making the tea and the sandwiches and emptying the dishwasher. I was beginning to get used to the contrast between Jack's and my styles. If we were going to make this work, then I had to allow him to stamp his own personality on the place, and it was actually rather nice to have appliances that worked and crockery that wasn't too ashamedly chipped.
I twirled around to dump the used teabags into the compost bin and caught sight of him leaning casually in the kitchen doorway, watching me with a satisfied smile. I did a double take, slightly thrown to realise that I had a spectator, but his enraptured smile didn't put me off: quite the opposite. My grin grew even wider as I threw my head back to deliver the next verse. *Now that she's back from that soul vacation, tracing her way through the constellation, hey.*
While I finished off the teas, Jack came forward, slid his arms firmly around my waist and settled his hands on my

hips, pressing his body against mine, joining in with my fluid movement to the music and chuckling softly against my neck.

"I knew there was a reason I moved in," he said happily. "I could get used to this." He placed his hands on the counter in front of me, our bodies touching, pinning me in place while he breathed me in. He kissed my neck softly and buried his face in my hair.

The energy of Jack's emotions, his love and happiness, drifted into my consciousness like a warm breeze. My mood lifted higher as my emotions responded to his, echoing his feelings.

"How did I get to be so lucky?" he wondered out loud before stepping away from me with a sigh to take his drink. "You really are stunning, you know? And you're mine. I get such a thrill knowing I'm the one that gets to wake up with you every morning. Do you know that?" He sipped his tea, still smiling.

I smiled right back at him. It was an incredible confidence boost, being admired so openly, especially at this time in the morning when I knew that my face was still flushed with sleep and my unruly caramel hair resembled, at best, a chaotic wild bird's nest. I looked down at my baggy pyjama shorts and my yellow vest and back up at Jack. He was staring at me with adulation, and the energy of his infatuation continued to roil around us, whipping up the air between us. I flashed him a coquettish smile and placed a chaste kiss on his lips on my way past, back upstairs to get ready for work.

"Thank you, Jack, but I think it's time to see about making myself a little more presentable for those who might not fully appreciate the just-woken-up-and-needing-a-wash look. Four-year-olds can be rather discerning, you know, and the parents, well, you'd think the playground was a fashion show, the way some of them strut around. Although I have also noticed one or two in their slippers on occasion," I laughed. "I think I'd better find some underwear. That'd be a start." I laughed again as Jack groaned playfully. I blew him a kiss through the bannisters.

Back in the bedroom, I washed the sleep from my face, teased a brush through my wayward hair, applied a little mascara and turned to my wardrobe. The weather was getting cooler as it progressed through September, and it was important that I was comfortable in the classroom. I had plenty of messy activities planned to get the new children motivated and relaxed, so I opted for a dark green long-sleeved top that would hide any inadvertent stains and some loose-fitting casual black trousers. I would wear my long brown flat, comfortable boots today. I wore my long brown flat, comfortable boots every day.

As I got dressed, I found myself thinking about Jack, a smile playing on my face. Moving him in seemed to be working better than I'd anticipated. We'd been in a relationship for over eight years and best friends for as long as I could remember, but I'd still struggled with the idea of sharing my space, my sanctuary from the world and all of the emotional noise out there with anybody and perhaps especially with Jack. Sometimes his emotional energy was exhausting, my body and mind's reactions to it draining, and I just needed to be by myself. In the end, though, he had won me over with his determination and persistence. His enthusiasm was highly infectious, and he was there most of the time anyway. He was right: it made sense.

I'd had to make certain alterations to my life in order to make the transition from boyfriend and girlfriend to cohabitors successful. I had more to consider than normal people because ... I wasn't normal. Still, with a bit of careful planning, somewhere to get away from the world and everyone in it, including Jack, we were making it work. He didn't truly understand the challenges that I had to face every day and I couldn't explain it to him, but he loved me and supported me with patience and consideration, and despite my initial hesitation, coming home after a long day at school

9

to a freshly cooked meal and the occasional foot rub was worth it.

It was the third week of the new school year; the children were starting to settle down and I was beginning to remember all of their names and get the measure of them. I still sometimes had sudden, stomach-lurching moments of panic first thing in the morning, accompanied by an almost paralysing, adrenalin-fuelled instinct to flee, but I always kept it in check. They were just so young, and some of them, so small. It was a massive level of responsibility to be entrusted with these inexperienced, innocent lives, to have a hand in moulding them into proper human beings.

The variation in capability and potential was huge in a class of children who were just beginning their school career, and the difference between a young, nervous four-year-old and a mature, confident almost five-year-old could be immense. That morning, I watched the children file into the classroom and saw the innocence and inexperience plain on their faces. One little boy was struggling to shake his arms out of his coat while another inadvertently spilled the entire contents of his bag onto the floor.

I got down onto my knees and gave Paul a reassuring smile. I glanced at the smeared toothpaste stain around his mouth and his sloppy untucked shirt and my smile widened, but his bottom lip was quivering and there were unshed tears in his eyes. My heart went out to him. He was frightened and confused, and it didn't take more than a normal level of human empathy to recognise it. He had only been in school for a couple of weeks and the transition was proving difficult for him. He was looking around in panic, no doubt searching for the familiar figure of his mother, who had already left the building. She had learned early that staying with him for those first few minutes of each day didn't help to settle his nerves and that it was best to get him safely through the door and disappear unnoticed. It might seem cruel and could be tough on parents too, but for some children, having Mum or Dad hold their hand only made matters worse.

"It's OK, Paul," I soothed. "Let's just get everything picked up and back in your bag. A little spillage is nothing to worry about." I summoned a sense of calm and reassurance, nudged it into his mind and was rewarded with a slight relaxing of his features and a weak smile. It was a start. I collected his books, his gloves and his hat and stuffed them back inside his bag while he scrambled around under the bench gathering up the scattered remnants of his precious collection of stones.

I looked up and sighed. "Louis? Sweetheart? You can't get your coat over your arms with your book and water bottle in your hands. Why don't you put them down for a moment, take your coat off and then pick them back up and put them in the box?" I was already scanning the room for other impending disasters.

"Jane? Do not pick up that paint brush until you have an apron on. Go and see Mrs Bishop. She'll help you. Karl? Do you need a wee, sweetie? It looks like you might need a wee."

Karl shook his head but continued to jiggle on the spot, his hand tightly gripping the front of his trousers.

"It's OK. I've got him," said the matronly Mrs Bishop, my indispensable teaching assistant and all-round superhero. She looked at Karl, her eyes narrowed in suspicion and a stern expression on her face. "No? Are you sure, Karl?" she asked. "I think you might. All the clues are there. How about we just go and see if we can squeeze one out, hmm?"

I smiled with relief as Mrs Bishop led Karl to the bathroom. The children were all in and the classroom was calm, if only for a moment. Everyone was accounted for, and most of the children had either found a seat at an activity table or were playing nicely with the toys in my Imagination Nation corner. I emptied my mind and took a deep steadying breath. I focused on the ebb and flow of emotions in the room, embracing and assessing the children's moods. A reassuring calmness and control radiated from Mrs Bishop, contrasting sharply with the vitality and excitement of nineteen exuberant minds.

Nineteen children in the class, projecting a profusion of super-charged energy. Anyone would be buoyed by such a mood. Anyone would find their spirits lifted by the proximity of so much joy, but not everyone would be able to sense the emotions as tangible things, taste them, almost touch them in the air. They danced around me like phantoms borne out of living energy, colliding with one another and sometimes plunging inside my mind. It wasn't an intrusion on my part or a deliberate theft of emotion. They came to me unbidden as they always did. I had precious little control over my interaction with the emotions of others, but that particular morning, I didn't resent it at all, happy to be carried by the children's contagious enthusiasm as I called them onto the carpet for the register.

"Little Owls, Little Owls, time to gather round," I sang. "Little Owls, Little Owls, let's not make a sound." I put my finger to my lips as the children gravitated towards my voice and took their places around my feet.

Mrs Bishop herded the stragglers over and sat at the back, keeping her watchful eyes peeled for signs of disruption or distress.

I was saddened to feel that there was a child among the rest who was out of sorts, a single strand of deeply negative emotion in the room in direct contrast with the joy and excitement of the other minds. I glanced over at Paul, wondering if it was his anxiety that I was sensing, but he was now engrossed in an entertaining conversation with Sarah, one of the more confident children, and looked totally at his ease, the distress of separation from his mum entirely forgotten. I couldn't quite identify the source of the malevolence, but I could feel it clawing at my own happiness, striving to drag me down. It felt more sinister than the energy of an average four-year-old missing his parents but not so acute or intense that I couldn't withstand its energy.

I proceeded with the morning register. As each child answered their name with a *Good morning, Miss Bliss*, and a *Good morning, Little Owls,* I met their eyes, connecting with each of them in turn, ensuring that they all felt special and noticed. I let my natural, happy warmth and quiet authority settle over them, not to artificially manipulate their feelings but simply to comfort and calm their minds in the same way that all teachers do. As I moved down the register, I was gradually rewarded with a group of quiet, content youngsters ready to face the day.

This early in the new school year, however, there were bound to be a couple of children who still found it a little bit harder to be away from their grown-up, and one who needed that little bit of extra support that morning was Melissa.

"Good morning, Melissa."

She sniffed. "Good morning, Miss Bliss." And then Melissa's sniff turned into a choked sob as she worked to finish the reply. "Good morning, Little … Little … Little …"

"It's OK, Melissa. We got through yesterday, didn't we? You managed just fine. Today will be even easier, I promise."

I looked the adorable, slightly snotty, blonde-haired, blue-eyed four-year-old in the eye and smiled again. She relaxed a fraction, her lip became firmer, and her countenance brightened as she discovered that she had the inner strength to finish her response. I didn't have to do anything. She looked slightly more confidently around at the rest of the class. "Good morning, Little Owls," she said quietly, and a smile lit up her face as she realised that she could do this and that perhaps today wouldn't be so bad after all.

Melissa had been a little sad and frightened, but she wasn't the source of the intensely negative emotion that I had sensed.

"Good morning, Joshua."

No response.

I looked up from the register to where the neat, tidy, polite form of Joshua Nelson sat, slightly apart from the other children, his head hung low, staring abjectly into the carpet. There was something amiss, and I was surprised and disappointed that I hadn't noticed it before. This was where the unwanted energy was originating, and there was more to it than the average normal upset or agitation of a four-year-old worrying about who he might play with today. Perhaps he was unwell, but I didn't think so. He looked healthy enough, but something was eating at him from the inside. Whatever was causing his distress had distracted him entirely from the here and now. He appeared to be lost, enveloped in his own world, and by the feel of his emotions, it was not a world in which any of us would choose to be.

"Josh?" I called again. "Josh!"

On the third attempt, Josh jumped as he recognised his name and was instantly back in the room. A couple of the other children giggled, but he didn't seem to notice. He looked up, reluctantly met my eyes, and at the moment of contact, a surge of anguish crashed into me. For a fraction of a second, the air around me became tight and I couldn't breathe. I felt horror, fear, revulsion. The intensity brought my own spirit crashing down and I couldn't prevent the gasp that escaped my lips. Mrs Bishop looked at me sharply and I hastily rearranged my features.

"Good morning, Miss Bliss," came a low, monotone response from Josh. "Good morning, Little Owls."

I fought to get hold of myself and tried to balance the frightening distress that was coursing through my system with my own sense of calm and some deep breathing. I looked away from Josh and channelled the buzzing positivity of the rest of the class. I couldn't afford to let myself be debilitated in front of the other children. I had to remain constant and dependable for them. With some effort, I was able to push the malignancy aside and move on with the register, but there was no denying the depth of poor Josh's wretchedness, and I promised myself that I would find a way to help him, or at the very least, discover the cause of his pain.

I cast my mind back over the last few days. I hadn't noticed anything like this level of distress from Josh before. He had always been punctual and well-mannered, and he performed well in tasks, but he was one of the children who didn't seem to be settling in quite as well as the others. He had been a little aloof and slow to make friends, but it had only been a few weeks and hadn't caused me any concern. Maybe I had missed something. Perhaps there were real problems in Josh's life.

At the end of the register, I was left with eighteen children happy and ready to learn and one causing me grave concern. I had my own emotions back under control and led my Little Owls through the class song. With just two weeks behind them, the children were already beginning to sing along. Some even sang the right words, and a couple actually sounded tuneful. I split the children into small groups and set them tasks to complete before break and snack. Mrs Bishop approached me, beaming.

"I don't know how you do it. You have them eating out of the palm of your hand. It's lovely. I've been in this school a long time and I've never seen another teacher able to command such focus from a group of children at this age. They adore you," she said.

I was delighted to receive such praise. People had been consistently drawn to me my whole life, especially children. Being more in touch with and more open to the emotions of the people surrounding me and not ignoring or dismissing what children were feeling meant that they could draw strength and confidence from me.

"Thank you," I said sincerely. "It means a lot."

After lunch I gathered the children together to do some

research into their first class project: Our Families.

"Little Owls, Little Owls, time to gather round," I sang. "Little Owls, Little Owls, let's not make a sound." With my finger on my lips and a bit of arranging and rearranging so that everyone was settled, I got them back on the carpet.

"Right, children, let's continue with Our Families. Yesterday we spoke about our parents and our brothers and sisters. Some of you, like me, have one mummy and one daddy, others have just one parent or three or more parents, and lots of you have brothers and sisters, half-siblings, step-siblings or baby brothers and sisters on the way. All families look different, and no family structure is right or wrong. Today I want to think about another important group in our families, our pets," I said.

Lots of little arms immediately shot into the air. Children were always enthusiastic to talk about their animals. A couple of them couldn't help shouting out, and I had to quieten them down again.

"Just a minute," I continued. "Don't forget, we don't shout out in class, please. Settle down. We'll get to specifics in a minute. First of all, I want a show of hands. A *quiet* show of hands. If you have a pet, please put your hand up." I was rewarded with a sea of arms and smiling faces and three glum looking children. "Wow, that's a lot of pets. You guys are so lucky. Sarah, David, Kerry? You don't have any animals?" They shook their heads sadly. "Well that's OK, neither do I at the moment. You can help us talk about what our pets need, and when we start drawing our animals, you can draw the pet that you would most like to have, OK?"

"Yes, Miss."

"OK. Everyone, put your hands down please. Karl? Karl, put your hand down, sweetie. I'll say a type of animal and I want your hands back up if you have that type of pet. We'll draw up a chart on the board and see how many animals we have between us."

I went through all of the common pets and drew up my

chart. Eight children had dogs, five had cats, and ten had other small furries. Lucas had three snakes, Melissa had a pony, and Amy had an African grey parrot.

"I'm trying to get him to say my name," she proudly told the class, "but he just always says *good morning, good morning* over and over again."

The class laughed.

"Wow," I said when we had finished. "Including Serena's fish, we have sixty-one animals between us. That's amazing. Now, who else wants to tell the class about their pets in more detail?"

As I had hoped, no one could resist, which meant that I had also got Josh's attention.

"Yes, Josh?" I said.

"I have a white rabbit called Bossy because he stamps his feet when he's hungry and a Jack Russell dog called Clementine," he said proudly.

"Bossy and Clementine. That's lovely. And who looks after your pets?" I asked.

Josh puffed out his chest. "I do, Miss," he said. "I feed and clean Bossy and give him lots of love, and I feed Clementine, and me and Mummy take her for a walk every day after school. At night, he sleeps in his bed in the kitchen."

I was delighted that Josh had opened up a little. The distraction had helped, but something still wasn't right. The sharp, debilitating anguish was gone, but left behind was an inner turmoil bubbling away inside. When I concentrated on him, the sourness of his emotions put my own mood on edge, although he was able to join in the class discussion, and on the outside, he appeared entirely collected. What I was sensing were not the regular simple emotions usually experienced by such youthful minds. There was something dark lurking inside Joshua Nelson and I didn't like it one bit, not in a four-year-old boy and definitely not in one of my Little Owls.

My feelings about my own emotional abilities were mixed

at that time. Even to describe it as an ability would have felt wrong. It wasn't something that I had any control of; it just happened to me and it was debilitating more often than it was in any way helpful. That morning was a prime example of my frustration. I had this vague awareness that something was wrong with Josh, but I couldn't control it or understand it. I could feel a problem, but I couldn't read his mind and had no idea what was causing his distress. Children are impulsive creatures, and for all I knew, Josh's mum had given him the wrong cereal for breakfast, but even on that day, the day that it first started, I knew that something was seriously wrong in Josh's life. The strength and intensity of his emotions hit me like a physical blow every time we came into contact, and at the end of the day, I could still feel a kind of insidious poison dripping out of him, trying to snake its way into my mind. Without any real idea about what I was dealing with, I took Josh to one side.

"Josh? What's wrong, sweetie? You seem unhappy. Are you feeling unwell?"

Josh looked startled at first, and I sensed fear before he got his features under control. With no expression on his face at all, he answered me in that same flat, monotone voice that he had used at registration.

"No, Miss Bliss. I'm fine, thank you, Miss Bliss."

He was unable to meet my eyes, and the calmness of his tone and the careful lack of expression contradicted the taste of his emotions. *I'm fine* was not a normal response for a four-year-old boy, and I couldn't understand why my concern might have generated fear in him, but unless he wanted to talk to me, I was totally helpless and had to let it go for now.

"OK, Josh, but you know I'm here for you, don't you? If there's anything you want to talk to me about, you just let me know. Anything."

Josh still didn't meet my eye and replied robotically, "Thank you, Miss Bliss. I'm fine, thank you. Can I go now?"

"Of course you can," I replied, and with a weight on my heart, I watched him walk away.

Chapter 2

At quarter past three, as the last child departed from my class, I was ready to go and followed them straight out of the gate. I needed to be alone. I could cope with six hours surrounded by a class of children, but afterwards, I had to have space and time to rid myself of the side effects of the excess emotional energy. I was able to manage my condition most of the time. I had become better able to spend time with strangers, and I found children, with their less complex emotions, easier to deal with than adults, but I still avoided crowds wherever possible and had never recovered from my fear of hospitals.

I used to find solace at home, but Jack's presence made that impossible now, so I headed for my other sanctuary, my secret place. It was a quiet space where I could always find solitude and time to think without interruptions, without other people's noise or emotions invading my mind. I drove straight to the familiar car park a short walk from the shores of the local lake, Ramsay Pool, and made my way up the steep hill along the overgrown path that I knew so well. I already felt better just being out there on my own.

After about a quarter of a mile, I came to a small clearing and a beautiful carved wooden bench overlooking the lake. There was a gold plaque on the bench which read *For Susan. My best friend, wife, lover and constant companion, who adored this spot. From your eternally loving husband. May we ever meet again.* There was no date on the plaque, and I couldn't guess its age, but the area surrounding the bench was unkempt and almost forgotten. I think that I was the only person who ever came here. I came here a lot and never met another soul. It might have once been Susan's favourite spot, but it was my place now. I took a moment as I always did to appreciate the kind of relationship that could span a lifetime. I pictured Susan and her husband sitting hand in hand, gazing over the water. I briefly placed my hand over the plaque in reverence to their love and then turned towards the lake and sat on Susan's bench gazing at the view as she and her husband must have done so many times during their long lives together.

I came here almost every day, whenever I needed tranquillity to recover from the emotions that invaded my mind. My time at the lake was precious. The sight of the darkly mirrored surface of the pool, the expanding ripples from surfacing fish or windblown leaves, the soothing, lapping sounds of the water against the shore and the rustling and chirping of the birds in the trees never ceased to help me to unwind and reflect, to find peace.

The incident with Josh that morning had worried me for two reasons. I was, first and foremost, concerned for Josh himself, but my reaction to his emotions had also been significantly more intense than I would have hoped. I thought that I had my emotional responses more under control.

I sat on the bench and stared out across the shimmering water. The sun was low in the sky, casting a celestial golden light in its path. I closed my eyes and took deep breaths, in through my nose and out, slowly, through my mouth. I sank further into the bench, feeling its solid strength beneath me. I felt the cool breeze play on my face and the weak sun beat down upon me, and I began to look inward at the extraneous emotions and energies trapped in my mind from the day.

Still breathing slowly and deeply, I released each fragment of unwelcome energy from my psyche one by one, casting them away and leaving me feeling clearer, cleaner. The malignant energy that I had absorbed from Josh had left a foul stain on my mind, which I examined dispassionately so as not to fuel its dark power. I slowly peeled it away and released it, allowing it to fade, no longer energised and not dangerous to me. I remained seated with my eyes closed for a few moments longer, relishing the feeling of relief, the regaining of my inner peace.

I wished that I had someone to talk to, someone who

might understand, but Mum and I had agreed long ago that it was better that I kept my differences to myself. Jack knew that I had my oddities. He understood that I reacted differently to people and struggled with my emotional responses, but it wasn't something that we talked about. He didn't push, not anymore. I had chosen not to share that part of myself with him, and although it hurt us both at times, he accepted that.

Sitting on the bench tonight, I remembered another early episode around the same time as the incident at the hospital, another truly distressing experience, when I really began to understand how different I was. *Special,* Mum had called it. People were not understanding. I hadn't felt *special* on that day.

I had always been a perceptive child, sensing the emotions of the people around me and being influenced by them. In my earliest memories, I became confused by my feelings, which could change instantly and dramatically without warning. Not only did I sense what other people were feeling, but depending on the strength of their emotion, I would experience it physically too. In my childhood, I had no control at all.

Mr Fitzgerald was my Year 2 teacher, so I must have been about seven years old at the time. It was a cold red-brown autumn day, and the ground was saturated from the rain. Mr Fitzgerald walked into the classroom looking tired, pale and sad. He had been crying and it didn't take an overly sensitive child to see that something was deeply wrong. All of the children noticed and were particularly sombre and attentive as we took our seats. It took longer than normal for Mr Fitzgerald to begin the class, like he was struggling to find the words. The sadness emanated from him in waves, and it affected me. It made me feel sad. Not in the usual sympathetic way a person relates to another human being in pain but in a way unique to me. His sadness entered my mind, and I was filled with a grief that I couldn't comprehend. Tears welled up in my eyes. I felt empty inside. When my name was called during the register, I couldn't even speak. Mr Fitzgerald looked up and caught my eye.

"Isabel?" he repeated.

The agony barrelled into me as our eyes met and I was hit with the full force of his emotions. It felt like a physical blow, and I had no defence for it. I doubled over and cried out. I couldn't breathe; I couldn't speak. I felt his pain as if it were my own, a sadness like nothing I had experienced before. The grief and anger made me howl in desperation. It was too much emotion for a child to command and I lashed out, knocking my chair to the floor and curling up in a ball in an attempt to block out the torment. I caught Mr Fitzgerald's eye again and saw the misery reflected in them before he broke down and fled from the room, abandoning his class.

Mr Fitzgerald was sent home, and Mum was summoned to the school. I was removed to the school office, where the staff watched me as if I might spontaneously combust. The pain receded quickly but the memory of it remained, and the sympathy and confusion of the teachers and staff only added to the emotional baggage swirling around inside, reducing me to tears. When Mum arrived, she held me in her arms.

"Shhh. Izzy, it's OK, I've got you."

I let her hold me and erase the pain. Enveloped in the soothing warmth of her arms, the ache of Mr Fitzgerald's misery was washed away. She spoke to the teachers softly and calmly, and whatever she said seemed to console them too. She took me home and put me straight to bed, but the following day we talked it through.

"It hurt, Mummy. He was so sad. He looked at me and I was sad. It hurt."

"I know, baby," Mum soothed. "I know it hurt. Mr Fitzgerald had some very, very bad news. His wife's going to die. They don't have long. He couldn't help the way he felt, and when he looked at you, you felt it too, even though you didn't understand."

"But why, Mummy? Why me? No one else felt it. What's wrong with me?" I asked.

"Oh, baby, there's nothing wrong with you," Mum sighed. "All the other boys and girls could see Mr Fitz's sadness on the outside, but you're the only one that could feel his sadness on the inside. You're special. You're more sensitive to other people's feelings, that's all. But you must learn to block it out, my love. You must learn to only acknowledge your own feelings. You're so full of warmth and love. Other people don't … won't understand. You must try not to let other people see how special you are. You must try not to feel it so much. Try to shut it out."

"I will, Mummy. I won't do it again. I promise."

"Good girl."

After the initial whispering and giggling, my classmates soon forgot all about the incident, and when there were no more episodes, everything went back to normal and it was never mentioned again. Mr Fitzgerald took some time off work, and I tried to forget and to follow Mum's advice, but it never went away. I remained sensitive to the emotions of those around me and sometimes couldn't help being overwhelmed by them. I always told Mum about the episodes, and she would wrap her arms around me, make the bad feelings go away and give the same advice.

You're special, but you must try to block it out. People won't understand. People don't like different.

I understood Mum's desire for me to live an ordinary life, and so I rarely spoke about it, not even with Jack, but I couldn't and wouldn't block it out like she asked. I did find that with dedication and hard work, I could control my emotions to some extent and enjoy the positive aspects of my ability. To be able to read the mood of a room, understand what people needed and desired and influence their emotions could be amazing. I could calm an agitated child and lift someone's mood on a bad day. Most of the people I met found me to be thoughtful, insightful, warm and perhaps a little quirky. I stopped talking to Mum about it most of the time because I didn't want to quarrel, but it wasn't going to go away, and ignoring it wasn't the answer.

I spent time studying myself and discovering certain techniques to help overcome my challenges. Gradually, I became more capable of controlling how much or how little I was affected by the emotions of those around me. I learned to avoid places full of negative emotion. Funerals were impossible for me to bear, and traffic jams filled me with an indescribable anger. It's shocking how much violent passion exists in situations in which people have no control. There had been terrifying occasions where I was struck by an overwhelming desire to cause pain, but on the other hand, I could be the life and soul of a party, embracing the rapturous energy of those around me and living in the moment, taking and supplying joy like a drug that I controlled with my mind.

I always had to be careful: careful to stay in control. I learned to avoid the dark corners of the parties, the haunt of the angry drunk or the ladies' toilets full of heartbroken young women. Violent strangers could send me into a frenzy, and newborn babies could literally leave me weak at the knees. Continuous concentration was emotionally exhausting, so I needed space to ground myself at the end of each day, and so I went to the lake.

The new living arrangement hadn't really been a problem. Jack had been an integral part of my life for so long, I didn't have to worry or be extra vigilant around him. He was consistent and loving, and I didn't need any exceptional skills to read him. He was an open book, with every feeling emblazoned across his face for the world to see. Jack adored me. Our being together made him happy and fulfilled my desire for life to be uncomplicated. I didn't want to be challenged or surrounded by fiery tempers or passions. I needed straightforward honesty, and with Jack, I had found my constancy, which along with my own dedication and hard work, kept my erratic, distressing emotional responses better under control. Sometimes I wished that I could let go, really let go and discover a deeper part of myself, but I was too frightened about what I might find hidden deep inside. Jack allowed me to keep those parts of me locked away. He made me feel safe.

All of this was why the incident with Josh had been so frightening. I thought I had things better under control. I knew that I was still vulnerable to extreme or complex emotions, but the troubles and concerns of a four-year-old boy should not have triggered an episode like I had experienced today. Either I didn't have as much control as I thought or Josh's feelings were unusually intense, and if it were the latter, then no matter the cause, I had to help him. I had to take his pain away. It was my duty as his teacher and my calling as whatever it is that I was.

Despite my instincts telling me that there was something serious troubling Josh, I had nothing to substantiate them, which meant that there was only one person whom I could talk to. Mum wouldn't tell me what I wanted to hear. She might not be of any practical help, but she would listen, she would put her arms around me, and in her own way, she would take away some of the pain. She was the only person who had any idea about what I went through. She was my mum.

I didn't need to visit the house to know that she wasn't at home. At that time of the afternoon, Dad would be pottering around in the kitchen, preparing dinner, and Mum would be pottering around her allotment. My parents were creatures of habit. The allotment was only a short drive away, and I had a pair of wellies in the boot, which I pulled on to navigate the muddy path. There had been no rain today, but everything was still wet and the ground was heavy.

As I approached, Mum was sitting on a canvas camping chair with a scruffy white bantam hen on her knee. She was stroking the hen absently.

Two little yellow birds were perching on the handle of her spade nearby, cute little things with a green tint to their wings and brightly coloured stripes on their heads. A pair of goldcrests, I recalled, smiling at the vivid memories of all of the wild bird, flower and plant lessons that Mum had given Stephanie and me throughout our childhoods. She knew every leaf, every flower and every wild creature and spent all of her waking hours outside, rambling the countryside or tending to her garden and allotments.

Mum had taken on her first allotment plot over twenty years ago. She had gradually acquired the three adjoining patches and yet her allotment, four times the size of the rest, put the other gardeners to shame. It was full of colour and vitality all year round. In pleasant weather, she would dig, plant and work the ground, and in inclement weather, she would be kitted out in full waterproofs, preparing cuttings or seedlings in the greenhouse, pottering in her shed or pruning and tidying her plants. Even when the ground was covered in snow, she would clear the bird baths, provide fresh food and water and talk with her hens.

The hen on Mum's knee appeared to be taking a nap, and the goldcrests were regarding her intently, heads cocked with interest. She preferred the company of animals to humans. She said that they were less complicated and easier to trust. She had an air of Cinderella about her, eccentric and innocent. She would simply smile and say *animals don't mind different.*

It was approaching the end of September and autumn had set in. The other allotments were looking bare and brown, and there was a general air of abandonment across the site, but not Mum's patch. Her vegetables flourished and her flowers bloomed splendidly.

I trudged over, waving and calling as I grew near. Mum looked up, beaming with delight.

"Izzy! Darling girl. Oh, what a wonderful surprise, "she gushed. "Come in, let me find you somewhere to sit and get

27

us both a drink." She disappeared into the shed and came back with another canvas chair and two cups of water.

I manoeuvred my way through the maze of little paths and walkways, marvelling at her success. She had it all: a self-excavated, modest wildlife pond with trickling waterfall fountain, wildflowers, manicured borders and an abundance of fruit and vegetables. The hens lived in a stunning palatial residence on stilts, where they were confined at night, protected from adverse weather and prowling foxes.

"What brings you here? This is a lovely, unexpected visit," she exclaimed, opening out the chair and inviting me to sit. "Oh ..." Her smile drooped. "You're upset. You need a cuddle from your mum. Is that why you're here? Bad day? Do you want to sit on my knee like you did when you were little?" she prattled.

I nodded and laughed. "I think I'm getting a bit big for sitting on your knee, Mum. Especially on one of these chairs. A hug would be nice, though, please. It's been a bit of a rough day."

Mum instantly put the drinks down, opened her arms, and I stepped in, wrapping my arms around her and pressing my head against her chest. Mum's arms went around me, and I was enveloped in her warmth and that indescribable strength that had been there for me my whole life. I felt like a child again. Mum gave the sort of hugs that make all of your worries disappear, and I felt better instantly. I breathed her in, absorbed her love and felt myself breathe out, settle and relax.

"You always make me feel better, Mum. Thank you. I really needed that," I said.

"You don't have to thank me. I'm your mum. It's what mums do," she replied. We sat down. She smiled. "It's taken a lot of practice, but my life allows me contentment these days. It's so important to be content. I'm where I want to be. Your father looks after me and I get to spend as much time as I like every day, here, with my girls." She nodded at the hens, who had come over to investigate me to see if I had brought treats. "Nobody really bothers me here," Mum went on, "and life is so much better when you're not being bothered by people. Now, do you want to talk about it?"

I smiled. I honestly believe that she would have been happy if she never had to deal with another human being for the rest of her life, apart from Stephanie, me and our dad.

"There isn't really anything to talk about, I don't think," I said carefully. I didn't want to make a big deal out of it, and I definitely didn't want to get into another argument with her. "Just a long day, lots of new people and new challenges, and I needed a hug."

Mum looked at me sideways. We both knew that I hadn't come here randomly for a hug, but she didn't push.

"Well, now you've had one, so how about you give me a hand with my pond netting before too many of these leaves fall in? Oh, and you can dig up the last of the potatoes too. Might as well make use of you now you're here."

I laughed and nodded. Mum never sat still for long, and we would catch up while we worked. I figured that it might be easier to bring up the Josh thing while we were otherwise engaged too, which was most likely her plan all along.

The next hour saw me digging and Mum cleaning and spreading the potatoes and the two of us covering the pond with protective netting. We talked about my dad, Max, and his present ill-fated decorating project, and my sister, Stephanie, who had graduated from her teaching degree last year and was currently taking time out, volunteering to help worthy projects in Senegal, of all places. My little sister was a grafter, a campaigner. She wanted to dedicate her life to people, especially children, who were less fortunate than her. She was brave and adventurous, and she was doing it all, following her heart. Stephanie is the sort of person who wants to save the world one day at a time, and it doesn't hurt that she is beautiful inside and out and that everyone who meets her falls in love with her on the spot.

"Is she still planning on being home for Christmas?" I asked.

Mum nodded. "Yes. Her mission finishes the week before and she's home for a couple of weeks before jetting off again. It'll be so lovely having you both round. And Jack, of course."

"Yes, it will." I couldn't wait.

I filled Mum in about some of the antics of my new class, and we chatted about Jack and his work at the hospital.

"He's a good man," Mum said with amusement.

"Yes, he is," I replied. "And I ought to be getting back to him." I realised that I'd been gone a while and had not let him know where I was. I felt a little guilty. "Thanks for this, though. I know I wasn't here long, but it has helped, Mum."

Mum narrowed her eyes at me. "You're not really going to leave without telling me why you came here in the first place?" she asked.

"Oh, honestly, Mum, I feel much better. It's probably not even worth mentioning now," I dodged.

Her eyes narrowed even further. "Nonsense," she said. "Out with it."

I sighed. "It was at school today," I began. "There was this … this energy in the class that I couldn't ignore." I looked at her. She didn't look happy, but she nodded for me to continue. I went on. "It was just … At first, I didn't know where it was coming from and I tried to ignore it. I tried to block it out, I really did." I didn't meet her eyes. "But anyway, it was stronger than any feeling I've felt from a four-year-old before. It was nasty and dark and … It wasn't that he … Josh … the boy. It wasn't that he was *feeling* nasty. It was more that he was … I don't know … upset … distressed … frightened about something. Honestly, Mum, I don't know. It was probably nothing, but I just felt … I don't know what I felt, but when I asked him …"

"You spoke to this boy about his emotions?" Mum cut in sharply.

I looked up. She definitely looked unhappy with me now.

"I didn't …" I tried to explain. "I just … I just asked him if he was OK," I said.

"Hmm." Mum made a noncommittal noise. "And …?"

"And nothing," I said. "He said he was fine and that was that, but I … I couldn't help … It was so intense. It wasn't normal for a little boy. It got to me. It got to me and it made my skin crawl. I couldn't keep it out."

"But he said he was fine?" Mum asked.

"Yes," I replied.

"Then he probably was," she said firmly.

"But …" I began but I couldn't finish the sentence.

"But …?" she repeated.

"I don't know," I shrugged.

"Izzy?" Her voice sounded softer now and I looked into surprisingly sympathetic eyes. "I … I never … but you … just … trust your instincts," she said.

I was shocked. I had been certain that she was going to tell me to suppress it, not to think about it.

"He's a child," she went on. "If … if there's something … if you can help this boy…" Her voice trailed off and there was a heavy silence in the air. "But Izzy?" She paused. "Just be careful," she said in the end.

I nodded. "I will, Mum. Thank you."

Mum closed the gap between us and threw her arms around me again. The ferocity of the hug caught me off guard, but as usual, being wrapped in her arms filled me with warmth.

She stepped away and was back to business. "Well, thank you for stopping by," she said, indicating that the matter was closed. "You saved me a real struggle, trying to get that net on by myself. The hens are lovely company but very little practical help," she said. "Go on, then. If you don't leave soon, you'll end up stuck talking to Mrs Plot Five. She's due any moment and she'll have her new little rescue dog with her: cute, yappy little thing. She'll want to fill me in on the latest on his digestive system." She rolled her eyes. "You don't want to be here for that, trust me."

I laughed. Nobody passed Mum's allotment without stopping for a chat, and as Mum's was at the top of the walk, nobody could get to their allotment without passing. Despite her vociferous protestations that she didn't like human company, everyone adored her. She always had treats in her pockets for the local dogs and she knew the intimate secrets of everyone in the village. People found Mum different but charming. She was part of the furniture.

"You know, Mum, I'm not entirely convinced about you," I said. "You might just be the exception to your own rule. Maybe people do like different."

"Get away with you," she said, smiling.

Chapter 3

Things settled into their new routine for me over the next few weeks. I shook off the haze of the summer holidays and relaxed into teaching again. After watching one class of children mature and graduate into Year 1 in July, it was always daunting starting again. I had a couple of girls in this class who were almost five, could read some letters, write their names and get themselves changed for P.E. and others who had turned four in August and were noticeably behind a lot of the others in their maturity and independence.

There was one little boy in particular, Sammy Harris. He was a sweet, kind child who got on famously with everyone he met. He was popular with his peers and a favourite among the staff already because of his sunny disposition and winning smile. When he arrived on the playground each morning, he greeted everyone that he saw with a smile and a cheery wave, but despite my being just as won over by his personality as everyone else, I could see that I had a battle heading my way. He was undeniably charming, but every time that I gave him a pencil and something to write on, he would hold it in his fist, scribble something unintelligible on the page, look up with his charming smile and announce, *Don't worry, Miss. I'll learn to write when I'm bigger.* This was nowhere nearly as reassuring as I think he believed it to be.

Fridays were good days. I took the children out for their Forest Schools session on a Friday afternoon, and just a few weeks into the first half term, the children were already thriving in the natural environment. It was clear from the start which children were used to outdoor play and which had spent their early childhoods glued to a screen and never been exposed to nature. Some tugged their wellies on and flew to the copse to start their games or search for mini-beasts, while others procrastinated and dilly-dallied and had to be firmly encouraged to walk across the grass and into the woods to play and learn.

Of course, at this age, just getting them into their coats and wellies and to and from the forest could be quite a challenge.

"Karl, have you been for a wee?" I asked as Karl made a grab for his coat.

"No, Miss. I don't need one," he replied, and I watched his hopeless attempt to stuff his right arm through the left sleeve of the jacket that he had left hanging inside out on his peg that morning.

"Give me your coat, please, Karl," I said, reaching for it and pulling the sleeves the right way round. "I'll sort this out for you. Mrs Bishop is at the toilets helping everybody go before we head outside."

"But I don't need one," came the petulant response, and Karl stood his ground, bottom lip out and hands on his hips.

"No exceptions, Karl," I said firmly. "Go and see Mrs Bishop. Go to the toilet, wash your hands and then you can come back and put your coat and wellies on. We will not have a repeat of last week, where I let you go out and we had to come straight back in." I pointed him in the right direction and he looked me up and down, assessing my resolve, and defeated, he reluctantly dragged himself to the waiting Mrs Bishop and disappeared into the bathroom.

I scanned the room to see which children were ready to go. Melissa was doing well. After a shaky start to the term, she seemed to have found her feet and was now at the front of the queue with her wellies and coat on.

"Excellent work, Melissa," I said. "Could you now be a special helper and help Caroline with that welly she seems to be struggling with?"

"Yes, Miss," said Melissa, and she set to it.

The two girls giggled together as they tried to push Caroline's wellington boot onto her foot.

"It won't go on, Miss," said Melissa. "Push harder," she instructed Caroline.

Another concerted effort and another giggle but no progress.

"There's something in it!" said Caroline, and she tipped it upside down and started shaking. "It won't come out, Miss," she said and held the offending article out for inspection.

I put my hand inside Caroline's welly, and with a little effort, retrieved a small green tractor and two plastic cows. I held them out to Caroline, who was delighted.

"Wayne's farm!" she shouted. "He's been looking everywhere for those."

"Excellent news. Mystery solved," I laughed. "Now, go and put Wayne's farm in your book bag and you can return it to him tonight. And tell your little brother to stop putting his toys in your school wellies."

"Yes, Miss," said Caroline happily. She ran to her peg and safely stored the tractor and the cows in her bag before returning to stand beside Melissa in the queue.

I looked at my queue of primed, excited children. There were now eight out of nineteen with wellies and coats on, waiting patiently, seven children in various stages of dress and four still in the toilet with Mrs Bishop. I fervently hoped that I could get them all outside before the first one announced that they needed another wee.

I was pleased to see that Sammy was well on his way to getting his coat on by himself. He had a rather interesting technique: spreading it out on the floor, lying on top of it, putting his arms through the sleeves and standing back up looking pleased with himself. It was a novel approach, but any sign of independence was progress, and I was proud of him.

"Well done, Sammy. Let me get that zip for you," I said. Zips are tricky when you're four. I fastened him up and sent him to join his friends.

Paul was not doing so well. He was sitting on the floor, staring into space. His coat was still on his peg and his wellies were abandoned on the floor by his side.

"Paul?" I walked over and stood in front of him. "What are you doing?"

"Waiting," came the response.

"What are you waiting for, Paul?" I asked.

"Someone to put my coat and wellies on," he said patiently, as if it were obvious.

"I see," I said. "I think it's time you started trying to do things for yourself, don't you, Paul?" I asked. "You're at school now. We like you to work on your independence."

There was a short pause, and he looked around as if searching for a second opinion on the matter.

"Now?" he asked, his eyes coming to rest upon mine.

"There's no time like the present," I said, and I took a deliberate step back despite being sorely tempted to pop him into his coat and wellies so that we could get outside and get something done.

Paul contemplated his coat for a few more seconds, apparently hoping that it might magically put itself on. He sighed loudly and stood up. He held the coat upside down and put one arm slowly into the hood, watching me out of the corner of his eye. I had the distinct impression that he knew exactly what he was doing, but I didn't have the time to enter into a contest with him. I sighed loudly too, giving in and accepting that I might have to tackle this another time. The rest of the class were waiting.

"Paul," I said, "it is really, really important that you start trying to do things for yourself. Putting your own coat on would be a good thing to learn. I'll help you this time, but we'll be working on you being able to fetch your coat and wellies and put them on all by yourself in the next few weeks, OK?"

"Yes, Miss," said Paul, turning his back to me and spreading his arms out wide like a king awaiting his royal dressers. I put his coat on for him, helped him into his wellies and went back to the queue to do another head count. Sixteen ready and Mrs Bishop on the way with the last three.

"So, we all know the drill," I said. "When we open the yellow gate, we'll all make our way across the field to Forest Schools. Mrs Bishop will go ahead with the leaders, and I'll stay at the back. No dawdling, no stopping for a chat on the way and no sitting down on the grass. It's wet. Walk in twos, please. When we get into the trees, I'd like you to arrange yourselves into small groups of three or four and look for interesting things to report. You can hunt for mini-beasts, collect interesting leaves or conkers or find funny shaped sticks. It's up to you. I'll gather you all together at the end to show each other what you've found. OK?"

"Yes, Miss Bliss," the Little Owls chorused.

"Good. Mrs Bishop and I'll be right there with you and we'll help you look or answer any questions you might have."

I nodded to Mrs Bishop, who opened the yellow gate. The children filed out.

"Joshua," I called as he passed, "will you be my walking partner?"

Josh nodded, and I fell into step beside him. I had arranged a meeting with Richard Beaumont, the head teacher, and Chrissy Brooks, the safeguarding coordinator, about him that afternoon and I wanted one more chance to see if he would open up to me first.

I had been watching Josh closely and I was growing more and more desperately worried about him. He was full of anxiousness all of the time. Some days it was worse than others, but at the beginning of each day, I would meet his eye during registration, and the feelings that radiated from him were still raw and unusually painful. I had come to dread that moment each morning, but I felt that it was part of my duty as his teacher. I had stopped fantasising that it was my imagination or that he was just an overly sensitive child. I knew that there was something seriously wrong. I knew that Josh was carrying a painful burden, but until I had concrete evidence or an admission to act upon, I was powerless to do anything. I had taken him aside and spoken to him over and over again, always reassuring him that I was on his side and always trying to encourage him to open up to me, but he continued to assure me that he was fine. All that I could do for now was to use my influence to gently improve his mood a little each day. I just tried to take the edge off his distress, which I hoped was helping, but it was a great struggle. The intensity of the negativity and fear surrounding him was a difficult force to fight against and I wasn't strong enough to do much for him.

I had, of course, tried to speak to both of his parents informally at drop off and pick up, but I had been faced with blank faces and emphatic denials that there could be anything wrong. Mr Nelson seemed relaxed and confident in his corroboration of his son's assurance that everything was fine. Mrs Nelson was quiet and reserved and difficult to draw out in conversation but she, too, assured me that she couldn't think of anything that would be causing Josh to be upset at school. Mrs Nelson had a strange sort of nervous energy about her, but after speaking to them both, I was no nearer to finding an explanation for Josh's palpable distress.

Josh had become drawn to me more and more as time went on, comforted by the way that I could ease his mood, and he seemed to be happiest when he was by my side. I think that I made him feel safe, and I was hoping that building his trust would encourage him to talk to me, but so far, he had remained resolutely silent on the cause of his distress. I had started keeping a mood diary for him where I recorded the emotions that I elicited from him each day, but there didn't seem to be any patterns.

His dad dropped him off every morning on his way to work, except on Wednesdays when he worked away and left early. His mum dropped him off on a Wednesday and picked him up every afternoon. Both of his parents were punctual, smart and friendly. Mr Nelson would nod and smile at me as he put Josh's water bottle in the tray each morning, and Josh flew into his mum's arms for a cuddle each afternoon.

He was a serious little boy, very quiet, studious and well-behaved. I never had cause to tell him off for shouting or playing when he should be concentrating on a task. His numeracy and literacy skills were high for his age, and I knew that his mum read with him every morning before school. He was always clean and smartly dressed, his uniform neatly ironed and tucked into his trousers, his dark hair cut short and kept tidy. He had big, serious eyes and he was always polite. He was too good. Too serious for a little boy. I wanted him to come out of his shell and let go on occasion, and I was sick of hearing about how he was always fine. I needed to find a way to break through if I was going to get to the bottom of his problems and help him because at the moment, the only signs of his suffering were on the inside, and I was the only one who had any idea of how deeply he was being affected by the invisible burden that he was carrying.

The one time that Josh did seem a little more at ease was on a Friday when the class were outside during their Forest Schools lesson each week, which was another reason for me to relish it too.

I looked at Josh now, walking by my side. He was looking straight ahead, and I could feel his characteristic worry bubbling away under the surface. There was also a hollow feeling of sadness clawing at me as we approached the woods. I heard him take a long, shaky breath and let out a shuddering sigh, but I decided not to tackle his problem right now. This wasn't the time. I wanted to see him have some fun.

"Right, Josh, what are you going to look for today?" I asked.

He thought for a moment and then he looked up at me and smiled. I relaxed a fraction in response. "I think I'll look for some footprints in the mud," he said. "There might be foxes or badgers down here at night."

"That's an excellent plan," I said. "Do you know what an animal is called that comes out at night?"

"Nocturnal," said Josh immediately, puffing out his chest.

"Excellent word, Josh. Well done. There might also be rabbit footprints, like Bossy. Do you know what a rabbit footprint looks like?"

Josh stopped in his tracks and his mood plummeted suddenly, shocking me with its force and almost causing me to cry out. I stopped with him and fought to right myself. This wasn't my grief. I couldn't allow myself to buckle under its weight. I steadied myself and looked at Josh. He was fighting back tears.

"Oh no, Josh, I'm so sorry. What happened? Is it Bossy?"

"He got broken, Miss. He's dead."

Josh was struggling to keep himself under control. It was a valiant effort for one so young. Usually, if a pupil's pet died, it would be the first thing that they told me when they arrived at school. It was rare for them to keep anything like that to themselves.

"Broken?" I asked. It was a strange term to use to describe the demise of an animal. "You mean he got poorly? I'm so sorry. I know how much you loved him."

"Yes, Miss," Josh sniffed. "It's fine."

I bristled at the familiar phrase.

I tried to get him back on track straight away. This was the one time during the week that he could be positive and enjoy himself. Dwelling on bad news wasn't going to help. I vaguely wondered whether the death of his rabbit had anything to do with his general feeling of anxiousness, but I didn't voice my concern. That could wait. I turned to him with a reassuring smile.

"Let's concentrate on finding these footprints, shall we?"

He nodded.

"Can you pick a few other children to help you? Who would you like to play with today?"

Josh pointed to two boys ahead of us.

"I think Ben and Oliver might be able to help," he suggested.

"I'm sure they would," I replied. "Go and ask them."

Josh stood still for another beat before venturing towards the boys, who were closely examining the end of a stick in Ben's hand. As we got closer, I could hear their conversation.

"It's poo," said Oliver. "You put the good stick in poo! It was my favourite stick."

"It's mud," countered Ben. "Look, it doesn't even smell," he said, thrusting the stick under Oliver's nose.

"Oi! Don't put the poo stick up my nose!" cried Oliver.

"It's not a poo stick," Ben insisted. "What do you think, Josh?" he asked as we approached. "Mud or poo?"

Josh looked at the stick. Ben held it still for him to examine. There was an expectant silence as the two boys patiently awaited his verdict, and with almost no hesitation, Josh put his finger into the brown substance in question and then popped the finger into his mouth.

"Josh!" I shouted.

"Urgh!" Oliver moaned.

"Ha. Nice one, Josh," Ben laughed and held up his hand for a high five. Josh hit it and grinned, not fazed in the slightest. I breathed a sigh of relief. I didn't think he would be so calm if it had indeed been poo.

"It's mud," he declared, and all three of the boys began to laugh, the infectious, genuine, carefree laugh of children at play. Josh asked the other two if they would help him look for footprints.

"Yeah, 'course," they agreed, and they ran off together happily without a backwards glance in my direction. I was happy to be forgotten.

I was pleased with Josh's progress overall. Taking the children out of the classroom was making a real difference. It wasn't a cure for whatever was going on in his life, but if I could give him a break from the anxiousness eating him up inside, it would give him a chance to be happy for a while. I loved having the class outdoors. Some of the other teachers complained about it, but it reminded me of being a child myself, and I tried to instil the same wonder of nature in my Little Owls as Mum had done for me.

Seeing Josh play with his friends made me feel a little lighter as I lifted moss-covered stones so that the children could check underneath for creepy-crawlies, and I made my own collection of fallen leaves of various colours. Josh didn't find any fox or badger prints, but he did find lots of bird prints in the soft ground. He spent the remaining time tearing around with the other boys, and he looked a little happier, more relaxed, his mind distracted from his pain.

Before we knew it, it was time to head back inside, remove our coats and wellies and settle down for the last session of the day. As I passed his chair, I focused on Josh's state of mind. The distress had been dampened by the liberating session outside, but it was still very much present, and I could still feel it trying to poison my own mood. I couldn't sit by and let this gentle child be consumed by an invisible enemy. If Josh couldn't open up about his problems, I would have to find another way to help him. I left the children in the capable hands of Mrs Bishop for story time and set off to the office for my meeting. I took a deep breath. I knew how it was going to sound. It was not going to be an easy sell, but I also knew that I had to try, for Josh.

"Isabel, I'm sorry, but I just don't know what you're expecting us to do. You've not given us anything here," said Richard, our good-natured, professional headteacher. He was looking at me kindly but was clearly bemused. "What is it you're actually basing your concerns on? A hunch?"

"I know there isn't much," I struggled, feeling utterly embarrassed but still determined as I tried to defend my position. "But something just isn't right. I know it."

Richard's look of bemusement began to turn to impatience. He opened his mouth to speak but Chrissy stepped in.

"You might be right, Izzy," she said. "I really hope you're not, but there might be a problem here. I've seen cases that start with a feeling. They can turn nasty, and often a teacher's intuition turns out to be right, but Richard's also right. We can't act on a feeling alone." She sighed. "He comes to school every day?"

"Yes," I said.

"And he's always on time?"

"Yes."

"Always presentable?"

"He's always clean and his uniform's neat and tidy, yes," I said, feeling the fight slipping away.

"Have you noticed anything that might cause concern during P.E? When he gets changed, I mean?" Chrissy asked.

"He doesn't have any marks or bruises that are out of the ordinary, no," I said.

"And when you've asked him if there's anything upsetting him?"

"He always says he's fine," I admitted reluctantly. "But that's part of the problem. He always says *I'm fine, Miss*, like a robot, like it's the only answer he knows. And I know he's lying. I know how he feels and it's wrong, but I don't know why." I felt tears sting the back of my eyes and furiously wiped them away. I had known exactly how this was going to go. It meant so much to me, but I was helpless.

"He comes to school every day, well-dressed, polite, healthy, and he tells you he's fine. He's on target with his work. Come on, Isabel, you know there's nothing we can do." Richard was dismissing me.

"Yes," I accepted. "Of course, Rick, but there is a problem. I know there's a problem and I've raised it with you. I'd like you to make a record of my concerns for the future, just in case."

"Yes, of course," he agreed. "We've documented this meeting and your concerns. I don't want you to feel like we're not taking you seriously." He was sensing my frustration and was trying to placate me. "You spend a lot of time with the boy. If you think something's wrong, you may be right. However, there's a process. This is the first step, and we've got no evidence to act on. Now, who's collecting Josh this afternoon?"

"His mum always picks him up," I said.

"Then, if you feel it's appropriate, you can gently, informally, bring up your concerns with his mother after school again. Let her know your concerns, but gently," Richard repeated firmly. "Don't go making any unfounded accusations."

"Of course not," I said, ruffled by the suggestion. "I wouldn't do that."

"Then that's the end of the matter, for now," he said with a tone of finality. "If Mrs Nelson says something to add to your *feeling*," he said, reminding me of his opinion on the matter, "please bring it to our attention."

"Yes, of course," I said and rose to leave. "Thank you for hearing me out."

The meeting had transpired exactly as I had predicted it would. It was extraordinarily frustrating, but I knew that I had been right to present my concerns formally. Now at least the other staff might have their eyes open when Josh was around, and if there was anything to see, hopefully someone would see it.

I knew with absolute certainty that there was a problem. I couldn't be mistaken about Josh's emotions and there was no simple, child-friendly explanation for their intensity and negativity. If he had burst into tears when I confronted him and told me that his dog was dying or that his grandma was ill, I would have put it down to him being a sensitive child with justifiable feelings, but I couldn't understand why any four-year-old child would lie about innocent problems or keep secrets. Whenever I asked him how he was feeling, he just straightened up, focused his gaze anywhere but into my eyes and told me that he was *fine*. It didn't make sense when I knew that he was anything but *fine*. It felt rehearsed. Four-year-olds weren't *fine,* and they talked openly about their feelings. They loved their friends, they were good or bad, happy or sad, lively or tired, but they were very rarely, and certainly not consistently, *fine*.

Pondering the meeting and my planned discussion with Mrs Nelson, I was absorbed in my thoughts and had my head down when I felt an odd and strangely familiar flutter deep within my mind. Before I could interpret the sensation, I rounded the corner of the building and walked headlong into a man hurrying the other way. We collided with considerable force, and the solid briefcase that he was carrying swung upwards on impact and struck my shin as I stumbled forwards, dropping me to my knees and causing an intense, sharp pain to course through my leg. I landed heavily and awkwardly on the floor, grazing and bruising my knees on impact with the unyielding playground.

"Owww!" I cried, grabbing my leg and sucking in a breath at the pain. "Oh, I am so sorry. I wasn't looking where I was going. I'm so sorry."

"Watch it," the man said roughly at the same time.

"I …" I was stunned and stared at the stranger, my mouth open wide. *Watch it?* What kind of person knocked another person to the ground with a heavy object, even if it was totally the other person's fault, and didn't apologise out of sheer British politeness, or at the very least, offer a hand and ask if they were all right? *Watch it?* I couldn't actually remember the last time that I had been spoken to like that. The man's voice was deep and harsh. He sounded unjustifiably angry. I looked up and met his eyes. Nothing. No apology, no concern for my pain and injury, but that wasn't what struck me. He wasn't giving off any emotion. None. There was just an empty space. It was no wonder that I had crashed into him. It was like he wasn't there. I was so used to sensing people from their radiating emotional energy that I was utterly confused by this hominid-shaped vacuum. Everyone felt something, ceaselessly. No one can just not have an emotion. Perhaps he wasn't human.

At that thought, my lip curled into a hint of a smile through the pain, which the man standing over me noticed and which apparently was enough to make him even more angry. He was a tall, muscular man with thick dark eyebrows over deep-set brown eyes. He had dark hair, tanned skin and an athletic build, but it was his expression that I noticed above his appearance. He looked absolutely furious, and I couldn't for the life of me comprehend why he would be angry that I was on the floor with a bruised knee. Even more confusing was that if he was as outraged as he appeared, then I should be able to feel it. I usually read a person by their emotional energy before I even noticed their expression and the other physical cues that normal people navigate by. This man gave me the creeps. I had definitely never seen him before. He was not somebody that I would forget, and yet that strange, familiar flutter remained deep inside my mind, a hair-raising sense of déjà vu. He was enormous, rude and utterly devoid of emotion, and I did not feel at all comfortable in his presence.

I tore my eyes away from his frosty gaze and picked myself up with a wince. There was no doubt that I would have some nasty bruises and would need an ice pack to prevent swelling, but my priority at that moment was removing myself from the vicinity of this thoroughly unpleasant, intimidating man. I dusted myself off and gathered my thoughts. I considered confronting him about his attitude, but when I looked up, he was gone, without a word, without a trace. I had no idea how such an enormous man could appear and disappear without a sound or even a breath of air or emotion. I was mystified.

In the next moment, Helen Young, the school receptionist, came hurrying around the corner. "Oh, hi, Izzy." She paused. "What happened to you? You look a bit ruffled."

"Yes. I just took a bit of a tumble," I replied. I stopped short of mentioning that I had just crashed into an unnerving goliath.

"Did you see a man come this way?" Helen asked. "Big, beautiful, gorgeous eyes?" She practically sighed.

"You mean a big, scary guy? Angry looking?" I suggested.

"Yes. Daniel," said Helen. "I think it's more moody than scary, though. Don't you? Gorgeous man."

"Can't say I noticed."

"No? Well, he's an IT guy. He was checking the computers in the office. Apparently, the school's getting an upgrade. I need to catch up with him before he leaves. There's something else Rick wants him to look at. Was he heading for the car park?" she asked.

"Oh, good," I said. "Yes. Probably. I didn't see where he went."

"They're new in town and causing quite a stir," Helen said as she hurried on towards the car park with a smile.

I hobbled slowly back towards my classroom, praying that I would get there before the bell went and the children needed to be dismissed. I was in agony. I hoped that it was just a bruise and I wasn't going to have to cancel date night tonight. I would see the children off, have a word with Mrs Nelson and then return to the office and put an ice pack on it. My mind wandered back to that horrible man and the striking difference in the ways in which Helen and I had seen him. Helen had only seen the exterior package: the muscle-toned body and chiselled jaw. She hadn't been affected by his lack of emotion, but of course, she wouldn't be. Most people were oblivious to the emotional energy of others and relied on more typical social cues such as facial expression and tone of voice, but I knew that what most people saw did not always paint the full picture.

I contemplated how much more difficult it must be to get to know a person without my awareness of their feelings, their mood, their emotional state of mind. I could see so much deeper than a person's expression and behaviour. I could sense what most people could not, and I realised now that I had always taken that awareness for granted. Despite promising Mum that I would try to avoid deliberate use of my extra sense, I could not get away from the fact that it was an integral part of me, providing me with a more profound understanding of a person and their openness, their honesty. I knew when someone's smile was false or their indifference faked. It was an inescapable aspect of every human that I encountered.

Sometimes I wanted nothing more than to be rid of knowledge that could be painful or embarrassingly intimate, but it was also what I used to judge a person, to get to know a person, and the basis for all of my human relationships throughout my entire life. Without it, I was blind. I had never before encountered a person that I couldn't read, and I didn't like the way it made me feel at all.

I hobbled into the classroom just in time to see the children lining up at the door. Parents were already milling around on the playground.

"Oh, Mrs Bishop, thank you so much. I was a little longer than I'd expected," I said.

"That's no problem, Miss Bliss. Oooh, what have you done to yourself?" she asked, noticing my limp.

"Oh, it's nothing." I brushed off the concern. "Just a bruise from a little fall. Right, class, all ready to go?"

"Yes, Miss Bliss," they sang.

I could feel the children humming with the excitement that always built up at the end of the day, the anticipation of seeing their parents. It was contagious and I smiled with them, temporarily forgetting my pain.

"Josh?" I searched him out and beckoned him over. "Can you just stay at the back, sweetie? I want to have a quick word with your mum before you leave."

Josh's mood crashed immediately. The bubbly, innocent

emotions of nineteen children were replaced by the cold, hard fear of one. He was terrified, and if I hadn't been watching for it, and if the positivity of the rest of the class hadn't been there to even it out, it might have incapacitated me yet again with its intensity. Why would the thought of me speaking to his mother cause such a drastic decline in his mood? Perhaps he thought that he was going to be in some sort of trouble. I was certain that he was not afraid of his mother. I had seen them together many times and I had felt the love between them. I took his hand and offered my reassurance.

"It's OK, Josh. You haven't done anything wrong. I just want a chat, that's all," I said calmly, trying to steady his mood.

We stood at the gate together as I released the children one at a time to their waiting parents. Melissa was at the front of the line again, shining with her newfound confidence and independence.

"Can you see your mum, Melissa?" I asked.

"Yes, she's right there, Miss," replied Melissa, waving.

"Off you go, then."

I released the next few children. Some were still struggling into their coats as they ran across the playground and threw themselves into the arms of their loved ones. Others dawdled, heads down, devastated at being separated from their playmates for a whole weekend.

"Whoa, hang on a minute, Karl, what's going on here?" I asked as Karl whizzed past with his bag gaping open at a dangerous angle, contents about to spill all over the playground. I straightened him up, fastened his bag and sent him on his way.

Sammy was next, already jumping up and down, unable to contain his excitement and pointing at his mum. "Mummy, Mummy! That's my mummy. Mummy, I've got a stick from Forest Schools!" he shouted.

"Yes, there she is indeed. No, wait until you get to her before you start taking things out of your bag. Good boy. Off you go, then, see you on Monday." I waved him off.

Before long, Josh was the only child left. He stayed glued quietly to my side as I called Mrs Nelson over with a friendly wave. I could feel the anxiousness rolling around inside him, but I didn't let it get a hold of me and I didn't let go of his hand. I needed all of the strength I had to give me the impetus to tackle this difficult conversation.

Mrs Nelson was a pretty little thing, always well-presented and very quiet. She never spoke to any of the other parents on the playground but stood a little way apart, eyes cast demurely down, keeping herself to herself. Today she was wearing a pale brown turtleneck jumper and black jacket, scarf, hat and gloves. It wasn't a particularly chilly day for the beginning of October, but she was slight and probably felt the cold. To those less perceptive, Mrs Nelson would appear poised and dignified, but I could feel the similar level of anxiousness that I felt from Josh radiating off her as she approached me at the gate.

Josh grabbed hold of his mum and hung on tightly. They both looked at me expectantly, nervously.

"I just need a quick word, if that's all right?" I said.

"Yes, of course. Is there a problem?" replied Mrs Nelson.

"No ... well ... yes. Nothing serious, I hope." I ushered Mrs Nelson inside the gate, out of hearing of the other parents and staff on the playground. "I just wanted to check that everything's OK ... again." It was so difficult saying something without saying anything, offering support without any idea of what the problem was. "It's just that Josh has been a little quiet at school, much more so than the other children. A little preoccupied, perhaps, or worried, and I wondered if there was anything that might be worrying him at home. Anything at all that I should know about?" I stopped.

Mrs Nelson didn't say anything. She just stood there looking at me as if she was trying to decide something. The silence became uncomfortable.

"So I can support him, I mean," I continued.

"No," she said finally. "There's nothing. He's fine. We're fine." She steered Josh towards the school gates, making it clear that the conversation was over. "Thank you," she added as an afterthought.

I felt both mother and son relax a fraction as they walked away together hand in hand. Their love for each other was unmistakable, like a cord tying them to each other and giving them strength. I was comforted by the sight of it and the feeling of unity that they shared. Maybe I was wrong about Josh. Maybe the Nelsons were just a highly strung family, deeply sensitive and naturally anxious. I played the conversation over again in my mind. Something niggled at me. Something still felt amiss. *He's fine. We're fine.* That word again. *Fine.* I simply wasn't convinced.

I limped slowly back to the office to retrieve my phone and sit with an ice pack on my swollen knee. I usually left early on a Friday so that I could get ready to go out, but I didn't feel capable of driving just yet. Once a fortnight, Jack and I went out for a meal together, and on alternate Fridays, I met up with my best friend, Donna, for girls' night. On girls' night, Jack would get together with his brother or some friends, and occasionally, the two groups would meet for drinks or a dance later on. Tonight was date night, and I was looking forward to a quiet romantic meal. I was glad that I was going out with Jack tonight. I could rely on him to be stable, consistent. Donna could be pretty intense, and I didn't think that I could cope with a lot of noise or a heavy night. I promised myself that I would try to put Josh out of my mind and enjoy the evening. No one would gain anything from my worrying.

I was alone in the staffroom, and it was quiet now that the children had left the school. Most of the teachers chose not to hang around on a Friday, so I was able to take a few moments to relax in peace and let go of the swirling emotions crowding my mind. I wouldn't make it to the lake tonight, which meant not having the opportunity to heal myself properly. I rested my head back on the comfortable chair and closed my eyes, trying to imagine that the agitation, excitement and anxiousness of the day were physical presences, bubbles trapped inside my mind that I could release and cast away. I wished that I could meet somebody like me, somebody who experienced the world like I did, somebody that I could talk to and share my world with, but I accepted that I had to deal with it on my own, keep it to myself and be careful, like my mum had always said.

As I began to unwind, I was struck by the powerful sensation that someone was in the room with me, standing too close, leaning into my personal space, intruding in my mind and examining the tangle of emotions that they found there. It was a horrible, creeping, invasive feeling, and it was accompanied by that strange but familiar flutter. I snapped my eyes open, suddenly breathing hard. I was still alone, but the cold, eerie feeling of being watched persisted. My eyes were drawn to the window, where an unfamiliar black van was crawling past and the man — the big, rude, emotionless man — was staring out of the driver's window, staring right at me with those deep, dark, scary eyes. It felt like he was gazing right into my soul and he didn't care that I could see him and feel him and that I was scared. I had the distinct impression that he knew what he was doing and that he was enjoying making me squirm. He held my gaze and his expression never changed. I had been right earlier. He was creepy. Helen had said that he was causing quite a stir in town, that *they* were causing quite a stir. If his attitude today was anything to go by, it was no wonder. *Callahan* was written in large silver letters across the side of the van. The Callahans. Welcome to Ramsay Bridge.

Chapter 4

"Hi, I'm home!" I called as I entered the house. I removed my boots carefully and padded gingerly towards the kitchen.

"Hi, honey. I heard your car, so I put the kettle on. Fancy a cuppa?" he called back.

"That's exactly what I need," I said, relieved to be home and happy to be looked after.

He was finishing the drinks as I came into the kitchen. He turned, enveloped me in a comforting hug and delivered my tea. I hobbled the short distance to the oak kitchen table and perched on the corner.

"I really needed this. It's been a bit of a tough day," I said.

"Are you limping?" he asked, concerned. "What happened?"

"Yes, a bit," I admitted. "It's just a bruise. I'll tell you about it later. First, tell me about your day while I sit quietly for a moment."

Jack looked uneasy not to be allowed to fuss over me, but he did as I asked. I sipped my tea and listened as he filled me in on his day. He worked in the hospital kitchen and had been up and down from the wards delivering meals to patients. He told me about his colleagues and some of the patients that he had seen, and I was reassured by his stability and the normality of it all. He was already dressed for our date in dark blue fitted jeans and a pale shirt, and as I drank my tea, I appreciated his soothing presence and how the affection shone out of his soft hazel eyes.

Jack was my best friend. He was constant, dependable, even-tempered and kind. He could be trusted to do anything he was asked and everything he committed to, and it was always a pleasure to be in his company. His gentle nature was a source of reassurance to me because I was in constant fear of causing pain or anger in someone I loved. Although it's normal for couples to lose their temper and be angered or hurt by their partners, my sensitivity to emotion meant that I found arguments particularly difficult to cope with. I would sense, absorb and often reflect my adversary's anger, which heightened my own reactions as well as theirs, resulting in unpleasantly inflammatory episodes. I put a lot of effort into avoiding situations with intense emotions. Jack and I never argued. We had similar dispositions and a shared desire for equanimity.

We had been best friends forever and had shared all of the big events in each other's lives. The three of us, Donna, Jack and me, had lived within a couple of streets of each other growing up. We played together at primary school, walked to school together as teenagers and had invariably spent our evenings and weekends in each other's company. I'm not sure exactly when Jack's feelings for me had become romantic. They had developed over time until it was blatantly obvious to everyone that he was totally in love with me. Our families and friends had assumed that we were a couple a long time before I began to return his affections. I really didn't have romantic feelings towards him. I just wanted to be his best friend, but this became more difficult as his infatuation developed until I was unable to escape the acute awareness of his feelings whenever he was near.

He was very patient with me during our teenage years and didn't ask me out until we were sixteen. I turned him down. My rejection hurt him badly, and in turn, his distress upset me, straining our friendship for a time, but it would have been unfair to profess feelings that I couldn't be sure were my own, and my confusing, complicated emotions had frightened me. When our friendship got back on track, his feelings resurfaced, and about six months later, he asked me out again and I rejected him once more. I hated hurting him because he was so important to me, and being around his misery caused me pain in response.

By the age of seventeen, I was so confused. Being a teenager was difficult enough without the added complexity of my sensitivity and response to other people's emotions.

When I spent time with Jack, I felt his adoration and I reciprocated, but I was frightened that I was mirroring his emotions, not feeling them for myself. I didn't know how to tell the difference. Sometimes I even wondered if there was a difference, but I didn't want to lead him on. Eventually, Donna stepped in. Donna always told it straight.

"I'm sick of you dancing around each other. I just don't understand it, Izzy," she said. "Any girl would die to have a guy like Jack after them. He's hot, he's kind, he's funny, and he utterly adores you. You clearly adore him too. Who wouldn't? What on earth more do you want?"

"It's not that I want more," I replied. "It's just that I love what we've got. You, me and him, together. The three of us. Best friends. I'm frightened it'll change things too much. And what if I don't love him enough or it gets too much and I end up hurting him?"

"Listen, Isabel Bliss," Donna demanded firmly. "If it was the other way round and it was me he was madly in love with, I wouldn't hesitate to dump our little threesome and have him to myself. But it's not. It's you, and you'll be throwing away your chance at happiness if you don't say yes. You'll be a fool. You can't live your whole life worrying about what might happen in the future. Saying yes will make him the happiest guy alive. And it's not like I'm going anywhere. The three of us are going to be best friends forever, no matter what. I promise you that. It would take more than you two getting your act together to get rid of me!"

Donna was right. Jack was too good to dismiss, and it didn't make sense to worry about causing him pain when my rejection was already hurting him and ruining our friendship. Deep down, I knew that I didn't really want to be with him romantically, but I didn't want to lose him as a friend, and it felt like I couldn't have both. He would make me feel safe and loved, and I could bring absolute joy to my very best friend.

The day that I finally made my move, we were on our way home from school. Jack and I dropped Donna off at her gate and continued alone. Although I lived furthest away from school, Jack went out of his way to collect me every morning and walked me home at the end of each day. It was a bright spring afternoon. The sun was shining in a baby-blue sky, and I felt glad to be alive. I was keenly aware of the radiance that surrounded Jack and the bounce in his step whenever we were alone together.

"Why do you always go out of your way to pick me up and drop me off every day?" I asked.

He didn't pause to think, not even for a moment. "That's easy," he said. "I get to spend an extra eight minutes with you every day. Four minutes before school and four minutes after school. I'd be a fool to pass up on an extra eight minutes of your company every day. You know, that's forty minutes a week and … twenty hours a year. I get nearly a whole extra day of you to myself."

He nudged me and flashed a mischievous smile, and I knew that he was being playful, but there's a difference between playful deceit and playful truth, and Jack wasn't lying to me. Part of my curse was that I always knew when someone was being dishonest, which had benefits but also often led to loneliness. Jack really did pick me up and drop me off so that he could spend an extra eight minutes with me every day. Being with me made him happy, and that was something that I wanted to be a part of. Did it really matter where the emotion originated as long as we were both happy? It was time to stop overthinking everything and get happy.

I stopped outside my house and turned to face him, leaning back against the gate.

"Jack?"

"Mm-hmm?"

"Do you think those extra eight minutes would be better if you were allowed to hold my hand?"

He stopped breathing for a moment, and I felt the shift in

his emotions. I felt the spark of hope, delight and passion a split second before his face caught up and I saw the smile.

"Really?" he asked. "Yes, I absolutely do."

"Well," I said, "let's see. You've been walking the extra four minutes to and from my house for nearly six years. Using your calculations, at nearly a day per year, we're talking about nearly a week altogether. A week. That's dedication. I think it's time, don't you?"

"Oh, Izzy," Jack breathed. "I knew it was time years ago. I've just been waiting for you to catch up." He took a couple of steps to close the gap between us. Pressed against the gate, I had nowhere to go, and he kept coming until his body was pinning mine.

"Is it OK if I stand this close?" he asked slightly breathlessly.

I smiled at his nerves and allowed my mind to absorb, reflect and respond to his unadulterated joy.

"I think," I grinned, "if we're going to do this, it's only right that you stand this close on occasion."

His smile was improbably wide. "That's really very excellent news," he said, and without another moment's hesitation, he bent his head and he kissed me. It was our first kiss. We were seventeen years old, and despite having known each other our whole lives, we were both jittery. I felt my own nerves mingle with his, but I also sensed his delight and adulation, and the combination was euphoric. It was a brief kiss, soft and tender and full of joy. I couldn't quite tell where his feelings stopped and mine began, but it didn't matter, and I suddenly didn't know why I had delayed for so long.

Jack held my hands by my side for a moment and looked me in the eye. "You've made me very happy," he said simply.

"I know," I replied, and I watched him turn and head towards home with a spring in his step. I watched him walk away, and as he reached the corner, he turned and saw me watching him and we were both happy.

That was eight and a half years ago. I hadn't always been the easiest person to be with, but Jack had remained patient and kind, and he was still my best friend. Being with him had never been difficult. I looked at him now as I sipped my tea and he told me about his day.

"What are you thinking about, Izzy?" he asked. "You're off in another world and I think you stopped listening to me."

"Sorry," I said. "You're right. I was looking at you and thinking about us, and I was remembering the day you kissed me at my gate."

"The day you made me the happiest man alive?" he smiled. "Well, in that case, I'll let you off. Right. Time to get changed, please. It's date night, if you're still up to it. And then I want a full account of what you've done to your leg."

Jack took my mug and put it in the dishwasher while I went upstairs. I picked out a black low-cut top decorated with pretty petrol-green flowers and my white linen trousers. The trousers were loose and comfortable, and the top was figure hugging and enhanced my cleavage. I pulled off my work trousers and examined my injured legs. Both knees were bruised, and the right one was swollen and decidedly tender to touch. There was a small graze, and it was already starting to turn a mottled purple colour. Where the briefcase had struck my shin, there was a nasty contusion, a lump and impressive discoloration, but the skin wasn't broken and would heal quickly. I would have some impressive bruises by morning but nothing to worry about.

I touched up my mascara and applied subtle lipstick and gloss. I let my hair down and ran the straighteners over it. I never spent a lot of time on my appearance. Jack and I both preferred the natural look. A dab of perfume on my neck and wrists and I was ready. I grabbed my thick black jacket and limped back down the stairs.

"I'm ready," I called. "Where are we going?"

"That was quick," he said, emerging from the kitchen. He

looked me up and down admiringly. "You look gorgeous, as always. We're going to Little Italy."

"Oooh, brilliant. Shall we go, then?" I said.

"Yes, let's," he replied, and he took my arm and escorted me out to his car.

Ramsay Bridge was an unconventional little town set around the south bank of the lake, Ramsay Pool, with its main streets running along either side of the river, away from the lake. The bridge itself was an old narrow stone affair built on the south bank at the point where the lake flowed into the river. Originally designed for wagons and carts, it retained its character, with the original lantern holders embedded in beautiful carved sconces at intervals along both sides. There was a new, wider road available now, but the old bridge was still passable if you didn't mind the delay that inevitably came upon meeting someone coming the other way.

Little Italy was a small family-run restaurant with a prime location right on the lake shore, its decking built on stilts in the water. It was a stunning place to sit in the summer and enjoy the view across the bridge, up the hill and into the woodland beyond. In the winter it was a charming, cosy affair and it was always packed, no matter the season.

It was Friday night and the restaurant was full. The atmosphere was relaxed and friendly, and the manager led us to a little table by the window, where we could look out across the bridge and the shimmering reflection of the lanterns on the smooth, dark water.

I ordered a glass of white wine, Jack took a coke, and we chatted freely whilst ordering and eagerly anticipating our food. We began with a sharing plate of antipasti with cured meats, olives, cheese, salad and bread. I took the olives, and Jack took all the spiciest meats. We didn't need to ask. We knew each other well enough by now. The meal was delicious as always and the atmosphere was delightful. I was able to relax and float happily on the feelings of pleasure and romance that filled the air.

"So, come on, then," said Jack halfway through the main course. "I can't believe you're going to make me ask. Tell me about your leg. What happened?"

I sighed. "Ugh, I'd almost forgotten about him."

Jack glanced up in surprise. "Are you calling your knee a him or is there someone else involved in this tale?" he asked with a playful smile.

"Yes," I replied, "one of the most ignorant, unpleasant, rudest people I've ever met." I said it with considerable feeling and a tiny bit too loudly for the surroundings.

"Blimey. Strong words," laughed Jack. "You don't let people get to you very often. I think I'm going to like this story. Go on," he urged.

"OK. So, you know how I was meeting with Rick and Chrissy this afternoon about Josh?" I asked.

"Yes, of course." Jack turned appropriately sober. "I assume that went as you expected."

"Yes. Not much to add on that front. I spoke to Josh's mum tonight, though."

"Oh, yes? How was that? Awkward?"

"Awful. I was awful. I just didn't know what to say," I complained. "Anyway, I basically said what's the problem, and she said there isn't one, we're fine, and that's all there is to it." My mind turned to Josh again and I almost let it ruin my mood. I closed my eyes and took a breath. There was nothing I could do about Josh tonight.

"I'm sorry, Izzy," said Jack. "I know how much you want to help this kid."

"Yeah, well, there's not much I can do for now," I said sadly. "But I do appreciate you being on my side. Anyway, this bloke."

"Yes, tell me," Jack urged.

"So, I came out of my meeting with Rick, feeling a bit rubbish, to be honest, and this bloke just barrelled right into me," I said. "I didn't even see him coming. He was carrying this big briefcase thing and it hit my shin as I went down, and I fell to the floor with a crash, on my knees. It's not funny," I said as I noticed Jack trying desperately to hold back his laughter.

"Well, it does sound a bit funny," he admitted.

"Yeah? Well it might have been, I suppose, if you weren't me," I continued. "Anyway, so this bloke knocked me to the floor with his briefcase and when I was down, I apologised because I'm a moron and he just said *watch it*."

"Watch it?" Jack stopped laughing.

"Yes. Watch it. He was so rude. He was a massive bloke, and he looked like he was cross with me when I was the one on the floor in agony."

Jack was laughing again. "I'm sorry, Izzy. That does sound awful. I don't know why I'm laughing, really." He covered his giggles with his hands.

"Neither do I," I pouted. "Stupid big bloke."

"Yes, he does sound like a bit of a stupid big bloke. Very eloquently put," said Jack.

"Yeah. Thanks. I'm feeling poetic. He was stupid, he was big, and he was a bloke. So, that's it."

Jack had the sense to look sympathetic although I could tell that he still found the whole thing hilarious. I wasn't sure whether it was the expression on his face or his emotions that I was reading most, but sometimes, it was rather useful having a built-in lie detector and other times, I just wished that I could have a normal interaction with someone, like a normal person. I looked down at my dinner. I felt a bit low all of a sudden and didn't want to spoil the evening with depressing thoughts. I was being silly. I was out on a date with Jack, and I couldn't let a stupid big bloke or my silly emotional baggage get in the way of having fun. I looked back up and caught his eye. He gave me a flash of his dazzling smile. I smiled back, allowed myself to draw on his unceasingly positive energy and on the emotions swirling around the room, where everyone was having a splendid time, and I felt better.

"So, who was he?" Jack asked. "The big bloke? Do you know? Do you need me to go and duff him up for you?"

That had the desired effect of making me laugh out loud. The thought of Jack being violent towards anyone was absurd, and the idea of anyone going up against Daniel Callahan was even more ludicrous. I had only met him once, briefly, but I had no doubt that he could handle himself physically, and he didn't seem like the sort to take prisoners. He was a powerful, cold man.

"I'd never seen him before. Helen said he was the new IT guy. Apparently, the school's getting new computers. Daniel Callahan's his name."

Jack sucked in a breath and let out a low whistle.

"Daniel Callahan? Of *The* Callahans?" he asked.

"*The* Callahans?" I repeated. "You say that like it's something I should know."

"Where have you been?" he asked in astonishment. "The Callahans are the new big thing in Ramsay Bridge. They moved into the old Ramsay place up on the hill. They must be absolutely loaded. Like, millionaires loaded." He sounded impressed.

"Oh, really? That's the first I've heard of it. I thought that house was empty. It's been empty forever."

I looked across the lake, up the hill and realised that I could see an extra light twinkling in the darkness. It was strange to think that the man who had had a hand in spoiling my day might be up there right now.

"It was," said Jack. "They've not been around long. Apparently, the other son is a builder. He's going to be doing the place up."

"Ugh," I groaned. "There are two of them?"

Jack laughed. "Yeah. The dad is some hotshot lawyer. He's been on the news. You must have heard of him. The one that never loses a case?"

"Nicholas Callahan?" I was impressed. "Yes, I've heard

of him. I didn't know he'd moved to Ramsay Bridge, though. He got some murderer off on a technicality, didn't he? It was all over the news. Apparently, everyone knew the guy was guilty. Poor family."

"Hmm … Maybe," Jack said noncommittally. "Although what if he was innocent? Surely we have to trust the system?"

"I don't know," I said. "Normally I'd agree with you, but the stuff I read was pretty convincing. It sounded like everyone thought the conviction was a sure thing." I thought for a moment. "Isn't that weird, though? I mean, if he's a hotshot barrister who never loses a case, wouldn't he want to live in the city, where all the action is?"

"Maybe he wanted to bring his family somewhere nice. You've got to admit the Ramsay Place is impressive. The land stretches right down to the lake. Daddy Callahan probably won't be around much anyway," Jack said.

"Yeah, I suppose." I was thoughtful. "Well, that probably explains Daniel's attitude. If Daddy's rich and he's used to getting everything, it must be a terrible inconvenience when one of the riff-raff falls over in your way, and you probably don't have much use for manners."

Jack laughed again. "Isabel, I don't think I've ever seen you take against a person like this before. And someone you've only just met. It isn't like you at all. I quite like it, though. This Daniel Callahan must be quite something."

Jack was right. It wasn't like me at all. I had conflicts with disgruntled parents and unruly kids and met my fair share of unpleasant people. I had been brought low and made to feel terrible by nasty, violent emotions of others, but I was usually able to put it behind me quickly. I couldn't remember ever coming away from someone with such a strong and lasting negative impression. It was his utter lack of emotion that had affected me so much. I could cope with anger. I could cope with pain. I could cope with all of the negative emotions that came my way with enough concentration, energy and time to process, but I couldn't cope with the void that I had encountered in Daniel Callahan. I didn't understand it, and it had upset me more than I had realised.

"I know," I said. "It's weird. I don't know what's come over me." I laughed it off. I didn't want Jack to see how affected I really was. "Anyway, enough about the stupid big bloke. Tell me more about your day, please."

We spent the rest of the evening enjoying each other's company, eating fabulous food and making one another laugh. By the end of the night, Daniel Callahan was just a bad memory and I had managed to put the Nelsons far out of my mind.

"I feel a bit sad that I have to wait two weeks before taking you out again," said Jack. "How do you think Donna would take it if you cancelled girls' night next week?"

"Are you kidding?" I laughed. "She'd actually murder me."

"Yeah. That's probably fairly accurate," he agreed. "OK, we won't risk it. So, what have you girls got planned?"

"Next week's movie night. Proper movie night at The Vestige Cinema in town. I love sitting in their comfy chairs and drinking my lemonade out of a real glass."

"Oh, yes. You know it's classy when you get your drinks in an actual glass made of glass," Jack agreed. "Although I'm still not convinced having a glass and a comfy chair makes those extortionate prices acceptable."

"I don't get to be posh very often. Just let me enjoy it without feeling guilty," I chided.

"Sorry. Of course," said Jack contritely. "It's your night. I'm sure you'll have a lovely time."

"We will indeed," I agreed. "What are you and Stu up to?"

"Not sure yet." He shrugged. "We'll just see how the mood takes us."

We lapsed into a companionable silence and I closed my eyes, enjoying the soporific feeling of the motion of the car, a couple of glasses of wine and a lovely evening spent in pleasant company. Jack put his hand on my knee, and I covered it with my own and gently stroked his palm with my thumb.

"Thank you, Jack," I murmured as I drifted off. He might have replied. He probably said something lovely, but I didn't hear him. I was fast asleep.

Chapter 5

I continued to monitor Josh closely after the frustrating meeting with Richard and Chrissy and the equally frustrating conversation with his mum. I also kept up with my diary of his mood and behaviour. I knew that it would become useful when we ultimately discovered what was causing Josh's distress because I was beyond trying to convince myself that I was seeing things that weren't there. Josh was in some sort of trouble, and it was only a matter of time before he opened up to me or I figured him out. For now, without his confidence, my hands were tied.

Recording Josh's emotions in a book that one day, ordinary people might read was difficult because of my sensitivity to what was going on in his mind. I tried not to write down things that other people wouldn't see and only to identify what he would look like to someone without my awareness of his emotional state. Unfortunately, I was forced to admit that for a four-year-old, he was a master of masking his feelings. He gave very little away, and it was no wonder that the rest of the staff weren't worried. Still, I knew that I was right, and I persevered.

As usual, Josh's father dropped him off at school on Monday morning. Mr Nelson never lingered or sought me out but always seemed good humoured and gave me a friendly nod every day. When I concentrated my senses on him, he seemed a little on edge at times but never in turmoil or pain, and his emotions were never as intense as those that I sensed in Josh.

My Little Owls were working on letter formation and finding out facts about dinosaurs for their next class project.

"'D' for dinosaur," I said. "I want you all to write a 'd' for dinosaur on your page, please, and then another one straight after it. Remember, around his bottom, up his tall neck, down to his feet." I hovered over Josh's work for a moment. "Wow! Well done, Josh. This is lovely. You've been practising, haven't you?"

Josh visibly brightened at the praise. "Yes, Miss," he said. "Mummy and me practise our letters every day."

"Well, the practice shows, Josh. That deserves a sticker." I stuck a gold star on his chart. My heart swelled when I felt just how much my recognition meant to him. The joy shone out of him, not replacing his characteristic churning anxiety but sitting on the surface of it, masking it while the distraction lasted. I had found that if I could keep him totally absorbed at all times, I could keep his distress at bay, but with a class of nineteen children who all needed me, it was impossible for me to focus on Josh enough to keep his emotional state under control at all times. However, I did remain hypervigilant and made a special effort to bolster his spirits whenever I could.

"Now, after you've each written five 'd's, I want you to come up to my desk, show me your work and then pick up a dinosaur picture to colour in. Then you'll take it in turns to come to the computer with me and we'll do some research and find out a dinosaur fact to share with the class," I explained. "I'd like to see some really nice colouring, please. Not just scribbling. Sammy, try to stay in the lines."

Paul's hand shot up.

"Yes, Paul?" I said.

"I already know lots of dinosaur facts," he announced proudly. "I know that Plesiosaurs lived under water and ate fish."

"Wow, Paul, excellent fact," I applauded.

"Does anyone else already know a dinosaur fact they would like to share with the class?"

"T-rexes had big teeth and ate people," said Ben.

I smiled. "Well, they did have big teeth and they were carnivores, but they didn't eat people, did they, because people didn't live at the same time as dinosaurs. Good try, though, Ben, but please remember to put your hand up and only share with the class when you're invited to."

"Yes, Miss," said Ben.

Jane had her hand high in the air.

"Yes, Jane? What's your fact?"

"Dinosaurs hatched out of eggs," said Jane confidently.

"Another excellent fact. I didn't know we already had so many dinosaur experts in the class." I looked around. "Yes, Melissa?"

"Dinosaurs turned into monkeys and monkeys turned into humans, so we all used to be dinosaurs," she said. "It's called evolution."

"No, Miss," Sammy interrupted before I had a chance to speak. "That's not right. Dinosaurs didn't evolve, they died."

"Well, firstly, Melissa, you have a good grasp of evolution, and that's a wonderful big word for such a little girl, but I'm afraid Sammy's right. The dinosaurs didn't evolve. They did, in fact, die. Well, it's actually much more complicated than that, but we'll stick with the basics for now, I think."

Melissa looked crestfallen.

"When we talk about evolution, I'll know who to come to, though, won't I?" I continued quickly, restoring her bruised pride. "Does anyone know what happened to the dinosaurs?" I asked. "How they died?"

There was silence in the class, but I could see Josh nodding his head. He hadn't raised his hand, but I picked on him anyway.

"Josh? Do you know what happened to the dinosaurs?"

"Yes, Miss," he answered.

"Could you tell the rest of the class then, please?" I encouraged him.

"A big rock called a meteor hit the earth and everything, including all the dinosaurs, died," he said dramatically. He was beginning to enjoy himself.

"Goodness me," I said. "Another fabulous fact." I looked at his page. "There are five excellent 'd's on this page, Josh. Would you like to come with me and be the first investigator finding out another fantastic dinosaur fact?"

"Yes, please, Miss," Josh replied. He was becoming engrossed in the topic and I could feel his anxiety ebbing away and his spirit lifting, breaking through his fog.

"Come with me, then," I said.

I knew that I should avoid favouritism in front of the class to prevent any division developing between Josh and his peers, but it was difficult not to make him the focus of my attentions when I was so wholeheartedly invested in his welfare and when I was the only person who could sense the conflict taking place inside his mind. I put my hand on his shoulder and guided him to the computer. He relaxed a little further under my charge and remained brighter and more settled for the rest of the day. He already had a keen interest in dinosaurs, so he was thoroughly absorbed in his tasks, and as long as he was occupied, I couldn't sense as much of the usual tension from him. Four-year-olds were always eager and willing to immerse themselves in the moment, and despite his troubles, Josh was no exception.

Mrs Nelson was on the playground at 3.25, and at first glance, appeared to be her usual pristine self in a long black coat with a faux fur hood, knee length brown boots and matching gloves. However, when I observed more closely, I realised that Mrs Nelson looked exhausted. She had done her best to disguise the dark circles framing her eyes by using pale makeup, but I could see that her smile was an act. In fact, even as I watched, I saw her sway with fatigue, unable to maintain her facade. As usual, Josh was thrilled to see his mum and charged across the playground for a hug. There was tension and agitation emanating relentlessly from Mrs Nelson across the playground, and watching her, I began to wonder whether it was actually Mrs Nelson that had the problem and if Josh's distress was perhaps as a direct result of sympathy and concern for his mother rather than his own burden. I fervently hoped that there was nothing seriously wrong as I watched the pair leave the playground, arms linked, radiating affection for one another.

On Tuesday I was doing some phonics blending with the children, working on their early literacy skills. I already had pupils like Melissa and Jane who were progressing admirably, able to successfully blend the easy consonant-vowel-consonant words and working on reading sentences, and I had others, like Sammy Harris, who weren't quite there yet but who were eager to learn and making great headway with letter recognition and blending. I was working with Sammy.

"Can you recognise these sounds, Sammy?" I asked him, pointing to the page on the table in front of us.

"'S'." Sammy pointed to the first letter.

"Excellent," I praised him, "and the next?"

"'A'," said Sammy. "That's a 'a'."

"You're absolutely right," I said. "And the last one?"

"'T', 't', 't'," he repeated, using the phonics skills that we had been learning, "That's a 't'. Down the tower, across the tower."

"Perfect," I said. "OK, Sammy. So, we have 's'...'a'...'t'. Can you say those sounds again for me?"

"'S'...'a'...'t'," Sammy repeated.

"That's right. And again, a little closer together?"

"'S'...'a'...'t'," Sammy said again.

"Perfect. Now, keep repeating those sounds and putting them closer and closer together until you recognise the word."

"'S'...'a'...'t'," chimed Sammy. "'S'...'a'...'t'. 'S'...'a'...'t'. 'S'..'a'..'t'. 'S'...'a'.'t', S.at. Mat!" he announced. "It says mat."

I stifled a groan. "No, Sammy, close but not quite," I said. "It can't say mat, look, can it? It starts with a 's'. Try again for me."

"'S'...'a'...'t'," said Sammy again, slowly.

"That's right, well done. Now faster again."

"'S'..'a'..'t'. 'S'..'a'..'t'. 'S'..'at'. 'S'.'a'.'t'. Pat! Does it say pat?" he asked with almost as much confidence.

"No, Sammy. Good try, but it can't say pat, can it? It starts with a 's'," I reminded him again, trying not to lose my patience. "You already told me it starts with a 's', remember?" I said the sound with him this time. "Together then, Sammy. 'S'..'a'..'t'. 'S'..'a'..'t'. 'S'.'a'.'t'. 'S'.'at'. Sat." I gave him the answer, fearing that I was beginning to lose the will to live and that we could be stuck on this word for all of eternity.

"Sat!" shouted Sammy. "It says sat. It says sat!"

"Excellent reading, Sammy. Well done. Now, can you try to cut these shapes out and stick them onto that dinosaur over there? Good boy. Josh?" I called.

Josh left his cutting of dinosaur shapes and came to sit with me. He had his reading record out of his bag to display proudly. I saw that his mum had filled it in that morning, recording that he had read his whole book over breakfast. She had drawn him a smiley face too.

"I see you and Mummy have been practising again," I said, "and it looks as if she's very proud of you."

His face lit up. "I like to make Mummy proud of me," he told me.

"Of course you do, Josh. Do you want to read it to me?"

He nodded and did a lovely job of reading the simple words from his book. The sadness continued to cling to him and threatened to infect me whenever we worked this closely together, but despite his disadvantage, he had settled nicely into the routines of school life and continued to find one-to-one work with me highly reassuring.

Once again, Josh's mood improved as it neared home time and he knew that he was going to see his mum, and once again, I watched closely as he ran to her across the playground. This time, when he threw his arms around her waist, Mrs Nelson visibly winced and doubled over with a pain that made her gasp out loud, clutching at her stomach. I immediately felt the reactive surge of emotional distress from Josh, a tremendous wave of guilt.

"I'm sorry, Mummy!" he cried. "I didn't mean to hurt you. I didn't mean it."

I was shocked by the force of Josh's guilt. It seemed like an astonishing overreaction. It was obvious that he hadn't hurt her on purpose and that Mrs Nelson was strangely weak. She was clearly in considerable pain and had turned a worrying shade of pale, but she tried desperately to mask it and reassure him.

"Of course you didn't, Josh. Don't you worry. I'm fine," she said, but Josh couldn't be consoled, and I watched helplessly as he cried out his self-reproach.

I took a step towards them to offer my support, but Mrs Nelson saw me and stopped me with a dismissive wave and a shake of her head. Josh and his mum fought to support each other as they walked slowly away.

Watching this display, I reflected over the past few weeks again. I thought about all of the times that Josh had seemed frightened or in pain but with no injuries or explanation on his body. Could his emotions be attributed to sympathy for his mum? Was he a frightened little boy with a physically failing mother, thinking the worst, terrified of what was going to happen to her as she deteriorated? Could she be seriously ill? The dark circles were more prominent. I realised that behind the nice clothes and the perfect makeup, Mrs Nelson actually looked awful. If she was seriously poorly, though, why wouldn't Josh talk to me about that? Why would it be a secret? I promised myself that, armed with this new clue, I would tackle Josh again tomorrow. It was time that I got some answers.

Wednesday was the day that Mrs Nelson routinely dropped Josh off at school while his father worked away, but this Wednesday Josh arrived with his dad, and there was no mistaking the fact that Mr Nelson was on edge too. He tried to force out a smile and give me his usual cheery nod, but I wasn't convinced. Mr Nelson was suffering. I could feel a mixture of unidentifiable emotions churning him up inside. I tried to reach him across the classroom in order to get a better read on him and to broach the subject of his wife's health, but on the way, I was intercepted by Melissa's mum, Mrs Willis, who wanted to show me Melissa's latest swimming badge. She was not the sort of parent to be dissuaded.

"Wow!" I exclaimed, turning my attention to the bouncing little girl. "Melissa, this is incredible. Level two already? What a star. Can we keep the certificate to show in assembly on Friday?"

Melissa's mum nodded. Melissa was skipping with joy and wearing a smile a mile wide. She had been dying to share her news and it was important that I gave her my full attention. I could see how much it meant to share her achievement with me. Melissa's delight was infectious, and I was boosted by it too. I glanced around, but Mr Nelson had already gone. My intervention would have to wait. Melissa was still tapping me on the arm.

"I got a badge too," she beamed. "Look, Miss. It's a starfish!"

"A starfish!" I repeated. "Well, that's amazing, well done, you. Right, that's a sticker on your chart, and we'd better put these away somewhere very safe so we can show the rest of the school in our celebration assembly on Friday." I put the certificate and badge in my drawer and added a gold star to Melissa's chart. "Oh my goodness!" I cried. "That's star number twenty-five on Melissa's chart. Little Owls, Little Owls, let's all gather round, please, and congratulate Melissa."

I had taught the children how to form a congratulation circle, which we did now while I led them in three cheers and a round of applause. Melissa could hardly contain her joy. Twenty-five stickers was a major triumph for a Little Owl. However, I couldn't help my focus veering to Josh again. He was on the edge of the circle, clapping along with his friends, but his heart wasn't in it. As I had suspected, things hadn't improved after yesterday's incident on the playground. His fear and sadness were as palpable as ever, and I could feel the weight of the emotional energy pulling at me, threatening to drag me down. It took an intense effort to push it away, and I couldn't imagine how a four-year-old was coping with such complex, oppressive emotions. It was little wonder that he struggled to appreciate the triumph of Melissa's swimming award.

I spent all morning trying to find an opportunity to speak to Josh alone, but it finally came shortly after lunch. I left the rest of the class cutting out and sticking dinosaur shapes with Mrs Bishop and took him into the corridor. I sat down next to him so that I could look him in the eye. His usual troubling emotions were bubbling away. I wanted to cry for him. It just wasn't fair.

"Josh," I began. "I'm worried about you." He stared at the floor. "Look at me, Josh. Tell me what's wrong." He looked up. I could see tears swimming in his eyes. He didn't speak. I gave him a few seconds to see if he could find the words and then I continued. "I'm worried about you, Josh, and I'm worried about your mum." His eyes widened and a tear slipped out of each and trickled down his cheeks. He wiped them away furiously with his sleeve but still didn't speak.

"Josh," I continued. "I want to help you but it's hard if you won't talk to me." I could feel the tears stinging my own eyes, responding to his pain and his fear. "Is it your mum, Josh? Are you worried about her?"

He looked at me then, really looked at me, shock written plainly across his face. "How do you know?" he asked quietly. "You're not supposed to know." He whispered this last sentence so that I only just heard. I had the urge to grab him and hug him and make the pain go away. He shouldn't be having to keep secrets that were so clearly tearing him up inside.

"I can just tell, Josh," I said. "I can tell there's something wrong and I think if you talk to me about it, I might be able to help."

I felt a surge of hope from Josh. He wanted to believe me. He wanted my help. He wanted to unload this burden. I held my breath, but the hope lasted only an instant and the wall came straight back up.

"You can't help, Miss. No one can help. Daddy said so. He doesn't want us to talk about it. He says it's not real if we don't talk about it."

I felt a welling of sympathy as well as anger towards Mr Nelson as I heard these words, convinced more than ever that the problem was a serious illness with his wife. It sounded like he was in denial. It must be difficult for him if his wife was poorly and he was refusing to deal with it or even acknowledge it or ask for help. I wondered whether he was forcing Mrs Nelson into silence on the subject too or if she agreed with this course of action, possibly even mistakenly thinking that it was the right thing for Josh, that, as he said, it's not real if they don't talk about it. I wondered how far they might take it and if there was a chance that Mrs Nelson wasn't even receiving proper treatment. She had looked so weak the previous day. She clearly needed help.

I knew that there was no right way to deal with situations like this and everyone had to find their own path. I also knew that denial was common. It couldn't be healthy, though, not in the long run. They must not have been aware of what a negative impact it was having on Josh. It was affecting his schoolwork, his relationships with his peers and his personality, and I couldn't allow it to go on. I was cross with the pair of them for putting him in this position. He was four. It wasn't right that he couldn't share what he was going through. He needed support as well. They were his parents and they were acting selfishly. It was their responsibility to put his needs above theirs, and if they couldn't, then I would have to help him myself. I resolved to tackle his parents again and to speak to Chrissy and find out who to talk to outside of the school. We could offer help, and social services could be involved if the Nelsons refused to accept our assistance, but things could not be allowed to continue on their present course.

That afternoon, Mr Nelson was waiting on the playground in place of his wife again. I called him over and took a deep breath.

"Mr Nelson, I'm worried about Josh. I'm worried about Mrs Nelson too, and you. I noticed she didn't seem too well yesterday when she came to pick Josh up, and she hasn't been here today. Is there anything the school can do to help you?"

Although he tried to hide it, at my questioning, Mr Nelson became angry very quickly. I felt the responding anger rise in myself, and as the energy spilled from him into me, I had to fight to stamp it down. Anger was a strong emotion, and Mr Nelson was carrying more than his fair share. It was a little frightening. He was a little frightening. He composed himself quickly, but the mask was beginning to slip.

"You're mistaken, Miss Bliss," he said firmly. "My wife is fine. She'll be fine. We do not require your help." He wasn't going to accept any assistance voluntarily, that was clear. "Josh, tell your teacher that we don't need her help," he barked.

"We're fine, Miss," said Josh quietly, looking at the ground. I could sense that he was frightened too, and I wished that there was a way to make it stop.

"OK." I held my hands up. I was defeated, for now. Pushing would only make the matter worse. "The offer is always there."

Mr Nelson didn't respond but turned his back on me, took Josh firmly by the arm and stormed angrily across the playground. I fervently hoped that I hadn't done more harm than good.

On Thursday morning, Josh arrived late to school. His dad dropped him off at the door and deliberately didn't make eye contact with me. No pleasant smile, no friendly nod, but I was highly aware of him from across the room. The stress was coming off him thick and fast. He turned on his heel and quickly walked away while I turned to Josh, whose feelings were so intense that I found it hard to concentrate on anything else. It was even worse than that first time, the time that it had taken my breath away. I wondered whether that had been a significant date for the family, a diagnosis perhaps. I tried to combat the negativity pulling him down, but all morning, Josh hardly said a word. I felt terrible. I knew that trying to talk to Mr Nelson yesterday had backfired and made things worse. Perhaps I had forced him to confront the issue, even just in his own mind. I hoped that I hadn't damaged Josh's confidence in me. I was out of my depth and more sure than ever that I needed guidance from a professional. I didn't have the skills or the authority to help the Nelsons with this burden.

Mrs Bishop commented on Josh's distraction. "Is he sick?" she asked.

"I don't think so," I replied. "Just worried and terribly sad." I hated to admit it, but maybe it was a good thing that other people had begun to notice that there was a problem. It might make it easier for me to garner assistance from elsewhere.

I ached to go and put my arms around him and make the pain go away, like my mum had always done for me when I was sad or hurting inside, but I knew that I didn't have that kind of power. My influence wasn't strong enough to make this pain go away. I continued to bombard Josh with all of the positive energy that I could muster and hoped that it was enough to make a difference.

More than anything, Josh just seemed exhausted all of that day. He was subdued and quiet. He wasn't concentrating on the tasks that I set for him, and he didn't mix with the other children at break or lunchtime. Even dinosaurs couldn't encourage him to engage. After lunch, one of the dinner ladies called in to let me know that Josh hadn't touched his food.

"It was cottage pie today," she said, "and he usually loves his cottage pie. Do you think he's poorly?"

"Thank you for letting me know," I sighed. "I'll talk to him this afternoon."

I had some numeracy planned with the children in the afternoon. We were working on one more than and one fewer than, and usually, Josh was one of the sharpest when it came to mental arithmetic and would answer my questions quickly. I gave out a box of counters and asked all of the children to count out five into a pile. I then asked them to make two other piles of counters, one with one more than five and one with one fewer. I walked around the room, helping those who struggled and pointing out mistakes or praising those that got it right. Mrs Bishop was also on hand.

"Right. Do we all have three piles of counters?" I asked. There was a general chorus of assent. I hovered at Josh's table. "Josh, you only have two piles, sweetie. One with five and one with one more than five. Can you also make a pile with one fewer than five, please?"

Josh promptly burst into tears. "I'm sorry, Miss Bliss," he cried. "I'm … sorry."

"It doesn't matter, Josh. Really, it doesn't matter." I tried to soothe him whilst fighting back the sadness threatening to engulf me. I wished that I could switch it off, that I could erect some kind of wall to block out the emotion. It was hard enough as it was trying to deal with Josh amongst a class of eighteen other children, without being bombarded by this languishing energy. It was exhausting, and it was all that I could do not to dissolve into tears myself. Josh was so tired and so sad, it appeared that he had simply let go. It was shocking to see, and I was being suffocated, dragged under by his misery. It would be too easy to give in to it and let it crash over me, but I couldn't allow myself that weakness. I had to be strong. It took everything that I had to fight off the encroaching despair, and I didn't have the strength left to help lift Josh's spirits. The other children in the class had started murmuring and a few had left their seats, walking over to Josh to see what was going on. I decided that I had to remove him from the classroom for a while.

"Josh? Come with me, darling. Let's take a break," I said, holding my hand out to him. He took it and seemed to draw some strength from it, but I could feel how churned up he was inside. I couldn't allow this to carry on. "Mrs Bishop? Can you just carry on with them for a bit, please? Josh and I are going to take some time out."

"Of course. Take your time," Mrs Bishop said with a reassuring smile.

I took Josh to the staffroom. All of the teachers were in their classes and the administration staff were busy, so it was refreshingly empty. I sat him down and crouched next to him, offering him my hand again. He took it and looked up at me with big, sad eyes. I felt myself welling up again in response.

"Josh," I began, "I wish you would talk to me. Can you tell me why you're so tired and upset today?"

Josh sniffed. "Sorry, Miss, I'm fine, Miss. It's fine, Miss."

"No, Josh, you're not fine, and it's OK to talk to someone when you're upset."

Josh continued to sniffle but didn't say anything more. His eyes were drooping.

"You look like you need a sleep, Josh. Are you tired?"

"Yes, Miss," he said.

"Are you not getting enough sleep at home?"

He just looked at me but didn't answer.

"OK. You just wait here for a moment. I'll be back in a minute." I left him in the staffroom while I knocked on the door of the Year 5 class.

"Sorry to interrupt, Kingfishers," I told them. "I just need to borrow Miss Brooks for a moment, if that's OK?" Chrissy came to the door.

"Is there a problem?" she asked.

"Yes," I replied. "It's Joshua Nelson. He's having a really bad day, and I wanted you to see for yourself."

"Of course," said Chrissy, and leaving her class with their teaching assistant, she followed me back to the staffroom.

Josh looked up. His agitation increased when he saw that I had brought another grown-up with me.

"Miss Brooks is going to join us for a minute, OK, Josh?" I said.

"OK," said Josh. "That's fine."

I turned to Chrissy. "Josh is very tired today, Miss Brooks. He couldn't concentrate in my lesson, and when I spoke to him, he began to cry. We stepped out for a break. As you know, I've been worried about him for a little while now, and I'm also worried about his mum."

Josh's eyes widened again. "I'm fine, Miss," he said, his wild eyes darting fearfully between the two of us. "I'm fine," he said again, but he couldn't hold back the tears, and they began to fall freely down his face. I fetched him a tissue, and he wiped his eyes and nose and fought valiantly to get himself back under control.

"I just want to talk to you, Josh," said Chrissy. "It's nothing to worry about. Is that OK?"

She smiled at him, but he looked to me for reassurance. I nodded. He reached for my hand but agreed with a hesitant nod.

"OK, good," she said. "Can you tell me why you're so tired today, Josh? Have you been having trouble sleeping?"

Josh looked at me again and I gave his hand a squeeze.

"It's OK, Josh. Just answer Miss Brook's questions. Just be honest," I encouraged.

"Maybe I haven't been sleeping very well," Josh admitted, "but I'm fine."

Chrissy smiled at him. "It's all right if you're not fine, Josh. You can talk to me about it. Is there anything you'd like to tell us?" she asked.

Josh glanced at me again before speaking. I was his

anchor. There was a long pause. "No, thank you. I'm fine," he said eventually, and I stifled a frustrated sigh.

Chrissy continued. "Miss Bliss said that she was worried about your mum as well," she said. "How is your mum? Is she having trouble sleeping too?"

Fresh tears threatened to fall and his face was pale, but Josh had his walls back up. He wasn't going to break his silence. "She's fine," he said, and he looked at the floor, a signal that the conversation was over.

"OK, Josh. Well, thank you for talking to me." Chrissy turned to me. "He isn't going to learn anything today, Miss Bliss. Do you want to call his parents and have them collect him early?"

Josh looked terror-stricken and I felt an ice-cold finger of dread prickle down my spine. His fear cut through my defences, and I felt and shared his panic, almost crying out myself. He jumped up from his chair, pushing it over in his haste, and shouted, "No!" There was silence. He quickly saw the startled looks on our faces and calmed himself down. "No, thank you," he said quietly. "I don't want to go home. I don't need to go home early. Please don't call my parents. I'm fine. I want to stay here. I'm fine … I am fine," he pleaded.

I swallowed the fear coursing through me, looked at Chrissy again and Chrissy nodded.

"OK then, Josh," I said. "You can stay at school, but I'm going to put some cushions on the floor in our classroom and I want you to take it easy for the rest of the day. Deal?" I offered.

"Thank you, Miss," Josh gushed. "Yes, I'll be good. I'll be fine," he said.

I escorted Chrissy out into the corridor. We spoke in a whisper.

"You're going to have to speak to his mum when she picks him up," said Chrissy.

"I know," I agreed. "But his dad's picked him up the last

couple of days. I tried to speak to him yesterday. It didn't go well."

"OK, well, just let whichever one know that Josh has been under the weather. You don't need to go into specifics. After school, come find me and we'll start a report. You can speak to Early Help tomorrow."

"Thanks," I said, relieved. "We really need to get the family some help. When you … when you suggested sending him home early, did you …? I mean, do you think …? He felt … I mean … he seemed scared. Did he seem scared to you?"

Chrissy nodded slowly. "Yes. He didn't like the idea of them knowing he wasn't fine, did he?"

It was my turn to shake my head.

"You're right, Izzy. Something's not right. Like I said, we'll start the report tonight and the referral tomorrow."

"Thanks, Chrissy," I said.

She nodded and returned to the Kingfishers while I fetched Josh from the staffroom and returned to the Little Owls, trying to get my trembling voice under control before I spoke.

"Everybody," I said when we arrived, "Josh is feeling a little under the weather. He's going to sit over here in the corner for a bit and have a rest. Let's all try really hard to be super quiet and caring for the rest of the day, shall we?"

"Miss?" It was Melissa.

"Yes, Melissa?"

"We should all be kind to Josh. He'll feel better if he has love in his heart," she said.

I couldn't help but smile. "Well, isn't that a lovely thing to say?" I looked at Josh with that smile. "We should all be kind to Josh, but let's do it quietly so that he can have some rest. OK?"

"Yes, Miss," replied Melissa, simultaneously making her fingers into the shape of a heart and pointing it towards Josh.

I made Josh comfortable and returned to my lesson. I

needed time to think about what I was going to say to his parent after school. I really hoped that it was his mum.

At 3.25, I had all of my Little Owls in their coats, lining up at the gate. I looked out around the playground and my heart sank. Mr Nelson was standing alone in the far corner. When it was Josh's turn to leave, I held him back and looked over with my brightest smile and beckoned to his dad. "Can I just have a quick word please, Mr Nelson?" I called.

He walked a little closer but remained too far away to manage a conversation, and he shouted back, "No, sorry, Miss, you can't. Josh and I are in a hurry tonight. I haven't got time to talk to you."

He stopped in the middle of the playground and beckoned to Josh. He clearly had no intention of coming any closer. I didn't have any choice except to let Josh go to him, but I followed Josh to where his dad was standing.

"Mr Nelson," I said, "just a quick word …"

But he pretended that I wasn't there and just walked away. I couldn't chase him out of the grounds, shouting at him, so again I had no choice except to let him go.

I called after them, "See you tomorrow, Josh. We can look for more footprints in Forest Schools if you like." And Josh turned and gave me a weak smile and a wave. I watched them leave and hcadcd straight back inside to talk to Chrissy and get the ball rolling with the referral to child services. I had to feel like I was doing something.

Josh didn't come to school on Friday.

Wrapped up against the cold in my thick winter coat and scarf, my gloved hands resting in my lap, I sat on Susan's bench overlooking the lake and I closed my eyes. I listened to the water as it lapped around the stones and tree roots. Driven in by the strong breeze, it splashed and gurgled noisily below the bank. The wind stirred the trees above my head, but I was sheltered from the elements, and I let my mind become settled by the natural sounds, distanced from human influence. I let the wind soothe my soul, my spirit floating upwards upon the currents. So often I craved this detachment from people, from traffic, from society: a disconnect from the emotions, the energy of the emotional world.

This haven had really saved my life over these last few weeks, with my uncertainty and my worry over Josh. I'm not sure if I would have survived without my sanctuary. I had been here every night, rain or shine, wrapped up against the cold, protected against the rain; it didn't matter, I didn't mind. I had to find a way to rebalance my mental health daily. I had to be vigilant over my state of mind, which I had felt slipping too often of late.

I found that day, that Friday, the day that Josh didn't show up to school, particularly difficult. I spent the first hour of the morning pacing the classroom, glancing nervously at the door, hoping that he would appear, frantically worrying about why he wasn't there. I knew that I had unsettled Mr Nelson by confronting him on Wednesday and that he had been avoiding me on Thursday. I had felt the tension in Josh increase when he joined his father on the playground, but I had no way of knowing how much of that was due to my involvement, how much was a genuine fear of his father and his temper or whether it was an anxiety about his mum and the reason behind her absence at school these last few days. What I did know was that the whole thing was turning me inside out, making me fractious, irritable and more susceptible to the stray emotional energies that seeped into my mind, catching me off-guard and fuelling my erratic behaviours.

I watched the other children running around the classroom, laughing with one another and playing as children should. For them, school was a playground, an opportunity to be with friends, let loose, hear stories, play and to simply be cared for and nurtured. The fact that they learned hundreds of new skills along the way was of little importance to them; it simply happened to them while they were busy celebrating life, which is exactly how I wanted my class to be. My ambition had always been for my pupils to reach the completion of the summer term having absorbed all of the information and the skills that I could impart without ever realising what had happened because they were too busy having fun.

I was normally proud of my teaching style. I was adored by the children, made them feel safe and secure, and I was usually fun to be around. I was enthusiastic about their progress and achievements, no matter how small, and had little need for punishment and discipline because they were so eager to please. In five years, I hadn't yet come across a child that I couldn't inspire to learn. I enthused children and parents alike. I put other people first. I listened and actually cared what people said, including those who were four years old, which is surprisingly uncommon. I had met individuals who had been teaching for their whole lives and still didn't care and some who apparently didn't like children at all.

That had never been me until Josh, until that week, that day when the stress over Josh changed me into an impatient, irritable monster. I couldn't stop thinking about him. He was tortured inside, and his torment was tormenting me. I had felt it for weeks and yet had been helpless to change the situation, unspeakably frustrated to know that there was a problem and unable to articulate it or explain it to anybody sufficiently, unable to help. I wanted so badly to take the wrongness away. I wanted other people to see it for themselves so that I could share the burden. I wanted Josh to be like these other children. I wanted him to be himself, to be free.

The fact that other members of staff were now beginning to see for themselves what I had known for weeks was partially satisfying because it signified an important change but partially terrifying because it meant that Josh's situation was worsening to the point that he could no longer hide it from the rest of the world. When he didn't come to school on that Friday, I experienced an awful, sick feeling in the pit of my stomach. What if I was too late? What if I had let Josh down by not rallying action sooner or made things worse by interfering in something that I didn't understand?

My ability to read emotions could be hugely rewarding. I used it to my advantage on countless occasions. It helped me learn how to approach a person or when someone was better left alone, and I could surround myself with people who radiated positive energy, fuelling my own mood and passions with those of others. Of course, it could also be a horribly unpleasant gift, causing me unwanted pain and anger that were not my own, but the majority of the time, I was able to limit those experiences and remove myself from those situations. One of the reasons that I loved teaching was children's amazing capacity for joy and their open, trusting honesty. Children were sad at times, and they could be frustrated and angry, but these negative emotions were invariably fleeting and easily combated with kindness and positivity.

The situation with Josh was a first: the first time that I had ever spent a prolonged period of time with someone who was suffering without being privy to the cause of their pain. It was confronting. My gift wasn't adequate under these circumstances. I had a glimpse, but it was not enough. Weeks down the line, I still didn't understand why Josh was suffering. The fact that he was a child in my care made it infinitely worse, and it was tearing me up inside. I couldn't focus on the rest of the class, which resulted in me feeling worse again because I was letting them down. My own emotions ended up being tangled up in knots and I didn't know how to feel. I even found myself snapping at Mrs Bishop, which was inexcusable, and I found it more difficult than normal to rebalance myself at the end of each day, especially today.

At about 10.00 a.m., Helen knocked on my classroom door and popped her head in. "I thought you'd want to know straight away," she said. "Mr Nelson's just been on the phone. He says Josh won't be in today. He's got an upset stomach."

"OK, thanks, Mrs Young. Thanks for letting me know."

I didn't know how I felt. I thought perhaps I felt a bit sick. I was certain that Josh didn't have an upset stomach, and my mind was filled with questions and concerns, but winding myself up wasn't helpful. It wouldn't do me any good, it wasn't fair on the rest of the class, and it certainly wasn't any use to Josh. I did manage to get back on track, and I made it successfully through the day. I worked hard with the children, threw myself into the fray, and we ended up having a great afternoon in Forest Schools despite the glaring hole in our ranks.

After Forest Schools, I handed Mrs Bishop the reins and took part in a telephone conference with a member of Early Help, *the first step in a coordinated multi-agency support network for families and young people in need.* I spoke to a lady called Sindi Wilkinson, who was wonderful on the phone. She seemed to really listen to my assessment of Josh and his family and to take it seriously, which was a huge relief, even though it was hard to communicate all of the things that I had seen or sensed without sounding crazy.

"I've known there was a problem with Josh for a few weeks," I said.

"Oh, really?" asked Sindi. "It looks like this is the first time the Nelsons have been referred for assessment."

"Yes, well, I did speak to my safeguarding coordinator and the headmaster last week, and I've been worried for longer. I've been keeping a diary, but they felt that there weren't grounds for referral before yesterday."

"Really?" asked Sindi. "What behaviours had you noted before this week, and why did your faculty take that view?"

This was the hard bit, the bit where I risked looking like a lunatic. "It's hard to explain," I tried. "I've been around reception class children for a few years now, and feel I'm tuned into them fairly well, and ... well ... Josh just hasn't

87

been right. I mean … he hasn't been feeling right. He's been upset and worried and … well … he just hasn't been right."

I wanted to scream that his emotions had been too intense for a four-year-old, that he had been full of gut-wrenching agony and that some days, his stress levels had been so high that I had had to leave the room because I couldn't get my own responding emotions under control, but I knew that it would be spectacularly unhelpful at that moment, so I bit my tongue.

"OK," Sindi said. "We put a lot of weight on a teacher's intuition, you know, Miss Bliss. What some people might think is your imagination getting the better of you, we often find can be very important information. Please continue."

I wanted to jump for joy. "Thank you so much," I said, and I went through the diary, detailing as much as I could up until the events of yesterday, including my attempts at conversations with Josh's parents and his failure to attend school today. Sindi seemed to take it all in.

"Thank you, Isabel," she said. "I'll put what you've told me into a report, and we'll be in touch with the Nelsons to arrange a meeting. We'll probably be contacting them on Tuesday or Wednesday next week to begin with. As part of our policy, we do ask that you report to the parents that you've spoken to us first. We find it makes maintaining good relations much easier in the long run, even if it can be hard for you. Parents who feel their children's teachers went behind their backs often find it much more difficult to get back to a meaningful relationship with that teacher down the line."

"Yes, I understand," I said, even though the thought of it filled me with dread.

"Great. OK, well, thank you again, Isabel. You've given me lots to think about. I'll get this written up and probably speak to you again on Monday. OK?"

"OK, thank you. Bye."

I hung up with a mixture of relief and terror. This was the

first time that I had reported a family in my career. I had no doubt that I had done the right thing and that this was the beginning of getting Josh and his family the support that they needed, but I felt physically sick when I imagined telling Mr Nelson that I had reported them to child services. However, Josh was my absolute priority, and hopefully, next week would be the start of a new chapter in his life. I hoped that it was a better chapter. For now, there was nothing more that I could do.

I sighed and focused on the present. I felt the sting of the wind against my cheeks and my hair being lifted and blown around my face. I felt the solid wood of the bench tying me to the physical world, supporting me and allowing me this time to reflect, absorb and let the emotions of the day be carried away on the breeze. I stood, stretched and walked to the edge of the lake. Darkness was approaching, and the evening light was casting strange, twisted shadows across the water. I felt like myself out here, with this time to connect with the earth, apart from people and all of their emotions and problems.

When I let go of the last of the jumble of feelings, I found myself almost at peace and ready for that peace to be shattered by a night out with my best friend, who was a fierce force of nature herself. It was movie night.

Chapter 6

An hour later, I pulled up outside Donna's flat and beeped my horn. Dressed comfortably in my black skinny jeans, knee-high brown suede boots and a red tartan shirt, I was also protected from the cold by my long black winter coat. I was looking forward to the evening and I felt all right, with all thoughts of Josh pushed firmly aside. I couldn't help him tonight.

A moment later, I felt like an aged, dowdy spinster as Donna skipped down the steps towards me with a huge, carefree smile and a wave. She was wearing an indecently short black skirt and low-cut sequin top. The outfit was totally inappropriate for the weather and the occasion, and I would not have dreamed of leaving the house in a single element of it, and yet somehow, Donna's confidence, personality and unadulterated beauty made it work. She always made it work and she never looked cheap or tasteless, just fearless and sexy as hell.

Donna was the life and soul of the party. She was a joy to be around, and she often unwittingly provided me with enough exhilaration to allow me to live on cloud nine for the rest of my life, if only it worked that way. In Donna's company, I could forget the stresses and strains of the real world and embrace her easy exuberance, which was exactly what I needed tonight. Before Donna even reached the car door, I felt my own spirit lifting, another step towards putting the remaining emotional turmoil and worry for Josh behind me.

Donna leapt into the car and threw her arms around me, giving me an enthusiastic hug and a kiss on each cheek. She leaned back, holding onto my shoulders, and looked into my eyes, concern etched across her face.

"How are you, gorgeous?" she asked. "You look a little tired and tense."

Donna and I had been best friends for a long time. She

knew me well enough to know when things weren't right, and although I'd never divulged the extent of my issues, she also knew that when things weren't right, they could quickly go from bad to worse. She always looked after me when I had an episode and trusted my instincts when I had a feeling about a person or a place. We always looked after each other.

"Gee, thanks," I responded with a short laugh. "I'm fine. Rough week at school but not something I want to talk about tonight. I feel better already for seeing you, though."

Donna took the hint. "My week's been full-on but really good," she said. "I've been in the city all week. I'm doing the regional links for the BBC now and getting airtime on the telly as well as the radio. On Wednesday I was at Broadcasting House in a team meeting with *Jeremy Vine*. It's all happening, Izzy. The hard work's paying off. I'm getting noticed and I'm starting to believe it might be for my work, not just my face."

I sighed. Donna had always had issues with the way that she looked. She was absolutely stunning, with long, wavy black hair, full lips, high cheekbones, dark brown eyes and rich, deep, flawless skin, but living in a rural village near the east coast of England, she was the only person of colour in our whole primary school. The numbers weren't much different at the secondary school in town, but none of the other kids ever cared. She was Donna Carpenter. She was clever, she was funny, and she was always popular, but being different had always been a problem for her. It wasn't that she was singled out negatively, treated badly or subjected to barbs or taunts. It was the simple fact that she was surrounded by people who all looked the same as each other, while she was the odd one out. It was impossible not to be aware of her difference and it coloured everything that she did. She called herself *The Poster Girl for Diversity,* and she was picked to be on the cover of the school prospectus, the front row of every choir concert, and college prefect. She always questioned whether she deserved her place or whether it was given to her because of the colour of her skin. Of course, the truth was that she was a straight A student with an exemplary school record and a beautiful singing voice, but Donna could never be sure, and the fact that she couldn't be sure tainted every achievement.

At university, she was no longer in quite such a minority, and being around people other than the white middle-class norm definitely helped, but Donna never really got over the feeling that she was ticking a box, and to prove to herself that she deserved the results, opportunities and accolades that she received, she put in twice as much work as her peers. She left university with a first in a bachelor's degree in journalism and a distinction in a master's degree in broadcast journalism. It was no surprise to anyone except Donna that she was going places in her career, but she was determined to go all the way, to ensure that her face would be seen by other children growing up like her who needed to see other faces like their own. She was spending more and more time away from the village, commuting to London on a semi-regular basis by then. I was happy for her but also a little terrified that I would be losing her to the city before long.

Donna and I both knew what it was like to be different. Perhaps it was our differences that drew us to each other. Her variance was on the surface and obvious to see, while mine was a little less obvious and a lot more complicated, but we always had each other's back and never belittled the other's angst.

"You know you're the best," I told her. "I don't think anyone thinks twice about the colour thing when they look at you. Why would they? You're so talented, and everyone falls in love with you at first sight. It's not the same in the BBC anyway; they recruit talent from that there London, and I've heard it's not at all like Ramsay Bridge down there."

Donna laughed. "You can say that again."

I laughed easily for what felt like the first time in a long time. Donna's charisma was infectious, and I relaxed.

I didn't have many close friends. I found it difficult to maintain relationships because of my sensitivity and my total inability to switch off the emotional radar when it became inconvenient. It meant that I often inadvertently reflected people's moods back at them, so if someone was feeling low, the mood could quickly spiral downwards, making me uneasy company. I tried to avoid anger and arguments for the same reasons, but what I found most demanding was that people's emotions often gave away their integrity, and I had discovered that there are actually surprisingly and saddeningly few genuinely honest people in the world. Jack and Donna, my two closest friends, were honest, reliable and almost perpetually cheerful, making them two of the only people that I could be around consistently without unpleasant incidents. I was lucky to have two such genuine people in my life. They were both also tirelessly patient with me because being around me did demand incredible patience, and although they didn't totally understand me, they gave me time and space without question and loved me in spite of it all.

I listened contentedly to Donna's stories on the drive, and it wasn't long before we left Ramsay Bridge behind and arrived at The Vestige Cinema on the edge of town. It was a beautiful old, listed building that had been converted into a cinema only about a year ago and was unlike any other, with grand, comfortable armchair-style seats and a choice of classic cinema rows, two-seater sofas and pods of up to six seats together. Somehow, no one got in anyone else's way. The angles and partitions were arranged so that each seat provided an unobstructed view of the screen.

There was a modern, classy bar downstairs that served snacks and drinks, and its extensive cocktail list drew many cinema goers to arrive early and remain late to eat and chat over liquid refreshments. There was an ordering system that attached food and drinks to seat numbers, and in homage to bygone days, the interval had been reintroduced, during

93

which customers could return to the bar or order drinks via the app and have them delivered to their seats.

I parked the car and followed Donna into the bar tentatively. I was always slightly on edge when going into a busy public space, but the high prices at The Vestige tended to attract a more refined, gentler customer, keeping the rougher clientele in the centre of town where they could find cheaper drinks, and more likely, an opponent for an argument or a fight. I couldn't afford to frequent The Vestige often, but when I did, I consistently found it to be a safe night for me, full of positive energy. Tonight felt like a good night, and as we worked our way to the bar, my head swivelled and my mind hummed as I took stock of the emotions floating around the room. I felt a heady mixture of anticipation, camaraderie, happiness and a trace of lust from the young couple in the corner who were leaning towards each other, whispering endearments into one another's ears. I glanced away, blushing at my inadvertent stumble into their intimate moment.

Donna reached the bar first and ordered a gin and tonic. "Are you going to have a drink tonight, Izzy?" she asked. "I can bring you back down for your car in the morning, no trouble."

"No thanks," I said. "I need plenty of rest this weekend. It's going to be full-on again at work next week."

"All the more reason to let loose a bit tonight," suggested Donna with a wink.

"Honestly, I'm not up for a big one. I'll just have a lime and tonic, thanks."

"Coming right up."

Donna didn't push. I regularly abstained from alcohol on a night out, but a drink only ever enhanced her joyful spirit and never brought her down. I had more to consider and would always assess the vibes of our venue first, but more often than not, I would remain sober, happy to observe and enjoy the inebriated pleasure of my companions, experiencing the effects of their emotions vicariously without the risk of a hangover the following day. I also found it more difficult to control the flow of emotional energy under the influence, making it more dangerous if I did come into contact with any particularly unpleasant feelings.

Donna set up a tab at the bar and ordered two boxes of sweet popcorn, and we made our way straight to our seats in front of the big screen. We always prebooked a luxurious two-seater settee, where we could kick off our shoes, put our feet up and chat over drinks until the film began.

As we neared the top of the stairs, an unusual prickling sensation made the hairs on the back of my neck stand on end. The familiar fluttering feeling was back, and I instinctively glanced behind me. Two men had just entered the bar, and the one in front was unmistakable due to his height, his build and the curious emotional vacuum that surrounded him. Daniel Callahan still gave me a weird sense of déjà vu, and it had reached me from the other side of the room. I couldn't comprehend how I could be affected so strongly by his *nothing*. It had no substance, no form, no taste, no smell. It seemed by its very nature not to exist, and yet I felt it. I sensed him, and I had the same uneasy feeling that I had had in the staffroom, the unmistakable awareness of being watched, of being scrutinised.

As if on cue, Daniel Callahan looked up in my direction. He didn't need to search me out. He could feel me just as I could feel him. He lifted his head, and his eyes latched onto mine instantly, reaching inside my mind and freezing me in place with his icy glare. He didn't hold my gaze for more than a couple of seconds, looking quickly away with an expression of distaste, but it was more than long enough. I felt violated. When I bumped into Daniel at school, I was highly aware of and unusually unsettled by his lack of emotion, but here, surrounded by normal people and normal emotions, it was even more peculiar and more than a little alarming.

I actually groaned out loud. It felt like all of the colour had drained from my cheeks.

"What?" exclaimed Donna. "Izzy? What's wrong?"

I rapidly tried to rearrange my features. "Oh. Nothing." I tried to reassure her, but Donna knew me too well.

"Don't give me that," she retorted hotly. "I know you, Isabel Bliss. You've got that look you sometimes get before something really crazy happens or before we have to leave in a hurry. What have you sensed? Is there going to be a fight? What?"

"No, nothing like that." I brushed it off with a laugh. "I just spotted someone I met last week, that's all. Someone I didn't like very much. Or who didn't like me, anyway."

"Whoa. Back up. You met someone you didn't like very much?" Donna had her hands on her face in mock horror. "Someone who didn't like you? Hold the press. This will make frontline news. You met someone who didn't like you?" She was laughing now. "Who is it? Everyone loves you. You've got to introduce me."

I laughed drily. "Very funny. It does happen sometimes, you know."

Donna just rolled her eyes skyward.

"It does! His name's Daniel Callahan. That's him over there by the bar, the big brute."

Donna looked to where I was pointing and her mouth dropped open.

"OK. Just a minute. I've got so many things to say right now, I don't know where to start." She pointed too and I had to grab her hand and steer her in the direction of our seats.

"Let me get this straight," Donna continued once we were seated. "You met Daniel Callahan … last week … and you didn't tell me? Daniel Callahan, of *The* Callahans?"

"Why does everyone say it like that?" I wondered.

"Er, because he's a big deal," said Donna as if it were obvious. "But I haven't finished," she continued. "You met Daniel Callahan, of *The* Callahans, last week and you didn't tell me and he's that hot? That great big, muscly sex god back down there?" She looked at me expectantly. "Well? What excuse have you got for that, Miss Bliss?" She looked angry but I knew that it was in jest. I rolled my eyes right back.

"Well, if you must know, it's because I wanted him all to myself," I said dramatically, making us both laugh noisily. "No, seriously, though," I said. "I didn't tell you because I didn't really want to think about it. When I met him, I had no idea he was *Daniel Callahan of The Callahans*. I just bumped into him, literally, at school, and I thought he was one of the rudest, most ignorant, unpleasant people I'd ever met. And later, when I found out that he was *Daniel Callahan of The Callahans*, it didn't really make that much difference because I still thought and still think he's one of the rudest, most unpleasant people I've ever met." I looked at Donna, whose eyes were shining and who was giving off an excitement that spelled trouble. "What are you thinking, Donna?" I asked, with a nasty feeling that I wasn't going to like the answer.

"I'm thinking," said Donna, "that you've got to tell me that story in detail and then you've got to introduce me."

"Er, no," I said.

When the film finished and the lights came up, I didn't move straight away. I didn't want the moment to end. The film was wonderful and had captivated every member of the audience. I had been swept away by the atmosphere and absorbed the rapture of the approximately three hundred other viewers mesmerised by the enthralling cinematic experience. From our left, where I suspect the young couple from the bar were ensconced in their own cosy two-seater, I had been bombarded by waves of sexual desire, which was mildly distracting but actually hadn't detracted from my enjoyment of the film. In fact, I had quite enjoyed the additional fervour it lent to the affair, the colour in my cheeks and the gentle heat between my legs. I was a little embarrassed to have inadvertently shared their ardour, but their ignorance of my awareness curbed my guilt. It wasn't something that I chose, I couldn't make it stop, and it had zero impact on the people whose emotions I shared, and so I had resigned myself to it a long time ago. Feeling shame over something that I had no control over could be a dangerous path.

There was something else, though. Something inside me, something new, was … humming. I don't know how else to describe it. It wasn't exactly a noise, it was more of a feeling, a trembling, deep inside my soul. It had persisted throughout the film, and I had to assume that somehow, I was reacting to being in the presence of Daniel Callahan, but it was different to before, different to the subtle flutter. This was more intense. It frightened me.

Donna was stirring in the seat next to me. She gave a loud yawn, a big stretch and a naughty smile.

"Oh, yes," she said, loudly. "Hugh Jackman could sing me to sleep any night of the week."

I laughed, and Donna continued, "And when I say he could sing me to sleep, obviously we wouldn't actually do any sleeping."

"Well, I hear he's back on the market. Maybe you should find him and introduce yourself?" I laughed.

"Yes, I am considering it," said Donna confidently, making us both laugh again.

On our way back down to the bar, Donna reminded me that I hadn't told my story about meeting Daniel. I had hoped that she might have forgotten, but it seemed that I couldn't avoid the subject.

"And don't leave out any juicy details," she warned.

I rolled my eyes again. "Trust me, there are no juicy details. It was just an unfortunate and unpleasant chance meeting." I thought for a moment. "No, it wasn't even that. We didn't even meet, come to think of it."

We ordered some more drinks at the bar, found a table,

and I filled Donna in. Her overly enthusiastic and mirthful reaction was even worse than Jack's. She couldn't control herself. She was crying with laughter by the time I finished my story, tears streaming down her face.

"That's pretty much what Jack said," I told her grumpily. "Why do my two best friends think it's totally hilarious that someone was mean to me?"

"Someone was mean to you?" Donna laughed even harder. "You sound like you're about seven years old."

"He was mean, though," I said, my arms folded across my chest. It was starting to sound pathetic, even to my own ears, and I had to concede.

"You're just so used to everyone loving you all the time, you don't know what it's like when you meet someone who hasn't fallen under your spell," Donna said.

I wondered if that was true. It was similar to what Jack had said to me last week. I did have a head start on most people, most of the time. Could my dislike of Daniel be down to the fact that I couldn't read him or influence him? That I was just missing my edge? I didn't think so. There was no doubt that he was rude and unpleasant, but Donna's blunt honesty did force me to think again. The fact that Daniel's emotions were not transmitted to me in the same way as everyone else that I had ever met in my life did not necessarily make him a bad person, just different. Either way, the whole thing was strange, and I was intrigued and troubled by him.

Donna slowly got her amusement under control. "Well," she said, "you might think he's a stupid big bloke, but I happen to think he's gorgeous, and he's rich, right?"

I nodded. "Millionaires, apparently."

"Right," agreed Donna. "And he's single?"

"How would I know?" I asked. "And why would you care? Aren't you promised to Hugh?"

"Well," she said, "I just think … maybe he's someone we ought to get to know better. It would do you good to spend time with someone who isn't in your fan club for a change, and it would do me good to spend some time with a drop-dead gorgeous millionaire."

I groaned.

"And," Donna continued, "if I'm not mistaken, he's just spent the last five minutes telling his drop-dead gorgeous friend the same story you just told me, and his friend thinks it's as funny as I do." She was looking towards the back corner of the bar.

"Are you kidding?" I asked, feeling my cheeks flush with embarrassment and turning in my chair to see.

"No!" Donna stopped me. "Don't look now, it's too obvious. He's over there in the corner talking to his mate, and they keep looking over at you, or at us."

I groaned again. "This night is going downhill badly."

"So, are you going to introduce us, or what?" asked Donna.

"Don't be daft. I've already told you; I haven't even met him myself. He didn't tell me his name and he sure as hell didn't ask for mine, and he's not a nice man and …"

Donna shushed me frantically. "They're coming over," she hissed.

I couldn't believe it. I didn't ever want to see Daniel Callahan again. I certainly didn't want to talk to the man, and I absolutely didn't want to spend the night watching Donna flirt outrageously with him. Why on earth would he come over?

"Oh, no," Donna said, not hiding the disappointment in her voice, "They're not coming here. They're going to the bar. Let's go too."

"What?" I was horrified. "Follow them to the bar? Are you insane? You know we're not teenagers, right?"

"Maybe not, but I'm on a mission," Donna stated boldly. "And I'm thirsty. Come on." And she gulped the last of her drink and tugged me out of my chair.

"Can't I just stay here with the coats?" I tried.

"The coats will be fine without us for a minute," insisted Donna. "Come on, or they'll be swallowed up by the crowd before we get there.

"Good," I said. "This is ridiculous."

I reluctantly followed Donna through the crowd towards the bar. I kept my head down and watched her feet. I was mortified. I didn't want to risk glancing up and seeing Daniel looking at me, knowing that I was following him. I didn't want to see him at all. I honestly couldn't believe that I was following Donna following him. We were supposed to be adults. I could only hope that Daniel would buy his drinks and move away from the bar before we got there.

"How did they do that?" exclaimed Donna, stopping suddenly.

"What did they do?" I asked, intrigued.

"They got straight through the crowd to the bar and got served in a matter of seconds. The queue just sort of parted and the barman went straight to them. I guess that's what happens when you're millionaires." She sighed enviously. "Everyone must have recognised him. Money talks, I guess."

"Ah, well," I said, relieved. "Can I go and sit back down, then?"

"Hang on." Donna grabbed my arm urgently. "They're coming back this way."

"I don't care," I hissed. "Let me go."

The next few moments occurred in painful slow motion. As I tugged my arm sharply out of Donna's grasp, I was jostled by a stranger on the other side. I felt myself falling off balance and reached out to grab onto something, anything, to keep me upright. The something that I grabbed onto was a jacket slung over an arm and the owner of the jacket pulled back on it hard, tipping me further off balance and sending me sprawling to the floor on my knees. I let out a pained cry as my still bruised knee struck the hard floor.

I ended up on my knees in front of a strong, long set of masculine legs in blue denim. I didn't know for certain to whom the legs belonged, but I could make an educated guess from the pitch of the gasp and giggle from Donna and the murmuring of the onlookers. I really didn't want to look up, but I knew that it was inevitable. I couldn't stay on the floor forever. My knee was painful, and I wasn't even certain that I could get up by myself. Slowly, grudgingly, I raised my eyes to find Daniel Callahan looking down at me with distasteful recognition and an unpleasant, disdainful smile. I looked him in the eye with as much dignity as I could muster. He continued to stare rudely. He didn't utter a word.

"Sorry," I muttered, and my hand flew to my mouth in instant regret. Had I seriously just apologised to him, again, for falling over, again? I was a total idiot, and I was more embarrassed than ever. What was it about this man that made me fall at his feet and behave like a stuttering moron with an apology tic?

"It seems like you're making a habit of falling on your knees in front of my brother. Here, let me help you."

In an instant, everything changed. My whole life turned upside down. Something inside me roared to life and I suddenly felt different, stronger, more alive. It came from the source of the humming, that place deep inside of me. Those simple words, that simple offer of a hand to my feet, the smooth, velvety voice. It was the sort of voice that could make a person weak at the knees with its deep resonance and gentle tone, but it was so much more than that. I didn't just like the sound of his voice. Something about the owner of that voice had just changed something fundamental about me, and somehow I knew, in that fraction of a second, that nothing was ever going to be the same again.

I wasn't sure if I could move or if I wanted to look into the face that belonged to those words, that voice. I was frightened about what I might find and what it might do to me, what I might become. However, I was still on the floor on my knees, so I put my hand out, took his and let him pull me to my feet.

Our eyes met, and without warning, a multitude of sensations overwhelmed me. I saw him, I felt him, I sensed him. I experienced things that I couldn't understand or explain, but it was like a fire had been lit in my soul, like fireworks exploding in the deepest recess of my mind. I couldn't just feel his emotions in the way that I normally do. This experience went further, deeper. It felt like in that single second, he was actually inside my mind, or I was inside his. I wasn't sure whether it was one or the other or if it were both. I couldn't process what was happening to me. It was happening too fast and exercising too many of my senses.

He looked at me with bewitching eyes that reached into my very core. Eyes a deep, rich brown, like swirling chocolate, shimmering with a layer of warmth. They glistened with a flame that matched the fire that had ignited inside me, as if his eyes understood and reflected the very essence of me. We saw each other in a way that I had never known before, a way that I had never even dreamed of, and as we looked into each other's eyes, the flames in his eyes grew larger, hotter. I took everything in, every minute detail. The dark hair swept back from his face, the healthy tan to his skin, the perfect line of his nose leading to full, rich lips surrounded by laughter lines, indicating a happy man: a joyful, confident, beautiful, magical creature.

The intensity of the moment wasn't limited to the visual. The way that he looked wasn't what captivated and thrilled my senses. When I sensed a person through their emotions, I usually felt that they were happy or sad, angry or hurt, but this was something new. This was a cacophony of feelings so loud that I felt as if my head might burst with the joy of it. Emotions that lifted me into the sky, swirling around me and through me — through my mind, through my heart, through my body — until I felt dizzy with the power of it. All that I could see were those eyes, those lips. All that I could hear was that voice, and yet I could feel and see and hear everything all at once, like I was awake for the first time in my life, like I had found the answer to a question that I hadn't known I'd been asking.

Donna cleared her throat and the spell was momentarily broken. I looked at her, blind and unable to think coherently, and she returned my look with a puzzled expression. I had to blink a few times to try to clear my head and drown out the roar that was still taking place inside. I turned back to the man in front of me and realised that I was still holding his hand. He looked a little dazed. I think I knew how he felt.

"Hi, I'm Scott Callahan," he said, and I wondered if this strong, athletic, handsome millionaire had just cast a spell on me or if I was the one who had cast the spell on him. I was reeling from the onslaught to my senses. I took a moment to steady myself, unsure if my voice would work.

"Hi, Scott. Isabel," I said. "Isabel Bliss."

"Nice to meet you, Isabel Bliss," he said in that deep, velvety voice. He smiled and his eyes crinkled in the corners. "Don't mind my brother. Daniel isn't exactly known for his social niceties. He gets by on his strength and his looks, not on his charm or personality."

I had actually almost forgotten Daniel's existence. He scowled at his brother, and Donna turned her sexy, happy smile on him, unaware of the exhilarating turmoil going on inside my mind, oblivious to the life-shattering magic in the air and as confident as ever.

"The Callahans," she said. "You're causing quite a stir in Ramsay Bridge, you know. That old house has been standing empty for a long time. You're big news. How about you boys come and join us for a drink and we all get to know each other?" She was already leading the way back to the table. She turned back around. "I'm Donna, by the way," she said.

It was the first time that I had seen Daniel smile. I actually hadn't thought him capable of it. He looked Donna over with arrogant, casual appreciation.

"Sure," he said, and he placed his hand familiarly onto her shoulder. "Lead the way."

I was taken aback. He spoke easily and fluently and was behaving like a normal human being. Perhaps he did have a personality after all. Perhaps the problem was me.

We were back at our table before I realised that we had never reached the bar and Donna and I were both without a drink.

"I'll go back and get us those drinks then, shall I?" I asked. "We forgot, in my clumsiness and the introductions."

Scott was already standing. "No," he said, "let me. You've hurt yourself. I could see you were limping."

"That's so kind of you," said Donna before I had recovered enough to reply. "A gin and tonic with ice and lime for me and a lime and tonic water for Izzy."

"No problems at all," he said, sweeping a shallow bow. "I'll be back before you know it."

I was left with Donna and Daniel, who were already chatting away as if they had known each other for years. They both seemed to have forgotten my existence, which suited me because I hadn't recovered from my reaction to Scott. I had never felt anything like it and had been unaware that I was living my life with a part of me dormant, that I was waiting for something, for someone, to wake me up, to make me feel alive for the first time in forever. I could feel it deep inside me, an awakened presence that was even now unfurling itself, stretching and promising me a new life, new experiences, new senses. It was full of unexplored potential and possibility, but despite the unparalleled wonder and unsolicited miracle taking place inside my soul, I knew that it was fundamentally wrong to react to another man in such a way.

As images of Jack came unbidden into my mind, I had a surge of intense guilt. This should not be happening. I should not be feeling this way. I resolved to put everything that I had into repressing the promise inside me and tried to focus on reality, on the present. I took a deep breath in, let it out and concentrated on the interaction between Donna and Daniel in order to distract myself from my own thoughts.

They seemed totally at ease in each other's company, and I could see how Donna might consider him to be good-looking and charming and why she would dismiss my concerns. I still didn't trust him, though. His emotional emptiness felt threatening. I was frightened of things that I didn't understand, and there were a lot of things happening that I didn't understand. Daniel still seemed to be treating me with open hostility, and I had no idea what I could have done to make him dislike me so intensely. Perhaps Donna might have a point, though. I wasn't used to people not liking me, and that in itself made me uneasy.

I tuned out Donna and Daniel's conversation but continued to watch their body language, and their overt flirting made me laugh. They couldn't have been more obvious. They were leaning towards each other, giggling and touching each other outrageously. I wish I could have just felt happy for Donna, but I couldn't help feeling uneasy and hoped that she wasn't going to get hurt again. She had a habit of choosing the wrong kind of men: the type who didn't treat her right and with whom she didn't have a future. Her dating history was the one aspect of Donna's life that didn't seem to be charmed.

From an objective point of view, Daniel was much more of a catch than the men that Donna usually went for. I studied him discreetly from across the table. He was laughing and looked totally relaxed. He was undoubtedly good-looking and he clearly worked out. He had a masculine, chiselled jaw and a winning smile. He was well-spoken, and he was the son of a millionaire, for goodness sake. Donna could and had done an awful lot worse in her time, but all of that was aside from the fact that I just didn't trust him. Even without the emotional void, he had been unforgivably rude to me twice in two meetings, and there was something else off about him. I could read people, and I didn't like Daniel Callahan.

Thinking about Daniel's lack of emotional signals soon

led me back to the intense, extraordinary moment with Scott, who appeared to be his brother's emotional antithesis. I had never felt such a staggering fusion of sensations and was still a little shaken up. It was as if he had been experiencing all the positive emotions at once and all of his emotional energy had been transferred into me at the same time as my emotions were being transmitted to him. The unity of power and feelings had consumed me, drawing an unparalleled response that we had both absorbed and reflected from each other, catching us in a spiral of echoing, bewitching emotions that reverberated through every fibre of my being in that one all-consuming moment. I was trembling again just thinking about it, and I tried to decipher what it might mean and if there was a link between my overpowering emotional reaction to Scott and my stone-cold reaction to his brother.

While I was lost in thought, Scott returned with the drinks. He set them on the table and sat down next to me, capturing my attention by staring into my eyes with a heated intensity that made me weak. The feelings that he was emitting were less jumbled now, slightly less confused, but still fiercely strong. There was no denying that I stirred a myriad of emotions in Scott Callahan, and he was doing nothing to hide the way that I made him feel. He smiled at me and I felt myself in grave danger of being bewitched by those smouldering eyes again. I looked back at him and felt his excitement, a fierce attraction and unadulterated wonder as he searched my eyes and my soul for answers to the unspoken question between us. I wondered if he was asking himself the same question that I was asking. Was he the same as me? Was he wondering if he had finally found something that he had been searching for his whole life? The way that my heart and mind responded to this man shook me to my core, and I had to force myself to look away and break the spell. It took all of my self-control not to impulsively do or say something that I would regret.

I picked up my drink instead, stared at the glass and took a large gulp, concentrating on the sensation of the cold liquid running down my throat, the solid reality of the glass in my hand, and wishing that I had asked for something stronger. I concentrated hard on the physical sensations, kept my gaze away from his and slowly started to feel more normal. I tried not to acknowledge his powerful emotions and the sensations that were whispering to me, demanding to be heard.

"Thanks," I managed finally. I put my drink back on the table and stared at my hands.

Scott, evidently aware of my discomfort, stopped staring so intently, and the intensity in the air seemed to dim a little. He cleared his throat.

"Sorry," he said. I looked back up at him with a question in my eyes. "I think I might have seemed a little ..." he offered, unable to vocalise the enormity of what had passed between us.

I didn't respond. I didn't know what to say. *A little?* sprang to mind.

"But ... the thing is," he continued, "I mean ... I don't want to ... I don't mean to suggest ... but I don't think it was just ... I mean it wasn't just ... Was it just ...? I mean ... I hope it wasn't just ... me. There's something about you ... Something about us. I don't know how to ... This really isn't like me. I've never ... I mean ... Sorry."

I still didn't respond, and he took a deep breath.

"We haven't even met properly yet." His eyes softened and he offered me another heart-stopping smile. I melted a little. "Can we start again?" he asked.

I still didn't trust myself to speak but I nodded.

"I'm Scott," he said.

"Yes," I agreed. I glanced at Donna and Daniel, hoping for a rescue, but it was clear that I wasn't going to get any help from that quarter.

Scott followed my eye. "It looks like your friend and my brother are getting along pretty well, doesn't it? Maybe you and I should try to get to know each other too."

I smiled, but the words still wouldn't come.

"I'll go first." He rescued me. "My name is Scott Callahan. I've recently moved to the area with my family." He paused awkwardly. "It might seem a little ... odd, two grown men living with their parents. The truth is, neither Daniel or I had any ties to the old area and we're both self-employed, and the old place our parents have bought needs a lot of work. We're both pretty handy. I'm a builder by trade, so Dad's kind of hired us to help, I suppose. He's brought us along to help do the place up a bit. It's not like there isn't room. It's a bit of a ... family project. Mum'll be making all the decisions, of course. Dad'll be funding the job, Daniel's the muscle, and I'm the skill." He smiled, starting to relax. "How about you?" he asked.

"OK," I said after a deep breath. "My name is Isabel Bliss. I know the place you're talking about pretty well. We're practically neighbours." I felt Scott's excitement accelerate and I talked quickly. If I didn't do it now, maybe I never would. "I've lived in Ramsay Bridge my whole life. I teach reception class at a nearby primary school, and I live with my boyfriend in my grandma's old cottage."

The world seemed to stand still. It was as if someone had thrown a grenade into the room, and there was a moment of silence before it exploded. I felt Scott's emotions nosedive, and the speed and depth of it shook me. The room was suddenly ice cold, and that something inside me that was alive for the first time ached at my rejection of him. Scott recovered himself quickly but not quickly enough. A normal person might have missed his reaction, but I wasn't normal and I didn't miss it. I felt his pain, a pain too sharp and too deep to have been caused by the words of a virtual stranger but real nonetheless; I felt the same pain and it wasn't a reflection of his emotions. This was all me. I was already mourning what could have been. I had an almost insuppressible urge to reach out to him, to touch him and take that pain away with a gesture or a smile. Instead, I took another deep breath and forced myself not to acknowledge it, to act as if it hadn't happened. Scott politely followed my lead and reined himself in. I was impressed by the way that he handled himself and how smoothly he managed his emotions because I knew what he was feeling and what it cost him to hide it.

"Of course you do," he said with a smile that didn't quite reach his eyes. "Well, maybe we'll see each other around town then, Isabel. It'll be nice to see a familiar face."

I nodded. "I'm sure all the faces will be familiar pretty soon. Ramsay Bridge is a small place, and most people know most other people's business. A family moving into the old Ramsay house will not go unnoticed, I assure you. It already hasn't."

"Yes, I suppose it does make us newsworthy," he accepted.

"You can say that again," I smiled. "I've heard the name Callahan mentioned all over town for the last week. Your family really is causing quite a stir."

That provoked a more genuine smile. "Quite a stir, is it?" he said. "I think I quite like that."

Once the initial awkwardness had worn off, and with the rules of engagement established, Scott and I fell into easy conversation. I filled him in on some of his new neighbours, and he told me a bit about the condition of the house and his plans for it. We were soon chatting comfortably and were even able to laugh at Donna and Daniel, who seemed to be so engrossed in each other, they had forgotten the very existence of their best friend and brother. It felt like we had known each other forever, and time passed quickly in Scott's company. After a couple more drinks, I looked at my watch and was surprised to see how late it was.

"Blimey," I said. "I need to be calling it a night. I'll just nip to the loo before we go." I spoke loudly, stood at the end of the table and looked at Donna pointedly.

Donna took the hint. "Hang on," she said, "I'll come too."

In the ladies, Donna let out a low whistle. "Oh my God," she said. "He's hot. He's funny. He's single. He's rich. I've hit the jackpot."

I couldn't let it go. "I still don't like him," I said.

"Yeah? Well, you don't need to," Donna said angrily. "You go home to Jack. Remember him? You've got a perfect man waiting for you. I've got this covered."

She was talking unnecessarily loudly, and the hostility was totally unlike Donna.

"Yes, thanks, Donna but I'm with you tonight. You've been drinking and you're my responsibility. I just don't trust the guy."

"You seem to like his brother all right." Donna was getting belligerent.

"Scott seems like a nice guy, yes," I said.

"And Daniel isn't?" Donna asked with a sneer. "Why? Because he likes me more than he likes you?"

I didn't understand where the nastiness was coming from, but I could feel a fierce anger burning inside her and it was beginning to contaminate me.

"Steady on, Don. I just think you don't know the guy. I have a bad feeling about him and I'm usually right." I said.

"I know enough," Donna said. "You take yourself home. I'll be fine."

"You're drunk and you've only just met the guy. I don't feel comfortable leaving you. I'd like to take you home."

"And we always have to do things your way, don't we?" said Donna unkindly. "If I want to make my own way home or I want to go home with someone else, it's no business of yours."

"Hey, that's unfair. I'm not trying to get my own way. I'm just worried about you. You usually trust my judgement."

"Yeah? Well, maybe I'm sick of my life being ruled by your *feelings*." She turned and stomped out of the toilets.

I was stunned. I had never seen Donna like this. She was

always so upbeat and loving. We never argued, and she had never walked away from me, not in twenty-two years of friendship. It made me even more determined not to let Donna make a decision that she might regret when she was in a better frame of mind, when she was more herself. I followed her out of the toilet and glanced over to our table. Scott and Daniel were both on their feet, pointedly facing away from each other with scowls on their faces. There was an unpleasant tension in the air. They had obviously also had a disagreement about something. I made my way over slowly, watching. Donna reached the table and looked beseechingly at Daniel, who was moodily staring at the floor. Everything about his body language and behaviour towards Donna had changed in the few minutes that we had been away.

When I reached the table, Scott tried his best to hide the tension.

"Right, well, we'd better be heading off," he said. "It was nice meeting you both."

Daniel still said nothing and didn't take his eyes off the floor. There was still no emotional output from him, but his mood was obvious.

"Daniel?" Donna said. She looked at him hopefully and took a step closer, but he turned his back and started walking towards the door without a word.

I stared after him, trying to figure out what had prompted the sudden and thorough change. As usual, I got nothing. He was a wall of ice, emptiness. He disappeared into the car park. Donna stared dumbly after him, her eyes filling with tears.

I picked up my coat. "Yes, well, we're heading off too," I said. "Nice to meet you, Scott."

Scott nodded.

I wasn't sure what to do, how to take my leave or how Donna was going to react to me. "Donna?" I said gently.

Donna flounced to the door without a word, and I

followed her to the car. She was obviously upset, but I could also sense a totally disproportionate, irrational level of anger in her. It seemed like Donna's outrage and animosity were mostly directed towards me. I got into the car, trying not to let myself manifest her feelings. Donna got in beside me, slammed the door and stared out of the window without saying a word.

As I pulled slowly out of the car park, I saw the same *Callahan* van that I had seen at school last week. Daniel was sitting in the passenger seat, staring straight ahead with a brooding, dark look on his face. Scott was standing outside, leaning against the van, watching my car as we drove past. I should have been too far away to feel his emotions, but they were coming through loud and clear. That part of my brain that I hadn't known existed until tonight was alive again, awake and excited by the intense, heated look in Scott's eyes. He didn't take his eyes off me, tracking me across the car park, and when I met those alluring eyes for an instant, the magic pulled at me again. Scott seemed to want me to see the depth of passion and longing in his gaze, and despite knowing how wrong it was, I'm afraid that I was unable to hide the answering agony in mine.

When I arrived home, my mind was reeling. The evening had thrown up too many questions and no answers. Daniel's behaviour was baffling. He was rude one minute, an outrageous flirt the next and back to hostile ignoramus by the end of the evening without communicating a single emotion. I had never seen Donna so hostile and couldn't understand why her anger had been directed at me, and then there was Scott. Part of me didn't want to acknowledge that anything had passed between us and part of me was unable to think about anything else. Whatever it was that he had awakened inside me was still there. I could feel it lurking but I couldn't identify it. I was emotionally exhausted.

Jack was fast asleep, and I sneaked around him so as not to disturb him while I got myself ready for bed. I sat on the edge of the bed and watched him sleep. I felt a deep fondness for this man who had been by my side for my whole life, my best friend who had loved me for so long. I stared into his sleeping face and I saw safety, friendship, affection and the promise of a future that we had planned together, but I didn't feel alive. As I climbed into bed by his side, he stirred, half waking, and he reached out for me.

"You're home," he mumbled, and he pulled me gently to him. It was then that I felt the love, the love that sprang from Jack. The emotion snaked around my mind, provoking a response, a love that I reflected back at him, and I realised the truth, a truth that I had suspected and smothered for more than eight years together. Our love, the profound emotion that went beyond mere fondness and friendship, was simply Jack's love augmented by my mind, by my power. I had asked myself whether it mattered many times, and before tonight, before Scott Callahan, I always told myself that it did not. I would have said that we were happy, but that was before. The awakening of the essence of whatever it was that now lay dormant again inside my mind was something that I simply couldn't ignore. I couldn't endure my life knowing that there was a part of me not living, not feeling, that I was not experiencing all of the sensations that the world had to offer. There might be someone else out there like me, someone who was different, someone who understood what it was like to be able to experience emotions like I did: someone extraordinary.

Sleep called to me, and as I drifted under, with Jack's warm presence by my side, silent tears of loss poured from my heart and dampened my pillow. Tonight may have been a beginning, a taste of something incredible, but all I could think at that moment was that it would also be the end of something beautiful.

Chapter 7

At 8.45 on Monday morning, I threw open the classroom doors and peered out onto the playground. The tide of enthusiastic children was flooding through the gate. It was a crisp, cold, clear autumn morning, and children and parents alike were in high spirits. The children called joyful greetings to one another and rushed together to share stories about their exciting weekends, and parents stood in small groups, sharing the latest gossip, complaining about their busy lives and applauding and grumbling over their offspring in equal measure.

The scene was replayed every Monday morning and was one that I usually loved. That morning, however, I felt twisted out of shape and couldn't find pleasure in the happy innocence of the children or the clarity of the crystal-blue sky. My experiences over the weekend had changed something inside me, but I couldn't even think about that. I was waiting for Josh, unsure of what I dreaded more — him being missing again or being here and my having to tell Mr Nelson that I had reported him to child services. Not that I would describe it in that way. I had been playing it over and over in my head. I would say that I had applied for support for the family. That was the line that I had planned, support for the family because I could see that they were struggling. I would word it so as to avoid any admission that I was accusing anyone of anything. There was to be no suggestion that the Nelsons weren't good, loving parents, just that they needed some assistance. I sincerely hoped that I could pitch it that way, but it was a hard sell when I couldn't even convince myself. It didn't matter how I packaged it; I was pretty certain that Mr Nelson was not going to thank me for my latest interference.

I beamed the happiest smile that I could muster at the children as they filed into the classroom. I showed them to the morning activity tables, helped them find scissors and pens and explained what they needed to do. I was taken aside by parents with stories of achievements and exciting news from their weekends, I cooed over a photo of Jane in her new ballet tutu, and I reassured Karl's mum that I always did my best to ensure that he got to the toilet before it was too late so that he didn't end up smelling faintly of wee. All of the time, I was privately fretting over Josh and his dad, frantically hoping that he would arrive so that I knew that he was OK whilst desperately panicking about the conversation that I had to have.

I felt a tug at my jumper and looked down. It was little Sammy Harris.

"Morning, Sammy," I sang, "and how was your weekend?"

Sammy was glowing. He puffed out his chest and pulled me to a table where his mum was hovering nervously with a pen and a piece of paper.

"I've been practising, Miss," he told me. "Do you want to see?"

"Of course I want to see, Sammy. I can't wait," I said. "What have you been practising?"

Sammy didn't answer but took the paper and pen from his mum and sat at the table. He put his left hand down to hold the paper steady and held the pen confidently and correctly in his right hand. His tongue protruded from his mouth a fraction in concentration.

'S'...'a'...'m'...'m'...'y', he wrote. The writing was faint and the lines were a little haphazard. The 'a' and the first 'm' were overlapping slightly, and the 'y' was occupying its own line completely, but it was, without a doubt, a 'Sammy,' and Sammy looked up at me with such pride and joy, it brought a tear to my eye.

"Oh, Sammy," I gushed. "You have been practising, haven't you? This is so fabulous, sweetie. You are my absolute star. Well done, you." I got down on my knees beside him and he threw his arms around me with the innocent abandon of a four-year-old who has jumped a hurdle that he believed was beyond his reach. I turned to Mrs Harris, who was glowing with maternal pride.

"You've worked so hard with him. No wonder you're proud. This is a real milestone for him, and I have no doubt that everything will start falling into place."

"Thank you," said Mrs Harris. "We have worked hard, but he did it for you. He adores you. Pleasing you is so important to him."

I laid my hand gently on Mrs Harris's arm. It might seem unimportant or insignificant to the average bystander or those ignorant of the needs of some children, but for a parent and teacher of a struggling little boy, it meant everything. Mrs Harris smiled, affectionately ruffled Sammy's hair and kissed his forehead goodbye.

"Well done, baby boy. See you later. Have a great day."

I felt an unexpected tremor of weakness shoot through my body and I spun around in an instant, searching for the source. Joshua Nelson was sitting, pen in hand, staring at his name plate on his table, and I had sensed his fragility from across the room. I lurched towards him without thinking, indulging the desire to touch him, grab him, feel for myself that he was here, that he was real, that he was all in one piece. I checked myself before I got to his table and looked around. I had to speak to his dad. I scanned the room. He wasn't there. I rushed to the door and checked the playground. He wasn't there. He must have deposited Josh and made a dash for the exit while I was distracted by Sammy. I cursed myself for having missed him. There wasn't much time before he would receive the communication from Early Help. I would have to speak to his mum after school.

I turned back to Josh, stood at a distance and watched him for a moment. He hadn't moved. He was sitting, staring at the table, lost in space. I focused on his emotions. I could see that he was tired again. His eyes were heavy. He was tired and sad and dreadfully worried. A three-day weekend at home hadn't improved anything. In fact, it might have made matters worse. I wished again that I could read his mind so that I could understand and help him. Instead, I did what I could, sat by his side and took his hand. I smiled at him, and he gave a weak attempt at a smile in return. I pushed as much positive energy into him as I could manage and felt him rally a little. His smile became slightly stronger. I squeezed his hand and silently promised him that he wouldn't be dealing with his burden alone for much longer. We would find a way to help.

Sindi from Early Help called at lunchtime to confirm that the paperwork was in place for the Nelsons' referral. She would put the letter in the post that afternoon.

"They should receive the initial contact tomorrow. It's fairly informal. They'll be asked to make contact to arrange a visit as soon as possible, at their convenience. We hope that families will engage voluntarily. If we don't hear from them by the end of the week, we'll follow it up in person. Is Josh in school today? Were you able to speak to the parent this morning?"

I was grateful that they were making progress. It felt good to know that things were happening, even though the reality made me nervous.

"Yes, he's at school, but no, I didn't catch his dad this morning."

"OK, well, try again this afternoon, then. We really do find that it's better in the long run if the teacher approaches the parents directly so everyone is on the same page."

"Yes, of course, I understand."

I spent the afternoon struggling to focus. I fervently hoped that Mrs Nelson was well enough to pick Josh up that afternoon, even though I knew that it made me a coward. I didn't feel quite right talking to Mr Nelson. He had never been openly hostile or unpleasant, but I strongly suspected that it was his will that was silencing the family about their issues, and there was something about him that I just didn't feel totally comfortable with. Josh was quiet all day. He was present physically, but his mind was elsewhere. I concentrated on the knowledge that he would soon be receiving professional help.

At 3.25 that afternoon, the children were all ready with their coats on and their bags packed. I kept Josh at the back of the line. Mrs Nelson was visible on the playground, on her own as usual, her head down. I felt a sense of relief that I didn't have to speak to Mr Nelson but also a moment of dread. After the last child had joined their grown-up, and when Josh hadn't run over to her as usual, Mrs Nelson was forced to look up and catch my eye. I was shocked by the decline that I saw. Mrs Nelson looked terrible. No amount of nice clothes or well applied makeup could hide that this lady was suffering. Her face was gaunt, almost skeletal, and there were garish purple rings around her eyes. She held herself upright and looked steadily at me, almost daring me to judge what I saw.

I waved her over and kept hold of Josh's hand, giving her no choice but to approach. Mrs Nelson hesitated for a moment but slowly made her way across the playground and followed me back into the classroom. I sat her down. Josh climbed onto his mother's knee and clung on with grim determination. They held onto each other, sharing their strength. I tried to ignore the anguish emanating from the pair as I launched into the speech that I had been preparing all day.

"Mrs Nelson, I'm worried about you. I know that things aren't right with you and they're getting worse."

Mrs Nelson didn't respond. She was holding onto Josh's hand tightly and studying the table with solid intent.

I ploughed on. "I'm worried about you, but my responsibility is to Josh and his well-being, and he's suffering and I can't let it continue." Still nothing. I took a deep breath. "Mrs Nelson, I have to inform you that at the end of last week, I made a referral to a child services team in the council. They're called Early Help."

Mrs Nelson looked up at that and I could see tears shining in her eyes, but she still didn't speak.

"Early Help have written to you and your husband. They'd like to arrange a meeting to get to know you and find out what's going on and how they can help you, and ultimately, help Josh, going forward." I couldn't quite decipher the mix of emotions playing out in Josh and his mother's minds. It was a jumble of feelings underpinned by a current of panic, but still, neither of them spoke. I tried the direct approach. "Do you understand?"

Mrs Nelson nodded slowly. "Yes, I understand, and I thank you for your concern." She was struggling to manage her emotions, but her outward demeanour was carefully controlled. Someone else might have been oblivious to her inner turmoil and judged her to be cold and unfeeling, but I knew better. Mrs Nelson rose to leave. This wasn't what I had wanted. I had hoped that Mrs Nelson might have opened up to me, that she might have given me something, anything.

I tried again. "Mrs Nelson? Is there anything you want to talk to me about? Anything you want to tell me, here, now? Is there anything I can do for you or Josh?" I worried that Mrs Nelson would pick up on the fact that my voice was becoming higher in pitch. The intense stress of the Nelsons was influencing my control, and I was finding it difficult to stay focused.

"No. Thank you," Mrs Nelson said carefully. "We'll be fine." Resignation, acceptance. She stood and led Josh from the classroom. They crossed the playground and they didn't glance back.

I watched them leave. I don't know when I began to cry but I could feel the cold, wet tears on my face.

At 8.45 on Tuesday morning, I threw open the classroom doors and peered out onto the playground. Once again, the weather was beautiful, the spirits of the children and parents were high, and my stomach was in knots. On Monday my worry had been over whether Josh would be in school and how I would go about approaching his father to break the news of the referral. On Tuesday I was dreading the moment that Mr Nelson entered the building again, this time knowing that I had referred his family to child services. I didn't know whether I should approach him or let him come to me, but I was not looking forward to the interaction.

When Josh arrived at school, accompanied by his father, the painful awkwardness didn't transpire as I had anticipated. Mr Nelson brought him into the classroom, gave me a terse nod, turned round and left again. He was there for a matter of seconds, and his attitude left me confused. I had expected confrontation, anger, an outpouring of betrayal or a hushed demand to discuss the matter in private, but Mr Nelson had been surrounded by his usual air of faint agitation. He displayed no fierce emotions, nothing out of the ordinary for him, no acute animosity towards me, no hatred. He behaved no differently than on any other morning, and it didn't take long for me to realise that he didn't know. Mrs Nelson simply hadn't told him. I sighed. I couldn't catch him now, and I didn't know what I would have said anyway. It was out of my hands now.

Josh had a marginally better day on Tuesday. He remained tired and unfocused, but the swirling pain that had been tearing at me wasn't quite as fierce. He had the same air of resignation about him that I had sensed in his mother the previous afternoon. Perhaps the knowledge that their burden was finally going to be shared had helped and they were quietly anticipating receiving some support. I focused on that hope and allowed myself a moment of relief. Time would tell.

When Mrs Nelson collected Josh that afternoon, I didn't make any attempt to approach or talk to her. The dark circles under her strained eyes were still prominent, but she held herself erect as usual and did seem slightly more calm and collected. I was relieved. I would talk to Sindi again before the end of the week and find out what measures were in place to begin the process of support, expecting that a meeting would be arranged between the family, child services and the staff here at school. I was eager to make progress quickly and for Josh to have an outlet for his emotions. I hoped that once matters were acknowledged, he would feel that he could open up to me and I would be able to help him deal with his problems.

On Wednesday I discovered that I had been foolish to let myself believe that things were any better. Wednesday was a bad day. It all came crashing down on Wednesday.

I was preoccupied with other children when Josh arrived on Wednesday morning, the day that his mum always brought him to school, when Mr Nelson worked away. I had hoped to catch her for a quick word to check that the communication from Early Help had arrived and that she understood the next steps, but Josh arrived when I wasn't looking, and although I ran straight to the door to grab her before she left, she was out of sight. I sighed and returned to my class. I wasn't having much luck with the Nelsons that week, but the situation was progressing; I would just have to be a little patient.

The morning was uneventful despite Josh being tired and preoccupied again. I could feel the weight of his burden pulling him down, but despite my best efforts, he still refused to open up. I continued with my lesson plan and tried to include him as much as I could, but as the day went on, he seemed to draw more and more into himself and I could feel his stress levels rising ever higher, setting my own on edge. A couple of times, I caught myself snapping at the other children with impatience, allowing Josh's emotions to influence me. I needed to get myself under control. At lunchtime I walked the perimeter of the field, away from the building. I breathed in the sweet, fresh air and the musky fragrance of the fallen leaves and focused on the joy emanating from the children at play, absorbing their spirit, letting them give me strength.

On my way back to the classroom, I was met by Melissa. She looked worried.

"Miss?"

"Yes, Melissa? What's wrong?" I asked.

"Miss, Josh is crying. He's in the classroom. I went to put my gloves back in my bag and I could hear him and then I saw him. He's just sitting on the floor, crying," Melissa said.

"Thank you for letting me know, Melissa. I'll go and check on him."

"Do you think I should come too?" she asked.

"No, Melissa, I think you should go and get ready to line up with the rest of the Little Owls. Leave this to me, sweetie."

I hurried towards the classroom. The rest of the children were already lining up on the playground, waiting to go back inside. There wasn't long before Josh would have an audience. Luckily, Mrs Bishop was coming from the opposite direction.

"Oh, Mrs Bishop. Could you bring the children in when the bell goes, please?" I asked. "I just need to go inside and take care of something."

"Of course," said Mrs Bishop.

I found Josh sitting on the floor in the corner of the classroom. Tears were spilling unchecked down his face, leaving dirty, wet tracks on his cheeks. His little body was trembling. He was trying to go unnoticed, crying quietly with little choked gasps and whimpers like an orphaned kitten mewling for milk. I could feel a deep, desolate sadness inside him, an emotion too intense for his years. He was a mess, inside and out.

I went to him quickly and sat on the floor by his side.

"Oh, Josh," I said, and he crawled straight into my lap, his arms snaking around my body, clinging to me tightly. I held him and rocked him slowly as his tears soaked my chest. He seemed to draw some comfort from my nearness, and his breathing slowly turned from wracked gasps to more even breaths. He leaned back a little and looked up into my face. His eyes were red and swollen.

"Will she be OK?" he asked.

"Who, Josh?" I asked, even though I already knew the answer.

"My mummy," he replied on a sob.

"Oh, Josh." I wanted desperately to be able to reassure him, but without knowing what was wrong, I couldn't give him what he needed. "I don't know, sweetie, but you can talk to me. Can you tell me what's wrong with your mummy?"

"Daddy says she's fine. He always says she's fine and that she'll be fine, but …" he checked himself again, afraid to share what was on his mind. He looked up with those same pleading eyes. "Do you think she'll be OK, Miss?"

"Josh, I don't know, sweetie. Without knowing what's wrong, I can't tell you what's going to happen."

My heart was breaking for him, but I couldn't just offer blind hope. I had to keep encouraging him to open up, and I had to be there to support him until he did. Social services support couldn't come soon enough. He buried his head back into my chest.

"Josh," I said gently, "I can hear the other children coming in. Do you want to stay in the classroom, or do you want to go somewhere else for a bit?"

"I want to be with you, Miss. You make it feel a bit better."

"OK, Josh. How about we head to the library? It'll be quiet in there. I don't think anyone's using it this afternoon. I always find that stories are a good way to take my mind off things."

Josh nodded. I stood and he followed me, clasping my hand tightly in his own. I looked down at our linked hands. My heart swelled.

"I need to go and speak to Mrs Bishop," I told him. He nodded but didn't let go. "Do you want to come with me?"

He nodded again.

We stood by the door as the rest of the class came tumbling in. I greeted them with a cheeriness that I didn't feel and asked Mrs Bishop to look after them for a bit while I spent some time with Josh.

"Of course, Miss Bliss," said Mrs Bishop. "We've got some spooky Halloween pictures to make, and the numeracy quiz is ready to go. You take all the time you need."

I had been relying on Mrs Bishop more than ever those last few weeks. I was lucky to have such a pillar that I could lean on in difficult times.

"Thank you, again, so much," I said, and I led Josh back through the hall.

I always felt at home surrounded by books. The school library was small but packed to the rafters with beautiful children's fiction, and I found something soothing and delicious in having all those stories in one place. The excitement and adventures that could be experienced in a book, the escapism, the freedom, the exercise of imagination. When adults think back to their earliest memories, they will often find rich, vivid images of bedtime stories read by parents, and the magical worlds and extravagant voices will come floating back. I knew that Josh enjoyed reading with his mother. We had discussed their extensive collection of books during his transition meeting in the summer, and I hoped that I might be able to use this knowledge to encourage him to open up now.

"So, Josh, anything you fancy reading? What does Mummy usually read to you?" I asked.

He smiled. "Mummy reads lots of books. My favourite is *The Snail and the Whale*."

"Then *The Snail and the Whale* it shall be," I said with delight and retrieved it from the shelf.

The next hour was full of sheltered reading and talking about books. I told Josh some of the stories that my mum used to make up for me when I was little, and Josh told me about acting out some of the best bits from his favourite stories with his mum at home.

"I'm the troll," he told me happily, "and Mummy is all the billy goats. She does different voices for them all, and when she's the biggest billy goat, she picks me up and throws me onto the bed." He laughed.

"Come on, then," I said. "Let's see your best troll. I'll be Baby Billy Goat, trip trap, trip trap."

"I'm a troll, foldy roll," shouted Josh, "and I'll eat you up for my supper!"

I laughed. "Excellent trolling, Josh. You made me quite nervous!" My distraction seemed to be working.

A little while later, I picked out *The Fantastic Mr Fox* by Roald Dahl from one of the higher shelves.

"We won't be able to read all of this today, but would you like me to start it?" I asked. "Then you can either book it out of the library to read at home with Mummy or we can wait until we have time to read some more of it together at school."

"Yes, please," said Josh. "I won't need to take it home, though. We have all the books by him. Mummy says she'll read them all to me one day."

"Excellent. Let's get comfy then, and I'll begin. *Down in the valley there were three farms. The owners of these farms had done well. They were rich men. They were also nasty men.*"

As I read, I maintained some focus on Josh's emotions. The sadness hadn't gone away, but I had managed to smother it a little and distract him for a while. As the afternoon wore on, though, it seemed as if the magic of the stories was wearing off, and he started glancing nervously at the clock on the wall. He peered at it more and more often, and I could sense him becoming more and more agitated. Usually, Josh became giddy towards the end of the day, but instead, his distress was getting closer to the surface, and as a result, I was also finding it harder to concentrate; his emotions were gnawing at me until I couldn't continue any longer. I managed to read to the end of the chapter and had to stop.

"How are you, Josh?" I asked.

"I'm fine, Miss," he lied and glanced at the clock again. "What time does it say, Miss?" he asked anxiously.

"It says two o'clock."

"How long is it until the end of the day?"

"School finishes at three twenty-five, so that's an hour and a half."

"How many minutes is that?"

"Well, it's actually one hour and twenty-five minutes." I did the quick sum in my head. "So that's eighty-five minutes altogether."

"So, if I count to sixty, eighty-five times, it'll be the end?"

"Yes, that's right."

"One, two, three, four ..."

"Josh?"

"Yes, Miss?"

"You're not really going to count to sixty, eighty-five times, are you?"

"I was going to, yes."

"I'd really rather you didn't."

"OK."

There was a thick, awkward silence. It lay heavily across the room like a cumbersome blanket, and I didn't know what to say or how to dislodge it. I could feel the turmoil inside him rising again, and the sense of panic made me want to run, to escape, to hide. It felt as if I was going to burst and I didn't know why, and even though he couldn't yet read the time, he just kept looking at that clock.

"Are you looking forward to seeing your mummy?" I asked him.

He didn't answer.

"It is Mummy picking you up tonight, isn't it?" I asked.

Still nothing.

"Josh?"

He had started to cry again, quietly this time. Silent tears were trickling down his face. "What if she doesn't come?" he whispered.

"What do you mean, Josh?" I asked, equally quietly.

"What if she can't get up?" he asked, piercing eyes looking straight into mine.

"Why wouldn't she be able to get up, Josh?" I asked, trying to remain calm but struggling to fight the fear — his, mine, and the terror attached to this new, vague comment.

"She couldn't get up this morning," he said. There was a weighty pause. "But she said she'd get better. She said she'd be here at three twenty-five," he told me, his voice rising slightly at the end of his sentence.

With my heart beating wildly inside my chest, I cast my mind back to first thing that morning. I hadn't seen Josh arrive, but when I had looked around, he was there. I had run to the door, hoping to catch Mrs Nelson before she left, but there had been no sign of her. The significance hadn't occurred to me before, but now I started to panic. My own emotions were beginning to fray. I tried to keep my voice even.

"Josh? Who brought you to school this morning?" I asked a little frantically.

"My dad went to work early," he said.

"Did your mum bring you to school, Josh?" I could hear that my voice was getting louder, but I couldn't stop it. "Josh, did Mummy bring you to school this morning?"

Josh didn't say anything, but the tears started falling faster. He let out a wracked, painful cry and turned to me, burying his face in my chest again. I pulled him away roughly and forced him to meet my eyes. All I could feel now was fear, but I didn't know whether it was his or mine that was punishing me the most.

"Josh, how did you get to school this morning?" I asked again. I was almost shouting, almost.

"I walked," he sniffed.

"Who did you walk with?"

"I walked by myself."

"Josh" — I needed to be absolutely sure — "it's a long way to walk by yourself. You have to cross a couple of really busy roads, and there's no way your mummy would let you come to school by yourself."

Josh's cries came harder, faster. He was losing control. "She couldn't get up!" He shouted. I held him close. "But she said she would be better and she would come this afternoon at three twenty-five," he repeated again.

"Josh, why didn't you tell me this sooner?" I barked. "No, sorry." Blaming him and shouting at him wasn't helpful. "OK. I need you to come with me to the office," I told him more calmly. "We'll give your mum a ring and see how she's doing. OK?"

"Yes, please," said Josh and tucked his hand back into mine as we walked to the office.

"Helen," I said when we got there, "I need Josh's parents' details, please. Now."

Helen took one look at Josh's tear-stained, swollen face and another at the panic in my eyes and quickly went to the computer and brought the record up. She handed me the office phone and turned the screen so that I could see the numbers. I dialled. It seemed like forever before the line connected and started to ring. Josh's hand, still in mine, gripped a little tighter. The phone continued to ring. Nothing. Then Mrs Nelson's cheerful voice asking me to leave a message.

"I'll try again, OK, Josh?" I said.

"OK," he agreed.

Again, the phone rang, and again, there was no answer. This time I left a voicemail. "Hello, Mrs Nelson, it's Miss Bliss from the school. When you get this message, could you please ring the school office as soon as you can? It's quite urgent. Josh is fine, but it's quite urgent. Thank you." I put the phone down and looked at Josh. "I'll try one more time."

He nodded. Again, there was no reply.

"I'll try your dad," I said quietly. This time, Josh squeezed my hand hard enough to hurt, but I didn't pull away.

"Yes, Miss," he squeaked.

I dialled the number on the record for Mr Nelson. This time there was no ringing. The phone went straight to his voicemail. I left another message.

"Hello, Mr Nelson, it's Miss Bliss from the school. Could you ring the school office as soon as you get this message, please?" I hung up.

"Helen, could you fetch Miss Brooks, please?" I asked without taking my eyes off Josh.

"Of course," Helen replied and hurried down the corridor.

I looked at my watch. It was 2.15. Only fifteen minutes since Josh had first asked me for the time and over an hour before Ms Nelson was due to pick him up.

Chrissy appeared at a trot.

"Miss Brooks," I said, "I think we might have a problem."

I led Chrissy and Josh into the staffroom, and we all sat down. I took a deep breath.

"I didn't see either of Josh's parents this morning," I said. Chrissy looked at me sharply. "It's always so busy first thing, and often, parents are in a hurry, so I didn't think too much of it," I continued. "In fact, to be perfectly honest, I wasn't that surprised because I thought they might be avoiding me." Chrissy nodded for me to continue.

"Josh has been really upset today," I went on. "We left the classroom this afternoon to spend a bit of time together and read some books. As the afternoon has worn on, Josh has become more upset. Josh, can you tell Miss Brooks what you told me about your mum? About this morning?"

Josh looked like a rabbit staring into headlights. He looked at me in panic, then turned to Chrissy, then back to me.

"It's OK, Josh. Please, just tell Miss Brooks what you told me."

Josh shook his head. "She'll be here at three twenty-five," he said, finally. "She said she would be fine. She's fine."

I thought that I might scream.

"Miss Brooks, Josh has just told me that his mummy couldn't get up this morning. He said that he walked to school by himself because his daddy was at work and his mummy couldn't get up. I've tried to ring both his parents, but there was no reply from his mum, three times, and his dad's phone went straight to voicemail."

Chrissy turned to Josh. "Josh, this is really, really important. We need to know if there's something wrong with your mummy."

"She's fine," he said.

"Did she stay in bed this morning because she was tired, Josh?" He shook his head. "Was it because she's poorly, Josh?" Another shake. "If we know what's wrong, maybe we can help her better."

Josh stared at the floor. "She's fine. She's fine. She's fine. She'll be here at three twenty-five. She is fine."

Chrissy gestured to me to follow her into the corridor.

"Try both of the parents again and then any emergency contacts listed on his file."

"There aren't any," I replied. "I've already checked."

"OK. If you can't get either of the parents, we'll go straight to MASH."

"MASH?" I repeated weakly. I vaguely remembered hearing the term before but couldn't work through the fog in my mind to locate its significance.

"It's the Multi-Agency Safeguarding Hub," Chrissy told me. "It's supposed to make it easier to get the right help from the right provider at the right time. They have police, social services, housing, mental health, that sort of thing. Try his parents again. We'll go from there."

I started back towards the office and then realised that I couldn't leave Josh by himself. I turned back, but Chrissy was one step ahead of me.

"It's fine, Izzy. I'll stay with him."

I thanked her. "Be gentle with him."

"Isabel, we're fine. It's two quick calls and then come back and check in."

I went back to the office and made the calls with exactly the same chilling result. Mum's phone rang out; Dad's went straight to voicemail. I looked at the clock. It was 2.25. I went back to the staffroom.

"Sorry, Josh. No luck with either of your parents."

Josh didn't say anything but ran to me and threw his arms around my leg. I had a feeling that he wasn't going to want to let go anytime soon. I sat down heavily.

"MASH, then," I said.

"Yes. You'll have to call them and go through everything. They'll decide what to do next," said Chrissy.

"I don't think it's a conversation I can have with Josh in the room," I said.

"No, I agree. Leave him with me. I know he won't like it, but we'll be fine."

There was a pause.

"I'm really beginning to hate that word."

Josh clung more tightly to my leg.

"I know you want me to stay with you, Josh, but this is super important. We need to get you some help."

"I'm fine," Josh said without letting go.

"We need to get some help for your mummy," I said softly, and it seemed to penetrate. Josh slowly released me, and Chrissy offered him her hand. He hesitated for a moment, but I nodded. He took it and sat back down.

"She'll be fine," he said.

I spent the next twenty minutes on the phone. The lady from MASH was polite and attentive but was clearly working from a script, and I didn't seem to be able to communicate the urgency of the situation fully. I was given a reference number, but ten minutes into the call, I wasn't convinced that I was making any real progress.

"I'm worried there's something seriously wrong right now and that delaying sending help to Mrs Nelson could result in disaster. I cannot overstate my concerns at this moment."

"Right, yes, thank you, Miss Bliss. So, let me see. The child is with you at school now?"

"Yes. Josh is at school."

"Right, and he is not hurt or in any physical danger now?"

"Of course not. He's at school, with me."

"Right. You're worried about the mother, but you don't know that she's unwell?"

"I know that she's been looking worse every time I've seen her for weeks. I have the word of a very troubled and worried little boy and the fact that she's out of contact."

"Right, but the child is now saying that his mother's fine, yes?"

I was grinding my teeth in my attempt not to lose my temper. I was kicking myself for having used that appalling word. This woman didn't need to know that Josh had said his mum was fine.

"Yes, but he's shut down now. Saying that things are fine is his way of coping. When he told me that his mummy couldn't get up, he was telling me the truth, I know it. When he says something's fine, we can't put any faith in it."

"Right, but no one has seen the mother today to confirm that she's unwell?"

Another deep breath.

"Josh is the only one who has seen her today. If she's too poorly to get up or to answer the phone, then no one will have seen her, will they?"

"Right, and you say the child has been referred to child services prior to today?"

"Yes, I spoke to Sindi Wilkinson from Early Help last week and again on Monday. She was writing to the Nelsons. They should have received the letter yesterday."

"Right, but Early Help haven't completed their assessment yet?"

"No, not yet."

"Right, I'll have to track down the report from Early Help to assist with assessing your concerns."

"Early Help haven't made a report yet. They only wrote to the Nelsons this week." My frustration was building.

"Right. So, you have the child, but you're worried about the mother?"

"That's right."

"Right, and the mother will be collecting the child at three twenty-five?"

"She's due to be here at three twenty-five, yes, but I am worried that she won't be here, and I think that someone needs to get to the house now, immediately, to check on her."

"Right, but it's now two forty-five and she is due to collect the child at three twenty-five? That's forty minutes."

"Yes," I said.

"Right, leave this with me please. I'll pass the information to the relevant people, and we'll decide what to do next. If you haven't heard back from us by three twenty-five and the mother doesn't arrive, please call back and let us know."

"Right. OK. Thank you,"

I hung up with a feeling of bitter defeat. I had no confidence that the lady had taken my concerns seriously enough and was certain that nothing was going to happen before 3.25 p.m. I did understand that as this was the first time that anyone had expressed this kind of concern and there was nothing concrete to back it up, waiting another forty minutes didn't seem totally unreasonable, but I knew in the pit of my stomach that Josh had been telling the truth, that Mrs Nelson was in serious trouble and that immediate action could be critical.

I returned to the staffroom. Josh was sitting next to Chrissy, still holding her hand. They were playing a game of I Spy, but he was watching the door and leapt up and ran to me when he saw me. He threw his arms back around my leg.

"So, I've spoken to somebody who should be able to help,

OK, Josh?" I told him. "Now we just have to wait." I smiled. I wished that I felt as calm as I sounded.

"OK," said Josh, and I took him to a chair. "Can I sit on your lap?" he asked quietly.

"Of course you can," I said, and he climbed up and rested his head on my chest and snuggled in.

"Miss Brooks? Could you just let Mrs Bishop know that I won't be back before the end of school? If she could dismiss the children for me, that would be great," I said.

"No problem," said Chrissy. "I'll go and sort that out and see to my class. I'll also have a word with Mr Beaumont, let him know what's happening. If you take Josh out to the playground at three twenty-five to meet his mum, I'll see you back here at three thirty-ish and we'll see where we are."

"Sounds like a plan. Thanks, Miss Brooks."

Chrissy left Josh and me alone in the staffroom. The hushed quiet descended over us and I didn't know what to say. Josh didn't seem to need me to speak, so I just held him close and stroked his hair gently as my mother had done for me when I was a child. I tried to offer as much comfort as I could to a frightened, sad little boy. I tried to get him to elaborate on his mum's condition a couple of times but couldn't coax him to say anything more than *she's fine* over and over again, so I just held him and hoped, reminding myself that my responsibility was to Josh and that he was all right.

We stayed like that for half an hour, holding each other tightly and watching the time creep agonisingly by. We didn't speak. There was nothing more to say. At 3.20, I ceased stroking, sighed and told Josh that it was time to go. We walked hand in hand to the cloakroom, where all of the other Little Owls were bustling around without a care in the world, oblivious to the potential tragedy in front of them, collecting their coats and bags and preparing for home. I helped Josh with his coat and his bag and tried to use the positivity of the other children to bolster myself as much as I could.

When he was sufficiently wrapped up, we went outside and scanned the playground thoroughly. It was quickly filling up with parents, but there was no sign of Mrs Nelson. I kept pressure on Josh's hand that was tightly gripping my own and hoped fervently that she would appear, but as the other children were dismissed and the playground slowly began to empty again, there was still nothing.

Josh and I walked to the gate after the last parent had disappeared, and we looked down the road. She wasn't there. She wasn't coming. We turned back through the playground, now deserted and eerily quiet, a single leaf swirling silently in the breeze. I shivered and held on tighter to the little hand in mine.

Halfway across the playground, Josh stopped dead in his tracks. He looked up at me, and his raw terror crashed into me. I staggered from the force of it and couldn't prevent it from taking hold. We were both terrified.

"She's not here," he said in a stunned, flat voice. "She said she'd be here." His voice rose until it was a cry. "She said she would be fine." His voice cracked on the last word, that awful word, and his face crumpled. He cried in earnest. Huge, wracking sobs that tore me apart to hear.

I scooped him up into my arms and looked him straight in the eye. "Right, Josh. You and I are going to be strong, OK?"

He sniffed and shook his head in misery.

"Don't give me that, Josh. You're a strong little boy. You're going to stay strong for me and for Mummy, OK?"

He wiped his sleeve across his face, smearing it with tears and snot that was pouring from his nose.

"OK," he whispered.

"Good boy," I said.

Back in the staffroom, there was a general murmur as teachers filed in and out. I filled Chrissy and Richard in, and they confirmed that they hadn't heard from MASH. I retrieved the phone and redialled both of his parents, again with no luck. I phoned MASH. The same woman answered and took my name, Josh's name and the reference number that she had supplied before.

"His mum isn't here," I said. "We can't get hold of her or his father and he has no emergency contacts listed. We need to get somebody down to the house … Now."

"Right, yes. I'll forward the message on, and we'll send a police patrol to the house and organise for someone to collect the child from school if his mother's not found or is not able to take care of him tonight."

Finally, something was happening. "Great. Thank you. How long will it take?"

"Right, yes. We can't give time frames just yet, I'm afraid. We'll have to establish when the nearest officers are available to attend. They're very busy, I'm afraid."

My hope faded again.

"OK. Please call me as soon as you know anything."

I ended the conversation and retrieved Josh from the staffroom again. I took him into the corridor alone and knelt in front of him, my hands firmly on his shoulders, looking him straight in the eye.

"Josh, look at me. I need you to tell me what's wrong with your mummy. Why couldn't she get up and bring you to school this morning? Please don't tell me she's fine. I need to know the truth so that we can help her. Please, Josh."

He looked at me. I could feel the fear inside him swirling like a flame in the breeze, burning him from the inside out, choking him and robbing him of reason. My fear threatened to match his and I struggled to fight the urge to run, to hide. I needed to do something, anything. I just needed to act. He still didn't speak. I gave him a little shake out of sheer frustration.

"Josh, please," I said again.

Josh opened his mouth. Nothing came out. He closed it and opened it again. The words came in a whisper.

"She isn't fine, Miss. She couldn't get up because it hurt

too much. She told me to go to school and she said she'd be fine, but she's not here and I don't think she's fine. She isn't fine, is she, Miss?"

He threw his arms around me again and poured out his fear. His sobs were muffled by my clothes, but I could feel him trembling against me, and I couldn't block out the fear and grief worming their way inside my mind. The emotions were building until they had nowhere to go. I couldn't sit here and wait for a phone call or ring again and go through another frustrating conversation with no relief. I couldn't do nothing. I felt like I was going to explode, and I couldn't fight it. I would have to get away from Josh to stand any chance of rebalancing my emotions, but I couldn't leave him, not now. I knew that my job was to stay here and stay strong and stay with Josh. I knew that I should wait for MASH or social services or the police to contact the school, but I also knew this little boy in front of me and I knew how he felt, and I knew that there might not be time. I let the walls down and embraced the fear. I let it flow through me and welcomed the adrenalin, giving me the strength to act, to do something and hang the consequences. I held Josh's hand tightly, and without a word, walked him down the corridor, out of the door and straight to my car.

Neither of us spoke while I fastened him in. Neither of us spoke while I started the engine and pulled out of the car park. At the car park entrance, I paused, took out my mobile and wrote a text message to Chrissy. *Sorry. Couldn't wait. I'm taking him home. He told me she couldn't get up. Call the police. I have to go.* I pressed 'send' and pulled out onto the road.

It was a five-minute drive to the Nelsons' house. I remembered it from my transition meeting in the summer, so I didn't need directions. We spent the journey in silence, wrapped in our own thoughts and fears about what might be waiting for us. I pulled up to the pavement outside and we got out and looked at the house. It was an ordinary house on an ordinary street. It showed no trace of the tragedy that might be unfolding inside. I started towards the front door. Josh gripped my hand and held me back.

"I didn't mean it," he said.

"What didn't you mean, Josh?" I asked.

"I was naughty. I'm always naughty. It's my fault," he said.

"What do you mean, Josh? What's your fault?"

"If I hadn't been naughty, he wouldn't have had to punish me. It would have been fine. But I was naughty, Miss, so he had to punish me, didn't he? He had to punish me and the best way to make me learn is to break things I love."

I felt the bile rising up my throat.

Josh continued. "There isn't much left, Miss. All my things are broken, but I still didn't learn. I was still naughty. I was naughty and everything was broken, and things weren't fine. You knew things weren't fine. I was supposed to make you believe that it was fine. No one was supposed to know but you knew and even when I said it was fine, you knew and then you told. He had to break her, Miss. She was the only thing I had left to love. I was naughty and he had to punish me, so he broke her. He broke Mummy and it's my fault."

I felt the cold dread in the pit of my stomach. How could no one have known? How could I not have seen what was happening? I knew that he was suffering, but I never thought for a moment ... I thought that Mr Nelson was also suffering because his wife was poorly. How could I not have known what kind of person he was? How could I have missed it? How could I have been so stupid? I reached for the front door handle. The door was unlocked and opened easily. It was cold inside, cold and deathly quiet. We stepped into the hallway and closed the door behind us.

Chapter 8

I paused in the dim hallway, reacquainting myself with the layout of the house. The kitchen was down the hall in front, the living room to my right. The cream-carpeted stairs rose to the left, up five steps, round a corner and then on up and out of sight. The whole place felt lifeless and hollow. All of the doors were closed. I tried to focus my senses, to feel the emotions of anyone who might be inside and might be in trouble. I assumed that Mr Nelson was still away at work but didn't want to risk being surprised by his unexpected and unwelcome appearance. He had made me nervous before, but after Josh's emotional revelations outside, I now realised that Mr Nelson was a very dangerous man indeed.

The problem was that all that I could hear was my own heart hammering in my ears, drowning out coherent thought. My terror was merging with the harrowing dread of the little boy whose hand I was gripping dangerously tightly in my own, flooding my system with adrenalin that was daring me to follow impulse over logic. My first instinct was to run and not look back, but I forced myself to breathe slowly, survey the house and try to make considered decisions. I turned my head to the side, listening, feeling my surroundings. I heard nothing apart from myself and Josh. I felt nothing, no regular sounds of life, no barking or scratching of a dog, no pain, no fear. I knew that there should be a dog. I remembered Josh talking about Clementine, but the house felt devoid of life and emotion. It only took my brain a split second to calculate what that absence of emotion might mean.

"Mummy?" Josh whispered. "Mummy?" he repeated louder. Nothing. No response. "Mummy?" he screamed, and he ripped his hand from mine and raced up the stairs, spurred into motion by his terror.

I was behind him in an instant, but he made it to the door first and burst violently into his parents' bedroom. I heard his tortured scream a split second before I reached him and grasped him to me, pulling his head down and away from the horrifying scene.

"Mummy!"

The agony of that ragged word was torment to my ears, and I wanted more than anything in the world to take his searing pain away. I felt it too and had to fight not to let it take over, not to succumb to the intense panic, to remain in control. I had to stay rational and act quickly and decisively. The next few minutes could be among the most important in my life. Mercifully, the figure in the bed was breathing, if you could describe the excruciating, panting sucking of air as breath. Mrs Nelson was alive, but she wasn't afraid and she wasn't in pain, which meant that she wasn't conscious, and considering the trauma in front of me, I had to count that as a blessing. I needed to assess the situation and get help immediately, and I had to hide the horror of the bloodstained sheets and what lay beneath from Josh. I pulled his head up and forced him to look into my eyes. He was struggling to get to the bed, but I held onto his shoulders tightly.

"Listen to me, Josh. This is very important. I need to look at Mummy. I need to help her. She's very, very badly hurt and I need you to be brave while I see to her, OK?"

Josh continued to fight me, but I held on tightly and forced him to hear. "It's important we do this as quickly as possible, Josh. I can't look after Mummy and you at the same time, and you can't help her like this. I need you to go into your bedroom and pack a bag with all the things you might need for a few days away. Can you do that?"

He stilled but now just stared at me with wide fear-stricken eyes.

"Josh," I repeated loudly, "Go now, to your bedroom, please. Close this door. When you have your things together, I want you to go downstairs, open the front door and wait for the ambulance that'll be coming to help. It's your job to show them where to come. It's a very important job. I don't want you to come back into this room. You've got to do this for me, for her. Go now, Josh." I turned him towards the door and gave him a little push.

"Yes ... Miss Bliss," he stammered, and with one last glance towards the bed, he left the room and closed the door. I took a deep breath and turned to face the bed.

I quickly took my phone out of my pocket before approaching the prone figure under the sheets. No matter what I found, I knew that the most immediate priority was to get an ambulance on its way. To my infinite relief, there was already a message flashing on the screen: *Police and ambulance on their way. They won't be long. You'd better be right about this.* Thank goodness for Chrissy. She was my hero. I felt the pressure ease a fraction.

As I approached the bed, I called out. There had been no movement or suggestion of awareness, and from the volume of blood on the bedding, that awful, rapid panting and the lack of fear in the air, I was certain that Mrs Nelson was unconscious, but I didn't want to startle her if I was wrong.

"Mrs Nelson? It's Isabel Bliss, Josh's teacher from school. The ambulance is on its way. I'm going to see what I can do to help you. Mrs Nelson?"

The horrifying sucking sound continued, punctuated occasionally with a harsh, dry cough. I didn't know how long the poor woman had been unconscious or how long she could continue to gasp for air before her body gave up. I stepped forward to the top of the bed and looked down. I couldn't hold back my own choked cry when I saw the unearthly wreckage of Mrs Nelson's face. It was an almost unrecognisable bloody mess. The entire left-hand side of her face was inflamed and distorted with puckered red and purple bruising from lip to eyebrow, and the eye was swollen shut. Her top lip was split open, jagged and distended, and her cheek looked strangely bent out of shape, as if an alien invader was trying to wear Mrs Nelson's discarded human skin. What remained of her face held a pallid bluish tinge, and there was blood trickling slowly from the corner of her mouth.

I automatically pulled a tissue from my pocket and gently dabbed at the blood. The ambulance was on its way and the patient was breathing. My critical first aid skills faltered after that point, and I had no idea what to do and was frightened to disturb the covers to examine any further.

"Oh, Mrs Nelson, I'm so sorry," I mumbled. "I should have known. I should have seen. I didn't realise. I didn't know." I was saved from any further investigation by the sound of sirens coming down the street.

"They're here, Miss," called Josh from the doorway.

I ran to the top of the stairs and saw him waving madly at the arriving crews. An ambulance and a police car pulled up almost simultaneously, and Josh was crying, although I wasn't sure whether it was with relief or fear. He was calling to them.

"She's in here. It's Mummy. She's upstairs. Please help her."

Suddenly, the house was filled with life and noise as two police officers and two paramedics came rushing through the door.

"She's up here," I called. "Please hurry, and don't let Josh see her."

One of the police officers gave me a nod — "Of course, Miss" — and guided Josh into the living room.

The paramedics and the second police officer continued up the stairs at a trot.

"She's in here," I said, and I stood aside to let them pass.

The paramedics approached the bed. "Shit," said the first one as he took in the blood-soaked sheets and the condition of Mrs Nelson's face. The other pulled the duvet all the way back without hesitation.

"Jesus fucking Christ. You'd better take a look at this before we move her." He motioned to the police officer hovering in the doorway, who came forward. I foolishly came with him, driven by a sort of dazed curiosity. What I

143

saw made me feel physically sick, and I stumbled backwards again. I felt the colour drain from my face and saw the matching reaction in the officer by my side.

Mrs Nelson was wearing a short-sleeved nightie that had ridden up above her hips, exposing her lower body grotesquely. It was light blue in colour and depicted a small flock of jovial sheep taking it in turns to jump over a gate. The heartless, perky sheep appeared to cruelly mock the figure that they danced upon. Every visible surface of her body was covered in injuries. There were fresh bruises, welts and a deep gash to her calf that was still oozing blood and accounted for much of the staining on the sheets, but there were also scars and healed wounds of all shapes and sizes over her legs and arms and deep purple bruising around her neck. I gasped again when I saw her wrists. They both had deep infected lesions running all the way around. They were old injuries where the skin had been torn over and over again in the same place, causing these deep, nasty burns, red around the edges, with yellow oozing, infected wounds in the centres. She must have been restrained, tightly and savagely, again and again, to cause these types of injuries that had blistered and burst and been defiled again.

My mind lurched back to all of the times that I had seen Mrs Nelson over the past couple of months on the playground and in the classroom. I had never thought about it before but now realised that she had always been totally covered, neck to toe. She wore high-necked jumpers or scarves and never removed her gloves, even inside. I couldn't believe how blind I had been. How could I not have realised that this woman was covering injuries from prying eyes, that she was in pain? All of a sudden, everything started to make sense, from Mrs Nelson keeping a distance from the other mums to Josh telling me that I wasn't supposed to know that there was a problem. *He says it's not real if we don't talk about it.*

I had missed all of the clues. I couldn't believe that I had been so stupid. I thought that I was one step ahead because of my ability. I thought that I would have known if I had been in a room with someone who was systematically torturing his wife and child, but the sort of man who was capable of this kind of sustained violence was not the sort of man who would exhibit normal emotions because clearly, he was anything but normal. He was a monster.

The paramedics were talking to Mrs Nelson in professional, soothing tones. They were reassuring her that they were here to help and that she would soon be receiving the care that she needed. Although they must have been horrified by what they saw, the professional way that they and the policemen handled themselves and their emotions was a great relief. The police officer asked the paramedics if he could take some photographs.

"Of course," said the first paramedic. "Anything that will help nail the bastard who did this, but we need to get her oxygen, fast, and we may need to relieve the pressure in her lung. She's got a traumatic pneumothorax where the bastard's broken her ribs and one's punctured her lung. She needs to get to hospital straight away. We haven't got much time. She's in a bad way, and if we don't get her there fast, you're going to be looking for a murderer. Take some photos quickly while we work. You'll be able to get more at the hospital later."

The officer nodded and started taking pictures while the paramedics continued their full assessment and emergency treatment.

"Miss? I'm going to have to ask you to leave the room please," said the police officer. "Please go and speak to my colleague downstairs."

I nodded my understanding and hurried from the room, relieved to be away from the scene of horror that I would never be able to erase from my memory. I rushed down the stairs into the living room, hurling myself towards Josh, who leapt off the settee as I came through the door and threw himself into my arms. Neither of us spoke for a moment. We just held each other and cried.

"I'm sorry," I told him over and over. "Shhh, Josh. Don't cry." I tried to soothe him through my own tears. "We're here now. Mummy's going to hospital and you're going to get all the help you need." I sat down heavily on the settee and pulled him onto my lap. He clung to me fiercely.

"Don't leave me, Miss," he whispered.

"I'm not going anywhere, Josh. Come here." And I held him to me and stroked him and made soothing noises until his breathing calmed and he was able to look up again, a little more under control.

The police officer introduced himself. "Hi, Josh, is it? And, sorry, you are?"

"Isabel. Isabel Bliss. Josh's teacher."

"I'm Paul," he addressed Josh. "I'm here to help you, and to do that, I need you to talk to me if you can. I need you to tell me a little bit about what happened to your mummy. Whatever you know."

Josh buried his head back into my chest and a fresh wave of tears ensued.

"It's OK, Josh," I soothed again. "I'm here and I'll help you as much as I can. How about we get a drink? That might make us feel a bit better and ready to talk." I stood to go into the kitchen, but Josh cried out.

"No, Miss. You can't go in there!"

The urgency of his cry stopped me, and I glanced at the police officer, a question in my eyes. The officer stepped in front of me and opened the kitchen door. He uttered a startled oath under his breath at the same time as Josh let go of me and ran past us both into the kitchen, crying out, "Clementine. Oh, Clementine. I'm so sorry I was bad. I'm so sorry this happened to you. I love you, Clementine."

I was there in a second and stood rooted to the spot when I saw Josh kneeling on the floor, trying to cuddle up to what must have once been his beloved Clementine. She had been a small dog, tan and white with curly hair, but she was now mangled, her body twisted at strange angles. Her life had been violently extinguished. I tried to make sense of the mess of fur and matted blood and gore, but something wasn't right. As I looked, I slowly realised that the problem was that the dog's head had been pulverised. Her skull had been crushed and her face had been beaten into a confused distortion, unrecognisable on the linoleum floor. Where there should have been shining eyes, a smooth coat and a wet nose, there was just a dark red congealed, furry mess. I thought that I could see brain matter in the mix, but I tried not to look more closely. It was like a scene from a horror film that I never wanted to see.

Josh was on his knees, trying desperately to find a clean piece of fur to stroke or to hold, as if his touch could put the poor creature back together. He was sobbing, his tears wetting the dog and the floor. He kept repeating, "I'm sorry. I'm sorry, Clementine. I'm so sorry," over and over again.

I thought that I might break at the heartrending sight and the outpouring of grief, but I couldn't allow myself that luxury yet. I had to be strong. I was all that Josh had right now. I went to him and pulled him away from the mess that used to be his adored pet. I picked him up and carried him back into the living room, stroking him and continuing to utter meaningless, soothing noises to try to take some of the anguish away.

"Don't you dare apologise for this, Josh. This is not your fault. None of this is your fault. Do you hear me?" I said firmly but softly. Josh nodded mutely.

The other police officer was coming down the stairs. He looked ashen and nauseated. He came into the living room and shut the door behind him so that Josh couldn't see his mum as the paramedics carried her out to the ambulance on a stretcher. He looked at Josh and then at me. He cleared his throat.

"She's going straight to the hospital now. He should go

too. Can you take him, or do you want us to call somebody?"

"No. I'm not leaving him. I'll take him to the hospital in my car," I replied.

"OK, good. We'll follow you down there when we've finished here. We've called for extra officers from Scenes of Crime to attend, and there'll be a duty social worker waiting at the hospital. We just need a few really quick details before you go, though, if you can manage?"

He looked at Josh, who was clinging to me again, fear and pain etched on his pale face.

"I'll help to answer anything you need to know," I said.

"Thank you," said Paul. "We'll need to speak to you both in much more detail later, but right now there are a number of priorities: getting Mrs Nelson treatment, securing the evidence in the house and catching the …" he paused. "Finding Mr Nelson," he said quietly. He looked at Josh. "Josh," he said gently, "can you tell me who did this to your mummy? Were you here when it happened? Did you …" He swallowed hard. "Did you see it happen?"

Josh sniffed and looked at me and then back to the officer.

"It was my fault," he stammered. "I knew I should be good but … he … I didn't mean to be bad," he whispered.

"Nothing's your fault, Josh," I said again. "You're not bad. You've done nothing wrong. Your father …" I didn't know what to say either. "Just tell the police officers what you told me earlier, Josh. Just tell them, and we can go and see the doctors who are looking after your mum."

Josh took another deep, jagged breath. I was only now starting to realise how tortured this little boy had been, and I marvelled at the cruelty of a person who could do this to his own child. I was also freshly and more deeply impressed by the resilience that Josh had shown, turning up to school every day, and in the main, behaving rationally and lucidly, whilst at home, he had been living in a vicious nightmare.

"I've always been naughty," he began, and I shook my head at him and held him tightly. "When I'm bad, Daddy has to punish me, to teach me," he continued between sniffs. "He broke my toys; he broke all my things. He broke Bossy." Josh faltered again and I gave him a reassuring squeeze.

"Go on, sweetie," I said.

"He broke Clementine too." He took a hard, shuddering breath. "Sometimes he had to hurt Mummy because she was my favourite and it was the only way I'd learn. Last night … or this morning … in the night … he broke Mummy. I heard her crying, but she always told me to keep away when he was like that, so I didn't go in. I didn't help her. This morning her voice sounded weird, but she told me not to go into the room. She told me to walk to school on my own. She told me that she would be all right. She told me through the door. She sounded hurt, but she said not to come in and that she would be at school at three twenty-five to get me … but she wasn't there. She didn't come."

On the last word, Josh's voice cracked with the effort and the overwhelming emotion. I could hardly bear the pain ripping through my body: pain that I was experiencing for myself and absorbing from Josh. I was overloaded with anguish, guilt and agony, and I could see that Josh couldn't go on.

"That's enough," I told him. "That's enough, isn't it?" I checked with the police.

"Yes. That's all we need for now," Paul confirmed. "Please could you help him gather enough clothes and belongings for a few days away? I'm not sure when he'll be able to come back to the house."

"Of course," I said, and I stood. Josh didn't move. I wasn't sure if he could move. I held out my arms and he came to me. I lifted him and settled him on my hip, like I might have done for a toddler. He was a little heavy to be comfortable, but I honestly don't think that he had the strength to manage for himself. He was totally drained. I suspected that he was going into shock. I suspected that I would probably go into shock soon too, but not yet. I couldn't let go yet. I carried him slowly up the stairs.

"Which one's your room, Josh?" I asked. "Could you show me your things? Did you pack a bag already?" I tried to keep it light even though there was no way to achieve any such thing. Josh pointed to the second door along the corridor and I pushed it open and stopped, open-mouthed, in the doorway, horrified to come face to face with yet another scene from another nightmare.

"Oh, Josh," I whispered, and I felt my legs give way. I crumpled to the floor with Josh still in my arms, and we sat looking at each other as I tried to keep my eyes from wandering around the room. Tears were still fresh in his eyes, and I felt a swelling of sympathy coming from Josh. He felt sorry for me. He was feeling sympathy because I had to witness the nightmare that he had been living. His strength was inspiring.

"It's OK, Miss," he reassured me. "They're just things. Daddy needed to remind me what happens when I'm bad. He did it to help me learn to be good."

The police officers must have heard me cry out or fall because they both came rushing up the stairs. They followed us into Josh's bedroom, stopped at the door and also stared at the horror in front of them. Paul gazed around with his mouth opening and closing like a fish, revulsion written plainly across his face. The other officer broke the silence first.

"What the …? Who would …? What kind of sick …?" He turned to me. "Just collect his things as quickly as you can and try not to touch anything that you don't need to. Don't move anything."

I nodded dumbly and continued to gaze, horrified, around the room. Everywhere I looked, there were eyes staring stonily back at me: glass eyes, felt eyes, plastic eyes. They had once been the eyes of innocent toys, but instead of sweet, entertaining or engaging figures and soft teddies, I was staring into hundreds of eyes of grotesque, disfigured monsters. Josh's toys hadn't just been broken; they had been deliberately and carefully torn apart and then painstakingly rearranged into contorted poses that made no sense except in this world of nightmares. There were hundreds of toys in that room, hundreds of toys that had all been attentively mutilated. Limbs had been torn from bodies, stuffing expelled from torsos, and some of the fragments of the toys still had the instruments of their torture impaled into their fabric. To have butchered these items of innocence in this manner would have been heinous in itself, but the dismembered bodies had then been reassembled to create Frankensteinesque monsters and arranged around the room so that there was no escaping their glare, and that was what was so appalling — that this had not been an isolated incident of passion or rage, but a calculated and sustained reign of torture.

It was tempting to presume a theory of madness in someone capable of this kind of abuse, but this behaviour couldn't be attributed to madness or a lack of control. This was deliberate, careful, intelligent, evil behaviour. This was a person who had calculated how to cause his own child the worst torment and had then purposefully set out to inflict that pain and horror. Labelling a man like this as mad or insane would be too forgiving, too easy. I had seen him in my classroom, morning after morning for months. I had felt his emotions. I knew that he had been a little anxious on occasion, but he had never been mad. I had never sensed that he was out of control. He had left this house, this scene of torture, with his son every morning and had smiled at me as he helped Josh remove his coat and hang it on his peg. He had smiled at me and nodded, and I had returned that nod and that smile, all the time unaware that this was the hell that was waiting for Josh at home. I had actually felt sorry for the man, believing that he was struggling to deal with the prospect of losing a physically failing wife. This man did not deserve my sympathy. He did not deserve a thing.

The police officers were still at the edge of the room.

They were looking at Josh and me, assessing if we had ourselves under control. I looked back at the officers in turn and probed their emotions, needing to regain balance and stability for Josh. I sensed the predictable shock and anger in the men, but they both also had the professionalism that kept the more extreme reactions wrapped up and under control. They had a job to do, and overriding their primitive emotions was a sense of steely determination. I could feel that these were sympathetic men, appalled by the crimes committed within this family, but they had a job to do. Paul and his partner wanted to gather all of the evidence quickly and securely and then use it to catch the man who had committed these crimes and bring him to justice. To do that, they needed strength and control, which is exactly what I needed at that moment and what I couldn't conjure on my own. I picked myself up, mentally shook myself off and drew deeply on their fortitude, bolstering my own courage. I gave Josh's hand another reassuring squeeze, stood and reached for his bag that was open on the bed. He drew on my emotional support, and together we proceeded to gather his things so that we could follow his mum to the hospital.

Josh had already made a start and didn't need much, so it wasn't long before we had his things together. I wanted to get out of that room and out of that house without delay. I would usually ask a child if he had a favourite toy that he wanted to bring, but in this situation, I thought that I already knew the answer. There was nothing in this house that would bring Josh any comfort, only reminders of the nightmares that he had endured.

"Right, is that everything, then, Josh?" I checked anyway.

He nodded but then stopped and whispered, "Actually, there is one more thing. One thing that's mine. It's in Mummy's room, though. Can we go in there?"

I turned to the police officers, who nodded, "As long as we come with you, that'll be fine," said Paul.

Josh bravely led the three of us back into his parents'

bedroom. He carefully didn't look at the bed, and I tried to block out the image of Mrs Nelson's prone, bloody form and the sounds of the woman's desperate, unconscious gasping for air. Josh got down on his knees and reached under the bed. He stretched up beneath the mattress and rummaged for a moment before pulling out a small, plain shoe box that must have been wedged carefully between the mattress and the frame. He opened the box reverently and smiled tenderly. Inside the box was a soft toy donkey, and he stroked it gently, lifted it from the box, held it to his nose and inhaled deeply. It was a black and white donkey with a red rope around its head and ears. It was all in one piece but appeared dog-eared and thoroughly loved. Josh gave it a squeeze.

"It's Dennis," he told us quietly. "Mummy made him for me with her sewing, and he could only come out when it was just the two of us." He hugged Dennis tightly and then glanced accidentally, instinctively, at the bed and blanched at the sight of the blood-soaked sheets. He pulled himself back into my side and looked up beseechingly.

"Can we go now, Miss?" he sniffed. "Can we go and see Mummy?"

"Yes, Josh. Let's go."

Josh and I walked back down the stairs in silence. I escorted him to my car, helped him back onto the seat and leaned over to fasten him in. Paul came to the front door. He took a few personal details and told me that he would see me at the hospital later, when they had finished at the house. He was a kind, gentle man with determination in his eyes and his heart.

"It sounds like he knew what was coming," he said. "It was inevitable after what he did. He didn't show up for work this morning. No one's heard from him all day. He's on the run, but we'll find him. We'll get him for what he's done here. For all of this."

"Thank you," I said, simply. "We'll see you at the hospital later." And I climbed into the car and pulled away from the curb, that house and all of its suffering.

Chapter 9

It was a subdued twenty-five minutes to the hospital, with the two of us lost in our own disturbing thoughts. I couldn't help replaying all of Josh's bad days at school during the last couple of months over and over in my mind: the days that he had been particularly quiet or distracted and when I had sensed the fear inside him but had failed to do anything to help. I had known that he was in pain, that he was tormented, even, but I hadn't known why, and instead of pushing, I had let him down. I hadn't fully understood the depth of his distress and had tried to write him off as an oversensitive or emotional child, and more recently, I had convinced myself that his mum was poorly and that his upset was caused by his worry for her health. With my ability to sense emotions, I should have done more, seen more, known more. I had fallen short in my duty of care.

It was obvious now that his bad days were the ones after he had been *punished* by his father, when he had had his things broken and destroyed. One would have been when Mr Nelson killed the rabbit, Bossy, and others when he had broken Josh's favourite toys or tied his mother up by her wrists and wounded her to exert some kind of sadistic control over his four-year-old son. I wondered when he had so diabolically and savagely murdered Clementine and whether Josh had been forced to watch. I realised with a jolt that something awful must have happened last Thursday night, after I had cornered him on the playground and told him that I was worried about Josh and his mother: the day before Josh didn't come to school. To think that I had felt sorry for Mr Nelson when all of the time he was inflicting the suffering, and I had only exacerbated the situation by divulging to him that Josh hadn't been playing his part. He had ruthlessly butchered Josh's beloved pet because Josh hadn't been able to convince me that everything was *fine*. Was it my fault that Clementine had lost his life? Was it my fault that Mrs Nelson had been savagely beaten and left for dead in her own home? The vicious circle of thoughts was dizzying and distasteful, and the rational part of my brain knew that putting the burden of guilt upon myself was unhelpful. There was only one culprit, one monster.

I called Jack on the drive. I explained where we were going and that I would be staying with Josh until he was taken care of and safe. I told him as much as I could with Josh present and Jack was wonderful, as always: understanding, patient and worried.

"You know you don't cope well at hospitals," he reminded me gently. "Do you want me to come, to be with you?"

"Thank you, but I'll be fine. It'll be hard, but I have to be there for Josh, and if you come, I might lean on you too much and not be able to stay strong enough for him. I'm prepared. Honestly, don't worry about me. I don't know when I'll be home. I'll try to call you again, but if I'm not home by bedtime, don't wait up. I'll see you soon."

I didn't really need reminding. The thought of entering that place again after all of these years was filling me with a hollow dread, but I needed to be there for Josh, and I didn't know what was going to happen or what the authorities would require from me. I wasn't sure whether I had convinced Jack that I would be all right. I certainly hadn't convinced myself. I never went to see him at work and did everything in my power to avoid ever having to set foot in a hospital. They were full of pain. They were full of suffering, sadness, heartbreak and grief, and I couldn't help absorbing and reflecting everybody else's misery. The thought of being surrounded by patients and worried, emotional, exhausted relatives and friends of patients terrified me, but I didn't have a choice. I would be there for Josh, no matter what. I could fall apart later.

I parked near the main entrance. I didn't know where Mrs Nelson would be or if there would be a delegation sent out to meet Josh, but the main reception seemed a sensible place to start. I took his hand and helped him out of the car. He looked so young and helpless as he climbed out and looked up into my eyes with absolute faith that I hoped I deserved. He was helpless and frightened and with good reason. I was all that he had right now. There were no next of kin or emergency contact details on his school file, but I still asked him if there was anyone else who I should call.

"A grandma or grandpa or an aunty? Anyone who could help to look after you?"

He just shook his head and continued to look at me with those innocent, beseeching eyes.

"There's just Mummy," he said in a whisper. "Grandma and Grandpa went away before I was born. We don't see them."

"Do you know where they went?"

Josh shook his head. "I don't really remember. Daddy said we were better off without them."

As we walked into the hospital hand in hand, with Dennis the donkey clutched tightly to Josh's chest, I kept thinking about the horrors in that house. I had witnessed it for just a few minutes and knew that it would stay with me for the rest of my life. I couldn't imagine what kind of damage that sort of prolonged torture would do to a four-year-old who had lived with it for his entire life and who had been mercilessly taught that the pain and the suffering was his fault. He was going to need a lot of love, a lot of time and a lot of therapy to have any hope of a normal life untainted by the inhumanity of his father. I desperately hoped that his youth and innocence meant that we might have been able to intervene early enough, but I knew how much he was going to need his mother to get him through. I didn't know much about medicine, but Mrs Nelson had been in a really bad way — a really, really bad way. Losing his mother on top of everything else could destroy him, especially when he would blame himself for that too.

We entered the hospital, and my stomach was churning. I was mostly worried for Josh, but this had already been by far the most challenging day of my life, and the fear, the pain and the horror of my experiences at the Nelsons' house had sent my emotions even further into overdrive. I was in a state of heightened anxiety and emotionally exhausted, but I had to find the strength to hold Josh's hand through his ordeal. I couldn't let him down. The torment could take me under later, when I had done what I needed to do. At that moment, I needed all of my strength. What I had seen and experienced over the last few hours would have been enough to send the most grounded, stoic of individuals into a spin. My heightened sensitivity to emotion was what had put me into this situation and ensured that Josh and I got to Mrs Nelson, hopefully before it was too late, but that same capability was just as likely to be my undoing.

I needn't have worried about finding out where we needed to be. There was a small group of people waiting for us in the fresh, spacious hospital entrance. There was a police officer in uniform, two professionally dressed women wearing identifying lanyards, and a casually dressed couple holding hands and glancing anxiously around them. One of the more official looking ladies approached Josh and me as we entered the building. She looked friendly. She had a warm, kind face and a pretty smile.

Her focus was all on Josh. Her body language and open, affectionate smile gave him everything he needed to know. She was there for him. He was her priority. I sensed it too and immediately felt lighter. At last I wasn't on my own. I caught the woman's deep brown eyes and focused on her mood. I connected with a calm assurance and let it wash over me, fractionally soothing and alleviating my fractured mind. We met halfway across the foyer, and the lady stopped, bent down so that she was eye to eye with Josh and addressed him directly.

"Hi. You must be Josh, right?"

Josh nodded nervously.

"My name's Sonya. I'm going to be in charge of looking after you while the doctors look after your mummy, OK?"

Josh nodded again, and I read the lanyard introducing Sonya as part of the council's social services team.

"Would you like to come and meet the other people that I've brought with me?" she asked him. "I know you're going to like them very much."

Josh looked unsure. "Can I see Mummy?" he asked.

I felt my heart tighten, but Sonya took the question in her stride. "Your mummy's with the doctors at the moment," she said. "But how about we make a deal?"

Josh didn't look ready to agree to anything just yet, but he didn't argue either, and Sonya continued.

"How about you come and meet these lovely people and then we go upstairs and talk to the doctors?" She waited for his response, not hurrying him but letting him come to it in his own time.

"OK," agreed Josh.

Sonya turned back around, walked a few steps towards the four people waiting, then stopped and glanced back at Josh, inviting. She held her hand out to him. Josh looked at me and then back at Sonya. He definitely wasn't sure. I had been his only safety net up until this point, but I nodded to him and released his hand. He only hesitated for another moment and then bravely stepped forwards and put his little hand into Sonya's outstretched one. Her smile subtly grew, and she gave the hand a welcoming squeeze. She and I shared a conspiratorial moment when our eyes met and we acknowledged the triumph of helping him take the first step towards trusting someone new. I felt a huge relief. Josh would be taken care of.

We walked to where the others were waiting, and everyone sat down. Josh let go of Sonya's hand, returned to me and climbed onto my knee. Sonya seemed happy to let him go, satisfied with baby steps. She introduced the rest of the group, talking to Josh all of the time.

"This is Amy," she said, pointing to the other official lady, who smiled at Josh and gave him a little wave. "Amy works with me at social services and will be getting to know you and working with you over the coming weeks. This is Stephen. He's a police officer like the ones that came to your house today. Paul, who you met earlier, will be here soon too. Stephen and Paul will be in charge of making sure you're safe."

Stephen nodded. Josh was looking at the couple who had yet to be introduced with interest, and I noticed that the woman had a green and brown cuddly dinosaur in her hands.

"These," Sonya continued, "are two very, very special people. This is Mark and Hope. They've got a bedroom at their house with no one living in it at the moment, and if it's OK with you, they would like to offer it to you for a little while while your mummy's poorly."

Josh looked fearfully at me. "Miss? I don't want to go anywhere else. I want to stay with Mummy."

"Oh, Josh," I replied. "Of course you do, but you also want your mummy to get better, don't you?"

"Yes, Miss," he agreed.

"That's what everyone else wants too," I reassured him, "and the best place for that to happen is right here with all the doctors who can look after her. She needs rest, and while she's being looked after here, these people are going to look after you. Mummy would want to know that you're being looked after too, wouldn't she? Is that OK?"

Josh was still unsure. These people were strangers after all, but Hope tiptoed over to our seat and crouched on the floor next to him. She was a naturally unassuming lady with delicate bearing. She exuded calmness and consistency, and I knew instantly that she would offer unwavering support if she was on your side. Her initial impression was one of cosy comfort. It reminded me of my own mother and made me think of warm home-baked apple pie. She oozed warmth and dependability in a similar way to Sonya, and I was impressed with the suitability of the team that had been put together so quickly for Josh in his hour of need.

Hope tentatively reached out a hand and put it gently on Josh's knee. He didn't flinch from that intimacy, and she smiled warmly at him. She nodded at Dennis.

"That's one good-looking donkey you've got there," she told him. "Have you seen my dinosaur?"

Josh nodded. Hope held the dinosaur up so that it was nose-to-nose with Dennis. "My dinosaur likes the look of your donkey," she said. She bit down on her bottom lip in mock concern. "You don't think he's going to eat him, do you?"

Josh laughed timidly. "No," he said. "That's a diplodocus. They don't eat donkeys. They're herbivores."

"Herbivores, you say?" said Hope, relieved. "Thank goodness for that. Hopefully, that means my dinosaur and your donkey can be friends. What do you think?"

Josh nodded.

"Does your donkey have a name?" asked Hope.

"Dennis," said Josh.

Hope frowned. "My dinosaur, my diplodocus, doesn't have a name. Maybe, if he's going to be friends with Dennis, you could look after him for me?" Josh nodded again. "And maybe you could give him a name too? If you give him a name for me, then I think he'll be your dinosaur. How about that?"

Josh nodded once more, emphatically this time, and Hope held the toy out for him to take. He slid off my knee and stepped forwards. "Thank you," he whispered.

"Oh, darling boy, you're very welcome," said Hope with a tear in her eye, and she opened her arms to him. He stumbled into her embrace and let her hug him tightly. I watched the exchange with delight and had to wipe a stray tear from my own eye. My emotions were all over the place, and it was wonderful to know that Josh was going to be looked after by these kind, loving people.

Our motley group of seven walked together to the lifts, and Stephen pressed the button for the second floor. He seemed to know where he was going. Navigating the hospital corridors was made considerably easier than I had anticipated by the team of confident, caring people surrounding me. I was able to concentrate on their stability and quiet calm, and for a time, I almost felt normal, although the burden of the last few hours had left my emotions confused and my mind and body exhausted. We stepped out of the lift and followed Stephen to a desk with numerous medical staff milling around behind it. At the sign, 'Major Trauma Unit,' my stomach clenched again. I had seen only a fraction of Mrs Nelson's wounds briefly, the ones visible on her face and arms and legs. I knew that there must have been other injuries that I couldn't see and assumed that there had been some internal damage too. One of the paramedics had talked about a punctured lung, and I remembered that awful panting, sucking sound that Mrs Nelson had been making in her instinctive effort to breathe, to stay alive. I was petrified about what the doctors were going to say.

We were led into a small, empty room by a middle-aged doctor in a white coat. He wore dark-rimmed glasses and looked owlish and serious. He gestured for us to sit. He cleared his throat and looked uncertainly around the group, unsure to whom he should be talking.

Sonya took the lead. "Hi," she said, "I'm Sonya. I'll be in charge of Josh's care for the time being. This is Josh. Cathy Nelson's his mum who the ambulance brought in. Hope and Mark are our emergency foster carers, and this is Isabel, Josh's teacher, and Amy from the social care team. I think you've already met Stephen."

The doctor nodded. "Hi," he said to the room. "I'm Doctor Atkins. I'm head of the Major Trauma Unit and will be following Cathy's … erm … your mother's progress." He cleared his throat again.

"Can I see her, please?" Josh asked.

"No, Josh, you can't see her yet. She's very poorly," replied Dr Atkins uncomfortably. He didn't come across as a man who was used to being around children.

There was a quiet knock at the door and Paul, the police officer from the house, came in.

"Sorry I'm late," he said. "I wanted to be here for the briefing."

Dr Atkins gestured for him to join them.

"Thanks," said Paul. "Mark's stayed behind with Scenes of Crime, but as I'll be working with the family liaison team, I wanted to be here. Also, we'll make sure there's an officer on the door of Mrs Nelson's room at all times, just until we're sure that no one who might want to cause her harm's anywhere near the hospital." He saw Josh's eyes widen and hurried on, "That's just a precaution, Josh. It's what we always do when someone has been hurt like this. There's no reason to believe your dad will come anywhere near the hospital. He doesn't want us to see him."

Josh nodded and looked back at the doctor. "So, when can I see her?" he asked.

Dr Atkins took a deep breath and glanced at everyone in the room in turn. He eventually settled on Paul, seeming happier to address another man. "Cathy's badly hurt, but we think she's going to pull through."

There was a collective sigh of relief, and I felt tears stinging my eyes again. I saw Hope's arms tighten around Josh, who had gravitated towards her when we had entered the room, and Mark put his hand on Josh's shoulder and gave it a little squeeze.

"The injuries she has sustained are very serious," Dr Atkins went on. "The most serious are the trauma to her face and her ribs, which has led to damage to her lung. She's also lost a lot of blood. She's in surgery now to fix her lung, and she's received numerous transfusions. Once she's made it through the operation and she's stable, we'll be able to start looking at the damage to her face and the more superficial damage to the rest of her body. My team will, of course, be putting a report together for the police."

Paul nodded. "Thank you, Doctor," he said.

Dr Atkins continued. "Josh, you won't be able to speak to your mother today. We'll keep her sedated, in a deep sleep, so her body has time to heal on the inside. There's still a risk while she goes through the operation, and we'll keep her in Intensive Care tonight. As long as there are no complications, she'll be moved to Recovery tomorrow, and hopefully, she'll be awake and you'll be able to talk to her then. I'm cautiously optimistic, but her recovery will be long, and she'll need a lot more work in the weeks to come. We may have to reconstruct some of her facial features, but we'll know more when the swelling goes down. At present, we've found no sign of other internal damage. She should be out of surgery in about an hour. I presume you'll wait in the hospital until then?"

Sonya nodded and thanked the doctor. He told us that we had use of the room for as long as we needed and that he would let us know when Mrs Nelson was out of surgery. Stephen excused himself to relieve the officer currently outside the operating theatre where she was being treated, and Sonya suggested that Mark and Hope take Josh to find something to eat.

"I'm not hungry," Josh said. "I want to be here when the doctor comes back."

"We will be," said Mark gently. "Don't worry. I bet your mum would want us to make sure you got something to eat and drink, though, wouldn't she?"

Josh nodded reluctantly.

"That's what I thought. We want you to be able to tell her that we've been looking after you properly so she hasn't got to worry about anything other than getting better, don't we?"

Josh nodded again. Hope held her hand out to him, and this time, he went to her without hesitation. He glanced back at me as they left the room.

"You won't go, will you, Miss?" he asked.

"Of course not, not yet, Josh. You go and get something to eat. I'll be here when you get back."

As soon as Josh left the room, I slumped forward and put my head into my hands. I was suddenly shaking all over. I had been holding onto my control so tightly for him and could now feel the repressed fear, horror and panic flooding my system. I put my head between my legs and tried to breathe, but my breath was quickly becoming more shallow, more rapid. The jumbled thoughts and fragmented images were careering through my mind at a hundred miles an hour, and my heart was hammering, trying to burst out of my chest. If I let the panic attack take hold, I knew that I wouldn't be able to pull myself back together. I tried to concentrate, to slow everything down, but I couldn't stop the rush of emotion like a tidal wave threatening to overwhelm me.

I felt a steadying hand on my shoulder and instinctively put my own hand over it and grasped it tightly, an anchor in the storm. There was a soothing presence close by, and I latched onto it with all the strength that I could muster and used it to slowly settle my breathing and push the darkness threatening to engulf me away again. I took a few deep breaths and opened my eyes to see Sonya standing by my side, holding onto me and offering her strength. I tried to smile but felt closer to tears. I nodded in gratitude.

"Thank you," I said emotionally. "It's been a tough afternoon." I could feel my bottom lip trembling and chose not to say any more until I could trust myself to speak.

"I'll say," agreed Sonya. "You've been through a lot. Don't underestimate how hard this is on you." She handed me a white plastic cup of cold water and I drank from it greedily, concentrating on the physicality of the icy chill flowing reassuringly through my body.

"Cases like this come along reassuringly rarely, and we can only thank God that Josh isn't physically hurt and Mrs

165

Nelson should pull through." She paused for a moment and then went on. "I'm so sorry to have to do this to you now, but we've got a bit of time while Mrs Nelson's in surgery, and the Hancocks have taken Josh for a while. Do you think you can talk about it?"

Paul nodded. "We need to take a statement from you, and the sooner we do it, the more detailed your memory will be."

"And we also need as much information as possible, as soon as possible, to help Josh," added Sonya. "The first few days will be critical, and the more we know from you, the more we can put together and the better equipped we'll be to help him." She put her hand back on my shoulder, and I covered it once more with my own, drawing again on Sonya's solid strength.

I took a few more deep breaths. Of course I could do it, for Josh. I nodded.

"Let's get started, then."

Sonya and Amy reached into their bags and brought out notepads and pens. Paul started up a laptop that had mysteriously appeared out of nowhere. It was Amy who spoke this time. She had been an unobtrusive presence until now but had been following everything closely. She leaned forward and looked at me kindly.

"I'm Amy," she said. "I'm a child psychotherapist with Child and Adolescent Mental Health Services. I'll be taking notes to help me figure out what Josh has been through. I'll be talking to Josh soon and will compare what you tell us with what he opens up to us about. Sometimes children talk about all the abuse once they're out of a situation. Some children never admit it or speak about it. Some children block it from their memories altogether. Some move on and live happy, healthy, normal lives. Some live in the shadow of their abuse for the rest of their lives. Some develop mental health problems but certainly not all. It'll make a big difference for Josh once Mr Nelson's in custody, and again when he's tried, and hopefully, put away for a long time.

Josh needs to feel safe. He's been controlled by his dad for a long time, probably his entire life. Dad will have told him what he can and can't say … what he can and can't feel. Josh feels safe with you. You'll be a big part of his recovery, and I hope you'll join us for some of our sessions."

"Of course," I said. "I'll do anything he needs."

Paul spoke next. "Your witness statement will stick to the facts of the case," he explained. "For Josh's recovery, the ladies want your opinions, but I'll be sticking to the facts. That doesn't mean we won't cover how some of the things you saw made you feel, but it does mean that we have to be careful not to include hearsay in your evidence. If you start from the beginning, the ladies and I will be writing down different parts of what you tell us because our records hold different purposes. Start from as soon as you noticed a problem with Josh and keep going until you get to now. If we need you to slow down, repeat or clarify anything you say, one of us will let you know. It doesn't matter if we don't get all of it today; we'll be speaking again over the next few months, but it's important to get as much as we can while it's fresh. If you think you can."

"OK," I said shakily. "I think I can do that."

"Take your time," said Sonya gently. "You're not the one on trial here. We're all on the same side."

"Thank you," I said. I think that she understood that it was all a little overwhelming.

I sat back in my chair and closed my eyes for a moment, thinking back to that first time that I had connected with Josh and felt his anguish besieging me. I remembered it vividly because it was the first time in a long time that I had been so intensely affected by another person and the first time in forever that I had felt that kind of emotion from a child. I was worried at the time. I wondered what could have upset him to the extent that his emotions caused me physical pain. I had been worried about him ever since and my concern had intensified over the last couple of weeks, but never in my wildest dreams could I have imagined the things that I had seen. I opened my eyes and took a deep breath.

"Some of what I say will probably sound really strange," I said, cautiously. "It started with a feeling. I've always been quite … erm … astute, I suppose … when it comes to how people are feeling. There was a day, I think it was in the second … No, I think it was the third week of term …."

I spoke for what seemed like a long time. The three witnesses interrupted occasionally and asked me to explain something again or clarify my meaning, but for the most part, they listened attentively and made their notes. I tried not to sound too unhinged when telling them that I just knew that Josh was feeling frightened or sad, even when there were no outward signs, nobody else saw it, and Josh assured me on multiple occasions that he was fine. I told them how that word seemed to be programmed into his vocabulary and how uncomfortable it had begun to make me feel. I told them about confronting Mrs Nelson and then Mr Nelson on the playground, referring them to Early Help, and I ended with my unsanctioned dash to Josh's house just a couple of hours ago. They listened intently as I described what I saw at the house, and I felt their emotions spike as I spoke about finding Mrs Nelson in the bed, discovering Clementine in the kitchen and the hideously disfigured toys in Josh's room.

When I reached our arrival at the hospital, I stopped. "And here we are." It actually felt rather cathartic to get it all out.

"Here we are indeed," said Sonya. "Thank you, Isabel. I know it's been awful for you, and you did really well. What you've told us is going to help immeasurably as we start talking to Josh and assessing his state of mind going forward. You clearly have a knack for reading children and a close bond with him."

I smiled ruefully at the understatement but was pleased that my account had been taken seriously and not dismissed as lunacy.

"And I don't think it would be wrong to say that without

your insistence and involvement with the Nelsons, this situation could have gone on for much longer and become even more of a problem for both Josh and Cathy," continued Sonya.

"I don't know," I said, voicing my deepest concerns. "I know it's not helpful, but I can't help feeling responsible for how things turned out for Clementine and Mrs Nelson. If I hadn't pushed Mr Nelson last week ..."

"Nonsense," Paul interrupted. "There's only one person to blame here and that sure as hell isn't you. People, monsters like this, always end up lashing out and doing serious damage in the end. If you hadn't acted when you did, it could easily be Josh lying in a hospital bed too, or worse."

Josh burst through the door at that moment. I had been talking for over an hour.

"The doctors have just came out of the room!" he cried. "They're smiling, Miss." He threw himself into my arms and I lifted him off the ground and spun him round in delight. Dr Atkins was right behind him, accompanied by a younger man, another doctor. They were both smiling.

"Good news travels fast, I see," said Dr Atkins. "This is Doctor Gotleib. He was the surgeon who worked on your mother, Josh. He's done a wonderful job, and unless there are any complications over the next twenty-four hours, we're confident she's going to be all right."

The eruption of joy and relief in that tiny room made me feel lightheaded. The excitement swirled around me and mixed with my already frayed emotions, and I had to sit back down before I fell. Sonya came over to me.

"Isabel, we've got it from here," she said. "You've been great, and we will, of course, keep you informed of any developments. I've written my direct number and Mark and Hope's number on my card, and you have Paul's details too. Please don't hesitate to call any of us, any time." She turned to Josh. "Josh? Dr Atkins says you can come back tomorrow morning and Mummy should be awake then, and you can talk to her and give her a very gentle cuddle. In the meantime, Miss Bliss is going to go back to her house and we're going to get you and Dennis and …?" She looked quizzically at the dinosaur.

"Dean," said Josh.

"Dean," she repeated.

"Dean the Diplodocus," he confirmed.

"Dennis the donkey and Dean the Diplodocus?" I laughed and pulled Josh in for a cuddle.

"Yes, Miss. Dennis and Dean."

Everyone laughed.

"They're certain to be best friends."

"Listen to me," I said. "You're one of the most wonderful, bravest, amazingest people I know. I've got to go home now, and you're going with Hope and Mark and they're going to look after you, but I'll speak to you tomorrow, OK?"

"Yes, Miss." Josh cuddled me before slipping his hand into Hope's. I could see that he didn't need me anymore, and that was OK. He was going to be all right. I said my goodbyes and made my way out of the hospital and back to my car alone. I needed to be alone.

Chapter 10

I pulled out of the dusky hospital car park in a bit of a daze. It was a busy evening. There were many people bustling around, coming and going. They passed close by my car, but I didn't see them, not really. I was aware of their presence, but I couldn't focus on anything. My mind was blank. It was as if I were moving through an impenetrable fog. Now that I didn't have to stay strong for Josh, I began to fall apart. I couldn't think. I didn't want to think. The blackness obscuring my thoughts was probably safer right now, so I embraced the gloom.

I felt numb, driving on autopilot, disconnected from my own body and mind. It was as if I were hovering above the Earth, watching somebody else driving my car, living this day: somebody who wasn't scared, who wasn't about to burst into hysterical tears or start screaming in order to drown out the roaring of the emotions that were clamouring to be released from my mind. The numbness was protecting me. I told myself that I wasn't really there, I hadn't really lived this day, all of this hadn't really happened, and I didn't have to think about it; I didn't have to deal with it. I couldn't hide from it forever, though. It had happened, and I knew that I would have to think about it and I would have to deal with it. I couldn't hold back the flood of emotions for long. I was going to have to stop, and I was going to have to let them out.

It was late. It was dark. It was cold. Until I began driving away from the hospital, I hadn't planned on visiting the lake. Any normal person would have searched for comfort at home, in the arms of their loved ones, but I found myself in remote darkness, and as I pulled into the deserted car park, I knew I was where I needed to be. I couldn't go home yet. I didn't want to see anyone, talk to anyone, be with anyone, not even Jack — maybe especially not Jack. I needed to be alone.

I had to allow the horde of emotions to come forward into my conscious mind so that I could sort through them, process them and exorcise them. It was going to be painful and confronting, but there was no other choice. If I didn't deal with them now, on my terms, they would pick the time and the place. They would hide in the recesses of my mind until such a time that I couldn't contain them any longer, and then they would creep out and incapacitate me. They would usurp my own emotions and render me helpless and unable to function coherently. I couldn't take the risk of that happening when I least expected it. There was never a good time.

I was thankful that I had been there and that I had been able to help Josh get through the day, but his desperate emotions had been fiercely assaulting me all day: the creeping, incessant clawing of the sadness and the vicious stabbing of the fear. Fighting to stay in control had been a challenge. Add my own distress and horror at what I had seen, the intensity of dealing with Mrs Nelson, the police, the paramedics, the oppressiveness of the hospital and my overriding worry for Josh, and it was astonishing that I was even remotely in my right mind and still on my feet.

I pulled on my hat and gloves and made my way along the overgrown path and up to my bench, my solace. I wrapped my scarf tightly around my neck to keep the wintry chill from seeping into my body. I breathed in the fresh, wild air and listened to the evening song, so different from the sounds of the lake in the daylight and yet familiar and soothing. The moon was bright, providing just enough light to see by, and because I knew the path well, I navigated it without difficulty. It was a clear night, and I marvelled at the infinite number of shimmering stars in the sky above. Along with the breeze whispering through the trees, I could hear the evening calls of the squeaking bats and the distant, soft hum of bustling insects. My feet on the uneven path and the snapping twigs underfoot were unnaturally loud in the muted night. I breathed in the night air, felt the crisp, icy freshness fill my lungs, and as I approached the clearing where Susan's bench waited, overlooking the water, I began to relax the firm grip that I had been keeping on my frayed tangle of emotions.

I quickly realised that something was wrong, different. A feeling that I couldn't quite identify crept over me, and as I reached the top of the rise, my relief turned to sheer panic. I let out a startled, piercing squeal when I caught sight of a large, hooded figure sitting on my bench. I had been coming to this spot for years and rarely met anyone on a clear, sunny day in the middle of summer, let alone after dark on a cold winter's night. My initial panicked thought was that Mr Nelson was here, lying in wait for me. He had discovered that I had taken the police to his house and was plotting his revenge.

The logical part of my mind dismissed this errant thought immediately. The figure was too slight to be Mr Nelson. There was no anger or agitation emanating from him, and there was no possible way that he or anyone could have known that I was going to be there tonight; I hadn't even known myself. No, this person wasn't waiting for me, but there must have been some power at work, something more than mere coincidence. The person on the bench was clearly startled too. My raw, penetrating scream alone would have unnerved him. He jumped up, turned to face me and held his hands low out in front of him, reassuring me that he posed no threat.

"I'm so sorry. I didn't mean to startle you. I mean … I wasn't expecting company. I mean … well … not that you're company … but … well, it didn't seem likely that … that anyone else would be out … here," he stammered clumsily. He took a step towards me, his head cocked slightly to one side as if he too was sensing something that he couldn't define. Recognition lit his face as he saw me in the moonlight. "Isabel?" he asked.

I think that I already knew. Something inside me had recognised something inside him, but I was so on edge that I hadn't been able to decipher the signs. However, when he spoke, my body reacted to him traitorously. We had only met once, but the knowledge of how Scott Callahan affected me came flooding back, heating my face and quickening my pulse. The shadows would hide my blush, but I was disturbed by my involuntary response and almost afraid to catch his eye. Those eyes. That voice. I was almost afraid, but the overriding impulse was too hard to resist. I didn't really have a choice.

I raised my eyes to his slowly and was instantly caught in the magical, swirling pools of flame. Time stood still. I stopped breathing. There was a deafening roar in my ears that became louder and louder until I was dizzy. It was too much. I felt the colour drain from my cheeks, and my limbs became feeble and somehow detached from my mind. I closed my eyes. I wanted to scream. It hurt. My head was going to explode. Then everything stopped and the world went black.

When I came to, I was lying on the floor, cradled in Scott's arms, and he was tenderly stroking the hair from my face and murmuring my name.

"Isabel? Isabel? It's all right. I'm here. You're all right … Isabel? Belle? Can you hear me? Belle? I'm here. You're safe." Nobody ever called me Belle, but somehow this time it sounded right.

His touch was warm and comforting. Being held felt so good. I hadn't wanted to be with anybody. I had come to the lake to be alone, but his embrace was soothing, his voice like a balm to my bruised mind. Lying there in his arms felt right. *He* felt right. I felt safe, like I was where I was meant to be. I leaned into his solid chest and breathed in his natural, perfect scent. I opened my eyes and saw him smile.

I leapt out of his arms in a flash, having recovered enough to fully appreciate where I was and to understand how wrong these feelings were. I shouldn't be thinking about how good it felt to be held by a virtual stranger. The chaos of the day had obviously addled my mind. I was going mad, but I couldn't escape that thing again, the thing inside me, deep inside my mind, that had roared to life once more and that was compelling me to go to him, to embrace these feelings, the knowledge that this man was born to be in my life. I fought it. It couldn't be real. Whatever it was didn't have power over me or my life. I made my own decisions, my own choices.

Scott remained crouching with one knee on the floor where he had been cradling me a moment before. He was looking at me as if he were scared, but scared of me or of himself, I wasn't quite sure. Probably scared of what I might do, scared that I might bolt or faint again at any moment — unless the same thing that was happening to me was also happening inside him. Perhaps he didn't understand it any more than I did.

He spoke again gently. "Belle? You fainted. You're frightened. It's OK. It's my fault. I didn't mean to startle you." He stood up and made his way slowly back to the bench and sat back down, but he kept his eyes trained on me and his movements slow and gentle, as if he were dealing with a frightened child or a wild animal that might take flight.

I tried to process what he said. I had fainted. I had never fainted in my life. I was frightened, though; he was right about that. Frightened of what I had seen and frightened of how I felt. I found myself standing still in the clearing, looking at Scott sitting on my bench, looking back at me. I wondered what my face was telling him. I couldn't make sense of my own feelings. I was disoriented. My legs were trembling. I couldn't get back to the car by myself if I wanted to. It had all been too much. I felt tears of exhaustion and confusion stinging my eyes and furiously wiped them away. I tried very hard to collect myself and to behave like a rational human being.

"No, I'm sorry. It's not you … it's me." I laughed shakily. I sounded ridiculous. "I mean … I'm not scared of you." Was I scared of Scott Callahan? I was scared of how I felt when he was near. "I mean … yes … I was scared. I am scared … of you … I mean … I'm not … not you exactly … I didn't expect anyone to be here. You startled me … that's all."

That definitely wasn't all.

"Yes, of course. I can quite imagine," said Scott. "But that's not all, is it?" he asked as if he read my mind. "I mean … I don't mean … I can feel … no … I mean … I can see you're troubled. You look exhausted. You've had a shock. Come and sit down for a minute, catch your breath."

I didn't have much choice. If I didn't sit down, I was going to fall down, and I didn't want to end up in the dirt again. I didn't want to end up in Scott's arms again either, with his large, soft hands stroking me and making me feel all kinds of wonderful, looking down on me with those smouldering eyes and speaking my name with that velvety voice. I shook myself back to reality, nodded dumbly at him and sat down on the bench by his side. He had said something about feeling … no … seeing. I knew that it was important, but I was too tired and too jumbled up to make sense of anything.

"It's been a tough day," I told him simply.

"I know," he said.

I looked at him sharply.

"I mean … I don't know ..." He reconsidered. "I just … well… you don't look … you look … you seem …" His voice trailed off. "The house is just up this hill." He changed the subject, gesturing up the slope to where the old Ramsay house stood, grandly presiding over the lake and all of its grounds. "You can't see it from here, even in the daylight, because of the hill and the trees, but our gardens lead right down to the lake. This path leads right up to my … the house."

The smooth baritone of his voice and the safer topic of conversation slowly made me feel calmer, more peaceful. I actually felt better than I had all day.

"I've been exploring, and I stumbled across this bench a

few days ago," Scott continued. "It's a wonderful spot. I haven't seen anyone else down here before, and I didn't ... well, obviously not. Why would anyone ... tonight? But I find it's a perfect place to sit and ... well, just be. I don't know how else to explain it. I know it must seem weird ... me being out here at night ... but ... well ... maybe it's not quite so weird," he smiled. "You're here too."

I nodded.

"I've been wondering about Susan and her husband," he said, gesturing to the plaque on the bench. "There's no date on it. Do you ... did you know them?"

I shook my head but didn't speak.

He looked at me closely again. "I know you said you've had a tough day. You're tense. Do you want to talk about it?"

"No," I replied. "I ... I feel ... I ... This isn't ... I just wanted to be by myself."

There was no way that I could explain to him what I had been through today, how harrowing it had been, how much I craved solitude and how confusing and frightening my response to him was. I wanted to be near him; I wanted it more than I dared to admit, and that, on top of everything else, proved to be too much. I couldn't hold back the tears. I was past trying to hold myself together.

Scott considered me thoughtfully. "I'm sorry," he said simply. "I honestly didn't mean to interrupt your alone time but I'm afraid ... now that I have ... I can't leave you. Not like this." He examined my face again, now streaked with tears. "I know what it's like to want to be alone. Trust me, I do, but it would be horribly irresponsible of me to leave you in this condition, and I can't do it. Actually, I think you need me to stay."

I didn't know what to say. I didn't want him to see me like this. I didn't want anyone to see me like this. I was uncomfortable having my emotions so openly on show. One of the main reasons that I came here was that I wanted my emotional recovery to be private. I wanted to be able to scream and cry and rage at the world and this was my space. I didn't know if I could go through it with an audience.

I looked at Scott, but words failed me. I couldn't get up and walk away, not yet, partly because I was too weak to move and partly because I had no idea where else I would go. I wasn't fit for company. I couldn't go home. I couldn't be around other people, and I still needed to get rid of all of the emotion clogging my mind, clouding my thoughts and making it impossible to think clearly or to do anything. I sighed.

I looked straight ahead at the water rippling under the stars. The light reflecting off the moon was creating beautiful shadows, and the sound of the water and the rustling of the leaves began to feel familiar and relaxing. If I just sat still, maybe I could forget that he was there, maybe I could have my moment of peace, maybe he would allow me that, and maybe, just maybe, he was actually the only person that I could go through this with.

Scott cleared his throat. "I'll just sit here next to you for a while," he said. "We don't need to talk. I just need to know you're OK before I can leave you alone."

I nodded to let him know that I had heard.

I sat there, trying not to be distracted by the bewitching man by my side. I took a deep breath, closed my eyes and concentrated on the natural sounds: the wind in the trees, the insects, the bats. I felt the breeze caress my cheek and I slowly let the breath back out, but all I could think about was him, and it was impossible to ignore the thing, the something inside my mind that was purring with happiness to be by his side. I tried not to think about what it meant, why I felt totally different around him than I had ever felt in my life, what it was that he had brought to life. I sighed again. Being near him felt good. It felt different. My heart skipped a beat as my mind wandered involuntarily back to the feel of his hands on my face as he'd held me in his arms a few moments earlier.

We were sitting dangerously close to one another. My right hand and his left hand were resting on the bench, almost touching, and I began to feel a tingling sensation in my fingertips, like tiny electric shocks. I felt a trace of excitement, and I wasn't sure whether it was his or my own. If it was his, I ought to leave, I ought not to encourage it. If it was mine, I definitely ought to leave. I knew it was wrong, but I didn't move, I didn't leave, and neither did he. I felt soothed and excited by him all at once and wondered whether being in his company would always be so confusing. My heart beat a little faster, and my breath caught in my throat.

I opened my eyes and surreptitiously glanced in his direction. He was sitting perfectly still with his eyes closed and a peaceful, composed expression on his face. He didn't look excited, and he didn't look as if he could feel my wayward nerves or my erratic heartbeat. Perhaps I was worrying about nothing. I took the opportunity to study him a little harder while he was unaware of my gaze upon him. He looked thoroughly at ease, breathing steadily in and out, content and relaxed, almost dreamlike, with a small smile on his lips.

I don't think that I ever looked like that. I always had to concentrate to maintain some modicum of control. I was always terrified that if I really let my guard down, things could go horribly wrong, so I spent all of my life holding back, holding onto restraint, monitoring my own emotions and my reactions to the emotions of those around me, even Jack. I would love to be able to just sit back and totally let go, totally relax. It's what I tried to do in my evenings here. It was what I was trying to do tonight, but it clearly wasn't going to be possible with Scott Callahan by my side.

I let out a little huff and closed my eyes again. I led my mind back to that morning, to my anticipation of Josh's arrival and to his stress and preoccupation that had built to a crisis point throughout the day. I remembered how tired he had been when he arrived at school and wondered if he had

had any sleep at all. I still didn't know exactly when Mr Nelson had beaten his wife so horrendously or whether Josh had been witness to the assault or had even known about it at all. I let the fear and the stress of that little boy from this morning enter my conscious mind, and I took that vile emotion, peeled it away and cast it out.

I felt the subtle tingle in my fingertips again, emanating from Scott by my side. His emotions, his spirit was trying to enter my body. It wasn't an assault, but a request, and I realised, to my surprise, that his presence didn't need to add to my burden. I felt safe in his company. I could be myself. There was something about him, some connection between us that I couldn't decipher but that we had both felt at the bar the week before, and in a different way, again tonight. I realised that I trusted him, and I stopped trying to resist. Something was telling me that he could help me.

I felt good when Scott was near, better than good. I felt wonderful when I was with him, and right then, I needed to feel good. I deserved to feel good after everything that had happened. I needed all of the positive energy that I could get if I was going to combat all of the poisonous emotions that were still trapped inside my mind. I relaxed. I let go, and even with my eyes closed, I felt his smile widen, as if he knew, and with that smile, I felt a surge of unsurpassed joy wash over my entire being. The connection that I already felt to him grew stronger as I opened myself up and invited him in, and I wondered again if I had finally found someone else like me, if I had finally found something that I had been searching for my whole life. I knew deep down that Scott was a good person. I knew that he didn't intend me any harm. He wanted to protect me. I could trust him.

Decision made, I stopped fighting, and the energy began to flow from Scott into me. It felt different to the straightforward emotions that I was used to, more difficult to translate. It seemed to enter where we were physically nearest and travel slowly around my body from the fingertips of my right hand, up my arm, into my shoulder and then outwards in all directions. It spread down my spine and up into my neck and my mind, and it spread like a warm caress, seeping into every corner of my being. This wasn't how I usually experienced people's emotions. They travelled straight to my mind and were much clearer, much simpler. I would feel immediate anger, grief, happiness or fear, and I could recognise the emotion, absorb the sentiment and experience it myself.

The energy issuing from Scott was more difficult to interpret. It wasn't distinct or defined. The emotions weren't regular. It was as if Scott's spirit was speaking an entirely different language to the one that I had been listening to for the last twenty-six years, but it felt warming and soothing. It felt like coming home, calming me from the inside. It felt as if Scott was supplying me with sympathy, strength and support from the inside, providing the reinforcement that I so desperately needed after a day of being overloaded with emotion that I couldn't deal with on my own.

With Scott's added protection, I could return to sorting through the corrupt emotions that were still choking my mind, and I could begin to set myself free. In fact, with Scott by my side, I felt stronger, more capable and more determined than ever. I kept my eyes closed. I took a deep breath. The breath seemed to fill my lungs more completely than usual, drawing warmth and strength from Scott. I felt good. I felt strong. I didn't stop. I embraced the power.

I was highly aware of his presence, both his physicality beside me and his emotional force inside. Our spirits seemed to have melded, and everything was suddenly easier than it had been before. I was able to harness our energies as one. I let my breathing become slow and even and the emotions swirl around me. I could feel the noxious energies from the day like contaminants. They were thick and black, clogging me up inside, but now it was easier to unwind the fear and the pain and to eliminate them from my mind.

I wasn't controlling it anymore. Scott's energy was doing the work from inside my mind. Hundreds of tendrils of energy were gently teasing out any emotions that didn't belong. I didn't understand how it was possible. It was unlike anything that I had ever experienced. This was not the detached emotions of a person unaware of the exchange. This was his energy, his life force, still very much connected to and a part of him. It felt alive inside me. It felt incredible. Without having to try, without having to relive the distress of the day, without having to examine and fight with each of the invading emotions, they were steadily being eliminated from my mind.

I wanted to open my eyes and look at him again. I wondered whether he was looking at me, whether his relaxed expression had turned to steely focus or whether this was entirely out of his control too. It didn't feel abstract or independent. I somehow knew that the energy that was inside me now was Scott's consciousness, as much a part of him as his physical body. I could actually feel *him* exploring my mind and my body, and I had little doubt that the experience was as remarkable for him as it was for me. I wanted to look, but I was terrified that if I did, it would break the spell. I didn't want it to stop.

It didn't stop. I allowed myself to relax and gave myself over to the sensations. I let down all of my boundaries and allowed him to explore. I emptied my mind of all of the doubts and worries, forgot about staying in control and just took pleasure in feelings that I had never experienced or even dreamed about. It felt like my body was turning to jelly as I was set free. I sank into a beautiful relaxation hitherto unknown to me.

Time seemed to slow down or stop or speed up, I wasn't sure which. I lost all track of reality as Scott worked his magic. He removed tiny fragments of invading emotions that may have been trapped in the corners of my mind for months or even years. I had been blind to the contamination and had learned to live with the monsters inside me, but now I was being released. Every last speck of detritus was being teased out and thrown away, and the feeling of liberation was unimaginable. I don't know how long we had been sitting there, but when the last of the poison disappeared, there was a wonderful weightlessness to my own energy. I felt lighter and more relaxed than I had done in such a long time. I felt more myself. I couldn't remember ever feeling so at peace.

It still didn't stop and nor did I want it to. Now that the poison was gone, the exploration changed. Scott turned his attention to me, to places inside me that were intimately my own: my positivity, my sensitivity, my laughter, my joy, my fears, my capacity to love. He was exploring me, body, mind and soul — searching me, learning me, touching me, and I welcomed it.

The world around me became clearer, crisper. The breath of the wind on my cheeks was sharper, the call of the bats more distinct. I could hear the water lapping powerfully against the shore, and I could feel the solidity of the wood beneath my hands and my legs. Every part of me became more sensitive, and every feeling became more intense. Scott embraced me, inside my mind, inside my body, and every fibre of my being burst into life. I had the most powerful sense that this energy inside me was supposed to be there, as if *he* was supposed to be there. It was the strangest and yet most natural thing in the world. I wondered if I was even really there anymore or if I was lost in some kind of dream. If it was a dream, I didn't ever want to wake up.

My breathing came a little faster, more ragged, as the energy inside me seemed to expand and fill every inch of me. A thousand magical hands caressed my mind, and all of my nerve endings were on fire. I could feel Scott next to me, and I could sense him inside me. I had never felt closer to another person, more intimately connected, and yet we weren't even touching. I had the urge to make the connection physical. I wanted to feel his touch, his skin on mine. I wanted to feel his breath on my face, his hands on my body. I didn't want any space or distance between us. All I had to do was to move my hand fractionally to the right. I could reach out and touch him, but I was afraid to break the spell.

Gradually, I became aware of a heat building up inside me, pooling, rising like a furnace, and my breathing came in shorter, sharper breaths. I knew that Scott could feel it too. Our breathing was in sync and the pressure was building inside both of us. I couldn't hold back a small gasp of surprise and pleasure. I had never let myself go like this. I never let myself feel to this extent because too much emotion was dangerous. I had always worried that I couldn't keep myself or anybody else safe. I had always been frightened and had always kept a lid on it, never letting go, but I wasn't frightened now. With Scott by my side and inside my mind, I was dangerously close to letting go. I moaned with pleasure, and the sound provoked an answering groan from Scott. I heard him take a deep, jagged breath in and out.

And then it was gone.

I was alone again on the inside, suddenly, coldly, cruelly alone. Scott was still there on the bench by my side, but his energy had withdrawn from me without warning, moments before the explosion that had threatened to shatter my soul. It happened so suddenly. One second, I was flying high and I could have sworn that he was right there with me and the next, nothing. I tried to gather my thoughts, and I felt bereft, lost, empty.

Despite the bitter disappointment, my mind was clean from invading emotions and whole again, for the first time in a very long time, thanks to Scott. He had taken away all of the beastly, foreign contamination, given me a sensual pleasure that I had never imagined and left me feeling like a new woman, even if the experience had been cut short. Despite the lack of physical contact or exchange of words, I had felt more open and more honest with Scott in the last few minutes than I had ever felt with anyone else in my whole life. I knew there would be an explanation for his sudden retreat.

Slowly I opened my eyes. I was still in my spot on the shore of Ramsay Pool, on Susan's bench. Everything was where it should be. The moon and the stars were still shining in the sky. The insects were still humming, the water was still lapping the banks, but I was different. He had changed me. In the last few minutes, Scott Callahan had changed my life irrevocably. I turned my head to look at him and saw those deep brown pools of fire, glistening with their flames, gazing at me with an intensity and sensuality that made me blush. He looked as if he had never seen me before, as if he were as shocked by the experience as I was. There was such passion in those eyes. He had been profoundly affected by the experience too. I wanted to touch him, to speak to him, to ask him what had just happened and what was going to happen next, but I couldn't find the words. I didn't know how to begin. Sott's eyes were searching mine. I didn't know what he was looking for and I didn't think that I would ever be able to look away.

I didn't have to. Scott seemed to recover himself, and he turned away from me and cleared his throat. I continued to stare at him, not moving, waiting, a little confused. I had so many questions, but he stood up and stumbled backwards, away from the bench, running his hands violently through his hair, shaking his head, a look of bewilderment on his beautiful face.

"I'm sorry," he said roughly.

He was sorry.

That wasn't right; it couldn't be. I didn't want him to be sorry: sorry for performing miracles inside my mind, sorry for making me feel things that I had thought I was incapable of feeling. He was sorry for that earth-shattering, life-changing experience and the undeniable, intimate connection. He was sorry. I didn't know what to say. I tried to make my brain work. I tried to work out how to make him not sorry. I didn't want his sympathy. I wasn't sorry. I wanted to go to him, to put my arms around him. I wanted him to comfort me, to hold me and to tell me that life would never be the same again.

Instead, in the same rough voice with the same bewildered look, he said, "I'm sorry, Belle. I shouldn't have … We shouldn't have … No, I shouldn't have … Jesus Christ, Belle … We haven't even … and you don't even … I didn't mean to … I wanted to … I mean, I meant to, but I never realised … I nearly… We nearly … I nearly … Jesus Christ," he stammered.

He was looking at me with something like fear in his eyes. He looked uncertain, vulnerable. I didn't understand. I didn't know what he was apologising for. I didn't even know if he was apologising or expressing regret. I wanted to scream at him that I wasn't sorry, that I didn't regret it, that it had happened with my invitation, my consent, my desire. I wanted to reach out to him. I wanted to go to him, to touch him, to tell him that it was all right and that he hadn't done anything wrong. I was ready to take a step towards him. I was ready to put myself out there and do something that would change my life, our lives, forever, but it was too late. I was too slow. That second of hesitation was too much. Before I could move, he spoke again.

"I'm sorry," he repeated. "That was unforgivable." And he turned his back on me and fled.

He disappeared into the undergrowth too quickly, running back up the hill towards his house, towards his family, and I was left alone, physically and mentally this time. I stared at the point on the path where he had vanished into the trees, and I didn't know what to do. I wanted to shout out, to chase him, to do something, anything. Instead, I sat on the bench and stared blankly into the night.

I tried to understand his reaction, but it didn't make any sense. I hadn't been alone in what I had felt. I had sensed his passion and his pleasure as I had experienced my own, and he must have been as aware of my emotions as I had been of his. I was more sure than ever that we were the same, that he shared my abilities, but I still didn't know what it meant. If he knew how I felt, then it didn't make sense that he would run. If I was right about the way he felt, it didn't make sense either. Nothing about this situation made any sense, but maybe it was simple. Maybe I was just wrong.

If he had reached out and touched me or had the courage to speak to me instead of running away, we might both have been able to learn about the experience, about our connection, about each other, together. That was what I had wanted. In that moment, if he had come to me, I would have thrown my whole life away for a man that I had only met twice and only had one proper conversation with because I knew that what had passed between us wasn't going to happen again for me with anybody else.

Scott's reaction had just proved how foolish I would have been. His apology and his flight could only mean that he didn't feel the same way that I did. I had been wrong to assume that he felt the connection or that it was special for him. If he had felt what I felt, he wouldn't have run away; he couldn't have. The truth was staring me in the face. He had left me alone in the dark. He had freed me of the foulness inside me, given me intimate pleasure and left me more alone than ever. There was no benefit of an earth-shattering discovery about yourself if you couldn't use it, share it, speak of it, even acknowledge it.

This was exactly why I had always held onto that control. I had always been terrified of being left alone and broken like this. I had been right. Mum had been right. People don't like different. I shouldn't show anyone who I really was or what I could do because when they got a glimpse, they ran away. I should never give all of myself to anyone. It wasn't safe. I had been right to listen to Mum and to choose to spend my life with a nice, sensible, normal man like Jack. Jack would never run away from me. Jack would never make me feel so alone. Jack loved me and was waiting for me at home. I had treated him horribly tonight and he didn't deserve it. He was a good man. I would go home to him, and I would bury this night in a corner of my mind and never look at it, never think about it, about him, ever again.

I let a few pitiful tears fall from my eyes. I cried for Josh and his mother, I cried for Scott, I cried for Jack, and I cried for myself and for the hollow exhaustion that I felt. Then I laughed cruelly at myself for being so stupid to think that I could trust someone I barely knew with the mess inside of me. I wouldn't think about it now. I just wanted to go home. I glanced up once more at the undergrowth into which Scott had vanished, amazed that I could ever have thought about throwing everything away for a moment of madness with a man who didn't even care enough to stay. I squared my shoulders and turned back down the path, back towards my car, towards home, towards Jack.

Chapter 11

It was late when I got back to the cottage, but rather than my coming home to total darkness, Jack had thoughtfully left the porch light on for me. I let myself in quietly and stood just inside the door, feeling the stillness and the peace beyond. I turned off the light and used the torch on my phone to find my way to the kitchen, where I discovered a covered plate with a note:

Wasn't sure when you'd be back or if you've eaten so I cooked.
Don't worry if you don't fancy it. It'll keep,
Jack x
P.S. Message from Richard on the answerphone x
P.P.S. I love you x

Shame stabbed me like a knife and brought a remorseful tear to my eye. I lifted the cover and breathed in the wonderful fragrance of the homemade lasagne, my favourite. I replaced the cover gently, stepped over to the phone and hit playback.

Isabel, it's Richard. I've left the same message on your mobile. Chrissy filled me in on everything, and I've spoken to the police. Sounds like you were a real hero today. I've arranged for a supply to cover you tomorrow and Friday. I took the liberty of assuming you wouldn't feel like coming in. From the sounds of things, there might be more for you to go through with the police and such anyway. Check in with Josh and social care tomorrow and we'll sort out the rest later. Well done for today. Speak soon.

Well done for today. The words seemed to taunt me, reminding me not of my accomplishment with the Nelsons but of my betrayal of Jack.

I pulled out a dining room chair and sat down heavily. I

was consumed by guilt. I could have walked away from Scott tonight. I should have walked away before it was too late, but I chose to sit on that bench. I chose to sit next to him, and I chose to allow everything that passed between us. I should have walked away. I should have run away as soon as I caught sight of him and my body began to betray me, but I couldn't ignore this thing inside me that had become part of me and that called to him. I could feel it even now, awake and unsettled.

I had been vulnerable tonight. My feelings had been in turmoil, my mind full of fear and pain, and the strain of the day had made me confused and weak. Scott had known that I wasn't myself; he had said as much. Maybe he had taken advantage of my fragile state. Maybe it wasn't my fault. No. I couldn't do that. It wasn't fair to blame Scott, no matter how much he had hurt me by running away. His presence, his energy, had revived and restored me, and I knew that he had done so from a place of good intentions. Scott had used his power, our shared potential, to enter my mind and ease my suffering, not to take advantage of me.

We had both been carried away by our undeniable connection and the insuppressible feelings that had followed. I couldn't kid myself that he had taken liberties. If I had put up any resistance, I know that he would have retreated. He had asked and I had invited, even if no words had been exchanged out loud. He had been inside my mind and my body with my full permission, and I had relished every second of it.

I was the one in a committed relationship with a good man — a man who adored me and would do anything for me. I was the one with the moral obligation to another. I was the one in the wrong. I had felt the connection with Scott last week and knew that he had felt it too. It had been impossible for either of us to ignore. I remembered keenly how he couldn't hide his disappointment when I told him that I was attached to another, and yet tonight, instead of walking away,

I had welcomed his otherworldly embrace. Not only had I met and matched his passion, I had allowed myself to believe that one breathtaking instance of awakening in a bar and one magical moment of desire on a cold, hard bench in the dark was enough to throw everything away for.

I was going round in circles. I didn't know which way was up, and nothing made sense anymore. I needed to take a good, hard look at myself. I needed a reality check. Perhaps I also needed to give myself a bit of a break. My mind was reeling from everything that had happened since I'd got up at 6.30 that morning. It was no wonder that I was churned up and confused. I had seen and saved a woman who had nearly been beaten to death and experienced a child's nightmares and tortures alongside him. I had encountered and absorbed more complex emotions in one day than it was possible for a human to comprehend, and I had shared the most intimate and soul-shattering moment of my life with a practical stranger with a mysterious connection to me and unimaginable emotional power. I couldn't think anymore. I couldn't untangle the web of my emotions. It was late. I was exhausted. I needed to eat, and I needed to sleep. Everything would look clearer in the morning.

About ten hours later, I woke up slowly and stretched languorously under the heavy winter duvet. I felt totally at peace with myself in a way that I hadn't for a long time. I couldn't quite recall the dream, but I had a sense that it had been beautiful and sensual; I had been adored, and there was a tenderness, a unity hitherto unknown. I felt like I had been set free, like parts of me were whole again that had been broken for too long. I indulged the sensation, snuggling back into that soft space between sleep and reality with my eyes closed, burrowing further into the sheets.

I stretched out my legs and pressed my feet and buttocks more firmly into the mattress, running my hand up over my smooth, flat stomach and stroking my sensitive skin. I was still dreaming and didn't want it to end. I moaned with pleasure as I rolled a delicate nipple between my fingers, my mind still mostly blank, my body delighting in the enduring pleasure from the hazy memory of the dream and the physical sensations shooting through my core. I embraced the feeling. I'd had one of the best night's sleeps of my life.

All at once, my mind became clear and my eyes shot wide open. It all came flooding back: Josh, Mrs Nelson, *Mr* Nelson, Scott, Jack. My moan turned from pleasure to pain as I recalled the meal and the note that Jack had left the night before and the drowsy memory of his tender kiss as he slipped quietly from the bed that morning. I remembered his whispered words as he crept softly out of the room, careful not to wake me.

I'm so proud of you. I love you so much.

His love had washed over me and into my subconsciousness, its purity settling me back into slumber, back to my dreams, but it hadn't been Jack's love that I had dreamed of. It hadn't been Jack's hands touching me, arousing my body and mind. The memory of the feelings that Scott ignited in me rushed to the surface. I groaned again. What had I done?

I sat up in bed, reached for my phone and checked the screen: 9.30 a.m. I blinked and checked again: still 9.30 a.m. This might be the first time in my adult life that I had slept past nine o'clock, and I had to admit that I felt amazingly refreshed and rejuvenated, especially considering what I'd been through yesterday. I didn't like to dwell on how much it had to do with Scott's magic spell because the answer was too frightening. All that mattered right now was Josh and his mum. The question of my love, loyalties and bewitching distractions could wait.

I padded down the stairs and found my jacket. Sonya's card was in the pocket. She answered quickly.

"Sonya Anderson speaking."

"Oh, hi Sonya," I said. "It's Isabel. Isabel Bliss. Josh's

teacher?"

Sonya laughed gently. "Of course it is," she said. "I've been expecting your call. How are you feeling?"

"Me?" I asked, surprised to hear the concern in Sonya's voice.

"Yes, of course, you," she confirmed. "You can't overstate the effect a day like yesterday can have on a person. You dealt with some pretty horrendous stuff. Things that most people won't ever have to face, and thank goodness for that. Of course, we're all worried about the Nelsons, but don't let that overshadow your own feelings. How are you, Isabel?"

I thought for a moment. Sonya was right. It would be weird if I hadn't been affected by the events of the day before, all of them. I examined myself carefully before giving my response. I felt good, physically and mentally, better than good. I shouldn't have felt so good.

"I'm OK," I replied noncommittally. "Really. I'm OK. I must have been tired. I slept … better than I expected. How's Josh? And Mrs Nelson? Have you heard from the hospital? Have they caught Mr Nelson?"

Sonya chuckled softly again. "It's almost all good news," she said. "I've spoken to the doctors, and Mrs Nelson's doing really well. She's out of intensive care and back in recovery. Josh is on his way to see her now. He can't wait."

I heaved a sigh of relief.

"Josh is a different thing altogether," Sonya went on. "What he's been through will stay with him for the rest of his life, and it's difficult to assess the extent of the psychological scars he's carrying. He's quiet. Hope spent the night in his room with him. He didn't want to be left alone, and she told me that he woke up three or four times in the night, crying. Not that that's all that surprising."

"No," I agreed. "The poor kid."

"Yes," said Sonya. "Anyway, he was OK as long as he knew someone was with him, and he's doing well, I think, all things considered. Often, when children are in these kinds of situations, it's so normal for them that they don't really know it's wrong until they're out, and then it can hit them really hard. He's going to see his mum, and when he sees her and understands that she's going to be all right and his father isn't going to hurt them again, I think he'll be able to start to heal, but we might also see him really struggle. As for Mr Nelson, no, I'm afraid they haven't got him yet, but they think they'll catch up with him today. They tell me he made it to Dover yesterday and tried to withdraw a large amount of cash. He won't make it out of the country. He's got nowhere else to go."

I swallowed hard. "OK, that sounds positive then, I suppose," I said. The thought of Mr Nelson still being out there, anywhere, was chilling, but I trusted the police and knew that catching him would be a priority.

"So, what happens now?" I asked.

"Now, today, we let Josh and his mum have some quiet time together. If she's well enough, Cathy'll be filled in on everything that happened yesterday. The doctors think she'll be well enough for a conference tomorrow."

"Conference?" I asked.

"Yes," confirmed Sonya. "A child protection conference. We don't normally have them in the hospital, but as Cathy will be recovering there for some time, we'll go to her. It'll basically be the same people you saw yesterday. The police will be there again. We need to get as much information as we possibly can from Josh and Cathy and then put a plan of action into place for them. We'll talk about what they've been through and who can help them and how we can all support them going forward. We hope you'll be there and your safeguarding coordinator too, Chrissy Brooks, I think?"

"That's right, OK," I said. "So, as for today? For me, I mean?"

"You don't need to worry about today. I'll be in touch this afternoon to confirm the plans for the conference, but if you can be available tomorrow, that'd be great."

"Yes, of course," I said. "Just let me know when and where, and I'll be there."

"Thank you, Isabel," said Sonya kindly. "Look after yourself today. Take it easy. You'll be tired, and tomorrow you'll hear things that aren't going to be easy. We'll all need to be strong."

"Yes, I don't doubt that," I agreed. "OK, well, thanks, Sonya. Thank you so much. I'll speak to you soon."

I hung up the phone and looked at the time again. It was almost ten o'clock, and Jack wouldn't be home until four. I would get myself clean and dressed, tidy the house and have something tasty waiting for him when he got in. I didn't get a chance to cook for him very often, and he deserved something nice. He was always there for me when I needed him and happy to give me space when I needed to be alone. Keeping myself busy and preparing for Jack's return would also be a good way to keep my mind off the Nelsons and the other distraction that I tried not to name.

By four o'clock, I was sitting bolt upright on the settee, tapping my foot impatiently on the floor, twiddling my thumbs and glancing anxiously out of the front window every thirty seconds. I had spent more than twenty minutes deliberating over what to wear and had discarded almost everything in my wardrobe. In the end I had gone for my pale blue jeans, a grey striped jumper and my fluffy pink slippers. The outfit was pretty but casual. It said *Welcome back, I've been home all day, tidying the house and preparing something nice for your tea.* It said *welcome home* without appearing like I had gone to too much effort.

It was, in reality, the outfit that I wore almost every day and, of course, I *had* been at home all day, tidying and making something nice for tea. On the other hand, I had undoubtedly gone to far too much effort and thought about it far too hard because I was apprehensive about Jack coming home. I was nervous and guilty and terrified that he would sense my nerves or my guilt or that he would notice a change in me, a spring in my step or a spark in my eye.

I had kept myself busy all day. I hadn't stopped, and the house was spotless. I had even cleaned the window frames in the conservatory. Sonya had said to take it easy, and I knew that nobody would blame me if I spent the whole day sitting in front of the telly and eating ice cream and chocolate, but every time I stopped, I started to think. My brain was in overdrive, but I wasn't thinking about Josh or worrying about Mrs Nelson. I wasn't troubled over whether or not the police had captured Mr Nelson yet. Every time that I paused in my work and my mind began to wander, it wandered right back to that bench and right back to Scott Callahan.

I began to wonder if I had been too hard on him after he had run away, leaving me alone in the clearing. After all, the experience had been unexpected, unfamiliar and more than a little terrifying. If, as I suspected, it had been as much of a shock or a revelation to him as it was to me, perhaps it was justifiable, maybe even forgivable, that he hadn't known how to react and that his instinct had been to apologise and run. I wondered whether it would do us both good to speak about the encounter, to try to understand the extraordinary power and our indisputable connection, but seeing him again, being with him again, would certainly lead to something dangerous or something sensational. All day long when my mind strayed involuntarily back to being near him and my heart began to flutter, I redoubled my efforts to scrub the house clean and look forward to Jack coming home.

Which is why, by the time that Jack's car pulled onto the drive at 4.10, I was sitting on the settee, trying desperately to keep my mind from wandering. When I saw him, I leapt up and ran to the front door, then checked myself and ran back to the living room and sat back down in as casual a pose as I could manage before deciding that sitting on the settee empty-handed with the telly off was anything but casual and running into the kitchen to put the kettle on and prepare two cups of tea with slightly shaky hands.

"Hi, honey, I'm home!" Jack called from the door.

"In the kitchen," I called back, and he came immediately through, took one look at me and opened his arms for an embrace.

I didn't hesitate. I stumbled blindly into his arms and let him envelop me in his love. I rested my head on his chest and breathed him in. Everything about him was reassuringly familiar, and I cried for what we had and for what I had undoubtedly destroyed. I let the tears fall between us, but his warmth and devotion soon dried my eyes. I opened myself up to his emotions, which were inevitably solid and soothing. He radiated affection and tenderness, and I absorbed them and let him calm my agitated mind. I let go of the worry and the guilt for now and sank into the familiarity of contact with this simple, honest, good man: a man that I could trust without hesitation, who had been there for me since I was a child and who would never, ever run away or leave me alone in the dark.

When I finally sighed and pulled away, Jack looked down at me quizzically.

"It felt like you needed that."

"I think I really did," I replied. "More than you know."

We took our tea into the living room, cuddled up on the settee, and he asked me all about yesterday and about Josh and Mrs Nelson. I filled him in on everything from school to my calls to MASH, the Nelsons' house, the horror of finding Mrs Nelson and Clementine, Josh's nightmarish bedroom and the hospital. As we talked, we finished our tea and pottered side by side, setting the table and dishing out the dinner. Everything was easy. There were no surprises with Jack, no surprises and no confusion. He was straightforward and reliable, and he loved me.

My phone rang. I leapt up quickly and snatched it from the coffee table. An unknown local landline number was displayed on the screen.

"Hello?"

"Hi, Miss," said a familiar voice that made me weak with delight.

"Oh, Josh," I gushed, "it's so good to hear your voice. How are you, sweetie? How's your mum?"

"I'm fine, Miss," Josh said automatically, and I felt myself tense in discomfort at his ready use of that dreadful word. "I mean, I'm good, thank you," he reconsidered. "Really good, actually."

I felt the tension ease. He sounded more positive than I'd expected and somehow more natural, more alive. "I've been to the hospital today and they let me sit with Mummy on her bed. She's tired and sore and her face looks awful, but she's Mummy and everyone says she's going to be all right. It's all going to be all right now, Miss."

"That's wonderful news, Josh."

"We're all going back to the hospital again tomorrow, Miss," Josh continued. "Can you come?"

"Yes, I think so."

"Hope's here," he said. "She wants to talk to you."

"OK, thanks, Josh. And thank you so much for ringing. It's wonderful to hear your voice."

"That's OK, Miss. Goodnight."

"Goodnight, Josh."

"Hi, Isabel."

"Hello, Hope. How's today been? How's Josh been, really?"

"He's amazing," she said. "There aren't many kids who could've gone through what he has and come out so good. Obviously, it's early days and we're only just getting to know him, but he's a good kid."

"I know."

"Sonya asked me to pass the message on that we'll be at the hospital after ten tomorrow for the conference at ten thirty. Is that OK?"

"Yes, of course. I'll be there."

"They're moving Cathy to a private room so we can talk freely. I'm not sure exactly where she'll be yet but we'll see you tomorrow then."

"Yes. No problem. I'm sure we'll find each other. Thank you."

"Thank you. See you then. Bye."

"Bye."

"That all sounded positive," said Jack.

"Yes. I'm going to the hospital again tomorrow. I think they want to talk it all through with Mrs Nelson and everyone that's going to be involved in Josh's care going forward."

"That makes sense," said Jack. "Are you going to be OK, going there again?" He was worried about me.

"Yes, I'll be OK. I'll be surrounded by really strong people, and it's for Josh."

"Of course," said Jack. "That doesn't mean I won't worry about you."

"I know," I said, and I gave his hand a squeeze across the table. "I really will be all right, though. I'm actually feeling quite strong."

"I know you will, Izzy. I'm so proud of you."

After dinner, we cleared up together and snuggled up on the settee to watch a film. I was soon dozing off with Jack's solid warmth around me. I felt safe. I felt secure and content with the natural order of things and carefully didn't think about anything else. At about nine o'clock, just as I was about to admit that I couldn't stay awake any longer, my phone rang again. It was Sonya's mobile number. I answered quickly.

"Hi, Sonya. What's the matter?" I asked without preamble.

"Isabel, hi. No, nothing's wrong. Quite the opposite, in fact. I just thought you'd want to know straight away. They've got him. Mr Nelson's been arrested, and because of the violence of his crimes and his attempt to run, they think he'll be remanded without bail."

My legs became a little wobbly, and I sat back down before I fell.

"Oh, Sonya. Thank you so much for letting me know. That's wonderful news. Does Josh know?"

"No. He'd already gone to bed when we found out. Cathy's been told, so she should be able to sleep more peacefully tonight. We'll tell Josh in the morning."

"Of course," I said. "Thank you again, so much, for thinking to let me know."

"Of course," said Sonya. "We can all go to bed a little lighter now, can't we?"

"Absolutely," I agreed. "Thank you, Sonya. Thank you. Good night."

"Good night, Isabel."

I put the phone down and beamed at Jack.

"They've got him," I said.

"So I heard," said Jack. "That's amazing. Such a weight off." He looked at me and smiled affectionately. "Are you ready for bed? You're not going to make it through the film, are you?"

I hadn't realised quite how exhausted I was, but I was suddenly dead on my feet.

"No, I'm really not," I said, and I leaned down and kissed him tenderly on the forehead. "I just need to sleep."

"I'll finish the film," he told me. "I won't be long."

I headed to the stairs and glanced back into the living room, over the bannister.

"Thank you, Jack," I said.

"I love you, Izzy," he told me.

"I love you too."

I wanted so much for it to be enough, but I wasn't the same person anymore.

Chapter 12

On Friday morning, I was just beginning to stir when Jack placed a cup of tea on my bedside table, leaned down and gently kissed the tip of my nose.

"I've got to get going," he said softly. "I'm on the breakfast shift again. It'll be weird, knowing you're there. You never come to work."

I smiled up at him. "Thank you. No, and I won't be making a habit of it either. I really don't want to be there, but I don't have a choice. I'll do it for Josh," I said.

"I know, Izzy, and I know how hard it is for you. I don't expect you to come for me."

"Thank you. I know you can't really know what it's like for me, but it's just not something I'm strong enough to manage. We're meeting around ten o'clock. I don't know how long I'll be. Maybe we could meet off site for a late lunch after?"

"You're strong. You can do anything. Lunch would be lovely, but I'll have to take the first break at eleven-ish, and then I'll be busy till the end of my shift."

"OK, no problem. I'll see you later, then."

"See you later. I love you."

I was up and ready in plenty of time, so I switched on the television and watched the morning news. There was no mention of Mr Nelson's arrest or of the attack and hospitalisation of Mrs Nelson. It wasn't even acknowledged on the local news, which, it seemed, was more interested in school league tables and an amber warning for heavy wind. I marvelled at how the whole world could be totally ignorant of a situation that seemed so significant to those of us who were involved, but the police probably wouldn't release any details about the Nelsons because of the nature of the crimes and Josh's age. It would be worse for Mrs Nelson if she thought that everybody knew.

The national news was as depressing as always. Another

public figure, David Brennan, some hotshot film director with some kind of association to or friendship with the prime minister, was being tried for having a computer full of indecent images of children and for alleged sexual assaults against multiple child actors. How these monsters ever became successful, I just couldn't understand, although, hopefully, with these kinds of allegations, he would never have a career again, even if he was found innocent. There was a guy who was found innocent of a series of rapes recently, but his face had been all over the news before the verdict and he looked weird, which was enough to damn him in the eyes of the public. I knew it was wrong, but he would be recognised as that rapist from the news for the rest of his natural life. The actual verdict didn't seem to matter.

I glanced at the time. I would rather be a little early than end up rushing and cause myself unnecessary stress, so I set off for the hospital. I was nervous about the day in many ways. Another visit to the hospital was going to be challenging, and meeting Mrs Nelson for the first time after discovering some of the truth about the extent of her suffering was going to be confronting for us all. What Mrs Nelson had to tell us so that we could properly understand and figure out how to help Josh was going to be hideous for her to say as well as distressing for us to hear. However, I was hugely excited about seeing Josh. Their lives could begin again now that the hell that they had been living in was over.

I wasn't sure what to expect from Mrs Nelson. We had never spoken much, and I had always considered her to be a bit of a cold fish. The truth was staggering. Cathy Nelson had been trapped in a hellish prison for years and probably didn't even know who she was anymore. She was going to have a lot to take in and a lot to come to terms with. I didn't envy her but hoped that with the right support, she and Josh would be able to rebuild their lives. There was a chance that she might resent me for my part in bringing about the exposure of her situation. She could be embarrassed or uncomfortable to have the spotlight thrown upon what she might see as an unforgivable failing as a mother. I was determined to show her that all I wanted was to offer support to a mother and son who had been the victims of a manipulative, violent monster and who had survived an unimaginable ordeal.

I met Chrissy in the hospital car park just before ten. I recognised her car as she came through the barrier and wandered over to meet her. Chrissy, who hadn't seen me since Wednesday afternoon, jumped out of the car and enveloped me in a warm hug.

"Izzy. Jesus, Izzy. I can't believe it," she said. "I mean … obviously I can … I mean … I do but … So … you were right all along. Not that we didn't believe you but … Well, I'm sorry we didn't act sooner. You did tell us. Worse than you knew though, hey?"

"That's an understatement," I replied. "If I'd've had any idea. You can't imagine what it was like in there, Chrissy. What they've been through."

"They've caught the bastard, though," Chrissy said with spirit. "I know we don't go in for corporal punishment anymore, but people like him make you think again. I can think of a few things I'd like to see done to that depraved freak."

I couldn't hide a smile. "Say what you really mean, Chrissy," I said.

"Don't pretend you're not thinking the same. Monsters like him should be castrated without sedation, for starters. I feel sick knowing he was on our playground all those times. We spoke to him, smiled at him, invited him into our school. Ugh, it's beyond belief. They'd better not ever let him out." She shuddered dramatically.

"I know. I can't believe I couldn't see it," I said. "Shall we go in?"

Sonya had messaged me the ward number, so we went straight up. The desk was manned by a giantess, a colossal woman with a thick neck and a loose double chin. Her hair was scraped severely back from her face, and her rigid, narrow eyes stared piercingly at us as we stood apprehensively in front of her. She reminded me of Miss Trunchbull, and based on first impressions, it was easy to imagine her picking up a little girl by the pigtails and swinging her high around her head. Her gaze was intimidating, and I could sense a simmering irritation that I definitely did not want to provoke. I took a subtle half step back, leaving Chrissy in the immediate firing line. There was an uncomfortable silence that Miss Trunchbull clearly wasn't going to fill.

Chrissy took a nervous breath. "Erm. We're here to see Cathy Nelson. We're supposed to be meeting some others ... police and social services? Are they already here?"

The nurse's eyes narrowed. She looked pointedly at the large clock on the wall.

"Visiting hours begin at ten thirty. It's ten twenty," she barked.

There was silence again.

"Right ... OK ... erm." Chrissy faltered. We appeared to be at an impasse.

We were rescued from further awkwardness by Sonya, who came bursting through a set of double doors to our left, followed by Amy, Mark and Hope, all carrying vending machine hot drinks in cardboard cups.

"Isabel," Sonya said happily, "and you must be Miss Brooks. I'm Sonya Anderson, children's services." She held out her hand.

"Chrissy, please," said Chrissy, taking the proffered hand and shaking it warmly.

"There are some seats just over here," Sonya indicated. "We can sit and wait patiently for visiting hours to begin." She smiled at Miss Trunchbull and was rewarded with a stony glare.

We retreated to the chairs.

"I'm so sorry," Sonya said under her breath with a grin.

"We meant to intervene before you encountered our lovely Ward Sister, but we had to leave for drinks."

"Yes," agreed Mark, "because visitors, especially those who dare to arrive before official visiting hours, *will not be offered drinks on the ward,*" he hissed, with a frighteningly good imitation of the unnerving nurse.

Chrissy giggled.

"She's a bit of a stickler for the rules, and we've already upset her twice this morning," added Sonya.

The others nodded.

"Where's Josh?" I asked. "He's not with you?"

"Ah, well, he's one of the reasons Miss Grumpy over there's already feeling a little grumpy," Sonya said. "He really wasn't interested in waiting for official visiting hours, and I have to admit, I wasn't in the mood for her jobsworth rules either. One patient's best interests are not the same as another's. Cathy and Josh need each other, and I'm afraid our disagreement on the matter got a little heated."

I was impressed. "You stood up to her?" I asked.

"She was amazing," said Hope.

"So, where's Josh?" I asked again.

"He's visiting his mum," whispered Amy loudly, with a wink.

"Well, good for him," I said.

At 10.31, Paul, the police officer, came strolling casually through the doors. He was on duty, in uniform, wearing a cheerful grin, accompanied by an officer that I hadn't seen before, and carrying a bag of freshly baked cookies. They smelled delicious. He breezed past our corridor chairs with a twinkle in his eye and marched straight up to the desk.

"Beatrice," said Paul smoothly. "It's a lovely morning."

"Beatrice?" mouthed Mark with glee.

Paul deposited the cookies on Beatrice's counter. Her previously icy countenance was instantly transformed into a beautiful smile, and she scooped them up without pause and secreted them into an invisible space under her desk. She beamed at him.

"Good morning, Paul," she sang. "It is indeed a lovely day."

"I'm here to see Cathy Nelson," he said. "Are we OK to go through?"

"Of course," she replied. "We've put her in one of the quiet rooms, so you won't be disturbed."

"Marvellous. Thank you so much, Beatrice. You're a star."

"Any time. Just sing out if you need anything."

Paul glanced at the waiting group with a wink. I'm afraid that I was staring, eyes wide, mouth agape. I turned to Sonya, who also appeared to be in shock. We laughed silently at each other. It was hard to believe what a good-looking police officer in uniform and a bag of biscuits could do. I suspected that Paul had dealt with Beatrice before.

Beatrice swooped from her desk and opened the double doors with a flourish. She held them open while everyone filed through.

"She's in room three," she told us, and Paul led the way.

The door to room three was slightly ajar, and as we approached, we were met by a heartwarming sight. Cathy Nelson was reclining on a large hospital bed that had been raised to a seating position. There was a tube in her chest, and she was hooked up to lots of monitors and machines. She had her right arm loose by her side and her left arm draped around Josh's shoulders. He was on the bed with her, curled up into her side, talking animatedly, Dennis the Donkey and Dean the Diplodocus in his hands. He was balancing them gently on Cathy's stomach, and it looked as if they might be dancing. Cathy had her eyes closed, but it was clear that she was awake and enjoying every second of this precious time with her son. Her left hand was gently stroking his arm, and I think she was smiling, although it was hard to tell.

Her face. I had known that there would be bruising on Cathy's face. I had expected it. I had seen the extent of the damage caused by the brutal attack for myself on Wednesday afternoon and had heard what the doctor said about her needing reconstruction, but in the forty-two hours since Cathy had been whisked away by the paramedics, the reality and true horror of what she had been subjected to showed on that face. There was barely a trace of the normal colour of her skin. Instead, patches of blue, purple, yellow and green vied for attention across a swollen canvas of dull grey where her cheeks and her eyes should have been. I had thought that Cathy had her eyes closed, but on second glance, I realised that with the degree of bruising and swelling covering the entirety of her face, it would have been physically impossible or at least unimaginably painful for her to open them. Seeing the infinite love shared by mother and son alongside the appallingly brutal injuries was jarring to the senses. I didn't know whether to laugh or cry.

There was a multitude of emotions emanating from my companions, but they were all overshadowed by the luminescence of the love and devotion radiating from Josh and his mum on that bed. They raised my spirits and sent my energy soaring. The effect was euphoric, but I wasn't the only one touched by it. We all recognised and appreciated the bond between these two extraordinary people who had lived through years of torture with only each other to love and to lean on. Now they were free, free to live and free to express their love for one another, and that love was a tangible force that filled me with rapture. I wanted to shout from the rooftops. No matter how excruciating those bruises appeared on the outside, they were worth it for Cathy Nelson, and she would have gone through that same pain a million times over if it led to being free and having her boy whole and by her side. There was a vague sense of reluctance from the small group at the door. We didn't want to interrupt this beautiful moment.

Sonya cleared her throat loudly and knocked gently on the door. She pushed it open a little wider.

Josh glanced up from his mum and gave us a joyful, beaming smile. His eyes locked on to mine and he leaped from the bed happily.

"Miss!" he shouted, and he threw himself into my arms, laughing. "It's good to see you, Miss. Look at my mum! She's sitting up. She's talking. She's going to be all right."

"That's wonderful, Josh," I replied as I hugged him hard and then let him go to run back to his mother's side. He sat on the chair at the side of the bed and held onto her hand, understandably reluctant to surrender their physical contact.

"Morning, Cathy," said Sonya. "Please don't try to open your eyes. It's Sonya here, with Amy, Hope and Mark, Isabel Bliss and Chrissy Brooks from the school and Paul and his partner from the police. It's quite a gang. I think you already know everyone."'

Cathy smiled uncomfortably. She licked her sore, damaged lips and tried to speak. The words came out a little indistinctly at first but became stronger as she went on.

"Yes. Hello." She was a little hesitant. "Miss Bliss? Isabel? Are you there?" she asked, quietly.

"Yes, Mrs Nelson, I'm here," I replied.

"Cathy, please call me Cathy," she insisted. "I need to thank you. I want you to know … I need you to know how … well, just how much you …" She faltered.

Tears were falling from her closed, bruised eyes. I winced in sympathy as the salty liquid trickled into the healing wounds around her mouth. I didn't know if I should speak or let Cathy finish, but the pause was only brief. Cathy collected herself and continued, "I can never really tell you how much what you did means to me … to us … but I know you … and then you … and when I heard your voice … Can I just say … thank you?" she said.

I could have told her that it wasn't necessary to express her feelings in words. The outpouring of gratitude and appreciation was already saturating me with warmth. I didn't want or desire her recognition. I had done what any decent human being would have done in my situation, and it was sheer luck that I had a tremendous advantage and that I had been in a position to put my gift to use. Perhaps most people would not agree that being a conduit for and participant in Josh's suffering for weeks without understanding was an advantage, or they might question whether my meddling had actually done more harm than good, but what Paul had said in the hospital on Wednesday was right. Monsters like Mr Nelson always cause serious pain in the end. If I hadn't interfered when I did, if I hadn't used my gift to help Josh and Cathy, things could have ended very differently. One or both of them could have ended up dead.

I stepped up to the bed and put my hand delicately over Cathy's.

"I don't need your thanks, but I appreciate it. I'm so glad you're going to be all right. I've been so worried about Josh and then on Wednesday … when I saw you lying there and I didn't know … I mean … I thought that maybe …" It was my turn to falter, and I had to wipe a stray tear from my cheek. I looked at Josh. "I'm just so relieved it's over for you. For you both."

Cathy was crying again, and she tried to lift a hand to her face but couldn't quite muster the strength. The salty, burning tears were sliding over the bruises and into cuts on her lower face, and her nose had begun to run. Sonya was there in an instant with a soft tissue and a gentle rebuke.

"Right, cut it out, you two. No more displays of emotion for Cathy. She doesn't need it and today is a day for celebration."

"Quite right," agreed Paul, "and on that note, I have an update from the station if you want to know? Can I speak freely in front of Josh?" he checked.

"Yes," said Cathy. "Josh and I are in this together. He's been through so much more than's right for any little boy. He's strong and I want him to know what's going on. Please."

"OK. You know that Mr Nelson … um … your father" — he nodded to Josh — "was arrested last night in Dover."

Everyone nodded.

"Well, he's been transferred back to our local investigation centre, where he'll be held until he's been interviewed and charged. He's facing a Section 18 GBH charge and serious crimes offences, and with the evidence on his person, clothes found in his possession and your statements, he'll be remanded in custody until his trial. He won't be able to hurt you anymore."

Josh didn't show any outward reaction to this information, but when his eyes met mine, I felt nausea, which could have equally been born from shock, relief or sheer horror. Most likely, Josh wouldn't have been able to define it if he tried. A world without the only father that he had ever known, who had tortured him mercilessly whilst claiming unconditional paternal love, must be a daunting prospect, which could easily fill a young child with a confusing mixture of dread and delight. Cathy's emotional reaction was considerably more distinct. She was, very simply, happy. I felt the surge of honest joy and relief from the abused wife and mother, although underlying it all was a profound sense of guilt that was dragging her down.

Paul went on, "The next few hours could be very painful for all of us but especially for Cathy and Josh. Things will be shared that are hard to say and hard to hear. We can stop whenever anyone needs to take a break. The main focus of this session is for the police to put together an interview plan from the information you give us. This will form the basis of Mr Nelson's charges, and eventually, the prosecution's case. Having spoken to Sonya, it became apparent that you guys need to have a similar conversation, so in order to avoid having to go over it all more than necessary, we decided to get the whole team together today."

Sonya took over. "We really appreciate your cooperation, Paul, and we know how hard this is going to be for you,

Cathy. The doctors have said that we've got to be careful not to wear you out, but I know you're keen to get this all out in the open and to only have to do it once."

Cathy nodded.

"What we really need … for Josh," Sonya continued, "is to understand what he's been through and what we can do to support him going forward. This won't be the last time we speak, but Josh's teachers probably won't sit in on any more of these meetings. We'll pass on to the school any information that we think will help them, if that's OK with you, Cathy?"

Cathy nodded again and took a deep, laborious breath. She was in serious pain, both physically and emotionally, and talking about her nightmare would be challenging. It pained me to sense that Cathy's overriding emotion was guilt. I hoped that she would eventually learn to see herself as a victim rather than an accomplice or facilitator of Mr Nelson's crimes, but this would inevitably take time. I centred myself and projected positivity in her direction, hoping that it would help get her through this ordeal.

"I don't really know what to say," she began.

"Take your time," said Paul. "I'll be making notes. Unfortunately, the more you're able to tell us, the better, so if you could start at the very beginning and tell us what your relationship with Mr Nelson was like, we'd really appreciate it. Obviously, if you're not well enough or there are things you can't bring yourself to talk about, we'll totally understand."

"Thank you," said Cathy. "I want to say it all. I really do. I've been frightened to speak for so long, and I want to be heard. The main thing I want to say is I'm sorry. I'm so sorry." Cathy reached for Josh and pulled him close. The apology was meant for him. "What I've put you through …" She stopped.

There was a hush in the room. Nobody knew what to say. Josh didn't say anything, but he hugged his mother tightly.

Sonya stepped forward with the tissue again and gently dabbed at Cathy's face.

"What did I just say to you?" she asked with mock severity. "No more crying, please. You'll ruin your makeup."

That made Cathy splutter with laughter, which in turn made her wince with pain.

"Listen," said Sonya, "this isn't your fault. Do you hear me? But if this is too hard for you, if you can't do it today, we can come back when you're feeling stronger."

"No, I'm sorry. Give me a minute to collect myself." Cathy took a few more deep breaths and began to recount her painful tale.

"Aaron was amazing at first," she said. "Looking back now, it's so obvious, and I can't believe how I let it happen to me but ... well ... anyway, when we were first together, he was my world. I was young and he was a few years older, and I think I was flattered by the attention. I liked how special he made me feel. He always wanted to be with me. He wanted to look after me." Her face was set with grim determination.

"He told me my friends were immature and that I was too good for them. Gradually, without me even really noticing, I ended up with fewer and fewer other people in my life. I always thought it was my choice. I was choosing to spend more time with him and less time with my friends and family. He was never violent. Not at first. But I suppose he was always controlling in a way. He liked to do things his way. My mum and dad warned me. They told me that he was cutting me off from the people who were important in my life, but I wouldn't listen. Kids never listen to their parents, do they? I started seeing less and less of them. He convinced me it was them who were trying to control me and he was setting me free. They tried, but over the years, I ended up shutting them out completely. He made me. He made me believe that what we had was more special, that we had a closer bond than me and my family and that I couldn't have both. I don't know how he convinced me. I can't believe I let it happen, but eventually, I had no contact with them at all. He changed my phone number. We moved house without telling them where we were going. They wouldn't have been able to contact me if they'd tried. I don't know if they tried. They've never even met Josh." This last sentence was said in a whisper, and Cathy's hand tightened around Josh's arm. "His own grandparents," she said.

"Aaron always liked to do things his way, but he trained me to think it was what I wanted too. I never felt like he was controlling me, only that I loved him and would do anything to make him happy. It started off with me thinking it was easier to do what he wanted than to deal with him getting upset. Over time, I stopped leaving the house altogether. He'd get jealous if I went out. He'd shout and rage about other people seeing me, speaking to me. If I ever questioned his anger or his actions, he somehow always convinced me that it was only because he loved me so much and that if I loved him as much as he loved me, I would do things his way, and that way, we would both be happy.

"Life settled into a routine over the years. I ended up only leaving the house to do the shopping, and I wouldn't speak to anyone. I would cook and clean for him and behave exactly as he trained me to. Even then, I honestly didn't even see that he was controlling me or using me. I thought it was what I wanted. I told myself I wouldn't have a child with him. By then I could see enough to know that it wouldn't be healthy. I told myself I would leave, but he took that choice away from me too. He threw my contraceptive pills in the bin. He told me that a baby would make us a real family. He convinced me that things would change when we had a child. He raped me.

"When I got pregnant, I wanted to see my parents. I asked him if it would be all right for me to tell them, just to tell them that they were going to be grandparents. That was the first time he hit me. We'd been together for years and he'd never been physically violent up until then." Cathy paused and licked her dry lips.

There was silence in the room. Sonya picked up a glass of water and held it to Cathy's mouth.

"Drink," she told her.

Cathy drank. She continued, "After that first time, he was so sorry," she said. "He said he couldn't believe what he'd done, that he never wanted to hurt me but that I had to see that it was my fault. There he was thinking that we were a perfectly happy couple, expecting a baby to make us a perfect family, and when I brought up my parents, it was like telling him that he wasn't enough, that I didn't love him enough. I ended up apologising to him. I ended up begging *him* to forgive *me* for making him do it." Cathy paused again, getting her breath back and struggling with the painful memories. "If I'd heard this story years ago, I would've condemned the woman as weak and stupid.

"After Josh was born, things started to get worse, and by then I could see what was happening, but I had nowhere to go and no friends or family to call on. By then he was in total control and I didn't know how to get out. I was so deeply under his influence and so frightened that if I ever spoke out to the health visitor or anyone else, that somehow, I would end up being the one in trouble and that *he* would end up with Josh. I couldn't bear the thought of losing Josh or of Aaron hurting my baby, so I just stayed quiet and tried to keep him happy. I stupidly hoped that the baby would change him, make him better.

"Of course, people like Aaron are never happy. You're always doing something wrong, and babies just don't behave all the time. He was horribly jealous of any time I spent with Josh, but I had to spend time with him; he's my boy. Every time Josh cried, if I couldn't quieten him immediately, Aaron felt like I was defying him. He would scream at me to shut him up, and he started locking the baby in another room. If I tried to go to Josh, Aaron would get violent. He hated it when

Josh kept crying but then he wouldn't let me go to him, so we went round and round in vicious circles. There were so many times when I would listen to Josh cry and I couldn't go to him. I was frightened of what he'd do. That's when he started hurting me physically, regularly. He was punishing me for not being able to make Josh quiet twenty-four hours a day. He couldn't cope with the fact that there was something in his life that he couldn't control."

Cathy took another deep breath, and Sonya helped her to take another sip of water. She continued. "I'm not a stupid person. I didn't use to be so weak, but by then I was trapped, and I was just relieved that it was me that he lashed out at and not Josh. He never hit Josh."

Josh snuggled into his mother's side again. He was stroking her arm, offering her the comfort of his touch.

"When Josh got old enough to understand a bit more, his father started to punish him instead of me. It was almost like a game. I think it was a power thing. He needed us both to know he was in charge. Josh was such a good boy. He's always been a good boy, and I tried to make his life as bearable as I could. I taught him that we had to keep Daddy happy. I bought into Aaron's control for as close to an easy life as we could get. Aaron still didn't like me going out, but he knew that we'd have to because of nursery and school and stuff. Like I said, he never hit Josh, but his punishments got harsher and harder. He seemed to get a strange sense of satisfaction from making Josh cry, and then he'd blame me if he didn't stop. That's when he really started hurting me, when Josh was about three years old. The scars … That's when he started breaking Josh's things, too. Every time Josh had something of his own, Aaron would find an excuse to break it to make Josh cry so he had an excuse to hit me and tell Josh it was his fault, but Josh was still so good. He was always so good. He didn't deserve it, any of it. Neither of us did.

"The physical violence stopped for a while when he

developed this new game. He could upset us both without the physical stuff, and it was obvious we'd be going out more in public, so he couldn't have me bruised. He kept his temper under control for a little while, and I thought things might be better, but unfortunately, when Josh started school in September, things got really bad again, really quickly. It was the first time Josh had mixed properly with kids his own age, and he was excited. He was still never badly behaved, but he was a little boy, and little boys can't always be quiet. They can't always be seen and not heard. He just wanted to tell us what he'd done at school and who he'd played with, but Aaron couldn't handle it. I think he was jealous again. He couldn't bear that Josh had a life outside of home and him. Every time Josh said something Aaron didn't like, he would break another one of his things, but eventually, there came a point where that didn't work anymore. Josh became numb to it, and school was exciting. He couldn't contain his joy at things he'd seen and learned.

"That's when he killed Bossy, a few weeks ago … I lose track" Cathy hugged Josh closer again as if she could see the tears shining in his eyes through her closed, puffy lids. "It wasn't your fault," she told him. "He loved that rabbit," she said to the room. "That broke a little piece of me, to see what it did to him. I begged Aaron to stop punishing Josh and to punish me instead, and Josh screamed at me not to be silly. He said he didn't mind his things being broken but he didn't want to see his mummy getting hurt, and something seemed to light up in Aaron that day, when he realised that by hurting me physically, he would hurt us both. He never laid a finger on Josh. I think he knew that that might be the one thing I wouldn't tolerate. Maybe he knew that it might tip the balance and give me the strength to leave, but he made Josh watch while he beat me whenever Josh did something that Aaron considered bad. This last month or so, it'd got really bad. The beatings got worse and more frequent. He was always angry."

Cathy stopped talking. She was obviously exhausted. Reliving the details of the last few weeks was going to be too much for her. Everyone could see it. Sonya opened her mouth to speak, but Josh took over the story for his mum, and the determination in his young voice made her stop and listen.

"After Daddy broke Bossy and started hurting Mummy, things got worse and worse. Daddy was always cross with me, and I tried so hard to be good. Every time I was bad, he would hurt Mummy. First it was just one hit, but he hurt her more and more each time. He'd tie her up by her hands or strangle her, and he'd hit her over and over again."

Everyone was looking at Josh, and there wasn't a dry eye in sight. I think everyone had stopped breathing. This was the first time he'd really spoken about it. Part of me wanted to rush to him and hold him and tell him that he didn't need to say it, but the bigger part, the more rational part, knew that it was good for him to get it out. Cathy was still holding his hand. Tears were running down her face, but Sonya's attention was all on Josh.

"It got harder and harder to be fine. Daddy wanted us to be fine, but we weren't. We had to go to school and be fine … act fine … tell everyone I was fine and Mummy was fine. But you could see that things weren't fine, couldn't you, Miss?" Josh looked at me. "I don't know how you knew but you knew things weren't fine, and when Daddy found out you knew, he just got crosser and crosser and hurt Mummy more and Clementine and …"

Josh's words had been coming faster and faster, and at this point, Cathy put her other hand over his and shushed him.

"It's OK, Josh. That's enough." She addressed the rest of us in the room again. "I think Aaron got scared. He realised he couldn't get away with it anymore. It was all going to come out because of Miss Bliss … Isabel. She wasn't going to leave it alone. When he … Clementine …" She swallowed hard. "He made us both watch, and it was awful. It was so awful. It was too much. Josh couldn't go to school the next day. He was a mess. We both were. I honestly don't know how we got through last week.

"When the letter came saying social services wanted to see us, he just went mad. I knew it was coming, but there was nothing I could do to stop it. I know you must all think I'm so weak and stupid. I know I do. Why didn't I just take Josh and run away? Why didn't I talk to someone? Why didn't I go to the police?"

Nobody spoke. There was no answer. Cathy wasn't expecting one.

"I can't answer any of those questions, and I've been asking myself over and over again. I suppose ... I was so young when we got together, and he cut me off from everybody. He was all I had, and despite everything, a part of me loved him and felt like I couldn't cope without him. God, I hate hearing myself say that."

Paul spoke up. "Cathy, you absolutely can't blame yourself for anything. You are the victim. Nobody thinks you're weak."

Cathy put her hand up to stop him. "That may be true, but I don't know when or if I'll ever really believe it. What kind of mother lets her child live that kind of life?"

Paul tried to speak again but Cathy cut him off. "No, Paul, let me finish. I'm almost there. I know what he did to me on Tuesday's important for the case. I need to get it out and then I can rest."

Paul was quiet.

"Thank you," Cathy said. She didn't speak for a moment.

"The letter came on Tuesday. I could've burnt it. I could have kept it from him, but I knew that there'd be another letter and another, and eventually, a visit. Maybe I wanted it to end, and this was the only way. Miss Bliss knew there was a problem and she wasn't going to stop."

I couldn't take it anymore. The guilt was crushing. I had

suspected that I was the cause of the attack, but to actually hear Cathy say it out loud was too much.

"Oh Cathy," I cried out, "I'm sorry. I'm so, so sorry. I can't believe I put you in that danger, both of you. I knew something was wrong, but I never guessed … I should have known. I should have done things differently." I was crying, and answering tears were streaming down Cathy's face.

Sonya stepped forward again with her tissue and the water. Cathy took a drink and held her hand out to me, searching.

"Miss Bliss? Isabel? No. Don't do that. I'm not blaming you. How could you possibly have known? Come here. Take my hand. Let me hold you while I finish this."

"Of course," I sniffed, and I stepped forward to the edge of the bed and took Cathy's outstretched hand. Josh adjusted his position so he had one hand on his mum's arm and the other on mine. I was trying to hold it together. This wasn't the time to have an emotional breakdown. I couldn't be that selfish.

Cathy started speaking again, and her voice was a little stronger.

"I sent Josh to his room early on Tuesday afternoon. He was in bed when Aaron got home. I was sitting in the living room with the letter on the coffee table. I didn't say anything, but we both looked at it in silence. Then he stepped forwards and picked it up. He read it through silently and then folded it and put it in his pocket. He looked at me and his eyes were weird … like … all the colour had gone and they were just black. Neither of us spoke for what seemed like ages but was probably only a few seconds. He just stood there, looking at me with those weird eyes. Then he said, really calmly, *Go upstairs*. I just went.

"He didn't come up for hours. I don't know what he was doing. In the end, I got ready for bed. It seemed like all I could do, and I just lay there, awake, just waiting. Eventually, I heard him coming up the stairs. I felt helpless.

Lying in bed made me somehow more vulnerable, so I got up … but there was nowhere to go … so … I just waited again. He walked into the room and started shouting. It was different to normal. When he was hurting me as a punishment for me or for Josh, it was usually fairly controlled, if that makes sense. Like … he knew what he was doing and how many times he was going to hit me, depending on the crime … like it was normal … like it was how everyone behaved, but this wasn't normal, not even for him. He wasn't meting out a punishment this time. He was out of control. He was shouting … screaming that me and Josh had ruined our family, that things could never be the same again. He kept saying all he'd ever done was love me and that we'd ruined everything. He kept shouting, *Why did you do it? We were fine! Everything was fine!*

"I didn't speak. I knew from experience there was nothing I could say. When he came towards me, I backed into the corner of the room, but he kept coming. He hit me in the face … a fist … right in the mouth. That was different too. He'd never hit my face before. He split my lip, and the pain exploded in my head. I could taste blood. Then he hit me in the stomach and then in the face again. He'd never left marks that people would see before, and I knew he was going to kill me. I just kept thinking, *Please just let it be me. Please don't hurt Josh,* but I didn't say it out loud. I didn't want to give him the idea. He just kept hitting me until I didn't even know where the pain was anymore. Everything hurt. Then everything went dark. I don't know how many times he hit me. I don't know how long it went on. I don't know how long I was out for, but when I came to, I was on the floor in our room and my whole body was on fire. The pain in my face and my chest was unbearable, and I couldn't get my breath in and out. Josh was knocking on my bedroom door, calling me. I didn't know where Aaron was. I didn't know if he was still in the house. I managed to call to Josh that I was fine and he should go back to bed. I didn't want him to provoke his dad any more and end up getting hurt himself. Somehow I managed to drag myself into the bed and I just lay there, fighting to ignore the pain, fighting to breathe.

"I must have drifted off in the end. I don't know whether it was sleep or unconsciousness, but the next thing I was aware of was Josh calling to me again. Telling me it was time to get up and go to school. I couldn't move. I was frightened, but I didn't want Josh to see my face. I couldn't see it, but I knew it was bad. I told him not to come in, that I was poorly and he'd have to go to school by himself. I told him I'd be fine. I don't know why I didn't let him come in or ask him for help. Of course he would've helped me. For some reason, I think I thought I was strong enough to get help myself and I was protecting him from the upset of seeing me that way.

"After he'd gone, I reached for my phone. I knew I needed to get to the hospital, and I was going to call an ambulance, but when I reached out, a stabbing pain ripped through my chest and I couldn't move. I guess that was the rib … the lung the doctors told me about, and it was then that I realised I couldn't see. I don't know why it hadn't occurred to me before. I tried to get to my phone again but ended up knocking it on the floor. I heard it go and I couldn't get it. I couldn't see. I couldn't move. The pain in my chest was like … awful, and it was getting harder and harder to breathe. I just lay there, totally helpless, waiting. I suppose I was waiting to die. The next thing I knew, I heard your voice, Isabel … and then … I was here, in the hospital."

There was a stunned silence in the room. Nobody spoke. Nobody moved. Cathy lay her head back on her pillow and breathed a long sigh. It must have been a huge relief to her to get it said. She was still holding my hand. She gave it a squeeze and spoke again, very quietly.

"Isabel. I want you to know … you need to know that you saved us. It's not your fault he did what he did to Clementine or to me. If it hadn't been for you, we'd still be living it. Who knows when or if we'd've got out? I could see that you were different … that you could see there was something wrong, and it gave me hope, it really did. I was so close to telling you that day you spoke to me in the classroom. I wanted to, but I was too scared. But you didn't let it go. You saw a problem, and you cared enough to help. I'll recover from this. We'll both recover, and we'll never forget what you did for us. Thank you. Thank you."

She sank back onto the bed again and her breathing slowed down. She was exhausted. It was time to let her rest.

"Time for a well-earned break," said Sonya. "Cathy, you've done so well. That was really brave. Get some sleep. We'll be back later."

Cathy didn't respond. She might not even have heard, but she looked more peaceful than she had before.

Josh leaned over the bed. "I love you, Mummy," he said quietly, and he took my hand and let me lead him out of the room.

Out in the corridor, we were quiet, thoughtful. Although I had seen for myself what Mr Nelson had done and was expecting to hear some awful things, somehow hearing it directly from Cathy like that had been harder than I'd imagined. It was a lot to take in. We all stood awkwardly outside the room. No one seemed quite sure what to say. Mark and Hope were holding hands, and they looked rather pale. Even Sonya seemed slightly less than her usual confident self.

It was Josh who broke the awkward silence.

"I'm hungry," he said with a smile. "Can we get some chips?"

Sonya laughed, Mark ruffled Josh's hair, and the spell was broken.

"Yes, Josh. Yes, we can get some chips. I think you've earned some chips. Would you like a sausage with those chips?" Hope asked him.

Josh's smile widened and he skipped along the corridor at the suggestion. "Can I? Yes, I'd really like a sausage."

With the mood lightened, we went down to the cafeteria together, found a table and sat down. None of the adults could face food, but we each ordered a drink, and Josh got a sausage, chips and beans. I hung around the door to the kitchen until someone saw me and came over to ask if I needed help.

"Hi. Sorry. Is Jack in the kitchen?"

The young girl nodded and withdrew without a word. A few seconds later, Jack was at the door. His face lit up when he saw me.

"Izzy!" he cried and wrapped his arms around me in his customary bear hug. "You came to see me." He was genuinely happy, and that happiness was exactly what I needed. It burst through some of the emotional sludge inside me and buoyed me up. I hugged him back.

"Josh wanted chips," I told him.

"Is he here now?" Jack asked. "Can I come and say hello?"

"Of course."

Jack disappeared into the kitchen for a second and then returned to accompany me over to the table. He beamed at the assembled group.

"Everyone, Josh, this is Jack," I told them.

"Hi, Jack," said Josh shyly.

"Hi, Josh," Jack replied. "I live with Miss Bliss. She's my girlfriend." He winked at Josh conspiratorially. "She's told me so much about how brave you are and what a fabulous boy you've been. I really wanted to meet you."

Josh blushed happily. Jack reached into his pocket and pulled out a purple lollipop.

"Do you fancy this after your chips?" he asked.

"Yes, please, if that's all right?" Josh asked Hope.

"Of course that's all right," said Hope. "I think the least you've earned is a lolly!"

Josh took the lolly and beamed at Jack again.

"Thank you," he said.

"My pleasure," said Jack, and he turned back to me. "I'll leave you to it. It was wonderful to see you. I'll see you back at home." He gave me a quick peck on the cheek and retired to the kitchen to finish his shift. I sat down, feeling a little bit stronger.

The group soon relaxed, and conversation moved on to less exhausting topics. Once the shock of hearing Cathy's story had worn off, we all felt relieved. If Josh could cope with everything and enjoy his chips, things couldn't be that bad. When we had finished and Josh had licked the last of his bean juice away, Sonya cleared her throat.

"Right, well," she said, "I think the police need to go over some details with Cathy after she's rested, and I know Josh wants to see his mum again before heading back to Hope and Mark's, but I think our part is pretty much done, so if you two are ready to go, we won't keep you. We'll be writing up reports and things, and I know you'll be having meetings at school and you'll be speaking to Hope and Mark when Josh returns to school. We'll all keep each other informed."

Chrissy and I looked at each other and nodded. I thanked Paul and Sonya and turned to Josh. "Can I have another cuddle?" I asked him.

He jumped from his chair and threw his arms around me. "Always," he said. "And Miss?"

"Yes, Josh?"

"I hated lying to you, Miss. All those times I told you I was fine, I hated it. I'm glad we don't have to lie anymore."

"Oh, Josh," I felt myself welling up again. "I'm glad too, for that and so much more."

"Miss?" Josh asked again.

"Yes, Josh?"

"Before, me and Mummy always looked forward to Wednesdays because that's when Daddy was away. We would get Dennis out, play and go to the park. We don't have to wait for Wednesdays anymore, do we, Miss? When Mummy's better, every day can be Wednesday."

I thought that my heart might burst.

"Yes, Josh," I murmured. "From now on, every day can be Wednesday." I gave him an extra squeeze and said my goodbyes. Chrissy and I walked out into the car park, blinking at the bright sunlight.

"Wow," said Chrissy.

"Yes, wow," I agreed. There was nothing more to say.

We walked in silence to the ticket machine, each lost in our own thoughts. When it was time to part, we shared a brief hug.

"See you on Monday," I said.

"No, you won't," said Chrissy. "Next week's half term."

"Oh my goodness," I said with a laugh. "I'd totally forgotten. Oh, and I left my class alone for the last days of their first half term. I haven't been there for them at all." I suddenly felt guilty.

"Don't be daft," said Chrissy. "You know what kids are like. They're four. They probably haven't even noticed."

"You're probably right," I said, and we drifted apart.

"See you a week on Monday, then," I amended.

"Have a nice holiday."

I walked to my car. I should have been thinking about Josh, but I found my mind wandering to the bench by the lake. I was tempted to go, sorely tempted, even though the cottage was empty and I had time for peace and contemplation at home. My mind conjured images of Scott sitting on that bench — his eyes, those swirling pools of flame, the feel of his hands caressing my face and the sound of his voice as he held me and told me that he was there, that I was safe. Something was telling me that he was there now, sitting on our bench, waiting for me. I felt compelled to go, drawn by an invisible connection between us that was almost impossible to resist. I yearned to be near him again, to feel his presence, his touch.

I wouldn't do it. I couldn't do it, not to Jack. We had a good life. We were happy. It was uncomplicated and I didn't want to throw that away. I didn't admit, even to myself, that the real reason that I wouldn't go to that spot on the lake tonight was because of the dread, the sickening sense of disappointment that I would feel if Scott Callahan wasn't there.

Chapter 13

I peeked discreetly from the classroom door. The hall was packed. The murmuring crowd was bubbling with anticipation. My own jitters were magnified by the giddiness of the children, and the joy and excitement in the air combined to provide me with a heady mixture of emotions and a healthy dose of adrenalin. I cast my eye over the children one last time: costumes on, ready smiles in place, jiggling around in their eagerness to get on stage. They knew their words, they knew their moves, and we were going to deliver a fabulous show. I looked for Josh and held his eye for a moment. He answered my questioning smile with a confident nod. He was happy. The old anxiety and turmoil were gone. He was ready to shine.

One last check before taking them out. I searched the row for Karl and pinned him down with my eyes.

"Last chance, Little Owls," I called. "Has everyone been for a wee?"

There was a general chorus of assent and no admissions to the contrary, but I needed to be absolutely sure.

"Karl?"

"Yes, Miss?"

"Do you think you should try for one more wee?"

"No, Miss. I've just been, Miss. Ready to go, Miss."

"Excellent. Let's do this, then. Good luck, everybody. Have fun. Be brilliant. And smile!"

I took one last deep breath and opened the door confidently, leading my cast out into the hall. The crowd erupted into spontaneous, enthusiastic applause. I led my four twinkling Stars and orchestra of two to the far side of the hall, where they sat on a bench overseen by the indomitable Mrs Bishop. The Shepherds filed in behind. My Angels and the Narrator filled the bench on the near side of the stage with the Wise Men behind them, and Mary, Joseph, the Donkey, the Innkeeper and his Wife took their positions on centre stage.

I stood at the front and settled the enthusiastic audience so that I could be heard.

"Ladies and gentlemen, boys and girls, parents, grandparents, aunts and uncles, guardians, carers and friends," I said. "Thank you so much for being with us and showing us your support this evening. Your encouragement has got us this far, and we're going to honour your hard work, dedication and practice. Ramsay Bridge's very own Little Owls are excited to present to you our classic and heartfelt rendition of the Christmas Nativity story. We'll start with a song to get you in the mood, the children will wow you with their acting skills and their enthusiasm, and we will leave you with the heartwarming message that Christmas really is a magical time of the year. Take it away, Little Owls."

I turned and raised my hand to the children, who all stood up on cue. The audience cheered again. I nodded to Helen, who was accompanying the children on the piano, and we were off:

It's a magical time of the year,
It's the time to enjoy the celebrations,
There's a wonderful song in the air,
The message of Christmas for the world to hear.

The children were in full voice, and with Helen's piano, Lucas and Amy's skills on tambourine and triangle and Mrs Bishop's tuneful soprano to guide them, I couldn't have been more proud. As I sang along with the children, I scanned the audience and was thrilled that every child in the class had someone in the crowd supporting them.

On the front row, I had reserved seats for the supporters of the lead roles. Serena's parents were puffed up, looking as proud as peacocks as their little girl sang her heart out; Jane's mum was already crying, dabbing gently at her eyes with an embroidered handkerchief, and Karl and Melissa's families were singing along at the tops of their voices. I couldn't imagine how many times these poor people must have heard and sung this song since I sent the music and lyrics home a few weeks ago.

Right in the middle of the front row, my eyes rested on the trio whose attendance tonight made this year's nativity that extra bit special. Cathy Nelson and Hope and Mark Hancock were sitting together, holding hands, and already had unshed, poignant tears shining in their eyes. They couldn't take their eyes off Josh, who was standing centre stage, singing with gusto and without a care in the world. Cathy's face was still colourfully bruised, but the wounds had almost completely healed. There was a darkness under her eyes that she hid with sunglasses most of the time, a jagged scar across her top lip and surgery scars on her left cheek from the repair of the cheekbone fractures. She would always carry the scars of her ordeal, but I marvelled again at just how strong she and Josh had been during the last seven weeks of recovery as they began to adjust to lives without their abuser.

My contemplation was interrupted by a feeling in the back of my mind, an emotional signature that I would know anywhere. I knew it almost as well as I knew myself, and it excited me. I hadn't even known that she was back in the country. I wasn't expecting her until next week. I looked up from the front row and scanned the remainder of the audience. First, my eye alighted upon a small group of people, almost hidden in the back corner of the hall, whose presence made the song catch in the back of my throat. Paul, the police officer, was leaning against the door, casually out of uniform, and next to him were Sonya and Amy from children's social services. I was thrilled that they had used the tickets I had sent on the off chance that they could come along to support Josh.

A little further along, also in standing room, were my mum, dad, Jack, and almost hidden from view, I glimpsed the lustrous shock of strawberry blonde hair before catching the dazzling eye of my beloved sister. Stephanie was home. We looked into each other's eyes and saw into each other's hearts. Stephanie's eyes shone with the same happiness that I felt upon seeing her. She raised her hand in greeting, and I nodded with a grin that nearly split my face in two. It meant so much that Josh's friends and family and my family were all here, and I was more excited than ever to show everyone what my Little Owls were made of.

As the opening number came to an end, Serena, the narrator for the show, stood and began to deliver her first line hurriedly, without pause. She was completely drowned out as the enthusiastic crowd whooped and cheered for the song, and her little face fell as she strained to make herself heard above the din. I quickly gestured to Serena to stop and wait. I put my fingers to my lips until the noise had died down and then gave her cue. She started again and ran with it like a true performer.

"Once upon a time," she began, "a long, long, time ago in a land far, far away, Mary and Joseph went on a long journey to Bethlehem. They had travelled far, and they were tired and hungry and looking for a place to stay for the night and a stable for their tired little donkey."

Right on cue, Josh linked his arm through Jane's and Caroline threw up the hood on her brown onesie, instantly becoming the cutest donkey in Ramsay Bridge, complete with ears and a long swinging tail. Mary, Joseph and the donkey slowly walked around the stage as the whole class sang a beautiful rendition of *Little Donkey*, accompanied once again by Helen on the piano, Lucas on tambourine, Amy on triangle and with vocal support from Mrs Bishop and me.

As the song came to an end, and this time with a slight hesitation to let the applause lull, Josh stepped to the front of the stage, dramatically wiped the back of his hand across his brow and declared, "Oh, Mary! We have tried all the inns and there is no room. Will no one find it in their hearts to give us a place to stay? Our donkey has carried you for miles and miles and is very tired, and you are going to have a baby."

Jane stroked the cushion under her dress lovingly and replied, "Oh, Husband, look! There is one more inn." She pointed convincingly to the back of the hall. "Maybe they will have room for us."

Karl and Melissa stepped to the front of the stage in their dressing gowns and slippers. Karl was in a blue and red Spiderman dressing gown and Melissa was wearing pink covered with rainbows and a hood with a unicorn horn. The audience giggled at the modern take on biblical nightwear while Josh theatrically knocked in the air and stamped his foot on the stage, transporting us all to the last inn in Bethlehem.

Karl opened the invisible door. "Yes?" he demanded sharply. "What do you want? It's the middle of the night and we're full." He quickly turned to his mum in the front row for a wave. She returned it with an enthusiastic thumbs up.

"Oh, but is there nowhere we can stay?" wailed Josh dramatically. "My wife is going to have a baby soon and my donkey is tired."

Melissa stepped forward, moved by his emotional plea. She tugged on Karl's dressing gown and said in a loud whisper, "We could let them sleep in the stable."

"The stable?" scoffed Karl.

"Yes. Look," said Melissa, "they're tired and their donkey needs some hay."

"Oh, all right then," said Karl, grudgingly. "You can sleep in the stable around the back."

Karl and Melissa both took the opportunity to wave to their parents again before melting to the back of the stage.

Serena was on again. She stood up with a flourish.

"Mary and Joseph were happy to have somewhere to sleep. They gave the donkey some hay. Mary had a baby.

They decided to call him Jesus." She fished a doll out from under her bench and passed him clumsily up to Jane, who tried to take him by the legs but fumbled and dropped him headfirst onto the stage. The audience began to laugh but soon quietened each other when they realised that Jane was going to cry.

I nipped onto the stage, collected Jesus from the floor, handed him carefully to Jane and gave her a quick squeeze. "He's OK. Don't worry," I whispered. "You're doing great."

Jane took the doll and wiped her nose noisily on her sleeve, placed Jesus lovingly into the manger, and she, Josh and Caroline knelt by his side. I gestured to the stars and the angels, who ran onto the stage. I nodded to Helen and raised the rest of the children to their feet for the next song. The stars and angels danced their steps beautifully and everyone else swayed in time to the music.

It was on a starry night,
When the hills were bright,
Earth lay sleeping,
Sleeping calm and still.
Then in a cattle shed,
In a manger bed,
A boy was born,
King of all the world.

As the angels sang for him and the bells of heaven rang for him, I encouraged the audience to sing along with the chorus. The audience in question required very little encouragement to join in, and as they sang, four little angels and four bright stars twirled around the stage with glee. While the audience applauded the song and dance, there was a reshuffle on stage and the angels appeared before a trio of shepherds tending to their flock.

In unison, the angels declared, "Don't be frightened, we are angels. We have come to tell you that Jesus has been born in Bethlehem. Go and see him." And they pointed to the back of the stage, where the stars were beckoning brightly.

I directed the play from the sidelines, helping the children along when they needed a gentle reminder or a word of encouragement and watching the enraptured audience's faces. The children performed better than I had even hoped, hardly dropping a line and singing and dancing with aplomb. Karl and Melissa put on a wonderful comedy double act as the disgruntled innkeeper and his wife disturbed throughout the night by uninvited shepherds and Wise Men desiring to visit their stable, and Jane played a wonderful doting mother. The songs were sung in something that closely resembled a tune, most of the words were spoken clearly, and everyone enjoyed themselves thoroughly.

The performance approached its conclusion, and the entire cast came onto the stage and formed a semi-circle around Mary, Joseph and Jesus in the manger. I had been looking forward to this number. Josh and Jane had been practising the duet covertly at school, so even their parents didn't know what we had in store. I gestured for the rest of the cast to sit quietly, facing the couple at the centre of the stage. Helen began the accompaniment, and together, Josh and Jane sang a heartrending lullaby to their miracle baby, surrounded by their guests.

Little baby, sleep, for you've had a busy day,
Little eyes closed, sweet dreams are yours,
Little baby, sleep.

Little baby, rest, for we are watching over you,
Safe in our care, we'll always be there,
Little baby, rest.

Sleep, sleep, sleep, little baby, sleep,
Sleep, sleep, sleep, little baby, sleep.

Their voices were beautiful, and they hit every note. The song was modest and moving in its simplicity, and as the last chord faded, there was a stunned silence in the hall. I looked around. As I had predicted, there was barely a dry eye in the place. Cathy, in the centre of the front row, let go of Hope's hand to fish a tissue from her handbag and dissolved into a soggy mess. There was a moment of stillness, and then the audience erupted into tumultuous applause. The whole crowd were on their feet, cheering, clapping and crying. Josh and Jane looked slightly bemused by the reaction.

I raised the class to their feet once more to take a couple of dramatic bows, and the audience continued their adulation. We rounded off the evening with a raucous encore rendition of *It's a Magical Time of the Year,* and all of the parents and friends sang along. When the applause and excitement finally began to die down, Richard took his place at the front of the stage.

"Wow!" he exclaimed. "What a show! It's hard to believe that these little stars are just four and five years old and have been rehearsing for a mere matter of weeks. It's times like these when I'm most proud to be head teacher of such a special village school and so grateful to you all as parents and friends of the children for all your hard work and support." He paused and glanced at me. "Of course, we have a very special person to thank for tonight's performance. Miss Bliss's hard work, dedication and passion is what has made tonight happen. I would like us all to give her a special round of applause and also to thank Mrs Young on piano, Mrs Bishop for all her help, and what can I say about that beautiful duet from Josh and Jane? So, one more round of applause, please, for Miss Bliss and the whole team, and then you can help yourselves to tea, cake and mince pies provided by The Friends of our school and served at the back of the hall and take the opportunity to mingle before making your way home. Thank you all again, and I hope you all have a very merry Christmas."

Richard started the final cheer and pointed the audience towards me. I felt myself blush with all of the eyes upon me, and I was dizzy with the power of the delight reverberating around the room. The volume of the applause had more to do with the children's, especially Jane and Josh's, performances than mine and was magnified by the school's shared appreciation of the Nelsons' trauma.

After being advised by Amy, Josh's psychotherapist, that Josh would benefit from being able to talk to his peers about his father and his traumatic past, Cathy had very bravely taken the decision to share some of their story with the other parents and children in class one evening, thus making Josh's starring role extra special for everyone. The fact that he possessed the voice of an angel and had just produced Oscar-worthy acting skills was the icing on the cake.

After the ovation had come to a natural end, I released the children from the stage and they all rushed to be congratulated by their respective families. I followed Josh to Cathy and the Hancocks, who were beside themselves with pride and delight. Josh was laughing excitedly as Mark swung him high around his head.

"Wow, Josh! I knew you were amazing, but that was even better than I'd hoped," he told him.

"Well done! You must be so proud," I said to Cathy.

Her smile lit up her bruised, scarred face, and her eyes sparkled with joy. "Miss Bliss," she said, "when I think about where we were two months ago … Well, it hardly seems real. Yes, of course I'm proud. I would've been proud if he'd just stood on the stage and smiled. This was more than I could ever have imagined."

Josh was back on the ground, and he wrapped his arms around his mother's waist while she smoothed her hand tenderly through his hair. She looked down at him with adoration and then back up at me, tears shining in her eyes again.

"The hospital have signed me off today. Fit to look after

myself and have my boy back," she said happily.

"Oh, Cathy, that's such wonderful news," I said. "And just in time for Christmas."

"Yes," said Cathy. "I'm not quite back to full strength yet, but it'll be amazing being together again."

"I'm so happy for you both," I said.

"There's more," she went on, her eyes shining brightly. "Everyone's been amazing. Sorting out somewhere to live and my finances is a long, complicated process, but for now at least, we're OK." She paused. "We're going to be staying with my parents," she said emotionally. "I'm going home." The tears were falling freely now. Tears of joy.

"Oh, really?" I was thrilled, and I put my hand on Cathy's arm. "Oh, Cathy, I couldn't be happier for you. You've seen them, then?"

"Yes," said Cathy. "I contacted them from the hospital, and they came straight in. They've been amazing. We've been seeing them almost every day and they've been getting to know Josh. They would've been here tonight, but they've been away. They're on their way back, though, and tomorrow it's all happening. They've been so supportive and understanding. I wouldn't've blamed them if they'd wanted nothing to do with me."

"Nonsense," I said firmly. "They're your family."

"Yes, that's what they said. They never stopped loving me. They'd been trying to contact me for years, but Aaron had blocked them everywhere. They'd just about given up. They were convinced it was what I wanted." She looked at her feet and shifted uncomfortably. "I'm trying to let go of the guilt," she said. "It's one of my challenges, but it's hard to believe I let him cut me off from my own parents, and they've missed out on so much of Josh growing up because of it."

"Don't think about that now," I said. "Just concentrate on all the good times ahead and wallow in the glory of being the mother of a super star!"

Josh looked up and laughed. "Yes," he said, "and Grandma and Grandpa say they've got a lot of making up to do, so I think I'm getting extra presents this Christmas!"

I winked at him. "Every day's a Wednesday."

"That's right, Miss. Every day's a Wednesday."

He spotted Sonya, Amy and Paul coming towards us. "You came!" he shouted and ran forward to meet them.

"As if we'd miss it," said Paul. "Thanks for the tickets, Miss Bliss."

"Of course," I said. "I wanted to make sure all of Josh's fans were here. When he's collecting his Oscar in a few years' time, we'll be able to say that we were there when it all began."

Everyone laughed, and I wished them all a merry Christmas and excused myself. I left the group singing Josh's praises and discussing their respective plans for the holidays, and I made my way around the hall, congratulating parents and children and being congratulated and praised for all of my hard work and the incredible performances.

Everyone was happy. I was surrounded by the enthusiastic chatter of children and grown-ups alike, and there was a wonderful festive atmosphere in the hall. Already buzzing from my own pride and excitement after the incredible show, I could hardly contain my delight as I was enveloped by the delicious high-spirited emotions around me. The volunteers had put together a lovely selection of cakes and biscuits. It was the perfect way to end an emotional term.

My family was waiting for me at the back of the hall. They wanted everyone else to have the chance to talk to me first, and while I was grateful for their patience, I was also desperate to get to them and to throw my arms around my little sister. I drifted around the hall, making sure to miss no one out. I wished everyone a happy Christmas and was wished the same a hundred times in return.

Eventually, I was free of all the parents and children. People had started drifting off into the night and the hall was quietening. I looked around. They were still waiting patiently. Mum, Dad and Jack were in conversation, but Stephanie was standing very slightly apart from them, people-watching but mostly waiting for her moment with me. Our eyes locked together. The force of the love that barrelled into my chest almost knocked me backwards. It was like coming home. I hadn't realised how much I had missed her until this moment. I hadn't realised how much I needed her, and suddenly, there was no one else in the room. We flew together and threw ourselves into each other's arms with an impact that nearly sent us both flying. We laughed with glee.

"Stephie," I said at last as I pulled away to look at her properly. "I wasn't expecting you until next week! It's so good to see you."

I looked deeply into the face of my little sister, a face that was so familiar despite her propensity for extended travel in recent years. I was struck, as always, by her elfin beauty, defined by the tips of her pointed ears that peeped from under her hair. Prolonged exposure to the sun in foreign climates had accentuated her caramel freckles so that there was hardly an inch of her pale skin left untouched. Her vivid blue eyes shone from under long dark lashes, leading artistically down over that cute button nose and full pink lips. Her hair, natural in its voluminous waves, framed her face with a thousand shades of gold, giving the impression of golden sunshine in a warm, gentle breeze.

Stephanie always looked relaxed. She could fit into any situation and drew people's eyes with her natural beauty and magical smile, which radiated warmth and drew strangers and friends like moths to a flame. Tonight she was stunning in a simple outfit of jeans and an off-the-shoulder grey cashmere top that displayed her naturally prominent collar bone and slim, toned figure. She was as delighted to see me as I was to see her. The pleasure of it lit her up like a flame.

"You look amazing," I continued. "All that sunshine and hard work is obviously good for you. Why didn't you tell me you were coming home early?"

Stephanie smiled modestly. "Thanks, but what about you? You were in your element tonight. Those kids adore you. And all the parents for that matter. You have everyone eating out of the palm of your hand as usual. I didn't tell you because I didn't want to distract you from the performance of your career," she teased, "and I was right. You were amazing. They were amazing."

"It's a reception class nativity," I replied with amusement. "Let's not get carried away."

"Hey, don't sell yourself short. It might be a reception class nativity, but for some of these kids, it'll be the most scary and exciting thing they've ever done, and for some of these parents, it'll be one of their proudest moments so far. And as for Mary and Joseph's duet at the end? Seriously, Izzy, there wasn't a dry eye in the place. I nearly went and I don't even like kids!"

I laughed and linked my arm through Stephanie's, steering her back to where our parents and Jack were waiting. They were all beaming. They had really enjoyed themselves.

"Hey. Thanks for coming," I said. "Did you enjoy it?"

"It took me back," said Mum. "I remember your first nativity. It's something a mum never forgets." She smiled. "Well done, darling. It was a triumph."

"I wish everyone would stop getting carried away," I laughed.

It was Jack's turn to give me a proud smile. "See?" he asked. "I told you it would go without a hitch. You had nothing to worry about. It was fabulous. I hope someone's got it on video."

"Yes. Serena's dad was filming it for us. He's going to make it available for any parents who want to download it to embarrass their kids with on their wedding days," I laughed. "And I don't know about without a hitch. Mary dropping Jesus on his head wasn't in the script," I confessed.

"Oh, I don't know," said Dad. "I thought that was the best

bit."

"Dad!" I hissed.

"What?" He shrugged. "You've got to have some comedy in these things or they can get a bit dry."

Mum shot him a disapproving look.

"Not that this ever felt dry," he continued with a glint in his eye. "Anyway, it added a bit of realism, if you ask me. Angels talking to shepherds and Wise Men worshipping a random baby in a manger underneath a really bright star all sounds a bit far-fetched, but you show me a parent who hasn't dropped their baby on its head a time or two. Never did you two any harm."

"Right. That's it, Dad. Let's get you home before you offend someone." Stephanie took Dad by the arm and led him towards the door, still laughing. She turned back, "Are you coming, Izzy?"

I surveyed the hall. "I just need to help get everything tidied up, but I'll come round as soon as I'm done. We can have a cup of tea and a proper catch up."

"Sounds good," said Stephanie. "We've got two weeks, so there'll be plenty of time before I head off again. See you in a bit."

"We'll leave Jack with you then, Izzy, all right?" Mum asked. "We picked him up on the way, so he doesn't have a car."

"Of course that's OK," I replied. "See you later."

"See you later. Well done again for tonight. You make me very proud."

I looked around. The volunteers had already almost finished clearing the hall and the stage of chairs and props. There were just a few stray items left to gather and stow away.

I turned to Jack. "I'm just going to make sure I've left the classroom fit for its Christmas holiday and check the kids have taken everything off their pegs. We don't want a mouldy banana skin at the bottom of a P.E bag causing a stink for January. Do you want to come?"

"Of course, whatever I can do to help," Jack replied, "but first …" He took me by the hand and pulled me in for a quick kiss. "I've been wanting to do that all night," he declared. "You were amazing, you know? Those kids are lucky to have you. I'm so lucky you're mine."

"Thanks, Jack." I blushed slightly, feeling the edge of his physical desire and my body's response to his emotion.

"I mean it," he said, looking me straight in the eye. "And one day, hopefully not too far away, you're going to make an amazing mum too. And our kids will be even luckier." He kissed me again, more thoroughly this time. I smiled, turned and made my way thoughtfully into the classroom with Jack by my side.

Chapter 14

We were at the beach. It was a gloriously hot, sunny day, and I could see for miles along the hazy shore. Miles upon miles of unspoilt sandy beach stretching alongside the open water. We were walking hand in hand at the edge of the surf, and the chilly water lapped around my ankles as my feet sank into the wet, yielding sand. There was a warm, gentle breeze caressing my upturned face, lifting and blowing my hair into my mouth, where I could taste the salt on it. I laughed, prompting him to turn to me, gently tease the hair out and tuck it tenderly back behind my ear, and every time he touched my face, he stopped and stared into my eyes with that intense, fiery gaze that set my insides aflame. He kissed my lips gently, with a hint of passion and promise.

The beach was deserted. There wasn't a soul in sight, and we were just walking — walking and touching and laughing. Every time I looked at him, a feeling of peace and belonging descended upon me and I felt whole. I felt happy.

After an indeterminate length of time walking lazily and happily side by side, Scott steered me away from the sea, up the beach towards the softly rolling dunes. The sand transformed from moist and cool to warm and dry, and the gentle, velvety grains flowed between our toes. He led me to a blanket spread out in a hollow, sheltered from the wind by rolling sandy mounds and long grass. He lowered himself onto his back and pulled me down with him, and at that moment, nothing mattered except being there, lying beside the man of my dreams.

Scott lay back on the blanket and I lay by his side looking up at the brilliant blue sky. I turned and propped myself onto my elbow so that I could look down at his face: that handsome, tranquil, perfect face and those deep, fiery eyes. I took a finger and traced it gently across his top lip, then around until I reached the centre of the lower one. I paused there and his tongue darted out and wrapped around my finger, drawing it into his mouth, where he sucked on it gently, staring deeply into my eyes. He groaned around my finger and heat shot through my body. I moaned in response. I was powerless in his presence. Whenever we were close, an unstoppable force drew us closer and closer and deeper together. Our feelings wrapped around each other, feeding off one another, the exhilaration climbing higher and higher and the desire building like a volcano that would surely erupt when we inevitably joined, body and soul.

Scott lowered me onto the blanket. Now it was his turn to look down on me and to trace his finger lightly across my face. He closed my eyes with his fingertips and traced a featherlight touch across my eyelids and down to my mouth, where I drew him in and sucked on his finger, hard and deep into my mouth. Scott groaned again and swiftly replaced the finger with his tongue, kissing and exploring my mouth deeply. His hand slid to my shoulder and slipped the straps of my top and bra down over my elbow while he continued his passionate assault on my mouth. I raised my hips in invitation, confirming my desire.

"I'm here," he told me, coming up for air. "I'm here, Belle. I'm here and I'm yours."

He was there. He was with me physically and inside my mind emotionally and spiritually. I could feel our souls unite. I was inside his head and he was inside mine, and words were no longer necessary because we could read each other's minds. The flames of desire licked around us where our bodies touched, and I gave myself up to ecstasy.

I surfaced from the dream mid moan, my hips raised from the bed, grinding into an empty space. My eyes flew open and I was back to reality in a second, staring in horror at Jack, still slumbering peacefully by my side. Thank goodness that I hadn't woken him. My cheeks were flushed, and they burned hotter still at the memory of the dream and the memories of all of the dreams that had gone before. Despite my determination to banish Scott Callahan from my waking thoughts, he had become a frequent headliner of my dreams, and I honestly didn't know whether I relished or abhorred his nightly visits. My latent self revelled in the involuntary visions, and the evidence of my body's traitorous response was undeniable on waking, every single time. I could still feel his touch on my skin and had to fight to regain control of my breathing. The fire that he inspired in my sleep was still burning in the cold light of day, and the dreams were only becoming more frequent and more intense as time went on.

I slipped quietly from the bed, careful not to disturb Jack. I grabbed a towel that Mum had left out for me and crept down the corridor to the bathroom, where I endured yet another cold shower. Once I had regrouped and was clean and fresh, I wrapped myself up and padded back towards the bedroom. I met Stephanie on the landing.

"Happy Christmas!" she yelled.

My mind clicked into gear. It was Christmas Day. Of course it was Christmas Day. That's why we had stayed at our parents' house last night — so that we could wake up as a family, all together on Christmas Day. I hurriedly arranged my features into a suitably festive smile and gave my little sister a hug.

"Happy Christmas, Stephie." I returned the greeting. "I wonder if Santa's been."

Every year, Dad gathered up all of the gifts from everyone to everyone else before the big day and he laid them all out under the tree after we had gone to bed. Even at the ripe old age of twenty-six, it was still magical to go to bed on Christmas Eve with an empty space under that tree and to come downstairs on Christmas morning to find a plethora of gifts. The actual existence, or lack thereof, of Santa had never been broached. We all embraced the magic.

"He always does," beamed Stephanie. "As long as you've been a good girl, of course."

Stephanie laughed innocently, but I couldn't help a

tightening of my chest. The vision of Scott Callahan's hands on my body and the taste of his tongue in my mouth was fresh, and even the memory of the fantasy drew a spontaneous warmth to my core and a flush to my cheeks that I hurriedly tried to hide.

It was too late. Stephanie's eyes narrowed in on me and I felt that familiar prickle probing at my mind. I forced it back out immediately but could feel Stephanie's troubled gaze burning into my eyes. I looked away guiltily.

"Are you OK, Izzy?" she asked. "You don't seem quite … right."

"Yes, of course," I replied quickly. "Just excited about Christmas."

I knew that I couldn't hide anything from her for long, so I trotted quickly back to the bedroom and swiftly shut the door behind me. I leaned back on it, eyes closed, breathing fast. I didn't know what Stephanie had seen in my eyes or sensed in my mind, but I didn't want her to know. I was ashamed. I had never hidden anything from her before. I didn't want to lie to her, but I couldn't tell her the truth either. Not that there was even a truth to tell. I hadn't seen Scott Callahan since that night on the bench eight weeks ago, and even then, nothing had actually happened — nothing physical, at least. I had done nothing wrong. I was not to blame for the uninvited dreams that were haunting me. I hadn't acted on my desires. I was innocent. I was innocent.

"Happy Christmas, darling!"

I jumped at the sound of Jack's voice. My eyes flew open. He was sitting up in bed, regarding me thoughtfully. "I woke up and you were gone," he said. "I'm glad you're back." He smiled. "Come here. I want a Christmas kiss."

As usual, Jack's honest, guileless warmth and love enveloped and grounded me. He was so good, so uncomplicated. I let go of the tension and went to him. I perched on the edge of the bed and let his emotions ease my mind. I looked into his eyes, the eyes of my best friend and

245

lover, the eyes of the man who had adored me unquestioningly for my entire life. I leaned in and kissed him, deeply, honestly. There was no question in my heart that I loved him too. I pushed the dream firmly out of my mind and resolved to start the day again, from this moment, with my family by my side.

It was a wonderful day. The five of us laughed together, played together and ate together. Mum made a beautiful breakfast of scrambled eggs on toast, fresh from the hens on her allotment, and we opened our presents from under the tree. We spent the rest of the morning playing silly games and chatting a bit about everything and a lot about nothing and prepared the Christmas dinner together. Dad was the executive chef, and he gave each of his assistants a job to do, but as most of the food had been prepared over the previous few days, it all went without a hitch, and we sang and danced happily to Christmas music as we worked. I set the table, pouring everyone a large glass of wine and distributing the Christmas crackers. Mum even got the best tablecloth out for the occasion.

The food was fantastic. Mum made her famous chestnut stuffing, and Dad prepared the roast potatoes to perfection with crispy shells and gloriously soft centres. We had homemade Yorkshire puddings and deliciously rich gravy and all indulged in too much Christmas pudding for dessert. After dinner there was a brief lull while everyone sat quietly, feeling uncomfortably full but content, just like millions of people up and down the country and across the globe on Christmas Day.

On top of the gifts from my family, I had put a pile of presents from the children in my class to one side. While the others busied around in the kitchen after dinner, I sat and opened them one by one. I had presented each of my Little Owls with a rainbow-coloured glow-in-the-dark star to stick on their bedroom ceilings and invite a little extra magic into their lives, and I had received, in turn, an impressive collection of mugs, pens, candles and bath bombs. One of my favourites was a cream fabric bag for life from Melissa. It had a message on it which read *This is what the best teacher in the world looks like,* with an arrow pointing upwards, and I planned on parading around the supermarket with it very soon.

I left the present from Josh until last and opened it slowly, with care. Cathy had warned me that it was fragile. It was small and light, and I eased it slowly from the colourful paper. It slipped out onto my knee. It was a homemade bookmark, a superhero bookmark. The body of the hero was made from a wooden ice-lolly stick painted yellow and glued to a red card cape. She was wearing a black face mask and had a badge emblazoned with *Miss Bliss* across her chest. On the back of the cape, Josh had written *Thank you for saving our lives. You are my hero.* It was perfect. I would cherish it forever.

I held the bookmark over my heart for a moment before slipping it inside the front cover of one of my new books. I always received books for Christmas, and I was always delighted. There are more books in the world than I could read in a thousand lifetimes, but it had always been my mission to get through as many of them as I could, and I derived pleasure from each and every one. This year, Stephanie had given me *The Moonstone* by Wilkie Collins, my classic, grown-up choice and a book that I had been meaning to get around to for years. *Go Tell the Bees That I Am Gone* was the latest in the *Outlander* series by Diana Gabaldon: a specific request because it afforded me the opportunity to continue my great romance with the fiery Red Jamie Fraser. Last in Stephanie's typically eclectic selection was *The Daughter of the Blood* by Anne Bishop, 'an intense and gripping dark fantasy novel' concerning witches, prophecies, magic and darkness. It wasn't something that I normally would have chosen for myself, but that was the point of allowing someone else to do the choosing. The world is full of adventures waiting to be explored, and I might discover a surprising new passion or new author to adore.

I put my presents carefully into a pile and went to join the others in the kitchen.

"Oh, that's right," scoffed Jack. "Just in time to watch us putting the last of the pots away!" He laughed and flicked me gently with a damp tea towel.

"Oi," I replied. "You know very well I had extremely important business to take care of." But I laughed with him.

"Of course you did," he replied. "So, how many *Best Teacher* mugs did you get this year?"

I laughed. "Well, OK, I'll admit I got a few more mugs to add to the collection, but I also got some other lovely things too. I got a snazzy bag from Melissa and a beautiful homemade bookmark from Josh. He said I'm his hero."

"Well, he knows what he's talking about," said Jack. "You happen to be my hero too."

I pushed him gently with the palm of my hand, but he grabbed it and pulled me towards him. "I mean it," he said.

"I know you do," I replied, leaning into him. "I love you."

Mum finished wiping down the work surfaces.

"Right," she said, "who's coming to give the girls their Christmas supper and find the perfect spots for my new friends before starting on the evening's entertainment and more eating?"

Dad raised his hands in surrender. "I just can't," he declared. "I can hardly move. I need to sit very still for a bit. I might even close my eyes for a few minutes."

Stephanie groaned. "Oh my God, Dad, you're getting so old!"

"Yep," Dad agreed, "and if an old man can't have a bit of shut-eye after his Christmas dinner, what's the world coming too?"

"Are you coming, Jack?" Mum asked.

"Hmm," he pondered. "I think I'd better stay behind and

keep an eye on the old man."

"Very wise," I said, "and nothing at all to do with the fact that you wouldn't mind shutting your eyes too?"

"Hey," Jack feigned offence. "I'm just doing my duty, looking after the host."

I shot him a knowing look.

"OK, I'll also admit I think I might have overdone it a bit on the turkey. And the stuffing. And maybe the Christmas pudding."

Everyone laughed.

"OK, well, I'm in," I said.

"And me," said Stephanie. "Christmas wouldn't be Christmas without visiting the girls."

"Lovely. Just us girls, then," said Mum. "Grab your coats and wellies. I'll find a bag for the fairies."

There had been a heavy frost overnight and the temperature hadn't risen above freezing all day, so the air was icy on our lungs, and the pale winter's sun cast a bleached light across the crisp ground. As we set off towards the allotment, our misty breath rose before us and our eyes burned with the cold. It was a family tradition to take a walk to the allotment after dinner at Christmas, and we strolled together happily, side by side, our feet crunching on the dry, frozen grass, the occasional call of the robins amplified in the gloom.

We arrived at the allotment at quarter past three. The sun was beginning to sink in the sky, casting an otherworldly pink and purple glow on the fluffy clouds over the horizon. Mum always wanted to spend a few minutes with the hens before closing them up for the night. She had the only animals on the allotments, so there would be no other gardeners venturing out today, but nothing would prevent Mum attending to her girls, come rain or shine. She had been out at first light to get them out of bed, collect eggs for breakfast and wish them a merry Christmas, but as we approached the gate, they heard our feet on the gravel and came running to the fence to greet us, gabbling noisily.

"Well, hello, ladies, and merry Christmas to you again," Mum said.

She disappeared briefly into the shed and returned with three foldaway chairs that she handed to me to set up. She disappeared back into the shed again and came back with three mugs that she handed to Stephanie. Then she disappeared into the shed for a third time, this time emerging with a bag full of fat balls and the leftover Christmas dinner that she had prepared for the hen's supper.

We entered the hen's enclosure and settled on the chairs. Mum poured us each a cup of tea from her flask and placed the food in a tray on the floor. The hens wobbled over and tucked straight in, clucking and cooing happily to each other over the feast. We relaxed, teas in hand. We were wrapped up against the cold, sporting thick coats, gloves, scarves and hats, so we were comfortable despite the wintry chill. Mum reached out a hand and stroked a couple of hens as they ate noisily by her feet.

"I could never admit it to your dad," she said guiltily, "but I think I might be getting old too. I wouldn't mind half an hour with my eyes closed after Christmas lunch either, but I find it so much more relaxing and peaceful to do it down here." We smiled at her fondly. "The fresh air and birdsong just help to take it all away, don't they?"

I murmured my agreement. I felt exactly the same way and suspected that Stephanie felt it too. It was like my trips to the bench by the lake. Being away from the hustle and bustle of the world, away from all of the people in it, connecting with nature. It just did something to me, cleared my mind, helped me find peace. Stephanie was nodding too. The three of us sat quietly together, lost in our own peaceful thoughts, with the breeze whispering in the trees and the clucking and scratching of the hens at our feet.

About twenty minutes later, Mum began to stir. I opened my eyes. I'm not sure, but I suspect that I might have dozed off. Those few minutes of total peace had been refreshing, especially with Mum and Stephanie by my side. There had been no strong, distracting emotions but a pleasant, companionable harmony. I suspected that they had been in a similar trance to me. Mum cleared her throat loudly and I smiled to see Stephanie flinch and her eyes spring open. I was right, she had been asleep.

"OK," said Mum. "If we don't get going soon, we're not going to have any light left. We need to find homes for these beauties and let the girls get some rest." She gestured to the stone figures that we had carried with us.

Mum always received gifts for her allotment for Christmas. If there was anything that she needed for herself, she would buy it herself. Her allotment was her one true love and her luxury, and the only way to make her really smile at Christmas was to buy for her garden. This year we had chosen a fairy theme and each bought her a stone statue. Mine was a small wild-bird bath with the water located in the enchanted fairy's cupped hands. Stephanie had bought a miniature stone fairy door, and Dad had given her a statue of an ethereal beauty with delicate wings, sleeping peacefully with her head resting on a toadstool. Mum was utterly charmed by them all and was eager to choose their new resting places before returning to the house.

We wandered around the plot together, trying different positions until Mum was satisfied. She filled up the bird bath, topped up the feeders and went back to check on the hens. Dusk was upon us, and they had finished their supper and put themselves to bed. Mum slipped into their enclosure and closed the henhouse door.

"Good night, ladies," she said softly. "See you in the morning. Happy Christmas."

Back at the house, we threw ourselves into our traditional Christmas board games session. Stephanie and I beat the boys in a game of Articulate, whilst Mum pottered in the kitchen. While Stephanie and I whooped, tears of laughter streamed down Dad's face. He was laughing so hard that he couldn't get his words out. He just kept pointing at Stephanie and me and waving his hands in the air.

"I don't know what's tickled you so much," said Stephanie.

"You can't …" he struggled, "That isn't … You can't …" He dissolved into hysterical laughter again, his sentence unfinished.

Jack was laughing too, although he was slightly more under control. "I think what Max means to say is, 'Hang on a minute, there must be some kind of rule against crazy sister mind-reading tricks!'" he said.

Dad nodded through the tears.

"If we'd've known there was going to be cheating going on, we wouldn't have agreed to girls against boys," continued Jack.

"Whoa," I said. "When did we cheat? There's been no cheating. I didn't say any of the words on the card!"

Dad was finally able to form a coherent sentence. "Isabel, you said, 'Some big stones in Scotland,' right?" he asked.

"Yes," I replied, bemused.

"And Stephanie said, 'Stonehenge'." He began to cry again.

"Yes?" Stephanie said with her hands on her hips. "That's right. That's what I said and that's the answer on the card. How can that be cheating?"

I turned the card over. "Stonehenge. See?"

Dad couldn't speak again, so Jack tried gently. "It's just that … well … Stonehenge isn't some big stones in Scotland," he pointed out. "It's in Wiltshire."

"It's the other end of the country," Dad spluttered. "They're four hundred miles apart!"

Stephanie and I looked at each other, blushed and joined in with the laughter.

"Ah," I said. "Well..."

"I blame the parents," Stephanie declared. "If you didn't

teach us our geography right, what hope have we got?"

"Great argument, dear," said Dad, "but you know your sister's a teacher, right? And you're heading that way. And how come not only did you both not know where Stonehenge is but you both thought it was in Scotland?"

"Like Jack said. Crazy sister mind-reading tricks," said Stephanie.

"And it doesn't matter how you get the answer, only that you get what it says on the card," I said. "And while we're at it, you can hardly talk. Have you forgotten that Jack thought a beagle was a large bird of prey and you thought Dr Livingstone was the alter ego of Mr Hyde?!"

We all broke down laughing again as Mum appeared at the door.

"What on earth's going on in here?" she asked. "I left you to play a nice game, and you've all gone mad!"

"Oh, Mum," I said. "You should have played. It's been so much fun."

"Hmm," she said. "It always makes me nervous. I can't cope with the stress!" She laughed. "And besides, somebody had to clean up. Who won?"

"We did, of course," said Stephanie.

Mum looked at the table where the boys' piece was almost halfway around the board and our piece was at the finish line. She laughed again. "I told you you shouldn't let them play together. They're a dangerous combination."

Dad had just about recovered. "I do love watching them, though. The way they read each other's amazing."

"We must remember next time," said Jack. "I want Isabel on my team."

"No way," I said. "You would never've got my Stonehenge clue! Only Stephanie would have got the double bluff I did. Or was it a triple bluff? I was relying on her knowing that I would give the wrong clue on purpose."

"Ha," snorted Dad. "A likely story."

Jack stood up. "Well, folks, it's been a wonderful day, but

I for one need to go and sleep off some of that fabulous food. I can't believe I ate so much cheese and chocolate after that massive lunch. I can't cope with any more fun. Good night, everybody."

"Good night, Jack," we chorused.

"I won't be long," I said. "Warm the bed up for me."

He smiled at me fondly. "I will," he said and kissed me softly on the lips. "Good night, Izzy. Happy Christmas."

It wasn't long before Mum and Dad drifted off too, and then Stephanie stood, gave a huge, noisy yawn and announced that she was also exhausted.

"It's been a lovely day, hasn't it?" she said.

"Yes," I replied. "It's been lovely all being together this last couple of weeks."

"You know I'm off in a couple of days, right?" Stephanie checked.

"Yes, I know. I'll miss you."

She had arranged to tour the country visiting university friends between Boxing Day and New Year and was travelling out to Thailand in just over a week. She planned to explore the world, teaching English and enhancing her CV as she went.

"I hate to sound like Mum, but you will be safe, won't you?" I asked.

Stephanie laughed. "Well, you actually sound just like Mum, and you don't need to worry. It'll be great. I'll meet some brilliant people, and if I hate it, I'll just come back. The whole point of getting my TEFL was so I could make some money whilst travelling, meeting people and seeing the world. I can't wait." She came over and laid a hand gently on my shoulder. "I'll miss you too, though," she said. "I love you so much."

"I know. I love you too."

I stood up and put my arms around her. I felt Stephanie's love, sure and strong, and met it with my own. Within a moment, it felt as if we were less two individuals and more one united, fluid existence. We had never spoken about our extraordinary connection; it was just something that existed between us, a part of who we were. I didn't even know whether Stephanie felt other people's emotions like me or if she also struggled and couldn't explain why. It didn't make sense that we could be so close and never have discussed such a fundamental and complex aspect of our lives. It should surely be something that we shared, and yet it went unmentioned between us. What I did know was that we shared an incredible bond which went deeper than that between most siblings. I also knew that I missed Stephanie terribly when she was gone. I would never ask her to stay. I wouldn't be so selfish as to expect her to give up her dreams for me, but I did find life just that little bit easier when she was near, and I was dreading having to say goodbye again.

Stephanie ran her hand gently through my hair, offering comfort.

"I know I'm supposed to be the big sister, but I always feel like you're the strong one," I admitted.

"You're stronger than you know," Stephanie said. "Just look what you've done this year. That kid, Josh. And not just that but all the kids. Every year you make them all fall in love with you, and you give them everything. I think you're amazing, Izzy."

Her words made me feel stronger.

I took a deep breath. "Sorry, Stephie, I'm getting all silly. I just don't want you to go."

"I know, but the world's a much smaller place now, you know. We have this thing called the internet. They even have it in Thailand!"

I laughed. "I know. It's not quite the same, but I know."

"Is there anything else?" she asked. "Anything at all you want to talk about? You've been … You've been a little distracted. You know you can talk to me about anything."

I did know that, and part of me wanted to open up to her and tell her everything that I was thinking, everything that I was struggling with, but I couldn't bear the thought of her being disappointed in me. I smiled.

"Thank you. I'm all right."

Stephanie straightened up. "OK, well, don't forget I'm always here. Even if I'm not here. Right. It's getting late. I'm going to bed. Good night."

"I won't be far behind you. Good night."

I was left on my own. I sank back into my favourite armchair and pulled my knees up to my chest. I was horribly tired but didn't want to go to bed just yet. I didn't want the magic of Christmas to end. It had been a wonderful day. I adored my family and was surrounded by warmth, love and laughter, so why did I feel this gnawing, empty space inside? I didn't feel totally at peace. Something was missing. I had that feeling that you get when you suddenly realise that you have forgotten something vitally important although you can't quite remember what that something is: that lurch, that gut-churning, hollow feeling in the pit of your stomach. It was always there, lurking in the shadows. It had been for months. As long as I was busy and surrounded by activity, I could ignore it, but at times like these, it snuck up on me — quiet times when I was by myself and couldn't hide from the truth. The truth was that I wasn't happy anymore, that I needed something more, something else. I needed to find the missing piece of my life. The unknown part of me, deep down inside, was alive and unsatisfied, demanding that I didn't settle for less.

As I gazed out of the window into the clear black sky littered with stars and the silvery glow of the moon, I let go of the control that I was keeping on my heart. I thought about another clear, starry night, the night that haunted my thoughts and the man that haunted my dreams. I was still fighting to deny the fact that I already knew the answer to the question, that I knew exactly what, or who, was missing from my life and causing the ache in my soul. I thought that if I pushed him out of my mind, if I refused to acknowledge my desires, he would gradually fade, and that moment, that night, would become a distant memory, but if anything, the ache was getting stronger and my attempts to banish him from my mind were getting weaker.

He was the reason that I didn't want to go to bed. He was the reason that I stayed up late even though I knew that I needed rest. I had to give in to the inevitability of slumber, but when my subconscious took over, I would once again succumb to the dreams. I was failing miserably in my attempts to block him out. In fact, the more I tried, the more vivid the dreams became. I wouldn't be able to deny it, even in my waking hours, for much longer. I already felt so guilty. Admitting it, even to myself, in the cold light of day would surely break something inside me. I couldn't go on like this.

I'm here. I'm here, Belle.
I'm here and I'm yours.

I stared out of the window into the night and shook my head, trying to clear the aberration. There was no one there.
I'm here. I'm here, Belle.

I wasn't asleep and yet it was his voice and the words that filled my dreams. Perhaps I was going mad. Part of me was desperate to embrace that voice and those words. I wanted to throw caution to the wind and go to him, to run now and find him or at least go to bed and embrace the dreams. I was happiest in my dreams. I felt safe. It felt right when we were together in my sleep, when I let him speak those words, and I knew that they were true. He was there. He was mine. In reality, though, we had only met twice. We had only had one proper conversation. How could I even be thinking this way? I had no idea whether he even remembered me, whether he knew my name, whether he ever thought about me.

No, that wasn't true. I knew.

I drew in a raw, jagged breath. I absolutely shouldn't be

thinking like this when Jack was sleeping peacefully in my bed. Jack, who loved me without reason, who had loved me for as long as I could remember and whom I loved in return. I couldn't go to bed and give in to the sleep that would bring the dreams and Scott Callahan to me, but something would have to give soon. It wasn't right. It wasn't honest, but I don't think I knew what honest was anymore. I hadn't fallen out of love with Jack, had I? Or had I?

I felt a tightness in my chest. My breath came in shorter gasps as I struggled to make sense of my thoughts. I was heading for a panic attack. Stephanie appeared in the doorway, a frightened look on her face.

"Izzy?" she whispered. "What is it? What's wrong?"

I hadn't made a sound. Stephanie must have felt my panic from upstairs. I looked into her worried face. If there was anyone I could talk to, anyone I could open up to, it was Stephanie. If there was anyone who would listen, who would understand the confusion in my heart, it was Stephanie. I needed to talk. I needed to share. I needed to rid myself of this intolerable burden. I had thought about opening up to Stephanie many times over the last couple of weeks, but it had never felt right. There never seemed to be a right time. Perhaps this was it. Perhaps I needed it after all. I took a deep breath.

"Girls?" Mum was suddenly at the top of the stairs. "What's going on? Why are you up so late? I heard you moving around."

I could have cried.

"We're fine, Mum," called Stephanie. "Too much of that stinky cheese keeping us awake. Go back to bed."

"I'm not going back to bed until you two get up these stairs. I'm still your mother and I can still tell you to go to bed."

She came into view. She sounded stern but she was smiling, and she was right. It was late and I was awfully tired. I smiled at Stephanie. The desire to share was gone. I was just tired and needed to go to bed. Things would look better in the morning.

"Mum's right," I said. "It's time to go."

Stephanie smiled back. "You're right. Let's get some sleep."

We bid each other good night on the landing. I gave Mum a quick cuddle and Stephanie a slightly longer one and quietly pushed open my bedroom door. I climbed into bed next to Jack, snuggled under the sheets and waited for the dreams to come.

Chapter 15

It was below freezing out on the street. I could see the white vapour of my breath rising into the darkness, but I didn't feel the cold. I was surrounded by the heady anticipation of a throng of revellers energising each other with their enthusiasm. Fuelled by the powerful combination of excitement and intoxication, they were flying high, and I was right there with them. Standing on the pavement, the songs reached the crowd as vibrations through the ground, a muted echo of the music itself, muffled by the fabric of the building and the heavy double doors. Each time the bouncers opened the doors and welcomed another group of giddy patrons in, a fleeting blast of a familiar tune roused the rabble further, increasing their volume and excitement, and in turn, increasing my warmth and exhilaration.

As we reached the front of the queue, every fibre of my being was electrified. I had only had a couple of glasses of wine, but I could feel the alcohol flowing through my blood, emboldening me and feeding my excitement. I didn't allow myself this sort of abandon very often, but I could see how these feelings could become very addictive very quickly. I felt alive with a kind of nervous energy that reached all the way to my fingertips and made them tingle with unharnessed power.

The bouncer pulled open the door and nodded us in. I let out a little squeal of excitement, squeezed Donna's arm and literally skipped through the entrance to the foot of the stairs. Inside, music filled the air and all I wanted to do was dance. I put my arms in the air and dashed up the stairs and straight onto the dance floor. Donna was right behind me.

"I'd forgotten how much fun you are when you're drunk," Donna shouted over the music as she joined me in the centre of a swarm of writhing bodies.

I laughed. "I'm not drunk," I insisted, "just enjoying letting my hair down for a change. I'd forgotten how good it feels to just let go, and I want to dance."

Donna smiled. "I love this side of you, Izzy. Wish we saw it more often. However, you might have lost all your inhibitions after two drinks, but I need shots if I'm going to dance." She laughed again. "I'm going to the bar. Want anything? Tequila?"

"No thanks. I've had enough. I just want to dance. I'll wait here."

"You really are a cheap date," Donna shouted over the music, and she left me to it while she headed to the bar for more liquid courage.

I continued to dance. I let the music control my body, relinquishing any conscious authority over my limbs and opening my mind to the euphoria of the crowd. The joy of the music superseded rules, friendships and self-consciousness, and I was content to swirl and sway by myself or to join in with other dancers while I waited for Donna. I danced as if no one was watching, just a little fuzzy with intoxication. It was like a mysterious part of my personality was let loose. A secret part of myself that I normally kept locked inside was allowed to burst free, and tonight I simply wanted to have a good time.

I needed this. I was always nervous of it because there was so little space between a drunken, happy nightclub customer and a drunken, angry customer, and being around angry people could be dangerous for me, especially when I had a drink, because my guard was down and my mind was further open to emotional assaults, but I had been feeling frustrated and stifled of late and I needed to get out of my own mind. I needed to get out and to let my hair down, and a Friday night girls' night with Donna was the ideal opportunity.

After a couple of songs, Donna was back and we danced together. We danced and sang at the top of our voices, and we laughed together. In a nightclub, the lights are so dim, the music so loud and the clientele so absorbed that even a normally insecure individual can hide in obscurity, dance without fear of ridicule and sing their heart out, safe in the knowledge that no one can hear them and that even if they did, they wouldn't care.

I had gone straight to Donna's house after work. We ate an Indian takeaway, Donna drank a bottle of wine, and we caught up on our respective family Christmases. We headed into town and visited a few bars, where Donna drank cocktails, I enjoyed a couple of glasses of wine, and we chatted some more. It had been great feeling relaxed in each other's company and reconnecting after a few weeks apart, and with all of the talking out of the way, we were now free to shout at each other over the loud music and dance. The couple of drinks and the buzzing energy of the throng had a similar effect on me as a bottle of wine, three cocktails and a few shots of tequila had on Donna.

After some time, I held my hands up in defeat. I cupped them around my mouth and shouted into Donna's ear. "OK, that's it. I need a rest and I need water, stat."

Donna laughed. "I so knew you would cave first."

"This isn't caving. It's simply taking a breather before coming back and wiping the dance floor with you some more."

"Oh, is that what you've been doing? I thought you were having some sort of seizure!"

I laughed again and pointed to an empty table in the corner of the club. "Go and sit over there. I'll go to the bar. Water? Or does madam require more tequila?"

"All right, bossy, I'll go and sit over there, but I'll tell you this." Donna's words were slightly slurred, and she levelled her finger right into my chest to make her point. "It's because I want to and not because you told me to. And water will be just fine, thank you."

Donna's slightly bleary eyes sparkled. She turned and headed for the table. I marvelled at the fact that she could still walk in a straight line. Half of what Donna had drunk tonight would have had me on my knees.

A trip to the bar later, armed with a bottle of still water for myself and sparkling water for Donna, I arrived at the table and sat down.

"Urgh. I'm not as young as I used to be," I complained, slipping off my shoes and rubbing my sore feet. "Either that or we don't do this often enough anymore."

"Definitely the first one," laughed Donna. "You're what? Fifty-five, is it now, fifty-six? I think you aged about a decade in the last six months and two in the six months before that."

"Yeah, all right, so we don't do this often enough," I conceded. "Seriously though, it's been so great tonight. I always get frightened, drinking and letting go, but I've had so much fun."

"Yeah, me too. We should definitely do it again soon. We need to make the most of the time we've got before you're married with kids."

"Steady on," I laughed. "My dancing days are far from over, thank you very much."

"Ah, yes, but it won't be long," Donna assured me. "You and Jack are cut from the same cloth. Marriage and kids can't be far away."

I smiled noncommittally and concentrated on my drink to avoid the conversation going any further in that direction. After the last few months and my increasing certainty that I wasn't where I wanted to be, I really didn't want to be thinking about my future with Jack right now. He was at his brother's house this weekend, which was one of the reasons that I had been so keen to come out. It felt a bit like freedom. I steered the conversation away, and we spent the next few minutes companionably drinking water and people-watching.

I was just about to suggest that we return to the dance floor when Donna grabbed my arm hard and let out an excited little squeak.

"Don't look now but you'll never guess who's just walked

in!"

"Who?" I swivelled round, but the prickle in my mind and the way the hairs on the back of my neck stood up told me that I didn't need to guess.

"I said don't look now," hissed Donna.

Daniel Callahan was standing on the top step, surveying the dance floor. He looked cool, calm and totally in control. He gave the impression of a king assessing his subjects and being rather disappointed. I had forgotten quite how large and imposing a man he was, but he stood easily a couple of inches taller than any other man in the club, and I had to admit that he had quite a presence. He was a difficult man to look away from, and I noticed that there were an awful lot of people in the club currently having that difficulty. Not that Daniel noticed. He was probably used to receiving admiring stares and wasn't fazed or impressed by them at all.

What caught my attention wasn't his stature or his commanding presence, though. I was struck by the normality of his aura. He felt like a human being. I couldn't tell exactly what he was feeling from this distance and with the interference of hundreds of intoxicated, happy people between us, only that it wasn't an especially intense emotion. Probably disdain, judging by the look on his face, but he definitely appeared to be decidedly more human. His eyes continued to track around the room as if scanning for alien lifeforms, and when he reached our corner, he saw us and immediately stiffened.

His eyes met mine for the briefest of moments and he looked away instantly. If it had been anyone else, I wouldn't have even been sure that he had seen me, but it wasn't anyone else, and I was sure. I knew that Daniel Callahan had seen me because at the very moment that our eyes met across the crowded dance floor, that void, that eerie emotional emptiness, returned. I didn't understand. It had been obvious that Daniel Callahan had taken some kind of dislike to me when we had encountered each other on the two previous occasions. I seemed to have an unfavourable impact on his personality, but I had never considered that it was actually my presence that somehow created or contributed to his total lack of emotional signal. With this indication that his reaction to me was more than a simple dislike, my misgivings about him intensified, and I was even more distressed by the dreamy sigh that escaped Donna's lips as she stared longingly across the room.

Scott strolled casually up the stairs behind his brother, and now it was my turn to gasp as my heart did a little summersault and the thrumming in the back of my mind roared to life once again. I hadn't seen him in the flesh since that night in October, but I had seen him in my dreams countless times and heard his velvety voice whisper to me, telling me that he was mine. I had felt his presence during waking hours too. At random moments, something deep within my mind would whisper to me that he was near, and my body would ache with the desire to see him again. I don't know how many times I had whirled around, certain that I would find him watching me, only to find myself alone, and as I looked at him now, I questioned whether my subconscious had even done him justice. It was true that Daniel had a commanding presence about him, but he had nothing that could touch the sheer magic of his little brother.

Scott reached Daniel's side, and he looked totally at ease in a light grey shirt and dark jeans. He smiled at Daniel, said something and pointed towards the bar. I couldn't tear my eyes away from him as Daniel shook his head and jerked his thumb towards the stairs at the other side of the club, clearly insisting that they head down to the other room. Scott nodded his consent. Donna and I never went downstairs. It was darker down there. The music was slower and more sombre, and the clientele always seemed to have a more forbidding, rougher edge. No one danced downstairs. People sat at dingy tables and talked or just drank. They called it The Pit, and it made me nervous. As the Callahans made their way towards the stairs, Daniel said something to Scott with a scowl and pointed right at me.

Scott looked over. When his eyes landed on me, everything about him changed just as it had with Daniel, except that nothing about the way that Scott looked at me was in any way similar to his brother. I was struck again by how I could have such a drastically contrasting impact on two people so closely related and how they could have such a drastically contrasting impact on me. When Scott looked at me, I instantly flushed and my heart began to beat faster, in an erratic rhythm. I actually saw his pupils dilate from the other side of the room, and impossible as it seemed at this distance, I could have sworn that I saw the fire inside them ignite. He had been devastating before, but his spirit seemed to come alive as he drank me in with those eyes. I stopped breathing. I think that I saw him take an involuntary step towards me. I think that I moved towards him too, drawn by the same invisible force, but the spell was broken when Daniel grabbed him roughly by the shoulder and propelled him to the stairs. They were out of sight in a moment, and I was left staring into an empty space, reeling from my body's reaction, feeling lightheaded but this time definitely not from the alcohol.

"Oh my God," sighed Donna. "Did you see the way he looked at me?"

I had to shake myself back to reality and turn my focus to my friend. I hadn't seen how Daniel looked at Donna. I had only seen how both of the men had reacted to me. I was fairly certain that neither of the men had looked at Donna at all, but perhaps I was being incredibly self-absorbed. I looked at Donna and was disappointed by her lovelorn expression.

"Do I need to remind you what happened last time you looked like that at Daniel Callahan?" I asked.

Donna just sighed again.

"You spent the entire night flirting with him, and then he upped and left without a word. He didn't even say goodbye,"

I reminded her. "And he put you in a foul mood. I thought you were going to fall out with me properly that night."

"You're crazy. I'd never fall out with you," protested Donna. "Haven't we been best friends forever?"

"Yeah, I know, but you were weird that night, and that look on your face worries me. Right, no more talking or thinking about Callahans, starting now."

I slammed my hand down on the table a little harder than I had intended to, making Donna jump. I wasn't sure if it was the heat between myself and Scott or the blindness of Donna's crush that unsettled me more, but I didn't want it to ruin our night. We sat quietly for a while, each lost in our own thoughts. Despite my determination for the Callahans not to impact on girls' night, there was no mistaking the fact that the atmosphere had changed. There were still hundreds of people on the dance floor, and the room was still full of high spirits, but the moment was lost. We didn't seem to have anything to say to each other anymore.

Donna took matters into her own hands. "Wait here," she told me.

I gave her a disciplined salute and did as I was told. Before long, she was back with a small round tray loaded with three shot glasses full of gold liquid, a sachet of salt and two slices of lime.

"Tequila!" she announced dramatically and unnecessarily.

I groaned. "Don," I complained. "I haven't done a tequila slammer in about five years. You know I can't handle spirits."

"You used to be good at them, though, remember?" Donna wheedled. "Anyway, it's one shot. Well, one for you, two for me, and you had your last glass of wine, what, three hours ago? Come on, Izzy. Don't pretend you don't know the drill. Lick your hand. That's right. OK. Salt, tequila, lime, ready? One, two, three."

I licked the salt off my hand, downed the shot and quickly stuffed the lime into my mouth. My initial reaction was to grimace as I felt the tequila shudder through my body, but soon after, I felt the heat spreading through my veins and the alcohol pulsing in my fingertips. I considered Donna, who now looked smug, and I couldn't help a smile spreading across my face.

"See? Donna knows best. Now, let's dance."

She led me back onto the dance floor. It wasn't quite the same, but she was right about the tequila, and I concentrated on the warmth it infused me with and was soon enjoying myself again, but I could not shake off the awareness that Scott Callahan was in the building. Every time the thought surfaced, I tried to push it to one side, but it wouldn't go away.

Donna tapped me on the shoulder. "Just going for a wee," she shouted. "Be back in a few."

I nodded.

While Donna was gone, he came back. I felt him before I saw him. Something in the air changed subtly, the thrumming in my mind intensified, my senses heightened, and I knew exactly where to look. I stopped dancing. I turned. There he was, leaning on the rail near the top of the stairs, staring right at me. He made no attempt to hide the fact that he was watching me, and when our eyes met, his gaze didn't waver. In fact, when our eye s met, he smiled with satisfaction, and I saw him expel a heavy breath. My insides melted. I knew that this particular smile, this heart-stopping, jaw-dropping, intimate smile was for me, and I lost all sense of reason, all rational thought, and was immediately and utterly caught again in his powerful magic and by his deep, fiery eyes.

Without thinking, I took a step towards him. I was compelled by some invisible force, but when he saw me move, he shook his head. It was the tiniest of movements, but I understood his meaning. It wasn't a dismissal. He wanted to look at me. He wanted to watch me dance. I would have done anything for him as long as he kept looking at me like that. I wanted to feel his eyes on me. I wanted him to see me.

This time, when I began to move to the music, it felt different to the anonymous, lighthearted dancing as part of the crowd. This felt intimate, exposing. I held his gaze and let the music speak to my body, no longer needing the emotions of the strangers in the room but feeding from the energy of our connection, the incredible power of his presence and the link between his eyes and mine. The room became both smaller and larger at the same time. Everyone else faded away until there was only him and me. Sounds and shapes became less distinct, somehow muffled and hazy, while he alone remained sharply defined. I didn't need to be told that the same thing had happened for him. He saw me and only me, but he didn't just see me with his eyes. He saw my spirit: the me inside of me. Despite the distance between us, I knew that he saw the complexion of my skin and the swirling green and blue in my eyes. He heard my heartbeat and he tasted the passion in my soul.

I danced for him. I put my arms above my head and I moved my hips slowly, seductively, to the music. My eyes never left his. To dance for him was freedom. It was passion. It was power. It was, quite simply, right. I felt more alive, in the same way that I felt alive when we connected in the bar on that first meeting and on the bench by the lake and every time that he visited my dreams. The most incredible part of the emotions that he inspired in me was that I had no doubt that he was feeling them too. The connection between us flowed both ways, and despite the fact that he was still on the other side of the room, I could feel his power and his emotions more clearly than I had ever felt anything from anyone before. I looked right into his eyes, and he stared deeply into mine. I felt a profound sense of awe, of joy and of belonging. I felt at once excited and at peace.

There was a voice inside my head, an entity that was part of me and yet separate from the me that I had always known, and that voice was shouting that life is short and that this is all that matters — that this is what I've been waiting my whole life for — and I asked myself, as rationally as I could, whether I should go to him. I asked myself what I wanted, who I wanted to be, how I wanted to live. He knew that I was making up my mind, and I think he knew what I would choose. He waited patiently for me to find my answer. He didn't ask me to come. He didn't tell me to come but I was in no doubt about what he wanted. Still, he allowed me to make my choice. I saw the passion and the fire in those eyes, felt the pull of desire, and I knew that if I went to him, I might never leave. I had dreamed about him every night for the last three months. I woke up with my body and mind on fire and I heard his voice in my head. Of course it was what I wanted.

As I came to my decision, I saw a flash of knowledge, of deep understanding, in his eyes, and his smile widened.

I'm here. I'm here, Belle.

I'm here and I'm yours.

The words came to me as clearly as if he had spoken them into my ear, as if we were close enough to whisper and as if there were not another soul in the room. They were the same words that he spoke to me as he cradled me in his arms at the lake. They were the same words that he spoke to me in my dreams every night and in my waking visions. He hadn't spoken the words out loud. I was looking right at him and his lips hadn't moved, but I heard him clearly, and as the words came to me, my eyes widened in surprise. Scott reacted too and a look of shock and of terror flashed across his face.

It was the same fear that I saw in his eyes at the lake after our earth-shattering connection. I saw that same vulnerability in him and felt him pull away from me, out of my mind. His eyes held the same note of apology, and I wanted to scream at him not to do it, not to go, but I couldn't get the words out quickly enough. I wasn't close enough to stop him. Before I had a chance to move, he turned from me and he fled, again. He left me, again. I watched him disappear quickly down the stairs, and I felt my stomach dive and my control slip as I found myself alone after another moment of connection with the man who was playing havoc with my life.

I fled to the toilets, hot tears of shame streaming down my face. Why would he do this again, and how could I give him that power? I gripped the edge of the sink so tightly that my knuckles turned white. I stared at myself in the mirror. I was such a fool. I didn't understand the spell that Scott had put me under, but it was breaking my heart and contaminating my entire life. It was inconceivable that a man that I had encountered only three times in my life could have such a profound effect on me, and without even an exchange of words, leave me feeling so fragile and so bruised. These feelings were not one-sided. I wasn't imagining our connection or the depth of the passion in his eyes, but there was also no denying that I was alone again, this time crying in the ladies' toilet. I was so confused. I felt sick.

I looked at myself in the mirror again and tried to gather my thoughts. I concentrated on my breathing and cast my mind back to the moment that Scott had fled from me at the lake, and just now, when he had run away from me again. I felt certain that the overriding emotion emanating from him on both occasions was fear and not rejection. I had been wrapped up in Josh, Mrs Nelson and in my own sense of abandonment last time, but this time I saw things a little more clearly and realised that this tendency to vanish might not be as simple as it first appeared. I couldn't ignore the incredible and tumultuous feelings that Scott ignited in me, the awareness that he awakened in me and the fact that he had become lodged firmly inside my mind. I could not go back to my life like this, and I could not allow him to be such a coward. We had to talk.

Scott had fled down the stairs leading to The Pit, not the stairs leading to the exit, so I knew that he was still in the building, and I wasn't going to leave without a conversation with him, at the very least. I deserved an explanation, and it was entirely possible that an honest conversation was exactly what Scott needed too. I would go after him. I just had to let Donna know that I was going downstairs.

I looked around the bathroom. The cubicles were empty. Donna wasn't here. I must have missed her coming out. I wiped my face and rearranged my features as best I could and returned to the dance floor. Donna wasn't there either. I looked at the bar. I searched the entire room, but there was no sign of her anywhere, and my chest tightened and my anxiety rose every second. I needed to follow this through quickly, or I would lose my nerve altogether.

After two circuits of the room, I had to admit that Donna was not there. She would never have left the club without me, so there was only one other place that she could be and only one reason that she would be there. In all of the years that we had known each other and all of the times that we had been out, Donna had never dumped me for a man — well, not without telling me first. Daniel obviously had some sort of strange power over my best friend, and I didn't like it. Now I had two reasons to get downstairs and to get down there quickly.

I paused at the top of the stairs. It looked dark and uninviting. I had lost all of my alcohol-infused courage and was drained from my encounter with Scott. My emotions were in a state of depletion, but I needed to get down there, find Donna, find Scott and have two difficult conversations. Finding both Donna and Scott also meant, most likely, another encounter with Daniel, which filled me with even more dread than before.

Stupidly, going down those stairs suddenly seemed like one of the most difficult challenges that I had ever had to face. I was frightened about how I would feel and how the conversations might go. A group of inebriated men staggered past. I was blocking their way. One of them bumped into me and stumbled, almost falling. "Bitch," he grumbled at me. I mumbled an apology and slowly began the descent. The further down I went, the more anxious I became. I didn't like it down there. I didn't like the music or the atmosphere. I didn't want to see Daniel Callahan, and I wasn't looking forward to seeing Donna with him either. My unease may have stemmed from my own legitimate fears or from the atmosphere and emotions in the air gnawing at my mind. I left the party atmosphere upstairs and descended into The Pit.

At the bottom of the stairs, I looked around. I didn't see them at first, but on second glance, there was Donna sitting at a table in a dark corner of the room, and as expected, she wasn't alone. She was leaning in towards Daniel Callahan, who was wearing a smile a mile wide and stroking the top of her thigh intimately. They looked as if they didn't have a care in the world. There was no indication that Donna had any qualms about leaving me alone upstairs. She looked as if she had totally forgotten about my existence, and seeing it hurt me. Donna was my best friend. I felt betrayed that she could throw our loyalty, our code, away so casually over a man, over Daniel Callahan, but guiltily aware that I may have done the same for Scott.

I felt myself becoming angry. I was already upset by my encounter with Scott and his apparent rejection or cowardliness, and I was tense because of my dislike of this place. Now that I could see that Donna was having such a wonderful time, my anger intensified. I was totally ignorant of the emotions of everyone else in the room because I was wound so tightly. I forgot to hold onto my control and was unaware that I was letting the malignancy creep in — unaware that these feelings were not my own but the combined emotions of all of the people in that dark, dingy room. This was the danger that I always avoided so carefully. I wasn't like other people. I couldn't just come out and have a good time, but at that moment, I didn't understand. It felt real to me, and all that I could think about was my own hurt, my own shame, my own anger. I even forgot that I had planned to find Scott and talk to him like a grown-up. I let the anger of The Pit take control. I trembled with it, and my breathing was rapid and shallow. I was only vaguely aware that my fists were clenched by my side. I started to walk towards Donna and Daniel's table.

As I passed the bar, a tall, dark stranger turned and blocked my way.

"Hi, darl," he slurred. "On your own? Can I get you a drink?"

I didn't look up or catch the man's eye, but his proximity fuelled my irritation.

"No, thank you," I said tensely but politely. "I'm on my way to see a friend."

"Oh, darl, that's not very friendly," the man said. "Surely you've got time for one drink with me."

I shook my head. He didn't move. I was forced to step to the side to make my way around him, but as I did, one of his friends manoeuvred himself to stand directly in front of me.

"My mate's just being friendly," the new man said with a snarl. "What's the matter? Think you're too good for our Kev?" Both men laughed.

I did look up this time. They hadn't given me much of a choice. The two men were standing shoulder to shoulder, looking down on me with an unpleasant gleam in their eyes. I felt rage inside the men, and part of me felt small, vulnerable and a little afraid, but as I looked into the second man's eyes, I also felt my anger rising in response to his. My fists were still balled tightly at my sides, and I felt an unfamiliar urge to use them. I tried to gather myself and stamp the urge down. I looked around for help, but no one was paying us any attention.

"I'm sorry," I said, loudly. "I didn't mean to cause anyone any offence, but please could you move out of my way so that I can get to my friend?"

I took another side step, and the second man matched my movement and remained firmly in front of me. The first man laughed nastily. They were playing with me and enjoying themselves, and it made me extremely uncomfortable. I felt another large presence at my back and realised that I was surrounded. The men smelled strongly of beer, and I had the distinct impression that they weren't here to make friends. They were drunk, and the air of excitement surrounding them suggested that they were enjoying upsetting me a little too much. The one behind me moved a step closer so that he was practically pressing up against my back.

"Making friends again?" he sniggered to his companions.

"Nah, this one's not friendly at all," said the first man, Kev. "Won't even let me buy 'er a drink. Stuck-up bitch."

All three of the men laughed this time, and the rage building inside me increased.

My natural reaction to adrenaline was usually flight, but at that moment, upset by Scott and unsettled by Donna's apparent lack of loyalty, I felt a burning hot anger and the instinct to stand and fight. My emotions were being fed by the obnoxious men, but I still had just about enough self-control to know that I didn't want to give in to the rage that was building inside. Getting abusive or physical with these men would not end well for me.

Out of the corner of my eye, I could see Donna and Daniel at their table. Donna never glanced away from him. She was totally oblivious to my presence, and her lack of awareness drove my anger to a new height. The men weren't going to let me pass, and I needed to get out of their presence before the combination of my own mood and their offensiveness drove me to behaviour that I would regret. Instead of making another attempt to move forwards, I twisted round and quickly pushed past the man behind me. I needed to get away.

I took a few steps before realising that I was heading further into the dark and that there was nothing for me back here. There was still no sign of Scott, and the only way to get to Donna or to the stairs and back out was to go past the horrible men, which I didn't feel ready for just yet. I felt angry, hurt and stupid, and I could feel the hot tears gathering again. I didn't want to cry, not in front of those awful men and not near Donna and Daniel Callahan. There was a slightly open door marked *Emergency Exit* to my left, and I stumbled towards it, spurred on by the promise of a chance to catch my breath and find a little solitude. Perhaps I could regain some control and drive away some of the darkness that was invading my mind. I pushed the door further open and found myself at a back entrance to the club, in a little concrete yard full of empty crates and wheelie bins, with the street beckoning through an alleyway beyond.

I stumbled outside. It was bitterly cold and I began to shiver as soon as the icy air hit my skin. The warmth of the party atmosphere and the alcohol in my system were long gone, leaving me weak and raw, and I wrapped my arms around my body tightly to try to keep the heat in. I considered running straight out to the road and making my escape, but in spite of everything, I couldn't leave Donna without a word, and I really did need to speak to Scott, so I stood in the little yard, shivering, trying to figure out what to do and how to feel. Images flashed through my mind: Donna and Daniel sitting together, touching each other and laughing, the three angry strangers leering at me, and the way that Scott had made me feel, first when he watched me dance and then when he left me on my own.

I struggled to cope with the conflicting emotions on top of the late hour. I was tired and I was cold. My vision became blurred by tears, and my body began to tremble more fiercely. Despite the rational part of my brain trying to calm me down, my heart was roaring in my ears, and I realised that if I didn't sit down, I was going to fall. I walked to the wall and crumpled to the floor between two wheelie bins in the dark, grimy yard, and I wrapped my arms around my knees, leaned back against the wall, and I cried. The night had gone from perfect to disastrous in the space of a few short minutes. I didn't really know why I was crying. It didn't really matter.

The emotion had all just got too much for me. I would give myself a minute. I would sit here and have a cry, and then I would straighten myself out and deal with Donna and with Scott.

The thought that I didn't want to examine but that I kept coming back to, and one of the reasons that the tears kept falling, was that my reaction to Scott had confirmed something that I didn't want to admit but that I already knew. No matter what happened now, my relationship with Jack was over. If I could even consider throwing his love away so easily when I thought that someone else wanted me, if I could react to another man like I did to Scott, I couldn't keep lying to myself or to him that what we had was enough or that he made me happy. Admitting it, even in my own mind, broke my heart. I hadn't fallen out of love with Jack, but I realised that I wasn't giving all of myself to him, and he was such a good man with so much love to give, he deserved to be with someone who could love him the right way. He deserved the kind of love that he gave to me, with his whole heart, the heart that I was going to break into a thousand tiny pieces.

I was startled by a noise close by. It was the sound of laughter, a door closing, then more laughter and loud, dissonant voices. The voices were familiar. It was the three men that had accosted me inside. I lifted my head and saw them walking towards me. It looked as if they were heading for the road. My first thought was panic that I wouldn't be able to get back inside if the door was closed, but that fear was soon replaced by a much more immediate danger. I hoped that they weren't looking for me. I hoped that they hadn't followed me. Either way, they were about to walk right past where I was sitting. All three of them were stumbling drunk, and I had to hope that if I just sat still and stayed quiet, they would walk past and not see me.

I wasn't so lucky. The first man, the one called Kev, the one who had offered to buy me a drink, glanced in my direction and stopped dead, staring at me with his mouth open for a moment. The others followed his gaze, and the one that I didn't recognise, who must have been the one behind me, spoke first.

"Eh up, Kev. It's that stuck-up bitch who didn't want to be your friend. Aww, look, she's crying. What's the matter, bitch? You realise your mistake and crying over our Kev?"

All three of them thought that this was hilarious, and they walked towards me, laughing at his boorish joke and leering at me. "How about you come with us now for a drink, sweetheart? Or better yet, back to Kev's? He'll make you so happy you'll've forgotten your tears in no time, eh, Kev?"

Kev nodded and took a few steps closer on his own while the other two hung back. I pushed myself to my feet and looked at him. He was only about a metre from me, far too close for comfort, and I looked straight into his eyes. What I saw there, what I felt, chilled me to the bone. Kev didn't look like he was joking anymore. Kev didn't look like he wanted to be my friend. Kev was looking at me with an intent that froze me to the spot, but it wasn't how Kev looked that frightened me the most, it was how he felt.

The moment that our eyes met, I was filled with a terrible rage, a rage that came with a desire to cause harm and pain, but it wasn't the rage and the violence that were most terrifying, it was the sickening combination of rage and arousal. The man standing one step away from me in a cold, dark, deserted yard, with his two friends standing by, wanted to cause me pain and was turned on by the thought of it. I had never been more terrified in my life.

I didn't speak. I knew from the connection with his emotions that pleading or begging him not to touch me, not to hurt me, would only fuel his excitement. I don't know if I could have spoken even if I'd wanted to, and there was no one to hear me scream. I was paralysed with fear, and at the same time, felt my own mind and body absorbing and reflecting his sick appetites. I tried to cling to the tiny part of my mind that was still my own, that was screaming that this wasn't me, that these feelings weren't mine, but the nauseating hunger for pain, for submission, for defilement, tore at my soul. I wanted to scream, but no sound came out. I wanted to block out the pain and the terror and the depraved cravings, but I couldn't move, and I was losing the battle over my sanity.

Kev inched towards me slowly, and I couldn't tear my eyes away from his. Until he touched me, I had no idea whether I was going to fight, run, submit to the inevitable attack or whether I was going to meet it with a depraved advance of my own. The emotions built up inside me: my fear, his excitement, my repugnance, his fury, until there was no distinction anymore. I was a ball of pure emotion, and my head felt like it was going to explode. Kev paused an inch away from my face and I could feel the warmth of his foul breath on my cheeks and smell the sweat on his neck, making me gag. He only stopped for a moment, a split second of stillness. The roaring in my head increased until I was only vaguely aware of anything except the fear and the noise and the pain. As Kev put his thick hand around my neck and thrust me back against the wall with frightening strength, following and pinning me to the wall with his body, his arousal was painfully evident, and I screamed. I screamed and I screamed, and I embraced the scream rather than consciously enduring what was happening to me, and mercifully, the jumble of emotions short-circuited my mind and the world went black.

Chapter 16

I'm here. I'm here, Belle.
I'm here and I'm yours.
Belle. I'm here.

I'm here. I'm here, Belle.
I'm here and I'm yours.
Belle. I'm here.

The words kept repeating over and over in my mind, the words of my dreams, protecting me from the pain and the trauma of the attack. If I just concentrated on the darkness and focused on those words and his voice, perhaps I could block it out.

Belle. I'm here.

I didn't want those words to be a part of this nightmare, though. They shouldn't be associated with something so foul and offensive, but they came to me unbidden, and they made me feel safe. They made me feel whole. They gave me something to cling to, and I was all right as long as I had that unseen protection and I was unaware of the cruel truth — as long as I could keep consciousness at bay. I didn't want to see. I didn't want to feel. I was safer in the darkness of oblivion.

"Belle. I'm here. I'm here, Belle.

It's going to be all right.

I'm here. You're safe now.

Open your eyes."

That bit wasn't quite right. He didn't usually deviate from the mantra. My exhausted, traumatised mind tried to make sense of the words and the possibility that this wasn't a dream. As I slowly climbed through the darkness towards consciousness, I probed the area around me and found that I could no longer feel the threat. I could no longer feel Kev's anger or excitement or the sickening presence of his disgusting friends. I wondered vaguely how long I had been out for. I wondered if it was really over. I wondered whether the soothing words were part of my subconscious desire for protection or if they might actually be real. I couldn't feel any pain, but I could hear a noise, a weak whimpering. It sounded strange, like a distressed, wounded animal.

"Shhh, Belle. Shhh, it's all right. I'm here."

He was shushing me. He definitely never shushed me in my dreams. He was shushing me, but I didn't understand why, unless I was making a noise. As the fog continued to lift, I concentrated on the whimpering noise that I could hear. That must be the noise that he was shushing. It was a cross between a cry and a moan, and it kept going on and on, pitiful and distressing. Someone needed to help the poor creature making that noise. I concentrated on it and tried to make sense of it. I tried to work out where it was coming from, but when I followed it, it led right back to me. I was the source of that painful whimper. That was why he was shushing me. I focused on Scott's voice, his calming, velvety voice, and tried to collect my shattered thoughts.

"Shhh. Shhh, Belle. I'm here."

I slowly became more aware of my own body and mind. Coming up through the fog of oblivion was like swimming through tar. It required a serious amount of effort, and it would have been easier to just stay lost in the fog forever, but I continued to listen to those words and that voice, and they called to me. He called me out of the darkness, and as I rose to the surface, I became aware of a physical, soothing contact that reinforced the words, anchoring me to the here and now, to reality, to safety. I felt my lungs expand with each breath, reassuring me that I was alive, and I felt strong, safe arms around me and a warm, gentle hand tenderly stroking the hair back from my face.

"I'm here. I'm here, Belle.

I'm here and I'm yours."

The words seeped through the fear and the panic, and I continued to rise towards them. Gradually, my body stopped trembling, and mercifully, the pitiful whimpering ceased. I lay still, feeling more human again but still a little afraid to open my eyes. The biting edge of the crisp air penetrated my consciousness, and the shivering returned, my body's acceptance that this was real and that the world was cold, distinct from the earlier psychological reaction to my trauma. I embraced the knowledge that I wasn't dreaming or actively being attacked. I opened my eyes.

I was lying cradled in his arms again. It struck me in an abstract way as interesting that I had only fainted twice in my life, and upon waking both times, had found myself wrapped in Scott Callahan's powerful arms. I gazed straight up into the smouldering flames of his eyes, and a flood of emotions hit me all at once. My confusion and fragility combined with his warmth and affection, his fear for my safety, but overall, his reassurance, came washing into my mind, calming and restoring my shattered sanity.

"That's right. You're all right. I'm here, Belle."

I wasn't quite fully conscious yet, but I slowly began to take stock. I wasn't in any pain. I was fully clothed with my clothes intact, half sitting against Scott's solid chest with his jacket draped over my legs, safe in his arms. I was all right. I wasn't hurt or defiled, or apparently damaged in any way, and I had the man of my dreams, literally, staring down at me with seeming reverence. I tried to recall what had happened. The last thing that I remembered was Kev pinning me up against the wall, his arousal terrifyingly physical against my stomach and his hand painful around my neck. The anger and fear had simply been too much for my fragile mind and my heightened emotions, and something had snapped inside, rendering me unconscious. It was little wonder that Scott looked so troubled if he had found me out cold, senseless and whimpering.

"I'm here, Belle. I've got you. You're fine. He didn't hurt you. I'd never let anyone hurt you. Look at me. That's right. Look at me, Belle. I'm here."

I did as I was told. It was my only option. I looked at him and processed what he was telling me. He was here and I was all right. I hadn't been hurt. Scott had stopped Kev from assaulting me. Kev and his revolting friends were gone, and I was lying in Scott's arms while he whispered sweet words to me and stroked my hair and face softly, tenderly. I carefully looked around. We were still in the yard behind the club, but the threat had gone. It was just him and me. It was over.

"That's right. I'm here."

He smiled down at me now that he could see that I was fully awake again. His concern eased slightly and was replaced by relief and affection. I could sense that he had been genuinely and deeply worried. I smiled back. I couldn't help it. I felt a rush of feeling towards the man who had stolen my heart three months ago and rescued me tonight. All of the negative thoughts about him abandoning me had disappeared. My gratitude connected with his relief, and we both absorbed the potent mixture of emotion flowing between us. It washed over me in waves, and I drank it in and allowed it to repair and strengthen my soul.

As I bathed in his generous, genuine affection, I became more physically aware of my position and was suddenly extremely sensitive to the fact that I was lying cradled in his arms again, my face mere inches from his. However, this time my instinct was not to jump up and run away. The man who haunted my dreams had just rescued me from a horrific assault and was looking down on me with those magical, bottomless, fiery eyes, aflame with passion and warmth. I met his feelings with my own eager sentiment, baring myself to him totally, emotionally. I relinquished control, looked into his eyes and invited him to see how he made me feel.

There was a swelling of gratitude that he had saved me tonight, but my emotional response to him went so much deeper than that and I didn't want to hide from it anymore. My encounter with Kev had reminded me how precious life can be, how easily it can be destroyed, and I suddenly wanted to grab it and hold onto everything that life had to offer. I had been suppressed for so long without even realising, but now it was time to embrace the truth. It was time to set myself free. There was a terrifying danger that if I let Scott see how I truly felt, the depth of my longing, he would run away from me again, but I had to take that risk because all at once, lying there on that cold, dark night in that dingy, dirty yard, surrounded by wheelie bins and beer crates, I felt happy in his arms. I felt a deep peace, and I knew without hesitation that it was where I belonged. I looked into his eyes, searching, and saw that he was no longer hiding either.

We stared into each other's eyes, and the magic that had connected us at the lake was back, only this time, instead of his energy entering my mind and exploring me, I was offering my spirit to him and exploring what it could mean. I sat up and twisted around in his lap so that we were facing each other. He kept one hand around my shoulder, but he let me move, and he accepted my gift. I let all of the emotions that had been pent up inside me for the last three months come pouring out. I remembered how he had made me feel at the lake before he had run away, and I thought about all of the times that I had imagined him and all of the times that I had dreamed about him, and I didn't hide any of it. I made myself totally vulnerable to him.

His eyes widened as he drank me in. There was surprise on his face, understanding and realisation, and I felt his spirit respond to me. We were communicating without the need for words. I wanted to kiss him. It hit me like a bolt of lightning. I craved the feel of his lips on mine and the awakening that I knew that it would bring, and I didn't want to wait, not for another minute. I glanced at his lips, then back to his eyes, and felt a fire begin to burn inside me. I had never wanted anything like I wanted to kiss this man. It was an all-consuming hunger. As Scott sensed my longing, he answered it with the same longing of his own. I wasn't mistaken. I could see it in his eyes and taste it in the air. I knew beyond any shadow of a doubt that he wanted to kiss me as much as I wanted to kiss him, and it made my heart sing. If I hadn't been certain before, the low, guttural groan that passed his lips was all the confirmation I desired. It fanned the flame of my passion, and I bravely reached up, put my hands around his neck and guided him gently towards my mouth. I parted my lips very slightly and I closed my eyes. I could feel the desire leaping between us like fireworks.

At the last moment, Scott stopped and pulled sharply back. Our lips didn't meet. He took my arms from around his neck and held me slightly away from him. My eyes opened and I looked at him in absolute horror. There was no kiss, only distance, emptiness. He groaned again, this time more like the growl of an animal in pain. I closed my eyes again but this time in shame. This couldn't be happening, not again.

"Belle..."

I didn't want to open my eyes. The feeling of disappointment and shame was so strong that I thought I might cry. I was so confused. I knew that he wanted me, and I sensed the remorse that he felt for causing me pain and the regret for pulling away from me once again, but I couldn't keep taking this rejection. I felt him flounder, and the echo of the wanting was still hanging between us, confounding me.

My emotions were all over the place. I was still reeling from my encounter with Kev. I felt a staggering amount of relief and gratitude, but there was also affection, arousal, sexual frustration, shame and guilt, to name a few, and I could feel a similarly bewildering jumble of emotions pouring from Scott. The hordes of entangled feelings were flying around, making me dizzy, bouncing off each other and fusing together. The energies were wild, and I lost track of which were mine and which were his, and I didn't understand what was happening, but I knew that I couldn't sit there with my eyes closed forever. I wondered whether I was strong enough to just run and never look back.

"Belle," Scott repeated. "You're killing me."

There was frustration and amusement and fervour in those four words, and it came as enough of a surprise to make me open my eyes. I looked into his eyes again and saw the same fire inside them, the same passion. I saw desire, vexation and compassion fighting for supremacy. I watched those flames living and dancing in his eyes, flickering, ever-changing from red to yellow to gold. I was mesmerised by those flames, hypnotised by them. I forgot my humiliation and my impulse to run as I stared into them with wonder.

"Your eyes ..." I said.

"Please, Belle," he begged. "Stop looking at me like that. Stop feeling ... everything, all at once. I don't know what's real. I know what you're feeling and I want to trust it, but I don't know how much is relief ... or gratitude ... or even how much you're aware of. I can't think straight. When you look at me like that and you feel ... Belle, please. You're making it really, really hard to ... not to ... Jesus Christ ... and I want to ... Believe me, God, I want to, and it would be so easy to ... but ... not now. Not yet. I'd never forgive myself if I took advantage of you again. If I ... and you didn't ... or you ... because you ... Please ... not here ... not like this ... Please."

That was a lot to absorb. I tried to make sense of what he was saying. He wanted me. That was good. He wasn't sure what I wanted. That was probably fair. He felt like he had taken advantage of me before and could be doing the same again. That went some way towards explaining a little of his reaction at the lake and earlier. He said not now, not yet, not *not ever*.

I had a pang of pure guilt when I realised that Scott might in part be alluding to my relationship with Jack. He didn't want me to be unfaithful, and he didn't want to be part of a betrayal. I was mortified that it was Scott and not me who had considered Jack first when he had been such a huge and important part of my life for so long. I had loved him, I really had. I still did in many ways. I didn't want to cause Jack pain, but it was inevitable now. There was no going back. I was going to break his heart. That thought was sobering. The fact that Jack hadn't even entered my mind until he had been taken into account by someone else was crushing but indicative of the truth.

Scott was watching me closely, quizzically. "Don't be too hard on yourself either. Your mind is buzzing. You're running on shock, adrenaline and instinct. It's understandable that you don't know how to feel or what to process first. You just narrowly escaped being ... well, being ... Urgh, I can't even think about it. That arsehole. What he would have done to you."

Scott absently rubbed his knuckles, and I noticed that they were bruised and sore. I detested violence but couldn't find it in me to condemn whatever Scott had done to prevent my inevitable attack. I would not waste any pity on Kev or his friends. I looked around the yard. He was right. I had no idea how to feel, but being reminded of Kev and his depraved intentions certainly took my mind a little further away from my intense connection with Scott. I shuddered. I suddenly didn't want to be there anymore. I was still sitting where I had collapsed when I passed out, surrounded by bins, crates and the faint smell of vomit. I pushed myself up and stood, feeling a little dazed and confused. Scott rose with me, stood next to me and put his arm back around my shoulder, offering unconditional support.

"Thank you. At least I can think more clearly now," he told me. "Although I think perhaps I preferred it when you were feeling ... better." He smiled gently.

There was renewed concern in his eyes as he looked at me, and I felt a fresh wave of reassurance settle my agitated mind, allowing me to process some of the other things that I had seen and heard. Scott had said that he knew how I was feeling. I felt sure that he meant that he was the same as me, that he shared my gift. I wondered how far the similarities went and whether it was the reason for the incredible connection between us. This prompted considerably more questions than answers, and I had no idea where to start.

"You're confused. You have questions and I want to answer them, or at least I want to try to answer as many of them as I can. We need to talk, Belle, but not here, not like this. Will you come with me?"

I wasn't surprised that he had read me so well, and I didn't hesitate. I didn't even need to ask where he was taking me. I would have followed him anywhere.

"Yes." I took his hand. "Oh, no… Wait. I can't leave Donna."

Last time that I had seen her, Donna had been sitting at that dark corner table, flirting outrageously with Daniel and obviously unperturbed by the fact that she had left me alone. Presumably, she had no idea about what had happened with Kev. It wouldn't have mattered how loudly I had screamed; no one could have heard me over the music in that place. Add to which, the door had been closed and there's no way anyone could have known that I was in trouble, but I still felt a little disappointed in my friend.

I forgot Donna as quickly as I'd remembered her as that thought turned over in my mind.

"Did you see me come outside?" I asked Scott.

"When? No. I didn't even know you'd come downstairs."

The cogs continued to turn. "And you couldn't have heard me scream?"

Scott looked slightly less casual now as he realised where my mind was going. "I didn't hear you scream, no."

"If you didn't see me come outside and you didn't hear me scream, I don't suppose it was an incredible coincidence that you happened to come through that back door, that closed emergency exit, just at the right time, was it?"

I was looking at him intently now and could see him shuffling his feet, trying to avoid my gaze. I could feel his unease.

"No, I don't think it was a coincidence," he said quietly.

"Scott, look at me," I demanded. He lifted his gaze, and I saw worry and doubt gnawing at him.

"How did you know to come to me? How did you know I needed you? How did you know where I was?"

There was an uncomfortable silence as Scott struggled to find an answer.

"I'm not sure," he said slowly. "Or I … Well, I … I just knew."

My mind was still a little slippery, and rational thoughts wouldn't stick properly. The only times that I had felt someone's emotions when they weren't immediately near was with Stephanie. There were times during childhood that I had known that Stephanie was hurt. I had felt her pain, but I just thought it was because she was my sister. I never connected the knowledge to my gift. Now I was less sure. I was less sure about everything. There was so much that I didn't understand. I felt on edge. I was doubting everything and confused about what was happening to me.

"You were thinking about Donna," Scott reminded me.

I tried to focus. "Yes, that's right. She'd worry terribly if I left without her."

As soon as the words came out of my mouth, I found myself wondering if they were true. I had never doubted Donna before, but I was still hurt over being dumped by her earlier, and I remembered the change in her attitude last time she had spent time with Daniel Callahan. I knew, rationally, that it wasn't Donna's fault that I had ended up outside with Kev, but I couldn't help wondering whether I would have been there at all if Donna had stayed with me. My mind was still jumbled. I didn't know whether I was angry with Donna or worried about her.

"She's OK," Scott tried to reassure me. "She's with

Daniel."

I smiled ruefully. That was exactly what I was afraid of.

"Yes," I replied noncommittally.

He smiled. "You're not much of a fan of my big brother, are you?" he asked.

I didn't want to offend him but knew that I couldn't get away with lying. "Not really, no."

He laughed softly. "I can understand that. He can be a little …"

"Rude?" I offered. "Unpleasant? Cold?"

"Ha, yes, I suppose he can be all of those things," Scott conceded. "But he is my brother. I trust him. I've already texted him. He'll make sure Donna gets home safely."

I wasn't totally convinced, but my legs felt like jelly, I was cold and tired, and I really didn't want to go back into the club. I certainly didn't fancy trying to drag Donna away from Daniel. Scott had said that he wanted to kiss me and that we needed to talk, and right now, I needed answers, and nothing seemed more important than that.

Scott stared in wonder at my face as I sorted through these thoughts.

"Did you know that your face shows almost every emotion … every thought you have?" he said.

I blushed. "OK, let's go," I said. "Where is it we're going?"

"Somewhere warm where we can talk without being disturbed."

Despite everything, I couldn't help the blush to my cheek and warmth to my core at the thought of going somewhere warm with Scott Callahan where we wouldn't be disturbed. He caught my stray emotion and answered it with a blush of his own. He covered it with a short cough.

"Please, Belle. You're pushing me here."

I was embarrassed that he hadn't missed my vagrant emotion and then felt an immediate stab of guilt because the image had come unbidden, without a thought for Jack yet again. Somehow, the thought of Scott thinking that I was a terrible, disloyal person made me feel even worse, which in itself seemed horribly unfaithful to Jack and set me on another spiral of anxiety and confusion.

"Wow, there's a lot going on in your mind," said Scott. "I know this is hard and I know you're confused. I can't promise that I can make it right. In fact, I might end up making things much worse before they start to get better, but I can promise to be honest with you, and hopefully, things will at least start to make a bit more sense."

Considering the situation that I found myself in, I felt like a bit more sense was probably the best that I could hope for. I was grateful that he hadn't promised too much. I looked at him, narrowing my eyes in as stern an expression as I could muster under the circumstances.

"Stop reading my mind. And you know, no one calls me Belle. No one's ever called me Belle."

"I do."

"Yes, you do."

Chapter 17

It was a short, quiet walk to the public car park where Scott had parked the van. My mind was spinning and I couldn't form a coherent sentence, so I just walked in silence by his side. I'm not certain whether it was exactly a comfortable silence for either of us, but I was so focused on trying to get my own emotions in order, I had no energy left to process how Scott might be feeling.

Once in the warmth of the van, I felt mostly revived, and the drive back to Ramsay Bridge can only be described as surreal. Being in the Callahan van was peculiar in itself, but being in it alone with Scott, after everything, was very strange indeed. We didn't talk much. I spent the time lurching between trying not to think about anything so that Scott didn't accidentally read my mind and being unable to think about anything except him. I was acutely aware of his physical proximity. He seemed to fill the van with his thrilling presence, and although I tried to keep my eyes on the road and my mind totally blank, I noticed every detail: the movement of his hand when he changed gear or altered his grip on the wheel, the sound of his breathing, his masculine, inviting scent.

Many times, I took a breath and opened my mouth, prepared to ask him a question and then changed my mind at the last moment and closed it again. Many times, Scott did the same. At times, the image of Kev's face, dangerously close to mine, and the intent behind his attack threatened to lead me off into another panic attack, but more intense and in some ways more terrifying than these were the moments in which I lost my focus and control and my mind slipped unbidden back to the lake, into my dreams or onto the dance floor tonight. Images of Scott exploring inside my mind, making love to me in the dunes or watching me dance played out in glorious technicolour in my imagination, and even though I tried to drive them out as soon as I became aware of their existence, I couldn't prevent my body's powerful, wanton response to the visions. At these moments, the passion that I couldn't defy fed straight into Scott's psyche, evoking an ardent response of his own which met and connected with mine, driving us both higher and more dangerously into a state of provocation and intimacy which I tried vainly to contain and resist.

I carefully breathed in and out, keeping my eyes forward and my hands to myself, but every time my mind wandered, my fervour increased, and I felt his emotional response to me, I had a desperate yearning to turn and search his face. I wanted to see for myself whether his desire was reflected in his eyes, and I longed to look at him again, to look, to touch, to explore. My hand itched to reach out and take hold of his hand or caress his face, and I could feel the equivalent craving from him. I could taste his yearning in the air, but his hand never moved towards me and his eyes never veered from the road. His knuckles were white with the force of his grip on the wheel, and it seemed that if either of us gave in to the temptation, even infinitesimally, we would lose ourselves, and our relationship would escalate from practical strangers to passionate lovers in an instant. We didn't give in to the temptation. We stamped down the sparks before they caught alight, and our journey continued in an intense silence with deliberately blank minds until the next time that my mind wandered without caution and the spiral began again.

I had only ever been with one man. My relationship with Jack had been warm and tender. I had never had reason to doubt Jack's love for me, and I had loved him back sincerely and honestly since the day that he kissed me at my gate when I was seventeen. We had always had a healthy physical relationship, but the love, the passion and the romance had always originated with Jack. I loved him dearly, but many of my feelings towards him were derived from a reflection of his feelings towards me. It was exactly what had worried me all of those years ago, before we first became a couple. I found it difficult to tell if the attraction, the love and the passion that I experienced were my own feelings or if they began as and were enhanced by the feelings that I absorbed from him. Until recently, I didn't think that it mattered. I thought that I was happy.

These feelings, these intoxicating, heady, all-consuming emotions that I felt for Scott were absolutely, without any shadow of a doubt, originating within me. This was different. They were joining with and being intensified by similarly libidinous emotions that originated within Scott, and the two were meeting and enhancing each other exponentially. This was nothing like anything that I had experienced before, ever. Scott and I were communicating via our emotions. There was him, there was me, and there was that beautiful space in between. I could almost read his mind, and as that thought entered my head, I accidentally envisaged how it would feel to be physically intimate with Scott Callahan, and before I knew it, Scott had once again sensed and matched my desire and we entered another spiral of wanting, yearning and concertedly, studiously suppressing our feelings without either one of us once glancing at the other or saying a word.

By the time that Scott pulled the van to a stop and switched off the engine, the energy between us could have been cut with a knife. Neither of us spoke for a few seconds. Scott's hands remained solidly on the steering wheel and his eyes pointed firmly forward while he composed himself. I took some long, deep breaths before turning to look at him. That was a mistake. I was struck anew by my instinctive response to him and was unable to tear my gaze away. Scott lowered his head slowly until it was resting on the steering wheel, his eyes closed. He groaned wretchedly.

"Belle, I can hardly breathe, I can hardly talk, and I'm frightened of what I might do if I look at you right now," he said through gritted teeth. "I daren't look at you ... I can't ... you're ... this is ... I'm going to get out of the van now and go for a walk. I won't be long. I'm not running away; I'm just getting some air and some distance. Please stay in the van and try to think about unimaginably dull things while I'm gone."

Before I could process his words, he leaped out of the van without glancing my way and closed his door hard. I was alone again, but this time I didn't feel empty or rejected or lost. I allowed myself a little smile. My life had changed irrevocably, and I had never felt this way before. I didn't know what was going to happen next, what I was going to hear or how I was going to feel, but it didn't matter. Nothing mattered because Scott wasn't running away. He wanted me, and that little empty space inside me didn't feel so empty anymore.

I stayed exactly where Scott had left me. It was pitch black and freezing outside, and I wasn't quite sure where he had brought me. We had driven back to Ramsay Bridge and turned into the grounds of the old Ramsay House, but instead of heading up the drive towards the main house on the hill, we had turned onto a rough track heading east along the perimeter of the land. I was a little relieved. There had been a moment when I worried that he was taking me to the family home. I definitely didn't think that tonight was a suitable occasion to be meeting the parents. I shuddered at the thought.

I stared through the windscreen into the gloom but couldn't see anything beyond the trees on either side of the track. I gave up and concentrated on keeping my mind away from salacious thoughts, although as it turned out, I needn't have worried because now that Scott wasn't there and the feelings that he inspired in me had cooled, things began to feel very different. Now that I was alone, I suddenly felt very alone. I didn't have Scott's presence protecting me anymore, and it was dark and it was cold, and my feeble mind stumbled back to being alone in that dirty, dingy yard behind the club not so very long ago. I recalled the anger and the hurt that I had felt even before going outside and how I had sat on the floor and cried. I remembered Kev's face and my utter lack of control, allowing Kev's filthy, violent appetites to take over my own energy, corrupting and defiling my mind. My own mood had been supplanted by Kev's rage and desire, and I had felt those emotions more strongly than any of my own. The fear, the horror, the anger, the frenzy had all combined to the point that I had been unable to do anything. I had been unable to think clearly. I had been unable to fight, and as those feelings came back to me in my memory, I felt out of control again. I felt sick. I felt sick and scared and ashamed that I hadn't fought him off. I hadn't even tried. My body began to shake with cold and delayed shock, and I put my head into my hands and cried.

Scant moments later, the passenger door was jerked roughly open and Scott was there with his power and reassurance, holding his strong arms out to me and lifting me out of my seat. I went willingly, like a child. I put my arms around his neck and curled up into his chest. He held me like a baby and he soothed me.

"Belle. Belle, I'm here. I'm sorry. I'm such an idiot. I should never have left you alone out here in the dark … in the cold. I should have realised. I'm such a selfish twat. I'm so sorry. I'm here … I've got you … Urgh … I keep getting everything so wrong with you. How could I let myself get all worked up like that when you needed me to be strong? I'm a selfish, ignorant fool. Oh, Belle. I'm sorry. I'm here now."

He held me securely in his arms and I felt him take some of the pain away. All earlier thoughts of attraction and sex had gone. I just needed him to be there, and he was. A feeling of calm washed over me and I leaned into him, absorbed his strength and took some deep, steady breaths.

"You're not a twat," I said with a grin. "But I … I didn't even fight," I confessed haltingly. "I should have hit him … scratched him … done anything to get away. It might not have worked, but at least I would've known I tried. I just stood there. I let his anger and all the disgusting feelings take over and I just let it happen. When he pushed me against that wall, I wanted to do something, but I couldn't move. I couldn't … do anything. If you hadn't come … I would … he would … and I would have just let it happen … enjoyed it … maybe!"

"Shhh. It's OK, Belle. It's not your fault. He's a sick monster and your system was overwhelmed. Your mind was flooded with feelings, and you couldn't process them all or stay in control. You did nothing wrong. You couldn't have fought him off if you tried. He was twice your size and bloody strong… and I did come. I was there. You weren't hurt and I was there and I'm here. I'm here."

Scott continued to shush and soothe with gentle words. He was right. I knew that he was right, but it was difficult not to judge my own behaviour and dwell upon what might have happened. After a few moments I felt much calmer and a little embarrassed by my needy behaviour. I lifted my head from his chest and smiled weakly.

"I'm sorry," I said. "You must think I'm deranged. Fainting and crying and … stuff … every time we meet. I'm not usually such a mess."

Scott smiled back. "I don't think you're deranged. I think you're dealing with some pretty heavy emotional baggage that you don't understand. I think you're confused, understandably, and I think you're wonderful. I'm going to put you down now because you're heavy and I'm not sure I can carry you over the rough path down here. Are you OK?"

My smile broadened. He'd said that he thought that I was wonderful. "I don't think it's polite to tell a girl she's heavy," I said.

"Ha, yes, sorry. Perhaps heavy wasn't quite the word I was looking for." He looked flustered, and his discomfort made me giggle.

"I'm kidding," I said. "I wouldn't want to carry me anywhere, especially not on a rough path in the dark. Where are we, anyway?"

"We're on the edge of our land. There's a cabin just down here. No one else uses it. It's my space. A place to get away from the family, to get away from everyone."

"I have seen your house, you know?" I replied. "Only from a distance, but I can't imagine the four of you getting under each other's feet too much. Haven't you got a wing each?"

"Funny. It's not quite that big, but you're right, we don't get in each other's way if we don't want to, but sometimes … well, sometimes, you need a bit more space, don't you think? No matter how big a house is, if there are other people in it, you're never really alone."

His explanation echoed exactly how I felt. When I needed peace and quiet, it wasn't enough if everyone else didn't speak or wasn't right there in the room with me. Just their presence or even the knowledge of their presence was enough to make me feel crowded. When I needed to be alone, I needed to be totally on my own. Scott was lucky to have a place to retreat to, even if it was a shed at the bottom of his parents' garden. I had a bench by the lake, but it wasn't quite the same on a cold, rainy night.

Scott reached past me and retrieved a torch from the glove box, which he handed over. He gestured down the slope to the right of the track.

"It's not far," he reassured me. "Just watch your step."

I followed him down a steep path through the trees. Within a few minutes we came to a clearing, and an old wooden cabin stood before us. It was difficult to see clearly through the gloom, but I got the impression of a quaint, rustic affair with a moss-covered roof and a chimney stack. There was a small window in the top half of the structure and a larger window downstairs. There was no lock on the door, and Scott pushed it open easily and invited me inside.

I quickly adjusted my impression of the cabin from a shed in his parents' garden to a dream retreat. It was stunning inside, and everything looked brand new and fresh but in keeping with the age and style of the building. There was no electricity, but there was a sink with taps, so I assumed that there was running water, and there were numerous gas lamps and a gas stove with four rings and a kettle. One main room occupied most of the floor space, and there was a smaller room behind an interior door. There was a set of stairs on the left leading to a mezzanine style sleeping area. From the entrance, I could see the foot of the bed.

As I got my bearings, Scott kept himself busy. At the rear of the ground floor, there was a huge fireplace, and he first lit a couple of lamps and then crouched down to it. There was a fire already prepared in the hearth. I was relieved when it caught immediately because I had been promised somewhere warm, and currently, it was hardly any warmer inside the cabin than it was outside. There was a small table with two chairs, a bench settee under the window and one solitary, comfortable looking armchair facing the window on the other side of the cabin, overlooking the tree-covered slope towards the lake.

I stood for the time being, unsure where to go. We didn't speak immediately. Scott lit the stove and offered me a cup of tea.

"Mmm. I'd love one, please. White with one."

I hovered near the doorway until Scott gestured to the chairs at the table, and I took the one nearest the fire, hoping that its warmth would soon begin to thaw the chill in my bones. The silence that stretched between us felt more comfortable now. We were both calmer, and the heightened energy between us had been dulled by my memory of the attack and Scott's concern for me. He finished the drinks and sat at the chair on the opposite side of the table, using the table as a barrier between us. I took my drink and sipped it appreciatively. I smiled almost shyly at him. This was the first time that we would have a proper conversation, and despite my determination to appear sane, I felt nervous about what was to come.

Scott cleared his throat and smiled as he gestured at the table. "Sorry. It seems a bit weird … sitting like this … considering … well, I just thought it might be best … for now."

I agreed wholeheartedly. The only other option would have been to sit together on the settee bench, and it was probably better if there was a little distance between us.

"It's fine," I said.

Scott cleared his throat again. He shifted uncomfortably in his chair.

"You're nervous," I told him sympathetically. He looked surprised at my insight and then smiled again.

"I guess I'll have to get used to that," he said. He ran a hand through his dishevelled hair. He looked vulnerable and endearingly uncertain of himself. I had an urge to reach my hand across the table and take his, offering my support. I didn't act on the impulse, but perhaps the desire to help was sufficient because of the magic between us. I saw him gather strength.

"I'm not sure what to say," he said. "Where to start. I've been dying to talk to you … properly … ever since that night at the lake when I behaved so abominably. Well … even before then … but I didn't know how … I didn't know if you … and then tonight … when you danced … Wow … I … Did you? … Could you? I didn't mean to … I'm so sorry."

I sat quietly for a moment, aware that he hadn't really said anything yet and wondering whether he was going to continue, but it seemed like that was all he could manage right now. I looked at him, directly into his eyes, and held his gaze.

"What is it, exactly, that you're apologising for?" I asked.

Scott shifted under my gaze but maintained eye contact with me as he answered. "That night … I … we ... no, I … I took advantage of you in the most intimate of ways … I should never have … It made me … I was as bad as …"

This time I didn't resist the urge. I placed both of my

hands on the table, open in invitation, and Scott didn't hesitate. He put both of his hands into mine and I instantly felt the power between us, a settling or a joining of energies. It wasn't as profound as what had occurred at the lake, but there was no mistaking that when we touched, we became more than just two people holding hands. The strength of it took me by surprise, but I didn't let it unbalance me. I didn't let go. It was a wonderful feeling: deep, intense and magical. I saw the answering surprise in Scott's face, but he kept his hands firmly in mine too and drew a deep, steady breath.

"Don't ever, ever suggest that you have anything in common with that idiot tonight," I told him. "You are good. I don't even … I mean … I don't know you … but I know you and I know that."

"Thank you," he said.

"I've no idea what's going on here," I confessed. "I get the impression you know more than I do."

Scott nodded and started to speak again, but I cut him off.

"No. Just a minute. I need to say something … to ask something of you before you say anything else."

He stopped and nodded at me to continue.

"Thank you," I said. "I don't know what's going on here, but I know this." I took a long breath. "There's something …" I took one hand back briefly to gesture between the two of us before returning it to the table, on top of his. "There's something between us. Something … different, something strong. Something that, in a way, I'm terrified to explore… but I'm even more terrified to ignore it." I closed my eyes for a moment and then opened them and looked back into the deep fire of his, staring straight at me. "Please," I begged him now, "please don't run away from me again."

I saw Scott swallow hard, and I saw the fire in his eyes begin to burn more brightly. "I'm not running, Belle. I'm here."

That phrase: *I'm here.* I'd heard it so many times in my dreams, but now that I heard it straight from his lips while I was looking into his eyes and we were holding hands across the table, it held a greater significance, and I felt my heart swell at the sound of it. The newly discovered thing inside my mind was also happy. Scott absorbed my reaction and gave an answering smile before looking sober again.

"I'm so sorry I ran from you that night. I couldn't face you after … I still can't believe I let myself … I should never, ever have … and when you were so vulnerable." He stopped again, but I could feel the remorse pulsing from him, and I needed to try to make him understand.

"Scott. That day was one of the worst days of my life. I'd seen things that no one should ever see and felt things that were hard to handle. When I went up to the lake, I wanted to be alone. I was all churned up with the foulness of the day. When I saw you, you gave me such a fright … but what happened then ... with you …" I blushed a little and looked down at the table. "What happened between us. You didn't take advantage of me. I wanted it. It was the most incredible feeling. Nothing like anything I've ever … You took the worst day and made it … well … for that short period of time, you made me forget and you made me feel things that I … well …" I looked back up. "But then you ran away."

"I was a coward," he admitted. "I felt so selfish and so wrong. When I sat there next to you, I could feel your internal struggle. The weight of all that poisonous energy was pulling you down and I just wanted to make you feel better. I wanted to take the pain away. But what started out as me trying to help you turned into me abusing the trust that you'd put in me, letting me in. It went from trying to help to taking what I had no right to take — what I hadn't asked for and what you didn't understand you were giving. It became about my own pleasure. My God, Belle, I nearly …" It was Scott's turn to look down at the table. His shame, palpable in the air, was written plainly across his face.

I considered what he'd said. "You said I didn't understand. You're right. I didn't understand it then and I don't now.

Does that mean you do understand it?" I asked.

"Not entirely, no," he replied. "I've heard about it … I mean I know … I know what … but nothing like that has ever happened to me before. Belle … I want you to know that. I need you to know that." He was searching my eyes for reassurance, and I gave it to him with a smile and a nod.

"Somehow I don't have any choice but to believe you. I can feel the truth behind your words. But you have to understand and believe me too. I don't feel like you took advantage of me. I think you're being too hard on yourself. I think you did ask. Not in words, maybe, but I never felt that you were inside my mind against my will and I felt … I knew … I know that if I'd wanted you to stop, I could have stopped you. I could have blocked you out. I could have. Look at me, Scott. Look at me and see that I'm telling the truth."

Scott looked deeply into my eyes, and whatever he found there obviously helped because I felt his tension ease. "Thank you, Belle. Yes, I can see it. I still think it was wrong of me, and I wonder whether you'll still feel that way when you learn a bit more about this, but I do believe you, and that helps."

"We'll see," I said. "What was definitely wrong was that you ... we … shared a life-changing experience and then you ran away and left me there alone, and that hurt … so much. I didn't know what to think … what to do, and on top of that, something changed inside me that night. It's like you left a little piece of you behind. You've been stuck in my heart and in my head ever since. You running away made me think it wasn't special for you. You just ran away and got on with your life."

Scott squeezed my hands hard, almost hard enough to hurt. "Oh, Belle. Nothing could be further from the truth. It never occurred to me that you thought I didn't care. Quite the opposite. I suppose you could ... No, I suppose you would think that, now I hear you say it. I made such a mess of things. I know it's a little late but let me put the record straight." He stopped for a moment, trying to find the right words. "I felt it at Vestige the first time we met. I'd never had that kind of reaction to anyone before. It was like … magic. Meeting you was like coming home. I was so excited, but then you told me that you were seeing someone and … even though I didn't know you, I felt that I knew you and I felt ... crushed. I was surprised because he's not … I mean … he can't … Anyway, I told myself to leave it, but I couldn't stop thinking about you.

"That night … by the lake … when I saw you struggling under the weight of the emotion you were carrying, I felt a burning desire to fix you. I wanted nothing more than to make you whole again … to make you … you again. When you passed out, I was so frightened. So much more than I should have been … than if you were a real stranger. You told me you wanted to be alone, but I couldn't leave you. I already knew … and I wanted to help. I wanted to take your burden away, so I … but then … when you were whole again … I … I just couldn't help myself. I wanted to explore you … to know you. I've never been inside someone's head like that before, and I thought I could control it, but the way you responded to me … it was more than I could handle. I lost myself and was taking my pleasure from you, and even though I knew you didn't understand, I didn't stop. When I felt your pleasure... My God, Belle … I've never felt anything like it … I've never wanted anything more … I can't tell you how hard it was for me to … to not … God, I wanted so much to reach for you … to touch you, to kiss you, to ..." He trailed off, staring into space.

I tried to speak, but he held up a hand to stop me. "Let me get this out, Belle," he beseeched me. I could see how hard it was for him, so I let it go for now. He continued, "When I felt … when I thought I might … Urgh … this is hard to say. I felt like an animal. I felt like I'd forced myself on you. I was so ashamed, I couldn't even look at you. I only thought that you'd hate me for what I'd done … for how I'd behaved, and I couldn't bear to see that or feel that from you, so I just ran. Like I said, I can see that that was cowardly now … But then … I couldn't think straight, so I ran away. I'm sorry.

"You said it was like a little part of me was stuck inside your head?" he asked, and I nodded. "I felt the same way. I haven't stopped thinking about you since. You're my first thought in the morning and my last thought before I go to sleep. I've spent nights lying awake, wondering if you're thinking about me and trying to stop myself from running to you. I told myself … if you came to me, I would grab you and never let you go, but if you didn't, then I had to accept that you chose him and let you go …. but even then, I … I've tried to stay away … To give you space but … I'm drawn to you … My … it clamours to be near you, and I've … I've … I needed to be near you to settle my mind … silence the roar … so I've … There have been times when I had to be near you …"

There was a short silence. I didn't know if he was waiting for me to speak or if he hadn't finished. We were still holding hands across the table, still looking into each other's eyes. He looked so vulnerable as he searched my face. I didn't know what he was looking for or if he found it, but he continued.

"Tonight … when I saw you in the club … it all came rushing back in a second. Just being near you … I felt … I just wanted … but I didn't know if it was what you wanted or if you wanted me to leave you alone, so I went downstairs with Daniel, but I couldn't stay away. I had to come back. I had to see you. When you danced for me … I could see in your eyes that you felt it too. I could feel that you wanted to come to me, and I wanted nothing more, but when you heard me … in your mind, I mean. You did … you heard me … didn't you?"

I nodded. I had stopped breathing. Up until that very moment, I hadn't been sure whether the voice inside my head had been real or my delusional imagination.

"When you heard me," he continued, "I panicked. I'm sorry. That's never happened to me before either. I've been waiting my whole life … looking … but of course, you haven't. You don't know. You're so … unaware, so … unfamiliar, so … I don't know if you even know what you are … what you can do … what I can do. And I know that running away again wasn't the answer. I don't ever want to run away from you ever again, but … I just panicked and I ran. I'm sorry. I didn't leave the club. I don't think I could have left, knowing you were there. I was going to come back … I think. I wanted you to know … I wanted to tell you … I would have done. But then I felt your fear from outside. It hit me like a truck. It was like nothing else. I felt you, paralysed with fear and anger, and it terrified me. It terrified me that I could feel it at all when you weren't so close, but it terrified me more because I knew you were in trouble. I just knew and I just ran … towards you this time. I don't even really understand how I knew where to go, but I could feel you and your … you called to me, and I just came to you and when I saw that … that … and he had you against the wall and he was … and you were … I just roared and ran, and he took one look at me, and he just dropped you. One swing and then he ran. I probably didn't have to hit him. I think he would have run anyway, but I couldn't help it. I don't … I never … but … coward. Filthy, disgusting …"

During the last part of his speech, Scott had begun to let his emotions rise with his memory of his reaction to my distress, and I was struggling not to let them affect me. I could feel the strength of his fear and his anger, and it was setting me on edge. I tried to tether myself, and I gave his hands a squeeze, reminding him of the present, reminding him that I was all right and that I was here. I tried to soothe him with my own reassurance, like he had done for me, and I saw his eyes widen in surprise and his shoulders relax just a fraction as he let me in.

Once he had himself back under control, he carried on.

"When he ran, you just dropped to the floor, and I couldn't feel you anymore. It was like the part of you that makes you you had … just … disappeared. I was so frightened. I pulled you into my lap and held you and I just kept thinking …"

"I'm here," I interrupted. "You just kept thinking, I'm here."

"Yes," he agreed. "And I am. I'm here, I'm yours, and I'm not running anymore."

I didn't know what to respond to first. Scott was looking at me with that fire in his eyes and his heart on his sleeve. I suspected that he was not prone to long, heartfelt declarations. I was moved, honoured and elated by his sincerity. In some ways, it was exactly what I had been hoping to hear, but some of what he said had confused and frightened me even more.

"I don't know what to think. I don't know how to feel. It's … You said that if I came to you … that I had made my choice. Except I had no idea there was a choice to make. No idea if you ever thought of me again after … after. If I'd have known, maybe I would have … but I didn't know. I didn't understand." My mind drifted off on a tangent. "I have literally no idea what time it is, and I'm tired and still a little in shock. Please bear with me while I try to sort through the jumble in my head. Oh, and don't tell me what time it is. I don't actually want to know."

Scott nodded. "Of course," he said. "I'm sorry." His thumb had started slowly stroking over the tops of my fingers, and it felt soothing. It felt intimate. It felt wonderful.

"You said one of the reasons you felt so bad was because I didn't understand what I am … what you are … what we can do."

Scott nodded but remained quiet.

"You make it sound like we're not human. Tell me you're not going to tell me we're not human." I was joking, but there was an edge to the humour, an edge of fear that either Scott was insane or that I was, or we both were.

"We're human," he reassured me.

I breathed a sigh of relief. "That's good." I laughed a little shakily. "But we're different."

Scott nodded.

"And you said it like … for some reason … you understand it better than me. You said I was unaware … unenlightened or something."

"I don't think I used the word unenlightened," Scott said, smiling. "But yes, that sort of thing."

"My mum's always said that people don't like different. I've never met anyone else like me," I said.

Scott's gentle face turned into a frown, and I could feel a trace of anger, which caught me by surprise.

"You must have talked to your mum about it, though?" he probed gently. "I mean, when you were little. You must have been frightened when you felt things you didn't understand. You must have gone to her?"

I thought back. The incident with Mr Fitzgerald floated to the surface, the old lady in the hospital. "Yes," I said, slowly. "I knew I was different, even as a very small child, but if I mentioned it, she'd just tell me it was better not to think about it and it was definitely better not to talk about it because people are frightened of what they don't understand, and people don't like different."

"But didn't she explain it to you … help you understand it yourself?" Scott insisted.

I thought about that. "I don't think she understood it herself. She never wanted to talk about it. When it was bad … when I had an episode, she would sit me on her knee and make me feel better. She would sing to me and talk about something else and take my mind off it. We never really talked about it except for her to tell me to try to ignore it. As I got older, I tried to talk to her a few times, but it usually ended in a row, so I stopped trying. I looked it up online. Some people call themselves empaths, people who can feel other people's emotions. I guess I'm ... we're empaths? I never took it any further. I try not to think about it most of the time although it's always with me. Sometimes … like with this little boy in my class who was having trouble at home, I think it's a wonderful gift, but other times … like with Kev tonight, I think it's just a curse." I shuddered at the thought of Kev. I felt Scott's grip tighten on my hands and instantly felt stronger, better.

"Belle …"

There was a confusing mixture of emotions churning in Scott's mind, and I wasn't quite able to untangle or decipher them. He paused for a long time. I didn't know if he had decided not to speak or if he was trying to work out what to say.

"Go on," I urged him.

"Belle," he repeated, "you're not an empath … or rather … you're not just an empath. Empathy is part of it but it … what we can do goes much deeper than that. Empaths experience emotions in rather a passive way. They experience the feelings of others, but they have very little control. There are individuals who have a much more complex … immersive gift. Please don't ask me where it came from or how it manifests itself in our DNA because that's not my field of expertise, but we have the ability not only to passively experience the emotions of others but to choose what we experience, what we block out, and to actively and deliberately influence and alter other people's feelings. And we *can* control it. We can decide when to … what to … to absorb energies. How much and how and when to transfer energies to others."

I put a hand up to prevent him going any further. He was hurting my brain. "Whoa, just a minute," I said. "You're saying we ... I … could switch it off? I can't. It's always there. And I don't have control. If I did I … I wouldn't …"

"Not switch it off, exactly, no, but sort of … yes. It's always there, but you can control it to a certain extent. You can stop it getting to you … I mean we can … you could …

you ..."

"So, tonight ... Kev? You're suggesting that instead of curling up into a ball and passing out, I could have, what? Just blocked it out? Just like that?" My voice was rising in pitch. "I couldn't." I was shouting now. "Don't you think I would have? If I could have ..."

"More than that, Belle," he continued calmly. "You could have blocked his anger and his vile excitement, and you could have turned him into a placid puppy dog."

"I couldn't!" I shouted. "I couldn't stop him! I couldn't even figure out what was him and what was me. Don't you think that if I had the power to stop him, I would have done?"

I was shaking with anger, fear, frustration. I didn't understand. Scott leaned forwards, still holding my hands and stroking them gently. He forced me to look into his eyes. I felt his calming influence flow into my mind, and I let myself fall back under his spell. I let him take some of the anger away.

"I'm sorry, Belle. I didn't mean you could have done today ... not ... not with your inexperience. Of course not. I didn't mean to imply that you should've or could've done anything differently. I'm sorry. I shouldn't have said that."

"No, it's OK," I said more calmly. "I shouldn't have shouted. This is such a lot to take in." I changed direction. "So, how come you know all this? How come you have control and I don't? And how can you be sure I really have this magic gift? I don't feel magical. I don't feel in control. I rarely feel in control of anything. Is there some kind of club? What do you call yourselves? I've got so many questions and it's late and I'm so tired and I need to sleep. Explain it to me. Please?"

"I know. I know you're tired. I know it's a lot. I know. I understand it because it's been explained to me ... my whole life. It's a huge part of who I am. It was instructed in me and practised and talked about and embraced from the moment I was born. There's nothing magical about it. Some people can do ridiculous mental arithmetic, some can hear a piece of music once and immediately play it on the piano… savants, I think they are. Some can absorb and control emotional energy. It's a sense … a part of our brain that we can access that most people … most ordinary people … can't. Is it that difficult to believe? My parents … they guided me. No, there's no club … exactly … well … although most families know each other … by reputation, at least, and we … I suppose. As for what we call ourselves, there have been many names throughout history: bellwethers, guides, ascendancers. Other people, people who don't understand, have used terms like witch, enchanter, demon. You've heard them all, but we don't possess magic powers. We're not supernatural beings. Your mum's right in one sense; people don't tend to like different, so it's not something we advertise. The most commonly used name now amongst our people is fluencer."

"Fluencer?" I tried out the word. "So, you're a fluencer? That's something to do with magic, isn't it? I'm sure I've read it somewhere. Somewhere in a fantasy fiction full of witches and wizards."

Scott smiled. "The term has been … appropriated, shall we say, by writers of fantasy fiction and sci-fi. The concept lends itself to theories of magic, but it's actually more to do with the transference and storage of energy. Emotions have their own energy signatures and can be manipulated in similar ways to heat, movement and sound. It just happens to be a rare gift for someone to be able to sense them and influence them. One that's becoming rarer all the time."

"I see. I think. And your parents are fluencers too? That must be nice," I said.

"Well, they would be," he said gently. "It's passed down to children. Everyone who has the gift is a direct descendant of two fluencers."

He gave me a minute with that one. I thought my brain might explode.

"You mean … you're trying to suggest that my mum … my parents… that they have this … this … this gift … this ability. That they're fluencers too? I don't get it. I can't … I can't …"

I stopped talking and thought about it. I knew, in the same way that I had known that I was different my whole life, that Scott wasn't lying to me. I could feel the honesty, could hear the ring of truth in the words. What he was saying actually made sense to me. In fact, now that I thought about it, I wondered why I had never considered it before.

"So, Mum's been lying to me for twenty-six years? Even if she wasn't told or taught by her parents, like me, she'd know something. It's not something she might not have noticed. She could have sympathised with me. She could have at least told me that she knew how I felt. She let me think it was just me. She told me to pretend it wasn't happening." I felt a bit numb. I didn't know what to think. I couldn't process this truth. It felt like such a monumental betrayal. "She … she always made me feel better. She was … she was … I don't … but Dad …?"

"I'm sorry, Belle, but yes, your mum is a fluencer, and she knows a lot more than you realise. Your dad … I don't know …"

"What's that supposed to mean?"

"It's not my place, Belle. You need to talk to her."

"What? You can't tell me all this and then choose to keep secrets about my own family."

"I'm sorry, Belle. I could tell you more, but I don't think it'd be right. There are things you need to hear for yourself … from her. It's not my place."

I was exhausted. My head felt heavy, and everything was beginning to look a little blurry. I could feel tears of exhaustion and grief threatening to overwhelm me. I looked back into Scott's eyes, trying to draw from their strength.

"I'm sorry. It's not your fault. You're not the one who's lied to me my whole life. I can't … Why?" I whispered.

"Why would she ... they ...?"

"I can't answer that," he said softly.

I tried to consider everything that he had said. I was sure that there was more: more information, more questions, but I couldn't get them to stick inside my head.

"You're tired," Scott said sympathetically.

"Yes. Tired, confused, angry. I don't know what to think, I don't know how to feel. There's so much I need to know, but I don't think I can do it anymore."

"There's no rush. I'm here now. I'm a part of your life, if you'll have me. We can talk again. If that's what you want?" he added a little hesitantly.

I didn't really process that. My mind had latched onto something else that he had said.

"There was something else. You said you already knew. You've been waiting your whole life. Waiting for ... what have you been waiting for?"

Scott was about to answer when another thought struck my mind, and I changed direction again. "Why can't I feel Daniel?" I asked instead. "Is he like you?"

"Like us," he corrected gently. "Yes, he is."

"But whenever I'm near him, I can't feel his emotions," I explained. "It's such a weird feeling. Tonight in the club, he was normal until he saw me, and then his feelings just disappeared."

"Yes. He's a very private man. He wouldn't want you to be able to read him, so he blocks ... shields his outgoing emotional energy."

"I see. So, he was hiding from me on purpose? He knows about me too?"

Scott nodded.

"Could you do that?"

"Yes, if I wanted to. You could too, with practice."

"I couldn't ... but I see what you mean. Could you influence me? Make me feel things that I don't really feel? Block some or all of your emotions from me?"

"It's different with me and you," he said slowly.

"Different how?"

"It's hard to explain," he said evasively.

"OK, I'm too tired for riddles. Please, I need to know that you haven't … tampered with my head. That when we … when I … You said you felt guilty about what happened on the bench. Was that because you …?"

Scott's reaction was a little frightening. His eyes became wide and dark, and his face turned a deep shade of red. At the same time, his shock and outrage barrelled into my mind without concession, nearly knocking me off my chair. He was horrified. It was all the answer that I needed, and I realised immediately that I had already known the truth and that I should never have said what I said. Scott was opening and closing his mouth like a fish. I wanted to do something, to take it back or reassure him that I realised my mistake, but I had no idea how, so I just sat in silence and watched his face. He gradually managed to get himself under control enough to form an answer.

"Belle. I have never, nor will I ever tamper with your head. I'm sorry you felt you needed to ask, but I suppose you don't know me that well, and perhaps it's natural to wonder. That isn't to say that I won't ease your mind when you're troubled or take away some of the pain when you're hurt. It also isn't to say that I won't … well … that what happened at the lake or … that my emotional energy won't ... but … I mean … only if you … if you … but I promise you that I'll never, ever deliberately alter or manipulate your emotions like that. I wouldn't. I couldn't.

"Belle. I've never felt this or anything anywhere nearly … remotely like this connection with a person before. I can't get you out of my head. I can't stop thinking about being with you in every way it's possible to be with a person, and I want that honestly. I've thought about you every day since I met you. You're … you're my … I tried … I asked you a moment ago if you wanted to talk to me again, to spend more time with me … I mean ... You dodged the question and asked me about Daniel. Is that your way of saying no?"

I smiled apologetically. "Did you? Did I? That was my way of being so tired I can only think of one thing at once, and I may have got them in the wrong order. Ask me again."

Scott smiled now, his shock mollified. "Would you like to spend more time with me?"

My heart skipped a beat. "Right now, that's just about the only thing that I'm certain of," I replied. "That and that I do trust you."

Scott looked uncomfortable again. "I need to ask. I need to say it straight away because we can't … not if … I know this is all a lot for you and you've got a lot to think about and other important conversations to have. I don't want to put you under any pressure but ... I won't be the other man." He put his hand up to stop me as I tried to interrupt. "No … Belle … you don't have to answer immediately and if … I'll understand, but I can't ..."

I didn't wait for him to say any more. "I don't need time," I told him defiantly. "I thought that was clear. It's going to be one of the hardest things I've ever had to do, but there's no way I can stay with Jack. I'm lying to him, and he doesn't deserve that. I'd already realised that before … before tonight and … I've known for a while. He's home … Sunday afternoon. I'll tell him then, straight away. After this long, I can't do it while he's away, and I don't want to call him home just to break up with him.

"I don't understand a lot of this, and I know it's going to take time and it's going to be hard, but … I feel … and I know this is going to sound totally ridiculous, but I feel as if a little part of me has been missing my whole life and I didn't even know I was missing it. When I'm with you … God, this sounds corny. You know we've only met three times? When I'm with you, it feels like that little piece is here … where it should be. I feel whole."

I couldn't believe I had just said that to him. I studied the table in an effort to hide my embarrassment, but Scott began to smile, properly now. I could feel it even without looking: the surge of joy that my words had given him. I slowly looked up and saw the flames in his eyes dancing and flickering with heat and passion, and I smiled back. I knew that no matter how hard and how complicated this situation was, this thing between us was real and it wasn't going away.

"Thank you," he said. "That didn't sound ridiculous, and even if it did ... a little bit, I liked hearing it. Listen, I'm not going to hold you to anything. You still have so much to learn, and you might change your mind when you've had time to think about what it really means, but Belle ... I'm here."

"Thank you." I looked at our hands. They were joined on the table again, and Scott's thumb was skimming my fingers, but despite the connection, despite how much I had been dreaming of a moment when we could sit and talk and touch, I was too overwhelmed, flooded with too much emotion and too exhausted to be happy for long, and as I watched, remotely, abstractly, tears started splashing onto the table in front of me.

"I'm sorry," I sniffed, staring at the table again. "I can't sort my head out. Part of me is so happy. I've dreamed about you every night. I've forced myself not to come looking for you even though it's all I wanted to do. I've sat in my living room and heard your voice and those words in my head, and now you're here and it might really, actually happen, but in order to make it happen, I've got to ... I've got to ... I'm sorry. Jack's a good man. He's a kind, genuine, good man and he loves me. I've felt it. I've felt the love he has for me every day since we were seventeen ... before, even. We've talked about our future. We've talked about having a family. How can I be happy about something that's going to cause someone I love so much pain? And then there's my mum ... my ... the lies ... Kev's attack. I don't even know where to start." The tears kept falling.

Scott's hands left mine, and for a moment, without his touch, I felt utterly empty and alone. I looked up to see that he had left his seat and was coming round the table to me. He crouched down next to me and took hold of my chin with his finger and thumb. He lifted my head so that we were level, looking each other in the eye, and all I could feel from him was strength and affection. I stared into those deep brown eyes once again. The flames were gone but their power was real. I felt a little stronger.

"Oh, Belle. I'm sorry you have to go through this and it's because of me. I think in time you'll see, although it's hard now, in the long run it'll be the best thing for everyone."

I nodded and sniffed again. "I know you're right. I already feel it, really. I've realised that it was never as real as I thought it was, and now that I know, I can't pretend. Scott? I'm so tired, I can't think anymore."

"I know, sweetheart, I know. Do you want me to take you home?"

I thought for a moment and glanced up at the mezzanine above our heads. "I don't want to be alone," I said quietly. "I mean … I don't mean …" I floundered.

Scott smiled into my eyes. "I know what you mean," he assured me. "Go and get cleaned up. The bathroom's just through there. You can stay here tonight. I'll sleep down here but I'll be near you. You don't have to be alone."

I was grateful for his compassion and understanding. I shuffled to the tiny bathroom and cleaned myself up as much as I could whilst feeling so tired that I thought that I might collapse again. After a minute or two, there was a gentle knock on the door.

"I thought you might want something more comfortable to sleep in," he called softly. I opened the door. Scott had found a large plain-white t-shirt and was holding it out to me. I took it and retreated back into the bathroom.

"Thank you."

I took off my clothes and slipped the t-shirt over my head.

It came about halfway down my thighs. It was comfortable and smelled sublimely of Scott. I took a deep breath in, let it out again and made my way slowly back to the main room. Scott gestured to the stairs, and I climbed them sluggishly. He followed closely behind, and at the top of the stairs, I found a cosy space containing a small chair, a bedside set of drawers and a double bed made up with a chequered green and cream duvet. Scott pulled back the duvet and I slipped into bed. The clean sheets felt soft and so good. I rested my head on the pillow. I was so tired that I could hardly think. Scott tiptoed back to the top of the stairs, but as soon as he moved away from me, I felt afraid.

"Scott?"

He paused and looked back, a question in his eyes.

"Don't go. Don't leave me."

He returned to the side of the bed, sat in the chair next to me and took my hand in his. He held it and stroked it. "Thank you, Scott," I said. I could feel sleep calling to me, and the comfort of his hand and the knowledge of his presence made me feel safe and calm.

"I'm here. I'm here, Belle.

I'm here and I'm yours."

Chapter 18

I was back in the grimy refuse yard being held against the wall by Kev's thick, sweaty hand, and I could feel his erection pressing against my stomach. I closed my eyes against the assault, imploring the darkness to claim me, knowing that my brain couldn't cope with the pressure and that I was going to pass out under the strain, but this time I didn't faint, the darkness didn't descend, and the dream continued beyond reality. I was unable to move and unable to make a sound. I was paralysed.

Kev began to undress me roughly, and my worst fears came to life. I should have blacked out by now. It should have been over. Kev still had one hand around my neck, and he thrust his other inside my top, reaching viciously for my breast. I tried to scream but no sound came out. I tried to kick out at him, but I still couldn't move. He reached my breast and freed it savagely from my bra, ripping my top and grabbing and kneading my flesh painfully. He pulled it free, and I felt the cold air skim across my flesh.

Kev was laughing, a cold and mirthless laugh. He laughed at me and his face was almost touching mine as he whispered with glee.

"You want this. I can feel your excitement. I can feel your desire."

"No!" I tried to scream. "It's not me. They're not my feelings, they're yours. I don't want this. I don't want this!"

My efforts were in vain. Although I wanted to scream, no sound came out, and Kev was blind to my resistance. I asked myself if he might be right. Once I absorbed somebody else's emotions and felt them for myself, perhaps that did make them my emotions, my desires. His words taunted me and provoked a deep-rooted terror. Did I crave the violence of this attack?

I felt tears streaming down my face. Kev's face continued to torment me, his hands were bruising my body, and I couldn't make it stop. I tried to scream again. I tried to scream again and again and again, and although I tried to fight him desperately, my body refused to respond and I just hung there, defenceless and exposed, while Kev continued his assault.

He let go of my breast, leaving it uncovered while he reached down and undid his trousers, pulling himself free and pressing himself up against me with more vigour, more intent. I was beside myself, trying to scream and to thrash my body from side to side, but it still did not respond. I was powerless to make it stop.

Scott hadn't come. He should have been here by now. He should have saved me, and I should be lying on the floor in his arms. This shouldn't be happening. This wasn't happening. It's not real. It's only a dream.

I thrashed and screamed and kicked with all of my might, but Kev was pressing himself against me and his hands were tearing at my clothes. I called out.

"Scott. Scott! Please! Scott!"

"I'm here. I'm here, Belle. I'm here and I'm yours."

Faintly at first, but rapidly becoming louder and more insistent, I heard it. He heard me. He had come.

I struggled towards his voice, away from the torment. The familiar words gave me an anchor and I was able to block out Kev's loathsome face and the feel of his hands on my skin. I began to feel warmth and support. Instead of Kev's clumsy, violent, intrusive hands, I felt Scott's gentle fingers on my face, stroking, soothing. I sluggishly emerged from the dream, my cheeks wet with tears and my body bathed in cold sweat. My feet were ravelled tightly in the sheets where I had been kicking and flailing in my sleep. My heart was pounding, but I could already feel the fragments of the nightmare slipping away.

"I'm here. I'm here, Belle. I'm here."

I ever so carefully opened my eyes, and fresh tears of

relief fell as I quietly took in the rustic charm and solidness of the cabin and the cleanliness and comfort of the bed. I looked across to Scott's worried face and down to the pleasure of his warm, solid hand holding mine. He was sitting in the chair by the bed, shushing and soothing me. I squeezed his hand in gratitude and tried to form words. They came out a little confused and faint.

"Scott. You came. You're here."

"Of course I'm here," he assured me.

"He … Kev … He …"

"Shhh. Shush now. I'm here. I'm here."

I felt a wave of reassurance and contentment wash over me and I accepted it with relief and gratitude, sinking into it and letting it soothe my tired mind. It was the middle of the night. I was still so tired.

"Don't go," I asked him, clutching his hand tightly as I drifted back to sleep.

"I'm here," he replied.

Soon the blissful darkness of dreamless sleep faded to be replaced by a new vision, a new dream, a new memory, but this time it was Mum who I dreamed about. All of the times that I had gone to her seeking answers, seeking acceptance and guidance were now distorted by Scott's revelations. My subconscious mind took these distortions and plagued me with image after image of me sitting on her knee, begging her to help me, to help me understand what was happening to me, why I was so different, and every time she took me onto her knee and she soothed me with her words, really, she was just lying to me.

The dream became dark and scary. Mum kept shouting at me, *People don't like different. People don't like different. People don't like different,* and her shouts were overlapping each other until I couldn't hear myself think.

Faintly at first, I heard a different voice amongst the noise. I tried to focus on it, to listen to it over the clamour. It became increasingly more insistent, and when I fixed on it, the voice broke through. *"I'm here. I'm here, Belle. I'm here and I'm yours."*

I concentrated on his voice, and I moved towards him. I blocked out the sound of my mum, and I reached for his outstretched hand. "Shhh. I'm here," he soothed, and I could feel him drawing me back to the real world.

I blinked into the soft light of the cabin. I looked down at my hand in sleepy curiosity and saw that it was still held by him, in waking as in my dream. He really was here, holding my hand, pulling me from another nightmare. I looked up into his eyes and saw worry and affection shining there. I was still groggy from sleep but was so grateful for him being there, watching over me. It was still pitch-black outside.

"Shhh," Scott continued to soothe. "I'm here. I'm here, Belle. Just close your eyes. You need to rest. I'm here." And I felt that already familiar, comforting warmth settle over me again, but I couldn't quite block out the images of Mum calling to me, reaching for me, and the confusing mixture of memories and dreams. Thinking of Mum brought a trace of panic to my mind, and I began to cry softly. I was frightened to go back to sleep, frightened of what the dreams might bring and what other demons the night had in store. I didn't want Scott to let go. I kept my eyes open, fighting his hypnotic influence, and I looked at him imploringly.

"Don't go," I whispered. "Hold me, please?" I lay on my back and shuffled across the bed a little, making room for him, still holding his hand but now inviting, pleading.

Scott looked unsure and perhaps a little afraid. His emotions were difficult to read, but he nodded and slipped into the bed beside me. I was still drowsy and sighed in torpid pleasure as he wrapped himself around me, giving me his warmth, his safety, his strength. Leaning back into him, I almost immediately drifted back to sleep with a contented smile on my lips. I slid into darkness.

We were at the beach. It was a gloriously hot, sunny day,

and I could see for miles along the hazy shore. Miles upon miles of unspoilt sandy beach stretching alongside the open water. We were walking hand in hand at the edge of the surf, and the chilly water lapped around my ankles as my feet sank into the wet, yielding sand. There was a warm, gentle breeze caressing my upturned face, lifting and blowing my hair into my mouth, where I could taste the salt on it. I laughed, prompting him to turn to me, gently tease the hair out and tuck it tenderly back behind my ear, and every time he touched my face, he stopped and stared into my eyes with that intense, fiery gaze that set my insides aflame. He kissed my lips gently, with a hint of passion and promise.

The setting was familiar because we had been here before. My mind had conjured this beach and this walk many times in my dreams. It was one of my favourites. Dream or not, I was happy to embrace this vision. The beach was deserted. There wasn't a soul in sight, and we were just walking. Walking and touching and laughing. Every time that I looked at him, a feeling of peace and belonging would descend upon me and I felt whole. I felt happy.

After an indeterminate length of time walking lazily and happily side by side, Scott steered me away from the sea, up the beach towards the softly rolling dunes. The sand transformed from moist and cool to warm and dry, and the gentle, velvety grains flowed between our toes. He led me to a blanket spread out in a hollow, sheltered from the wind by rolling sandy mounds and long grass. He lowered himself onto his back and pulled me down with him, and at that moment, nothing mattered except being there, lying beside the man of my dreams.

Scott lay back on the blanket, and I lay by his side looking up at the brilliant blue sky. I turned and propped myself onto my elbow so that I could look down at his face: that handsome, tranquil, perfect face and those deep, fiery eyes. I took a finger and traced it gently across his top lip, then around until I reached the centre of the lower one. I paused

323

there and his tongue darted out and wrapped around my finger, drawing it into his mouth, where he sucked on it gently, staring deeply into my eyes. He groaned around my finger and heat shot through my body. I moaned in response. I was powerless in his presence. Whenever we were close, an unstoppable force drew us closer and closer and deeper together. Our feelings wrapped around each other, feeding off one another, the exhilaration climbing higher and higher and the desire building like a volcano that would surely erupt when we inevitably joined, body and soul.

Scott lowered me onto the blanket. Now it was his turn to look down on me and to trace his finger lightly across my face. He closed my eyes with his fingertips and traced a featherlight touch across my eyelids and down to my mouth, where I drew him in and sucked on his finger, hard and deep into my mouth. Scott groaned again and swiftly replaced the finger with his tongue, kissing and exploring my mouth deeply. His hand slid to my shoulder and slipped the straps of my top and bra down over my elbow while he continued his passionate assault on my mouth. I raised my hips in invitation, confirming my desire.

The caress of the sea breeze on my face gradually died down and was replaced by the touch of heat from the flames of a fire. The softness of the sand beneath the blanket was replaced by a deep, sumptuous rug, which I wriggled into, enjoying the feel of the plush weave against my skin. When I opened my eyes, Scott was still looking down upon me, but we were no longer at the beach. We were in his cabin, lying together on a beautiful deep-grey rug, and Scott was undressing me, kissing and caressing my body as he went. I was overwhelmed by the mixture of physical and metaphysical feelings engulfing my being. There were the tangible sensations produced by Scott's hands and mouth on my skin, inducing my body to arch from the floor, and the dreamlike, abstract feelings developing in our minds, joining and combining in an unparallelled pleasure as he kissed me like I had never been kissed before.

"I'm here," he told me, coming up for air. "I'm here, Belle. I'm here and I'm yours."

He was there. He was with me physically and inside me emotionally and spiritually. I could feel our souls unite. I looked into his eyes and saw the flames reflected from the fire. I was inside his head and he was inside mine, and words were no longer necessary because we could read each other's minds. The flames of desire licked around us where our bodies touched, and I gave myself up to the ecstasy. I felt his name burst spontaneously from my lips, "Scott," I called out. It was the most natural and wonderful feeling in the world. "Scott," I cried louder.

As his name passed my lips for the second time, I opened my eyes and blinked into the bright sunlight streaming into the cabin from the windows downstairs. I took in my surroundings and closed my mouth hastily. I was in Scott's bed, in Scott's cabin, wearing Scott's t-shirt with the smell of Scott lingering on it, and I could still hear the echo of my impassioned cry reverberating around the rafters. I lay very still for a moment, listening for evidence of him moving around downstairs. It was quiet and still. Perhaps he was still asleep. I fervently hoped that he was a deep sleeper and that my cry hadn't woken him. I blushed hotly at the thought.

I was hot, and my breathing was coming fast from the passion of the fantasy. I could feel the arousal of the dream still clinging to my body, and I had a vague, groggy memory of begging him to get into the bed with me, to hold me, to comfort me with his strong arms and masculinity. My blush deepened.

As I surfaced into the real world, I recalled the earlier nightmares that had haunted my sleep. The details were already beginning to fade, but images and impressions remained vividly etched on my mind. The combination of alcohol, fear and all of the revelations and emotions had combined to leave my subconscious mind sore and confused. I was grateful that Scott had been with me and that I had somehow contrived to summon him into my dreams.

My breath caught in my throat as I remembered the feel of the ice-cold air on my breast when Kev had ripped into my clothing and exposed my flesh. I gingerly ran a hand across my chest, checking for tenderness or bruising. There was nothing. I reached for my clothes and checked for tears in the material. Nothing. I breathed a sigh of relief.

I thought about the dream about Mum, my brain's way of processing a truth that was hard to accept. I felt angry and betrayed, and the knowledge that our entire relationship had been based on lies was hurtful and distressing. I knew that I would have to confront her and that it was going to be a painful encounter.

I remembered Scott's voice and his words penetrating my dreams and his soothing presence throughout the night. I recalled the feel of his hand stroking my skin and the comfort of his embrace. My mind turned again to the last dream, triggered by his proximity and the lingering effect that he had on my body and mind. I blushed hotly again, took a deep breath and roused myself from the bed, trying to tame my tousled hair, dishevelled from the agitation of my sleep.

I crept slowly downstairs, steeling myself for coming face to face with him after the emotional outpourings of the previous evening, all of the revelations and the dreams. How on earth was I supposed to behave around him now? I didn't know what we were to one another. Nothing had really been defined. It was one thing baring your soul to a person after an emotional evening, riding the echoes of the passion of the night, but it was quite another thing facing someone in the cold light of day when everything seemed so solid, so normal and I felt so human, so ordinary.

The cabin was warm. The fire had been carefully banked and was giving out a gentle heat, keeping me comfortable in Scott's oversized shirt. On my way down the stairs, my eye was caught by the rug on the floor in front of the fire: the deep-grey rug that had featured so recently in my dream. Its existence must have lodged in my subconscious to become a part of my fantasy. I blushed again and forced myself to look away and scan the rest of the cabin. There were no other signs of life. The cabin was empty. My heart plummeted. I had that lurching, queasy feeling in my stomach, wondering if he had left me again. Perhaps he regretted the confessions of the evening and it was him that couldn't face me in the cold light of day.

On the table in front of me, I saw a note, folded with my name on the outside. I opened it carefully, my hands trembling slightly.

Don't panic.
Gone to fetch more wood.
Put the kettle on. I'll be back before it boils.
Xxx

My whole body relaxed, and my mouth curved into a smile. He hadn't deserted me. Of course he hadn't deserted me. Not only had he not deserted me, but he had left me a note because he knew that I would worry, and he had signed it with a kiss. With my heart infinitely lighter and a silly, goofy smile on my face, I made my way to the gas stove and kettle. There was already plenty of water in the kettle and two mugs out on the side, tea bags and a bowl of sugar in easy reach. I lit the stove and walked over to the cabin door, stepping out onto the deck.

I stretched my arms above my head and breathed in the fresh, fragrant air. The cabin was in a small, flat clearing in the trees on what was otherwise a steep slope leading down towards Ramsay Pool. I could just make out the far shore of the lake. The water was shimmering in the golden early morning rays of the sun. It was peaceful and still here, a heavenly retreat from the hustle and bustle of the world. I felt like I had stepped back in time to a simpler, cleaner world. The only sounds were the sweet music of wild birds calling to each other with joy on this beautiful winter's morning and the faint hum of the kettle as it heated the water for our morning tea.

The fresh sun lit the moss-softened rocks and illuminated the verdant greens of the trees and grasses all around me. I felt like I had stumbled upon a small slice of heaven, unspoilt and remote. I could understand why Scott would use this place to get away from everybody and everything. It was exquisite in its simplicity, and I could feel myself relaxing moment by moment, just standing on the deck of this old, ramshackle cabin in the woods.

As I savoured my surroundings and listened to the melody of the birds, Scott emerged from the trees on the downward slope. He was wearing casual jeans and a long-sleeved cotton shirt and looked totally at home and relaxed. He caught sight of me and paused for a fraction of a second as if taken by surprise by my presence. His face lit up with that dazzling, heart-stopping smile. He quickened his pace and was quickly standing in front of me, closer than any decent company would allow, and without warning or preamble, he took my chin in his fingers, tilted my head gently upwards and settled a short, firm, delicious kiss on my lips. I lost myself for a moment as I enjoyed the honest tenderness of his touch, and the goofy smile borne by his note now took a firmer hold of my face as I stared deeply into his fiery eyes. I no longer had to wonder how we would behave around each other; this was how.

"Sorry," he said with a smile that belied his words. "I just couldn't help myself. God, you looked good as I came into the clearing just now. Since moving here, I thought the cabin was perfect, that it was designed just for me and that I felt totally happy and at home here, but now I see you standing there, crumpled from sleep and ravishing in that old white shirt, I realise that the cabin had nothing before. You were missing, and I never even realised it."

I just stared at him with my mouth slightly agape. I wanted to tell him that he never had to apologise for kissing me like that, that that kind of greeting is something that a woman dreams about her whole life, but I couldn't find the words. His words would have sounded corny and unreal in almost any other circumstance, but today, this morning, standing here looking at him, it seemed so perfect and so right that I wondered if I was still dreaming. I didn't know how to respond at first but realised with wonder that words weren't necessary. Scott drank me in, feeling and absorbing my happiness, and I felt his joy in return. The goofy smile grew even goofier.

I glanced at his empty arms, and with a shrug, to the wood store at the side of the cabin, packed to the rafters with neatly split logs. When I looked back to his face, I saw a faint wave of embarrassment flicker there as he realised that he'd been caught out, but at that very moment, the kettle began its shrill whistle and he smiled. "Saved by the bell," he announced and slipped quickly past me into the cabin.

I smiled and followed him in. He was at the stove, staring at the kettle with intense concentration, trying not to catch my eye and see the question that he knew that he would find there. Despite his studious embarrassment, there was no real awkwardness between us at all. I had been worried for nothing. I felt totally at ease in his company.

"Your note said you were going out to get firewood," I challenged him.

He looked up and laughed softly. "Fair cop. Full disclosure?" he asked.

"Of course. Absolute honesty," I replied.

He shifted uncomfortably for a moment while he finished the tea. I sat on the settee in the window, and he brought my drink over and settled next to me. Our legs were just touching, and the contact felt right.

"I couldn't be near you," he confessed.

I hadn't expected that. I looked up in surprise.

"It wasn't something I was expecting either," he admitted. "But your dreams … Jesus Christ, when you dream, I can *feel* you. I didn't know it would happen like that. I felt your fear when you dreamed about that monster outside the club, and I tried to wake you, to reassure you. And then later, after you'd gone back to sleep, I left your side and you had another nightmare. I felt your anger and you were shouting in your sleep. Your mum?" he probed gently.

I nodded.

"After I woke you the second time, you begged me to stay. You asked me to stay close, to hold you."

I nodded. I was right, he had been in my bed. The strength that I felt had been real.

"But then … This morning …" Scott swallowed, and the realisation hit me and I felt the hot blush return to my cheeks. He had felt my dream. He had felt my desire.

"As the sun came up this morning, you started to dream again … Only this time, I don't think it was a nightmare."

I was mortified. I shook my head and stared studiously at the floor. Scott leaned over, took my chin in his fingers gently again and lifted it so that I couldn't avoid his eye.

"You don't have to be embarrassed," he told me. "I know this is horribly new and strange for you, but if we're … I mean, if me and you are going to … well … if we're going to spend a lot of time together, I'm afraid we won't be able to keep many secrets from each other when it comes to affairs of the heart." He continued to look me straight in the eye, and his frankness took the edge off my embarrassment.

"I don't want you to think …" he continued. "I mean … I didn't want to take advantage of you, but you … well … you were … I think you were rather enjoying yourself, and I could have … so easily …" He laughed a little, and my cheeks grew even hotter.

"OK, thanks," I said. "Now I know. How about we change the subject?"

Scott laughed. "OK, just a minute, though. Like I said, I didn't want to take advantage of you, but like you said, absolute honesty, right?"

I nodded.

"After the last few months and last night and … well … how well lodged into my brain you've become. When I felt your desire in your sleep and when your body started to respond … well … I couldn't help but respond to you. I was so turned on. So ... well, you get the point?"

I nodded again.

"I never, ever want to feel like I've taken advantage of you again … like I did before, but there was literally no way I could stay under the same roof with you while you were … well … you know … and not ... so I had to get out. I had to put a little distance between us. Do you understand?" he asked.

I nodded again, too embarrassed to speak.

"You don't have to be embarrassed around me," he said again, and I looked at him sharply, caught off guard by his easy translation of my feelings.

"You're going to have to get used to that too," he reminded me. "Although Blind Freddy could see you're a bit embarrassed right now." He laughed. "While you're embarrassed already, can I ask you something?"

I thought about that. "I don't know. I'm not sure I can take any more," I confessed.

Scott laughed again. "Was it …? I mean, were you …? I mean who …? I mean …" He faltered. It was his turn to look embarrassed.

When I realised what he was trying to ask, my cheeks could not have got any redder, and I closed my eyes tightly for a moment. When I had gathered myself, I opened them and looked back at him and felt his hesitation, his vulnerability, his surprising insecurity, and I had to rescue him. After the number of times that he had rescued me in the last few hours, it was only fair.

"You want to know who I was dreaming about?" I said.

"Yes ... I mean, no ... I mean ... It's none of my business if you don't ... sorry ... I mean ... you don't have to ... I don't want to assume ... if ..."

Now it was my turn to laugh. "Absolute honesty?" I checked.

He just nodded. He was adorably unsure of himself.

"You really have to ask?" I said.

His smile returned a little, but I could still feel his genuine uncertainty. I told him the truth. "The dreams started about three months ago. After we ... after you ... no, after we ... well, you know ... after that night at the lake."

He nodded for me to continue.

"This is so embarrassing," I said, but he nodded at me again, silently asking me to go on, and I could tell that he needed to hear it even though it was excruciating to say.

"It might have even been before that ... I mean ... I ... I've never ... before then ... before you, I mean ... I've never ... even though ..." I stumbled. "Of course I was dreaming about you," I told him simply. "It's always you."

His smile returned in full force and the flickering flames were dancing in his eyes. We held each other's gaze for a moment, and he put his hand gently on my knee.

"Thank you." he told me. "I know that was hard to say. I hoped ... I mean, I thought ... but I think I needed to hear it. This is new for me too. I'm not sure I could have handled it if someone else was ... I mean ... if you ... I know I have no right to tell you what or who you can dream about .... but ..."

I could have stopped him there, but I was quite enjoying his discomfort. He felt my amusement and he relaxed.

He stood and offered me his hand. "Come here. I want to show you something."

I took it, and he led me back to the door. He opened it and we stood on the deck together. He pointed down the hill to the edge of the lake that was just visible in the distance.

"See there, that tiny bit of lake?" he asked.

I nodded.

"I know it's probably not, but since that night, I've stood here so many times looking at that little bit of lake and the shore beyond, wondering if that's where the bench is. It must be round about there somewhere, don't you think?"

I nodded again.

"Well, I've stood here and looked over there and wondered if you were down there. I've wondered if you were down there sitting on that bench, and I've wondered if you were looking up here and thinking of me."

Scott's admission was honest, vulnerable and adorably sweet. He put his arm affectionately around my shoulder and I snuggled in close. We stared out over the trees at that point on the lake together, breathing in each other's feelings, relishing our connection and marvelling at the ease that we were already coming to share in each other's company.

We enjoyed a modest breakfast together, and as the morning wore on, became more and more comfortable with each other, chatting together easily and temporarily forgetting about the rest of the world and the challenges that lay ahead. We kept the conversation light. My doubts and concerns slowly ebbed away as it became undeniably obvious that this was where I was meant to be. Not here, physically, in this cabin, but here, in essence, by Scott's side. I could see a future with this man, which gave me a warm glow inside and a feeling of becoming whole, of peace, of belonging. There were moments when the depth of this conviction terrified me because I was falling so thoroughly and so fast, but when the feeling of terror hit, Scott would sense my unease, look me in the eye with the very conviction that I was scared of, and the moment would pass because like it or not, fast or slow, there was no doubt that my heart was his.

After a time, it became harder to repress the inevitable. There were important topics that Scott refused to talk about until I had spoken to Mum, and we couldn't sit here and pretend that the rest of the world didn't exist forever. I needed to confront Mum about last night's revelations, and as that knowledge crept in, I began to lose focus and become twitchy. Tomorrow afternoon Jack would be home and I would have to face another impossible conversation. I needed to get this one out of the way before I lost my nerve.

Scott sensed the shift in my mood. "Do you want me to take you home?" he asked.

"I left my car in town last night. Donna was going to give me a lift back for it this morning."

"OK, that's fine. I'll drop you in town," he said. "Do you want me to come with you to see your mum?"

I was touched by his offer. "Thanks, but no. She doesn't know anything about you … Yet … And we've got enough to talk about as it is. Besides, this is a conversation I need to tackle on my own."

"Of course. If you need anything, though, I'm here. Anytime. Always."

"Thank you. I can't tell you how much that means right now. I think I'm going to need you a lot."

"I'll be here," he said with a gentle smile. "You know, though, I just thought, we don't even have each other's numbers."

"Well, that's easily fixed." I held my hand out for his phone. He unlocked it and placed it in my palm. I typed my number in and saved it under 'Belle.' It made me smile to use his name for me, a name that I'd never associated with myself before but that now seemed so right. I called my phone from his and smiled again as it rang. It felt like another small step on our journey together. I looked out of the window wistfully.

"Belle," Scott began a little hesitantly.

I looked at him, wondering what had caused his uncertainty. He stood and moved to stand beside me.

"I don't want you to think I'm moving too fast or putting any pressure on you or anything, but I think it's hopefully

OK to say that I can see that you like it here. Here at the cabin, I mean."

"I love it," I replied honestly.

"Good," he smiled. "No one else ever comes here. It's mine. I'd like you to feel like maybe in time, it could be yours too," he suggested. "I don't mean hey, let's move into the cabin together," he quickly clarified. "It's a bit too rustic for permanent living. But what I mean is that I'd like you to feel that you can come here anytime."

I smiled. It felt like a wonderful gift.

Scott went on, "I think the next couple of days are going to be hard for you."

I nodded. "I think 'hard' might be an understatement."

"Yes," Scott agreed. "I just want you to know that there's somewhere you can go, somewhere you can get away and be by yourself … or with me" — he shrugged, adorably uncertain again — "if you want. There's plenty of room on the track for two cars, and no one other than me would ever need to know you were here … if you didn't want them to. If you want to hide here and be alone, you can just let me know and I won't bother you. Or if you want to be here and you'd like my company … well, you could always let me know that too. If you want … Or don't … Or ..."

I stopped his rambling with a reassuring hand on his arm. "Thank you, Scott, so much," I said sincerely. "For everything. For last night, for this morning … for this." I gestured around the cabin. "That's an incredibly generous and wonderful offer and I think … I mean, I'm pretty sure that I'll be taking you up on it. I love it here and it really does feel ... away from things. Thank you."

I looked up at him and our eyes met and held. A frisson of excitement passed between us and the flames in Scott's eyes ignited again. We both stood up. There was almost no space between us and we stood still, locked in place and absorbed by each other's eyes and the depths that we found there. He had kissed me this morning in the doorway, and it had been a moment that I would never forget, but this felt different. This felt like the culmination of three months of wondering, of wanting, of pent-up desire and of the revelations and discoveries shared last night and this morning. This felt like a moment that I had been waiting for my whole life.

As this notion stumbled through my head, I glanced nervously at his lips and back up to his eyes. He caught the glance, felt my jitters and matched them with a tremble of his own. We continued to stare into each other's eyes, and our nerves dissolved and transformed into eager anticipation. Scott reached for my hands, and we smiled at each other. As the gap between us closed, I felt that sense of belonging intensify and a deep certainty that after this, nothing would ever be the same again. As our lips finally, achingly came together, we became so much more than two people. Our connection was infinite, unconditional. It almost felt as if we were reading each other's minds.

The kiss was everything that I could ever have hoped for and more than I could ever have dreamed. We fitted together like two pieces of a puzzle and we melted into one another. His hands came up, his fingers entwined in my hair, and he held me tightly to him. My hands moved to his back and held him close. Our lips moved gently against each other and parted, consenting, as we increased our exploration. I felt his tongue gently caress my lips and I responded with the barest touch, a graze of my own tongue against his. The passion between us ignited a flame somewhere deep inside, a flame that grew in intensity and licked up around us, engulfing us in a blaze full of promise and belief.

The rest of the world melted away. The worries, the uncertainties, everything ceased to exist as we were suspended together in that moment of time. The kiss was demanding and yet gentle, yielding, comforting, a surrender to inevitability, and it was magical. We stood in that cabin, our bodies pressed against each other, our lips locked together, and we became more than two individuals in contact, so much more than the sum of our two parts. Our hearts beat in time, and the impassioned thrill saturated our bodies and minds from our hearts to our fingertips.

Scott's fingers tightened in my hair, and he deepened the kiss even more. I pressed my body more firmly against him and he groaned his pleasure into my mouth. I moved my fingers across his back, into his hair and stroked his neck, his shoulders, his arms. I didn't think that I would ever be able to get enough of this man and the feelings that he ignited inside me. I let my energy delve into his mind and felt him inside mine. Our passions and emotions came together, cementing our connection, sealing, binding us to each other, inspiring emotions that I had never even imagined.

When we broke apart, we leaned back to look deeply into each other's eyes. We each saw the fire reflected there and felt the passion and the promise, a spark ignited with shared secrets and desires. A warmth had settled into my being, ignited by that kiss, and something had begun that could never be undone. A pledge unspoken and yet no less consequential in its silence. A promise of hearts and minds: The Essence of Bliss.

Chapter 19

I returned home for a shower and a change of clothes and then picked up my phone to call Donna. We'd had no contact since the club. To my shame, I hadn't even checked that she had made it home safely, but then she hadn't checked on me either. I had second thoughts about the call and decided to send a message instead. It would be impossible to talk to her without saying something about what happened last night. It wouldn't be fair to talk to anyone else until I had done what needed to be done.

The thought of the inevitable conversation with Jack made me feel physically sick. Although Donna had always been my best girlfriend, it was Jack who had always been there for me, Jack who I had gone to whenever I was sad, confused or angry, and Jack who had loved me unconditionally from the moment that I let him kiss me outside my parents' gate almost nine years ago. I had honestly thought that we would be together forever. We had talked about our future. We had talked about our children.

Tears sprang into my eyes when I thought about all that would never be, all that we had dreamed of sharing together. Our relationship was over. The feelings that I had for Jack were not enough; they could never satisfy me now that the previously dormant part of me was awake. I could not deny my feelings for Scott or fail to explore the potential of my passion and power and the possibility of a life with someone the same as me. I couldn't stay with Jack knowing that it was a lie, but my love for him hadn't just disappeared. He had done nothing wrong, and there was no escaping the fact that he was going to be devastated, heartbroken, crushed. I was frightened for him and terrified that I would be losing my best friend, possibly forever.

I sat down heavily on my bed and my phone lay limply in my hand. I stared at it absently. I still needed to message Donna, the third side of our triangle, best friend and confidante to us both. Donna wasn't going to take the break-up well either. She loved Jack too, and it had always been the three of us. We played together, learned together, laughed together and lost together. We had always been there for each other. The Three Musketeers, The Three Stooges, The Three Tenors. I smiled sadly to myself. After tomorrow, I feared that we would never be a three again. Nothing would ever be the same.

I had no idea what I was going to say in my message to Donna. I had never had to think about it before. Everything with Donna had always been easy, but everything had changed. A simple message checking that she was OK felt awkward and dishonest because I wasn't telling her the whole truth. Part of me wanted to ring her and confide everything, but a bigger part knew that would be wrong, and a tiny part of me was still upset that she hadn't checked on me. She had left me alone on the dance floor in order to spend the night with Daniel Callahan. We had left the club separately, a first for girls' night, and she hadn't even sent a message to ask if I made it home all right.

Daniel Callahan. I was certain that he wasn't a good guy and even more certain that he wasn't good enough for Donna, but after this weekend, I suspected that my opinion on the matter would not be one of Donna's main priorities. Donna most likely wouldn't want to know what I thought about anything ever again.

Hi Don. Hope you had a good night and got home OK. Sorry the night didn't end as we planned. I'm home and I'm fine. Speak soon, Izzy x

Message sent. I couldn't put off seeing Mum any longer. It was time to go.

When I pulled into the tiny gravel car park at the allotment site, mine was the only car, which was a relief. I turned off the engine and sat unmoving for a minute, staring straight ahead but not seeing anything. My mind had been full of all of the things that I wanted to say, all of the questions that I wanted to ask, but now it was completely and horribly blank. I forced myself to get out of the car, grab my wellies from the boot and trudge over to Mum's plot. She glanced up from her pruning when she sensed my approach. Her face split into an unaffected, wide smile. She waved her empty hand in greeting and deposited her secateurs on a handy fence post.

"Izzy! What a wonderful surprise. What brings you down here today? Jack's away this weekend, isn't he? Weren't you out with Donna last night? Girls' night? I thought you'd be having a quiet day at home, recovering."

I didn't say anything and I didn't smile. I couldn't control all of the thoughts and emotions that were racing erratically around my head when I saw her smiling face and heard that cheerful voice. Now that I knew that she could read my emotions, I desperately wanted to hide them or at least to remain in control so that I didn't give too much away, but despite Scott's assurance that I had the capacity for control, in reality, I had no control and could do nothing about my emotional effluence. I was hurt, I was angry, and I was frightened. Most of all, I was extraordinarily sad, and Mum could sense it all. Of course she could. The recognition of my previous ignorance and stupidity only fuelled my pain and anger.

I marched straight to where she was standing and looked her steadily in the eye. Her smile faltered, and she regarded me with worry bordering on fear. Disconcertingly, I couldn't read her. I focused on the aspect of my ability that came naturally, the ability that I used, knowingly or otherwise, every day — the ability that influenced all of my interactions throughout my entire life — the ability to sense another's emotional energy. I felt nothing, not a whisper. It wasn't quite the same obvious, offensive emptiness of Daniel Callahan, but there was a deliberate, considered barrier preventing me from accessing Mum's feelings. She knew how to control her emanation and was doing so now. She must have been doing so for twenty-six years. The knowledge intensified my anger even more.

All of the thousands of days, the hundreds of thousands of hours that we had spent together while I grew up, playing, learning, laughing and crying. Had she always been hiding from me? I couldn't remember. She was just my mum. She had always been my mum. Everything about her was just how it was, how it had always been, the natural order of things. I had never analysed it before. I had never thought about it. I had never needed to think about it or analyse it because it had never occurred to me, in all of those hours and all of those days and all of those years, that she might be lying to me, might be hiding from me, might be suppressing her emotions to keep me in the dark and altering my own emotions to prevent me from seeing the truth.

I saw Mum's face fall, and I didn't even try to hide anymore. I wanted her to sense my emotions. I wanted her to see exactly how upset I was, to feel it all — my pain, my frustration, my anger — and I didn't hold back.

"Izzy?" Mum asked warily. "What's wrong, sweetie. What's happened?"

She closed the gap between us and tried to lay a hand on my arm. I flinched.

"Don't touch me," I said sharply.

Mum grew pale, and tears immediately began to shine in her eyes. I was never fractious with her. I always treated like a fragile child, but not today, not anymore.

"Izzy, what's happened? What's wrong? Come here." Mum held out her arms to me. "Let me make you feel better."

Alongside those familiar and now enraging words, I felt a subtle nudge, a soft blanket of reassurance slowly infiltrating my mind. It felt so natural, such a normal part of being in Mum's presence, that I had never knowingly been aware of it before. It was different today. I had woken up and could see clearly for the first time. I could sense exactly what Mum was doing. I used all of my strength to summon the power to push the suggestion back out. I wasn't going to let her take control.

"Stop it, Mum. Don't."

She looked genuinely confused. "Don't what, sweetie?" she asked, but I felt the intrusion, the suggestion, back off a little.

"Just don't," I said. "I don't want to feel better right now. I want to talk to you. I want you to stop lying to me."

The last few words came out through gritted teeth, and I had to force myself to breathe and to calm down.

Mum continued to look at me with something like fear in her eyes, but I still received no emotional signal from her at all. I realised with a start that she was powerful, practised, that she knew exactly what she was doing. The knowledge only incensed me further.

"I met someone," I said quietly.

"You met someone?" Mum repeated. "Who did you meet?"

"I met someone who was more honest with me in one night than you have been in my whole life," I said calmly, slowly.

"Honest? I don't know what you mean."

"Drop the act, Mum. Don't lie to me. I think you know exactly what I mean. I met someone who told me the truth about what I can do … about what you can do … about what I am … what *we* are and what it means. About how you've been lying to me … my whole life." I couldn't keep my voice even. I felt it rising and wavering involuntarily.

The little nudge was at the corner of my mind again, trying to snake its way in. I forced it back out.

"Stop it, Mum! Stop it! Don't hide from me. Don't try to control me. Don't try to influence me, or *fluence* me, or whatever you like to call it. You need to be honest with me today. You can't hide from it anymore."

Mum's face crumbled with devastation when I used that word. She knew what it meant. The realisation and truth struck home before her face hardened again with close-lipped anger.

"You met someone?" she asked again, almost a whisper. She walked a few paces away, staring intently at the ground, thinking hard. She turned and came back. "Callahan," she spat. She didn't phrase it like a question. She knew. Her face had turned pale. "Isabel, you can't trust that man. He's not a good man. He's a dangerous man."

"Is he?" I asked. "And how could you possibly know that, Mum? How could you possibly know anything about him? They've only just moved to town. Right now it feels like he's less dangerous than you. He hasn't been lying to me and playing mind tricks on me for my whole, entire life. You're more of a stranger to me than he is."

Mum's face fell again. She realised that it was too late to try to hide anymore, too late to try to control my emotions in order to avoid the difficult truth. She blinked back tears and sighed deeply. She looked imploringly at me, hands out in front, begging me to step into her arms, but one more glance at my stony features and she quickly accepted that the situation was not going to be resolved with a hug. She nodded.

"I thought it was for the best," she said quietly. "I thought not knowing would give you a chance at a normal life, a happy life without any of the … without the games, the choices, the intensity … the hassle."

"The hassle?" I couldn't control the outrage in my voice. "I'm sorry, did you say *the hassle*? You thought that lying to me, controlling my mind and hiding the truth from me every day for twenty-six years would save *the hassle* of me knowing the truth?"

She tried to placate me. "No, sorry, hassle wasn't the right word."

I laughed drily. "No."

"OK," she gathered herself. "You're right. We need to talk. Let me get chairs and drinks and I promise we'll talk. I promise I'll be honest with you."

I nodded. Mum shuffled into the shed, and I took the opportunity to try to regain control of my disordered thoughts. I hoped that she was not a bad person. She must have had her reasons. She must have convinced herself that her choices had been for the best, but so far, I hadn't heard anything enlightening and couldn't think of a single excuse that would convince me that she had been right. I tried hard to concentrate on the fact that Stephanie and I had always been loved. Ours had been a happy childhood, a pleasant, comfortable life. I had always adored my parents. We were close, and I didn't want to quarrel, but at this moment I struggled to imagine how she might appease me. I felt like I had been trapped in a lie for my whole life, when the truth would have set me free. Maybe I didn't know her at all.

Mum returned with two of her canvas chairs, which she set up in silence. She then disappeared back inside and returned with two cups of water. I noticed that her hands were trembling. I didn't thank her. This was not the time or place for niceties or worrying about bad manners. I sat down. The chairs were facing each other, but Mum didn't look up. We sat in silence for a few seconds. Those few seconds felt like a long time.

"When … where did he find you?" she asked.

"What?" I was confused. "Who?"

"Callahan." Mum said the word with a shudder, as if it left a bad taste in her mouth. "I knew he was … I mean, I knew he would … but I didn't think he would actually … He … he always wanted … but I thought … I should have made sure. What does he want from you? Is he here for you …? Did he tell you …? What did he …? How much did he tell you?"

This was not how I imagined this conversation might go. This was strange. Mum sounded weird, paranoid. She was not making any sense.

"I've no idea what you're talking about, Mum. Nobody found me. We met by chance, and we … I've never met anyone like me before. Or at least I thought I hadn't. I felt it immediately. He felt it too and …" I trailed off. I hadn't come here to talk about my feelings for Scott. "What am I saying?" I shook myself, literally. "Why am I …? What does it matter how we met or when? I'm not here to talk about him … to answer your questions. That's not what's important here. I'm here to talk about me. About you. About my life and why it's all been a lie!"

"I don't know how much he told you, but you can't trust him," Mum continued, almost as if I hadn't spoken. She didn't sound normal, rational.

"Stop it, Mum! You sound mental. You don't even know him!" I shouted.

"I haven't seen him for a long time, but you have to trust me, Izzy, I know him … I knew him … I know him. Please, Izzy, stay away from Nicholas Callahan."

"Nicholas? Nicholas Callahan … I haven't ... It wasn't … I haven't even met … What do you know about Nicholas Callahan? I didn't know you ... How do you …? What's your connection to him? Not that it matters; you're just trying to deflect the attention from your own lies. Stop it. Stop avoiding the subject. And in answer to your other question, I know enough to know that your lies and control have seriously affected my life. That my whole life is, in fact, a lie!"

"Oh, Izzy," Mum sighed. "All the choices I made, I made for you. I thought it was right. I thought you'd be better off. I thought you … I just wanted to protect you from what I … I mean … I love you … and you know he … your dad, I mean… he loves you too. He doesn't … he doesn't need … I didn't think you ever needed to know."

"I've struggled with it my whole life, Mum," I said. "You know that. You've seen me struggle. You've seen me cry.

You've seen me scared. You've seen me at my worst. I always came to you. I always asked you. You said you didn't know. You said you didn't understand it, but it was all lies. All of it. You're the same as me. We're the same. You, out of everybody … you knew what it was like, and you did understand it. You did know. I presume you've always known … Grandma?"

Mum nodded.

"So, you've known your whole life! You were brought up knowing? You learned how to control it as a child? You were given a choice!"

Mum nodded again.

"You must have known how hard it was not to know … not to understand. You must have known, and you saw it in me. I don't get it. I don't get how you could have hidden it from me all this time. I don't even know where to start. Please tell me something that might help me understand because at the moment, I just feel … well, I don't need to tell you what I feel, do I? You know. You've always known. You can feel my … me … you knew … you know."

Mum had the sense to look ashamed. She nodded. "You're right. I do understand, but I also know the damage it can do, and I wanted to spare you that. I thought I was making the right choice for you. After Dad … my dad, I mean. After he … after your grandma … after …" She drifted off and stared into space. I didn't want to interrupt if she was going to actually say something, but I could have screamed in my frustration.

The silence stretched on, and I waited for her to continue. Just as I was about to explode, she went on.

"They were so wonderful." She looked wistful, captivated by her memories. "Mum and Dad. Everybody loved them without them ever having to will it. They were beautiful people and a wonderful couple. They were good. They did good things. They achieved so much together. They were so in love. Their love, it sort of … radiated out of them. You

346

just had to be around them to feel it … to see it. Growing up surrounded by that kind of love is … That's how it is with our … with us. True love between two … fluencers, it's so strong, so powerful. Anyway, there was an … an accident … an incident … they … he … your grandpa, he …"

She stopped talking again and stared absently into the distance. I waited for her to continue, spellbound. She never spoke about my grandparents. Whenever they were mentioned, she would skilfully change the subject, and Dad always said it was hard for her and that we shouldn't push. He was always looking out for her, protecting her, but I realised that neither Stephanie or I had ever properly pursued the matter. It would be normal to be curious about your own grandparents, but after the initial vague responses to our questions, it had never seemed that important. That horrible sick feeling in the pit of my stomach returned again as I realised that more of my life than I had suspected must have been manipulated by Mum's power. She had suppressed our interest, curbed our curiosity. She had been toying with the minds of her children throughout our entire lives. There were just so many lies, it was hard to comprehend.

Mum seemed to recover herself a little and she went on, "After your grandpa … Mum just fell apart. I don't mean she was upset … grieving. I mean … she was, but it was more than that. She … well, I don't know how else to explain it. She just fell apart, totally. There weren't even enough pieces for us to put back together. She was just a shell and then … she … she …"

She blinked back a tear, and just as I thought we were getting somewhere, I watched as her face closed down again.

"It doesn't matter," she said instead. "After … when I'd lost them both, I promised myself that it would never happen to me. I would never let the power, the fluence, claim me, control me. I would never be at risk of that kind of collapse … of doing to my children what my parents did to me. So I turned away from it. I didn't want it in my life. It's impossible to get rid of it, but I did everything I could to ignore it and to live without it. And I met a ... I met your dad. But then when we ... I wish I hadn't had to go to him, but I had no other choice, and now he's here and you know, and I didn't want this for you ... Oh, Izzy."

I tried to understand what she had just said, but I couldn't wrap my head around it. I knew that Grandpa died relatively young, but I didn't know the circumstances. Grandma hadn't died until fairly recently, although I never met her. Mum never spoke about her, but I didn't know why. I think Mum had been raised by her aunt, Aunty Susan, but again, the details were strangely vague. I had always assumed that there had been some sort of a family feud, but it had never occurred to me to look into it or at least ask the question, especially as I was now living in Grandma's old cottage. Now that I thought about it, of course I was fascinated by my family history and the story behind Grandpa's death, Grandma's apparent mental breakdown and Mum shunning her ability and her birthright for an eccentric, unconventional life lived between her family and her allotments. Perhaps there was more to Mum's peculiarities than I had ever imagined, but the fact that this was the first time that I had ever glimpsed these complexities and also happened to be the first time that I had deliberately prevented her from fluencing me was enlightening and even more enraging.

As for the ambiguous implication that Nicholas Callahan was villainous, connected to Mum in some way from her past, and that she had gone to him for some kind of a favour, the whole thing sounded absurd, irrational and nonsensical. I had never heard the name Callahan before they moved to town. I would have remembered.

"You're not making sense, Mum. You're talking in riddles and not finishing sentences. I have no idea what you're talking about. What did you go to him for and why do you think he's here?"

"It doesn't matter." Mum's tone was flat.

348

"It doesn't matter? It doesn't matter?! I don't believe you just said that. Of course it matters! It all matters! You haven't said anything that makes any sense. You've told me half of nothing about Grandma and some weird nonsense about Nicholas Callahan. I'm no closer to understanding any of it. I need something, and I thought you might actually tell me something that might help, but you just ... and now you're saying it doesn't matter! Please, Mum, please. At the moment, all I can see is that you've been lying to me about who I am and who you are forever. I can't ... we can't get past this unless I understand it or at least some of it. Please."

"It's poison," she said vehemently.

"What is?" I asked.

"All of it," she said, raising her hands in the air. "It poisons, it corrupts, it ruins lives. I didn't want that for you. I didn't want it for me, and I didn't want it for my girls. I didn't need it. I met your dad, and he was enough for me. He's a good man ... an honest man. I thought that maybe one day ... that when you got older, you might ... that I might have to ... but then there was Jack, and he's such a good boy, and he loves you so much, and I saw that you were happy ... happy enough ... I thought the two of you were strong enough to manage without. Not all families need children ... do they ...? You could've ... you might've not ... I honestly didn't think you needed to know."

I watched Mum as she spoke. She was wringing her hands together, and her eyes had a wide, frenzied quality about them. I wondered whether she had always been this unsettled and whether I had been blind, or if the subject had triggered something hidden deep inside that she had been striving to bury for as long as I could remember, perhaps longer. I struggled to understand her confused ramblings, but there was no missing the last revelation. My blood ran cold.

"What?" I asked.

"What?" she repeated.

"You just said you thought we could manage without

children. What did you mean by that? What have children got to do with it? What are you saying?" My mind rewound the conversation. "And before, you said Dad … You said Dad loves me and …"

Mum looked frantic. "You mean he didn't …? But you said he … I thought you knew …"

"Knew what, Mum? Knew what?" I couldn't bring myself to say it, to think it, but I felt as agitated as she looked.

Mum looked into the air as if she was searching, wringing her hands together even more furiously. I'm not sure if she was searching for the words to tell me the truth or if she was looking for another lie to cover it up. I wasn't sure whether I was more worried about her or angry with her at this moment, but I couldn't let it go.

"One thing at a time and no more lies, Mum," I said slowly. "At this point, I can handle a lot from you, but I cannot handle one more lie. First, you said Jack and I could manage without children. Tell me what that means. Tell me what it means."

Mum looked straight at me, and even though she still had the emanation of her emotions under a tight rein, she couldn't hide the anguish in her eyes. The next words came out almost as a whisper.

"Fluencers. You … we … we can't … we can only … Jack isn't … so you couldn't … you and Jack could never have children."

I had seen it coming, but hearing the words still sent me reeling.

"Jack and I could never have children because he's not a fluencer?" I said slowly, ensuring that I was absolutely clear.

Mum just nodded.

"Jack and I could never have children. We … and you've known this forever? You knew as a child? You knew you needed to find a fluencer to have a family. You had a choice, and you took that choice away from me when you decided to lie to me. And to Stephie. And you let me… you let Jack …

350

knowing ... knowing that we could never ... knowing that he could never ... and you were never going to tell us? You condemned me ... us ... him to a half life because ... what? Because your mum fell apart when her husband died? Lots of people struggle with grief. It's not a reason to ... to ... I might never have ... he could have ... I ..."

My voice had risen to fever pitch. I tried to bring it down, but I was crying and couldn't go on. I hadn't believed that anything that Mum could tell me would have made me feel more furious or hurt, but this was another level. With a moment to compose myself, I went on.

"We've talked about our future, Mum. We've talked about having a family. You knew it was what we wanted. Jack ... Jack could have ... with somebody else, he could have ... he's always wanted to be a dad, and if we'd known ... if I'd known ... What gave you the right, Mum? What gave you the right to take that choice away from him ... from Jack? He's a good man. He could have ... he should have ...it's cruel. You're cruel. That was cruel, Mum. You didn't think I had the right to know, to make my own decisions. You thought you had the right to control me without my consent. You thought you had the right to take the truth from me. But Jack? How could you?"

Tears were streaming down my face. I had come here knowing that my relationship with Jack was over, but to discover that so much of what I believed was based on a lie felt like torture. If I had known the truth, I could have prevented it ever getting to this point and I could have avoided the heartache that I was going to cause him tomorrow. To discover that Mum had known all along, had deliberately kept it from me, was almost more than I could take. I wanted to turn away, find a small hole and just curl up into a ball and cry, but we weren't finished yet.

Mum was holding her hands out, beseeching, but I didn't want to see it. She didn't deserve my comfort. I hung my head down low, thinking, seething, sobbing.

"Izzy, I'm sorry. I thought … I honestly thought it was better."

"Shush, Mum, please be quiet. I'm thinking."

But she didn't shush. She went on. "Look at me and your dad …"

My head snapped up again. "Look at you and my dad," I repeated slowly. "Yes, look at you. Look at me. Look at Stephanie. So, Dad ... you said you didn't want it, but you must have chosen to have it … to have us. Even that was a lie. You're still lying." My mind was churning, joining the dots. "So it wasn't just you. You weren't the only one lying to us all this time. Dad … no. That doesn't make sense. Dad isn't … he couldn't … you said … just before, you said that Dad was enough, like he wasn't … As soon as he told me, it made sense… about you, I mean. I could see it. I can see it. You're … but not Dad. Not Dad too. But he must be ..."

Mum responded with one quiet word. "No."

I stood up. I couldn't sit any longer. "No?" I repeated.

"No. That wasn't a lie. Your father isn't … he isn't …" Mum stopped again, seemingly unable to complete the sentence.

"He isn't?" I asked.

Mum just shook her head. Tears were streaming down her face too.

"He isn't what, Mum?"

She didn't respond.

"He isn't what?" I shouted. Still nothing. "Just say it!" I almost screamed.

She continued to shake her head.

"No, you don't have to answer that, do you? You've already told me. He isn't a fluencer, is he? I know he isn't. He couldn't be. He's too … Dad could never … he would never …" I sat back down heavily, the final cog grinding into place. "But if he isn't a fluencer, he can't be ..." I looked into Mum's eyes and saw the truth shining there. "He isn't my dad," I said quietly.

A stunned silence fell between us. Tears were still falling, but neither of us made a sound except for the raggedness of our breath. Mum didn't need to confirm it. I could see the truth. I had expected tears, I had expected anger, I had expected some sort of confession of betrayal and a reluctant explanation for Mum's behaviour, but I had never expected this. The silence stretched between us, but a roar set up inside my head. I felt like I had been sucked into a black hole where everything was backwards and inside out. Nothing made sense and nothing was real anymore. Everything was a lie. Dad wasn't my dad. Dad, who had made me feel loved every day for twenty-six years, whom I adored completely. It was too much to take. How was I supposed to deal with something like that?

"Does he know?" I asked in the end.

Mum shook her head. "He doesn't know anything … any of it. He's a good man."

That simple, honest statement caused me to see red, and I found myself shouting again. "I know he's a good man, Mum. He's a good man that you've been lying to for over thirty years. You've lied to everyone. You've cheated, you've lied, you've manipulated. You let him believe … he thinks … he thinks … we … everyone, Mum. You've lied to everyone! Our whole lives. It's all been a lie. Dad ..."

I faltered again, but the cogs were still turning. There was something that was still gnawing at me. I still hadn't quite got to the bottom of everything and probably never would, but a thought struck me that caused me to stumble backwards, tripping over my chair, which fell to the floor with an unnaturally loud clatter.

"Wait." I held out my hand as if I could physically block the direction of my thoughts. "No." I felt the colour drain from my cheeks as the thought took shape, a distorted, abhorrent shape. "You said … you were worried about … you said ..." I couldn't bring myself to utter the words. I took a deep, shuddering breath. "Nicholas Callahan. He's a … you said you went to him. You said he came to find me … you … he … no … he's not my … is he my …? He can't be." I almost didn't say it out loud, but not saying it didn't make it any less horrifying. "Nicholas Callahan cannot be my father!"

I thought that I was going to be sick. I doubled over. I couldn't breathe. In my panic, my chest became tight and I had to fight for each ragged breath. All that I could see were images of Scott's perfect face, his deep, fiery eyes and the way that I knew that nothing would ever be the same after our extraordinary kiss that morning, just a few short hours ago. I recalled the promises that we had made to each other, the way that he had looked at me, the way that he made my insides melt, and I had to force the images away. My stomach clenched, and I could feel the bile rising up through my throat. I sat on the floor, put my hands on my knees and dropped my head between my legs, trying to breathe.

"No."

It was spoken so softly that I wasn't sure if I'd even heard the word. I looked at Mum, who was staring back at me with sharp intent.

"No?" I asked.

"No. Nicholas Callahan is not your father."

The tightness in my chest eased very slightly. I stood up slowly, collected my chair from the floor and sat back down, hoping with every fibre of my being that this time she was telling the truth. The nausea was passing, but I still felt faint.

"Nicholas Callahan is not my father?"

"No."

We each took a moment to collect ourselves. In twenty-six years, I had never noticed that I couldn't read her emotions, but it was distinctly apparent to me now. In the space of the last few minutes, that insignificant void had become a vast abyss, and I despised it. It felt as if Mum and I had never shared a single honest exchange. I had no idea whether I could believe a word that she said. She was sitting very still and her face was unreadable, but she was looking at me, studying me, and I hated the fact that she could read my every emotion without giving anything away herself.

"If you're lying to me now ..." I began.

"Nicholas Callahan is not your father. I'm not lying to you ... but he did help me." I didn't fill the silence. I waited for her to continue. "Your dad and I ... I mean, Max ... I mean ..."

I didn't offer to help her to fill in that blank either. She deserved to flounder.

"We... he... he wanted a family. I knew we couldn't. I ... Nicholas has a reputation amongst ... he's a powerful man. He has a lot of influence." She laughed insecurely at the word, but at my sharp look, she carried on. "I went to Nicholas and asked if he could help. He found me a ... he arranged ... he arranged it all, and the ... and the doctor and ... he would never have ... I would never have ... Georgia ... he ..." She trailed off again.

"So, let me get this straight. Nicholas Callahan arranged some kind of a fluence sperm donation? In secret? This just keeps getting better. So, who is he? Who is my father?"

Mum studied the floor. The words came out faintly. "I don't know."

"You don't know? You don't know. Really, Mum? Really? Great. That's just great, Mum. Great. But you're sure that he, Nicholas, I mean, that he can't be?"

"No." She sounded certain. "I wouldn't ..."

I looked at her scathingly at that and she shook her head firmly. "He was already married to Georgia. They had Daniel and she was pregnant again, and they were so in love. If you ... you'll see ... he would never have done anything to jeopardise that. You could see it in him. The love. The bond. No. He's not your father."

"But he would know who is," I said. It wasn't even really a question. I had no idea if I even wanted to know.

"I suppose so, yes. He would be the only one who would."

"You suppose so. You suppose so. Don't try to tell me you were never curious."

"No, I ... I didn't want to know. I didn't want anything to do with it ... with him. I was married to your ... to Dad, and he was enough. I couldn't risk ... I didn't want it."

"So, the donor, my father. Does he know that he has children? Does he know about me and Stephanie? Tell me we're sisters, Mum. Tell me we have the same father."

"Yes, you're sisters. He got two. I asked for ... we wanted ... I don't know how Nicholas did it. I didn't ask. I don't know if the donor knows. I didn't want to know him. I don't want to. I don't want anything to do with any of it."

As I studied my mother, trying to comprehend this latest bombshell, it struck me that she looked and sounded like a petulant child. She had always seemed a little eccentric, a loner. We always indulged her, and her oddities kept the other allotment keepers and local residents entertained, but this was the first time that I questioned whether there might be more to it. This wasn't normal, none of it. It wasn't the behaviour of a sane, reasonable person, and she didn't seem to recognise just how harmful her actions had been. Perhaps she had been damaged by the death of her father and breakdown of her family, but I was too invested in the fallout to feel sorry for her. This was personal, and I wasn't inclined to be sympathetic or forgiving.

"But you can't decide that, Mum." I spoke deliberately, clearly. "You can't just decide to be someone you're not. Surely you can see that? And if you really meant it, you shouldn't have ... not having children was part of the life you chose. You just wanted everything. Shun your ability, turn away from people like you, but go to them when you need something, when you want something. And then have children and lie to them, to everyone that matters, every day. It's so wrong, Mum. It's so messed up. It's ... is this why you're so ... why you ... why you come down here and hide amongst your plants? You hide away from the real world in case you meet someone, in case you feel something … in case you let something slip and we find out the truth.

"You knew you would … could … never truly be properly in love with someone without it. You chose to live half a life, to not experience what you could have had because you were scared. But then you chose that life for me … for us, and that wasn't your choice to make. You were scared to live in case you got hurt. Then you chose to cheat and steal and manipulate to get what you wanted and then you lied and lied and controlled and lied.

"Oh, shit. You did it to me and Stephie, didn't you? To stop us … you did! We would have … we could have … shit, Mum, you've been stopping me and Stephie learning together … being … manipulating us. I can't believe this is happening … that you've been doing it to us all for so long. You're a coward, Mum. You're a coward and a liar and I … I don't … I can't …"

I was frightened that if I finished that sentence, if I really told her how I felt, there might be no going back. Our relationship might not ever recover, and I didn't want to lose my mum. There was already a chance that the rift created by all the lies was irreparable, but I didn't want to let my emotions get the better of me and say something that I would regret. I knew that she could sense my emotions, but that doesn't mean that hurtful words wouldn't have caused her pain. I looked at the floor, gathering my composure. Neither of us spoke.

I felt numb. I couldn't wrap my head around it all. I had known that this conversation was going to be difficult, but the scope and the depth of the lies was staggering. The idea of Mum lying to me for all of these years was always going to test our love, but the addition of the impact that her lies would have on Stephanie, Dad and Jack massively exacerbated the burden that I now had to bear.

When I reflected on my life, it was so obvious that Mum's behaviour and attitude towards my gift had always been strange. It wouldn't have been the normal reaction of a mother to tell her daughter to ignore and hide a huge aspect of herself. If she didn't understand, a normal mother, a loving, nurturing mother, would have helped me to find answers. She would have listened and explored it with me. The more I learned, the more that I realised that the lies were only a small part of the control and manipulation that Mum had been practising on her entire family every day. It was horrifying.

I thought about Jack. I wouldn't be able to tell him the whole truth. It wouldn't be of any benefit to him to know. I didn't know what I was going to say, but learning that our relationship had always been doomed to dissatisfaction and infertility and that Mum had kept this from us, letting us believe that we had a normal chance at a happy future with a family, seemed unnecessarily cruel. I thought about Stephanie too, of how she would also struggle with the truth. Of course, I could now see that even my relationship with my own sister had been manipulated in ways that I had never imagined. It couldn't be a coincidence that we'd never shared the wonder of our gift with each other. We shared everything else. I thought about this Christmas and remembered my desire to talk to Stephanie about my encounter with Scott and the feelings that it had left me with. Mum had come downstairs at that moment and the desire to share was gone, replaced by a drowsy calm and acceptance. It was so obvious now. We had all been blinded by our love and our trust. Our good natures had been abused by the one person that none of us would ever have suspected.

I thought about Dad, the only dad that I had ever known and the kindest, gentlest man alive. His marriage was a lie. He didn't know who his wife really was, and his children weren't his children. I wanted to weep for him. I wondered what learning the truth would do to him. I didn't go so far as to wonder whether or not I would tell him or if I would force Mum to come clean. I was too worked up to make those kinds of decisions right now, and it could wait. I did ponder how many millions of times she must have fluenced him over the years to prevent him discovering the truth. My head was swimming.

Mum's voice broke into my thoughts. She had obviously been thinking too.

"So, if it wasn't Nicholas," she said slowly, "it must have been one of the boys. Daniel?" She paused for a moment.

I didn't answer but couldn't prevent a tiny sense of aversion at the mention of his name.

"Or Scott?" she finished the question. I still didn't speak. I desperately didn't want to give her any more information, but she was watching me closely, she knew me better than anyone, and she could read my emotions. I didn't stand a chance.

"Scott. Right."

"Don't do that, Mum. You have no right."

"I can't help it, and no matter what you think of me right now, I'm still your mum, I still love you, and I worry about you. And I love your dad. And Stephie."

"Love us? Worry about us? I don't think I can talk to you anymore right now, Mum. I can't even look at you."

"How far's it gone?" Mum carried on as if I hadn't spoken. "With Scott, I mean?"

"What's wrong with you?" I asked. "You're not normal. As if I would tell you anything now, after what I've just found out. You think we're going to have a heart-to-heart?"

"OK. I understand that you're upset."

"Upset? Mum, seriously? Upset doesn't cover it."

"But just let me say this …"

"No. Don't say anything. I can't … Me? Steph? Dad? Jack? And now Scott too? I don't want to hear anything you have to say. I can't trust anything you have to say. I have to go, Mum, before I say something we might both regret."

"Be careful." Mum continued to speak as if she was unaware of my outburst and the level of my distress, which was ironic because I knew that she was very much aware of my feelings. That was the problem. I started to walk away, out of the allotment towards my car. I couldn't stand to be there a second longer. I didn't want to listen to another word, but I couldn't help hearing the warning that she called after me as I stormed across the field.

"The closer you get, the harder it will be to leave. If you let him in, you won't be able to get him out. The Callahans are dangerous. Please, Isabel. Please be careful."

Chapter 20

I pulled out of the car park in a hurry, desperate to put some space between Mum and me. My mind was spinning, and I could hardly see for the tears streaming down my face. I turned onto the main road at speed with my head down and my left hand outstretched, rummaging through the glove box for a tissue to staunch the flow. I felt a lurch, glanced up and screamed in alarm as I caught the car swerving off the road onto the grass verge. I sat up instantly, jerking the wheel back to the right and narrowly avoiding slamming headlong into a tree in an accident that I would never have survived. I managed to straighten the car up again just in time to avoid hitting another car speeding past on the other side of the road, but my heart was in my mouth and my whole body was trembling as I realised how close I had just come to writing myself off. Nothing was worth that. Both hands back on the wheel and facing forwards, I regained full control of the car and tried to focus on the road. My head was full of all of the things that I had just heard, things that could never be unheard.

It was a short journey to the cottage and a route that I had driven countless times before, but when I found myself back on the drive, staring at my home, I couldn't recall a single moment of it. I had been so lost in my thoughts and distracted by trying to make sense of everything that I had driven on autopilot, unaware of speed, direction or my surroundings. I was lucky to have made it home in one piece. I sat on the drive, looking at my front door, but I couldn't get out of the car. I didn't want to walk back into that house alone. I didn't want to be greeted by silence and spend the evening with my erratic thoughts for company, waiting for Jack to come home tomorrow so that I could break his heart.

This house had once belonged to my grandma and it was now my home, but I knew almost nothing about the life of my mother's mother. The cottage had remained empty for a long time before I moved in after graduating from university. I didn't even know if Mum had been born in the cottage or if she had lived there in her youth. Grandma had left it jointly to Stephanie and me in her will, which was a complete surprise. Stephanie was already bound on a lifetime of travel and adventure, so we agreed that I should move in and we would work out the details later. It was a small two-bedroomed cottage full of character, and I had suggested that we take a room each, but Stephanie decided that she would keep her room at Mum and Dad's and that this place would become mine alone. I couldn't help wondering now whether it was really Stephanie that had come to this conclusion or whether Mum had somehow manipulated the two of us in order to keep us apart and oblivious to her lies.

This train of thought led to so many other depressing and damaging images: all of the times that Mum had encouraged Stephanie to travel abroad and how much she had supported my relationship with Jack and the idea of him moving into the cottage with me. I thought again about Jack, about Stephanie, about my dad. I thought about our family and all of the love and the good times that we had shared, and I wanted to rewind the clock back to before I knew the truth. There were so many unanswered questions, but mostly there was sorrow and anger, and in my anger at Mum, all of my memories became lies in my bruised mind. All of the times that I had been happy here with Jack were based on dishonesty. All of the family get-togethers, all of the meals, all of the games, all of the good times suddenly felt like they hadn't really counted because they were all based on this colossal deceit. It seemed like nothing I knew was real anymore, and now that I knew the truth, at some point I would have to decide what I was going to do with it.

I couldn't sit on the drive forever. I had to go inside, I had to sort myself out, and I had to wait for Jack to come home tomorrow. I glanced at my phone; it was only lunchtime, but I felt totally drained. It had been extremely late by the time I got settled at the cabin last night, and my sleep had been fitful and littered with intense dreams. On top of a lack of sleep, there was the strain of everything that had happened, the emotional toll of what had just taken place with my mum and the hollow pit in my stomach over what I was about to do to Jack.

I went inside, made myself a cup of tea and sat on the settee, willing my mind to settle down and give me some peace. I don't know how long I sat there, but I must have fallen asleep because when my phone rang about an hour later, it woke me with a start. It was Jack.

"Hello?"

"Hi, baby. How are you? Did you have a good night last night? I just thought I'd check in."

"Hi, Jack, I'm ok … I mean … we did but … not really, I … no, I … no, not really."

"Izzy? What is it? What's wrong?" He was instantly concerned.

"I … I'm OK. I just …" I couldn't keep my voice steady, and I couldn't talk to him without crying. There's no way that I could have made him think that everything was all right until tomorrow. I was a mess and I needed to get it done, for both of our sakes. If I waited until he returned home tomorrow, he would only have one night to process what had happened before going back to work. It would be kinder to do it today, and I didn't want to lie to him. I didn't want any more lies.

"What's the matter, Izzy?"

"I … I need to talk to you. Not on the phone. I … we need to talk. Can you come home?" My voice wavered. There was a short silence. *We need to talk* was still hanging in the air.

"What's happened, Izzy? What's wrong? I … you need to tell me."

"Please, Jack. Can you come home now? We'll talk when you're home."

"Yes. Of course I can." Jack's voice was quiet, flat. "They

don't need me here. I'll just get my stuff and I'll leave. I'll be back in less than an hour."

"OK. I'll be here. See you in a bit."

"See you soon Izzy. I … I … I'll see you soon."

"Bye."

"Bye."

I hung up and burst into tears. He didn't say *I love you.* We didn't say *I love you.* He heard the tears in my voice and that awful sentence, *we need to talk,* and he already knew that something was very wrong. It didn't take a genius to work it out. There were hardly any conversations that we wouldn't have had over the phone. I would have rung to tell him if I had been poorly or injured, if I had fallen out with Donna or something had happened at the house or with Josh or work. There was only one conversation that a couple can't have over the phone, only one thing that even halfway decent human beings won't do by phone or by text. He was packing his bag at his brother's house, packing his bag to come home to hear me break his heart. I felt like a piece of shit.

I must have checked my phone a hundred times over the next hour. I checked it again: 3.04, one minute since I last checked and nearly an hour since I had hung up the phone. He would be here any minute. I usually had a cup of tea waiting for him when he arrived home. I would normally put the kettle on when I heard his car on the drive, but I had considered it carefully and I had decided that this wasn't a cup of tea kind of conversation, and so I sat on the settee doing nothing, and I waited. After putting the phone down, I had packed an overnight bag for myself so that I could get out of the house and allow him some space if that's what he needed, but I didn't know if that was right or wrong. I didn't know anything. I lit up my phone screen again: 3.05.

I could have put the television on. I could have listened to the radio. I could have done some cleaning or some laundry, but I didn't. I didn't do any of these things because I was too jittery, too preoccupied. Nothing would take my mind off what I was about to do, the conversation that I was about to have, and so I sat and I waited. I still hadn't got any idea about just exactly what I was going to say or how I was going to say it. My mind was a jumbled mess of emotions and anxiety. I was counting on the vain hope that when I saw him, everything would become clear and I would instantly know how to get it right.

The next few minutes dragged on for hours while I waited impatiently, but at last I heard his car on the drive. I glanced at my phone: 3.09, as good a time as any. I stood up, walked across the room and sat back down again on a single armchair. It had just occurred to me that I couldn't risk him sitting cosily by my side and that standing to greet him would put us at risk of familiar physical contact, so I sat on the chair and anticipated his entrance with dread. The front door handle creaked and the door opened and closed with its familiar report.

Jack didn't say anything when he walked through the door — no cheerful greeting, no announcement of his arrival. I didn't say anything either. I heard him drop his bag at the bottom of the stairs and I held my breath until he entered the room. I waited for him to come to me, and he came, looking like a man on death row. Jack Somers didn't have a bad or a miserable bone in his body. He was a beautiful person, inside and out, his smile could light up a room, and his ceaseless positivity was usually irrepressibly infectious. Not today however, not now. I didn't need reminding of all of Jack's wonderful qualities, and my own anguish could not be allayed. I let out my breath on a mournful sigh.

Jack stood in the doorway and looked at me. He took in the pallor of my face and the solemnity of my expression. He remained standing.

"What's wrong?" He looked at me and I looked back at him. I didn't answer straight away, but tears sprang spontaneously into my eyes. I think that in that moment, that barely perceptible beat of time, when I didn't immediately ease his fear, he already knew. I absorbed his terror. I had promised myself that I wouldn't cry, but when his eyes swam with tears in response to my own, it was like the world had stopped turning for a fraction of a second, and a single tear spilled from my eye and trickled slowly down my cheek.

"Izzy?" he asked.

"Sit down, Jack," I whispered, not trusting my own voice and gesturing to the chair on the other side of the room.

"Izzy?" he asked again more passionately, not moving, glued to the spot.

"Please Jack," I begged him. "Sit down so we can talk."

"I don't want to sit down," he said coolly.

"Please?" I begged him.

Jack stumbled across the room. He had to hold onto the arm of the chair to stop himself from falling, but he sat down and then looked at me with unconcealed terror. I could see him trembling, and his bewildered shock and fear were attacking my mind, making it difficult to keep my focus. The feeling of nausea was strong, and I concentrated on what Scott had told me before I left this morning. In order to ensure that I only had my own emotions to deal with in a difficult situation, I must concentrate on that part of me deep inside, my fluence, and hold onto it with my mind, protect it, keep it safe.

Jack's eyes were wide open. He tried to cut me off before I had even begun.

"Izzy," he croaked. "Whatever's happened … whatever you're feeling … whatever I've done, we can work it out together, can't we? Whatever it is … just talk to me and we can work it out."

I shook my head. The tears had started rolling down my cheeks.

"Izzy? Don't cry, Izzy. It's OK."

"No," I said quietly. "No, Jack. Don't do that. Don't be nice to me. You haven't done anything wrong, but it's not OK, and we can't work it out. I'm so sorry."

"No," he said. "You don't mean that. You can't mean that. Don't say that." Tears were now streaming down his face too. He knew that this was real. We looked at each other across the room and cried silently together. The pain in my chest was strong and tight. It felt like someone was squeezing my heart in a vice, strangling it, choking it. Concentrating on my own core, my own essence, was of no real help because in breaking Jack's heart, in so many ways, my heart was breaking too.

"Jack," I started, but he interrupted me before I could say any more.

"No," he said. "You don't have to say it. I don't want to hear it. Please."

"I do have to say it, Jack. I have to say it and you have to hear it. I'm so sorry Jack. I'm so sorry but I … I just … I don't … I can't be with you anymore. It's over, Jack. I'm sorry, but it's over. We're over."

I took a deep, shuddering breath in and blew it back out. I had done it. I had said it. Now I just had to keep myself under control. I was the one that was choosing this. I was doing this for me. Jack was the one that it was happening to. I had to stay calm and allow him to react however he chose, however he needed to react. I had to let him have this moment. I couldn't make it about me.

He didn't say anything for a few seconds. He seemed to be concentrating on getting his breath in and out, but the tears were still falling. After a while, he seemed to find some inner composure. He nodded.

"Right," he said. There was silence again. I waited for the questions and the accusations or recriminations, but they didn't come. I didn't know what to do. The silence stretched on.

"Right?" I repeated. "Don't you want to talk about it? Don't you want to ask me anything?"

Jack considered that for a moment and shook his head.

"No," he said. "I know you, Izzy. You haven't made this

decision lightly, and you've made it firmly. If there was room for discussion … room for changing your mind, you wouldn't be here … like this. We would have … you would have… there's no going back, and I won't beg. I don't need to know why. I don't think I want to. I've seen it. I've watched you this last few months. Something's changed in you. You've not been … you've been …" His voice cracked. "I couldn't bear to hear you tell me you don't love me anymore or that you've met somebody else." He looked at me and he smiled softly through the tears. "You know how much I love you, baby. I've only ever wanted to make you happy. If I can't, if I don't …" He shrugged in defeat.

"Oh, Jack, I know, and I'm sorry. I'm so, so sorry."

"I know you are, baby. I know you are."

He didn't attempt to hide the pain in his heart or the tears on his face, but he took a few deep breaths and stood up slowly. He looked around the room in a daze and came back to me. He sighed deeply. "I'll go and get a few things and head back to Stu's. We can sort the rest out another time." He walked to the door.

"Jack?" I asked in a panic. "Is that it? Are you going? Now? Don't you want to talk about … well, about … about it? I packed a bag so I could go. You can stay here tonight … if you like."

He gave a short, low laugh. "Why would I want to do that?" he asked. "This is your place, our place. There's nothing here for me without you. You're everywhere. Your things, your clothes, your smell. And no, of course I don't want to talk about it. There's nothing to say. Maybe in a few days but not now. I can't … not without …" He shrugged, turned his back on me and walked out of the door slowly, as if his feet were weighed down by the sorrow of his heart. I heard him pick up his bag and head up the stairs.

I sat still, rooted to the spot in silence, a strange kind of calm washing over me. I was stunned. I was in shock. I had done it. He hadn't shouted, he hadn't begged. He had just accepted it and walked away, vacant but composed. This wasn't what I had expected. I don't know what I'd expected but it wasn't this. This was horrible. This was empty, hollow. My breath caught in my throat, and I let out a strangled cry. It felt like a little piece of my heart had been scooped roughly away, leaving a sore, jagged gouge that hurt when I breathed. I let the tears fall for a moment and then wiped them away. If Jack could retain his composure, then the least that I could do was keep mine for him. I owed him that. I would make sure that I let him choose the tone. I would follow his lead.

I sat in the chair and listened to the muted noises coming from upstairs. I pictured him collecting his things and looking around at the house that he had briefly called home. I heard him in the bathroom and then in the bedroom again. I heard drawers open and close and then silence. He was no longer moving. He had stopped. I sat there and listened, but there was no sound for some time. When I checked my phone again, the time on the display read 3.31, twenty-two minutes since he had arrived home and about fifteen minutes since he had gone upstairs.

I tiptoed out into the hall and listened intently. Nothing. I took hold of the bannister, pulled myself onto the first step and then quietly crept up to the landing. Our bedroom door was open, and Jack was sitting on the floor, leaning against the bed. His head was in his hands and his whole body was shaking. He wasn't making a sound, but he was sobbing silently. His heart was breaking. Of course he wasn't calm. Of course he wasn't composed. He had wanted to be. He hadn't wanted me to see him fall apart, but he was without doubt falling apart in front of my eyes. He had tried to make this as easy for me as he could because he knew me and he loved me and he didn't want it to hurt me any more than it had to, but by being so good, by protecting me from the pain, he just reminded me what kind of a person he was, what I was losing, what I was throwing away.

I ran to him and sank to my knees. "Jack," I soothed. "Oh,

Jack, Jack." He looked up with tear-filled eyes and he grabbed my hand hard.

"Izzy," he pleaded. "Izzy, don't do this. Whatever it is. Whatever I've done. However it's changed … I love you. I'll do anything for you. Please, baby, please. I'll do whatever I need to do, but please, Izzy, please."

"Oh, Jack." I didn't know what to say. There was nothing that I could say that could make this any easier.

"I know I said I wouldn't beg, but I've changed my mind. I thought I could do it. I thought I could stay strong and walk away with my pride intact, but I can't, and my pride doesn't matter."

"Oh, Jack." I was stroking his hair now, soothing him like a baby. "You'll be fine. You don't need me. You'll find … I'm so sorry I'm doing this to you, but there's nothing you can do. There's nothing you can say. It has to be this way. I'm sorry."

He nodded and took a few long, shuddering breaths. I felt so helpless kneeling there on the floor by his side. I wanted to give him something to cling on to, but I couldn't. I had nothing to give. I tried to explain.

"You deserve more than this, Jack. More than I can give you. It's changed for me and I can't … I can't pretend, and it's not fair on you. You deserve someone who can give you everything. It's over, Jack. It has to be."

"I know. I do already know that. I meant what I said downstairs. I know you wouldn't … not if you weren't sure, but I just … I couldn't help it. I had to … I have to … when I came into our room and started packing my things …" He gestured to the room hopelessly.

"I know," I said. "I know."

I stopped stroking him, but he didn't let go of my hand. It was an anchor point, and as long as he held it, he didn't have to move, he didn't have to leave, this didn't have to be real. After a few minutes, he seemed to have himself back under control. He looked up, composed again.

"Can I …? Can we …? Do you think I could stay? Could we stay together …? Just for tonight? Could we pretend this isn't real …? Just for tonight? I just want to hold you in my arms one more time. Spend the night holding you … one more time. I'll leave in the morning and it can be real then, but do you think …?

"Oh, Jack, no," I was quick to cut off this train of thought. "Of course not. Oh, Jack, it just wouldn't be right. We can't pretend. It wouldn't be fair on either of us. It would be a lie and we'd both know it, and you'd regret it. We'd both … no, Jack. We can't. It's over. It has to be over tonight. It just has to be."

Jack nodded. "Of course. I just thought … well, I just … no, of course you're right." He stopped talking. I wasn't sure if he had finished, but I let the silence hang between us until he spoke again. "It's just that if I'd've known … If I'd've had any idea … the last time I kissed you … really kissed you … I don't even know when it was. I can't remember it." He sounded panicky, confused. It was hard to see, hard to hear. "If I'd known it was going to be the last time, I would've made it count. I would've made everything count. I …" He looked at me with those wet, pain-filled eyes.

"Shush, Jack, shush. Please." I couldn't bear to hear the pain in his voice and see the desperation in his eyes. "Please don't torture yourself like that. I know how … it's horrible, but you will ... with time you'll … we'll … people …"

Jack seemed to recover himself then. He nodded and he stood, looking around for his things. "I know," he said. "People do, don't they? Move on, I mean. They have to."

I nodded. "I'll go back downstairs. There's no hurry. Just come down when you're ready," I left him there, composed but alone.

Back downstairs, I allowed myself a moment of self-loathing and reproach. I kept it quiet and brief, but I was struggling to contend with the crippling agony that was assailing me from Jack's grief. I cried bitterly but fleetingly

371

and then refocused on my essence and my breathing, like Scott had said. I had known that this would be painful. I had known that Jack's heart would break, but in the long run, this was the right thing for everyone. I couldn't and wouldn't condemn Jack to a life without the possibility of a family or sentence him to a life shared with someone incapable of loving him as he deserved to be loved.

Although it was one of the most harrowing things that I had ever had to do, the things that I had learned about myself over the last few months, and more particularly in the last twenty-four hours, had to be explored, and I had to give myself the opportunity to really feel, to really love and be loved in a way that I had never dreamed possible, and that was beyond the bounds of reality as long as I remained with Jack.

Jack would suffer, but in time he would get over this heartache and he would fall in love again. Humans have a great capacity to recover from loss. They have to. He would find somebody worthy of his adulation and somebody who could love him back with every fibre of their being. He would find somebody who could give him a family and the fulfilled life that he deserved. If I stayed now because of the residual love that I still felt for Jack or because of the love that he felt for me, we would be destined to fall apart in the end, and I couldn't allow our relationship to become loveless, stale and resentful. This was the way that it had to be.

When I heard Jack coming down the stairs, I prepared myself for an excruciating goodbye. I controlled my breathing. I focused on the inner strength that I had to possess for us both. Jack approached me purposefully and stopped a few feet away. He had washed his face and looked fresher and more composed. His breathing was regular and slow. He kept his voice even.

"I know I said I didn't want to know, but I have to ask. Not to … I just need to know. Why, Izzy? Why? What is it that's changed? Please explain it so I don't go insane guessing because I know you loved me."

He was right. I owed him an explanation. I had expected the question and had agonised over my reply. The whole truth was far too complicated and hurtful and would be impossible for him to understand. I didn't need to hurt him any more than was necessary, but I also didn't want to lie to him after ten years of love and honesty. He didn't deserve that, and I had to accept the role that I had given myself. There was no doubt that I was the bad guy here. I had to own it.

"I never … of course I loved you, but I … I've realised that you … it … this … it isn't enough for me. I'm so sorry Jack, but I need something else, something more, and once you realise that, you can't carry on, can you? You can't. It would be like living a lie, and it wouldn't be fair on either of us. My feelings for you … I haven't stopped loving you, but I've stopped loving you enough. I've stopped loving you the right way. You deserve more. You deserve someone who can give you what you've given me. Someone who can give you everything, and that's not me. It can't be. I can't. I'm sorry.

"I feel like we've become best friends … I mean, we've always been best friends, but sometimes … now, when I look at you, that's what I see. My best friend and not my … I need … you need … I think I … I think you'll find something … someone who's more … a passion that's missing…"

Jack nodded thoughtfully. "I've always known … well, we've always been … you've always been … I've always known that we're unbalanced. Let's face it, I practically had to beg you to be my girl, but I've always treasured what you gave me, and I've never asked for more. Haven't I always been there for you? Haven't I always given you space when you needed it and let you cry on my shoulder at night? Haven't I let you have your strange ways? Not questioned all the time you want to be alone? Haven't I always loved you? Don't dress it up as if you're doing me a favour here. This isn't about what I want or what I deserve, but you're right about one thing: once you know, you can't go back. No matter how much I love you, no matter how hard this'll be, we could never go back now, not after hearing those words. We're over. It's over. I hope ... I hope one day we can learn to be friends again. We've always been ... you've been everything to me, but I'm fairly certain that it won't be one day soon. This hurts. It hurts too much, and it won't stop hurting anytime soon. I don't know when ... I don't know if ..."

I had to blink hard to force back the tears. He was right about everything. He had every right to be angry and feel hurt by me. We had planned a future together and I was destroying it. He had always been there for me. He had always loved me. I never meant to hurt him like this, but that didn't mean anything. He didn't deserve it, and it was horrible.

"You're right," I said. "You don't deserve this."

"Stop telling me what I do or don't deserve!" he shouted.

"I'm sorry," I said.

"No, I'm sorry," he apologised unnecessarily. "I shouldn't shout. Or maybe I should. I suppose I can do whatever I like, but I don't want to shout at you. I don't want to feel angry, but I do. I feel angry, I feel hurt, I feel confused. I should just go, but I don't want to. Once I walk out of the door, that's it, isn't it? I mean, that's really, actually it? You're my best friend, Iz. I thought we'd be together forever. I thought you ... I thought ... oh, for goodness sake, just get a grip and go," he told himself in frustration, but he still made no move towards the door.

I took a step towards him, my arms going out in front of me in invitation. I didn't know what the etiquette was during a breakup, but I didn't care. What I wanted right now, what I needed and what I thought that Jack needed too, was a hug, pure and simple, a physical comfort and release. I took another hesitant step. I wouldn't push it if he didn't want this, but he stumbled blindly forwards to meet me and we came together with force and threw our arms tightly around each other.

It was a painful embrace, an embrace that marked the end of something beautiful. I buried my head in his chest, and he clung to me for dear life. I desperately wanted to impress upon him how important he had been to me, and he just didn't want it to end. He buried his face in my neck and breathed me in one more time. It wasn't a denial of the truth but a reminder for us both that we had been each other's first and only loves until now. I could feel Jack's grief all around me, and for a moment I wished that I could harness the power that I held inside to ease his pain, but the torment that he felt was a natural, honest part of the awful process of ending a relationship, and instead I welcomed his pain, fuelled it with my own and allowed us both this moment of agony and relief.

At last I pulled my head away slightly and whispered, "I'm so sorry, Jack. I'm so sorry." And Jack looked down at me with tears swimming in his eyes.

"Oh, Izzy," he gasped, and he pulled himself away from me roughly. He grabbed his bags from the bottom of the stairs, rushed to the front door, jerked it open and ran out of it without looking back. I watched him leave and heard his strangled sob as the front door closed behind him. He had gone. It was over.

I listened to the sound of his car starting and moving off the drive, and then I sank to my knees and I cried. I cried for myself, and I cried out the weight of the sadness and heartbreak that I had absorbed from Jack. It was an outpouring of emotion for the end of something that I would never have again. Jack would always be my first love. The memories of everything that we shared and all that we had learned about ourselves and about each other together would stay with me forever, and I hoped fervently that one day, Jack would be able to look back on our relationship and remember it fondly too, without the agony that came at the end.

I let myself cry until I was spent. I wasn't wallowing in self-pity, but I needed to release the surplus emotions, and it was normal to regret an ending, even if it was my choice. I knew that I had done the right thing and that by ending my relationship with Jack, I was giving myself the chance to live the life that I was destined to live and that I had been denied until now. I had a power inside me that I needed to harness and explore, and Jack would have to grieve until it wasn't so hard anymore, but he would love again. He would find someone, they would be blissfully happy, and he would be a husband and a father, I had no doubts.

Tonight I would be sad. Tonight I would mourn the loss of a huge, meaningful chapter of my life. Tomorrow I would begin to pick up the pieces and allow myself to dream of possibilities and plan my future. I wasn't naive enough to imagine that my next adventure was going to be all plain sailing, magic and unicorns, but despite the pain and the sadness, I already felt the lifting of a pressure and a cautious excitement that I had no doubt would grow with time.

Jack would find someone who loved him the way he deserved, who didn't need his love to ignite their own. I had convinced myself that what Jack and I shared was enough, but it never had been, not really. I had always thought that I needed to be kept safe, that I couldn't afford to let passion into my life, that it was dangerous because I couldn't control my emotions, but for the first time, I hoped that maybe that wasn't true. Jack had kept me safe, and I would forever be grateful to him for that, but it was time that I freed the hidden parts of my soul and gave myself up to all that life as a fluencer had to offer. After all, that was what I was now, that was what I was born to become. I breathed a long, deep sigh, and I made myself a cup of tea.

Chapter 21

On Sunday morning I woke up in my bed alone. It felt wrong. It wasn't really being alone in my bed that felt wrong. There were plenty of nights that Jack had stayed away, but it was the first time that I had woken up in my bed alone and he wasn't coming back. I felt his absence and I missed him. I worried about him. I wondered if he had slept, how he was feeling, what he had told Stu and what Stu must think of me. I wondered when I would stop thinking about Jack and worrying about Jack and when the ache in my heart and the hole in my life would mend.

It was a relief to me that he had somewhere to go, someone to look out for him who would always be on his side. Jack would be all right at Stu's house. He had the space and actually lived closer to the hospital than we did. He would look after his little brother. They were close. Stu and I had never really been friends. He was a few years above us at school and we didn't mix with the same people, but we had always got on pretty well. I suppose I had lost that too. There were probably a lot of things that I hadn't considered that I had lost in losing Jack, like Jack's mum and dad. That thought struck me like a slap to the face. Lauren and Des had been like second parents to me. I had gone round to their house for dinner at least once a week since I was about ten. They had taken me on family holidays and treated me like one of their own. It had always felt like they were my family too, but they weren't anymore. So much had changed.

Jack hadn't lived with me at the cottage for long, but we had made a real effort to make it feel as much like his home as mine. Unfortunately, that now meant that his things were everywhere. I went downstairs to make a cup of tea, and that shiny black kettle seemed to be glaring at me. I never liked that kettle. It didn't go with any of my things or match the character of the cottage, but it was Jack's, and having shiny new things had made him happy.

As I pottered around the house, listening to the oddly strange silence of Jack's absence, in some ways my heart felt lighter than it had done for a long time. There was a deep sadness for what I had lost and an even deeper sympathy for Jack, but there were reasons that I had made this decision, and I didn't doubt that it had been the right thing to do. It had been the right thing since I met Scott in the cinema bar back in October, when the thing inside my mind had roared to life. Something had changed in me that night and it could never be unchanged. Jack and I had never had the perfect relationship that I had liked to believe while I was keeping intrinsic parts of my identity a secret from him and spending hours on my bench at the lake, avoiding going home because his presence was not what I required. I don't know why I had thought that it was all right to live like that. I think it's because I viewed my ability as something that was wrong with me, something that I should turn away from and that I should keep from everyone else, all of the *normal* people in my life, even Jack.

That night at Vestige, something extraordinary had happened. Something passed between Scott and me that was special, magical, and from that moment on, my relationship with Jack was over. It was doomed to fail because I could never go back, I could never unlive that experience. I could never not be me. Something inside me had been unlocked, and at that point, it was only a matter of time.

I could feel it now. Ever since that night, my fluence had been alive. I was still not entirely sure what that meant, but I knew that it was thrilling. It was not something to hide or run away from, and I needed people in my life who could help me learn about who I was and who I could be. I had potential that I had not even skimmed the surface of, and my life, my future, could be exciting.

That second encounter with Scott at the lake had been so many things — unbelievable, arousing, terrifying all at once — and the memory of it still brought heat to my core and a blush to my cheeks. I wanted the opportunity to learn, to understand what had passed between us, and that was what I had given myself. I had lived with that memory of Scott and the things that he did to my mind for months, and it made my life, the one that I was trying to live, the one with Jack, where I hid from who I was, a lie.

Perhaps I thought that it was all right to live a lie because of what I had been taught as a child. My mum, who, as it turns out, knew exactly what I was going through and who should have helped me to understand, had instead made me feel like I was wrong, that something inside me was broken and that I should hide it, shun it and keep it out of my life. I had now discovered that they were her issues, not mine, and perhaps, if I had been armed with all of the information from the start, I would have made different, better choices. She had not given me that option, and I wasn't sure if I could ever forgive her for that.

I had loved Jack, and even if that love had been borne out of his love for me, it hadn't always been a lie. I had loved him, but things had changed, and I had a chance now, a chance to discover what I could do and who I could be. Scott was a part of that chance, part of my new life, and although I hated myself for what I had done to Jack, it was the right thing, for all of us.

I would have gone insane trying to hide such a huge part of myself for the rest of my life. We would never have been able to have children, and I would have condemned both of us to a half life. That is not the way to live; it is a route to unhappiness, to resentment. We are on this earth for such a short time. We must grab hold of what this life has to offer and live our best life. For me, that best life was not a future with Jack, and for Jack, it was not with me. That time was over, and I felt, in some ways, calmer for that. I didn't have to hide anymore, not from myself and not from Scott. Scott had set me free, and there was excitement and endless possibility in my future.

I had asked Scott not to contact me after I left him yesterday morning. I didn't want the distraction, and I couldn't risk him interrupting things with Mum or with Jack. A lot had happened since then, and I knew that he would be thinking about me. He had been on my mind every day for the last three months, and I suspect that after the things that had passed between us, I had been on his too.

I wanted to talk to him. He was the one person who might be able to comprehend some of what I was going through. I also longed to hear his voice. The future could begin today. I smiled. I picked up my phone. I hadn't even saved his number yet, but it was on my recent calls list and I saved it now. Even that felt good. He answered on the second ring.

"Belle."

With that one word, he managed to convey everything that I needed to hear. He was there, just like I knew that he would be. He sounded happy to receive my call. He sounded anxious and protective and intense. He sounded like Scott, *my Scott*, the thing inside my head purred. I was suddenly lost for words. There was no way to sum up the traumas of yesterday or the relief that I felt upon hearing his voice. I became emotional. I was choked up and I hesitated.

"Hi," I managed in the end.

"How are you?" he asked gently. "How did it go?"

"Yesterday turned out to be pretty eventful," I told him. "It was a tough one."

"Your mum?"

"Mm-hmm. And Jack."

"Jack too?" He hadn't expected me to see Jack until that afternoon. "Did you see him?"

"Yes. After Mum I … I asked him to come home early. I couldn't … I wouldn't … it didn't seem right to … I couldn't lie to him anymore, and I couldn't hold on. I had to do it … get it done … tell him …"

"It's OK. You don't have to explain it to me. So, how are you? Do you want to talk?" he asked.

I smiled at the concern in his voice. "I think, all things considered, I'm all right," I said.

"Did you …? Do you …? I mean, do you need …? Do you want to talk about it?" he asked again.

"I don't know. I wasn't sure last night. I wasn't sure if I wanted to … I nearly … but in the end, I just fell asleep. I think it was all just so much. And today I feel … I mean, I don't feel … the … Jack … I thought … It hurts. It feels weird, like there's something missing, like I forgot to do something, but I don't feel so… yes, I'm all right. Better than I expected, actually. I think after all the … after the … it was time."

"I'm glad," Scott said. "I mean … I'm not … I don't mean … I meant I'm glad you're all right, not …" His clumsiness was endearing.

"I know what you mean. Don't worry. I'm glad too."

There was a short silence. He waited for me to go on.

"It was awful … Jack, I mean. Painful and sad, exactly as I knew it would be. He cried. I cried. We hugged each other and he left. He didn't make it harder than it needed to be, but he was devastated. I feel sick that I caused that kind of pain and even sicker that part of me's happy. I don't know if we'll ever … he's been my best friend for so long, and I don't know if we can recover anything after this."

"Of course," Scott said sympathetically. "It's going to be hard. It's going to be harder for him because it wasn't his choice, but you know you had to do it. It would have been crueller on you both in the long run if you hadn't."

"I know you're right," I said sombrely. "I do, and I don't regret it, not really, but I still wish there had been a way to do it without breaking his heart."

"I know. I'm sorry," he said. There was a short silence. "How was your mum?"

I gave a short, humourless laugh. "How's my mum?" I repeated. "Good question. She's mad, that's how she is. I went there to find out the truth and all I got was more secrets and lies. There's so much to sort through. So much to unpack. She talked about me and Jack, about how we couldn't … did you know about …? And then there's her mum and your dad…"

"Her mum and my dad?" Scott interrupted.

"No, not her mum and your dad … like, together. I mean her mum, your dad, Jack, me … and Dad. That's … I think that's the hardest part … that Dad … that Dad's not …"

I heard Scott sigh. "Do you want to see me?" he asked gently. "I could come round, or you could come here. There's stuff I could help you with. Stuff I could explain. I think we … I think we should …"

"Not today," I said quickly. "It's too soon. It's not right. It's not that I don't want to see you or I don't think you could help, but it's … I really do, but … only yesterday … if I saw you, I know I'd feel happy and forget, and then I'd feel horribly guilty all over again. Perhaps I could see you tomorrow after work? No, actually, I was thinking I ought to go and see Dad. I think … I don't know. I want to see you, I really do, but there are things … I don't know if we should be alone. Does that sound stupid? I don't want to rush things, and I don't trust myself around you. It was hard enough before, but now that I'm … and yet, I do desperately want to be alone with you."

"Oh, Belle, I know how confusing this all must be. I can't tell you how much I want to be with you, near you, but you have to … I wouldn't want to …. Do you think …? When …?" Scott tried.

"Also, we can't go anywhere local," I said. "You know … in public … so soon. It's such a small town … so many … what if we bump into …? What If …? And it's too soon. I don't want anyone going running back to Jack with stories of me being out with another guy."

"Whatever you need, Belle. I'm here. Whenever you need me, I'm here, but I do think … I mean … we do need to get together, though … soon. Not to … but there are things … so many things. We've got a lot to talk about that can't be said in public. There are things you need to know. Things I need to tell you before … well, before … I don't want you to feel like I've been lying to you."

My stomach plummeted at his words. "What do you mean?" I didn't want any more secrets, any more surprises. "What do we need to talk about? What lies? Are you lying to me too? Because I can't … I don't think I can take …"

"Belle … no. Belle, I'm not lying to you." He tried to reassure me. "Please … I'm sorry, please. I just meant …"

I had started to cry again.

"Belle. Don't cry. Listen to me, Belle. I'm not lying to you. I just … there just … like you said, there's a lot … we need …"

"I know," I said. "I know we do, and I want to, I really do. I'm excited most of the time, and then I suddenly just get scared or sad or … I broke up with Jack last night. Like … It was only yesterday. But then all the stuff Mum said. I haven't got my head round it. I want to talk to you about it … and about us. I mean, I want … I don't want... I need … Can you tell I don't really know what I want?" I laughed awkwardly.

"I totally get it," Scott said. "Your head's all over the place and it's hardly surprising. Why don't you try not to think about it today? Put some telly on, something that'll make you laugh. If you need me, I'm here. Call me, text me, whatever, anytime."

"Thanks, Scott. I just need … Yes, I'll do that. I'll speak to you later, OK?"

"Of course. And Belle? I hope this doesn't sound patronising, but I'm proud of you."

"No, it doesn't sound patronising, and it was horrible, but it had to happen, and I suppose I'm a little bit proud of me too. I'll speak to you soon, then."

"Speak soon. Get some rest. Don't beat yourself up."

"I won't. I promise."

"Good girl. Speak soon, then."

"Speak soon."

"Bye."

"Bye."

I didn't put the telly on. There were no films or programmes that could take my mind off everything. Instead I nipped out to the shop to buy some chocolate because chocolate helps every situation, and while I was out, I drove up to the lake, parked in my spot and walked around the perimeter, beginning and ending at Susan's bench. It was a beautiful walk, and it helped to blow some of the cobwebs out of my mind.

I sat on the bench looking over the water, and I felt a kind of calm settle over me. I had a lot of wonderful memories with Jack to look back on and a spine-tingling future to look forward to. The memories would be raw and painful for a while, but that didn't mean that I couldn't begin to move on with my life, slowly. I looked up the hill, through the woods, towards the Ramsay estate. I couldn't see the big house or Scott's cabin because they were hidden by the trees, but I knew approximately where they were, and I smiled to myself as I thought of Scott sitting in that cabin looking down this way and thinking about me as I sat on the bench looking up that way and thinking about him. I finished my second chocolate bar and pulled my phone out of my pocket. He answered quickly again.

"Belle,"

"Hi, Scott."

"Are you OK?"

"Yes. Actually, I'm much better. I decided to come out and get some air. I'm sitting on the bench looking up the hill and thinking about you."

"I hope … thinking about me … in a good way?" Scott said.

"Yes, in a very good way," I breathed.

"That's good, then," Scott said, and I could hear the smile

in his voice. "You sound better. As it happens, I'm sitting in the cabin looking down the hill, thinking about you."

"I hope … in a good way?" I countered.

"A good way?" he said. "I can't ever imagine thinking about you in any other kind of way."

"That's good, then," I replied. "I think I might have made a mistake earlier. When I said it was too soon. The truth is, in some ways I've been waiting for this moment since October, perhaps longer. Perhaps I've been waiting my whole life. Anyway, the thing is, I don't want to wait anymore. I've got to work, obviously, and I want to see Dad tomorrow, but … after …? Or maybe on Tuesday …?"

"No, after sounds good," Scott said quickly. "Or … no. See your dad tomorrow and let's get together on Tuesday after work. I was thinking too, and you were right. We should go out … in public so we can maintain some kind of … but I'll take you … we can go somewhere out of town and have a proper … a proper … but then will you come back with me? Not to … not … but we do need to talk. There are things … will you come back to the cabin with me so we can talk properly?"

"Yes," I said firmly. "Yes, Scott, I'll go out with you on a proper date on Tuesday, and yes, I'll come back to the cabin with you. Scott?"

"Yes, Belle?"

"Thank you."

"What for?"

"I don't know. Being … just … just thank you."

"You're welcome. Any time."

"See you on Tuesday, then."

"Yes, you will."

"Bye, then."

"Bye, Belle."

"Bye."

"Bye."

"Bye."

I hung up the phone before it got ridiculous. I was smiling. I felt lighthearted. I was already looking forward to Tuesday. There was an incredible, fascinating man waiting for me, who already knew parts of me that I hadn't even known existed. He made my insides do acrobatics at the mere thought of him, and he could teach me about a strange new world that I was born to be a part of.

Chapter 22

I threw myself into routine and work the following morning. I arrived at school early, avoided my colleagues and went straight to my classroom to set up for the day. The topic for the term was pirates, and I had printed sheets with body parts and effects for the children to cut out and stick together. I put a pot of scissors and a couple of glue sticks out on the tables and laid a pirate worksheet at each seat. The children would design their own pirates from the choices on the sheets and could choose whether they would be accompanied by a parrot or a rat as their pet. They also had a choice of hats of various shapes and sizes and whether their pirate would have a wooden leg or a hook, amongst other things. I was happy with the variety on offer and hoped that each child would come up with their own ideas and inspiration. Pirates was a universally popular topic.

Mrs Bishop arrived at 8.35 a.m. and was surprised to find that everything was set up and ready to go. Although I generally had a wonderful way with the children, I was not known for my punctuality. I was usually in a hurry and relied on Mrs Bishop's organised mind to get things done. Mrs Bishop looked around the classroom in wonder and then turned her discerning eyes to me.

"Good morning, Isabel," she said.

I avoided her gaze. I couldn't get much past this astute woman. "Morning, Mrs Bishop," I replied with forced affability.

"You're all set up and ready to go, I see."

"Yes. Thought I'd get a head start."

"Everything OK? Good weekend?"

I did look up and catch her eye this time, realising that I might as well get it over with. We would be working together all day, and I wasn't sure if I had the strength to hide my disquiet for that long.

"My weekend was … eventful. Not the best, to be honest.

Jack and I broke up." My bottom lip trembled a little when I said it out loud for the first time. I held Mrs Bishop's eye long enough to see the shock and sympathy register.

"Oh, Isabel, I'm so sorry."

"It's OK," I replied with a sigh. "It was my decision, so …" I attempted to shrug it off. "The children will be here soon, though, and I don't really want to talk about it, if that's all right?"

"Of course," Mrs Bishop replied. "If you need anything, though …"

"Thanks. I'm fine."

We spent the next few minutes in quiet preparation. At 8.45 a.m. Mrs Bishop opened the doors and the keenest and most punctual of the children and parents began to file in. As soon as they arrived, I felt better. Their innocent zest for life and enthusiastic greetings to one another lifted my spirits. I opened up my mind and absorbed their energy, buoying my own mood and relieving thoughts of the breakup. One of the joys of working with children was that they simultaneously required every ounce of focus and were a delight to be with. It was easy to dismiss the unfavourable emotions in the presence of such happiness.

Most of the children found themselves a place to sit, and their parents hovered around, reading through the instructions with them and discussing how their pirates were going to look. Some picked up scissors straight away and began furiously cutting and sticking, while others took their time. Some just sat staring into space, while a few attacked paper with scissors without any idea of what they were supposed to be doing at all.

I hovered near Sammy Harris. His concentration was improving and he was always eager to please, but his dexterity with scissors still left a lot to be desired. He struggled with his fine motor skills, so the morning activities were always a challenge, and his mum usually had to drop him off and rush to work, so he was on his own. I handed him the spring-assisted scissors and knelt by his side.

"Right, Sammy, have you decided what you want your pirate to look like?" I asked. "First of all, do you want a boy pirate or a girl pirate?"

"He's going to be a boy pirate, of course, and he's going to have this big black hat with the skull and crossbones on it and he needs a peg leg. There's no lobster, so he can have this green parrot wearing the same hat so they're matching," said Sammy. I was impressed by his vision.

"Ooh, Sammy, excellent pirate words. How did you know it was called a peg leg?" I asked.

"I saw the peg leg," said Sammy.

"Yes. I can see the peg leg too, but I didn't tell you what it was called. You must have heard that word somewhere. Did you read it in a book? A book about pirates?"

"No, Miss, I saw it on a film. The one with the muppets and the pirates and the singing. Long John Silver had a peg leg. Daddy told me."

"Ah, the one with the muppets. I know the one. A classic pirate story," I said.

"Yes, Miss," agreed Sammy.

"And that'll be where you saw the lobster too," I remembered. "I never thought of a lobster when I was putting the sheets together. I thought of parrots and rats, but I didn't think of lobsters. Silly me," I berated myself.

"It's OK, Miss," said Sammy generously. "He'll be OK with this green parrot."

"Thank goodness for that. Right, are you going to get cutting and sticking? Look, Melissa has nearly finished hers!"

"Yes, Miss," he said, and he began to attack the paper with gusto. His cutting was rather haphazard even with the spring-assisted scissors, but he was holding them correctly in his right hand, with the paper in his left, and making some sort of an attempt at cutting around the pictures, which was a huge improvement from where he had been just a few months ago. I was satisfied and gave him a pat on the back and a smile.

I moved to the front of the class and retrieved my tingly bells from my drawer. I gave them a little shake, and as if by magic, the last of the parents slunk away and the children downed tools, put their fingers in the air and wiggled them around like tiny silent tingling bells of their own.

"That's right, Little Owls. Quiet tingly bells. Come and gather round on the carpet and we'll take the register, and we'll see ... let me see. Whose turn is it for show and tell today? Caroline? Of course it is! Did Mummy give your show and tell thing to Mrs Bishop this morning? Is it hidden away in my secret box? OK, come and sit down now, then, and Mrs Bishop will get it ready for you to show us all in a minute. OK, Little Owls, shush please. I'm talking to Caroline. No one else should be talking, should they? Sitting quietly please. Let's see who's here."

I sang my way through the register and the children sang back. The normality of it and their infectious enthusiasm settled my agitation, and I was soon so engrossed in Caroline's collection of Frozen figures and the rest of the children and the pirates that I didn't have the time or the energy to dwell on any other part of my life. During morning break, I tidied up and reset the classroom for decorating pirate flags, and at lunchtime I stayed in my classroom again and set up for the afternoon's lessons. I was just finishing off my sandwich at my desk, pleased that I had avoided any difficult conversations with my colleagues, when there was a knock on my door and Chrissy Brooks popped her head through.

"Hi," she said, a little bit too cheerfully. "I didn't see you in the staffroom, so I thought I'd pop in for a catch-up on the weekend."

I eyed her suspiciously. "I often don't come into the staffroom at lunchtime, and you don't usually pop in," I said.

"No, well ... but it's Monday and I know you were going

out on Friday, so I thought I'd just … you know … come and see if you had a good time. You know, see if you have any stories to share."

"Well, there's not really much to tell," I said, but I couldn't catch Chrissy's eye.

Chrissy came further into the room, deliberately not taking the hint that I wasn't in the mood to talk. She perched on the edge of a desk and studied me quietly. I could feel the curiosity flowing from her, curiosity and sympathy. Chrissy didn't speak again straight away, but she clearly wasn't going to leave without something. I looked up, resigned.

"You've been talking to Mrs Bishop, haven't you?" I asked, surprised and a little disappointed that the rumour mill had begun so quickly.

"She didn't tell me anything," Chrissy was quick to point out. "But she did say she was worried about you and suggested you might need a friend. I don't think she's really the shoulder-to-cry-on type, and when you didn't come over for lunch … well, I just thought I'd come and offer mine … if you need it."

I was quiet for a moment. I knew that Mrs Bishop's heart was in the right place, but I had hoped that I could come to terms with things for a few days before my life became the hottest topic of gossip for the staffroom. I finished the last bite of my sandwich. A chat with a friend wouldn't hurt.

"Thanks," I sighed. "It was eventful. Yes, Donna and I went out on Friday night, I fell out with Mum on Saturday and then broke up with Jack."

Chrissy let out a shocked gasp. "Whoa, what? You and Jack? When she said … she never said … I never thought … No wonder she was worried. Oh, no, Izzy, oh, I'm so sorry. I can't believe it. You were … I mean you're always so … I mean ... but he adores you. I mean you … I mean… what happened? I mean … no … sorry, it's none of my business if you don't want to talk about it, but I'm just so … well, it's so … he just … well, I'm just really sorry."

Tears sprang unbidden back into my eyes. It turned out that talking to a friend hadn't been what I had needed at all. Not this friend. Not now. I didn't want to cry at school, but Chrissy's shock and dismay had floored me. I wondered if this was how everyone was going to react. Everyone adored Jack and would have to be blind not to see how much he loved me. I knew that it would be hard for people to understand, and they couldn't hide their true feelings from me. Every time that someone else found out, I would feel their searing condemnation.

"I know. He did. He does. You know, you're supposed to be on my side."

Chrissy backtracked. "Oh, Izzy, of course I'm on your side. If it's right for you ... of course. It was just a surprise, that's all. I had no idea you were unhappy."

"I know. I don't blame you. I didn't expect it either but ... well... it's the right thing. I'm sure about that."

"Well, that's all that matters," said Chrissy, "and of course we're all on your side."

"I know. Thanks."

"And you fell out with your mum too. Now, I do know what that's like! Mums, eh? Your biggest fan and your harshest critic. Was that about Jack? No, sorry, that's none of my business either, but if you ever do want to talk, I just want you to know I'm here for you. Anytime."

"Thanks, Chrissy. I do appreciate that. The thing with my mum was about a lot of things, really. I think maybe I'm just finally growing up and seeing things for what they really are. Seeing her ... I haven't even told Donna yet ... about Jack, I mean. Not yet. I don't know how she's going to take it. I don't know if he's told her yet, but I assume not because she hasn't come down here banging on my door, demanding an explanation." I sighed. "I'm terrified I'll lose both my best friends ... forever."

"Oh, Izzy. These things are never easy, and it's always hardest in the beginning, but you'll get through it. People just do. I know it must have been the right thing. We all know you. We know you wouldn't … not if you weren't sure."

"Thanks," I said again. "I don't want to go into it any more now. I'll only cry, and the kids'll be coming back in soon. Look, I might avoid the staffroom for a few days. I don't want to see everyone's sympathy and have to go over it again and again. Do you think you could spread the word so I don't have to? Hopefully, that way, by the time I'm ready to face everybody, I'll be feeling stronger and they'll have gotten used to the idea, and they won't all gawp and gasp about what an amazing guy Jack is and how obvious it was that he adores me."

"I'm sorry." Chrissy was humble. "You're right. That was so insensitive of me. Of course I'll mention it. Totally get it." She hesitated. "Do you want a hug?"

My soft smile was a little wobbly. "Thanks, but no. A hug'll set me off, and I'm not going to cry. The kids are lining up on the playground, look. Maybe in a few days, but no. I don't want a hug, thank you."

Chrissy nodded her understanding. She hopped off the desk and briefly put her hand over mine, giving it a squeeze. "If you ever need anything," she offered. "Anything at all. A chat, a hug, a gin." she smiled. "I'm here. Anytime."

I had thought that I was composed, but the generosity behind that offer moved me to tears again, and one big, fat drop spilled from my right eye and rolled slowly down my cheek. "Now look what you've done," I chastised Chrissy with mock severity as I wiped it away. "Clear off, would you?"

When Mrs Bishop led the children back into the classroom a few minutes later, she looked at me with a questioning smile and a slight shrug of the shoulders. It was a confession and an apology, and I smiled back, letting her know that everything was all right between us.

We had a busy afternoon. The pirate theme had captured everyone's imaginations, and the classroom was filled with pirate ditties and heartfelt *shiver me timbers, ahoy me hearties* and *heave-hos* that rattled the windows, earning the class some worried looks from other children who happened to be wandering past. I planned to end the term with a pirate-themed party for parents as well as children, who could all get dressed up. The next few weeks would be spent making decorations, learning songs and planning pirate-themed food. With any luck, the children would be having too much fun to even notice that they were learning.

As the end of the day approached, I started to feel nervous. I found myself glancing at the clock more often than usual, and there was an uncomfortable gnawing sensation in the pit of my stomach. I focused on the children and managed to ward off the feeling temporarily, but as home time loomed and I helped the children into their coats and started to tidy up at the end of the day, the gnawing became stronger. I was nervous and feeling churned up and out of shape as a result of my intention to visit my dad. He was still my dad. Mum would be at the allotment for another hour at least, and I wanted to see him without her there. I needed to see him, to reassure myself that nothing had really changed even though everything had changed.

It was the house that I had grown up in and called home for twenty-two years. It would always be my home in many ways, and yet, sitting in my car on the drive today, I felt like I almost didn't recognise it at all. The revelations on Saturday and everything that I had learned had had a powerful impact on me and had distorted my feelings about my family and our home. I had always felt safe here. I had always felt loved. I had two parents who adored me, a beautiful sister and a good life. Now all of that had been tainted, and I felt like everything had changed. Now I had one parent who had lied to me throughout my whole life and one who had been lied to and who, it turned out, wasn't really my parent after all.

I almost didn't get out of the car. I almost reversed off the drive instead of facing Dad, who wasn't my dad anymore, who never had been my dad, who had always been and would always be my dad. I was so confused. I felt tense. I felt sick. I felt like I was about to cry again. I didn't want to cry. Crying seemed to be my response to every situation at the moment, and I needed to tell myself that this was nothing out of the ordinary and definitely nothing to cry about. I had just come round to visit my dad.

The butterflies in my stomach wouldn't cease their frantic fluttering. Their wings were flapping so hard and so fast, it felt like my stomach itself was twisting and churning. I was in full fight-or-flight mode and my palms were damp with sweat. I forced myself to get out of the car and walk to the front door. The driveway had never seemed so long or so quiet, my footsteps impossibly loud on the gravel. It was a matter of a few metres and yet my feet seemed to drag, laden with invisible weights, and I felt strangely detached, like I wasn't really here at all. A thin bead of sweat was forming at my brow.

I paused at the door. I lifted my hand to knock and then caught myself and lowered it again. I felt like a stranger visiting an unfamiliar house, but I wasn't a stranger, and the house was my family home. I had never knocked at this door in my life and wasn't about to start doing so now. I reached for the handle, pushed the door open quickly and walked straight in. I called from the hallway.

"Dad? Dad? It's Isabel."

His surprised and delighted voice wafted from the kitchen to greet me.

"Isabel? Hello, love. Come on in, then. To what do I owe this pleasure?"

I didn't suppress the natural smile that sprang to my lips at the sound of Dad's voice. I felt the tension ease immediately. I stowed my shoes in the rack by the door, and the familiar feel of the thick carpet between my toes transported me back to happy times. I padded into the kitchen and took in the sight of him preparing dinner, regular and reassuring.

He was my dad. Of course he was my dad. The biology, the lies, the secrets — none of that mattered. He was my dad, this was his home, and I would always be loved here. Suddenly I had absolutely no idea what I had been worrying about, and the relief was incredible. I felt so light that I thought that I might fly. He turned to greet me and smiled his gentle, caring father's smile. I smiled too. It was just so good to see him. I had worried that it might be different, that somehow he would be different or that I would feel differently about him, but I hadn't realised how much I needed him. He opened his arms, and I flew into them. He hugged me fiercely, knowing without having to be told that I needed an extra tight squeeze. He held me for as long as I needed to be held, and when he felt me relax, he stepped away and looked into my eyes.

"Not that it isn't just wonderful to see you, Izzy, but what's the matter, sweetheart? You're out of sorts, and don't give me any nonsense about just feeling like dropping in. That doesn't happen and we both know it. Mum's been off since Saturday too. She said you had words but wouldn't tell me what about. It doesn't take a genius to see that you've come here when you knew she wouldn't be home. You shouldn't fall out with her, Izzy. You know how sensitive she can be, and yes" — he held up a hand to prevent me from interrupting — "I know she can also be terribly insensitive, but that's just her way. You know that. You don't usually let it get unpleasant with her. She's been really out of sorts. And now you're here and ... well, I'm worried about you both."

I was taken aback. It hadn't occurred to me that I would have to defend my behaviour towards Mum when she was so obviously the one in the wrong. I was unbelievably angry and hurt by her behaviour, but I couldn't mention any of it to Dad without revealing the impossible truth. One thing that was certain was that he was totally innocent in all of this and he didn't deserve to be hurt. Instead, I ignored that part of the question and I told him the news that was mine to tell.

"Jack and I broke up."

Dad froze on the spot and stared at me with his mouth open wide. He looked like a fish out of water. His mouth began opening and closing, but no sound came out. He looked totally confused, like he couldn't grasp what I had just said. Jack was like a son to him. He had been coming round to play since we were four years old and was almost as much a part of the family as Stephanie and I were ourselves. Dad had probably never even considered that Jack wouldn't be in our lives forever. Perhaps I had underestimated what kind of impact this was going to have on the other people in my life. Perhaps I should have broken the news more gently. I had been so caught up in Jack's feelings and my own that I hadn't really considered how hard it was going to be for others.

Dad gathered himself as much as he could and tried to piece together a coherent sentence.

"You mean …" he started. "I mean … you mean … for real? For good? Forever? Broke up like … like ...?"

"Yes, Dad. Forever."

"Oh, Izzy," he sighed. "I'm sorry. I'm so, so sorry. I didn't … I mean … you didn't … can you …? I mean, did you …? I mean, did he …? I thought, maybe at Christmas you weren't quite so … it wasn't … but I never thought … it didn't occur to me that … Why?"

Why? The question that would be on everybody's lips. To all observers, Jack and I were the perfect couple. His love for me radiated out of him, and there had never been any suggestion of a problem. Explaining how unfulfilled I had been was going to be impossible. Introducing a new man into my life was going to be even worse.

"Yes, Dad," I said patiently. "Forever. It was my decision, and it was the right one. Don't … I know you won't get it, but as for why …"

Before I had a chance to go on, he stopped me.

"Wait," he said. "I'll make a cup of tea. We need a cup of tea. Go and sit down and I'll bring it in."

"OK." I could see that he needed a minute to compose himself. "Thanks, Dad."

I retreated to the living room and sat in my usual spot, leaving Dad to wrap his head around the news while the kettle boiled. He soon came through with two cups of tea, gave one to me, put one on his usual coffee table and disappeared back into the kitchen without saying a word. He returned a few seconds later with a third cup, which he set down next to his own. I eyed it suspiciously.

"I called Mum. She's on her way," he confirmed. "We're a family. No point in saying it all twice." I nodded even though it was the last thing that I wanted. I supposed that it wouldn't do me any more harm to see Mum today, with Dad here. Leaving it would only make things more awkward, and at least with Dad in the room, there would be no danger of the arguments of Saturday afternoon being rehashed. We could all concentrate on the bombshell of the end of my relationship with Jack. I might even have an ally in Mum, who knew more about the reasons for my decision and must feel guilty for her own part in it.

Our tea was still hot when the footsteps on the gravel outside heralded Mum's arrival. She must have downed tools and hurried straight home as soon as she received Dad's call. I felt nervous again. My mind was full of conflicting emotions, but the choice to see her had been taken out of my hands. I didn't move when she walked in, which was unusual in itself. It was unheard of for us to not embrace. Mum stood awkwardly in the doorway for a second, and I knew that she was probing the emotions in the room. The fact that I could do nothing to prevent the unwanted intrusion while Mum could block my gift without effort made me prickle with anger. She had been instructed in controlling her ability since she was a baby and had taken that choice away from me, but

I sat still and kept my face blank so as not to alarm Dad.

"Hi, Isabel," Mum said quietly, and she sat down next to Dad, who hadn't failed to notice our unusual behaviour and was looking between the two of us in bewilderment. "I wasn't expecting to see you again so soon. Dad said it was urgent, so I came straight back." Her words were short and stilted. She was uncomfortable, and the atmosphere was tense.

I realised with a jolt that Mum was nervous. She hadn't rushed back because she was worried about me at all. She had rushed back because she was terrified that I was about to tell Dad the truth about her lies. I felt a surge of anger towards her and a sliver of grim satisfaction when her eyes widened in response to it. Now that I knew that Mum could read my emotions, at least I felt that my anger wasn't in vain. It was right that Mum knew how hurt and angry I was at her betrayals.

"I hadn't planned on coming here to bother either of you with this, really," I said, looking directly at Dad. "But when it came down to it, I didn't want to go home and be by myself, and I realised that I just wanted to see my dad."

"Be by yourself?" Mum repeated in a vague voice.

"Isabel and Jack have broken up," Dad told her gently, like he was talking to a child. "That's why I called."

Mum let out a sigh of relief that made Dad look at her sharply and made my anger spike again. Added to my irritation was the fact that Mum was still keeping her own emotions hidden. She had probably been doing it for so long that she didn't even know that she was doing it anymore. It was going to be a long time before I could even begin to recover from the enormity of her deception. I doubted that our relationship would ever be the same again.

I decided that for now I would just try to pretend that Mum wasn't here. It was important that I talk to Dad properly. I needed his support, and he had loved Jack for so long, he deserved a proper explanation.

"I'm sorry, Dad," I told him with feeling.

"You're sorry?" He sounded shocked. "Gosh, Izzy, I don't want you to feel like you have to apologise to me. I'm sorry. It's just ... well, it's just come as a bit of a shock." He looked at Mum, who was avoiding his eyes. "To me," he amended. He had obviously worked out that the tension between Mum and me had something to do with the breakup. He couldn't know that that was only a tiny part of it. "But I'm here for you, sweetheart. You're my family. You're my priority."

"I know, Dad. It's not been right for a while, to be honest. I've been having doubts for months, and over time I've just realised that I wasn't happy. Or not as happy as I should've been anyway. I didn't feel that spark anymore, you know? I didn't feel excited about being with him. I didn't miss him when he wasn't there. In fact, sometimes, I was relieved when he had to stay late at work or when he went over to Stu's. It'd become ... I need more."

"Relieved?" Dad repeated.

"Yes. It sort of started to feel like a chore to be in love with him, and that's just not right. He was more a ... more a friend. You can't base a future on a relationship that isn't quite right, can you? We both deserve more than that. He didn't do anything wrong, and worse than that, he didn't stop loving me, so it's going to be awful for him, but my feelings weren't there anymore, and it felt like I was lying to him ... to everyone ... to me."

"Well, when you put it like that," said Dad.

"I know it's going to take you a while to get your head round it, Dad. I know you love him too."

Dad nodded.

"You know, if you want to ring him. If you want to check on him or just talk to him, that's OK with me. I won't feel like you're being disloyal or anything. I know how important he is ... was ... is ... to you."

"Oh, Izzy, no. You're my girl," he said.

"I know, Dad, and I love you. I don't mean you should

ring him right now," I smiled. "I just mean … I don't want you to ever worry about hurting my feelings if you do see him or speak to him or stay in touch or whatever. He's done nothing wrong. He might appreciate it one day. I hope that maybe we can be friends again one day."

"OK, but like I said, you're my girl," Dad repeated. "You're my …" He glanced at Mum again. "*Our* priority. Are you sure you're OK?"

"Honestly, Dad? I'm so glad I came. I'm OK. I really am. I wasn't sure but saying it out loud to you has made it feel a bit better. It's so easy to let it go round and round in your head and worry about whether it's right, but yes, honestly, I'm all right. I know it's the right thing for both of us. He probably won't be able to see that for a long time, but … yes, I'm all right."

"Well, that's the main thing, isn't it?" Dad nudged Mum back to life.

She came to with a start. "Oh, yes, that's the main thing," she said quietly.

I wasn't sure if Mum had been listening at all, but it really didn't matter. Seeing Dad had made me realise what was important. It didn't matter that it wasn't his blood running through my veins. He was my dad. He loved me and I loved him and always would. This conversation had also made me realise that I really was all right with my breakup with Jack. I would carry the guilt of hurting him forever, but knowing that he was now free to find his real true love and have a family actually made me feel lighter. The fact that Mum had sat by and let us spend nine years together still horrified me, but that wasn't something that I needed to dwell on now. Watching the way that Dad treated Mum like a child prompted me to speculate about her mental health again. I sipped the last of my tea and regarded her with slightly detached curiosity.

My phone beeped a notification. I opened it, and my heart did a little somersault when I saw Scott's name on the screen.

I opened the message immediately and eagerly. It was short and to the point and it was all that was needed to inspire a genuine smile.

Hi. Are you OK? Just thinking of you x

Yes. Yes, I was OK, and I loved knowing that I was on his mind. I replied at once. *Yes I am. Just told M&D about Jack. Thinking of you too. See you tomorrow x.* I looked back up at Dad.

"Right. I've got to go," I told him.

He glanced suspiciously at my phone and then back to my smiling face. I wasn't going to discuss it with him now. One bombshell was enough for today. I stood up. Dad stood up too. Mum remained sitting. I walked to the front door with Dad right behind me. He pulled me into another tight hug.

"I love you, Izzy," he told me. "I only ever want you to be happy."

"I know, Dad. I really will be OK," I reassured him.

"Yes, I think you will," he said. "I don't know what's going on between you and your mum. One of you would've told me by now if you wanted me to know, but don't let it go on too long, will you, sweetie? You know she's not as strong as she makes out. This thing's really bothering her. She isn't herself."

I hugged him again. "Don't worry, Dad. She'll be fine. I'll be fine." For some reason, I couldn't quite bring myself to say we'll be fine.

"Hmm ... OK for now but don't be a stranger."

"I won't, Dad. I love you." I opened the front door and stood in the doorway.

"I love you too, Izzy. See you soon."

"See you soon, Dad. Bye, Mum," I called.

I closed the door behind me without waiting for a response. I glanced at my phone, still in my hand, and felt that goofy smile begin to return as I thought about seeing Scott again. It really was going to be all right.

Chapter 23

There were so many emotions flying around my mind, it was hard to sit still. I was excited, scared, aroused, a little guilty, but I think agitated is the best way to describe how I felt: agitated mostly in a good way. I was ready to go. I had been ready to go for thirty minutes and there were still another fifteen minutes before I needed to be ready to go.

A proper date, that's what this was. The only person that I had ever been on any kind of a date with, proper or otherwise, was Jack, and now I was prepared to go on a proper date with Scott Callahan. I thought I might be sick. Up until now, every time that I had met Scott in the real world, it had been unplanned and unpredictable, but this was real. This was organised and calculated. I was going to see Scott and spend the evening with him on purpose.

We were meeting at the cabin. I didn't want him coming to the cottage, we didn't want to drive to dinner separately, and there was no way that I could have been persuaded to go to the big house and meet his multimillionaire fluencer parents so soon. We were leaving my car at the cabin, he would drive to dinner, and we would return to the cabin, where we could talk properly without eavesdroppers or interruptions. I'm not sure what I was most giddy about: seeing him again for the first time because I had no idea how to navigate that, being alone with him in the van again after last time, being on a proper date with him, or the planned, uninterrupted time at the cabin. I don't suppose it really mattered which — the whole thing had me twitching in anticipation.

I wished I had someone to call, a girlfriend or someone to share the excitement with. I hadn't told Donna about Jack and me yet. I wasn't brave enough. We weren't due for another girls' night until a week on Friday, but I would have to tell her soon. I couldn't let her find out any other way, but the thought of ringing her and telling her brought me out in a cold sweat. I wasn't going to think about Donna tonight. I already had enough reasons to break out in a cold sweat.

Eventually, it was time to go. I took one last look in the mirror, and satisfied, I set off, driving up to the Ramsay Estate, through their gates, and pulling off the drive along the track to the clearing. Scott was waiting for me. I knew he was there even before he came into view because as I crawled along that track, I could feel him, I could sense his nearness. My fluence began to ramp up its excited babbling, letting me know that it could sense him and that it was delighted about it too. I was starting to get used to this strange presence inside my mind, a part of me but not entirely me, keeping me company and running an otherworldly, almost intelligible commentary on my life.

When I rounded the final bend, I saw him leaning casually against the front of his van, looking staggeringly gorgeous and totally at ease. His face burst into a spontaneous smile at the sight of me. Scott pushed himself up off the bonnet, sauntered over and opened my car door. I stepped out in my most capable manner, put my foot straight into a rabbit hole and stumbled a couple of steps before managing to right myself and look up with as much dignity as I could muster. Scott looked at me, mirth shining in his eyes. I looked back, trying desperately to keep the blush from my cheeks, and when our eyes met, we burst into laughter together.

The ice was refreshingly broken, and when Scott opened his arms and offered his embrace, I didn't hesitate. He wrapped his arms around me, and I buried my face in his neck, my warm breath tickling the edge of his throat. When he held me close, it felt perfect, natural, like coming home. My fluence agreed, purring contentedly inside my mind. We didn't stay locked in the embrace for long, but it was a sublime moment in which something new passed between us, something real and raw and untarnished by anything that had gone before. This was our time, starting now; this was where life would begin again for both of us.

404

I stepped back and looked into his eyes. The flames were burning, and I thought I saw a tear shining there, but he blinked and it was gone. He held one of my hands in his and nodded, apparently satisfied that I was here, that this was real.

"Good," he said and then, "Sorry, hi."

"Hi," I replied. There didn't seem to be anything else to say. It seemed that words were not always necessary between us. Scott seemed to get a grip of himself, nodded again and opened his van door, gesturing for me to climb aboard. He nodded again.

"Good," he repeated. "Let's go, then, shall we?"

It was my turn to nod. "Yes, let's go."

The drive was surreal, and it was happy. We didn't talk much, but this time, I was able to relax in his company. We made a little small talk and he asked me how I was coping. I told him honestly that I felt better at that moment than I had done for a long time. He seemed content with that, and we continued the drive in relative silence, extraordinarily aware of each other's presence. Every now and again, Scott would glance sideways as if checking that I was real, that I was still there, and his mood would lift and his smile would widen when he saw me and caught me smiling too. I could not contain the goofy grin because we were together, this was allowed, and we were on the same page, right where we wanted to be.

Before long, we pulled into the car park of a quaint village pub. I had never been here before, but the sign outside said that they served homemade food all day, and it looked rustic and charming. Scott opened the van door for me and gave me his arm for support. I jumped down without stumbling this time. We walked into the pub and found a small table in a quiet corner, immediately opening our menus and choosing what we were going to eat. Scott ordered at the bar and bought our drinks.

"Thank you," I murmured.

He put his own drink down and passed mine into my hand. Our fingers brushed lightly as I took it from him and a spark ignited where we touched, shooting into my heart and heating me from inside. My fluence did a little summersault and I looked up, stunned, and found the same dumbfounded expression on his face that I knew was adorning mine. The smouldering flames in his eyes were alight.

"Your eyes ..." I said, staring into them and needing to ask, to understand. "When I ... when you ..."

"Nope. Sorry." Scott cut me off, apparently blinking the flames away. "I'm afraid that's one of the forbidden topics. This meal is for getting to know the ordinary things about each other, the mundane, the human."

"But ..." I tried to interject, but Scott held up his finger in admonition.

"No buts," he chastised. "There'll be plenty of time for that later. I'll answer all your questions later. No, that's not necessarily true. I'll answer most of your questions to the best of my ability. I'm not sure we'll get through it all tonight, but I'll give you as much as I can. For now ... for here, let's concentrate on the other stuff, shall we? I want to know about you: your life, your childhood, your family, your job. I want to get to know you, all of you, but not the other stuff, not yet. No talk of" — he leaned in and lowered his voice dramatically — "fluencing or what happened with your mum the other day or what's happening here." He tapped his index finger gently on the side of his head and then leaned across and tapped on mine, "And here. It's too early and it matters too much to try to have those conversations in public. We're together, and you're still so ... it's raw and painful and confusing for you and you have little control over your emotional output. You could easily inadvertently upset innocent passersby, and I doubt you'd be able to talk about it discreetly. I don't know you ... well, not intimately ... well ..." He blushed. "Not as well as I would like ... yet ... but I do know fluencers and I know a little bit about you and your mum and the whole situation, and I want you to have a safe space where we can talk it all out and you can shout and rage if you need to, and … let's face it, you probably will … and that's not here. You need to be able to ask freely, express freely, and I need to be able to answer. It might get a little" — a frown crossed his face — "a little … confronting … emotional … difficult, and I don't want you to have to hold back, and you would, here. Do you understand?"

I nodded slowly.

"OK, good," he said. "Now, go."

"Go?" I repeated, confused.

"Yes," he said. "Go. Start. Begin. Tell me something. Tell me everything."

I shook my head.

"No?" he asked.

"You first," I said. "Tell me about you. I want to learn too. You said … when we … you said you were self-employed. You said you were the … the skill in the renovations at the house. What does that mean? What do you do?"

That was it. From that moment, the conversation flowed freely. It was so refreshing getting to know somebody new, and we talked and we talked and we talked. There was barely a lull in the conversation and no awkward silences. We hardly even paused to eat our food, talking and laughing between mouthfuls. He told me about his building business and stories about some of his friends. He talked about his parents.

"What about Daniel?" I asked. "What does he do?"

"Daniel? Well he … he … he does computer stuff. I don't understand it at all. He wasn't really … he never wanted to … Dad sort of … took him on … so he still does computers, but he also helps Dad with … well … I don't really know what he does for Dad, but he … he does stuff … to help. Mum does a lot of the bookkeeping and secretarial work and Daniel … Do you know …? Dad always wanted it to be a family affair … you know … all go into law or work for him.

Daniel wasn't good enough at school to ... not except in IT. He always loved technology. Not that he wasn't capable, but he didn't have to ... he didn't exactly apply himself to his studies, but I guess it didn't matter ... like he knew it wouldn't because Dad took him on anyway. I mean, he's family after all, but I ... I just wasn't ever interested in ... in that type of life, I suppose," he said thoughtfully.

"I was capable too," he continued. "I could have studied law, but I liked real things, you know? I like to make things, change things, build things, improve things ... physical things. I like watching a project take shape, finding things in old properties, working out the best way to make use of a space. It just ... it just suits me, I suppose. And I was lucky. We both were. Dad's ... Well, Dad's the best, the best at what he does, and his success meant we were always safe, secure. Dad would always look after us, so we could ... follow our dreams, I suppose. But it turned out that I was rather good at my dream, and I found a couple of lads who I knew ... I trusted, to go into business with me, and between us ... well, we do all right, and they're keeping the business going down there while I help Mum and Dad with their ... with this ... with the house here. It's fun, actually, the four of us being back together again in the same house. It feels a bit like being a kid again except now I'm the one telling Mum what she can and can't do, what will work and which of her plans might cause the whole house to cave in."

We both laughed. His eyes were alight with joy when he talked about his family. He obviously loved them very much, even Daniel, which I couldn't understand but I could relate to. I told him about growing up with Stephanie. I told him stories from when I was little, and I told him about work and my class. I told him about Josh, about that day three months ago.

"So, that's when ... I took him home ... to his home. I sort of ... kidnapped him, I suppose, and we got in my car and I drove him home, and that's when we... he... we found her and… and that was when … that night … after the hospital was when I … I came to the bench, you know …? When you were there."

Memories of that night came flooding back, and as always, my body flushed with heat at the thought of it. Scott must have caught my errant reflection or emotion, or perhaps the memory had the same effect on him because he blushed too. He smiled, almost shyly.

"Yes," he said. "Yes, I do know. I think about it often." His blush grew deeper, and he cleared his throat. "That and what that … what we …" He coughed again. His discomfort was adorable, and I could feel my heartbeat speed up as we both thought about how we made each other feel. "We ought to … perhaps it's time to go," he suggested.

I looked at the table. Our empty plates had been cleared away and our glasses had been drained. I had work tomorrow and we still had so much to talk about. The thought was sobering. I'd had such a wonderful time over the last couple of hours, chatting. I was relaxed in his company. In some ways, I was desperate to get back to the cabin, to be alone with Scott and to have some of my questions answered, but in other ways, I never wanted to leave. I just wanted it to be easy and normal, like this.

Being with him tonight had been exactly what I needed. Being with him just felt right. My whole life had changed because of him and this connection, this feeling of rightness, but I had to keep reminding myself that I didn't really know him at all, not yet. I knew that he was like me and that I was drawn to him. I knew that he could make me laugh, but I also knew that he could make me cry. He was inside my head. He was inside my heart. I did know him, part of me insisted, that feral, alien part. Although we had met only a handful of times and it made no sense, I felt like I had been waiting for him, that I had known him before I met him, that he and I were meant to be — two halves of a whole, two people destined to share our lives — and when I looked into his serious face and nodded my agreement that it was time to go, he held out his hand and I took it. We walked from the pub holding hands and I acknowledged that feeling of rightness, and although I hadn't said a word, Scott's smile grew as if he knew what I was thinking. Perhaps he did. Perhaps he knew.

The drive back to the cabin was different this time. After Scott rescued me from Kev on Friday, I had been running on adrenaline, out of control and confused, a slave to my emotional impulses, but this time I was more aware and more in control of myself. We had spent a lovely evening in each other's company, and there was no ignoring the sparks that crackled and flew between us, but this time we were heading back to the cabin for a reason. We had a purpose that I was equally excited and terrified about. I was going to learn what I was, what we were, and he was going to explain some of the unsettling revelations that Mum had made to me on Saturday. I wanted answers and I needed to know the truth, but I was also afraid of what I might discover, and there was a knot in my stomach that I couldn't ease.

Scott sensed my unease but was unable to relieve it himself because he was beset by an anxiety of his own. I could feel it disturbing his usual poise. Between leaving the pub and setting off in the van, his demeanour had changed, and he was no longer the sparkling, charming man who made me laugh but was now thoughtful and preoccupied. The drive was subdued, and Scott's introspection added to my own disquiet. What did he have to tell me that worried him enough to distract him so thoroughly from our chemistry?

When we arrived at the cabin, he led me quietly inside and turned to look at me, his gaze intense.

"Belle?" he asked tentatively. "Now that we're … before … now … could we …? Could I …? Could I just hold you for a moment, before we …? Could I just hold you? Please?"

I sensed his fear, and the thought that whatever he had to tell me was frightening him terrified me, but I couldn't say no to him. I wanted so much to wipe that uncertainty from his face, but what I wanted more than anything in that moment was to be held by him.

I moved into his outstretched arms, wrapped mine around him and buried my face in his chest. His strong arms surrounded me, and he lowered his chin to rest on the top of my head, instantly enveloping me in that warmth and security that felt like coming home. His powerful arms were protective yet gentle, and he held me close with our bodies pressed together so that I was cocooned in his embrace from head to toe. I melted into the clinch until it was impossible to tell where I ended and he began. We fitted together perfectly, two parts of a single essence, connected body, mind and soul. He tenderly, slowly stroked my back in a soothing motion, and being held was enough to ease us both. I felt safe and whole, and I know that he felt it too.

I don't know how long we stood there locked together, but we drew strength from each other. It was time. I had questions and he had answers, and the time had come to discover the truth. We moved into the main room and sat together on the settee, facing each other, our knees touching. I think we both needed that connection, that reassurance, even though I didn't know what was coming.

"OK," Scott said. "We're here and you have questions. You want answers and I want to give them to you. Where do you want to start?"

It was a good question. I wanted to start by asking him what he was doing to me, what kind of spell he was putting me under, but I decided that that should wait for a little while. I took a deep breath and let all of the questions and the thoughts that I had been repressing since the weekend rise back to the surface.

"It all feels like so much more than I knew. I feel like I don't know who I am anymore. I'm not who I thought I was. Even when you told me on Saturday morning ... you told me about the fluence, and I need to know, but ... there's still more, isn't there?"

Scott was nodding.

"This thing between us. It's more than being the same, isn't it? That's what's frightening you. I'm frightening you or … not me but …"

Scott continued to nod. "Yes. I'm frightened. I'm terrified," he admitted.

"Of me?" I asked.

"Yes … no … not of you but …"

"Wait," I said.

Scott stopped.

"She … Mum … said she made the decision to move away from … away from the … you know, the … the …" I couldn't find the word.

"The fluence?" Scott suggested softly.

"Yes. Sorry. It feels so weird using a word I'd never heard before the other day in relation to Mum and me. I haven't gotten used to it yet."

"I'm not surprised you're finding it tough," Scott tried to reassure me. "I've never met anyone of our age who didn't know before. There are plenty who agree with your mum's way, plenty of people who choose not to use it, not to live with it actively in their lives, to surround themselves with ordinary people and ordinary lives, but I don't know of anyone who didn't have the choice. It makes you kind of special."

I gave a short laugh. "That's one way to put it," I said. "It doesn't feel special. Not in a good way anyway. I'm not sure not knowing who you are makes you *special*. Deluded maybe."

"Belle. Stop that. You're not deluded."

"Mum spoke about her mum, my grandma. She said that Grandpa died and that Grandma fell apart."

Scott smiled sadly. "They were bonded?"

"Bonded?" I asked curiously. "I don't even know what that means. She didn't … I guess so. She said … well, I don't even know what she said. She said she was left with no parents. I got the impression Grandma had some kind of a breakdown."

"It happens," Scott said. "Especially if the death is unexpected, sudden."

"She said there was an accident ... no ... she said there was an *incident*. It seemed odd at the time, but everything about the conversation was strange and I don't even know if I took it all in. I was too busy being angry and upset with her. Bonded? Go on ..."

Scott shifted uncomfortably. He put his hands out open in front of him, inviting. I placed mine into his without question and looked him in the eyes, waiting.

"I didn't know how to ... I mean, I know you need to ... you need to know," he said quietly. His thumb gently brushed over the top of my hand. "What did your mum tell you about relationships between ... people like us?" he asked.

"I don't know. Yes, I do. She said we can't have children with ... without ..."

"That's right. Fluencers can only have children with other fluencers. I don't know why. I don't suppose anybody knows, really. The thing is, there aren't that many of us around, and because of the baby thing, there are less and less all the time. The pool of potential life partners isn't that big."

I smiled. "Like Sarah Kennedy."

Scott raised his eyebrows in question. "No, she's not like us ... not a fluencer. She was like some kind of born-again Christian type thing ... or her parents were anyway ... and she could never have a boyfriend at school because she could only see people from her church. I always thought it was kind of sad, you know, that she couldn't choose out of everyone, she could only choose out of the few people her parents and her church approved of. What if she met and liked someone who wasn't ... you know? That must be hard."

"Exactly," Scott agreed. "Like Sarah Kennedy, except that if Sarah Kennedy decided to leave the church or she fell in

413

love with a random heathen" — this made me smile — "she could actually, biologically speaking, I mean, go and have a baby with Joe Bloggs. You and I? If we want children, we're kind of stuck with each other." He blushed adorably. "Not me and you. I'm not tying you down to having children with me right now." He tried to recover. I laughed at his clumsiness, but he didn't laugh. "Except…"

"Go on," I urged. "Except what?"

"What your mum said about your grandma?"

"Yes?"

"You know, on Friday night you said that since that night at the lake, it feels like a little part of me has been stuck inside your head?"

"Yes?"

"And I said that I felt it too?"

"Yes."

"Well …"

I began to feel uneasy. "Go on."

"I think that maybe … after … there's a chance … no, more than a chance … I mean … I think … a little bit of me might actually be stuck inside your head or … well, inside your … you."

I impulsively snatched my hands away from his and shot to the other end of the settee, putting some distance between us and severing the physical connection.

"What?" I asked.

I immediately felt remorse when I saw Scott's eyes widen and felt a rush of panic from him because of my desertion. I very slowly inched forwards again and carefully put my hands back into his, which had been left open and empty on his knee. He closed his fingers around mine and held them tightly.

"Sorry," I mumbled. Scott's panic eased slightly, but his anxiety was still palpable. He must have been able to sense my fear.

"No," he said, "You've got nothing to apologise for. It's

414

me who needs to apologise to you. Again."

He took another deep breath and stared intently into my eyes. His eyes were open and earnest, the flames burning with a shallow intensity. He seemed to be trying to convey the importance and the sincerity of what he was about to say. "Please don't run away," he asked me.

"I'm not going anywhere," I said and gave his hands a tiny squeeze in reassurance.

"We'll see."

"You're scaring me again."

"OK, so, when two fluencers find their bond ... their ... when they ... like me and you ... they tend to ... they tend to ... to ... well, to stay together."

"Right?"

"Well, I mean, it can be quite hard to ... well, to ..."

"Just say it," I told him.

"OK," he said and took another deep breath. The next bit came out very fast.

"The thing is that the more time they spend together, the closer they become. I mean, the more bonded they become. When they're, erm ... when they're ... when they're really intimate, either physically or emotionally, they actually do kind of leave a little bit of themselves inside the other. I mean their ... their kind of ... well, their... their ... sort of ... their essence, kind of thing. And every time they ... well, you know ... they get close to each other, that part of them inside the other, well, it sort of ... it sort of grows and they sort of bond and they, well, they ... they sort of become more ... together ... you know ... more ... well, more ... they can sort of feel each other more. They become more ... bonded ... you know? Well, you don't know, but when they ... when we ... when we're actually ... well, actually, a fully bonded couple ... we sort of become less of two ... and more kind of ... more like ... well, more like ... one. And it can be very difficult ... actually, it can be quite dangerous, I mean most people don't ... I mean ... once you're bonded, you don't really … well, it's hard to break that bond. Really hard. I mean … well … you know."

I stared at him. My mouth was open. I looked into his eyes and I knew that what he said was true. I knew because I could see it and I could feel it. I could feel him. Not the feeling that I get when reading a stranger's emotions. I could actually feel him inside my mind, and that part of him that was inside me was begging me not to be scared, not to run away, not to leave him. Now that he had said it out loud, I could see it. I could see the truth. This is what I had been feeling, why I was drawn to him. I was carrying part of him, part of his essence, his fluence, inside me.

Scott was begging me to remain calm with his eyes, but I felt a moment of pure terror. I felt trapped. This was too weird. It was too much to take in. I was back in that black hole where nothing made sense or followed the rules that I had played by for the last twenty-six years. I pulled my hands out from his again, more deliberately this time, and I stood up from the chair. I stood up, turned my back on him and walked to the window, where I stared out into the darkness. I needed a moment to think.

"Belle?" Scott hadn't moved, but I could sense his uncertainty, his fear. I continued to look out of the window, keeping my back to him as I spoke.

"When we were in the club and I danced for you. When you looked at me and I heard your voice inside my head?" I said quietly.

"Yes, that's the bond."

"When we were on the bench at the lake and you … we … you …"

"Yes."

"That's when. That's when you put it there? You did this! You knew it would happen. You knew it would connect us. You knew and I didn't know!" I was horrified. "You knew and you didn't give me that choice …"

"Yes."

"That's why you ran away! That's why you felt so guilty! Because you knew that I didn't know, that I didn't understand."

There was a silence. It felt empty. It felt hollow.

"When we kissed? On Saturday morning. Jesus Christ, you kissed me. You let me kiss you … knowing that it was … that we were …!"

"Yes."

"Jesus Christ, that's what Mum meant. That's what she meant when she said that if I let you in, I wouldn't be able to get you out. That's how I knew you were here when I arrived today. I didn't understand it, but I knew. You're inside my head!"

I felt like someone had kicked me in the stomach. I was aware of Scott in the room and I was aware of him inside my head. I didn't turn around. I couldn't, not yet. I knew that if I looked into his eyes, I would see passion and hope and fear shining there, and I knew that I would get lost in those eyes and that I wouldn't be able to look away again, but I was frightened. This was big. This was huge. Six months ago, I would have laughed in someone's face if they had told me what Scott had just said. I would never have believed it. Five days ago, I probably wouldn't have been that impressed either, but not now. Now things were different and I knew and I could never go back.

"Belle, listen to me, please. I don't want you to feel like I've lied to you as well. I know this is a lot to take in. Belle, please come back. Please come and sit with me and let me explain. Please, Belle, look at me. I can't talk to your back. Please, come here, sit down and hear me out, and then if you want to turn your back on me, if you want to leave here and never come back, never see me again, then I won't stand in your way. But please, Belle. You've got to believe that I didn't mean to … I didn't want to … I didn't know … Please."

I couldn't bear to hear the pain and the fear in his voice. I could feel his desperation across the room. I slowly turned around and walked back to the settee. I sat at the opposite end to Scott, out of his reach, but I did look him in the eye. Those hypnotic, beautiful, deep, fiery eyes. They were at full force. He was looking at me with an intensity bordering on anguish. He held out his hands, open in invitation. I looked at them with trepidation.

"If I hold your hands …?"

"No, Belle. We won't … it can't … not from holding hands. I promise. Please."

I took his hands gently and looked into his eyes. I would hear him out. He held my gaze as he spoke.

"I've grown up my whole life knowing exactly what I am … who I am and what it means. My mum and dad, they're like your grandparents. They're a bonded couple, I mean. They're the best. When you see them together, when you're near them, the love sort of … well, you can see it … you can feel it. Some fluencers, most, never see it … their whole lives. Some see it in others but never find it, but everybody knows about the bond. Fluencers can be together and be a couple and have children without that connection. They can just … be … and it can be great because of what we are, but that connection … the true bond is rare. It's getting rarer. Some people … like your mum … they don't want it. They choose to be with an ordinary because they're frightened of the kind of bond that forms between two people like that. They're frightened of the power. They're frightened of what might happen to them if they find it and lose it, like your grandma. Some people search for it their whole lives.

"Daniel and I, we're very different … I guess you've noticed. We've got the same parents. We've both seen their love and the strength of it, and he's terrified of it. He would never admit that it's fear. He would say it's foolish to be so reliant on another person. He doesn't want it. He doesn't want love. He shuts himself off from it so that he never has to worry about it. I think that's sad. I've always wanted to find

418

what my parents have.

"My mum and dad, they know a lot of people. We've known a lot of people, a lot of people like us, I mean. Some fluencers choose to live amongst others like them, others choose to live amongst ordinaries for a simpler life. I've never ever felt anything for any other fluencer … not like this … not like with you. I'm not saying … I'm not … well, I've been with girls. I mean, I've found girls attractive, and I've had some good … never mind." Scott coughed a little to cover his awkwardness.

"When I first met you, the first time I saw you in that bar at the cinema, I knew immediately. I felt it … that moment when I saw you on the floor at my brother's feet. You felt it too, but you didn't understand it. I don't think I really, properly understood how much you didn't understand it or how much it meant to me. And then you told me you were seeing someone. I tried to keep away from you after that. I did keep away in the main, but I didn't stop thinking about it … about you. The way I felt in that one tiny moment … and I knew that if that's how I felt then … after one …just seeing you … well, I knew our bond would be strong.

"That night at the lake, I honestly, honestly … I honestly didn't mean to begin the bond … the … but when I was inside your head … I just couldn't stop. When I realised … as soon as I realised what might … I tried to get away. I stopped before I … I thought … I hoped that I hadn't … and by then I knew that you didn't understand any of it. You had no idea what you are, and you had a boyfriend and … but I couldn't keep away from you … I couldn't … I can't … I couldn't stop thinking about you, and on Friday night at the club, you heard me in your head and I felt your fear in that yard, and I knew then. I knew it'd already … that I must've … because you could hear me and I could feel you, so I must have … but how could I tell you?

"I was always going to tell you. I wasn't trying to trap you. I would never've let it go any further. That's why I wanted to talk to you tonight, but I felt there were things that you needed to hear from your mum first, and I wanted to break it to you gently when you weren't so … when you didn't have so much going on and … selfishly, I wanted to spend time with you before so you could see … so you could see how well we get on … how good we could be. On Saturday morning, when you looked at me like that and … and you wanted … and I knew you wanted to kiss me, and I've never wanted to kiss someone as much as I wanted to kiss you … I should have known, I should have thought. I should have stopped, but all I could think about was how much I wanted you, how much I needed to feel you in my arms and kiss you at that moment.

"I've never felt a bond before. I've never felt anything remotely like it. When I left you at the lake that night, I honestly didn't know it had begun. Perhaps I should have. Of course I should have. Over time, when I couldn't get you out of my head, I began to realise, but I thought if I ignored it, it might go away. On Saturday morning … the kiss … that was the only time I knowingly risked strengthening the bond, but I couldn't tell you then … I couldn't. You were just about to go and see your mum. You didn't need that adding to your stress, but I couldn't … I couldn't not kiss you. Not when you stood there and you looked at me like that, and you felt … you wanted me … you wanted to kiss me, and after that dream and … I knew you wanted to because I could feel your … and I wanted to … so much … and it was just a kiss … or so I told myself, but it wasn't just a kiss, was it? What a kiss it turned out to be." His eyes flashed with fire as he recalled the passion and the power of our embrace.

"Perhaps it was selfish of me … no … it was selfish of me … of course it was, but I felt that you needed it, and God knows I did too. Perhaps it was dishonest … it was … but it didn't come from a bad place. It was instinct. It was the same instinct that drew you to me … that made you want to … but yes, I knew, and you didn't know, and that meant … I'm

420

sorry. Please know … you have to know that this doesn't mean that anything you felt isn't real. Your feelings are yours. I'm not lying to you or controlling your mind in any way, I promise. You can trust me and you can trust your own emotions. I want to … I want you to … I want … I …"

During this speech, Scott had gradually been squeezing my hands tighter and tighter and leaning in towards me. I was drowning in those eyes again, and despite telling myself to get up and run, I found that I was leaning in too. Scott glanced at my lips, and his tongue darted out and wetted his own. He had stopped talking and was staring at me with adoration and desire. If he kissed me, I knew that I would kiss him back. I understood that the force drawing us together was not within his power to control. I felt it too. I believed that he hadn't been trying to trap me, and I had to admit that I could understand his dilemma. He had been waiting for me his whole life, but I hadn't. I hadn't been looking for him. This was all totally unexpected and terrifying for me, and yet despite the unexpectedness, despite the fear, despite the fact that I hadn't been waiting my whole life to find this bond, I still would have kissed him.

Scott didn't kiss me. He continued to stare into my eyes, but he kept his hunger under control. There could be no doubt as to how he was feeling or what he wanted to do, but he didn't do it. He didn't kiss me. Instead, he inclined his head a fraction, sat back up a little straighter, gave my hands another gentle squeeze and let me go. That act, that control, the fact that he would curb his instinct in order to let me choose, that made my decision for me. I nodded in recognition of his restraint and I didn't run away.

"What do you see when you look into my eyes?" he asked quietly.

The question took me by surprise, but the answer was already on my lips. "I see flames," I told him. "The flames ignite when you look at me and they grow hotter and stronger when you … when we …"

"When I look into your eyes, I see water," he said. "The ocean. I see waves rolling into the shore and the more ... when you ... the waves get higher when you look at me and you want ... do you remember when you first saw the flames?"

I did remember. I remembered every minute detail. "Yes, of course. They were there the first time I looked at you. The first time I saw you in that bar at the cinema. The first time I looked into your eyes."

"Yes!" he almost shouted. "That's right. It was already there. I didn't plant anything in you. I didn't create the bond out of nothing ... nowhere. It was already there. We were already made for each other. Our bodies, our minds, our fluences, they already knew. Nobody's eyes have ever shifted for me, and they never will because it's you ... it's only you. We're meant to be together, Belle. We're meant to be together. We just had to find each other ... we just had to find each other. You have to believe me. I didn't ... I didn't do anything to you. It was already there. You're my ... you're my ... it was already there, and I couldn't ... I didn't want ... we would never have been able to ...I simply can't resist you.

"I meant what I said," he told me, although I could see that the words were difficult. "It's not too late. The bond isn't too strong ... yet. If I go away ... if we don't see each other again ... if we put some distance between us, with time it'll fade. In time, it won't be there anymore and it won't do you any lasting ... harm." He looked at the floor, trying to hide the fear and the hope in his eyes, but I wasn't fooled for a moment. I could see how much I already meant to him, and I couldn't deny how much he meant to me. "I was always going to tell you," he said.

"I know," I said. I looked at him. I really looked at him. From the depths of his enchanting eyes and the curve of his beguiling smile to the gracefulness of his every movement. He was sensitive. He was strong. He captivated me with the

422

smooth velvet of his voice, and the mere touch of his skin against mine quickened my pulse in a thrilling way that I fiercely wanted to explore. I was already in grave danger of losing my whole heart to this bewitching man.

He was right that I had felt our connection instantly. It was undeniable. Not a single day had gone by since that first encounter that I hadn't thought of him. When I arrived at the cabin tonight and sensed him near, my heart had soared with the power of it. I had ended things with Jack and changed the course of my life forever because of the way that Scott made me feel.

I thought about how it felt when he put his arms around me and how my world had tilted when we kissed. He was it for me too. I was certain. I might not have consciously known about the bond before but putting it into words didn't really change anything. It felt good. It felt right. This was what I wanted. He was what I wanted. As I sorted it all through my mind, the inescapability of it was a little disturbing, but more terrifying than anything else was the idea of not exploring this connection, this bond, of letting it fade and never knowing what we could have shared. There was no choice to make, really. It had already been made. I simply could not contemplate walking away.

Scott was watching me intently, waiting. I could feel the fear rolling off him, but he kept himself composed. I put both of my hands back out in front of me, open in invitation. He looked at them and then he looked back at me to make sure. I smiled and nodded. He placed his hands inside mine, and I felt his spirit lift instantly at the contact. I felt it too, a lightening of the tension, an amalgamation of our strength. I saw his smile begin to return. I felt his tentative delight.

"If I wanted to leave, you'd let me?" I asked deliberately.

Scott swallowed hard but he nodded. "And if I decide to stay?" I felt the hope rise in him again.

"And if I decide to stay but change my mind later and want to leave?"

"I would never do anything against your will," he told me. "I will never force you. If you stay and we give this a try, and later you decide you want to break the bond" — he hesitated — "I won't stand in your way."

I could see how hard that was for him to say, and if everything that he had just told me was true, then I could hardly blame him. I might be his only chance at a true bond, at the kind of love and happiness that he had heard about in stories as a child and seen and envied in his parents for his whole life. I could see how hard he was working to try not to put any added pressure on me and I felt the weight of that pressure anyway. If things didn't work out and I decided to leave him, now or later, I wouldn't just be breaking his heart, I could actually be condemning him to a life alone, broken.

I smiled. "You know this is insane, right?"

He raised his eyebrows again.

"I mean, for me. This is totally insane. It's like … in the last four days, the Earth has turned on its axis and is spinning the other way. There's this whole other world I should have been part of my whole life, but I didn't even know it existed. In some ways, it explains so much and makes me feel like I finally belong. It answers some of the questions I've been asking forever. And in other ways, it just totally scares the crap out of me. There's all this stuff I never knew and never would've imagined in a million years." I laughed softly. "You know, I never would've thought anything could be as weird as what my mum told me but you being … you being actually inside my head? Forever?

"OK, here's the thing. I believe you didn't deliberately mislead me. I believe you didn't mean to trap me, and I believe you mean it when you say it's up to me. I also know you're right. I've felt the connection between us right from the start." I could feel his eyes burning into mine and see his smile becoming wider. "But" — I tried to give him a firm stare — "you have to understand how crazy this is for me. This is new and absolutely bloody terrifying. You're going to have to bear with me. You're going to have to go slowly. You're going to have to make sure you spell everything out to me so I don't accidentally do something that might cement this bond thing before I'm ready, right? Absolute honesty, OK? We do this my way, at my pace, but yes, we do it. Of course we do it." I couldn't stop that goofy smile returning to my face. I felt genuinely, giddily happy.

The relief and happiness that flooded Scott's system and barrelled into me was powerful and infectious. I thought that he might actually leap up and whoop with joy. My own silly, wide grin could not compete with his. I hadn't realised quite how much tension he had been under, but I felt the release like a champagne cork. He had been keeping it tightly under control, but now that he could let it go, I saw the unrivalled joy shining in those eyes, with flames that were sparkling, gleaming and dancing in the muted light of the cabin. He pulled me roughly towards him so that our faces were only inches apart. He looked at me like he had just discovered the most precious thing in the world.

"Thank you, Belle. Thank you. I've been searching for you. I've been searching forever, and I'm so glad it's you. I know this is insane for you. I'll try to do all those things you just said. I really will, but … Belle?" he asked.

"Yes, Scott?" I replied, even though I already knew from the heat in his eyes and the soaring of his heart exactly what he was going to say.

"Belle? Can I kiss you?"

"I think you'd probably better."

This kiss was different from the last. That had been full of passion and promise, two people succumbing to a temptation that had been driving them wild, giving themselves to one another physically and spiritually. By contrast, this was delicate and tender, a promise of a different kind. Scott's embrace was gentle and slow, undemanding, bestowing. It felt like an offering, a supplication. It felt like he was pledging himself to me with patience and understanding. Our hands were still joined between us, and it was me who slowly pulled one away to cup the back of his head and draw him in closer and deeper, giving the consent with my body that I had already given with my mind. We each closed our eyes and kissed each other deeply and thoroughly with a sensitivity that spoke of affection and devotion, and when he pulled away gently, he took my face in his hands reverently and rested our foreheads together with a deep gratitude and appreciation that required no words.

I felt as if my whole body had turned to jelly. I was fairly certain that if I tried to stand now, my legs wouldn't hold me, so I remained exactly where I was, my forehead leaning on his, and I smiled shakily against him. I was stunned at how easily I was falling for this man with his incredible kisses and profound insight into my heart and mind. I sat up slowly, still facing him, and smiled into his eyes. I felt a peacefulness of mind in his presence that I had never known before. I felt, genuinely for the first time in my life, that I could be totally myself with another human being and not have to make an apology for or hide from my failings or my complexities, and in return, I wanted to know all of him, body, mind and soul. The fact that I could countenance peace and happiness after the turmoil of Mum's revelations and my guilt and sadness about Jack was virtually a miracle in itself. I turned around on the chair with his arm protectively and possessively draped around my shoulder and settled back into him with a sigh.

Afterwards, we talked like two people who have got the rest of their lives to get to know each other. He told me about growing up as a fluencer, with stories of playing mind tricks on the ordinary kids at school. I was appalled.

"We were just kids, and we could, so we did. It's not that bad. It didn't last and we never really hurt anyone. You know that kid at school? The one who's unbelievably annoying because he's so cool and popular and in with the in crowd, but actually he's just a total idiot? Imagine how funny it would be if he inexplicably developed a crush on the captain of the Lego club," he said, laughing.

"You didn't! You wouldn't!" I was truly horrified. "The weirdest thing about that story isn't the emotion control, it's that you actually had a Lego club at your school," I laughed.

"You'd better believe it. And what about when you did badly on a test or forgot to do your homework and the teacher happened to be in such a good mood, he didn't notice?"

"Well, I suppose that does sound pretty handy," I said.

"Like I said, never anything serious. There are so many rules about what we can and can't do to ordinaries. It has to be treated with respect."

"I should think so too. So, who makes these rules? Who enforces them? Can you fluence each other? Oh, wait, I know you can. My mum's been doing it to me my whole life."

"Well, yes, she has, and you can, but the reason she's been able to do that is because she kept you so clueless about it all. Honestly, I've never heard of anything so … well, anyway … forget your mum for now … yes, we can fluence each other, but it's not as effective as it is on ordinaries. It depends how strong you are and how strong the person is that you're trying to fluence and whether they're aware of you. Most of us can block it out. It's not like we go around all day messing with people's minds. We don't live off it or anything. Think of it kind of like a sixth sense. Some people have a more delicate sense of smell than others, some people have perfect eyesight, while others just don't. There are different levels. It's just something that's there, and we learn to control it and live with it as we grow. Because not everybody has it and not everybody would understand it, it's just not something we talk about with ordinaries. My parents …"

I stiffened at the mention of his parents. It brought back the other things that Mum had spoken of.

"Yes, do tell me about your parents."

"Why do you say it like that?"

"My mum told me… warned me not to trust them … you. She said the Callahans are dangerous. You don't feel dangerous, although you have got yourself stuck inside my head." I smiled. I was so OK with it that I was already making jokes.

Scott smiled too.

"She said … she told me …" I looked at the floor as it all came crashing back into my mind. I felt so guilty that I had been laughing, kissing and chatting with Scott as if I hadn't just found out about Dad and hadn't just ended a nine-year relationship.

"What? What is it, Belle?"

"Talking to you about us … about you … has taken my mind off it, and it's been wonderful, but ... but she told me that my dad isn't my dad. Of course he can't be. He isn't a fluencer. She also told me that your dad … God, Scott, when she first said it, it sounded like your dad was my dad. I nearly had a heart attack! She said that your dad helped her. That he got her the … you know … that he arranged the donation and the doctor and everything. She said he was powerful and influential. She said he was dangerous."

"Wow, that's a lot to take in," said Scott gently. "I kind of assumed … well, knew … about your dad, I mean. But I couldn't say anything. You understand, don't you? You had to hear that from her. Not about my dad though! Blimey. I had no idea they even knew each other. How weird. But then, she's kind of right. Dad is influential. He knows people who know people and can make things happen, so he would be someone to go to. He's the best at what he does, and he's good at other stuff too. He would never have told me about something like that, though, of course. Why would he? Dangerous, though? That seems a bit strong for someone who's just been caught out lying to her family for years. What she's done to you … put you through … it's genuinely dangerous, Belle. People can … people do … go mad when they don't understand. You're strong, Belle … I can feel it.

Don't underestimate yourself.

"Listen, Dad can be pretty ruthless, and he's stepped on a few toes to get where he is today. I don't always agree with him, but I love him, and he's the best at what he does, and I think you should make your own mind up about him, don't you?"

"Yes. I think that sounds like a great idea. Thank you, Scott. Probably not just yet, though. There's already enough going on in my mind to last me a little while. I'm all over the place. One minute I feel so happy and safe, snuggled up in here with you, and the next minute I feel sick with guilt about Jack and everything else."

Scott squeezed my arm in reassurance.

"Listen, Jack's going to be hurt and confused, but you had to do it. It was the right thing, and he will get over it. I don't mean to sound heartless, but he'll move on with time. That's what ordinary people do. You've given him the opportunity to find someone who can really love him with everything. You can't give him that, and you can't give him the family he wants. And this is for you. You have the opportunity to learn about who you really are, who you can be. Concentrate on that. Concentrate on the future that you want. And I'm here. I'm here, Belle. I'm here for you."

"Thank you, I know, and it helps, but ..." I felt tears stinging my eyes. I was tired and getting emotional. My eyes felt heavy and sore.

"Hey. Don't give me that. You're strong, Belle. So strong."

I gave a short laugh.

"I'm serious," he went on. "You're out there saving little boys and worrying about everybody else. God, you're an impressive woman, Belle. I can't wait to get to know you. I can't wait to teach you."

I turned back in his arms so that I could see his face. His admiration and support were holding me together. I knew that he was right about Jack, but I was just so tired. The happiness that I felt in being with him was not enough to combat the exhaustion that was taking over. It had been another long day, and I had learned a lot. I wiped the tears away with my sleeve.

"I'm tired, Scott. I'm going to have to go. I have to drive home, and I have school in the morning.

"Of course, sweetheart." Scott leaned in close and stroked my hair back from my face. It felt soothing. It felt nice. It would be so easy to just stay here and be touched. He rested his forehead against mine again in a tender, intimate gesture. "I know. Let's get you home."

"But Scott?"

"Yes, Belle?"

"I want to see you again. I need to see you again … soon. I know what I said about taking it slowly, and I don't want … but … I don't know how we're going to get the balance here because I want to get to know you. I need to … I want to spend every minute with you, and at the same time, I'm scared that every time we spend time together, it means it's going to be harder to ever stop."

"Well, that's OK, sweetheart, because you're never going to want to stop. We're never going to have to stop. I know it's terrifying and thrilling and so many other things, but it's OK. This is where it starts for us. We've found each other. We don't have to be scared anymore."

The conviction in his voice and his absolute certainty and strength was infectious. We rose together and he walked me to my car. He kissed me with heartfelt tenderness.

"It's strange," I told him. "It feels so … easy with you, and yet everything feels so strange. I wonder if anything will ever feel normal again."

"Who wants normal?" he asked. "I don't. I've got you."

Chapter 24

He had got me, there was no denying it, and the next chapter of my life began immediately. The cottage felt strangely empty without Jack, and being there alone was depressing, so as Scott and I were eager to spend time together, I met him at the cabin every day, where we spent long evenings after work getting to know each other and talking about absolutely everything. We learned extensive, sweeping and intimate details about each other, told endless stories and made one another laugh. I began to really understand what it could mean to be a fluencer and to have the power to control the ability that until now had controlled me. I began to comprehend how much it could change my life.

"You might find you have more control when you're with me," Scott told me. "My fluence will sort of bolster yours."

"Right. OK," I said. "So, is that the same for all of us? We have more control, more power, when there are more of us together?"

"Sort of, yes," Scott said, "but for me and you, because of the … our … because of the …"

"The bond?" I supplied. It had been a couple of weeks, but Scott was still tiptoeing around my reservations. "You can say it, you know. I'm not going to run away and hide."

"I know, sorry," he said. "I just … I don't want you to feel like I'm going on about it or putting pressure on you. But, yes, the bond makes us stronger together. The closer we become, the more of each other's fluence we have access to. Fully bonded couples have more power, more control."

"Right, OK," I said. "Well, that is a bit scary," I admitted. "So, you can, what? See more …? Feel more? Fluence more when you're with me?"

Scott nodded. "Being with you just makes me feel … well … stronger, I suppose. And happier and healthier and …"

"Yeah, all right, I get it, Romeo," I interrupted.

"Sorry," Scott said, blushing. "It's true, but I know it

makes you uncomfortable.

"Mum and Dad, they're amazing. They charm everyone they meet. The power just sort of oozes out of them. It's so … effortless for them. When you're with them, you … you just … you can't help loving them and wanting to be with them … wanting to have what they have. Everyone does. I always have."

"Hmm." I wasn't so certain. "I'm not quite sure I like the sound of that. It doesn't sound real. Doesn't it get boring? Being perfect all the time? In fact, I think I might have gone off meeting them." I smiled.

Scott laughed. "That definitely wasn't the intention," he said. "And I'm not saying they're perfect, but they do have a certain … you'll love them, and they'll love you. I just know it."

"We'll see," I said. Meeting the parents still felt like a big step. "So, if you're … like you are, and they're like you say they are, what went wrong with Daniel?" I asked. "He's … hmm … how can I put it politely? Not like you."

Scott smiled. "You don't need to be polite. I'm aware of his failings. To most ordinaries, he's a good-looking, charming kind of guy because they don't sense the difference, the emotional ... emptiness. There's lots of girls who like a bad boy, so he does all right in that regard. However, to most fluencers … well … let's just say he's not really … too … popular with people like us."

I smiled at his turn of phrase. I don't think that I had ever been *people like us* before. I had been loved by my family, adored by my pupils, admired by my colleagues and friends, but I had always felt like an outsider because there was so much of my life that I couldn't define. Being *people like us* felt warm, it felt special, it felt like acceptance for something that I had thought would render me alien and lonely forever. I felt a glow of happiness spread through my body. Scott felt it too and it stopped him in his tracks. He stared into my eyes with wonder.

"It's very distracting when you do that," he said huskily.

"Do what?" I asked.

"When something makes you happy like that and I feel the warmth of it. It demands I look at you, and then … when I do …"

"You were talking about Daniel?" I reminded him with a sharp nudge to the ribs to get his mind back on track.

"Yes. Sorry." Scott got himself under control with some effort. "So … when you spend your life bouncing off emotions, connecting and interacting with mood and temper, even if you don't do it deliberately or if you don't understand it … dealing with a brick wall isn't much fun, and it definitely doesn't promote trust. We work on instinct so much of the time, and our instinct is based on the emotions we sense from others. Daniel doesn't feel … honest … genuine, I suppose."

"No, I'd noticed. It's horrible, but why do it? If he knows it makes people dislike him? Why's he so closed off? Are his real emotions so awful that he can't bear to let anyone feel them? Is he mentally ill?"

"I don't know," Scott sighed. "I honestly don't. He's been that way for as long as I can remember. Well … no, that's not quite right. It's got gradually worse. He doesn't even let me in anymore, and we used to be quite close. I think … and this is in total confidence, OK?"

I held out my hands in mock offence. "As if you have to ask. Anything you say to me's between us. It's not like I'm going to go running to Daniel and say *hey, guess what your brother told me about you.*"

"No, I know. Sorry." Scott paused. "He says he doesn't need people to like him. He says being close to people is for fools, but I think he might be scared."

"Scared?" I repeated. "He doesn't seem scared. Far from it. He turned me into a stuttering fool twice and it didn't seem hard for him. He oozes confidence."

"Yes, but I think that's all part of the act. He can have

relationships … flings with ordinaries and can be whoever he wants to be. He can be strong and suave and charming and has them eating out of his hand, but the relationships never last. He chews them up and spits them out every time. You can't do that with fluencers. We see through each other because we know how the other person really feels, so it's almost impossible to be dishonest … or to be dishonest consistently, at least. Daniel doesn't want people to know what's going on inside his head, so he suppresses it around us or chooses to spend time with ordinaries who he can manipulate instead of fluencers whose insight scares him away."

I thought about Donna with a pang of guilt. "You're not exactly selling him here. I thought you were going to convince me he's a good guy. I still don't know what it is he's so scared to let anybody see."

"I'm being honest with you." Scott shrugged. "That's all I can be. I don't think he is necessarily a good guy, but he's still my brother, and I love him. I don't … I can't think it comes from a bad place … if you know what I mean? I don't think he's trying to hide what he's feeling. I think it's more that he's trying to hide that he's feeling anything at all."

"Erm, sort of. No, not really." I shrugged.

"I think he's scared of getting hurt. I think he's scared of letting anyone in and becoming vulnerable."

I considered that for a moment. "You're talking about fluencers? He doesn't want to let fluencers in, you mean? Not even his family?"

Scott nodded. "Because he can't lie to us," he said. "He's still close to Dad. I think they're open with each other when they're together. Dad trusts him to help with his work and stuff, but he's not open or honest around other people. Not even me."

I could feel that the admission caused Scott pain. I reached out a hand to take his. He squeezed it gratefully and went on.

"When someone can see your feelings, they know an

intimate thing about you that you didn't necessarily want to share. Fluencers get used to that as kids. Our parents can see right through us, and we learn early on that it's best just to be honest. It'll be harder for you now, learning it at your age. You've been able to see other people's emotions, but you've not really experienced it the other way round. Or not knowingly anyway. As a community, by our very nature and the nature of those around us, we're open and honest in the main, but we forget that not everybody's like that. Of course, most of us can control what other people can sense, as we can control what we sense in others, but Daniel's the only person I know who takes it to such a degree."

"Do you know if he's seen Donna since ... do you know if he's planning on seeing her again?" I asked. I would have loved to be able to ask Donna myself, but she wasn't speaking to me. When I rang her to let her know that Jack and I had broken up, she was really upset. She had rushed me off the phone, saying that she needed to speak to Jack, that he would need a friend and that she wanted to be there for him. I was glad. It was a comfort to know that he had her to talk to, but I really wanted to talk to her too. She was my best friend. I wanted her to understand the decision that I'd made. I wanted her to know me well enough to know that it was right. I wanted her to want to talk to me, but every time that I'd rung since, she hadn't answered the phone, and she wasn't replying to my messages. She obviously felt like she couldn't maintain a friendship with both of us right now. I needed to give her some space.

"I honestly don't know," Scott replied. "I doubt it, but I'll try and find out for you. Not that he'll tell me anything, but if he does or I hear anything, I'll let you know."

"Thank you," I said.

"I do sometimes worry about what people ... ordinaries, would think about it if they knew," Scott said absently. "We read people's emotions like they're ours to take, ours to use or abuse or just sample as we pass by, and most of the time, if they knew, they'd be horrified. Ordinaries grow up knowing that no matter what else they lose, they'll always have that private part of themselves that no one else'll ever know. It's just biology ... Or is it physics ...? Or chemistry ...? Or ... something, to them. Anyway ... it's science. When they get cross with someone but they manage to keep it bottled up inside, or ... at least they think it's bottled up. When they have feelings for someone that are inappropriate... of course, it's not like we're reading their minds ... their thoughts. It's much more fundamental than that, and it's not like we care most of the time or that we even do it on purpose. Most of the time, I'm totally oblivious to most people's emotions. Most of the time, I don't even look, but ... sometimes ...

"Think about your teacher ... the one you told me about ... Mr ... Mr ..."

"Mr Fitzgerald?" I supplied.

"Right. Sorry. Mr Fitzgerald. His wife was dying, but he thought he could hide the worst of his pain from everybody, and he could ... from most people. Other ordinaries, especially those who knew him well, would've seen that he was sad or there was something on his mind, but they wouldn't ever, ever have been able to grasp the extent of the utter agony he was feeling, not unless he told them what was going on, and that was his choice. If he thought people would know what was going on in his head, I bet he wouldn't have gone into work that day. Those kinds of emotions are private because most people have lived their whole lives securely in a world where their emotions are private ... their own secret.

"So, there's Mr Fitzgerald, dying on the inside because the love of his life was dying for real, but he thought he could get through the day by acting as normally as possible, and if anyone asked him what was wrong, he could just smile and say he didn't really want to talk about it, and they'd go away. But you didn't go away. You were only ... what? Five or six? You were a kid in his class, and you couldn't go away.

The rest of the class could see there was something wrong with Mr Fitzgerald that day, but they couldn't *feel* it. When you felt it and he felt you feel it, that shattered his shell, the wall he thought was solid. It shattered the barrier he'd erected, and it shattered him and frightened him. He couldn't bear the thought and couldn't understand that anyone, let alone a little girl, could read his mind. He didn't want you to. He didn't give you permission to, but you did it anyway."

I was horrified that I had unwittingly invaded Mr Fitzgerald's privacy like that. Scott was right. Emotions are amongst the most secret, private, intimate possessions people have, and I had violated him when he was at his most vulnerable. I was stunned into silence. My earlier glow vanished completely as I considered how many times I had purloined the intimate feelings of strangers and friends. I felt like a monster. Scott rushed on.

"No, Belle. Not that what you did was wrong or that you had any kind of choice. I just meant … I was just trying to … oh, Belle, I'm sorry. I didn't for one minute mean to make you feel bad. I was just thinking out loud. You did nothing wrong. You do nothing wrong. You had no control … no control at all, and it was as horrific for you as it was for him. You were a child and a child who didn't understand what was going on. It must have been awful for you. No, Belle, you weren't to blame for that or for anything else you've accidentally experienced in your life. Even those of us with complete control use our ability every day. You didn't ask for this. You can't feel bad for something you didn't choose. In fact, you should feel proud and thankful for your gift.

"Blind people wouldn't ask the sighted not to look, and deaf people wouldn't ask the hearing not to listen. It'd be cruel. It'd be senseless, but people, ordinaries, wouldn't like what we can do, partly because they wouldn't understand it and people don't like things they can't explain but also because it's in people's nature not to appreciate an advantage that only affects a minority. They would see it as unfair,

437

unjust. They'd want to know why you …? Why me …? Why not them? It's something you have … a fundamental part of you, a sense that you were born with, and it's yours to use. I'm just giving you something to think about … perhaps a reason to keep what we can do to ourselves. If the ordinaries knew … well, have you seen the X-Men? They'd be so scared of us, they'd want to round us all up and experiment on us or just eradicate us from the earth." Scott was smiling now, but I wasn't seeing the humour. "Oh, Belle," he pleaded. "I'm sorry, this has all got really heavy. I didn't mean to come on so strong. We were having such a lovely time."

I smiled back at him softly. "No, you don't need to apologise. I just feel so awful that it had never really occurred to me that I was invading people's privacy in such a horrible way. You're right. They don't want me to know how they're feeling. What right have I got to know?"

"No. It's not about right, Belle. And there's no easy right or wrong about any of this. You're so new to it all. There's so much you'll never have considered because no one's taught you. We … most of us … have the morality of every possible scenario drummed into us as children. What we shouldn't do. How we shouldn't behave. When it's OK to fluence. When it's forbidden. You haven't thought about any of this for two main reasons: one, because you didn't know you had any choice because your mum didn't teach you." He rolled his eyes to the sky, and I could sense his infuriation. "And two, because of that … because you didn't know … you never had any control, so you couldn't make decisions about when to sense things or when to fluence people because you didn't know how. Please, Belle, try not to feel guilty about something out of your control. I'm sorry I said that … said it like that. And … try not to make any hasty decisions about how you'll use your ability when you can control it, not till you've really got to know it better. Some people do decide to try to live without it, but many, many

438

more live happier, more fulfilled lives because of it."

I was surprised that my thoughts had been so easy to read, but Scott had articulated almost exactly what had been going through my mind. For the first time since finding out the truth, what Scott had just said made me consider that Mum might have been right, not about the lies and the cheating, but perhaps she was right to strive not to use her ability in a world full of people who are oblivious to the truth and cannot give their consent to what is essentially an invasion of their most private selves.

Scott smiled sadly. "I've told you before, sweetheart. I don't need to be able to read minds to know what you're thinking. You're like an open book. Every thought plays out across your face, and I can feel your guilt ... your uncertainty. It doesn't take a genius to figure out that you're sitting there thinking you'll never use it so you never accidentally learn something about someone that they didn't want you to know. Honestly, Belle, we're so unbelievably lucky to have this gift. You're right, we shouldn't abuse it. It'd be wrong to deliberately tune into the emotions of someone's private moment just as it would be unforgivable to peek into someone's bedroom window, but you're wrong if you think we should never use it either, just as people should keep their eyes open. Fluencers do amazing work. Some dedicate their lives to helping ordinaries deal with their emotions. Doctors, therapists, priests — the list is endless. Think about what you did for that little boy in your class last year. Josh, right?"

I nodded.

"Where would he have been without you? If you'd switched it off and shunned your ability to feel his pain? If you hadn't known that something was seriously wrong? If you hadn't kept at it like a dog with a bone until you saved him from that monster. Where would he be now? And his poor mother. You've been given a wonderful gift, Belle. We have to use it carefully, but I firmly believe we have to use it.

Learning to control it's the key, and that's where I come in. I'm going to help you. You're going to see what you can do. It'll change your life, and you'll use it to improve the lives of so many others. You know, you already do; you're just not always aware of what you're doing."

I mulled over Scott's words. His comments about Josh really resonated. I wasn't sure how I felt about the bigger picture, but there was no denying the truth about that. Things could have been much worse for Josh and Cathy if I hadn't stepped in when I did, which I wouldn't have been able to do without the fluence. If I had had full control prior to Josh and had chosen to suppress it, he might not have had anyone in his corner until it was too late.

Scott's talk of fluencing professions was also interesting and something that had never occurred to me before. From personal experience, it made sense that fluencers would choose caring professions where they could use their gift to make a real difference in the lives of innocent people. I had always had to hide from people in pain, choosing to spend my time with children and avoiding intense and destructive emotions in order to keep myself sane, but I was now beginning to see the world in a totally different way. Perhaps I wouldn't have to hide anymore. Perhaps I could use my gift to help those people instead of running away.

The fluence was an intrinsic part of me, not something that I should choose to use or to ignore at will but something that shaped my identity. Without it, I wouldn't really be Isabel Bliss. I wouldn't be me. I couldn't ignore it. I couldn't banish it. The doubts were gradually slipping away, and I yearned to connect with it fully, to learn its potential and to embrace the part of myself that had been a mystery for so long. Without it, I also would never have found Scott and wouldn't be here, standing on the edge of this staggering precipice.

Every time we spent an evening together, Scott and I grew closer, and despite my protestations about wanting to take things slowly and my terror of the predetermined nature of the bond, I couldn't hide the fact that I was loving this time and relishing the lessons in which he taught me about myself and my abilities. I also couldn't, and quite frankly, didn't want to get him out of my head. People at school had definitely noticed the change in me, and although no one said anything, I did catch the odd knowing glance that passed between my colleagues when they caught me singing in the corridors or wearing that goofy smile.

Scott was true to his word, and he didn't push. After promising that he would respect my pace, there were no more passionate kisses and no pressure for our relationship to become more physical. I was certain that physical acts would cement the bond beyond the point that I felt I had any control, and I liked to try to convince myself that I was still in control. At the end of every evening, we would embrace on the deck, share a lingering look, and I would take myself home to the cottage. Neither of us could have been trusted to spend the night together without those limits being stretched beyond endurance. Sometimes one or the other or both of us would catch a stray emotion sparked by a look, a comment or an innocent touch, and a moment would pass between us in which the attraction became so intense that I thought that I might burst if I didn't close that fragile gap between our bodies and our minds, and usually, during those supercharged moments, it would be Scott who pulled away, Scott who severed that connection, and I would ask myself why I was fighting against being with this smart, funny, gorgeous, sensitive man who was already connected to me in a way that I could never even have dreamed of.

February half term came around quickly, and there was no question about where I would be spending my week off and who I would be spending it with, long days spent together, longer nights spent apart.

"Aren't you supposed to be doing up that big house at the

end of this long drive?" I asked him halfway through the week. "What do your parents think you're doing down here every day?"

Scott looked at me, surprise written clearly on his face. "What do they think I'm doing?" he asked. "They don't think … they don't wonder. They know exactly what's going on and who it's going on with. They know me, remember? They can read me like a book. We have no secrets, and they're beyond thrilled that I've found you, although I'm pretty sure they're even more frustrated than I am about the whole taking it slowly thing. They can't wait to meet you. They're the best."

They couldn't wait to meet me. I was embarrassed by Scott's lack of discretion but knew by now that he didn't feel that any subject was taboo and that he and his parents shared everything. I was a little bit thrilled that he was confident enough about our relationship to be talking to his family about me and perturbed that I hadn't as yet mentioned Scott to anyone. That omission would have to be rectified soon if I didn't want him to start thinking that I was ashamed of our relationship, and I knew that I couldn't put off meeting his parents for much longer either. I was saved from vocalising that thought, however, by Scott's next question.

"So. Are you ready, then?" he asked.

"Ready for what?" I replied.

"I think we've talked around it enough for now. We've talked about me, we've talked about you. We've talked about the fluence, and you've felt it inside you. You're beginning to be more aware of yourself and your ability, but the only way to really, truly understand what you are and what it means is to feel it, to dive in and connect with it properly. Up till now, it's been inside you, and you couldn't deny its existence or its strength, but you haven't acknowledged it, explored it, connected with it. You need to surrender to it, relinquish the barrier that you're unconsciously keeping it behind. Let it in. Let it out. Let it become part of who you are, a part of you, Belle."

I was instantly nervous and excited. I felt a trembling and a tingling in my fingertips, and my heart beat faster. I had known that this was coming. The thing, the fluence, inside me had been getting stronger since I had become aware of its presence and stronger still since I had been spending so much time with Scott and learning about the fluencing world. He was right. It was time, and just the fact that I was open to the possibility seemed to wake up the entity inside my mind. We were ready.

"Do you remember at the lake when we connected?" Scott went on. "When I helped to balance you and then ..."

His words trailed off, and I felt a fresh wave of guilt assault him. I smiled softly. "You know you can stop feeling guilty about that now? Of course I remember. While you think about how awful it was and how you *took advantage* of me, I remember how incredible it felt. I'd never felt anything like it before. It was like someone had taken the blindfold off and I was seeing the world in its full technicolour glory for the first time in my life."

Scott blushed. "That's a lovely way to put it, and I can assure you it wasn't awful for me. Quite the opposite. Far too much the opposite, in fact, which is why I still feel guilty." His blush deepened as he remembered. There was a crackle of electricity in the air, and the magic and intimacy of that otherworldly connection sparked again inside the cosy cabin. We looked deeply into each other's eyes and allowed the memories of one of the most intense experiences of our lives to shape the present, causing a surge of emotion to burst from us both, meeting and combining in the air between us, giving rise to a more profound sensation that was both a part of each one of us individually and a construct of our bond. It took my breath away, and I didn't resist the temptation to reach out my hand and place it gently on his cheek, adding a physical element to the connection and further enhancing the excitement and the spark.

We stayed locked in that position, staring into each other's eyes for a brief moment before Scott placed his own hand gently over mine, took a deep breath and deliberately closed his eyes, severing the visual facet of the connection. With his eyes still closed, he spoke.

"As much as I want to stare into your bewitching eyes forever … drown in those waves and fall under your magic spell. As much as I desperately want to put my hands on you and kiss you until you can't see straight … this is important. You have something to do."

I laughed. "My bewitching eyes? My magic spell? You know you're the one doing all the bewitching around here."

"If that was true, I wouldn't be the one standing here with my eyes closed, now, would I?" He peeled my hand slowly away from his face and let it go. "Now, are you still looking at me, or is it safe to open my eyes?"

I laughed again and turned to look out of the window. "OK," I told him. "It's safe."

Scott opened his eyes. "Phew," he said. "Now, let's get on with this before we get distracted again. Not that I'm complaining about being distracted by you. You're by far the best distraction around."

It was my turn to blush. "Well, I have to admit, being kissed until I can't see straight does sound rather nice."

"Rather nice?" Scott exclaimed. "Rather nice? Right, you know I'm going to have to kiss you now, just to show you how much of an understatement that is."

"Oh, yeah?" I said, turning back from the window. "Is that a promise?" I took a step towards him, amusement and wanting in my eyes.

Scott groaned, took hold of my shoulders and held me back. "Belle," he growled. "Stop it. Focus."

I laughed again. "OK, sorry. I'm on it. What exactly is it you want me to do?"

"Sit down here with your hands in your lap," he said.

I did as I was told.

Scott continued, "Close your eyes. I want you to turn your consciousness inwards, tune out the cabin, me, all the outside world, and search inside yourself. Control your breathing and dive into your mind. Try to find that part of you that controls your emotional energy and the emotional energy of others, the part that responds to my fluence, our connection. Find and focus on the part of you that controls your power. It's always been there, and you can't keep living separately from it anymore. It's part of you. Connecting with it will make you feel more whole. Find it, greet it, accept it, invite it to share your soul. It already does; you just don't know it yet."

"Oh, that's all?" I said. "Well, that shouldn't be a problem at all, then. I'll just do that, should I? I'll just do that now. Although … wait … come to think of it, if it was that easy, wouldn't I already have done that sometime during the last twenty-six years?"

I couldn't help the tinge of sarcasm in my voice. I think it was fear. I was frightened that the experiment might fail, that I might fail. I didn't want to disappoint him. I didn't want to disappoint myself.

"Don't worry," he told me gently, ignoring the derision and soothing my nerves. "You can do this. You've already begun to acknowledge it and accept its existence. You're ready for this. Up till now, you've actively pulled away. You've been taught to ignore it, and you've felt like it only ever caused you pain and misery. Now you know that not only can you exert your will onto it and use it with control but also that it can contribute to amazing joy and … the most incredible sensual pleasures. Now, suddenly, it's worth the effort to find, don't you think?"

"Well, when you put it like that …" The tingling had returned to my fingertips, and now it was joined by a warmth that spread slowly throughout my core. I ignored the trepidation, focused on the ambition and excitement and closed my eyes. "I'm ready."

"OK," he said. "Think of it a bit like meditation. You need

to put all other thoughts out of your mind. Breathe slowly and deeply. Forget about the world around you and concentrate on you. Look inside and find the part of you that makes you Isabel Bliss. Remember that night on the bench? I was there. The part of me that makes me me was inside your mind and connected with your spirit. That's where you need to be. That's what you want to find."

Scott became very still. I knew that he was there because his presence continued to sustain me. He was standing beside my chair, lending me his strength, but there was nothing physical to give him away, no movement and no sound. With my eyes closed and my mind focused, he had effectively disappeared, and without his distraction, slowly I was able to tune everything out and do precisely as he had asked. I bypassed all conscious thought and breathed slowly and deeply, in and out, in and out. I felt my heartbeat slow down and I separated my mind from my body, concentrating on pushing on, past my consciousness, past my subconsciousness, to reach for my spirit, my fluence, my innermost self.

Scott's advice to recall that night helped to focus my exploration. I would never forget how it felt when his spirit had been inside my mind, and I could almost sense a trace of that encounter now, drawing me towards the entity that I desperately longed to engage. Gradually, everything else fell away until I was deep within myself, alone, staring into a black hole — a deep, dark chamber of my mind. It was a part of my mind that I had never known, that I had never had reason or inclination to discover, but I knew now that this was where my spirit, my fluence, the essence of me resided.

As I stared into that space, adrift from the corporal world, I sensed a presence which was impossible to define but which I recognised was as much a part of me as my eyes, my voice or my smile. As it came into focus, a feeling of wonder suffused my being. It was as if something that had been lost forever had finally been restored, like the missing piece of a puzzle finally falling into place. It wasn't anything that I could see, exactly, but an entity that I was simply aware of. It's hard to describe because words for this kind of miracle of enlightenment simply do not exist, but just as I became aware of it, it seemed to become aware of me, and the miracle expanded beyond all reckoning.

The fluence was fluid, malleable, *alive,* and it was quivering with untapped potential and a faint luminosity. There was a *being* inside my mind, and when I focused on it, it burst into life. It began to unfurl and expand, and it greeted me with the absolute, unparalleled joy that Scott had promised. I smiled inside and out as I gazed upon it and breathed it in. It thrummed and purred in response. The level of power and energy inside me was thrilling and absolutely terrifying, but I continued to breathe slowly and deeply, in and out, in and out. The fluence started to pulse in time with my breaths until we were moving, living and breathing as one. I was in total awe of this energy, the entity inside me.

I had done it. I had connected with the part of myself that I had been running from since before I could remember. I no longer had to fear it. I no longer had to hide. The time had come to embrace the fluence and learn from it, learn with it. It was time to harness my power and start living my life, the life that I was born to live. Any concerns about whether or not to use the fluence melted away at that moment. There was no choice to make. I would never deny my nature again.

I spent a few precious moments on the inside, savouring the pleasure of our newfound accord, and then, as I began to slowly return to the present, to consciousness and reality, letting myself drift away from the core of my gift, I sensed a second presence, a less substantial power but no less existent, inside my mind. This was also a spirit that I was familiar with. Not so much a part of me but a link to another soul, a link to Scott. This discovery would have sent me into a tailspin before my epiphany, but at this moment, I was strong enough to take on anything and anyone, and I actually revelled in the fact that there was a part of Scott inside my mind, existing alongside my own energy. So, this was the bond: a part of him, a part of his essence, inside my head and inside my heart, exactly as he had told me that it would be. Our souls, our spirits, were united in a way that took my breath away, but incredibly, I realised that it didn't scare me in the slightest.

I slowly opened my eyes. The world hadn't changed in any notable way. There were no fanfares, whistles or fireworks exploding in the cabin. Gravity still held my feet firmly to the ground and the cabin still stood in its clearing on the hill, surrounded by trees and earth and birdsong that drifted in through the windows. I, however, had changed. I was still myself, still Isabel Bliss, but I was filled with a new sense of peace, a sense of belonging, a sense of completion. I didn't have to search for my fluence anymore. I would never have to run from it, hide from it or fear it because it was a part of who I was. I could still feel it, its energy, thrumming quietly, happily, in the background of my mind, and I was connected to it, connected through it. It was now thoroughly a part of my soul and a part of every movement and every decision that I made. I felt a blanket of peace and satisfaction shrouding me, saturating every atom of my being, and my first instinct was to turn and thank the man who had guided me to this moment, the man who had made this possible and who, I was beginning to accept, would be by my side for the rest of my life.

Scott was staring at me with thinly veiled excitement and a measure of trepidation of his own, but as I turned to him, the trepidation vanished, and his own delight burst forth.

"You found it!" he exclaimed. "You did it! First time. I can already feel the change in you. I can feel your connection with it and the peace it's given you. You feel stronger. Our connection feels stronger. Can you feel it? Oh, Belle!"

I was thrilled and emboldened by his enthusiasm. His eagerness reminded me of an over-excited puppy that simply couldn't contain itself. He appeared to be having difficulty keeping still and was staring at me with undisguised wonder. His exuberance combined with my giddiness at the illuminating discovery of the power inside me, and I chose not to resist the temptation to rush into his open arms. I gave him a dazzling smile and threw my arms around his neck, and he welcomed me with passion. He bent his head to mine for a delicious celebratory kiss that enhanced my sense of delight with the world. I even think that the newly discovered part of me, deep inside, purred more thoroughly in response.

"Yes," I told him gleefully as I came up for air. "I found it, I connected with it, and now I can feel it humming away inside me. And it can feel me. It knows me. It's been waiting for me. It's like a paralysed limb come back to life, like I'm fully aware, fully awake for the first time, and yes" — I couldn't help the blush that crept into my cheeks — "I can feel you too. All your talk of the bond, our bond, has really scared me up till now, but now I can feel it, I don't think I'm scared anymore. It feels amazing. I feel amazing. Everything feels amazing." And I tipped my head up to his once more, and with my hands firmly around his neck, drew him in for a deeper, more earth-shattering kiss.

This time I was in control. I chose the pace, the pressure and the intensity of the embrace. I kissed Scott thoroughly and hungrily and put all of my newfound power and freedom behind the task. This time it wasn't just the reaction of my body and mind that I could feel but the ecstasy of my fully engaged fluence, which was now singing its rapture. I closed my eyes and relaxed into the pleasure of Scott's lips against mine and the feel of his skin under my fingertips. I sensed his instant, fevered reaction to my touch and felt the trembling of his body against my own. He pressed himself firmly against me and I matched his pressure. With the power between us, it felt like my whole body was about to burst into flames. The heat was rising from the ground, through my toes and up into the pit of my stomach, spreading throughout my veins. My knees became weak and I felt myself swaying unsteadily as the passion threatened to knock me off my feet. Reluctantly, I pulled away before we fell to the floor.

"Wow," said Scott. He looked a little dazed. He had to put his hand out to the arm of the chair to keep himself from falling. He blinked rapidly a few times as if to check that he wasn't dreaming, and then he looked at me with such intensity that I thought the flames might actually leap from his eyes and set the cabin on fire. His chest was heaving, and the expression on his face was hard to read, but there was no doubting the emotions that were careering around the room. "Wow," he said again. "I ... I ..." He took a deep breath. "Wow."

As I watched, his emotions changed suddenly. I felt a jolt of fear pierce my heart. His smile fell, the flames in his eyes died, and I thought that I saw the shining of unshed tears replace the fire that led to his soul. He turned his back on me quickly and walked unsteadily to the door. He opened it and stood on the deck, looking out at the trees, taking deep gulps of air, steadying breaths, and holding onto the deck railing tightly with both hands.

I was confused. I knew that Scott wasn't unhappy. He had more than enjoyed the kiss, and he was proud of my achievement. The sparks of passion were still lingering in the air. I couldn't understand why he would walk away. I couldn't quite put my finger on what he was feeling, but I deduced that he needed my support. It was my turn to save him. I followed him to the door and stood just behind him on the deck, our bodies almost touching. I breathed in the same sweet, fresh air. I put my hand gently, supportively, on his back, letting him know that I was there for him if he needed me.

Scott immediately altered our position slightly, taking my support and manoeuvring himself so that he could put his arm around me. He pulled me in close to his side. I breathed a sigh of relief.

"I'm sorry," he said. "It's just … I think I'm a bit … well, a bit overwhelmed," he admitted. "I didn't realise it would have such an impact on me, but I feel … I don't know how I feel." He took a deep, uneven breath. "I can feel your power so much stronger. It's almost like I can taste you now, all the time. Even though it's only been a few seconds, I know it's here to stay." He laughed shakily. "It's like you're more … well, more a part of me … more … more everything. It's incredible. It's terrifying.

"It's been so long for you. To live that long without knowing it … I wanted to believe you could do it, but honestly, I had doubts. I didn't know if you'd ever be able to unlock it, and I wondered if we'd ever be able to … well, if our … if our bond …" He shook his head. "But I felt it. I felt it wake up when you found it, and I felt you come to life. The power felt so strong. I felt it roll through me, and the strength of it took my breath away. You're an incredible woman, Isabel Bliss. You're strong and determined and capable. So much stronger than you know.

"When I was worried you might not ever be able to connect with it fully, I wondered what that might mean for our bond … for us. I wondered whether we'd ever be able to bond fully, and I hated myself for worrying about that when it was so much more important for you, but I couldn't help it. It's selfish, but it's what I've always wanted."

I entwined my fingers with his and gave him a squeeze of reassurance. He gripped my hand tightly and swallowed hard before continuing.

"That worry, that fear, was nothing compared to the intensity of the feelings that surged through me just then when you found it, and then again when you kissed me with such … so much … I was overwhelmed by the strength of my feelings for you. I want to kiss you forever. I could have drowned in that kiss. I want to pick you up and carry you upstairs and throw you onto the bed and make love to you. I want to hold you close to me and never, ever let you go.

"You said you were scared of the bond before, but connecting with it made it easier?"

I nodded, my mouth slightly agape at Scott's spectacular confessions.

"I wasn't scared of it before. It's what I've always been waiting for. But now?" He swallowed hard again. "Now I'm terrified."

I was thrown. I didn't really understand what he was trying to say. "What are you scared of?" I asked him quietly. "You haven't … you haven't changed your mind?"

Scott laughed. "Never. I'm scared of just how much I want you … of how much I need you … of how much a part of you I feel. I've known you for such a short time. We're only just getting to know each other, and I know the idea of the rest of your life being laid out before you is still frightening for you, and I get that. Ordinaries talk about destiny and soulmates, but they haven't got a clue what they're talking about. Even though I've known about it my whole life, I don't think *I* really had a clue until now.

"I know you still need time. Time to get to know me. Time for us to learn about each other. Time to feel like you're choosing me … us … not that it's already been chosen for you and you have no choice. Choice is a big thing for people, especially people who haven't grown up understanding what we can be, and I know you value your independence. You don't want to feel like you don't have options, choices, but … when you kissed me like that just then, and when I felt the bond react and … well, I was just utterly terrified of the depth of my feelings, and I couldn't help a tiny moment of terror when it occurred to me that you might … that you might not … I … I feel like … I know I said … and I'm not … I'm not taking that back. I just … I don't think I could bear to lose you.

"Some people, even people who grew up with the fluence in their lives, rebel against the bond because they don't want to be forced into being with someone that they didn't choose for themselves, but I don't see it that way. The bond can be a choice. Some people never find it, some choose to walk away, some choose to hide, and others choose to embrace it. You *can* choose, but if you choose to follow this particular path, you're choosing happiness, and why would anyone want any other choice? If the path that's been chosen for you is the best path, the one that gives you the best life and the most happiness, why wouldn't you choose to follow that path? You *are* choosing. You're choosing to follow your destiny. I'm choosing too. I'd already chosen before I even met you, but now you're here, now I've found you, I'm still choosing you. I'm choosing you even more."

Before I had time to respond, Scott turned me in to face him and pulled me into a crushing hug. "I'm sorry, Belle. That was too much. I shouldn't have said that. Not yet. Today's about you. I just … I'm sorry."

I pulled my head away from him so that I could breathe and speak. "Absolute honesty, right?" I said.

He nodded. "Absolute honesty," he agreed.

"You're right. I hate feeling like I don't have a choice, that the path was chosen for me and it was always destined that I would walk this road, but … perhaps I'm beginning to realise that that's a very *ordinary* way of thinking. Honestly? You don't need to worry. I get it, what you're saying about choosing happiness. There's so much going on in my head, I don't know what to process first, but I'll tell you a few things I do know, if you like?"

"Yes, please," he said.

"I know I've just had one of the most incredible experiences of my life. Finding what's been hidden from me for all this time was just … is just … well, there aren't words, and that wouldn't have been possible without you. When I found it and I felt you there … well, I already told you … you already know it felt amazing."

Scott's smile returned, and he squeezed me against him even more tightly.

"When I opened my eyes, all I wanted to see was you, and when I saw you, all I wanted to do was kiss you."

The smile was now threatening to split his face, and the flames had reignited in his eyes.

I went on. "Because of the way I've lived and the world I've lived in for the last twenty-six years. Because of what I understand about love and life … you're right. At the moment I feel like it's too much to start making promises about how I'm going to feel next week or next month or next year, let alone the rest of my life, but I'm changing, and right now I want to learn about what I am, who I am, what I can do. I want to learn how the world looks now I've changed. I want to live this life and experience everything, and now … here … today. I want to do it all with you by my side. Can that be enough, at least for now?"

Scott nodded. "Yes. Yes, that's enough. Of course it is. I'm so happy for you. I'm so excited for you … for us. I can't believe how strong you are, Belle. I honestly didn't know how long it might take or if you would ever really find it after suppressing it for so long. You're strong, you're capable, you're amazing. I can't wait to teach you, to help you learn how strong you can really be. Doing it together will make it easier for you, if that's all right with you?" He looked at me, embarrassed again by his overzealousness but unable to tone it down. "Sorry, again. Tell me to slow down if you need to. Tell me to butt out. I won't be offended."

I suspect that he would have been horribly offended if I told him anything of the sort, but luckily, we wouldn't have to find out. I was just as excited as he was and couldn't wait for it all to begin. I turned to face him again and took both of his hands in my own.

"I'll never be able to thank you enough, Scott. You've given me the greatest gift, and I want nothing more than to explore it with you. It's hard to describe how it feels. You've been connected with it your whole life, and I've always had a piece of me missing.

"I felt it. I did. So many times I felt it, but I had no idea what I was feeling and no one to … well, no one who would explain it to me or help me. I feel different and yet totally me. More me than I've ever felt before. I feel like I can do so much, feel so much, and I could never have done it without you." I looked deeply into his eyes, trying to convey my sincerity. "Thank you," I whispered.

There were tears shining in both of our eyes. Tears of happiness, tears of relief, tears of gratitude.

Scott cleared his throat. "Cup of tea, then?" he suggested.

"A cup of tea sounds amazing," I agreed enthusiastically. "Have you got any biscuits? Or cake? I'm famished."

Scott laughed. "Hungry work, is it?"

I nodded.

"How about we call for a takeaway, then?"

"Perfect."

I padded over to the settee in the window. I sat down and leaned back into the cushions, curling my feet up underneath me and closing my eyes. I didn't mean to go to sleep. I only meant to rest for a moment while Scott made the tea, but as I leaned into those cushions, a sense of inner peace and contentment descended upon me. A light had been turned on inside. A light that warmed me from the inside just as the sun's rays warmed my skin on a cloudless summer's day. I was centred and relaxed. My breaths were fuller, deeper, and that light of happiness suffused my entire being. As I drifted from wakefulness, away from reality and towards the bliss of a deep sleep, I turned inwards and felt the power inside me stretch and relax too. We were connected now. We were whole.

Chapter 25

Over the coming weeks, I felt as if I had been reborn. I discovered that until now, I had been living my whole life through a muted filter, half-asleep or underwater, blind to the breathtaking capacity of my spirit, power and ability. Now that I was awake for the first time, I could appreciate the true warmth of the sun or the brilliance of a clear blue sky, the softness of the grass under my feet or the smell of the rain on the leaves. Scott pushed, challenged and thrilled me at every turn. He inspired me to delve deeply into my mind and soul in order to explore my uncharted potential. He began to teach me exactly what it meant to be Isabel Bliss, and in doing so, we learned by degrees exactly what our lives had been missing before we found each other.

I had never slept so well. Discovering and exercising the hidden parts of my mind that had lain dormant for so long left me feeling calmer and more peaceful at the end of each day. My sleep had always been haunted by an unsettled energy that I had shied away from, but now that I had connected with my potential and was working on harnessing its power, the agitated, nervous energy had left me. It felt like another miracle. I had become so used to feeling that a part of me was lost, I hadn't realised how much I was being plagued by the spirit that I had denied. I now went to bed physically and emotionally exhausted, and my sleep was deep and sound. My bed felt softer, the covers more comforting, and despite sleeping alone, I was wrapped in a residual warmth and security that spending time in Scott's company left me with.

Every morning I woke up feeling refreshed and energised. I skipped through my days at work, engaging the children with my infectious positivity and inspiring their most conscientious work and best achievements. I sang and I danced, I nurtured and inspired, and it was easier than it had even been. I had always been good with the children, but there was now a new depth and efficacy to my personality. It was easy to be the person that the children needed me to be. It came spilling out in response to their needs and desires. I was open and in tune to their emotions and energies, breathing it all in and responding instinctively. The children lapped it up and matched it with a vigour of their own.

By 3.30 every afternoon, I was buzzing with the anticipation of being in his company again. I remained resolutely at my desk until all of my preparation was done and then ran to my car and flew up the hill to the Ramsay land and his cabin, wearing that goofy smile and doing nothing to suppress my excitement.

I could feel his energy humming in the air the second that I stepped out of my car. His spirit spoke to me, and I knew that he was waiting. It began to feel as if he was an extension of me, that I was more whole when we were together, and that thought, that knowledge and the taste of his energy on the breeze simultaneously thrilled and terrified me. My tummy did a somersault, and my mind squirmed between embracing the thrill of it and abiding the warning, but the excitement always won and my smile only widened. I fully accepted that he was part of my life now, one of the most thrilling and exciting parts of my life. I suppressed the fear and I embraced the joy.

A subtle change, a pulse of energy in the air, told me that he knew that I was near. He reacted to my proximity in the same way that I reacted to his, and when he sensed me, our excited spirits flew together, entwining and joining in a sorcery that intensified the thrill and wonder of the connection. It meant that I was different but that we were the same, that we were special and that we were set on some kind of preordained path, a magical kind of destiny. I skipped from the track, down the path, feeling light and excited. Every afternoon without fail, he was waiting for me on the deck, and every afternoon without fail, my heart skipped a beat when I saw him. I paused and let my eyes rake over him,

457

taking in the sight of his perfect shape, his shining eyes and that heart-stopping smile. I'm sure that I saw his breath catch in a reflection of mine when he saw me too, and a bolt of electricity ran through my core at the knowledge that that smile and the fire in his eyes were for me and me alone.

When I reached him there on the deck, Scott stood impossibly close, gently took my face in his hands and stared deeply into my eyes. I'm not sure what he saw there, but the flames in his eyes ignited, danced and flickered in the light, his smile widened, and he drank me in. I felt utterly adored, and the feeling was mutual, and even though we had only known each other for a short time and there was still so much to learn, it felt so right and so honest that I gave into it and let the passion and the joy shine in my eyes for him to see.

In the days after that initial connection with my fluence and the mind-blowing kiss that followed, Scott was still a little unsure and asked my permission to kiss me when I ran to him and our faces were shining with the joy of being so near. When I saw the flames in his eyes and felt the mirroring response to my own, and when my soul was singing in tune with his and our spirits were dancing together, I couldn't say no. I didn't want to spend one more minute of my life denying what I was, who I was or what it was that I wanted, so I decided to listen to the instincts that were screaming at me to let go, enjoy these moments, embrace the strengthening of our connection and kiss him.

So I kissed him every day, and after a while, he stopped asking for my permission, and when I ran down that slope into his arms and he held my face and looked deeply into my eyes, I leaned into him and we let our instincts take hold. The kisses were full of wonder and yearning and promise. Every kiss was different, and yet every kiss held the same dazzling power and magic, and I poured my body, heart and soul into them and felt his body, heart and soul being offered to me in return. We connected in ways that ordinary men and women would never experience and could never understand, in ways that haven't even been imagined in the fairytales.

When we kissed, it felt as if my body was engulfed in the exhilarating fire that blazed in Scott's eyes, and the more time we spent together and the closer we grew, the more magical it became. I could feel the flames licking around my body, from the soles of my feet to the tips of my hair, and as we kissed, the flames lifted us from the ground so that we floated above that deck, wrapped in the embrace, oblivious to the solidity of the earth and impervious to the searing heat of the flames. Other times it felt as if my body was melting. The flames dissolved every cell of our beings into a liquid fire that fused us together and left us lying fragile and exhausted by the door.

Despite my misgivings, despite my fears born from a life lived oblivious to the enchantment of this secret world and the power inside my mind, I continued to run to him and continued to kiss him with abandon, and when we broke apart and looked into each other's eyes, I could see right into his soul, and I invited him to see into mine. Every day, I felt myself falling more deeply in love and giving in to my destiny.

Every afternoon after those first few weeks and that awe-inspiring moment and kiss, we entered the cabin hand in hand and spent our time learning even more about each other and more about ourselves together. We talked for hours, and there was now an equality to our conversations, a harmony, a togetherness. We spoke about our families, our lives, our childhoods. I told him of my hopes and my fears. I told him stories of times that I had felt like I had no control and times that I had been overwhelmed by the strength of the negative emotions of others. I told him secrets that I had never shared, that I had believed that I would never be able to share with another soul. I kept no part of myself hidden, and Scott reciprocated in kind, giving just as much of himself to me.

The fact that I couldn't hide anything from Scott, even if I tried, made it easier to let go and be myself. Normal barriers were absent between us, and he always knew exactly how I felt. The emotions that I inspired in him were reflected back to me, and he wasn't frightened to let me see just how much I affected him. In fact, it was more than a lack of fear with Scott. He had no doubts about our future, and that unqualified confidence meant that he was totally free, honest and refreshingly vulnerable. He was extraordinarily happy in my company, and his happiness was highly contagious.

We sat together on the settee in the window most of the time. We drank tea. It was too dark and too cold to be outside. There was no television in the cabin, but it would have been years before either of us noticed. Nothing was more important than simply being in each other's company. Sometimes Scott cooked a simple meal, other times I picked up takeaway on my way over, and sometimes we forgot to eat at all. Sometimes Scott would lean back on the chair and I would sit beside him, leaning into his warmth with his arm wrapped protectively around me. Other times we would sit and gaze into each other's eyes as we talked, telling particularly funny or poignant stories. I learned a different way of seeing myself and a different way of viewing the world, and I eagerly absorbed everything that he had to impart. I also learned to use my ability with control. He taught me exercises to strengthen my fluence so that I could learn to block the emotions of others creeping in and my own emotions spilling out.

When Scott told me about growing up as a fluencer and everything that it had taught him, I was envious of the freedom and security that he had known. The very things that had terrified me and set me apart from everyone else, the things that I had been told to ignore and repress, had been embraced in Scott's family and community, and I couldn't stifle a pang of jealousy. I told him about my fears of being abnormal and how growing up knowing that I was different and being prevented from discovering the truth had impacted my life. The knowledge that there were others like me, that there was a whole community that I should have been a part of, could have prevented so much of my suffering. I'd had to modify my life in so many small ways because of a lack of understanding of what was happening to me.

Contemplating what I had missed out on, I often found myself thinking about Mum. We had always been close, and despite her unwillingness to explore my gift, had shared almost everything. I missed her terribly during those weeks but realised more and more just how much had been lost because of the lies. I was torn between desperately wanting to share these profound experiences with her and never wanting to speak to her again because of the choices that she had made. I let out a deep sigh. Sometimes I felt less angry and hurt, but other times, the pain was still raw.

"Are you thinking about your mum?" Scott asked in his usual perceptive way.

"How do you do that?" I asked. "We can't read minds, remember?"

Scott smiled. "I'm not reading your mind, sweetheart. I just know you. I think … I'm beginning to get to know you. Am I right?"

"I'm thinking about lots of things." I nodded. "But yes. I want so much to forgive her for what she's done. Sometimes I think I feel more sad than angry, and I want to rush around there and tell her about everything … tell her about you. But then I think about how she sat by and watched me struggle for so long. It's cruel. She knew I was suffering.

"I don't think Steph found it so hard. I don't know why; she just always seemed to take everything in her stride. I don't know how she managed it, though, do I? Because of Mum. We could've been there for each other, but Mum took that away from us too. I just don't understand it. I always felt loved. I always thought she loved me, but she just sat back and watched when she could have helped. She could have taught me. She could have explained it to me. She could have been there for me even if she didn't want it for herself. Steph and I could have had each other if we'd known. How could any parent watch their children suffer, have the tools to help and not do anything?" Tears threatened to fall, and I looked at Scott for the answers that I craved.

Scott took a deep breath and sighed. He pulled me against him and began to slowly stroke my hair. It felt wonderful: soothing and understanding.

"OK, listen to me. I don't know your mum. I've never met her, but I have a lot to say about what she's done to you and how it's affected your life. What I do know a little bit about, though, is you. I've glimpsed inside your mind. I've felt your compassion and your generosity. I've seen the stunning sight of your smile and felt how much you worry about everyone else above yourself."

I smiled. It gave me a warm feeling inside, knowing that he saw me that way.

He went on, "Over the last few weeks, despite not being on speaking terms with your mum and without even realising you were doing it, I've heard stories and caught sight of a childhood full of love and of joy. I don't think there can be any doubt, seeing what I've seen and knowing what I know, that your mum loves you. As for the rest …" He stopped stroking my hair and angled himself so that he could look into my eyes while he spoke.

"I'm appalled that any fluencing parent could allow their child … children … to suffer in the way you have. You've experienced terrifying things and lived with crippling confusion. You haven't told me the half of it, but I can imagine some of the things you must have felt, and I can't believe that you've turned out so … so … I was going to say normal, but …" He laughed and I punched him gently on the arm. "No, I'm serious though, Belle. Never underestimate your strength. You're a fully functioning member of society. You have a job and a home, and your sister's travelling the world. The pair of you are inspiring. What you've overcome is nothing short of a miracle. Most people would have gone quietly, or more likely, noisily insane. There are probably frustrated fluencers like you in mental health facilities all over the world because they don't understand what they are and can't cope with what it does to them. I can't imagine how strong you both must be. Well, I can a little because I've felt you. I've explored a tiny bit of your mind, and I know how … how … I don't know how to put it into words, but what I wanted to say wasn't about how fabulous you are but how low your mum must have been to lie to you when she obviously loves you. You've mentioned that your dad treats your mum like a child?"

"Yes," I said. "He does pretty much everything in the house and shields her from everything so she can just hang around on her allotment with the plants and her birds." I had never felt resentment for the way that Mum lived before, but now everything seemed different.

"And you knew that?" Scott asked. "You saw that before finding out all this? Forget what she's done. Forget how cross you are. Think back to a few months ago. Did you treat her like a child too?" he asked gently.

I thought about all of the times that the family had rallied around Mum to make sure that she didn't have to deal with anything difficult. She was wonderful if you felt rubbish and needed a hug. She could make the bad feelings go away, but she couldn't cope with anything practical or any social event involving more than four people at a time, but that was just Mum. She was a bit weird, but she was Mum. The family made allowances and the locals smiled at her indulgently, but I had never really thought about it in any detail before now. When you grow up with a situation, it often doesn't occur to you to question the status quo.

I nodded thoughtfully. "Are you trying to say Mum's mentally unstable?" I asked.

It wasn't actually the first time that the thought had occurred to me. Even on that day at the allotment when it had all come out, I had noticed the frantic, frenzied look in her eyes and wondered whether there was something wrong, something more than just guilt or the fear of being discovered. I had always known that Mum was a little eccentric and didn't like people very much, but I had never imagined that she might actually be mentally ill. It wasn't a stretch now, though. I wasn't surprised by Scott's question, especially after everything else that I had learned.

Scott nodded. "I've suspected she might be suffering since the first time we talked. The things you say about her, things that to some people might just seem like oddities, but then you told me a bit about her parents and the fact that she was, to all intents and purposes, left … an orphan — an adult, granted, but an orphan nonetheless — an orphan and a fluencer. And she blames the fluence for the breakdown and abandonment by her mum. I'm sorry, Belle, but I suspect your mum's broken in some way. I suspect by not telling you and Stephanie what you are — what you can do — she's shutting it out in every way. I wonder whether it was even a conscious choice. You said she always said she didn't understand what you were going through?"

I nodded again.

"Sometimes when people's minds can't cope with the truth, they bury things away, deep inside themselves, and they sometimes bury them so deep, they almost forget what they've done. They forget the truth. They tell the lie so many times, they believe it themselves.

"You know she's different. You know she isn't strong. She's always been there for you, though, hasn't she? Not in the way she should have been, of course, but she's always been there. She soothed you when you cried. She made the pain and the fear go away because she loves you. In her own mind, I think she honestly thought you were better off not knowing. She thought the pain of not being able to control it was better than the pain you might experience if you embraced it."

I nodded again. I wanted to be able to accept this version of Mum and forgive her for something that perhaps she couldn't control, but it was hard.

"I hear what you're saying," I said. "You might have a point, but she's not a stupid woman, and some of what you say doesn't add up, does it? If she really didn't believe in it, if she really had buried it that deeply or if she thought that life's better without it, then how come she's spent my whole life using it to hide? She's fluenced me, my sister, our dad … every day. Every day, Scott. She's affected our relationships with her … with each other … with everyone — to hide the truth. Deliberately. That's not mentally ill. That's just lies. And if she was suffering, we would have helped her. We all loved … love her. One of her biggest things we were told when we were little was that lying's always worse than telling the truth. *If you do something naughty, we'll be cross, but if you lie about it, we'll be crosser.* Turns out she's just a giant hypocrite."

I wasn't ready to forgive. The whole thing still made my blood boil.

Scott tried to soothe me again. "I know," he said quietly. "I do know. I don't know your mum, and I'm absolutely not making excuses for her. I think what she's done's horrific. I'm really not making excuses for her, but I'm suggesting that you don't write her off completely. Not yet. She's brought up a kind, caring, compassionate, beautiful woman, inside and out. She must have done something right.

"Fluencers have a greater capacity to feel … to experience, and it can be the most wonderful thing, but don't forget, we also have greater capacity to suffer too. You've felt it yourself. Your mum was brought up with it. From the little you know, she was surrounded by the kind of love that I see from my parents every day, and then one day, that was gone. Her dad dead, her mum gone, and she blamed the fluence. That kind of thing can have a significant effect on a person's mental state. I'm not saying what she's done to you isn't awful or you don't have the right to be cross, but mental health is so fragile, and it sounds like your mum went through a traumatic time. I haven't got any answers. I'm just putting it out there. I look at you and I see and feel so much love. You've been loved. Don't ever doubt that."

I began to cry.

"Oh, sweetheart, I'm sorry," Scott said.

"No, please don't apologise," I sniffed. "These aren't really sad tears. You should already know that. I think … I hope you're right. Anger's easier sometimes, but I'll take it all on board and mull it over, I promise. It'd be nice to feel like I should … I could forgive what she's done." I was quiet for a moment before remembering something else that I had been meaning to ask. "The other day, we were talking about Daniel, and you said he was scared. Do you think that's part of the same thing?"

"Yes and no," he said slowly. "With Daniel, it's different. He doesn't shy away from his fluence. He's connected with it and uses it every day. He's strong, but he's also selfish. I told you that fluencers, especially children, are very often honest because we're surrounded by people who can read us and know when we lie."

"Yes, I remember."

"Well, Daniel would flout that rule, even really early on when we were children. He'd block his own emotions so people couldn't read him and he could get away with things. Other kids … teachers … even our parents. I remember it leading to some big rows with Dad. He was impressed that a son of his had such control but would be really angry if he hid himself from them. I never understood why he did it, but he never really changed.

"Most of us are open with our emotions and open to the emotions of others, most of the time. That way, if someone needs our help, we can be there for them. We're taught to respect our ability and use it kindly and wisely. Daniel doesn't see that as his responsibility. He doesn't want to use it to help others, only to help himself, but honestly? I think it's because he's scared that what happened to your grandma could happen to him, same as your mum is."

I thought that through. "So Mum was scared of the bond because she saw what it did to her mum when she lost it, and scared for me and Steph for the same reason?"

"Exactly. If you don't bond, you can't be ripped apart by losing it. You mum didn't think she was strong enough to go through what she saw her mum go through, and she thought by stopping you doing the same, she was saving you from the same fate. I disagree with her wholeheartedly and think the way she went about it was wrong, but I think I can understand her reasons, especially if losing her parents broke her mind in some way.

"Daniel's a loner. He doesn't want to rely on anyone else. He doesn't want to need someone. He doesn't want to need someone so much that it would break him if he lost them. I think he's scared to love."

Despite the gravity of the conversation, I couldn't help giggling. "Big bad Daniel's scared of love?" I laughed. "I'm so going to tell him you said that."

Scott laughed too. "No, you are not," he said. "I mean it, though. People like Daniel and your mum … not that Daniel's anything like your mum," he quickly clarified. "They close themselves off from everyone and everything and never really experience anything to avoid getting hurt."

Something else occurred to me. "What happens if this bond thing … if it happens … with someone you couldn't actually stand?"

"It happens," said Scott soberly. "Really rarely, but it does happen. Usually, if they trust fate, if they give it a chance, they discover something that changes their minds and live happily ever after, but other times, people fight it forever or just run away and risk never knowing what they could've had. Nature is constantly trying to reproduce to survive, so bonds are almost always compatible."

He looked at me with those deep, fiery eyes, and his face was intent, serious. "That's what I've always been most scared of. Of never finding it. I always knew I was meant to be somebody's everything. I watched Mum and Dad, and I wanted what they had. I've had affairs … flings with girls. I've had physical relationships. I mean … I've met people and had a good time, but I've never met anyone who challenged me, who could satisfy me, who I could love. I've spent my whole life looking for you."

I nodded once more and felt the powerful magnetic pull as I stared back into his intent face. I was in danger of being hypnotised by those eyes again. When he looked at me like that and said things like that, I felt myself falling headlong into his arms. I thought that I had known wanting before. I thought that I had been in love, but this was so much more than anything that I had ever known. This went beyond the physical, beyond traditional notions of love, and it would be so easy. It would be so easy to give myself to him without question, to trust what my heart was telling me and what my fluence was screaming at me, and to succumb to the sensations flooding my body. I began to wonder why I was resisting it, why I was holding back, and as the doubts fell away, Scott picked up on the shift in my mood, and my pulse quickened and my cheeks flushed at our bond's powerful response. I reached one hand out and placed it on his thigh. I ran it smoothly higher and felt his muscles tighten involuntarily at my touch. The air crackled with desire.

Despite the electricity in the air, Scott pulled away. He broke eye contact and stared at the floor, taking deep breaths.

"Jesus Christ, Belle. I don't know if you're aware of what you do to me. I feel … I know you would … if I …" He looked at me and there was pain and desire in his eyes. He gulped hard. "But we can't. You're not ready, and I won't let it be wrong. No matter how easy it'd be. I want you. God knows I do, but if I touch you now, I don't think I could stop, and we can't. Not yet. You haven't even met my parents yet.

Your dad doesn't even know I exist. I know this is … I want it … I want you, but until we've … I'm still traditional at heart. If you're not ready to tell … to share … to … then you're not ready to …"

He looked back at the floor again. He stared at it hard. I checked myself. He was right, and it turned out that he was stronger than I was. I smiled. He was doing this for me. I understood how difficult it was for him to deny his desire. I knew how much he wanted to claim me, to make me fully, irreversibly his, and I knew how much he wanted to share our love with the world. I gave him a moment.

"You do know that it's not that I don't want you, don't you?" I asked. "Or that I'm ashamed to be with you. You know how I feel, and I would, you're right. But you're also right … I'm still a little … if you were normal … ordinary … if we were ordinary … if this was just sex … you're right, I need to talk to Mum and Dad, and yes … I need to meet your perfect parents. Despite the fact that it all feels so right and so easy with you, I still kind of can't bear the thought that once we go there, I no longer have any control … any say."

"I know," he replied. "I do know. It's the choice versus destiny thing again. I totally get it. I'll wait as long as it takes. In fact, I want to wait too. The act of making love, of giving ourselves to each other in that way, will cement the bond. We'll be fully connected, body and soul, and that can't be taken lightly. I can't risk getting there if there's any chance you're still not sure. I can't risk having it … having you and losing you. Your mum? Daniel? They're not the only ones who are scared.

"It must seem so weird to you. We live in a modern world where sex is sex and doesn't have to mean everything. It shouldn't. I'm not an old-fashioned stick-in-the-mud or a religious zealot, but …. and for both of us … with anyone else, it wouldn't. But for me and you? It matters. And what makes it worse is that we're biologically totally geared towards sex. Me and you, I mean. All animals are programmed to procreate, to populate the world, and we're no different. The hormones, the chemicals, they're all there and stronger because of what we are. The genetic line needs continuing, and our instincts are to do it.

"You know, it's the real reason people used to wait for marriage to have sex. Before, I mean. Forget the Bible and the Christian faith, or any other faith for that matter. Forget sexual immorality preventing fornicators inheriting the kingdom of God, although in the past most fluencers would have seen their gift as a blessing from God. But no, it's much more fundamental than that. It's biology. Sorry … I'm rambling. I just mean I understand why you're scared, and I agree that we should wait."

I think Scott was rambling a bit because of the sexual tension in the air, but I thought about everything that he'd said. I was constantly learning about this new world. I was learning about my ability and control but also about the history, the stories, the community. Scott had been brought up surrounded by other people like him, shaping the person that he had become. He knew it all. He knew how we fit into history and culture. He was relaxed and comfortable with his power and the bond. For him, it was a natural part of life that he had always had absolute faith in. Although I had no choice but to accept it, for me it was still an alien concept, and the lack of freedom frightened me and challenged my modern sensibilities, despite the fact that, bond or not, ultimately, I already knew that I would choose to spend the rest of my life with this man.

"Do you want to …? There's … I mean … if you want to …" Scott said hesitantly. "It might … you know what …? When …? But it will … could … no, *would* deepen our connection without … I mean without … but you wouldn't have to …"

"Go on," I said. "Spit it out."

"Sorry. You might find it tricky, but you've already proved how strong you are, and there's only me here. It doesn't matter if you can't do it. I'll understand if you don't want to. You've … sorry. I know I'm not making sense. I'm nervous," he admitted. "When you normally sense someone's emotional energy signature, you're sensing the sort of … the output. What I did to you … what we did … shared … on the bench …" He blushed and coughed. "I mean, I'd like you to… I mean… well, would you try …? Would you want to …? It's like, you know… what's on the inside."

I tried to follow his halting attempts to explain his request. I slowly joined the dots. "You want me to go inside your mind?" I asked. "Deliberately? Like you did to me when we … when …"

Scott nodded.

"But not just then," I said. "You've … I've felt you since then."

Scott nodded again.

There had been times when our conversation had ceased and we sat in a comfortable silence together. Sometimes during these moments, I had felt Scott's presence inside my mind, in a similar way to the time on the bench by the lake when it all began. He wasn't trying to rid me of a miasma of foul, invading emotions; he was simply exploring my mind, getting to know the feel of my spirit in a way that until recently, I would never have been able to comprehend. At these times, I opened my mind to him willingly and delighted in the sensation of having the man who occupied my every waking thought actually inside my head. It felt sensual, loving and intimate, as if he were caressing my mind. It was a testament to the trust and the growing affinity between us.

Scott waited patiently as I considered his suggestion. The more that I thought about it, the more excited I became. I had connected with my own fluence and was ready to take this next step. He had warned me that it would deepen our bond, but I was happy with that, excited even. I felt ready. Scott deduced my decision from my emotions before I could articulate it. His eyes lit up. He took my hand.

"Are you sure?" he asked. "Don't do it for me. Do it because you want to."

I smiled back, letting my enthusiasm and curiosity shine through. "I want to."

He told me to think about the moment that I connected with my fluence and how it felt when he was exploring inside my mind. He told me to close my eyes again and use the connection that I had with my own fluence and the bond that I had with his to follow his emotions back to his mind, to sense with my fluence, to see into his soul.

I closed my eyes and slowed my breathing, slow and even, in and out. I emptied my mind of all other thoughts and imagined myself as an ethereal spirit unconnected to the physical reality of the world. I glided silently to the chamber of my mind in which my fluence resided, finding it more quickly and efficiently this time, knowing instinctively where to go. This time, it was already awake. It was already pulsing, breathing in time with my body, glowing, humming, anticipating my desires, making me stronger.

I felt myself unite with the power, and without any physical motion, I cast the energy out, away from my own mind, searching for Scott: his spirit, his energy, distinct and yet somehow already connected with my own. I recalled to mind the part of him that was already a part of me, and it didn't take long to find him. There was a hint of resistance as I approached, which quickly fell away, giving me permission, and my own energy was welcomed inside.

I had done it. I was — at least my spirit was — inside Scott's mind. I could feel his breathing. I could sense his essence, his fluence, the part of him that made him Scott Callahan. It felt so strong, so powerful. I felt as if I could absorb that energy and I would be able to do anything, be anyone. I could dance, I could fly, I could take on the world. It was a heady, intoxicating feeling, a lightness, a sensual, arousing pleasure like the caress of silk against naked skin or the popping of champagne bubbles on a parched tongue. This is where Scott's essence resided, and it was laid bare for me to explore, to learn, to taste, and I didn't hold back. It felt too good.

I began to feel strangely out of my depth, as if I could drown in the beautiful, delicious sensations all assaulting me at once. I had to struggle to keep my breathing under control, feeling it coming faster and being aware of a weakness, a trembling in my physical body. There was a burning desire to open my eyes, to reach out and touch him, to connect with him physically, rip off his clothes and put a stop to all of the waiting, the resistance, the sanity and the reason, but I determinedly held onto the last vestige of control and slowly, reluctantly withdrew, leaving a small part of myself behind, adding to our connection, strengthening our bond. The whole experience had only lasted a few seconds but would stay with me for the rest of my life.

I opened my eyes and took a moment to orientate myself in the present, physical world. I felt lightheaded, dizzy and hot, as if my skin was on fire, and memories of that night on the bench came flooding back. I recalled how it had felt for me when Scott had entered my mind and realised how much it must have affected him. It was no wonder that he had felt so confused and so guilty. I could appreciate why he had run. I looked at him now. He was sitting on the chair beside me and his eyes were tightly closed. He was sitting as still as a statue and his fists were clenched on his knees, his breathing coming hard and fast. I could feel his arousal and frustration, and I knew exactly how he felt because I felt it too. I tentatively reached out a hand to touch him, to let him know that I was there.

"No, Belle," he said through gritted teeth. "I don't think you should touch me right now."

I nodded my understanding, withdrew my hand, stood and took a few steps away from him and waited. Slowly, his breathing returned to normal and he opened his eyes. The flames were burning brightly.

"Well," he said. "Well, that was more ... I mean that was ... I didn't expect ... I mean, Jesus Christ. Wow. So ... you found it, then?"

I laughed unsteadily. "Yes, it seems I did. It was a bit ... I ... yes," I said. "You're beautiful."

"OK. This is getting ..." Scott began. "Well, it's getting harder all the time. I knew it would ... I mean, I knew, but I didn't ... hey, I'm not a saint." He flashed me a roguish smile. "Something's got to give, Belle. Spending all this time here alone together. It's not going to work. We need to find a way ... I need to find a way to be near you and not ... to control myself ... ourselves ... we need to ... change things up a bit. Especially now that you ... now that you can ... Jesus Christ." He was still a little shaken.

"Yes. You're right, and I agree," I said. "I want it, Scott. I'm certain. More certain than I've ever been of anything. I want it all. I want to be with you, I want to go out with you, I want to tell my dad about you, I want to tell the world, and I don't want to hide. And yes, I also want to meet your parents. Let's just ... can we ...?"

Scott could barely contain his excitement. "Really?"

I nodded and smiled.

"OK, then," he said. "Let's do this. Let's do it properly, starting with going out, surrounded by other people so I'm not so tempted to ... well, you know.

"And also, while we're about it, you need some ordinaries to practise on. It's all very well teaching you the theory, but you're never going to get it when you've only got me to play with because ... well, look what just happened. We're too close. We're already connected. I want to see you come across someone who's having a bad day and whose emotions are all over the place. I want you to stay strong, stop the emotions from getting to you, crippling you, and change their proclivity. You're so strong. I could feel your power. It was dizzying. And there's other stuff I want to teach you as well. Stuff you need other people for because you can't block me

474

out. I'm already inside your head." He flashed that wicked smile. "It's the weekend tomorrow. Let's go out. Let's go somewhere where there are other people. Let's mix with folks. It's time."

I had been nervous about going out with Scott in public because we lived in a small community. I didn't want to rub Jack's nose in my newfound happiness so soon. There was also my family to consider. I hadn't spoken to Mum since the night that I split up with Jack, and I had only spoken to Dad briefly on the phone. Despite everything, I had to be the one to break the news to Mum that I was in a relationship with a fluencer and that I had found my bond. I also owed it to Jack and Donna to speak to them first. I didn't want them hearing my news on the grapevine, but Scott was right; it was time. It had been a couple of months now, and it was OK that I needed to move on. We needed to get on with our lives.

It had been wonderful these last few weeks, sharing our secret, magical life, but we would have to leave the cabin sooner or later, and I would just have to bite the bullet and speak to my friends and family. He was right about the other thing too. The temptation to be together physically was growing stronger every day. We needed to get out. Once again, before I had time to articulate my answer, Scott knew. I opened my mouth, but he got in first.

"Marvellous," he said, a glimmer in his eye. "It's a date. I'll pick you up in the morning. Be ready by nine and bring a coat."

Chapter 26

Someone had been in my house. As I stepped through the front door, I sensed a slight disturbance in the air. There was no sign of forced entry or disorder, just a feeling, an illusive scent, but familiar and harmless. I recognised it immediately. Jack had been here. Entering the living room, I saw a single folded sheet of paper with my name on it on the coffee table, and when I picked it up, Jack's house keys slid out of the centre, hitting the table with a heavy, penetrating clatter that startled me. The note was short and simple.

I've collected the last of my things.
Here are your keys.
See you around,
Jack.

I sat down heavily, staring at the note in my hand. It was terse, to the point. It didn't sound like the Jack that I knew. He must have come while I was at work, knowing that he could avoid me and therefore avoid an awkward or emotional encounter. I hoped that the fact that he had felt up to returning to the house for his belongings meant that things were improving for him but was unsure if that meant that he would be open to hearing from me. It might be worse today, with his having been here. It might be better if I was already on his mind. It was a shame that he hadn't called before coming round. I would have liked to speak to him, even seen him, perhaps. I missed him. I wanted to know that he was all right. In the end, it didn't matter whether it was better or worse today. I had to do it. I had to do it now, tonight.

"Hello?"

"Hi, Jack. It's me. It's Isabel."

"Yeah, I know."

"Of course. I just … I …"

"You got your keys back all right?"

"Yes. I've got them. Thanks."

"Sorry I didn't call. Sorry I let myself in. I just didn't want to … I wasn't sure if I could … I thought it'd be better while you weren't there."

"It's OK, Jack. It's fine. That's not why I called."

"No? Why then?"

"How are you?"

"Honestly? I've been better, but it's better now than it was. It's getting better."

"Yes, of course. I'm sorry. I hope …" I couldn't finish that sentence. I didn't even know what I wanted to say.

"I know. That wasn't why you called either, though, was it?"

"No, I … I just wanted to let you know. I thought you should hear it from me." There was a weighty silence while I tried to find the right words, but in the end, there were no right words, but the message was simple. "I'm seeing someone, Jack. I … I've met someone. Someone … new. I just … I just didn't want you to find out another way. I thought … I mean, I owe it to you to be … I just wanted you to know."

I waited for him to speak. It was a few seconds before he found his voice.

"That didn't take long," he said bitterly. "Not that it matters, I suppose."

"Of course it matters, Jack. I don't want to cause you any more pain. I don't want to make it worse but … I had to … I needed to tell you."

"Well, you've told me. You've found someone else. That's great. I'm glad you're happy. Was there anything else?"

"No, that's all. I just …"

"You just wanted me to know. Yes. Well, now I know. I'll see you around, Isabel."

I kept the dead phone pressed to my ear for a few seconds. I felt horrible. He didn't sound like Jack at all. It had always been so easy, so warm and relaxed between us, but that had been painfully awkward, and his voice had sounded lifeless and cold, empty of emotion or filled with grief. I still cared about him deeply. I hated that I had caused him so much pain. I had a surge of anger towards Mum. If I had known the truth, if she had told me what I was, I could have made informed choices and would never have been with Jack in the first place. We would still be best friends.

I sighed. I also had to take responsibility for my own feelings, my own actions. The next call wasn't going to be much easier, but I had to try. I had reached out to Donna a few times since the breakup, but she had made it crystal clear that she wasn't ready to talk. This news was going to do nothing to help repair our relationship.

"Yeah?"

That was a bad start.

"Don? It's me."

"Yeah, I got that. Did you want something?"

"Oh, Don. Don't be like that. It doesn't have to be like this between us. I don't want to lose you too. You know me. You know I never meant to hurt him. I wouldn't have if …"

"I thought I knew you."

"Oh, Don, that's not fair. You do know me. We've been best friends forever."

"Best friends? You didn't talk to me. Why didn't you talk to me? If you were having doubts, if you were unhappy, you could've talked to me. That's what best friends do."

"Yes, I could have talked to you. I know that. But what would you have said? He's your best friend too. I didn't want to put you in that position."

"What would I have said? I would have reminded you how much he loves you, how much you love him, how it's been the three of us since we were six years old. The guy worships you, Iz, always has. I just can't believe you'd do this to him. I would've told you you were being stupid. I would've talked some sense into you."

I didn't reply immediately. Of course that's what Donna would have said, which is exactly why I could never have gone to her.

"Exactly," I said quietly.

"Exactly?" Donna shouted back. "Exactly? You sound like you think it makes me a shit friend because I would've told you the truth! I would've told you what you needed to hear. I would've stopped this. That doesn't make me shit. You're right. He's my best friend too, you know? I love him too. I love you both. And I was there for him when he was crying, when he told me he didn't know how to carry on without you. He begged me to tell him what he did wrong, what made you stop loving him, and I couldn't tell him, could I? I couldn't tell him because I didn't know. I don't know. I don't understand, Iz. It's not me who's shit. It's you."

Her words felt deliberately hurtful.

"Oh, Don, I'm sorry. I'm sorry I hurt him. I'm sorry I hurt you. I had to do it, though. Please can we talk properly? Please don't just be mad at me. Listen to me. Hear me out. You're my best friend."

"I don't know, Iz. I just don't know."

"You don't know what? If you'll talk to me or if we're … if you're still my best friend?" There were tears streaming down my face. I felt sick that Donna was so upset with me and sick that I didn't know if it could ever be fixed. The guilt stabbed at my heart. Jack had been crying and questioning his future while I had been at the cabin with Scott, happier than I'd ever been in my life, starting again.

"Like I said, I just don't know," Donna replied. "And I don't want to talk about it tonight. I'm not ready. Was there something you wanted, or can we save this chat for another time?"

I almost didn't do it. The thought of the added anger and pain my words would cause almost stayed my hand. I didn't know if I could tell her, but I knew that I had to, especially if there was any chance of her hearing it from Daniel instead of from me, and I had no idea if or when she might see him again.

"Yes, there was something. The reason ... one of the reasons ... I wanted to let you know that I'm seeing someone. I'm seeing Scott Callahan. I ... we ... I just ..."

"Right. Of course." Donna laughed, an unpleasant, humourless sound. "Of course. I should have seen that coming. Wow. That's just ... right. Wow."

"Don ..." I started.

"No, Izzy," Donna snapped. "Don't say any more. I don't want to hear it. I don't want to ... if we ... if I ... I might say something I might regret one day. Thanks for the call. Thanks for the heads up. Probably best if you don't ring for a bit, though. Thanks. Bye."

She was gone before I had a chance to respond, and I was left holding the silent phone again. I suppose it hadn't gone any worse than I was expecting. I had known that she was angry with me and that my revelation would only make things worse. It didn't make it any easier to hear that tone of condemnation from my best friend, though. I thought that she might be able to see both sides or at least make some effort to see things from my point of view. Even if she didn't agree with me, didn't our friendship count for something? It almost felt like talking to a different person. Perhaps I didn't know her as well as I thought I did. Perhaps she had changed. She had seemed different ever since the night that she got cross with me after the cinema, when we met Scott and Daniel the first time. I would give her time, but I wasn't about to give up on her, not without a fight.

I sighed. I had made the choice to let Jack go and build a life with Scott. The life that we were building together was going to make me happier than I could ever have been. It was a selfish choice, but it was my life. I deserved to live up to my potential, and Jack deserved someone who could love him properly. He deserved the chance to be a father.

There was one more call to make. I dialled Dad's mobile, still not brave enough to speak to Mum alone.

"Izzy, darling. Hi."

Just hearing his voice brought me to tears again. There was no mistaking the love that he had for me. I paused, searching for my own voice.

"Izzy? Are you OK?"

"Hi, Dad. I'm … yes, I'm OK thanks. In fact, I'm good. Only … I just rang Donna. It didn't go so well. She's so angry with me."

Dad sighed down the line. "Give her time, Izzy. She'll be hurting too, but she loves you. You'll work things out. Time heals. It really does. So, how've you been?"

"Honestly, Dad, I've been good, really good." It was such a relief to not have to hide it. "In fact, that's kind of why I'm ringing. Dad, I've met someone. He's … he's … he's really special, Dad."

Another silence. I hated the lack of emotional clues in a phone call. I had no idea what he was feeling. I couldn't even see if he was smiling. I tried to imagine his face.

"Yes," he said at last. "I wondered. It seemed odd that we haven't heard from you or seen you since the breakup, as if maybe you weren't alone at the house by yourself feeling sad and lonely."

"Oh, Dad, don't. You don't want me to be miserable, do you? I know it's quick but …"

"Of course I don't want you to be miserable, darling. I always want you to be happy. If this man makes you happy … but you're right. You said it. It is quick, darling. You and Jack've been together so long. He loves you so much."

"Urgh, Dad! Why does everyone keep telling me how much he loves me? Do you think I don't know? I know he loves me and I know I've hurt him. I know!" I didn't mean to raise my voice but I couldn't help it.

"I'm sorry, Izzy. That's not what I meant. I didn't mean to be insensitive. I'm sorry. Can we start again? Shall I go and get Mum?"

"No, please don't go and get Mum. Look, Scott and I are going out tomorrow and I just wanted you to know, and I wanted to hear your voice. I hoped you might be happy for me. You can let Mum know for me."

"Don't be like that, Izzy. We can talk."

"I'm not being like anything, Dad."

"Do you want to tell me anything about this guy, Scott? Are we going to get to meet him?"

"He's a good man, Dad. I'd like you to meet him, yes. I don't know. I just don't know."

"OK. Look, darling, I'm sorry this didn't go right. I'm worried about you, but I'm glad you're happy. I'll tell Mum for you, but you two really need to sort things out too. She's not been herself. She misses you."

"Yeah. I miss her too. I love you, Dad."

"Love you too, Izzy."

"Bye."

"Bye."

I sat still for minutes, my phone limply forgotten in my hand, my mind not really on anything. I stared sadly at the floor. Jack was suffering, Donna hated me, I wasn't speaking to Mum, and Dad thought that I was rushing into a new relationship after dumping Mr Right for no good reason. It was no wonder that I had kept to my safe, magical bubble with Scott in the cabin. While I was with him, I had temporarily forgotten that all of the other meaningful relationships in my life were in tatters.

I stood up slowly and dragged myself upstairs to bed. I felt really low. I felt guilty for breaking Jack's heart and even guiltier for moving on so quickly and so thoroughly. The trip to the beach tomorrow suddenly didn't seem so appealing. I didn't feel as if I deserved to be treated so well. I didn't deserve to be happy.

Not nearly long enough later, I groaned as my alarm startled me from an uncomfortable, restless sleep. I had been dreaming about Jack, about Donna. My feelings of guilt had seeped into my sleep and I had tossed and turned all night, waking once or twice from a nightmare, the details of which eluded me in the dark winter morning. I gripped the duvet tightly, my heart hammering in my ears, and I reached out for my phone to snooze the incessant refrain.

With the alarm silenced at last, I dragged the phone over to glance at the screen. 7.01 a.m. and a message from Scott flashing before my eyes.

Good morning my beautiful girl x

My humour was promptly restored. I smiled. I had been waking up to the same message every morning of late, and it was a practice to which I could easily become accustomed. As I crafted my reply, I roused myself more fully and reminded myself that Scott and I had plans today, plans involving more than the two of us in his cabin, plans involving Scott actually taking me out.

Good morning yourself x

He must have been waiting for my reply because his next message came instantly.

Missed you last night. I could hardly sleep thinking about today. Be ready by 9 x

My smile widened. Scott was taking me to the beach. I had let the anguish of the previous night's phone calls worm its way into my sleep, but I didn't have to let it ruin my day. Today Scott would take me out and I didn't have to hide. We were going somewhere together, deliberately, and people would see us as a couple. I was wrong last night. I had let the negativity infect me, but I was wrong. I did deserve to be happy.

The idea of being out in public with Scott Callahan was thrilling and a little unsettling. My tummy did a somersault and my pulse quickened. I was nervous as well as excited. My relationship with Jack had stemmed and evolved from a childhood friendship. It had always felt normal. This felt different. I felt like a grown-up going out with a real man, a man whose presence affected every ounce of my being. This felt special. It felt exciting.

Mood much improved, I sat up in bed. It was 7.02 a.m., which meant that I had two hours to get ready. I counted backwards from 9.00 a.m., allowing time for a shower, to style my hair, choose an outfit, get dressed and eat breakfast. I had plenty of time, but I didn't want to be flustered when he arrived, so I decided to aim to be ready by 8.50 a.m. I leapt out of bed and headed straight for the shower, humming tunefully to myself, the challenges of the previous night temporarily shelved.

Despite the fact that Scott had seen me, kissed me, explored my heart and welcomed me into his mind every day for weeks and weeks, there was something particular about being taken out that made today feel momentous. Clean and refreshed from my shower, I asked Alexa to play some uplifting music and shimmied around the bedroom getting dressed. I picked out my clothes carefully. It would be chilly on the beach in March. The forecast predicted a dry but cold and windy day, and I didn't want to spend the whole day blue and shivering, so I picked out trousers and a comfortable fitted jumper over a low-cut black top. I would wear my pink winter coat and sensible trainers, preferring comfort over fashion so that I could relax and enjoy the day. By 8.45 a.m. my hair was straight and shiny and I was sitting in the living room by the window, eagerly anticipating Scott's arrival.

At 8.47 a.m., his van passed the cottage. I watched bemused as he did a three-point turn a little further up the road and parked outside a house about four doors away. I watched him glance at his watch and turn off the engine and I laughed at the notion of my strong, confident man being embarrassed to arrive thirteen minutes early for our date, presumably not wanting to appear too keen, which had never seemed to worry him up until now. I pulled out my phone.

I can see you x

I watched, highly entertained, as he retrieved his phone from the glove box and read my message. Even from this distance, I saw the colour rise to his cheeks. He slowly scanned his eyes to my front window, where I sat waving cheerfully with a knowing smile on my face. He raised a hand in mock salute, started the engine and crawled back along the curb, coming to rest at the end of my drive. He leapt out of the car and sprinted to the door, all thought of playing it cool apparently forgotten.

Scott didn't need to knock because I also had no intentions of playing it cool. I jumped up and had the door open for him before he made it to the bottom of the drive. He looked down at me hesitantly for a moment as if unsure what to do, but when he saw me smile and sensed my open, guileless joy, it was enough. He swept me off my feet, planted a delightful kiss on my lips and searched my eyes.

"I didn't want to put any pressure on you to be ready, in case you weren't. I know I was a bit early, but I just couldn't wait. I know … I know I only saw you yesterday, but there was something so exciting about actually leaving the house and coming to get you. I can't wait to take you out. I can't wait to show you off and shout to the world that you're mine."

I laughed up into his smiling face, blushing slightly at the sentiment.

"I was waiting for you," I told him. "I couldn't wait either. I feel exactly the same."

We were soon in his van heading swiftly towards the

coast. We chatted all the way, enjoying lighthearted conversation about undemanding topics, easy in each other's company. We talked about films and television, books, music and food. We planned fictitious holidays and swapped celebrity crushes. Conversation flowed easily, and we were animated, fuelling and consuming the lively emotions bouncing around in the van. I enjoyed getting to know the little things about him and answering his questions, teaching him the little things about me. There was a different energy surrounding us outside of the cabin. The building sexual tension that had become overwhelming had dissipated to a dull roar, ever present but more manageable under new and different conditions.

We parked in a small, quiet car park alongside a modest harbour on a sandy creek where numerous pretty fishing and pleasure boats were moored, bobbing playfully in the water. I had never been to this part of the coast before and took great pleasure in the charm of my surroundings. Scott took my hand and steered me over a stile onto a path that led towards the beach, with the creek on our left and an enormous expanse of freshwater meadows on our right, forming part of a huge nature reserve running for miles along the coast. It was tranquil and unspoiled. It was beautiful.

The path ran along the top of the creek bank, with the marshes opening out below on the right-hand side. We walked hand in hand, and as I breathed in the fresh sea air and watched the wading birds paddling in the mud of the creek, Scott talked me through some of the things that he wanted me to practise.

"You've already achieved so much more than I expected at this stage," he told me happily. "I don't want to sound patronising … again … but I'm so proud of you."

I glanced at his face to make sure that he wasn't making fun of me, but the sincerity in his eyes and the rising feeling of delight reassured me immediately.

"We've talked about the three main features of the

fluence, but it's time you started putting theory into practice," he said.

I nodded, eager to learn.

"So, as you know, it's mostly about sensing and sharing other people's emotions, something you've always been able to do. It comes naturally to you, so naturally that you've had to share other people's feelings whether you liked it or not, and I know that often, you didn't … like it … but what you need to do now is learn to embrace it. Feel people's emotions, taste their mood and their passions but without letting the feelings take over *you*. You have the power to separate yourself from the emotions you're reading, to keep a hold of yourself and not be consumed by it. You just have to learn to control it."

"Yes. That's exactly what I've always wished I could do, but it was always just wishing. I wished so hard sometimes that I didn't have this cursed affliction, but actually, having it isn't the problem at all; it's the lack of control."

"Exactly. You should never've been left to try to deal with it without being taught about what you are and what you can do, and being told to ignore it and try to make it go away just added to your problems because if you're suppressing a thing, you can't learn about it or gain any control over it. But the power inside you's too strong to be suppressed totally, so it's been spilling out in an uncontrolled way for your whole life. We've already started. You're already much more in control. Now you've connected with your fluence and you're working with it, not against it, the rest will be so much easier. I'm excited for you." Scott squeezed my hand, and I squeezed his back, echoing his emotion.

"Not only can you read emotions in others, but you can also control how people feel, although that's a much harder skill and obviously comes with more responsibility," Scott continued.

I couldn't suppress a little laugh.

"You sound like something … wasn't it Spiderman who

said *with great power comes great responsibility?*"

"The Peter Parker principle, exactly ... although ... it was Uncle Ben, and obviously, the theory far predates Stan Lee. But while it's been connected to Spiderman and does sound like a bit of a cliché, it's still something we take seriously. We have the power to change people's lives without even knowing we're doing it, so it should always be done carefully, sensitively and only for good."

I couldn't suppress another giggle. Scott shot me a reproving glare.

"I'm sorry," I said. "I love what you're trying to do, and I'm so happy. I'm happy to be here with you. I'm happy to be learning all this stuff, but you do sound a bit like you're planning on turning me into the next Avenger or the next X-Man ... or X-Woman."

Scott laughed too. "You'd look great in Lycra," he said. "We should definitely see about getting you a uniform made up."

I punched him hard in the shoulder, and he winced.

"OK, OK, I'm sorry. Not PC enough?"

I just scowled, and he laughed.

"Where were we? Yes, reading emotions, fluencing emotions. The other thing's really just about control. Controlling what you feel from others, controlling what others feel from you, that sort of thing. You're really strong, Belle. I think you're going to get it all really quickly and be a fluence master in no time." He saw the funny side this time, laughed and stopped, taking a wide stance. "Daniel-san, Daniel-san, wax on, wax off, wax on, wax off."

"You know that's karate, right?" I said with a smile. "Not fluence? And no, I'm not going to wash your van. I'm certain it won't help my studies!"

We laughed together and continued on towards the beach.

About a mile from the harbour, the firm ground beneath our feet began to change into softer sand, and there was a section of boardwalk that led us into the heart of the dunes. Once there, the reinforced path came to an end, and on the sand, our progress slowed, the wind began to pick up, and we had to pause our conversation as we approached the beach. We reached the top of the rise at a gap in the dunes where the view suddenly opened up before our eyes. I found myself surrounded by the tall grass of the dunes, whispering in the breeze, and faced with the most beautiful expanse of unspoiled golden sandy beach that I had ever seen. The glittering flecks of sand and shell stretched out to meet the rippling sea, which in turn met with the clear blue sky on the hazy horizon. It was totally empty, deserted, giving the impression that we might be the only people alive in the world. I stood still at that gap and let out a sigh of surprise and delight as the wind whisked the salty air across my face.

I let out a whoop of joy and ran headlong down the slope with my arms flailing madly in the air. I ran out onto the beach towards the sea. I felt completely free. I could hear Scott laughing behind me, and as he caught up, he took hold of my hand and spun me round to face him. He looked into my eyes.

"I had a feeling you'd like it here," he told me. "It's usually quiet because of the walk, but it's totally worth it. You look so alive. Alive and beautiful with the sun on your face and the wind in your hair." He tucked a strand of hair behind my ear. It was a tender, intimate gesture, but it came untucked again immediately to continue blowing in the wind and made me realise what a waste of time it had been straightening and styling it this morning. We had been out of the car for less than an hour and I felt like Bridget Jones in the convertible on the way to her mini-break with the nefarious Daniel Cleaver.

It didn't matter in the slightest. I didn't care how my hair looked. I was out, we were together, I was free, and more than that, I was happy. One of the wonderful things about being with someone whose every emotion I could read as clearly as my own was that I didn't have to worry about whether he thought I looked silly or even whether he cared about how I looked at all. I was wrapped in the warmth of his affection and the undeniability of his adoration. I was able to bask in the absolute confidence that he cared for me deeply, inside and out, and if Scott didn't care that my hair was a mess or that my mascara might run from the salty spray, then I certainly wasn't going to. I could release all of my inhibitions, relax and enjoy myself unreservedly.

I took his hand, and we walked down to the surf. We turned right, and I marvelled at the sight of the miles upon miles of beach stretching alongside the open water. It felt so familiar, and yet I had never been to this part of the coast before. It suddenly occurred to me that this was the setting of my dream, the beach dream, the fantasy that I had been visiting since last October. The weather was not as warm and we were wearing more clothes, but there was no mistaking the scene. I glanced at Scott subtly to make sure that this was the fantasy version and not the nightmare from last night, but when the wind whistled bitterly around my exposed neck, it reminded me that this was no dream at all. This was reality, but knowing that I had dreamed this place staggered me and caused me to pause and stare around in fascination. Scott turned to me with bemusement.

"What is it?" he asked.

I was a little embarrassed. "This place," I said.

"I've never been here before, but I feel like I've been here before. I mean … I know I haven't … but I have … I haven't … but I've seen it."

"You've been here before, or you haven't been here before?" Scott checked. "You've seen it in pictures or on the telly, you mean?"

"Not exactly." I paused. "I've been here before … with you … in my dreams."

That piqued Scott's interest. His face lit up, and there was a fiery glint in his eye.

"Oh, yes?" he asked. "Do go on."

I laughed. "Do you remember when I stayed in the cabin that first night? After the club? After Kev?"

"Of course I remember," he said softly. "Every tiny detail."

"You remember after I had the nightmares? When I begged you to get into bed and hold me?" My face was becoming redder and the flush was heating my body, making me immune to the chill of the winter wind.

"Yes?" said Scott, beginning to respond physically to my embarrassment and the memory of how my physical reaction to the dream had affected him that night.

"You weren't there when I woke up," I reminded him. "I was so embarrassed, terrified that you would've heard me calling your name."

"You were calling my name?" he asked quietly.

"Yes, I think so. Yes." I laughed.

"Wow," he said. "I didn't hear you, but it sounds like I was right to leave when I did."

"Yes," I agreed. "Anyway, I was dreaming about you … about us. We were here … right here, on this beach, holding hands and walking in the water. It was much warmer in my dream. The sun was shining, and it was summer, and we were walking and talking and laughing together. It's the same dream I dreamed ever since that night by the lake. There were so many nights I dreamed about you but woke up next to … well, I dreamed about you at Christmas. I dreamed about you before we even knew each other. And almost every time I dreamed, it was here, and we were walking like this and …"

"And…?" Scott demanded, his body responding to the heat in my mind.

I laughed, embarrassed again. "Well, like I said, in my dream, it was summer and it was hot and … well … we would walk and talk and …"

"Yes, you've said that already. How about we skip to the bit where you're lying in my bed, calling my name?"

I flushed even hotter. "You'd walk me up to the dunes from the beach and there'd be a blanket lying in a sheltered spot in the dunes."

"A blanket?" asked Scott. "Whose blanket?"

I laughed. "I don't know. I guess I always supposed it was yours. You always knew where to go."

"My blanket?" he asked. "How did it get there? Did I put it there?"

"I don't know, do I?" I laughed again. "It was a dream. I never asked."

"OK, so there's a blanket up there in the dunes?" Scott asked, tugging me away from the surf. I pulled him back, laughing.

"No, Scott. I'm pretty sure it's not there today. It's not warm enough. This isn't the day of the dream. This isn't the dream, just the setting."

"Oh." Scott looked disappointed, but his eyes were shining with laughter. "You don't think we ought to just check?"

I shook my head.

"All right. So, I take you to this blanket …?"

"Yes, you take me to the blanket, and you pull me down and you kiss me and …"

I couldn't continue because Scott was kissing me. He took the passion of the dream and he poured it into a kiss that made me weak at the knees.

"Like that?" he asked.

"Something like that," I said, a little dazed.

He stared into my eyes again and the flames in his were blazing. He shook his head.

"Your eyes will be the death of me, Belle," he said softly. "They move and dance with your moods and emotions. The ripples on a pond or the crashing of waves in a storm. They glimmer and they shine, and when I look into them, I feel like I'm falling or being hypnotised. They're so intense, so deep. I can't look away. Sometimes it's a little frightening, in a good way."

"That's exactly how I feel when I look at you," I whispered.

We stood still for a few moments, lost in our thoughts and in the magic of each other's eyes.

I laughed again, feeling so free. "Do you remember why we came out today?" I asked him.

"What? Why?" he was startled out of his reverie.

"We'd spent so much time alone together, we were in danger of getting carried away," I reminded him. "So you said *let's go out. Let's go and surround ourselves with other people where we won't be tempted,* and then you brought me to a remote beach on a winter's day. There isn't a soul in sight, and it just happens to be the setting of my sexual fantasies."

We both laughed.

"Hmm … yes, maybe I didn't think it through. Or maybe this was all part of my evil plan." He let out an evil laugh and took my hand again.

"I've always wondered what it'd be like to be taken out by a millionaire," I mused. "I mean, what would you do if money was no object? Now I know. You go to a deserted beach in the middle of winter and get blown around in the wind, and it's … it's better than I could ever have imagined. It's magic."

Scott nodded in agreement.

"Come on," he said. "Let's walk, let's talk, and let's head back to civilisation. I really am going to take you somewhere where we'll be surrounded by other people and there won't be any temptation. You really get under my skin. I'm going to take you somewhere where we can practise your abilities, somewhere a little out of your comfort zone. This date isn't over."

We continued our walk along the beach for a mile or so and then made our way back up through the dunes and along a path through a thick area of woodland that emerged on the other side of the marshes, near the little car park by the harbour. Scott led me past the car to a cosy cafe where we sat inside and ordered two luxury hot chocolates with cream and marshmallows and two slices of freshly baked lemon drizzle cake. There weren't many people in the cafe, but I was keen to practise the exercises that Scott had described.

When the waitress brought our drinks, I focused on her aura. I concentrated on actively using the fluence to read the woman's emotions rather than letting her emotions pursue me. I practised tuning out the other emotions in the room and was thrilled with my progress. It seemed easy.

"It is easy when you know how," Scott assured me. "Now you and the fluence are working together, everything will be easier, but that doesn't necessarily mean everything will always be easy. You've got a lot to learn. In here there aren't loads of extreme emotions bouncing around, so it's easier to sense each one individually and manipulate that energy. Let them in, study them, block them out. This little kid bouncing in now. She wants an ice-cream. You can sense her energy from here. See if you can stop it before it breaches your mind. Look at her, sense her emotion, but hold it at arm's length and study it dispassionately rather than letting it get inside you and letting it manipulate your mood."

I looked at the little girl with her blonde ringlets and beaming smile. She was tugging at her mother's hand, and it didn't take any superpowers to sense that she was giddy with excitement. Her mum was laughing.

"You know it's February and cold enough to need your winter hat, right? Are you sure you want an ice-cream?"

The little girl just nodded and laughed, dragging her mum to the freezer.

I smiled at the child. I tried not to stare as I used my fluence to connect with her emotion before it hit me, but this one was much more difficult. The little girl's excitement was too strong for me to contain. The energy came barrelling into me, and although I could identify it and its source, I was unable to harness it and hold it away from my mind. The emotion was simply too powerful, and it flooded me with a feeling of irrepressible joy, that unique delight of childhood.

Scott laughed with me as he, too, took a hit of childish glee, and we savoured the feeling for a moment before I let my own disappointment shine through.

"Urgh. I thought I was getting it," I complained.

"Belle, you're amazing," he chided. "Don't be disappointed. Children's emotions are hard to control because they're so pure and sharp, and you're only just starting out. I know grown fluencers who've been dealing with it their whole lives and wouldn't be able to stop ice-cream excitement getting in. And let's face it, why would you want to, really? One of the many advantages of our sensitivity is that we get to experience emotions that don't exist for most ordinary adults. That little girl didn't lose anything because we shared her joy. There are only winners here."

I smiled at his assessment. He made a good point, but I had felt strong and wanted to prove to myself that I had control. My disappointment continued to churn.

"Seriously, Belle. This is going to take time, and you're making amazing progress. Don't be too hard on yourself. Do you want to give it a rest, or do you want to try something else?"

I thought for a moment. "There is something else that I meant to … I keep …" I said. "I can't get Daniel out of my head."

"Uh-oh, should I be jealous?" Scott teased.

"Ha, not likely. It's just … It's not that I want to block people out, but I want to figure out what it is that he does, especially now you said your parents do it too. And my mum. I just want to understand it better, I suppose."

"OK. It's not something I can help you that much with, to be honest. I don't do it, so I don't practise it, but I understand the theory behind it. Promise me, though, that if I teach you,

you won't ever try to block me out? One, it'll be difficult because of the bond. You're pretty much stuck with me, I'm afraid, and two, I already can't bear the thought of not sharing everything with you."

"You're so corny. It's kind of cute and kind of a bit weird. I'm not used to people being so open with their feelings like you. You wear your heart on your sleeve."

"Only with you," he corrected me.

I raised an eyebrow.

"OK, yes, I wear my heart on my sleeve most of the time with most other people too."

I laughed.

"But it's different with you. I don't ever want to hide anything from you, and I don't want you hiding from me either. I know you want your independence. I know my intensity probably terrifies you, but … well, you'll just have to get used to it. It's me, and I'm here to stay."

I shook my head. "I don't want to learn it so I can block you out," I reassured him. "I'm not scared of your honesty. It's refreshing and inspiring. Like I said, I just want to understand it all. Daniel really frightened me when I first met him. His coldness was sort of … inhuman. I thought there was something seriously wrong with him or seriously wrong with me. If I can understand what he's doing, it might make it seem less scary, that's all."

"Yeah, I get that," Scott conceded. "OK, so, your emotions occur naturally. To a certain extent, you can manipulate your own feelings. If you get scared, you can take deep breaths and try to calm yourself down. If you're sad, you can listen to happy music or go to your happy place … on the beach … on my blanket in the dunes." He winked. "Some people embrace every emotion they feel, while some try to suppress them, and some are considerably more capable of doing that than others. Some people see therapists, and other people take medication to alter the feelings they have. But that's not what this is about. When you block your

496

emotions from getting out, it's about stopping the flow of energy … not not feeling them at all.

"Remember, it's only fluencers who can read your emotions, so most of the time, it's not even an issue, around ordinaries, I mean. Daniel likes to surround himself with ordinaries mainly so he doesn't have to concentrate so hard on keeping his own emotions in check.

"So, blocking the flow of energy that can be read by another fluencer is basically like building a wall around your mind. It's hard, and it takes practice and strength to keep it up. You'll have to concentrate really hard at first. It's the same shield that'll stop a fluencer getting in to tamper with your emotions. They … we … shouldn't do it. Fluencing another fluencer is a big no-no, but unfortunately, it can happen. Didn't you say you pushed your mum out when she tried to fluence you at the allotment? You knew what was happening. You could feel it — her — trying to get in. Like when I … at the bench. I know you didn't understand, but I think you felt like you could have stopped me if you'd wanted to, if you'd really wanted to, I mean."

I nodded, and Scott went on. "So, yes, using that energy, the energy … the muscle that you used to push your mum out. You use that to build a wall around your mind. Imagine you and your emotions are behind that wall and the rest of the world is on the other side, and don't let them in. Don't let your emotions out, don't let their fluence in."

"OK," I said firmly. "Don't let them out. Don't let them in."

To tune everything else out, I chose a point on the opposite wall and stared at it steadily. I withdrew to the part of my mind that housed the fluence, and beginning there, I built a shield of energy around my mind. It rose slowly but surely. Scott could feel it.

"Good," he said, nodding. "Now pass me that spoon, please."

I glanced at the table for the spoon. The moment that I

allowed my eye to stray from the wall and my concentration to stray from the task, the shield collapsed. There wasn't even a spoon on the table.

"Hey!" I complained.

Scott just smiled. "Sorry," he said. "Just making a point. That was it, exactly right, but I wanted to show you just how much concentration it takes at first. While you're sitting still, staring at the wall, concentrating everything you have on the shield, it grows, and it might even stay, but as soon as you want to do anything else — move, talk, pass me a spoon — it's gone."

"Yes, I see," I said.

I turned away, tuned him out and began again. Staring at the same point on the wall, I started to build the shield back up. I could feel it obstructing the flow of emotional energy. It felt strong.

"Yes, that's it, very good," Scott praised.

He didn't interrupt any more. He sat back and left me to it, and after a few seconds, I turned to him with a proud smile, but once again, at the lapse in concentration, my shield crumbled, and my smile turned into a frown.

"It's amazing. I can get it up, but I can't do anything else. I can't think. I can't move without it coming crashing down."

"If you really want a strong shield, you just need to practise. It's all about strength and practise. It's like any other muscle or sense. You have to work on it if you want it to be strong. I've never put much effort into a shield. I'm not really interested in blocking emotions."

"I know." I smiled. "You're all about embracing it, letting it in. You're all about the love," I teased.

He smiled back and nodded. "Exactly," he said.

"Seriously, though. I can't imagine being able to do that and other stuff at the same time. Daniel's had his wall up the whole time I've been near him. It must be totally draining. How can he do that and live a normal life?"

"Normal?"

"Good point. How does he ever experience anything properly, though? I actually feel a bit sorry for him."

"He doesn't have the shield active all the time, just all the time he's around others like us. I told you he likes to spend most of his time with ordinaries."

"It's still odd," I said. "Wouldn't it be easier to just let us in?"

"I gave up wondering about Daniel years ago, but you're right: to remain fully functioning whilst maintaining a shield is a pretty impressive feat of strength. Don't try too hard, though, Belle. You don't need that. You're not like him. You're open. You're honest. You're more like me. Don't lose yourself trying to be somebody else."

I smiled. "Never," I replied.

We sat in the cafe for another couple of hours. It was quiet, but there was a slow, steady stream of customers for me to practise on. It was fun. I could feel it getting easier all of the time. The power was within me and I had the ability to use it. I just had to put the effort in now. In between exercises, our conversation continued until Scott glanced at his watch.

"Goodness me, it's time to go!" he cried.

I looked at the time. It was almost 6 p.m. "Time to go where?" I asked.

"The next part of our date, of course," he said with a knowing smile.

"There's more?" I groaned. I hadn't realised how tired I had become.

"You haven't worn yourself out, have you?" he asked. "It's the same as any other workout. You practise too much and you'll overdo it. All that fresh air won't have helped either. Come on." He held out my coat and escorted me out of the cafe.

Back in the car, I asked where we were going again.

"You'll see," he said cryptically.

Scott put the heating on in the car, and the warmth and the

vibration of the engine soon lulled me into a drowsy torpor. He was right. I had worn myself out. I thought about how difficult it had been to erect that shield and how quickly it had come crashing down. I couldn't imagine how much effort it would take to keep a barrier in place all of the time like Daniel did. I also couldn't imagine why anyone would want to. Mum had blocked me, Daniel did it, and Scott said that his parents did too. Despite his protestations, I couldn't help but feel that it might be a useful skill to master and promised myself that I would continue to work on it on my own.

I dozed comfortably in the car and had no idea how long we had been travelling when I felt Scott's hand squeeze my thigh and heard his voice through the haze of slumber.

"Wake up, sleepyhead," he murmured. "Wake up, we're here."

Chapter 27

I came to. We were in a brightly lit car park in a built-up part of town. I blinked to clear the fuzziness and took a better look. There were bright lights around a revolving door, and the name of the restaurant was carved into the stone above. I grabbed Scott's arm in panic.

"Scott, we're at Chez Chez." My eyes were wide as I watched impeccably dressed patrons handing their keys to the valets and striding confidently through the doors as if they owned the place.

"Yes. Yes, we are," he agreed calmly.

"We can't be here," I said quickly. "Not today. We can't eat here."

"Why not?" he asked, amused.

"Look at me!" I demanded. "I'm in my pink coat. I probably dribbled in my sleep. My hair's all over the place from the wind and the sea and ..."

"And I bet you're still the most beautiful woman here. I'm proud to have you on my arm, and we can go anywhere we want, but if it makes you feel better, you can leave the pink coat in the car."

He looked deadly serious. He hopped out of the van, walked round to the passenger door and opened it, holding out his hand for mine. I hesitated.

"If I'd known ... you could've warned me ... I would've ... I might've ... I could've at least ..."

Scott laughed. "Hush, Belle. Honestly, you're gorgeous. Get out of the van, take my hand, and let's go and get some dinner. I'm starving."

I shed the pink coat, cast one last helpless look at the safety of the van and took a deep breath. I accepted Scott's proffered hand and allowed myself to be escorted out into the car park and to the beautiful golden revolving door.

"I've never been here before," I whispered. "I know people who've come for special occasions, but ..." I stopped talking and my mouth fell open as we entered the enormous elegant dining room. My eyes were immediately drawn to the high ceilings, which had somehow been adorned with green foliage festooned with miniature silver flowers that were centred with tiny bulbs, making the ceiling itself shimmer and sparkle. The large chandeliers hanging below cast a warm glow on the exquisitely decorated space.

Scott put his hand possessively but gently on my lower back and drew me towards the maître d', who nodded his welcome and didn't appear remotely perturbed by my untidy hair and casual clothes.

"Callahan. Table for two," said Scott softly, with the conviction of someone born to frequent such establishments. The maître d' glanced at his rostrum and nodded respectfully.

"Of course, Mr Callahan. Follow me, please."

He led us across the flagstone floor to a small table set for two. The table was made of walnut, decorated with a classy single white rose and crisp white napkins that stood proudly next to the gleaming silverware. The sound of live piano music wafted softly through the air, and I meekly allowed myself to be seated, removed my jumper, hung it on the back of my chair and stared dumbly around the magnificent restaurant.

I began to feel the emotion of the place caressing my mind. It was alive with the buzz of romance and captivation. There were a few larger tables set for wealthy businessmen and women to show off to their clients, but the vast majority of the tables were intimate affairs attended by couples, courting and in love: couples talking, flirting, holding hands across the table and leaning tenderly towards each other. I opened my mind to the rapturous emotions and drank in the atmosphere. It was like a drug — exhilarating, provocative, dreamy.

It was as if Scott could read my mind.

"You never have to worry about negative emotions in a place like this," he told me conspiratorially. "No one comes here to have a bad time. You can relax, enjoy yourself, soak it all up."

I wasn't quite ready to let him off the hook. "It's amazing, Scott. I've always wondered … but seriously, look at me. I might be the only one in here not wearing hundreds of pounds' worth of evening dress. Everyone else might be buzzing and dripping with love and wine. I should be in the local chippy."

Scott snorted with laughter. "It doesn't matter where you are. You light up the room. Why don't you pop to the ladies, check yourself out in the mirror, powder your nose if you like, and then come back here to me, sit back, relax and enjoy a beautiful meal."

It was my turn to snort. "Powder my nose?" I laughed. "I seem to have left my powder puff in my other jeans."

We laughed together, but I stood and looked for a sign for the bathroom.

"Over there in the corner between the piano and the bar," Scott pointed.

"Thanks."

I made my way across the huge room, trying not to stick out like a sore thumb. I located the bathroom and pushed open the door. The toilets were like nothing I had ever seen, and if conceivable, possibly even more impressive than the dining room. They were luxurious, with thick, plush rugs underfoot and soft lighting. There was a row of heavy circular dark-coloured glass sinks on top of a wide marble counter with softly lit mirrors behind and a full-length mirror at the end of the room. I used the toilet and then stood, alone for a moment and able to breathe and relax a little. I nervously stepped forwards to wash my hands and check my reflection.

The girl staring back at me in that stylish mirror was, quite simply, radiant. Her soft, voluminous hair tumbled in perfect waves to rest lightly on her shoulders, and her simple black top had slipped off one shoulder to reveal a delicate, shapely collarbone bone and flawless skin. Her face was unblemished with no requirement for the makeup that had been obliterated by the wind and the salty sea spray. I looked natural and I looked joyful. Easily the most striking of my features were my eyes, which shone with incandescence. I smiled as I regarded the transformation that had taken place. There was no denying the informality of the trousers and the dirt on my totally inappropriate trainers, but I felt less out of place than I had expected. Happiness made me shine.

Back in the dining room, I squared my shoulders and shrugged away my concerns. I had always wanted to eat at Chez Chez. Now that I was here, I was going to enjoy it. I sauntered back to our table and smiled as Scott's face lit up.

"Good," he said contentedly. "You look happier, more relaxed, less like a frightened rabbit. Now, let's decide what we're going to eat, shall we? And no more exercises or practice. You've worn yourself out, and as this is our first … or is it second date? I just want you to sit back and enjoy it."

"Deal," I said with a smile.

"Do you want a drink?" he asked. "A glass of wine, perhaps."

"No," I said. "I don't drink much, and the last time I drank …" I faltered, not wishing to spoil the evening with a bad memory.

"Kev …" Scott guessed with a frown.

"Yes, Kev," I confirmed.

"Most of us don't drink much when we're out," Scott said. "There's no reason we can't, but the fact that it dulls the senses does make it that little bit more dangerous for us. Under the influence, it's harder to block extreme emotions, and of course, if you're on a night out, surrounded by other people who are drinking and having their senses dulled, you often find yourself surrounded by intense emotions, one way or another. If they're positive, it can make for a lovely time, but if they're unpleasant …"

"Like Kev."

"Exactly. Like Kev." Scott sighed. "That name is banned for the rest of the evening," he declared. "He's ruined enough nights, and we're here to have fun. One day, I'll buy us a nice bottle of wine to share at home."

The evening was incredible. The food was delicious, the atmosphere was delightful, and the company was perfect. I couldn't have imagined a better date.

"It still feels so weird … you know? Knowing that I'm not actually insane … that it's OK to feel the way I feel … to have the kind of reactions I have to people. I've enjoyed it in the past. Of course I have. It's given me pleasure, allowed me to help people … but I was always kind of running from it … kind of ashamed. Sitting here, allowing the feelings of everyone around me to just be and for that to be OK and not be a massive secret, it feels so different, so wonderful. I feel like a huge weight has been lifted from my shoulders. Thank you, Scott."

"I'm so glad. It's such a wonderful gift, and you're really strong. It's been a waste and a shame for you to hide from it for so long." He took my hand across the table and stroked his thumb gently across my wrist.

"I don't want to be frightened anymore," I said quietly. "I think that's why I want to learn the shield thing. I love the fact that you don't want it. Your openness is one of the things I … well, it makes you special, and I want to be like that too, but I feel like if I have a safety net, I won't be so frightened anymore. When I found out my mum's been fluencing me without my knowledge all these years, and when I came across Daniel, who seems so cold ... I want to be able to stop that. I want to be in control.

"I promise I don't want to block you out. I don't even know if I'll ever use it, but I want to feel like I'm the one who decides. I want to get the other stuff too, the stopping emotions before they get to me and examining them without letting them take over, and I promise I'll work on that. Every time I walk into a crowded place or even a not crowded place, my first instinct is to scan the room for bad energy or check out every face in case one looks angry or sad. I don't want to have to do that. Or not in such a negative way. You always seem so relaxed, like nothing fazes you."

Scott looked at me intensely.

"What?" I asked.

"You faze me," he said. "I had it all. Money, family, confidence. And you're right, I thought that too … like I was invincible. Not anymore. This thing … what you do to me … you make me feel vulnerable. All of a sudden, I'm not invincible anymore. I'm the one who's scared because I've found something I want more than any of the stuff I already had, and I don't know how to make sure I don't lose it. I'm not used to being scared."

I was touched. "Just keep doing what you're doing," I told him. "I'm not going anywhere."

Scott smiled, but then his attention was caught by something else. He looked around. I watched him for a moment. He looked like a dog that had caught the scent of a rabbit on the breeze. He was smiling.

"What?" I asked him. "What is it?"

"I felt something. I can feel something … an opportunity."

"What? What can you feel?"

Scott wasn't going to give it to me that easily.

"See for yourself. Cast your senses out," he said. "Work through all the happiness and the giddiness and the general good-time vibes. What else can you feel?"

I concentrated on the emotional energy swirling around the room. I had never really consciously searched for an emotion before, except with Josh, but then I knew who and what I had been looking for. Emotions had always come looking for me, not the other way around, so searching for an unknown emotion in a huge room full of strangers was a long way out of my comfort zone.

"I don't know what I'm looking for," I complained.

"You will when you find it," he assured me. "Look for the

odd one out. Close your eyes if it helps. No one will notice."

It did help. With my eyes open, I was distracted by all of the people in their fancy dresses and suits and confused by trying to interpret their expressions, but without sight, I was able to concentrate more fully on the emotions themselves. I tried to ignore the noise and the background babble of the patrons and staff so that the only thing that I had to examine was the emotional energy in the room.

I could sense emotions, like pockets of energy, and I could trace some of them back to their source. The room was buzzing with positivity, but after a few seconds of scanning, I felt it, the signature that Scott had sensed. There was one different energy pattern, distinct from the relaxed party atmosphere. I opened my eyes.

"Someone's frightened," I said. "No … not frightened … it's not bad like that. Someone's nervous. Nervous excited. Nervous terrified … but in an exciting way, not a monster or mobster kind of way."

"Mm-hmm," said Scott. "Who?"

I closed my eyes again. This time, it was easy to find the disparate emotion because I knew what I was searching for, and this time, when I found it, I also noted the location of the source. I opened my eyes again and used my sight.

"Him," I said loudly and proudly, pointing at a young man about halfway across the room, sitting on his own at a table set for two.

Scott laughed and pulled my hand down. "Don't point," he suggested.

I blushed. "Sorry," I said. I looked around to make sure that no one had noticed.

"Why's he so nervous?" Scott asked.

"I don't know. I can read his emotions, not his mind. He's not on his own, is he? Where's …?"

"No, he's not on his own," said Scott patiently. "You can use your eyes as well now."

"All right, all right … hang on. I'm not used to spying on

people in restaurants like you."

Scott chuckled.

"OK, clearly he isn't on his own because I can see there are two plates of food and two glasses of wine."

"Good," encouraged Scott.

"So his girlfriend … his partner is in the loo. And while she's gone, something's made him nervous." I thought for a moment. "OK, Sherlock, I give up. What's up with Mr Nervous Pants?"

Scott chuckled again. "When Mr Nervous Pants' girlfriend went to the toilet, he took something out of his jacket pocket. Look. It's on his knee. He can't leave it alone."

I craned my neck to see.

"Belle," Scott hissed. "How about some subtlety?"

"Sorry," I said again. "This is my first time, you know." I looked again, trying to be a little more discreet. When I found what I was looking for, I nearly jumped off my seat in excitement. "Oh, Scott, it's a ring!" I shouted, and I grabbed his hand hard.

Scott laughed loudly. "Shhh!" he told me. "I said there was someone we could help, not *there's someone we can draw the whole world's attention to.*"

I laughed too. "Sorry," I said again. "Yes, you're right. OK, I've got myself under control, I promise. So, Mr Nervous Pants is actually Mr Romantic and he's going to propose." I felt myself welling up at the prospect. "So … I can see how watching Mr Romantic propose might be nice for us, but what are we going to do?" I asked.

"Well, first of all, we can settle his nerves a bit. A few nerves are good, but his hands are sweating so much he can hardly hold the box, and he looks like he's about to throw up. Ooh, hang on, she's back."

A beautiful young woman had just approached the table. She sat down with a smile at Mr Romantic and continued with her meal. The man looked pale. He wasn't touching his food. He was still fiddling with the ring box under the table.

"Hang on. What if she says no?" I asked.

"Well, either way, we can make him feel a bit better. It's no good if he's sick all over his food whether she accepts him or not, but she's not going to say no," Scott said confidently. "She's madly in love and she's been waiting for him to ask all night."

"What?" I hissed. "You can't possibly know that."

"Look at her. Feel her. She's too excited for this to be just a date and too in love for this to be their first date. What other reason do people come to Chez Chez? You said you'd never been before. They're either trying to impress someone, celebrating something or just showing off because they're rich. He doesn't need to impress her — she's already smitten — they're too old to be graduating, too young to be rich, and her parents would be here if it was her birthday. The level of excitement emanating from her suggests something special. She knows he's brought her here to propose, and she can't wait."

"You just made a lot of assumptions," I said.

"But I'm right," he replied with a grin. "Let's help the poor sod get through his dinner."

I watched in awe as the colour gradually came back into the young man's cheeks and he was able to continue with his dinner. There was no sign from Scott that he was doing anything at all. He looked as casual as ever, but the man began to relax and the couple's conversation resumed. The ring box was still on his knee, and he continued to fiddle with it on and off, but his tension had eased.

"Nicely done," I said, impressed.

"Why, thank you," replied Scott.

When the couple had finished eating and the waiter had cleared their plates, the man's nerves returned with force and set me on edge. I glanced at Scott, who didn't appear to have been affected by the tension at all. He wasn't alleviating the man's nerves this time.

"Nah, we'll let him have these. It's part of the ordeal," he said.

I laughed. "So, what's second of all?" I reminded him. "First of all was settling his nerves …"

"Second of all is giving them a crowd of adoring fans."

At that moment, Mr Romantic left his chair and got down on one knee. His girlfriend's face lit up like a flame, and to my surprise, Scott started waving his hands and pointing excitedly in order to get the attention of the people at the tables nearby. People began to notice what was happening, and the news travelled fast. Within a few seconds, almost the entire dining room was watching with bated breath as the young lady said yes and her fiancé slipped the ring onto her finger.

Scott took my hand and squeezed it hard.

"Teamwork," he declared. "The happiest, most excited, most joyful emotions you can muster, everywhere. Go."

I caught on fast. Using my own strength and the additional power conferred upon me through Scott and the bond, I disbursed a wealth of positive energy. I could feel Scott, by my side and inside my mind, doing the same thing. It was an easy task because everyone in the room was already upbeat, and a large proportion were tipsy and therefore easier to persuade. What started out as a smattering of applause and kind smiles soon became a roar of appreciation. As everyone became enthralled by our energy, so that energy came bouncing back for Scott and me to enhance and resupply. People were soon clapping and whooping for joy. Even the professional staff of the establishment had paused their duties to join the frenzy.

I felt the raw power flowing through me and between us. It was a wonderful, magical feeling, and the euphoria of the diners became infectious. As they became happier, so did I. I laughed aloud as I saw strangers leave their own dinner to approach the couple, shake their hands and pass on their hearty congratulations. One lady even hugged them both.

When a portly gentleman in a suit ordered the affianced couple a bottle of the restaurant's finest champagne, Scott turned to me with a grin.

"Our work here is done," he said. He let go of my hand and turned his attention back to his dessert.

"Scott, that was amazing," I said, tears of happiness shining in my eyes. "What you did ..."

"We," Scott interrupted.

"Yes, we, but it was you who ... you didn't have to do that. You don't know those people. You don't owe them anything, but you ... just because you can and ..." A tear spilled out and ran down my cheek.

"Of course," said Scott, appearing genuinely surprised by my reaction. "I saw an opportunity to give those people a moment to remember, not that they wouldn't have remembered it always anyway. But if we can augment that happiness, why wouldn't we? It just seemed like a nice thing to do."

"It was, Scott. It really was. They'll tell their kids about the lady who hugged them and the man who bought them champagne. They'll never forget. I'll never forget either. I'll never forget the first time we did that together. I'll never forget this night, this whole day."

I sat back and watched Scott as he watched the couple celebrate their engagement. He hadn't done it for recognition or praise. He had simply seen an opportunity to use his fluence for good and had seized the moment. I was still looking at him when he turned back to me and smiled with a glint in his eye that had something to do with the company, something to do with the feeling in the air and something to do with the fact that he had just helped two total strangers have the night of their lives.

"Thank you, Scott," I told him quietly, thoughtfully. "Thank you for letting me be a part of that." I placed both of my hands on the table, open in invitation, and he put his firmly into them. I looked into his eyes, certain that mine were shining with emotion. I could see the flames flickering in his. I knew then. It hit me with absolute certainty and I knew without a shadow of a doubt. It had been quick, but there was no mistaking the feelings that I had for this man. I saw his eyes widen and the flames explode as he felt my realisation and the shift in my feelings. I smiled shyly.

"Why do I get the feeling that you can actually read my mind?" I asked him.

"I can't read your mind, but I can read you … I think … I hope," he said slowly. He looked at me steadily, and I held his gaze.

"You impress me, Scott Callahan. You're good and you're kind, and you make me feel things that I've never felt before. I've been so wrapped up in not letting the stupid bond dictate my feelings, I've neglected and ignored my actual feelings, but I know this is real. You've been so good to me. I know you've held back to let me catch up, but I have. I'm there, Scott. I know. I love you, Scott Callahan. I'm in love with you."

I felt numerous things happen at once, and it was difficult to grasp them all. There was a strange shifting in my mind, which felt peculiar and incredible, and a surge of emotion from Scott, which barrelled into me with its potent force and felt even better. The strength of Scott's love was immeasurable, and there was no mistaking it, just as there was no mistaking the exchange of energy between our minds. The amalgamation of our feelings for each other was almost beyond belief, but I did believe it and I trusted it. It felt right. The smile on Scott's face could not have been wider, and the flames in his eyes could not have burned more brightly. Something inside of us clicked into place, and I was not scared of it. I welcomed it.

"Oh, Belle I … I mean, I hoped … I mean, I … I didn't want to scare you away. I wanted you to realise it for yourself. I wanted you to … I mean, I didn't want to … oh, Belle, I love you too. My darling Belle, you know I love you.

I love you. I love you."

Once he had said it, he didn't seem to be able to stop. He was jiggling around in his chair. "My God, I can't tell you how much I want to kiss you right now. Can I kiss you? No, I can't kiss you in here, can I? Or can I? No, with all the euphoria already floating around, we'd probably have people buying us champagne too. No, I can wait until we leave. I think. But Jesus Christ, I love you, Belle, and … sorry … I just …"

I giggled. "You love me?"

"You know how today was supposed to be about getting away from temptation?" he asked. "Getting out and mixing with other people so that we weren't … You know?"

I nodded.

Scott's voice dropped lower. "It hasn't worked," he admitted. "I've never wanted you more."

This time, I blushed.

"I've come to a conclusion," he declared loudly. "There's nothing for it. I'm sorry, but it's going to have to happen." He paused dramatically.

"What?" I asked. "What conclusion? What are you going to do? What's going to happen?" I giggled again.

"You're going to meet my parents."

"Yes. Yes, Scott. I want that too. I want to meet the people who created you, who crafted you, who made you perfect for me."

Scott winked. "They're the best."

Chapter 28

"It's so weird," I declared. "I've been to the cabin so many times, and we've been so close to your parents and their … your house, but I've never actually been inside your house… or even to the front door. Not that I'm complaining. I love the cabin, but it's not actually where you live, is it?"

"No." Scott chuckled. "I don't live in the cabin. I live in the house. I have a bedroom with walls and everything."

I laughed too. "But it's still weird," I went on. "It's weird that we've been seeing each other for months now, and before that … and ... we've … well, we've grown pretty close."

"I like to think so," Scott agreed with a smile.

"But I've never been to your house," I repeated. I was rambling. I knew that I was rambling, but I couldn't seem to stop talking. It was the only way to keep myself from panicking. I was so nervous about meeting the famous *Callahans.* I continued. "It's also weird that you're nearly thirty and live with your parents."

"Hmm. You've got a point there. I haven't lived with them for long, you know. I did live in my own place. I did have my own place. Well, I still do."

"What?"

"What, what?"

"You have a house?" I hadn't heard about his house before. It made sense when I thought about it, but it had never come up, not specifically.

Scott chuckled again. "Why is that so surprising?" he asked. "You have a house. Yes, I have a house. It's nice. You'll like it, but I've no idea if I'll … we'll ever live there now. When Mum and Dad came here, I was at a bit of a loose end and they needed help doing the old place up. Although, to be honest, they didn't really need that much help. There was nowhere nearly as much to do as they'd made out. I think they were just using it as an excuse to get the family

514

back under one roof for a bit. Daniel was coming anyway, and it seemed like a good idea at the time. Now that you ... now that we ... it turned out that it was the best decision I've ever made.

"It never really occurred to me before that living with Mum and Dad would have its drawbacks. I didn't plan on meeting you and wanting to bring you home." He squeezed my hand and I felt myself blush. He went on, "I said I'd come for a year, and the house'll be looking great by the summer and I'll ... we'll ... well, I'm not sure what'll happen next."

We were walking hand in hand up the wide, sweeping driveway, having left my car on the cabin track. I didn't want to get drawn into a conversation about our future right now. I had enough to worry about being on my way to the Big House and dinner with his parents. Around the next corner, I saw the house for the first time. I paused for a moment, taking in its grandeur and beauty. Due to its position on the hill, hidden by trees, there was very little of it visible for anyone to appreciate unless they were here, right next to it, or approaching on the driveway. I hadn't truly appreciated its size or its elegance before.

The formal gardens had been somewhat neglected over time and were a little overgrown, but they were still impressive in their shape and design. There were beautiful borders, manicured hedges and an elegantly edged pond with an Italian fountain, all leading towards the front of the magnificent, imposing red-brick Victorian house with its steep roof topped with copper domes and spires. The sheer number and size of the windows was staggering, and the single storey white-pillared porch was festooned with lights that lit up the entire facade in the semi-darkness. It was stunning and daunting, and I clung more tightly to Scott's hand as we approached the front door.

Scott didn't knock. Of course he didn't knock; this was his home, but it felt wrong to me to just walk into the mansion. It made me even more nervous, if that were possible. Scott took hold of the enormous black handle, twisted, and pushed open the huge, heavy door. He ushered me into the spacious hallway, where he courteously removed my coat. Inside, the house seemed slightly less imposing. It had a comfortable air about it, and the soft, cushioned carpets felt lived in, used. There were signs of recent decoration everywhere. Everything looked fresh but in keeping with the character of the house.

"Mum?" Scott shouted. "Dad?" There was no reply. "They'll probably be in the kitchen. Come on. I know they're dying to meet you."

I allowed myself to be escorted down the hall, past a couple of large oak doors and towards the back of the house. It was little wonder that there had been no answer to Scott's call. It was a long way from the front door to the kitchen. As we approached the last door on the left, he called again, "Mum?"

He pushed the door open, and I was greeted with a scene of absolute domestic bliss. The Callahan's kitchen was one of the most beautiful rooms that I had ever seen. It was huge, but the large, heavy furniture filled the space and created an air of warmth. The surfaces were made of white marble, and black wooden cabinets served as a perfect contrast. There was a huge black double-range oven in the centre of the far wall, beautiful glass-fronted cabinets displaying impeccable dining and glassware sets, and a sunken brass sink sporting ornate brass taps. In the centre of the room was an enormous dark-oak topped island set with four brass-bordered chairs, with black and red checked gingham-style covers adding a splash of homeliness to the mesmerising space. The kitchen was obviously new. Everything looked shiny and state-of-the-art, and yet they had accomplished a perfect replica of an upper-class Victorian kitchen.

Talking of the most beautiful and impeccable things, as we entered the kitchen, a woman who must have been Scott's mum and who had been attending to something that smelled utterly delicious on the stove turned to greet us. She was the sort of woman who took your breath away. She smiled the kind of smile that stops strangers in the street and causes traffic collisions. It was a smile of absolute beauty, and the warmth and radiance in that smile captivated me completely.

Georgia was a petite woman, a couple of inches shorter than my five foot four, with a cute button nose and cheeks that dimpled charmingly when she smiled. She had rich, thick auburn curls that tumbled over her shoulders, and full subtly red-tinted lips, but it was her eyes that set her apart. There was a light shining from deep inside them that made her appear utterly and joyfully alive. I had never felt such a glow of warmth surrounding a person. I felt immediately and thoroughly at ease in her presence and simply happy to be alive. In a long-sleeved, cropped white top that showed off an unbelievable physique and red trousers fastened with a wide black belt, Georgia oozed confidence and effortlessness and displayed an instantly winsome charm.

"Isabel."

With that one word, she made my arrival seem like the most wonderful thing ever to have happened, and somehow I almost believed that it was. Georgia stepped forwards with her hands outstretched, and I found myself stepping forwards to greet her without conscious thought, following a spontaneous impulse. We met in the middle of the kitchen and clasped our hands tightly together.

"It's so wonderful to meet you, my dear. I'm Georgia. We've heard so much about you. So wonderful."

I felt a warmth rush to my cheeks, and for a moment I worried that I might cry. I felt so welcomed, so wanted, so genuinely, happily accepted by this small, beautiful woman, this practical stranger, that it hardly seemed real. I loved her already.

"Hello," I replied quietly. "Thank you."

The kitchen door swung open behind us, and I turned to

see a tall dark-haired man in about his mid-fifties enter the room. This must be Scott's dad, the notorious Nicholas Callahan.

"I thought I heard voices," he said, coming around the back of Scott and me and crossing the kitchen to stand by his wife's side. "I was just finishing off some business. You must be Isabel. Absolute pleasure. Nicolas." He held out his hand, which I took, and we shook warmly.

In contrast to Georgia's softness, there was a sharpness to his features and a rigidity in his pose. His dark, hawklike eyes were a little intense, but he also smiled, and his smile held the same genuine quality as his wife's. I considered him to be a handsome man, but there was a striking resemblance to his older son which I found disconcerting. His voice was smooth and rich. I could imagine it carrying authority and assurance in a court of law. He draped an arm around Georgia's shoulder and visibly drew strength from the contact. He was already an imposing figure, but the succour from his wife seemed to make him even more arresting. He was a tall, slim man, wearing dark suit trousers and a long-sleeved blue shirt with the top three buttons undone, revealing a powerful chest smattered with black curly hairs. The physical contact between them also had a visible effect on Georgia, and I saw her light up even more, seemingly blossoming under his touch. Scott had been right. They were a wonderful couple. I had barely exchanged a word with them, but within seconds of acquaintance, I could feel it already. The love shone out of them and lit up the room. It was infectious, joyous and intoxicating.

"Can I offer you a drink?" Nicholas asked attentively.

I panicked at the first hurdle. I didn't want an alcoholic drink during my first meeting with Scott's parents, but I felt that it was what was being offered. I wanted to stay sharp and in control, but at the same time, I didn't want to appear rude, so instead, I became tongue-tied and flustered and just stood there in the middle of the kitchen, opening and closing my mouth like a fish out of water and eventually looking up at Scott to save me. Scott chuckled quietly and patted my hand.

"I think we've got some fresh juice in the fridge," he offered.

I smiled and nodded gratefully. "That would be lovely," I replied.

"Why don't you two go and sit in the lounge while we finish pottering around in here," suggested Georgia, and Scott nodded.

"I might give Isabel the guided tour first," he replied.

"Of course, lovely idea." Georgia smiled.

"We'll call you if you're not back in time for dinner."

"Thanks, Mum," Scott said, and with a hand in the small of my back, he guided me into the hallway, where I sagged against him.

"I didn't know what to say," I whispered. "He offered me a drink and I just went stupid. Urgh, I must have looked like such an idiot. I couldn't even think of the words for yes or no."

Scott laughed quietly. "You were fine. They didn't even notice. Mum loves you already." He led the way back to the front door.

"She seems so lovely, Scott," I said when we were out of ear shot. "She just sort of made me feel welcome, I suppose. Welcome and wanted and … she just seems nice."

"She is nice. That's why," Scott assured me. "She's the best, and you are welcome, and she wants to get to know you. Right, the tour starts here."

Scott led me around the house, happily chatting about alterations and decorations that had been made to each room as we went. It turned out that he had been single-handedly responsible for the design of the kitchen. There weren't actually as many rooms in the house as I had expected having seen it from outside, but each room was enormous, and the walls were almost fifty percent window, with floor to ceiling glass and huge alcoves with window seats and heavy, draped curtains. The effect was that the house felt open and light, which was offset by the dark walls, floors and furniture, creating a graceful balance. The furniture and finishings were modern but had been chosen sensitively, in keeping with the energy of the building, and every room made me gasp with delight.

I was delighted by the enormous living room with its stunning fireplace and dramatic, low-hanging chandelier, and in the dining room, the classic mahogany table with its high-backed chairs. On the opposite side of the house, next to the kitchen, was another reception room, which Scott said he and Daniel used most often, and a closed door, the one door that Scott didn't open, explaining that it was his dad's office and library.

"That's the one room that's out of bounds," he told me. "Well, I probably won't show you Daniel's bedroom either," he smirked. "But really, Dad takes client confidentiality very seriously and doesn't like to have to keep his files locked away all the time, so instead, he keeps the whole office locked away so he can be as relaxed as he likes when he's in there. It usually looks like a bomb site anyway, with bits of paper strewn all over the place. Mum always tuts when she sees it, but Dad's determined that it's organised chaos and he knows exactly where everything is. He's always been the same. You wouldn't believe it if you saw him in court. Everything's impeccable when he's on stage."

"On stage?" I asked.

"That's what he calls it," explained Scott. "He says all courts are a theatre. All the characters have a part to play."

"Sounds like he plays his part pretty well," I said. "He's practically a celebrity."

Scott nodded and laughed. "He's worked really hard for it too. He's the best at what he does. Come on, let me show you the sun parlour."

"The sun parlour?" I laughed. "Is that Callahan for conservatory?"

"Well, why don't you come and see?" he challenged.

"Well, maybe I will." I laughed again.

I had to admit, the word *conservatory* wouldn't have done it justice. Stretching all of the way across the back of the property was a colossal domed solarium. The frame was painted a dark green and the ceiling was startlingly high. It was furnished with long, low wicker sofas and enriched with tall ferns and potted tropical plants. The crowning glory was a small round three-tiered stone fountain in the centre of the room with water bubbling and trickling from one level to the next. It stopped me in my tracks.

"Erm, Scott?" I said.

"Yes, sweetie?"

"Did you know there's a fountain in your conservatory?"

"Nice, isn't it?" he grinned. "More than a conservatory."

"I've never seen anything like it," I exclaimed.

I walked forwards and swept my hand under the water. I ran my palm along a couple of giant fern leaves reverently and stood against a window, looking out onto the huge immaculate lawn that sloped downwards and disappeared into the trees beyond, down towards the lake. I sighed.

"Scott, it's incredible. If I lived here, I'd spend my whole life in this room, curled up on one of these chairs with a good book."

"I knew you'd like it," he agreed. "When the sun shines, it's just amazing in here, and the sound of the fountain just sort of adds … I don't know … something."

I just nodded.

Scott sat on one of the wicker settees and patted the cushion by his side. "Come and sit with me?" he suggested.

"Yes," I replied.

We sat together quietly for a few minutes, looking out into the encroaching night. The sun had long since cast its last rays on the glass and the room had picked up the evening chill, but with Scott's arm draped around me, I didn't feel the cold. I felt relaxed here, totally at ease in this magnificent room in this incredible house. I sighed and closed my eyes, leaning against his chest. I could feel Scott's slow, rhythmic breathing against my back.

"I could get used to this," I murmured.

At that moment, I heard a door open somewhere in the house and was startled out of my reflection. A delicious smell wafted out from the kitchen.

"Scott? Isabel?" Georgia called out. "Dinner's almost ready. Do you want to come and sit down?"

I jumped up and hastily started to smooth down my top.

"What are you doing?" Scott laughed.

"I don't know," I said. "Do I look all right?"

"Sweetheart, you're gorgeous as always, and you know you're not on show. Mum and Dad have just made dinner. They just want to meet you, get to know you, that's all. Just be yourself and they'll love you like I do."

"Yes, all right." I tried to relax.

Scott gave my hand a reassuring squeeze.

"This way, m'lady," he said with a flourish, and holding my hand up high, he led me through to the dining room.

We sat next to each other on the side of the table furthest from the kitchen, and for the next few minutes, Georgia and Nicholas were in and out, carrying a plethora of wonderfully fragrant food. They had created a Spanish tapas-style dinner with no less than fifteen dishes. There were simple cold platters of olives, cheeses, breads, salads and cured meats, potato dishes with various herbs and dipping sauces, a couple of variations of croquettes and two impressive main dishes of Spanish omelette and paella.

Everything looked and smelled incredible. They must have gone to a huge amount of effort, but both looked totally at ease as they bustled around. They worked together effortlessly, weaving in and out of each other's space as they brought the various dishes from the kitchen onto the table. They moved like a dancing couple, separate entities flowing as one, and every time they met and stepped around each

522

other, I caught the slightest hint of a touch or a graze or just a private smile that united them, setting them out as a couple absolutely in tune with each other and very, very much in love.

When the last of the food was in front of us and there was a moment of hush before we tucked in, I took the opportunity to praise their efforts.

"This looks amazing," I gushed. "Just amazing."

"You wait till you see dessert," Scott said. "You haven't seen anything until you try Mum's crema Catalana and Dad's turon."

My eyes became even wider. "No way," I breathed.

"Way," he assured.

Georgia laughed. "Enough talking about it. Let's get eating," she declared.

Dinner was as delicious as it looked, and Georgia and Nicholas were wonderful hosts. Despite my earlier nerves, I felt relaxed in their company, and conversation flowed freely throughout the meal. They felt like family already. The subject of the fluence or anything relating to that aspect of our lives didn't come up, and I wasn't sure if I should introduce it. I felt sure that Scott must have spoken to them about my ability and my story, and knowing how strong their power was made me incredibly curious, but I didn't want to break the joyous spell. Sitting back and enjoying their company felt incredible, and so I happily allowed the conversation to remain on the little things: hearing embarrassing stories about Scott as a child and anecdotes about their lives and the house. We all smiled and laughed, and the evening flew by.

I watched Georgia and Nicholas and their transcendental love. They were clearly utterly enthralled by each other, which was surprising considering that they must have been together for well over thirty years. I didn't know anything about their life before the boys, but the way that they shone for each other after all of this time was a joy to behold. Scott had told me about the bond. He had warned me that it was strong in his parents, and now that I was seeing it for myself, I understood why he had been chasing it for his entire life. Nobody in their right mind would be able to grow up surrounded by this kind of connection and not be inspired by it. Georgia and Nicholas hung off each other's every word, and their eyes sparkled when they looked at one another. They seemed to be able to communicate without words, passing each other dishes or condiments before the other even realised they were in need. It was nothing as obvious or inane as finishing each other's sentences. They weren't displaying their affection like lovelorn teenagers. It was deeper and more fundamental than that. It was as if they were totally in tune with each other, totally in sync, and their lives just made more sense because the other was in it.

When we'd finished the main course and every morsel of food from every plate had been polished off, I stood to help them clear the table.

"Now, you need to sit back down, dear," said Georgia.

"You're a guest here tonight," added Nicholas.

"We want to look after you," said Georgia.

"So just let us wait on you," added Nicholas.

"And next time, maybe we'll let you do the washing up," said Georgia.

"Or fill the dishwasher, at any rate," chuckled Nicholas.

I sat back down and did as I was told.

They were like a well-oiled machine, and within a few seconds, they had all of the dirty dishes, plates, bowls and cutlery stacked up between them and whipped off the table. Nicholas stood in the kitchen doorway and held the door open for Georgia, who stepped adroitly over his foot and disappeared, Nicholas following closely behind. As they withdrew out of sight, I let out a long sigh. I turned to Scott.

"They're wonderful," I whispered.

"So are you," he replied.

"Am I doing OK?" I asked nervously.

"OK? They love you. I love you." He leaned over and kissed me softly on the back of my neck, just below my ear. "I didn't realise just how good it would feel having you here with them. I know I'm always in danger of getting ahead of myself, but it just feels right. Like you're family already."

"They really are great," I said. "And that food was incredible."

"Mmm," Scott agreed. "Mum's family are Spanish, and they spend a lot of time over there. Barcelona mainly. I wasn't kidding about dessert, though. You ain't seen nothing yet."

The kitchen door burst open again and Georgia and Nicholas reappeared, Georgia carrying two dishes and Nicholas carrying three. There were two huge portions of a beautiful yellow crema Catalana covered in a thin layer of sparkling burnt sugar, two slabs of a thick white nougat-type dessert striated with nuts, which I assumed must be the turon that Scott had mentioned, and a large bowl of cinnamon coated churros, which Nicholas placed at the centre of the table. Each couple ended up with a crema Catalana and a turon between them and two spoons each. I was speechless. I wasn't quite sure where to start.

"These are ours to share," explained Scott, pointing to the crema Catalana and the turon. "The churros are for everybody. Just tuck in. You'll have to be quick if you don't want me to finish the whole lot before you've even started."

He laughed and picked up a spoon in each hand, paused over the desserts for a second and then attacked. I laughed too and followed suit. I had never tasted anything so amazing. The crema Catalana was simple, clean and fresh, and the turon was beautifully sweet with the perfect balance between the chewiness of the nougat and the bite of the almonds. The churros were warm, straight out of the oven, deliciously crispy on the outside and soft in the middle. The whole thing was heaven, and the four of us said very little for the next few minutes. The only sound in the room was the singing of cutlery scraping on plates.

When the dessert dishes had been scraped clean, we all sat back in our chairs, sighed and laughed.

"Wow," I said. "That was just amazing. I don't think I'll be able to move for a while."

Georgia beamed at me. "That's what I like to hear, and don't you worry about moving. Nick's going to make us all a nice hot drink in a minute, aren't you darling? And we can take our time over it. We're not in any hurry, are we?"

"Absolutely not," I said. "That sounds wonderful."

"Tea or coffee?" offered Nicholas.

"Tea for me, please," I replied. "White with one."

"Coming right up," he promised and disappeared into the kitchen again.

"Shall we retire to the living room?" suggested Georgia.

"Absolutely," said Scott. "It's time to get a little more comfortable. You take Isabel in. I'll help Dad with the drinks."

Once we were all settled in the living room sipping our drinks, quiet and satisfied after our meal, the conversation finally turned to the fluence.

"So," Georgia began hesitantly. "I just … I just wanted to say … I wonder if … I mean, it seems wrong not to mention it at all. Fluence, I mean. It's who we are and it's who you are now too, sweetheart. Scott told us how new it is for you and a little bit about … well, about … well. Anyway, we didn't want to make dinner all about that, but I think it'd be wrong to ignore it altogether."

I wasn't sure what to say. I wondered for a split second whether Georgia was referring to Nicholas's involvement in my conception, but a glance at Nicholas told me that he was totally at ease, clearly not expecting that bombshell, and I realised that, of course, Georgia was talking about Mum's lies and my ignorance about it all for so much of my life.

Georgia took a deep breath and carried on. "I can feel your power, sweetheart. You're strong. I can feel it in you. I know you've got a lot to learn, but you've got a wonderful teacher here and a wealth of potential." She indicated to Scott.

I looked at him and smiled. "I know," I said.

"If you need anything," Georgia went on, "anything at all, you know where to find us now. Next time you visit, we can talk about it properly, see how your training's coming on. I don't want to overwhelm you now, but I just want you to know that we're here. You're family now."

"Thank you," I said, sipping my tea and not looking up in case Georgia's sensitivity and kindness made me cry. "Thank you so much."

We finished our drinks and sat in a companionable silence. The fire was roaring in the grate, heating the room with a warmth that lulled us into a drowsy stupor. I didn't want to leave, but it was getting late, and the combination of the food and the fire had left me in danger of falling asleep during my first meeting with my boyfriend's parents. That wouldn't do at all. Stifling a yawn, I stretched and announced that it was time for me to go. Scott said that he would walk me to my car, and taking my hand, led me to the front door, where he helped me back into my coat.

Nicholas arrived in the hallway just after us, with Georgia right behind him. She stood by his side, and he automatically draped his arm around her shoulder. I could already see, after just a few hours in their company, what Scott had meant when he said that losing one half of a bonded couple could be mentally and emotionally impossible for the half left behind. Georgia and Nicholas appeared to be perfectly normal, regular human beings on their own, but the presence of the other simply lit them up from the inside, making them more, better, stronger — making them whole — and once a person had accepted that kind of partnership and embraced that bond, I could see that the prospect of living without it would be devastating. The thought was at once electrifying and sobering.

Once I was in my coat and ready to go, Georgia came up close and took both of my hands in hers once again. She smiled that dazzling smile, which seemed even more sincere after the wonderful evening that we had just shared.

"This has been lovely, Isabel. He was right about you. We love you already. We want you to be part of our family. Please feel like you can come here anytime. We want to see you. We want to get to know you." Her voice dropped to a whisper. "He's been looking for you. Our boys turned out to be such different people. Daniel's happier on his own; he doesn't want to share his life with another, but Scott's always felt something was missing. I'm so glad he found his missing piece. I'm so glad he found you."

I was lost for words yet again. I wasn't sure if I could trust myself to speak, but I nodded my appreciation, tears shining in my eyes. I had gone from being a perfect stranger to having a sudden urge to throw my arms around this kind, beautiful, effusive woman and begging her to stay in my life forever.

"Thank you," I whispered. "You've been so kind, so welcoming, so ..." I didn't have to continue because Georgia was pulling me into that hug that I had craved.

"Oh, Isabel, you don't have to thank us," she cried. "It was our absolute, absolute pleasure, wasn't it, dear?" she asked, glancing at Nicholas, who stepped forward on cue.

"It's been a real pleasure," he said. "And she means it, as do I. Anytime."

"Thank you," I whispered again, and I followed Scott out into the night. I turned around one more time and put a hand up to wave goodbye. "Thank you," I whispered again. "Good night."

We began the walk down the drive in silence, hand in hand, watching our breath rising in front of us and gazing contentedly at the stars.

"I really wasn't sure what to expect, coming here," I said. "I mean, you've told me over and over how great they are but

… well … the house and the money and … Daniel … I just … I wasn't sure what kind of people they'd be, and I was so nervous, but … oh, Scott, I've had such a wonderful time. I never imagined they would make me feel so welcome, so much part of your family already. I love them."

I sighed again and lapsed into silence. "Are we going to be like that?" I asked a few seconds later.

"Like what?" Scott enquired. "Kind, welcoming, good cooks?"

I laughed. "You know what I mean," I said.

"So … so … you know, just so totally together? I mean, I love you and I want to … someday, but … I mean … I think …" I stopped, at a loss.

"Ha. Yes, I know what you mean. We won't be them. We'll be us. Every bonded couple is different just as every ordinary couple is different. We'll find our own balance, but to some degree, there will be an element of the extraordinary about it. How could there not be when we … the bond … when we …it … well, you know."

I just nodded in the dark. "I felt like I could be me, here, with them," I admitted. "I've missed that. I mean, obviously, I'm me with you, but since … well, sometimes I feel like I haven't got anyone else. There's this massive part of me that I always hide. I hide it at work, with Donna, with Jack. I even hid it from my own family to protect Mum from the stress of worrying about me." I laughed at the hypocrisy of that situation. "It feels so refreshing knowing that I can be open and honest with other people, that I could have a real family, a family who accepts me for who and what I am. I don't think I realised how lonely I've been until now.

"I had a wonderful time tonight and can't wait to spend more time with them, but I also can't help but think about my own family. I miss them so much. Dad's done nothing wrong, and Mum … well, I miss them both. I can't help thinking about how different things might have been if Mum hadn't made the decision to lie so horribly for so long.

"There were so many clues, Scott. It seems so obvious now, but when you're a kid ... and even when you grow up ... she's my mum. I wasn't looking for it. But she always knew when we were lying, even when there was no way she could've known. I just thought it was a mum thing, you know? I can't believe I didn't realise. And there were so many other things. And I keep thinking I'm getting over it and then something else'll pop into my head, some memory or something, and I'm just as mad with her as ever.

"In some ways, it makes me more cross when I see what you've got with your parents and when they offer to be there for me, no matter what. That's what Mum should've done. She should have been there for me. She should have trusted me. She should have let me be me." My voice had been gradually getting higher in pitch during this speech, and on the last word, I broke down.

"Belle, oh, Belle." Scott stopped walking and put his arms around me, soothing. "I'm here. You know I'm here, and your mum loves you and she's not going anywhere. You don't have to be over it right now. You can take as long as you need, and in the meantime, you've got me and my family for support. Shush, sweetheart. Come on, we've had such a lovely night."

"I know. I'm sorry," I sniffed. "There's things, though. Other things that I ... we need to think about at some point and they're ... it's on my mind."

"OK, what things?" Scott asked.

"Stephanie and Dad, mainly. Obviously, Steph needs to know, if she doesn't already. She needs to know what she is, what we are and what it means, but the rest of it ... the dad thing. Should I tell her? Should I make Mum tell her, or doesn't it matter? No matter what the biology says, Dad will always be our dad but ... and Dad. Where do I even start?"

"These are really big questions, sweetheart, and you're tired and emotional, and now isn't the time to make these kinds of decisions," said Scott calmly.

I started to interrupt, but he went on.

"I'm not saying we won't talk about it or I won't help you, I'm just saying not now, OK?"

I nodded reluctantly, allowing him to soothe my suddenly agitated mind. "You're right. Of course you're right. It just all got to me a bit, and all the emotion …"

"I know."

"I'm sorry. Tonight was lovely. I don't want to ruin that. I'm so glad Daniel wasn't there. How can two such generous, loving people have brought up you and such a … such a …?"

"Ha. Daniel wasn't keen on being a fifth wheel, and Mum was happy to let him off. As for how, I've no idea, but I hope you know he's the exception, in our family and in the wider community. Most fluencers are good, open, honest people, like me and Mum and Dad."

"I know. I do. And I want to get to know you … them … this whole life. I want to be a part of it. I had such a wonderful time. The food was amazing, the house is amazing, your parents are amazing, you're amazing."

"All right, steady on," Scott laughed.

"No, but I mean it. Your dad was lovely tonight and your mum … well, she's just wonderful, and together … no wonder you want what they have. You know I love you, right?"

Scott chuckled. "Yes, I know."

We had reached my car. Scott leaned against the door and pulled me into him, kissing me softly. "And I love you too."

I leaned into him again and we shared another soft, gentle kiss. Scott opened my door for me and I climbed inside.

"Good night, Isabel, my love. Sweet dreams."

"Thank you, Scott. Good night."

Chapter 29

As the freshness of spring dawned with its new life and warmth chased away the winter, plants began to bud and bloom, and so did my confidence and power. True to their word, Georgia and Nicholas welcomed me with open arms and made me feel every bit a part of their family. Scott and I spent more time in their house on the hill than we did at the cottage, and we rarely frequented the cabin anymore, preferring instead to sit out on the immaculate lawn behind the house or under the cover of the stunning solarium dome, enjoying the view down into the trees beyond.

I relaxed about being seen in public with Scott as time went on, and my faith in our love became unshakable. I didn't want to hide it anymore. I didn't want to feel guilty that I had found someone who made me truly happy. In fact, I wanted to shout it from the rooftops. We divided our time between going out together and using our dates to practise my fluence on oblivious ordinaries and spending time at the house. Sometimes we were joined by Georgia, and less frequently, Nicholas, who were invaluable with their help and guidance on using and honing my abilities.

I felt myself becoming stronger and more assured. I developed a control over my reaction to most external emotions and was better able to prevent them from breaching my cerebral defences without my deliberate consent. I could now, with relative consistency, consciously sense the emotions of a person nearby and examine them before deciding whether or not to allow them to penetrate my mind and affect my own mood. There were still occasions when a particularly intense emotion caught me off guard, infiltrating my psyche and altering my own feelings before I knew what was happening, and instances where I found myself surrounded by a multitude of heightened emotions that were difficult to manage, but overall, my competence was improving fantastically and continued to do so every day.

My connection with Scott also grew stronger and more profound. I felt the part of him that lived deep inside my mind becoming more intrinsically linked with my own sense of self, little by little, so that I was subconsciously aware of it wherever I went and whatever I did. Far from terrifying me anymore, the knowledge that a part of him remained with me even when we were physically apart became a comfort and a joy in my waking hours, and I embraced the knowledge that we were intimately linked through our love and the bond and that we were as aware of each other's emotions and desires as we were of our own.

My relationship with Daniel was another matter entirely. He did nothing to induce me to like him, and in fact, seemed to go out of his way to be rude or insolent whenever we crossed paths. I couldn't understand how three-quarters of a family could be so charming and such good, uplifting company, while the last member could have so few manners and be so intensely unlikeable, and a few days later, Scott and I were walking hand in hand across the lush green lawn of spring when I saw something that made me tighten my grip on Scott's arm and point frantically down the hill.

"Oh, Scott, look, that's Donna with Daniel, down there by the edge of the trees, isn't it? I'm sure it is. That's Donna."

Scott squinted down the hill in the direction in which I was pointing. "I'm not sure. It could be. I don't really know her. I've only met her once but she's ... there aren't many ... I mean, there aren't many ..."

I laughed at his awkwardness. "There aren't many people of colour in Ramsay Bridge? No, you're right, there aren't, and that's definitely Donna. I know her, the way she stands, the way she moves. Are they coming towards the house?"

Scott squinted harder into the sunlight. "I think they're walking along the top of the tree line. I don't think they're coming this way. Why don't you call to her? They should be able to hear you from there. They could join us."

I hesitated for a moment. As much as I wanted to make

things right with Donna, I wasn't certain if Daniel and Scott being there the first time that I'd seen her since the fall-out was the best idea, but I pushed my misgivings to the side when I looked at Donna and felt a rush of feeling. I missed her so much. She was my best friend. Of course I wanted to see her, talk to her, try to regain our friendship, whatever the circumstances. I cupped my hands around my mouth and shouted.

"Donna. Donna!" There was no reaction from the couple at the bottom of the hill. "Oh, Scott, I don't think she can hear me."

"No, the wind's blowing in the trees. It's probably drowning you out."

"Shall we go down there?"

"We'd never catch them, look. They're heading back into the trees, down towards the lake."

I was disappointed. I wished that I hadn't hesitated. Perhaps Donna would have heard me if I had shouted that brief moment earlier. I tried once more.

"Dooooonnaa!"

They heard me. The two figures looked up the hill towards my voice. They looked right at me. I saw them speak to each other, and then they both shook their heads. Donna looked away and continued her descent into the cover of the trees without looking back, but Daniel remained where he was for a few extra seconds, looking right at me. Although I couldn't see him clearly from that distance, I had the distinct impression that he was smiling before he turned and followed Donna out of sight.

"Did you see that?" I asked Scott.

"What?"

"They saw us but carried on into the trees. Why didn't they stop? Why? I didn't even know they were spending time together. Did you? How long's it been going on?"

Scott shook his head. "No. I had no idea. I don't know."

A theory began to form in my mind. "No wonder she

won't forgive me, Scott. Daniel hates me. If they're seeing each other, he'll have spent all this time encouraging her to ignore my messages and throw our friendship away."

Scott shook his head again. "He doesn't hate you. He's unfriendly to everyone. You're not special."

I laughed automatically, but I wasn't convinced. I had tried to speak to Donna numerous times over the last few weeks and had been shunned at every turn. Finding out that she had been spending time with Daniel made me feel sick. I was worried for my best friend. From what I had seen of Daniel and what Scott had told me about the way he treated ordinaries, especially women, I hated the idea of Donna being with him but knew that there was absolutely nothing that I could do. With our friendship in tatters, giving Donna advice about who she should and shouldn't see was out of the question. I was stuck, knowing my friend could be in trouble and helpless to prevent it.

I wondered if I had been naive to think that I could ever reclaim a friendship with Donna and Jack. Jack was a kind, generous, giving person, but I doubted if there was really anyone who would welcome their ex-girlfriend's new boyfriend into their life, and I couldn't see myself ever spending time with Jack without Scott now, either. The two aspects of my life were so distant from each other. In reality, very few people remain close to an ex after the relationship is over, but I had been convinced that the strength of our friendship before love would have made us an exception to the rule and that Donna would have been the glue that kept us together. Perhaps if we had been members of a bigger group of friends, it would have been easier, but it really had always just been the three of us. I had hoped that perhaps, with time, Donna would realise how much she missed me and remember that our friendship could overcome anything, but adding Daniel into the mix was a devastating blow.

Scott put his arm around me and pulled me in tightly. He could sense how much I was hurting.

"She'll come round," he assured me gently. "A friendship as close and as long as yours can't truly be broken. Give her time. She'll come round."

"I hope you're right," I said sadly, without conviction. "I really hope you're right."

It was the last night before Georgia and Nicholas went away. They were heading to London for a few days for Nicholas to meet with clients, and they were flying out to Barcelona at the weekend. It was also the night before the last day of Spring Term, and my class were holding our pirate concert and party tomorrow. I had roped Scott into coming in and helping out and had been excited about introducing him to the children and my colleagues at last. The incident with Donna had put a dampener on things.

Scott led me back to the house and into the living room, where Georgia and Nicholas were watching television and sharing a bottle of wine. They brightened as soon as we entered the room, and I felt immediately better in their company. Georgia sensed that I was upset and stood without hesitation to offer a great big hug, no questions asked. I was so grateful for the support, I nearly cried. They turned off the television, and the four of us chatted late into the evening. I felt a million times better when it was time to go. I might have temporarily lost some things over recent months, but nothing could beat finding a family.

"Have a fabulous holiday," I told Georgia and Nicholas as I stood to leave.

They both thanked me with more cuddles.

"We will," Georgia assured me.

"And you," I turned to Scott. "We have a party to go to tomorrow. I want you on your best and most piratey behaviour."

Scott grinned and offered me a pirate salute. "Aye aye, Cap'n. I'll go aboard the Little Owl and join in some sea shanties with the crew. Aye, you see if I don't, Cap'n, ma'am."

Humour restored, I was smiling as I left the house, heading for home and a good night's rest. I had a crew of young pirates and a new first mate to contend with tomorrow, and I couldn't wait.

Chapter 30

When Scott appeared at my classroom door the next morning, I hardly recognised him. He was dressed in full Jack Sparrowesque swashbuckling regalia, complete with breeches, doublet, knee-high black boots, a long black dreadlock wig and a brown-red suede tricorn hat. He even had a brightly polished cutlass slung across his waist, a large gold hoop earring dangling from his left ear and blackened teeth. The transformation was incredible, and his appearance and the effort and planning that he must have put in took me by surprise — a very pleasant surprise. Scott swept into the otherwise empty room, treated me to a swarthy smile, performed a deep bow and pulled me roughly to him with his right hand in the small of my back.

"First mate Scotty the Sea Dog reporting for duty, Cap'n. That I be." He said, in a deep, raspy pirate voice. He looked me up and down appreciatively and his voice lowered even further. "But you can call me Sea Dog."

I giggled girlishly as Sea Dog bent me backwards and treated me to a thorough, amorous kiss. His eyes were aflame, and my body and mind responded to him passionately. I instinctively pressed my hips against his eager body with a primal urge as I experienced an intense emotional response to his proximity, a rush of happiness, love and desire, matched only by the intense emotional response of his own. Heat flushed my skin in acknowledgement of our powerful emotional energies and the ardent press of our bodies through our ridiculous costumes. When he righted me with a small groan of pleasure and satisfaction at my wanton reaction, I felt the heat rise to my cheeks. When I noticed that Mrs Bishop, Chrissy Brooks and Helen Young were standing in the classroom doorway, staring at us with their mouths open wide, the blush deepened furiously.

Scott must have entered the school through the office and

been escorted to my room, but I hadn't noticed the women in the excitement of seeing his pirate getup. I pushed him off me and attempted to straighten my own hat and wig, mustering as much dignity as I could under the circumstances and laughing at their stunned faces.

I addressed Scott first. "You look amazing. I can't believe you went to so much effort. Thank you. Thank you so much for this."

Scott grinned. "What kind of first mate would I be if I didn't make an effort on me first day aboard the Little Owl, Cap'n?" he asked.

"What kind indeed?" I replied.

I beckoned to the ladies, who were still standing, staring, by the door. "I take it you've all met, then?" I asked. "In case introductions are still needed, this is Mrs Bishop, Chrissy and Helen." I pointed to each in turn. "And this … is Scott."

Scott bowed low again, removing his hat and sweeping it across the floor in a flamboyant gesture. "Scotty the Sea Dog at your service, ladies," he said with a wink, remaining stubbornly in character and voice. I laughed again and gave him a short, sharp jab in the ribs. He made a strangled yelp and quickly stood up straight, clearing his throat. "Sorry. Hi. As the lady said, I'm Scott."

He smiled at the women, and I think that I saw Chrissy and Helen blush under his piercing gaze. I felt a rush of pride that I could say that this was my man, and I sensed a pang of envy from Helen, who was looking at Scott with barely disguised hunger. I had to lower my face to hide the giggle when I picked up on the attraction that she felt for him, aware of the mortification that she would feel if she had any idea that her emotions were not as private as she believed.

Mrs Bishop was the most sensible member of the little group as usual and was the first to remind us all, with a clearing of her throat, that we needed to get back to business. She ushered Helen and Chrissy out of the room with assurances that there would be time for fraternising later. We had a little work left to do before the children stormed the classroom, ready for their pirate day. Helen and Chrissy left reluctantly, and Scott turned to Mrs Bishop with a salute, restored to character once more.

"I'd recognise the authority of a good quartermaster anywhere," he said astutely. "Put me to work, ma'am. Scrubbing the decks, manning the guns, digging for treasure?"

Mrs Bishop allowed a small smile to play on her lips. Even she was not totally immune to his charm. She looked around to hide the smile, set her mouth into a stern line and placed her hands firmly on her hips.

"We're mostly set, but if you want to make yourself useful, you could put nineteen shoe boxes out on desks with a selection of pen pots, scissors and glue," she suggested, pointing towards the relevant cupboards.

"Aye aye, ma'am," he saluted again, "We'll soon have this boat shipshape and ready to receive its crew." And he fell to work.

At 8.45 a.m. sharp, I threw open the classroom doors, stood on the threshold looking splendid in my own pirate costume and began to usher the children in from the playground. It was lovely to see the effort that they had all put into their costumes. Some had bought them from supermarkets or online, while others were homemade, but all of the children strutted in with enthusiasm and pride. Jane had her hair braided with colourful beads and was flicking them off her shoulders vigorously, parading them for all to see. The last day of term was always exciting, and a theme added an extra thrill to the eve of the upcoming holidays.

My efforts inside the classroom paid dividends as each child entered and marvelled, wide-eyed, at the transformation before them. Starting ridiculously early this morning, I had turned the classroom into The Little Owl, a majestic pirate ship, with rolls of blue paper towelling creating the waves of the ocean and tables lined up in the middle of the room with stiff brown paper hanging to the floor over the outside edges with portholes cut out of them. I had a giant skull and crossbones flag flying from the ceiling and had even created a sail and a crow's nest out of a large white sheet, an old curtain pole and an upcycled coat stand. At the back of the classroom, the Imagination Nation corner had been cleverly disguised as the entrance to the interior of the ship, accessed via a sparkly red curtain, behind which Scott was hidden with a golden treasure chest and strict instructions to remain unseen and unheard until it was time to play his part.

Most of the parents popped into the classroom when they dropped their children off, and a few commented on the anticipation that had been leading up to today.

"I hope it lives up to their expectations," I said to Mr Canning, Louis's dad.

"If the amount of effort you've gone to setting the place up is anything to go by, I'm sure you won't have anything to worry about," he replied. "You've never let them down before."

I smiled in gratitude. "I do my best," I said.

I turned to the rest of the room and raised my voice, hoping that I would catch all of the parents before they left.

"Don't forget, all parents are invited to join us for the last hour of the day," I called. "Come back at two o'clock if you can so the children can show you what they've been working on this term and today. We're very excited to share it with you. I hope you can come."

There was general assent from the departing parents and a few shouts of encouragement from the children.

"My mummy's coming," announced Melissa loudly.

"Excellent, Melissa. I'll look forward to seeing her," I called back. "I'll expect you to sing extra well for her."

Melissa grinned and nodded.

After ushering the last parents out of the door, I turned to the children and clapped my hands loudly. It took a few moments for them to settle down. They were buzzing with emotion, and I was happy to let all of the positivity buoy my own mood. I rang my tingly bells, and the children soon began to respond appropriately with their mouths closed and their fingers in the air, ringing their own silent bells. I gathered all of my young pirates onto the carpet, placing a finger to my lips. They gradually fell silent.

"Today's register's going to be a little different," I told them. "Who can tell me, what's the first thing all pirates need?"

Nineteen hands shot eagerly into the air.

"Yes, Sammy?"

"A hat?"

"A hat is good, but not every pirate wears a hat, and it's not what I'm looking for. Yes, Melissa?"

"A parrot?"

"A parrot certainly helps. Yes, Josh?"

"A sword?"

"OK, these are all good answers. Now, what does a pirate need so that other pirates know what to call him?"

The hands waved frantically.

"Karl?"

"A name?" Karl suggested.

The other children nodded and agreed enthusiastically.

"A name, exactly," I said. "Today, when I call your name on the register, I'd like you to stand up, go to the back of the ship and walk through the red curtain into the captain's chamber." I pointed and nineteen heads turned, murmuring eagerly. "There, you will receive your pirate name."

More murmurs from the children, who were beginning to get a bit over excited.

"Shush, Little Owls, shush. We can't get on if I can't hear myself speak. It's OK to enjoy yourselves, but we still have to listen to each other as well. Right. That's better. Let's begin. Paul?"

"Good morning, Miss Bliss, Good morning, Little Owls," said Paul obediently whilst visibly bouncing with excitement.

His eager desire to run to the back of the room was infectious.

"Good boy. Up you get, then. Into the captain's chamber."

Paul stood up and trotted to the curtain. He paused for just a fraction of a second and then threw it open and took another step forward.

"Ahoy, me hearty!" came the loud cry of Scotty the Sea Dog. Paul let out a high-pitched squeal in a mixture of fear, surprise and delight and dropped the curtain as if it had grown teeth, remaining firmly on the classroom side. He turned back to the rest of the class with his mouth open wide. He was pointing at the curtain and his mouth opened and closed like a fish out of water, but he seemed to be too agitated to speak. I breathed a sigh of relief when I saw that he wasn't upset. I had been worried that Scott might make the first one cry, but Paul was hopping with excitement despite the uncertainty on his face. He wasn't sure if he was brave enough to face the pirate. The other children were clamouring excitedly, wanting to know what he'd seen

"There's a pirate in there!" Paul yelled when he found his voice. "An actual pirate!"

A few of the children leaped to their feet, and all of them started to chatter excitedly again. I picked up my tingly bells and tried to bring them back under control. I had to resort to raising my voice in order to combat the furore.

"Little Owls?" I called. "Little Owls, please stay sitting on the floor until it's your turn to go into the captain's chamber for your pirate name. Paul?"

He was staring at me, unsure what to do.

"Go on in," I encouraged. He took a deep breath and marched through the curtain with all of the confidence that a five-year-old can muster.

The conversation that took place inside the captain's chamber was unclear from our end of the classroom, but it was peppered with Sea Dog's rough voice raised in pirate phrases and exclamations and the muffled responses of an

543

enraptured little boy. After about thirty seconds or so, Paul reemerged with a name badge written on a skull and crossbones flag stuck to his chest, which read, 'Peg Leg Paul.' Scott and I had spent hours over the last few nights coming up with a suitable list of names for the class. Peg Leg Paul returned to the carpet wearing the biggest grin that I had ever seen. He was spellbound.

He couldn't contain his excitement as he sat down with his friends gathered around him, desperate to know what had occurred in the captain's chamber.

"There's this pirate in there," he squeaked. "Like, an actual pirate. He talks funny. His name's Sea Dog and he asked me what my name was and he told me my pirate name was going to be Peg Leg and he wrote it on this flag and stuck it on me and said 'Aaaarrrggghhh' and 'Ahoy,' and stuff like that." He spoke so quickly that it was difficult to keep up.

The children were enthralled by Paul's recounting, demanding to know more and jiggling around in anticipation of meeting the exalted Sea Dog, but Louis was staring intently at me, knowing that his name was next on the register. I smiled at his earnest face.

"Go on then, Louis," I said, and he was at the back of the room opening the curtain before I had finished his name. He emerged from the captain's chamber a minute later, looking equally as impressed by First Mate Sea Dog and proudly wearing his pirate name badge announcing him as 'Long John Louis'. His chest was puffed out like a peacock, and he returned to sit down with his classmates and recount his own experience.

Gradually, we made it through the register and ended up with nineteen named pirates sitting in front of me. I called Sea Dog out of the chamber to join us.

"Aye aye, Cap'n," came the raspy voice, and Scott emerged from behind the curtain, took a sweeping bow to the assembled company and stepped over their heads to stand next to me at the front of the class.

"That's right, and for today only, I'm no longer Miss or Miss Bliss to you scurvy dogs. I'm Cap'n, and if I give you an order, you will address me so." I turned to Scott, who demonstrated admirably.

"Aye, aye, Cap'n."

I turned back to the children. "Is that clear, crew?"

"Aye aye, Cap'n," they chorused.

"Miss?" asked Savage Sammy.

"Yes, Savage? I replied.

"How do we know he's really a real pirate?" he asked, pointing at Scott dubiously.

"Leave this to me," Sea Dog replied. He pulled his cutlass from its scabbard with a flourish. "This is my cutlass, my pride and joy. I call her Sparrow. I sharpen her every morning on the deck of The White Pearl — that's me ship — because the morning sun cuts her sharper than the evening sun. That's how I get her so shiny and sharp. Only a real pirate would know that, now, wouldn't you say?"

The children stared at Sea Dog, then at Sparrow and back again. Their mouths were wide open. There were no doubts now. Savage Sammy nodded his head dumbly, and I seized the opportunity to regain control. I had planned a full day of pirate activities for the children to wrap up the term's topic, and I couldn't have imagined a better day. Sea Dog was the star of the show and thoroughly stole the limelight, thrilling me with his way with the children and seemingly boundless enthusiasm. The children adored him and vied with each other for his attention, so I had to work extra hard to ensure that there could be no complaints about fairness.

Each child made their own wave bottle with vegetable oil and food colouring so that they had a piece of the ocean to take home with them, and they each made and decorated a small treasure chest out of a shoe box for storing their special trinkets and most prized possessions at home. We did some island hopping outside, hopping into hula hoops and being careful not to fall into the ocean where the crocodiles and sharks lay in wait, and of course, there was a treasure hunt, which resulted in every pirate finding their own bag of gold chocolate coins.

A pirate-party lunch had been provided by the parents, who had each chosen an item to contribute from a list posted on the class noticeboard, and the parents, as always, had outdone themselves. There were chicken drumsticks, seaweed rolls, cheese cubes on skull-and-crossbones-flag cocktail sticks, and Caroline's mum had even dressed up nineteen bananas in pirate hats and striped t-shirts and given them faces complete with eye patches. There were cannonball crisps, cucumber and carrot stick cutlasses, pirate-flag cupcakes and a treasure map sponge cake that was an absolute triumph. I was touched by how much effort everybody had made.

By two o'clock, the children had completed all of the activities that I had planned for them and were standing behind their desks, quiet and alert, ready to receive their parents and perform for them. Most of the children had at least one grown-up who was able to attend, and those whose parents both worked or couldn't make it were spread out around the classroom, sitting with close friends whose parents were coming along to ensure that they all had someone to make a fuss of them.

Once the grown-ups had arrived and were standing quietly against the wall, I introduced myself and my crew.

"Welcome, me hearties, to my stunning ship, The Little Owl. I'm Captain Bliss, this is my first mate Sea Dog, our quartermaster Mrs Bishop, and this lot here are my motley crew. We'd like to sing you a sea shanty to get you in the mood, and then we'll show you all some of our treasures. So, avast ye, ye landlubbers, here we go."

On cue, Mrs Bishop started the music, and the class, with Sea Dog in particularly fine voice, treated the adults to the first of their pirate tunes.

When I was one, I played the drum, the day I went to sea,
I jumped aboard the pirate ship and the captain said to me,
We're going this way, that way, forwards and backwards, over the Irish Sea,
A bottle o' rum to fill my tum and that's the life for me.

When I was two, I buckled my shoe, the day I went to sea,

The children were in fine voice and bolstered admirably by Captain Bliss and Sea Dog, who, unsurprisingly, was not averse to performing in public. There were joyful faces everywhere, and Scott and I were riding high on the emotions of nineteen excited children and fourteen supportive, admiring, entertained grown-ups in the room.

I looked for Cathy Nelson, as I always did, and gave her a special nod when I caught her eye. I knew that I would be expected to be even with my affection towards the children and their parents, but our experience would always give us an extraordinary bond that went beyond the usual teacher-parent-pupil relationship. Cathy came to all of my little class events, and the joy that radiated from her was just that little bit sharper because of what she had gone through to get here. She and Josh had moved into a little house of their own and were now living closer to her parents and further from the school, but Cathy had made the decision to keep Josh at Ramsay Bridge Primary for the remainder of this school year while he was in my class. He would be moving to a new school in September. It gave me a lump in my throat when I thought about Josh leaving, but Cathy had promised that they would always stay in touch.

After performing the first song, I sent the children to fetch their grown-ups and show them their work, which was spread out on their desks. It included items that we had created today as well as some of the projects that we had been working on throughout the term. I wandered around the classroom chatting about the work while Scott thoughtfully took it upon himself to round up the few children who didn't have grown-ups and put them to work *swabbing the deck, battening down the hatches* and *looking out for land.* His little gang eagerly hung off his every word.

Just before three o'clock, I gathered the children back together, announcing to the parents that they had another couple of sea shanties to share. The children danced and sang joyfully to the rousing ditty.

We are the pirates, pirates of the ocean,
We are the pirates, young and free,
We are the pirates, ready for adventure,
Digging for the treasure, you and me,
We are the pirates, Yo ho ho

And outshone themselves in their emotional tale of a pirate's ultimate fate after a life of swashbuckling dishonesty, ending with a rousing chorus.

So ho heave ho the anchor,
Ho heave ho the sail,
All our pirate adventures,
We're going to all end up in jail.

The parents erupted into tumultuous applause, and Sea Dog ran around the children giving each of them a high five and using phrases like *Blow me down with a feather, By gum, lassie,* and *Shiver me timbers.* Pirate day was officially a triumph.

When the applause died down, I invited the children to gather their belongings while I looked on, ensuring that all of the pegs were empty and the cloakroom was totally clear for the holidays. I released those with grown-ups inside and escorted the remaining children out to their parents and carers on the playground.

Scott remained in character until the last child disappeared around the corner, standing against the railing, waving his hat and shouting at the top of his voice.

"*Fair winds to ye, mateys!*" was his last cry, and he sank to his knees dramatically. He let his character slip and beseeched me in his own voice once more. "Help me. Belle, help me. I'm so exhausted, I'm not sure if I can move."

I laughed. "Come on, Sea Dog. We've got all the cleaning up to do yet."

Scott groaned loudly. "Cleaning up? Seriously, Belle, I have a newfound respect for what you guys do. I mean, I always knew you worked hard and had the patience of a saint, but seriously, they're exhausting. All day every day? You're amazing. Seriously. Amazing."

He followed me slowly back into the classroom and began picking up all of the chairs and dismantling the Little Owl.

I smiled. "Thanks, it's hard work, but you also went above and beyond today. It's no wonder you're exhausted. Sea Dog's hyperactive. You were bouncing round like a lunatic all day. The kids loved you. I love you. You're wonderful."

I paused in my work to admire him. He had removed his hat, wig and cutlass and looked hot, tired, a little bit ridiculous and totally irresistible. He had demonstrated again just what a wonderful human being he was. He was perfect, and I knew beyond doubt that he had my heart. It wasn't because some prophecy had foretold it or the destiny of the bond had ordained it; it was because I'd met him, got to know him and fallen in love with him. The realisation inspired an elation that caught me off guard. This is what I had been waiting for. This moment was everything that I needed. I was filled with an unparalleled devotion to this man, my man, my bond, and I felt an immense physical and spiritual longing. I loved him, I wanted him, I needed him, and I didn't need to wait any longer to commit myself to him forever.

I felt a pleasant twinge in the pit of my stomach and a squirming pleasure deep inside my mind from my fluence, who had known all along and had been waiting for me to catch up. My fingers and toes began to tingle in anticipation, and my emotions transmitted my decision to Scott instantly. I saw the colour rush to his cheeks before he looked up from his task and caught my eye. His deep, dark eyes were on fire, and the flames in them reflected the desire in my own. Suddenly, the classroom felt too hot and too small, claustrophobic. Our hunger for one another was a palpable energy in the air, and I struggled to catch my breath while Scott studied me with eyes that were burning a path to my soul. I needed some air. I needed to concentrate on the task at hand. I needed to get Scott alone. I needed to remember that Mrs Bishop was standing right there, busy with the classroom and oblivious to the sudden increase in temperature. I tried to avoid Scott's gaze and redoubled my efforts to get the room in order, but I was helpless to ignore the sparks firing between our minds. My body was on fire. There was nothing more important than finishing the job and getting him home.

We didn't speak when we left the classroom and returned separately to our cars. We didn't need to. Our objective was clear: get back to the house and into each other's arms without delay. I glanced at Scott across the car park. He felt my look upon him and returned my gaze. Our eyes held for a fleeting moment and the heat that passed between us spurred us even more urgently towards the big house. By the time that I arrived, Scott was already out of his car and was holding the enormous front door open for me. I followed him inside without hesitation.

In the dim hallway, I paused. The emotional energy assaulting me was as strong as anything that I had ever encountered in my life. Scott was radiating a myriad of feelings: desire, anticipation, hope, fear, but above all, love. The same mixture of emotions were playing across his face, causing him to appear adorably defenceless. He held up a hand, asking me silently not to approach any closer until he said what he needed to say.

"Belle …" His voice trembled. "Are you sure? I mean are you really, truly sure? Before we … I mean before you … because if you're not sure, you need to tell me now while I still have some self-control because once we … once I … Jesus Christ Belle, I'm shaking. I want you so much. I love you so much." His fists were balled by his sides.

I moved towards him tentatively, as if approaching a frightened animal. I held my hands out in front of me and inched forwards until I was so close that I had to look up to see his face, but we were not touching. I gently but deliberately placed my hands on his chest and ran them slowly down to rest on his hips. Scott groaned but kept his own hands to himself. Even though he could feel it, he needed to hear me say it out loud, and I understood.

"I've never been more sure of anything in my life," I told him, looking into his eyes and letting him see the truth and the intensity shining in my own. The flames had never burned more brightly in his eyes, making it difficult to look directly into them. "I love you. I want you. I need you. I have no doubts or hesitations. I'm ready for this, Scott. I'm ready to be yours and I'm ready to make you mine. I've never wanted anything more."

I closed the last of the gap between us so that our bodies were touching at the hip. The physical evidence of his desire was undeniable, constrained between us, as well as the intoxicating mixture of emotions that he was projecting. I slid my hands underneath his shirt, ran them back up over his flat stomach and lay them out on his toned, taut chest. Scott took a deep, shuddering breath and bent down suddenly, roughly, seizing my mouth with a possession and a ferocity that he had never displayed to me until now, kissing me with passion and abandon, crushing our bodies so close together that it almost hurt. I kissed him back with the same abandon, tasting him with my tongue inside his mouth, eliciting an erotic groan from deep within.

I pushed him gently away, just far enough to allow me to take a breath to speak.

"Here, Scott? Here in the hallway? Or do you think we can contain ourselves enough to make it to the relative privacy and comfort of your room?" I asked with a grin.

Scott growled, reluctant to let go of me even for the few seconds that it would take to climb the stairs.

"Go on, then," he said roughly, giving me a nudge. "You've got a three-second lead. If I catch you before my bedroom, I'm taking you right there on the stairs."

I giggled and started to run. I heard him breathing heavily in the hall, and then his quick footsteps were right behind me. I sprinted for his bedroom door and managed to throw it open just as he caught up with me. He lifted me clean off the floor and threw me bodily onto the bed. I squealed and giggled again as I landed on my back on the soft sheets. He entered the room, closed the door behind him and leaned back on it heavily, breathing hard.

I lifted myself off the bed and stood next to it with Scott on the other side of the room, the bed a physical barrier between us. We communicated with our emotions and the fire and passion in our eyes, and then walked slowly towards each other, meeting at the foot of the bed. Scott's breathing was uneven. It seemed like now that we were here, he was confused; he didn't know what to do. I made the first move. I took hold of the bottom of Scott's billowing linen pirate shirt. He had removed his coat but was still sporting the low-cut white shirt and breeches. Fortunately, the black enamel paint had worn off his teeth.

I smiled. "Arms up, Sea Dog," I demanded.

"Aye aye, Cap'n," he replied quietly.

I lifted the shirt over his head, standing on tiptoes, balled it up and threw it to the floor. The sight of his flawless skin and defined abdominals served to intensify the fluttering in my stomach. I placed my hands on his shoulders and traced the line of his collarbone, sliding gently down over his perfectly formed chest smattered with short, dark, curly hairs. I paused on my journey downwards to circle each nipple with my thumbs, watching them pucker at my touch, and Scott made a tiny involuntary sound in the back of his throat. I slowly followed the trail of hair down over his flat stomach to the waistband of his trousers, but there, Scott took my hands gently in his own and removed them from his body, placing them purposefully back at my sides.

"No," he said in a strangled voice.

"No?" I asked.

"Not yet. My turn," he insisted, and he took hold of the bottom of my blouse. "Permission to undress ye, Cap'n?" he asked with a grin.

"Permission very much granted," I replied.

I lifted my arms obediently into the air and Scott pulled off my blouse and threw it on top of his shirt. He traced the same line with his fingers down my collarbone and gently stroked the swell of my breasts. He bent his head to my neck and very softly kissed the same trail, leaving electrified goose pimples in his wake. I couldn't help emitting a small sound of my own, and I felt a throbbing heat building inside me as my body prepared to welcome him.

"Your skin is so soft," he whispered. "Like velvet."

He spun me around so that I had my back to him and slowly, gently, undid my bra. I could feel his fingers trembling against my skin. He threw that, too, onto the pile of clothes and held me against his chest firmly, his hands on my hips. He slowly ran trembling fingers up over my stomach, and my breath came in a shudder. I didn't hide my quivering. I gasped when his hands reached my breasts and cupped them with fingers that were on fire, tracing his thumb slowly around my nipples just as I had done to him. They responded instantly to his touch, and the pleasure leapt from my breasts to my core. After a moment, he let his hands fall back to his sides.

"Turn round," he told me. "Turn round so I can see you. I need to see you."

I did as I was told, and Scott's breath hitched at the sight of me.

"Damn, you're gorgeous," he told me. "I'd like to ... I mean, would it be ok ...? I'd like to see ... well ... all of you. Would you feel comfortable ...? I mean ... can I ...? Would you ...?"

There was a moment of hollow panic, but I was only a few short steps away from him and I could practically read his mind through the flames in his eyes and the clamouring of his emotions. I had never felt so desired. I wanted him to see me because he wanted it so much. I didn't want to keep any part of myself hidden from this wonderful man who resided inside my soul. I nodded, turned my back on him again, removed my remaining clothes and turned slowly back to face him, revealing myself in all of my glory.

Scott's reaction was electric, his rapture emboldening. I smiled coquettishly, lifted my arms into the air and indulged him in a slow, sultry spin.

"Fuck, you're beautiful," he breathed. "Sorry, I mean ... well, yes, that's exactly what I mean. Fuck ... You ... Are ... Beautiful." He reached for his own trousers and fumbled with the belt. His hands were shaking so hard that he couldn't master the fastenings, and I could feel his frustration and embarrassment warring with his desire.

I stepped up close to him and put my hands over his. "Here," I whispered. "Let me." And I took his hands and placed them on my hips while I carefully undid his belt. Scott's hands didn't move as mine slipped inside his underwear, but his grip tightened painfully when I took him in my hand and stroked him softly. He hissed and pulled me sharply against his chest, crushing me and causing me to cry out in surprise. He released the pressure immediately.

"I'm so sorry, Belle, I just ... to feel your hands on me ... I've never ... your touch with your ... my ... and the fluence flipping out inside my mind... I can't think straight. I can only feel. I never knew it could be like this. I mean ... I imagined. Obviously, I imagined, but everything you feel, I feel. Your desire spurs me on like you wouldn't believe ... or maybe you would ... I feel like an animal. I'm frightened I'm going to hurt you or ... I'm frightened to touch you in case I ... or ... urgh, I can't even talk straight. I want to take my time with you. I want to worship you. There's so much I want to do. So many ways I want to explore you but ... today, can we just ...? I can't ... I mean, I don't think ... I mean ... I'm sorry, but I won't be able to ..."

"Shhh," I whispered gently. "I know. We've got our whole lives to get to know each other. Look at me."

He looked into my eyes.

"Feel my mind, my desires. Know I want this too."

Scott nodded dumbly.

I dropped his trousers and underwear to the floor, and he stepped out of them. We stood, our naked bodies touching and his arousal standing between us. I hadn't expected to have to take charge of the situation. Scott was usually cool and in control, but on this occasion, he needed leading by the hand, quite literally. I took him to the bed and climbed on, lying on my back, totally exposed. I beckoned to him.

"Come here, Scott. Come here and kiss me."

Scott nodded dumbly again and climbed onto the bed, positioning his knees between my legs and leaning over me so that the weight of his chest was on my breasts and I could feel his breath on my face. He looked into my eyes and I knew that he would find love and passion there, matching the flames burning brightly in his. He bent his head to kiss me and I kissed him back passionately, closing my eyes and losing myself to the assault on my senses. Our desire hung in the air, overwhelming our minds and bodies, reducing everything to nothing except our hunger. The room was filled with a static charge that crackled around us, and through the passion, I became intensely physically aware of every cell in my body, while the fluence, alive inside my mind, was screaming its appetite, begging me to claim him. I could sense the reciprocal urgency inside his own mind.

My body responded to the intensity of his touch, and I felt a liquid heat, a slick invitation between my legs. He sensed my readiness, and his hesitation, his fear, was gone. Suddenly, Scott was back in control, sliding a hand between my legs and groaning at what he found there.

"My God, Belle, you are the sexiest woman ... Isabel Bliss, look me in the eye and look now. Look here. See through the flames and see me and tell me that this is what you want ... that I'm what you want and you have no reservations because we're fast reaching the point of no return and I won't be able to stop. I can't ... I don't want to stop."

His hand was cupping me, the heated pressure against my sex scorching me and causing me to squirm against him on the bed. I could hardly form a coherent sentence myself, such was my need, but I opened my eyes and did as he asked, looking deeply into his once more.

"You don't need to ask me what I want, you can feel it. Feel it, feel me. You can feel it here" — I touched his heart — "and here." I laid my hand against his head. "There is no doubt. I want you. I love you."

That last assurance was his undoing, and he was suddenly bearing down on my body without restraint, pushing into me without control, gliding swiftly and easily inside. I felt him enter my body and my mind simultaneously, his power fusing with mine, and the combination of sensations was almost too much to bear. I rose to greet his every stroke and felt a fierce pressure and a heat building from deep inside me, becoming more intense and urgent by the second. I clung to his damp body, beading with sweat, ground myself against him and called out his name. His hands pinned mine above my head, his grip tightened, and an oath passed his lips when he heard his name on mine. The pressure and the heat inside me continued to build until I felt certain that I would explode. I was overwhelmed by the intense pleasure of the flesh and the equally intense, exquisite pleasure inside my mind.

"It feels like heaven. You feel like heaven," Scott said breathlessly, and he called my name, a hoarse cry of passion and possession, as he thrust more quickly and deeply into my body, and I watched his face with rapture, clinging to his hands for dear life. I looked into his eyes and through them into his soul, letting my eyes become his window into mine, lost in each other for all time.

"Belle!" he cried. "Belle, I'm here. Belle, I'm yours." And that familiar refrain unlocked something inside my mind, and the pressure that had been building began to erupt. The climax seemed to come from everywhere within me at once and felt like an extraordinary explosion of heat and sensation. When Scott felt my muscles tightening around him with my pleasure, he let go and thrust so deeply inside me that I cried out in ecstasy and we reached our peaks together, with one another's names bursting from our lips, our minds and bodies joined, staring into each other's souls. Nothing had ever felt more profound, sweeter or more right, and as our orgasms gradually dissolved around us, we stayed locked together in that embrace, not moving or speaking but breathing heavily and revelling in the sense that there was no longer a place where I ended and he began but that we were and would now be forever two parts of one whole. He was mine. I was his. We were each other's, and we shared a core that bound us tightly together for eternity.

This had been so much more than a joining of bodies. We were connected to each other in ways that most people could never imagine and that could never be fully explained. I didn't understand it myself, but I welcomed it without hesitation. I felt stronger, more powerful than ever before, and yet a profound vulnerability had been born. Being joined to a person in this way made him responsible for me and my happiness and me for his in a terrifying way, but the terror was overshadowed by the unsurpassed joy of our unity.

Scott rolled off my body and lay on his back on the bed next to me. I crawled up to him and lay my head on his chest. His arm snaked around me, holding me close. Our breathing was slowing, but we were unable to speak, so I concentrated on the feeling of security and love, and I listened to his heart beating quickly but steadily in his chest. Our hearts beat in time, and I had never felt more utterly satisfied, utterly complete.

Eventually, Scott recovered enough to speak.

"Well," he said slowly. "Wow."

I giggled. It was a brief analysis, to the point, but I felt that it covered everything.

"Yes," I agreed. "Wow."

Scott snorted under his breath and placed his hand on mine, trapping it over his heart.

"This is it, Belle. You know this is it, right? Body, mind and soul. You're mine. I'm yours. Truly, madly, deeply. You've got my heart, and I trust you to take care of it as I intend to take care of yours. Belle, I'm here. I'm here and I'm yours."

I felt a single tear slip from my eye and roll down my cheek onto his chest. The emotional energy being exchanged between my heart and his was thorough and thoroughly inspiring. I wanted to put my feelings into words but couldn't formulate a coherent thought, so instead I just nodded into his chest and repeated the words that he had offered to me.

"Body, mind and soul," I murmured. "I'm yours."

Chapter 31

"Do I look different?" I asked nervously.

Scott regarded me carefully, his head tilted to one side. "Mmmm … You look … delicious," he said.

"Stop it," I chided him. "You know what I mean. Do I look …? You know, different?"

Scott just laughed. "You look like you: wonderful, beautiful, mine."

"So, I do look different? I mean, will I look different to them? Do I seem … You know, do I *feel* different? My … our … Will they notice?"

"Belle, calm down. It's Mum and Dad, not an interrogation squad. They're not coming to test you or judge you; they're just coming home from holiday and they want to see us."

"I know, but you're … you're their … and we … well, we've ... just tell me, will they know?"

We were sitting on my favourite wicker chair in the solarium, and the sun was beating down on the glass from a cloudless sky, but I struggled to enjoy the warmth and comfort, too preoccupied by Georgia and Nicholas's imminent return. Scott took my hands and held them steadily in his own. The contact soothed me, but his answer did not.

"Will they know we've spent the week making sweet love in every room of their lovely house?" he asked with a straight face.

I felt the blush colour my cheeks. "Not helpful, Scott," I said. "You know what I mean … I mean us … the … the difference. Will they know?"

Scott smiled. "Yes, they'll know. Of course they'll know. Maybe not about the kitchen but certainly the solarium."

"Shut up! That's still not helpful," I complained.

"I'm sorry … no, really… I'm sorry. Yes. They'll know. They'll feel it as soon as they see us. It's not something we can hide from them. They know my signature as well as their own, and they'll sense the change. We don't need to hide it from them, Belle. Why would we want to hide it? I don't know about you, but I want to shout it. I want to put an ad in every paper. I want to plaster it all over social media. I want to change my Facebook status. You're mine. I'm yours. The world should know. Yes, they'll know. I'm connected to them. You're connected to me. They'll know."

That didn't help the blush in my cheeks. It was excruciating. I didn't understand how Scott could be so calm about his parents being about to discover that we'd had sex and were now, apparently, bonded for life, like it was a normal, everyday occurrence. It really wasn't normal, not for me. I put my left thumbnail into my mouth and started to gnaw on it nervously.

"Stop it," Scott scolded.

"I can't help it," I said. "What if they're upset?"

Scott laughed heartily. "Upset? Why on earth could you possibly think there's any chance they'd be upset? They adore you. They love me. They want us to be happy, and they already know that means me and you being together forever. They'll be thrilled. You're thinking too much like an ordinary. You don't need to be embarrassed about this."

Rationally, I knew that Scott was right. However, the fact was that I did think like an ordinary, and sex was an embarrassing subject in ordinary society. I groaned aloud at the image of Scott's dad's face when he saw me and knew that we'd been making love in his house. I would know that he knew, and that knowledge made me sweat. I stood up and walked to the fountain, dipping my hand into the cold water in the hope of distraction. Watching the water trickle over the stones always calmed me. I embraced the strange combination of the physical comfort of Scott's presence and the sense of his soothing spirit inside my mind. Being together made us stronger, and I could already see how quickly our bond was becoming an essential extension of myself.

My fluence saturated my mind with joy when it sensed my acceptance and newfound delight in our bond, and I felt Scott's fluence, through our connection, reflecting and expressing its own satisfaction. He stood and approached me slowly, like a predator stalking its prey, taking me firmly in his arms and eying me with a look of blithe delight.

"Mmm. You love me," he told me smugly.

"Yes, I do," I replied. "And you know it without me having to say it, and you can feel it, and I'll never be able to hide a thought or feeling from you ever again."

I meant to sound accusatory, but Scott saw right through it and his smile just widened. "That's right," he confirmed, "And you need to get used to it. You're stuck with me, and you love it."

I tried to look indifferent, but Scott caught my eye with his cheeky smile and I couldn't help responding with a smile of my own. Once he saw that I had dropped any pretence of nonchalance, his eyes began to glow with warmth, and my body and mind responded to him instantly. He chuckled under his breath at my silent answer to his unspoken question, the flames in his eyes ignited, and he pulled me in hard against his body and bent his head for a passionate kiss.

"I just can't get enough of you," he told me huskily. "I wonder if it will always be this way?"

At that very moment, we heard the front door close, heralding Georgia and Nicholas's return. I nearly jumped out of my skin.

"Oh my God, they're here!" I cried. I leaped away from him.

He just smiled, not ruffled in the slightest. "Scott," I said urgently. "They're here."

"Yes, my love," he said calmly. "They're here. We knew they were coming and now they're here. Shall we go and meet them at the door?"

I was frantically trying to get my head straight, but I was panicking and couldn't create order from the chaos inside my mind. I didn't know what to do. I touched my hair and smoothed down my top nervously.

"Stop it, Belle. Stop panicking. Relax," Scott told me patiently, and I lapped up his composure, allowing myself to be slightly mollified. He led me to the front hall.

Georgia was hanging her coat on the rack and Nicholas was carrying in the last of the bags when Scott and I reached them.

"Mum, Dad," Scott said warmly, "welcome home." He embraced his mother warmly. "Did you have fun?" he asked.

"Mmm, it was wonderful," Georgia replied. "Beautiful weather and too much food, exactly what a holiday should be. We even got out of the city, into the hills for a couple of days."

"Pretty darn good company too," Nicholas added smoothly, coming up behind Georgia and draping his arm around her shoulder affectionately.

"Yes." She smiled. "That too."

I hung back slightly from the intimate family scene, unsure whether I should go in for a hug or whether I should say something, anything, but my mind was blank. My palms felt clammy. Scott released his mum and returned to stand by my side, putting his arm around my shoulder in a mirror of his dad's familiar gesture, a signal of our union.

Georgia beamed at me. "And Isabel," she gushed. "So lovely to see you too. You look well. You both look …" She paused mid-sentence and stood still for a fraction of a second, contemplating Scott and me. I felt the briefest caress in my mind, a sweep of inquiry, and Georgia's face split into a huge, genuine smile, which flooded me with a rush of joy and warmth. She opened her arms wide, beaming.

"Oh, Scott. And Isabel. Congratulations. Oh, my boy, we couldn't be happier for you, could we darling?" She turned to Nicholas, who nodded his concurrence. "We knew it was only a matter of time before you … but we didn't know. We talked about it while we were away. We hoped you might.

Oh, my darlings, I'm thrilled for you. Oh, Isabel, you really are truly part of the family now."

She rushed forwards and grabbed me, embracing me with a maternal love that brought a tear to my eye. I hugged her back fiercely and tried to convey everything that I was feeling through that embrace. I looked with gratitude to both Georgia and Nicholas for their generosity of mind. I was a little overwhelmed and didn't know what to say, but the happy chatter between Scott and his mum gave me time to compose myself and find my voice.

I couldn't remember why I had been worried about the return of these good, kind, loving people who had become my family. Scott had told me as much and I should have known it, should have felt it inside. I felt yet another rush of warmth for these people who had accepted me without question or judgement. I cast aside all of my niggling doubts and worries and followed my new family into the kitchen, where Scott filled the kettle for tea.

"We should celebrate," Georgia declared. "Let's go out."

Nicholas replied, always the voice of reason. "We should celebrate," he agreed, "but let's not go out. We're tired from the journey, and I'm sure none of us really want to get ready to go out now. How about we order in tonight and crack open a bottle of champagne? We can celebrate here in the comfort of our home with the people we love and still be in bed by nine." He smiled at everyone happily, took Scott's hand and shook it warmly. He gave me a hug. "It's wonderful," he told me quietly. "Welcome to the family."

I blushed, and Georgia beamed again. "You're right as always. I don't really want to go out tonight. Yes, we'll celebrate at home and arrange a proper party later."

"Oh, I don't know about that," I said, panic-stricken. "We don't really need a party to announce that we … well, that we … I mean, we don't need to announce it to the world, do we? I mean it's not really … it's not like we … do you guys really throw parties for these sort of things?"

I was horrified at the thought of having a party to announce that I'd had sex with my boyfriend, especially a party thrown by said boyfriend's parents. The idea seemed absurd and a little obscene. Scott laughed at the expression on my face.

"I'll say it again. You've lived like an ordinary too long. Consummating your love isn't something to be ashamed of, it's to be celebrated, and it's not exactly the sex that we celebrate; it's what it means. Think of it like an engagement party. A celebration of the fact that we've made a promise to each other and accepted each other as permanent features in our lives."

This didn't mollify me, and I was reeling at the fact that Scott had just said the word 'sex' in front of his dad. "But we haven't …we're not ..." I stammered.

"No, I know sweetheart, we're not engaged, not exactly, anyway, but to me … to us, bonding is so much more than an engagement. It's a uniting of two souls, two fluences. It's one of the most momentous experiences of our lives, and yes, we usually do share it with our friends and family. Yes, it's common to have a party."

I wasn't convinced, and Scott let it go, for now. "Don't worry, no one's going to organise a party without your say-so," he offered. "If you don't feel comfortable, then it just won't happen, right, Mum?"

Georgia looked disappointed but nodded slowly. "Of course, dear. It doesn't matter who else knows, does it? The only people who truly matter are right here, and we're just thrilled to be a part of your lives."

I was relieved. "Thank you," I said. "For now, let's park the idea of a party, but I do like the sound of a takeaway and champagne tonight. Let's do that. We do want to celebrate with you."

I wanted to tell them how much their acceptance meant to me again and hoped that I was managing to convey it through my words and emotions. The atmosphere was exhilarating and I embraced the heady delight, but I also had someone else on my mind and something else that I needed to do. I turned to Scott.

"There are other people who should be sharing this news with us, though," I said.

He understood immediately. "Your parents?" he asked.

"Yes. Being a part of this family has been so wonderful, and you've accepted me and been there for me and I'll never be able to truly repay you, but it makes me realise that family and love is so much more important than anything else, and despite what she's done, Mum's my mum, and Dad, well, he's done nothing wrong, and I've cut him out of the last few months of my life because of her. No more. We need to sort it out. I need to forgive her or at least work on working on forgiving her. I need you to come and meet my family, Scott. They need to know you. We can't think about celebrating with strangers when my parents haven't even met you.

"We're family now," I said, gesturing towards the three of them, "and Mum and Dad ... and Stephie are part of that too. I can't be this happy and not share it with them. It's not really real until they know. You guys have shown me how important love and family is. I need to start letting go of the anger because I want Mum in my life. We need to go and see them."

"About time," Scott said with a smile. "Let's do it."

A couple of days later, my nerves were wound tightly and my mind was full of apprehension as we approached Mum and Dad's house, but I was reassured by Scott's emotions, my fluence and our bond supplying me with the instinctive awareness that Scott felt nothing but happy anticipation for the meeting. He had promised that he wouldn't prejudge Mum on her handling of my fluence and the lies and manipulation that she had employed to deceive her family, but it would be terribly difficult for him. His feelings towards both me and the fluence were fierce, and the immutable knowledge of his own ability and the fluence community had been integral to every aspect of his life since before he could remember. He loved me deeply and couldn't stand the thought of anyone causing me pain, but he had promised and was committed to an open-minded meeting. Actually, despite the many reasons for Scott to dislike Mum, I felt that it would be me who struggled to avoid judgement, not him. Scott had reminded me time and time again of his theory that Mum's decisions had their foundations in a genuine belief that she was doing the right thing, based on a deep suffering that began when she blamed the fluence for the loss of her parents. I understood the explanation in theory but was still struggling to come to terms with it in practice and had no idea how I was going to react today when I saw Mum for the first time in two months. I was also terrified about how she would react when she discovered that I had bonded with Scott, the son of a man that she despised, and that our bond had been consummated before they had even been introduced.

"Turn left here," I told Scott, "and it's just round the next corner on the right. That's it, right there with the cherry blossom tree. There's room on the drive."

Scott pulled into the driveway and turned off the engine but didn't move to get out of the car straight away. "Belle." He spoke to me calmly, taking my hand and looking steadily into my eyes. "I'm here, I'm yours. It's going to be all right."

I absorbed his strength and his love, took a deep breath and pulled myself together.

"Thank you," I said gratefully. "It helps a lot."

I undid my seatbelt, got out of the car and walked resolutely to the front door, where Scott stood by my side, holding my hand and lending me his strength. I almost lifted my hand to knock again but caught myself once more. I didn't want to start this visit on the wrong foot. I wanted Mum and Dad to know that I loved them and that I was here to make things right, not to continue the fight. Somehow, not knocking on the door seemed very important. I took hold of the handle, turned it and pushed.

"Mum? Dad?" I called, but I needn't have announced our arrival because before the door had even closed behind us, Mum and Dad were upon us in the hallway and Mum's arms were wrapped tightly around me, squeezing the life out of me. She didn't say anything at first, but she had deliberately lowered the walls around her mind and was allowing me to examine her emotions. The overwhelming outpouring of relief and love was impossible to mistake. It came barrelling into me, knocking the breath from my body, and although I had stiffened momentarily at the initial contact, I quickly accepted the display of affection and relaxed into the embrace. I began to let go of all of the anger and resentment that I had been carrying, allowing myself to be held and welcoming the affection and the absence of the indicating nudge against my mind that might disclose an attempt to manipulate me in any way. I felt my own emotions rising to the surface, allowing Mum to sense my own love and gratitude in return for this moment of emotional honesty, and we shared a silent communication. Although this had come far too late in my life, the progress in our relationship was momentous, and I allowed a few silent tears of joy to fall from my eyes.

Dad allowed us a moment, but it wasn't long before he was pulling Mum out of the way so that he could get to me.

"Izzy," he said quietly, "it's been too long." And he pulled me into an embrace of his own, an embrace that was shorter and a little less impassioned than Mum's but no less meaningful to me. I hugged him back as tightly as I could, trying to communicate to him that I loved him completely and that no matter what happened or what we discovered about each other, he was and always would be my dad. Of course, Dad being an ordinary meant that the intricacies were largely lost on him, but he understood that I was there and holding him close, and that was all that he needed to know.

Scott hung back while I embraced both parents. Although this visit was, in part, his introduction, he was highly aware of how important it was for us to reconnect and happy to give us all of the time that we needed to do that without foisting himself upon them before they were ready. It was Dad who addressed him first, no doubt wanting to make a good impression and not wanting Scott to think that we were a family of emotional imbeciles. He let go of me and took a step back, looking up into Scott's face.

"Sorry, you must be Scott. Come on through. We don't normally stand around in the hallway hugging all day. Come into the lounge where we can meet you properly."

Scott nodded affably and the four of us entered the living room. Mum and Dad stood together and I stood by Scott's side, my arm linked though his.

"Sorry, yes. This is Scott," I said, smiling affectionately towards him. "Scott, this is Max and Beth."

Scott held out his hand to Dad, who took it and gave it a firm shake.

He smiled. "Hi, Max, Beth. It's lovely to meet you."

"You too," nodded Dad. "And not before time." He gave me a pointed look, which softened quickly to a smile that he couldn't hide because there was no point in lamenting the last couple of months. I was here.

"Now, let me get everyone a drink. Tea?" he offered.

"Yes, please," Scott and I said in unison. Scott smiled. "White with one, please."

"Coming up." And Dad disappeared into the kitchen.

When the three fluencers were left alone in the room, I became aware of a strange tension. Scott and Mum hadn't moved but were staring intently into each other's eyes, and I realised that there was some sort of a silent communication going on between them. Scott was relaxed, smiling, but Mum looked intent as she examined him, using her fluence for an interrogation. I drew breath to interject, but Scott sensed it and shook his head ever so slightly, asking me to wait. The silence stretched on, and I became frustrated by the pair of them, but Scott held out his hand for me to take and I knew that he was consenting to undergo her scrutiny. I thought that I saw Mum's eyes narrow at one point, but then I definitely saw her relax into a smile before she looked away and the spell was broken. The interrogation was over. Mum stepped towards Scott with her arms open, and he stepped forwards for a hug. It was the last thing that I had expected, but Mum seemed to have accepted him, while I just stood staring at them dumbly and wondering what to say.

Mum relaxed and was all smiles as she invited Scott to sit. He sat next to me on the settee, but I was still lost for words after witnessing their peculiar fluence dance.

"Thank you, Scott," said Mum. "It was the only way."

"No problem," he replied smoothly. "I mean it. I've got nothing to hide from you, and we both want what's best for Belle."

Surprise briefly flashed across Mum's face at the unfamiliar abbreviation of my name.

"Of course. I've only ever wanted what's best for her." She turned to me. "For you. I love you, sweetie."

"I love you too, Mum." I looked at Scott with a question in my eyes, needing some kind of explanation.

"It's OK, Belle. Your mum and I were just getting to know each other. It's much easier than a whole lot of questions and answers."

Mum let out a short laugh. "It is, isn't it? I'd almost forgotten." She looked a little vague, dreamy. "It's nice."

Scott laughed too. "Nice?" he asked. "Yeah, I suppose it is."

I turned to Mum. "Did you find what you were looking for?" I asked.

"I didn't find what I was expecting, which is a huge relief," Mum replied with a smile. "I found a young man who's very much in love with my daughter, a young man who doesn't have a lot of secrets, and I found you inside his head. Are you happy?"

"Yes, Mum, I'm happy. Happier than I can say. Scott makes me whole. He makes me who I'm supposed to be."

"Then I'm happy for you," she said. "All I ever wanted was for you to be happy; I just didn't know how."

"It's OK, Mum," I said, stretching out a hand to cover hers briefly. "I love you."

Dad came back into the room with two teas, which he passed to Scott and me before returning for another two for himself and Mum. We all sat quietly and sipped our drinks. After a few minutes, I worried that the situation was becoming awkward, but Scott must have sensed it too because he came to the rescue.

"Did Isabel tell you about Pirate Day?" he asked.

Mum and Dad shook their heads.

"Honestly, this woman's a miracle worker," he told them. "I've never seen anything like it. The kids had such a wonderful day. There was this one little girl, Jane, right?"

I nodded with a smile.

"So, Jane comes in looking fabulous. Mummy's gone to some real effort there, braiding all her hair in these tight little plait things tied up with beads and stuff, and her costume is like this state-of-the-art fashion pirate getup, and she keeps flicking her hair over her shoulders all day, so happy, so proud of herself, and then just after lunch we hear this commotion coming from the toilets. Jane's screaming and this other little girl ..."

"Melissa," I supplied.

"Yeah, Melissa," Scott agreed. "She comes running into the classroom shouting, *Miss, Miss, Jane's hair's stuck in the toilet, Miss*, and I think, *boy, I've got to see this,* so Belle and me run to the toilets while the terrifying Mrs Bishop keeps all the other kids back, and there she is, half out of a cubicle with these braid things caught in the lock on the door. She must have been flicking them just at the wrong minute and they've sort of wrapped around the lock. Poor kid was beside herself, and it only got worse when Belle told her she was going to have to cut some of her hair off." Scott laughed and I giggled at the memory.

Mum and Dad laughed with us, and the tension was gone.

I took up the story. "Yes, poor thing was so upset. I tried to untangle her, but she must have been struggling before I got there because some of them were so badly tangled, there was nothing for it. Luckily, I didn't have to cut much, but she was so upset about it. It took two gold chocolate doubloons to calm her down, didn't it?"

"Two gold doubloons and something else if I remember rightly," said Scott.

"That's right." I was laughing harder now. "You sang to her. She loved it."

"Yeah, and then you had to write it in the accident book. How do you word that one? I'd love to have a good look through that accident book one day. There must be some great entries in there."

"A few great ones and an awful lot of *Child collided with peer on the playground resulting in a small red mark*," I said drily.

"Hmm … Maybe just publish the funny ones when you're writing your memoirs," Scott suggested.

The remaining tension died down as we caught up and Mum and Dad began to get to know Scott. Before long, he had the pair of them eating out of his hand. He was just that kind of person. Everyone who met him loved him, and fluence or not, people were happy in his company. I also relaxed. I had been nervous about seeing Mum and about Mum and Dad meeting Scott for different reasons. I had also been worried about my relationship with Dad, but I really needn't have worried at all. Mum and Dad were Mum and Dad. They loved me and wanted me to be happy, and I loved them. Nothing could change that, and Scott was the most positive thing in my life. His charm and obvious adoration for me was enough for them.

The afternoon flew by with stories and laughter until Mum announced that she needed to pop to the allotment to check on her hens and water the greenhouse.

"Do you want to come and see the girls?" she asked.

I looked at Scott. "All of us?" I asked.

"Well, I was hoping I could convince Scott to have a look at the damage on the bedroom ceiling," said Dad. "We've had a leak, and it's left a bit of a mess that needs sorting out. I know we've only just met and all, but Isabel told me as how you're handy, and I was hoping you might be able to give me some advice."

Scott looked at me and I gave him a nod. "Of course I'll have a look," he replied. "I'm sure I'll be able to sort it for you as well, save you getting somebody out."

Dad smiled. "I was hoping you might say that," he said. "Not much point in having a handyman join the family if I can't use him for my own gain, is there? Girls, you head down to the allotment, and we'll join you in a few so Scott can see your place, sweetie. Give you a chance for some girl talk and me a chance to grill Scott about his intentions towards daughter number one."

I rolled my eyes. "You know you couldn't scare a flea, don't you, Dad?" I laughed. "Don't pay him any attention," I said to Scott. "See you in a bit."

And Dad led Scott upstairs while Mum and I put on our coats and shoes and headed outside.

It was a cool spring day, but the sun was bright and the walk to the allotment was comfortable. We walked in silence for a time, feeling the awkwardness return now that we were alone.

"So," I said warily, "what do you think?"

The silence stretched on for what seemed like minutes, and I began to get impatient. It wasn't a difficult question. I just wanted to talk to her. I just wanted her support.

"Don't do that, Mum. Answer the question. You're making me nervous. Either tell me you like him or you don't, but know that he makes me happier than I've ever been. I really want your blessing."

Mum continued to walk at my side in silence for another few seconds before taking a deep breath. "You bonded with Nicholas Callahan's son." She stopped on the path, forcing me to stop too. We looked at each other. The barriers were back up, preventing me from reading her emotions, but it looked like there was anger and possibly, strangely, laughter in her eyes. "You bonded with Nicholas and Georgia Callahan's son," she repeated, and this time she did laugh. It was a short, hollow, unpleasant sound that held no real mirth and sent a shiver down my spine. It also made me immediately defensive. I started walking again, talking as I went. Mum had no choice but to follow.

"Yes. Yes, I bonded with Scott. I love him. He's my one … my soul mate. He also happens to be a Callahan. I take it you have a problem with that?"

We arrived at the allotment before Mum replied, and the silence stretched on as she entered the shed, fetched the hen food and filled the feeders. I waited for her response, my anger and frustration building as the silence continued. Eventually, she sighed.

"He seems lovely. He seems honest, smart, funny, good-looking, and he clearly adores you."

I let out a small sigh of relief of my own, but Mum hadn't finished.

"But … but he's a Callahan," she said with a note of finality and a shake of her head.

"Yes, he's a Callahan," I replied hotly. "And the Callahans have been nothing but good to me over these last few months. They've welcomed me into their family, their home. They've taken me under their wing and they've helped me learn and come to terms with everything that I am … with what I can do. They've shown me that the fluence is a gift, not a curse like you always wanted me to believe. They've accepted me … all of me. They've loved me when you

573

couldn't … when you wouldn't … when you couldn't love me for me. They're the best, Mum. The best."

Hot tears were streaming down my face. I hadn't realised how much I was hoping that Mum would apologise for her behaviour, that we would reconnect over my happiness, but it wasn't to be, and the disappointment was almost more than I could bear.

"Do you owe them anything?" Mum asked suddenly.

"What do you mean?" I said, sniffing. I didn't like her tone.

"Are you in his debt?" Mum pressed on.

"In his debt?" I asked. "What's that supposed to mean? Yes, of course I owe them. I owe them everything. I owe them love and kindness because that's what they've given me."

"Yes, yes, but has he asked for your help? Has he told you that you owe him anything? Has he suggested you're in his debt?" Mum continued to push.

"Who? Nicholas?" I asked.

Mum nodded.

"You sound crazy again, Mum. I was hoping it'd be different, but you're not making it easy. You're not making sense. No, Nicholas hasn't said I owe him anything. He's ... they've helped me 'cause they're good people, not because they want anything from me. Don't start with the conspiracy theories again. It's not them I can't trust.

"I don't want to fall out with you. I wanted it to be different this time. What are you talking about? Urgh, no, don't answer that. I can't do this again. I don't want things to be off with us. I just want you to love me and be my mum and be happy for me because I've found so much … I've learned so much about myself … about what I can do and who I am. Can't you feel it? Can't you be happy for me? Why do you have to be like this?"

Mum looked me up and down, took in the tears and my rising tone and stepped forwards, enveloping me in her arms.

I let her hold me. She spoke softly. "Shhhh, I'm sorry, baby, I'm so sorry. Let me ... let's just ... I'm sorry, Izzy. Let me look at you." And she stepped back, keeping hold of my shoulders and looking into my eyes.

I tried to erect a shield to keep my mind hidden from her probing fluence for a moment but relented when I saw the love shining in her eyes. Instead I tried to cling on to everything that Scott and I had talked about, reminding myself that Mum was broken in some ways and childlike in others. I tried to concentrate on the fact that despite all of the craziness, despite all of the lies and the deceit, Mum loved me very much. I gradually relaxed and let her in. I felt the familiar probing in my mind and saw her smile.

"You're beautiful, Izzy," she breathed. "Beautiful and stronger than I ever could have imagined. I always knew it was strong in you. You and Stephie, you were both so strong in different ways. It was one of the reasons I tried to protect you from it. I didn't want you to feel the pressure this kind of strength can bring, but of course I'm happy for you. If you're happy, I'm happy for you. I'm happy you've found your mate. I'm happy he loves you. I can feel his love inside you. I can feel ... he knows you're upset. He's on his way. He'll be here soon."

My eyes widened. I didn't quite understand what Mum had been sensing or how she knew what Scott was feeling, whether it was part of the bond inside me that she was reading or whether she could feel Scott's approach another way. It was a strength, an aspect of the fluence that I had yet to discover. I sighed.

"I wish you would've taught me, Mum. I wish I'd've discovered it with you. I wish you'd let me be me. I can see ... I can feel that you're strong too. It's still strong in you and it isn't too late. You could help me now. We could do this together."

Mum shook her head vehemently. "It's not that I don't love you or don't want to help you, but you're wrong, I'm not strong. I'm so weak." She pointed around the allotment, dazzling in its spring beauty. "This is all I have now. This is all I'm good for."

"Oh, Mum." I sighed again. "That isn't true at all. You have me."

She looked at me sharply.

"You do, Mum … if you want me. You still have me and Steph and Dad. You're loved. We love you."

Mum nodded slowly. "Maybe," she said. We heard men's voices approaching and her face suddenly looked wild. She grabbed my arm tightly. "They're coming," she said urgently.

I hastily wiped my eyes. I couldn't hide my feelings from Scott, but the last thing that I wanted was for Dad to know that we had fallen out again. He was so happy that things were going well.

Mum lowered her voice and whispered to me frantically. "I love you, but don't forget what I said before. Nothing's changed. Nicholas Callahan is dangerous. He and Georgia are too strong together. Just think about it, please. Think about what he does. Why do you think he dedicates his life to getting criminals out on the street? Think about how many dangerous people are in his debt. They'll manipulate you. They'll control you. Don't let him do you any favours, Izzy. Don't get in his debt. Don't let him take your power. Please … please just think about what I've said. Just think about it," she finished urgently and physically pushed me away so that we were standing a sensible distance apart, apparently admiring the hens, when the men arrived.

I tried to arrange my expression into something resembling normal, but I was reeling from the sudden urgency and fear in Mum's voice. Her desperation was frightening. I had known that she was struggling but hadn't realised that she had sunk into actual flights of outrageous fancy. Talk of danger, power and debt — this hostility towards Nicholas Callahan was out of control.

Scott, sensing my distress, came straight to me and took me in his arms, soothing my agitation with his love. "I'm here," he told me.

I looked up at him with gratitude and let him take charge of the situation, buying me a little time to compose myself for Dad.

"Wow," Scott said. He beamed at Mum, who plastered on a smile for appearances and beamed back. "This is some allotment."

Mum, always prepared to show off her garden to a willing audience, was instantly distracted.

"I mean, this really is something else," he went on. "You totally put all the other plots to shame."

Dad chuckled with pride. "Doesn't she just?" he said, moving to stand with her. "She lives and breathes this place, and her passion shows."

"You're not kidding," agreed Scott. "Can I have a guided tour?"

Mum nodded and started pointing out features of particular interest. They set off on the tour, leaving Dad and me standing by the shed alone.

"I like him," he told me simply.

"Good," I replied. "I rather like him too."

"You look happy together."

"We really are, Dad."

"That's all a parent ever wants for his kids, you know. I know I was upset about Jack, but I can see something different in you and it's good. You're shining. You look properly alive, and your happiness makes me happy."

"Thanks, Dad. I love you."

"I love you too, and it's been really good seeing you today. We've missed you these last few weeks … months even." He sighed. "I know Mum can be difficult, but she loves you too. It's been hard on her, not seeing you. And on me."

"I know, Dad, and I've missed you too. Do you think …?

Mum, I mean ... I'm worried ... Do you think she's ...? Well, she's ...? I don't know ..."

I wanted to ask him if he thought that Mum was crazy, to suggest that she needed help, but there was no way that I could even begin that conversation without sounding crazy myself and without immeasurable trouble. Everything began with the fact that Mum had been lying to him, to us all, for years: that he wasn't our father and that Stephanie, Mum, me and even Scott were, in an inconceivable way, more than ordinary. I couldn't go on.

Dad understood the basis of my concern, even if he couldn't comprehend the details, and he sighed again. "You know, she had it pretty tough after her dad died and her mum, your grandma, left. She never really understood why, and I think she always felt like she'd done something wrong. It was awful, you know, just awful. She was broken. I don't know whether you and Jack ... well, I think losing Jack or you losing Jack or you choosing ... well, I don't know, but she's not been herself since. The last couple of months she's been ... she's been more like she was back then. Maybe it brought up some stuff for her, but whatever the reason, she's not been right, and you staying away's made things worse."

"I know, Dad, and I'm sorry. I do love her, but ..." I stopped again. There was nothing that I could say that would satisfy him. "I love you both."

"I know, sweetheart. Let's put it behind us, shall we? Allow us to get to know Scott. Don't be a stranger."

"I won't, Dad. I promise. I love you."

When Mum had finished showing Scott around, the four of us walked back to the house and said our goodbyes on the drive. Mum and Dad stood close together to wave us off, and as we drove out of view, I breathed a sigh of relief. Scott took his hand from the steering wheel and gave my thigh a comforting squeeze.

"Max is wonderful," he told me. "You know he couldn't love you more, right?"

"I know." My eyes instantly filled with tears. "It doesn't even really matter that he's not my father, you know? He'll always be my dad, but ... I don't know. There's this whole other question rattling around in my mind. It's not just does he love me and do I love him. That's never in question. But does he deserve to know the truth? I don't know. It's not that he doesn't deserve it in a bad way, but what good would it do? And then there's this other guy. There's another guy out there somewhere who's part of me, a guy who's my biological father. Does he even know I ... we ... exist? Does he care? Do I want to know? Do I? I don't know."

Scott paused before carefully voicing a possibility that I had been contemplating but didn't quite know how to broach. "We could ask my dad. I know it's not something that we've really talked about since ... but you said your mum said he ... well, I don't know, but if what she said was true, then he'd know. Dad would have some of the answers, wouldn't he?"

I nodded.

"I've never mentioned it to him," Scott went on. "It's not my place to ... not without you ... without your ... and I assume he doesn't know you know, or he might have brought it up. He's never mentioned any connection with your mum, and I didn't want to ... not until you ... but it's an option if you want it. We could talk to him together."

I smiled shakily. "Thank you, Scott. Thank you. I know. It's something I've wondered about too. Is it odd that he hasn't mentioned knowing her or does he just think it better to keep quiet until I bring it up? I don't think I'm ready ... I can't ask the question because I don't think I'm ready for the answers. And Mum ... and Steph ... and Dad ... I mean, it's not just my decision, is it?" I stared out of the window blindly, overwhelmed.

"OK," said Scott gently. "Let's leave that for now. Do you want to talk about your mum?"

I let out a short laugh. "If it's not one thing, it's another," I

579

said. "I'm sorry I've got so much baggage."

"Hey," he said sharply. "Don't do that. I love you. I love your baggage." And he put his hand back on my thigh, offering stability and comfort.

"I know," I said. "And I'm not sure what I'd do without it right now." I laughed again. "So, yes, what did you think of Mum?"

Scott thought for a moment, choosing his words carefully. "You've been around her all your life, so she's normal to you …"

I scoffed.

"No, you know what I mean. She's really strong, Belle … I mean … she's not strong because she's broken, but if she could be put back together … her fluence is really powerful. It's actually quite thrilling. You have a lot of her inside you. The strength you've gained in such a short time is unbelievable, but I can understand it more now, having met her. You're your mother's daughter."

I scoffed again. "Great," I said sarcastically. "I imagine you feel like running for the hills right about now, then."

"Don't be silly," he said gently. "You know I'm not going anywhere. No, but really, meeting her was fascinating, and I'll tell you one thing for sure. She loves you too. She really loves you, Belle. The way she probed my fluence, the way she interrogated me … she's fiercely protective of you. I'm more sure than ever now … that what she did … the way she … the things she didn't … well, she honestly believed it was for the best.

"I probed her too, you know. She allowed me in. She made herself reachable to me so I could see how strong her love for you really is, which must have been hard for her, having been closed off to it for so long. I think … I hope your mum and I came to some sort of understanding today. We have something in common after all. You. We were right, though, Belle. There's something broken inside her. Something I don't know if can ever be fixed. And the way she's found of coping with the excess emotional energy after giving up the fluence is incredible. It's probably stopped her going totally insane, and I imagine she did that for you ... for you and Steph and Max."

"What are you talking about?" I asked.

He tried to explain. "Right, you haven't seen it because you weren't looking.

"Seen what?" I asked, confused.

"So, the fluence is all about the flow of emotional energy, right?"

I nodded.

"Your mum's fluence is strong, but she struggled to come to terms with her dad's death and the abandonment by her mum, blaming the fluence for everything, right?"

I nodded again, following so far.

"But she couldn't get rid of it. You can't just ignore it, and if you try, it gets stronger and stronger anyway because emotional energy is flowing all the time, all around us. You couldn't ignore it, could you? Despite your mum trying to get you to ignore it, you couldn't."

I shook my head.

"And your experiences were causing you mental and physical pain. It didn't matter that she told you to ignore it; it seeped in unbidden and you had to do something about it. You heard me inside your head. You felt other people's pain. You felt frustrated. You had to learn about it and begin to harness your ability in order to cope with it better."

I nodded again.

"Beth wanted to hide from it completely, to convince herself and everybody else that it wasn't a part of her, but it *was* a part of her, and she had a husband and two children to look after, so she needed to channel the energy somewhere else ..."

I was beginning to lose my grasp on his train of thought. "I still don't know what you're talking about. Where did she channel it?"

"Channel probably isn't the right word," Scott mused out loud. "It suggests a deliberateness that I don't think Beth had. She probably felt frustrated, but because she was suffering mentally and emotionally from loss and guilt, she didn't connect her feelings of frustration with the fluence. She needed something else, something to keep her occupied, to keep her sane."

I snorted again. "Well, whatever it was didn't work, did it?"

Scott smiled. "Maybe it did. Maybe without it, she would have gone completely insane and ended up being sectioned or on medication or in therapy for the rest of her life."

"Therapy sounds good right about now," I said drily. "So, what are you saying? What's your point?"

"The allotment," Scott said patiently.

"The allotment," I repeated blankly.

"Have you seen it?" he asked.

"Of course I've seen it," I said in exasperation. "She spends most of her life there. We've been traipsing down there since we were babies. Sometimes I think she loves those hens more than her family, and her flowers and fruit and vegetables are legendary, like they're her other kids."

"Exactly." Scott looked satisfied.

"Exactly what?" I asked.

"Beth's plot is so much better than the others. Like … sooo much better. I know she spends a lot of time down there, but haven't you ever wondered why her flowers bloom so much brighter, her vegetables grow bigger, her fruit tastes sweeter?"

"No. I can honestly say I've never wondered about any of those things."

"Well, I've only been there once, and knowing her story, knowing what she is, I could see it immediately." He let his words sink in.

I stared ahead, my mind filled with racing thoughts. He was right. I wondered how I had never seen it before, but then perhaps that was obvious too. If you live in a world without magic, you never look for magic to be the answer to any of your questions. I said the words slowly. "Mum's been … what? Fluencing the allotment …?"

Scott smiled. "Sort of. Don't look so horrified. It's not as crazy as it sounds. She needed somewhere to channel the energy. It flowed from her into the plants, into the soil. The allotment's kept her functioning because the emotions that might have broken her have fed her passion. Having heard her story and met you and her, I imagine she has no idea. She thinks she's successfully blocked the fluence from her life, which is why she believed you could do the same. But a fluencer can't ever really live without it, and trying is a sure-fire road to madness. I've heard about this sort of thing, but it's rare. I've never met anyone like her or seen anything like it." Scott seemed actually excited about the revelation.

I wasn't sure how I felt about it, but I wasn't happy. It was just another thing to process. At times, I felt like I was starting to belong in this realm of fluence. The connection that Scott and I shared and our ability to experience the world on a higher plane made me feel powerful and incredible, but at other times, the enormity of it all just seemed like too much to comprehend. Scott had had nearly twenty-nine years to live with and understand his fluence. It was a part of everything that he had ever experienced and everything that he was. For me, it sometimes still felt like there was an alien inside my mind, and sometimes I did wish that I could just suppress the magic, go back to living a more ordinary life, back to before.

As usual, Scott understood my reflection before I had time to process it myself. One of the benefits of an otherworldly affinity with one's partner was that it became unnecessary to vocalise difficult emotions, which was both frightening and comforting in itself.

"I know it's a lot to take in," he told me. "I don't expect you to be able to deal with it all straight away. It's OK to be overwhelmed, especially about things that concern your family, and even more especially, your mum. There's so much going on in your mind and in your heart. Give yourself a break."

I looked at him with gratitude again. It was a relief that he wasn't going to push it right now. My mind was already enough of a jumble. The fact that Mum had been unknowingly feeding her allotment with the siphoned emotional energy of strangers was yet another disquieting discovery. Scott changed the subject slightly, but the new one wasn't comfortable either.

"What did she say to you before me and your dad arrived?" he asked gently. "I felt your distress. You had me worried."

I nodded. "I know you did. Mum told me."

He nodded back. "Yes, I'm not surprised. She's very responsive to our bond because of her connection to you."

He didn't speak again, content to wait for me to decide if or how much I wanted to share.

"She was just … it was just … I asked her what she thought about you … about us, and she … she … she was … she was just …"

"Wait. She didn't like me, did she?" Scott asked with mock incredulity.

I laughed. "How could anyone not like you?"

"Well, it doesn't happen often, but maybe, under the circumstances …"

"No. She said you were lovely. Honest, smart, good-looking,"

"Thank goodness. She clearly has good taste after all," Scott interrupted.

I snorted. "Maybe … but then she just … Well … I'd hoped things would be different, but … like you said, she's damaged. She said some hurtful things. I don't think I want to talk about it. Not now."

Scott's hand gently stroked my thigh. "That's fine," he

said. "I'm here whenever you need me."

I felt guilty for not telling him the whole truth, the things that Mum had said about his family, but I couldn't bring myself to do it. I didn't want to damage the tentative progress that we had made today and the dawning of a positive relationship between Scott and Mum. Scott always saw the best in people. Despite Mum's deceit and unattractive behaviour, he viewed her as powerful, someone to empathise with, sympathise with, even admire to a certain degree. He wouldn't feel like that if he knew the truth, and I didn't want to destroy his fragile opinion.

What I did think about was my interactions with the Callahans, of how they had welcomed me into their family and helped me find my feet. They had been nothing but kind, loving and supportive of my fluence. My relationship with Scott and his family was precious. Mum was the dangerous one, fabricating obstacles in order to drive a wedge between the Callahans and me. I would not allow it. Mum was paranoid, and the Callahans were loving, beautiful and successful. They were the best. Perhaps it was jealousy that drove Mum to such unnecessary cruelty.

I pushed the seed of doubt firmly out of my mind and covered Scott's hand with my own. "I love you," I told him.

He smiled. "As it happens, I love you too."

Chapter 32

The summer term brought with it the promise of fine weather and high spirits amongst staff and pupils alike. Children's laughter, that eternal elevator of the soul, reverberated around the school grounds, igniting the inner optimist in everyone. Inherently infectious to ordinaries and fluencers alike, the stimulating mixture of emotions buoyed my vitality, resulting in spectacular results. Scott became a familiar face to my colleagues and friends, and my life fell into some semblance of normality and routine.

I awoke every morning enveloped in Scott's arms, feeling safe, warm and loved. We ate breakfast with Georgia at the kitchen table. I went to work inspiring young minds and returned to the big house at the end of each day, after my marking and preparations were complete. Daniel continued to be absent whenever I was at the house, and Nicholas worked away during the week or was ensconced in his office for most of the day, leaving the three of us to our own devices. When Nicholas did put in an appearance, Georgia visibly flourished in his presence, and I never failed to marvel at the intensity of their love.

My evenings and weekends were varied and engaging. Scott and I spent quiet nights together in the house's second, cosy lounge, chatting, eating and watching films. My fluencing lessons and training continued with Scott or Georgia or both, and at least once a week, Scott and I had dinner with Mum and Dad. Regardless of our schedule, the end of every evening found us back in his room, lying in each other's arms, exploring our bodies and minds with hands, lips, tongues and fluence and making love more frequently, more passionately and with a deeper connection than I could ever have dared to imagine.

The rapid and dramatic development of my mastery of the fluence was becoming almost a daily celebration with the Callahans. Now that I had given myself over to my new psyche and embraced the extra strength that the bond had bestowed upon me, I was becoming stronger and more skilful with every passing day. I hadn't honed the control that Scott and his parents possessed, but my raw talent and power surpassed everyone's expectations, and as my potential was realised, I grasped it eagerly and held on tightly with both hands.

Scott was incredibly proud of me and adored my spirit, but it was Georgia who seemed to get the biggest thrill out of seeing my fluence develop, always encouraging me to push myself and test my limits. Whenever Nicholas was at home, he was also demonstrably excited by the speed and extent of my skills. The Callahans quickly became my second family. I revelled in their pride and worked harder than ever to earn their love.

When they hosted a party luncheon at the house, they assured me that they weren't celebrating Scott and I having sexual relations, but I had my doubts. At least I managed to persuade them not to put it on the invitations.

They hired a marquee, caterers, a fully stocked bar and staff to wait on their guests. I watched in awe as the crew arrived and cases and cases of champagne and crates of silverware were unloaded from a large van. The lawn was gradually transformed into an upper-class gala event. At precisely 11 o'clock, after the van had been removed from sight, cars began to arrive and scores of impeccably dressed society elite descended upon the lawn. The hired staff were smart and attentive, ensuring that every guest was offered a glass of champagne or fresh juice on arrival and was never left with an empty glass in their hand. Georgia and Nicholas didn't have to lift a finger, which allowed them to glide gracefully among their guests, performing the role of perfect hosts with aplomb.

Scott and I were in the solarium looking out at the throng. Scott looked stunning in his black suit over an open-collared black shirt, and I felt slightly uncomfortable in the stunning floor-length burgundy V-neck dress that I had been persuaded to wear.

"Come on," he cajoled. "Let's go and try the vol-au-vents at least. They look amazing."

"I'm just not used to parties in the light," I complained again. "Usually, unless it's close family, parties happen after dark or in a dark room, somewhere I can hide in a dark corner. There aren't any dark corners on that lawn. Georgia's even ordered the weather. Does everyone always do everything she says?"

Scott laughed and looked me up and down with open admiration. "Yes, and she says you have to come to the party. Besides, the last thing you need is a dark corner to hide in. You're more than gorgeous. I want to show you off. I want all these people to know you're my girl."

I smiled. "Remind me again who all these people are and what this party's for … really?" I asked.

"They're mainly rich, important business folk and politicians Dad wants to schmooze, but there are also some of Mum and Dad's closer friends and one or two of mine, believe it or not. It's mainly because Dad thinks Mum's getting lonely out here in the sticks. And it's for us as well, of course."

He laughed at my horror-stricken face. "Don't look so scared. They … we want you to have the opportunity to spend some time with people like us. They want to show you the kind of world they live in, show off to you a bit and show you off to their friends. I know you don't want to hear it, but their son finding his bond is a big deal for them. And I want to introduce you to some of my friends too. It'll also give you some people to practise on."

"They had better not have spent all this money and invited all these people for … to … because we … You know that's insane, right?" I laughed.

Scott laughed with me. "No, I told you. You … we're just a part of it. Mum and Dad always have parties. It's been ages since their last one, actually, but enough of the house is done that they can let people see. They want to show off their new pad. I mean, wouldn't you? Trust me, they'll take any excuse for a party, and they do like to keep tabs on the influencers of the day. Like I said, any excuse. Don't worry."

"OK," I said. "So, how many of these people … the guests … are … like us? They all look so upper class, so full of their own importance. Haven't I …? I'm sure I saw … isn't that …?" I pointed to a lady on the edge of the lawn, close to where we were sitting. "Scott, do your parents know the Home Secretary? Is she at your party?" I was looking out with more interest now. "Is she a fluencer? How many other politicians …? And where are your friends? If you can find me someone a bit more … a bit less … someone I might actually be able to have a conversation with, that'd be a good start."

Scott laughed again. "Which order would you like me to answer those questions in? Yes, most of the people here will be pretty full of their own importance. Mum and Dad like the bigwigs, especially the ones they went to school with or the ones in our community. A lot of the top offices of the country are held by fluencers, and Dad moves in those kind of circles. Our talents and our charms tend to give us an edge. I'll definitely find you someone worth talking to, and as for how many of the guests are fluencers, how about you step outside and see for yourself? You'll be able to sense them. You always have; you just didn't recognise what you were sensing before."

"That's right," I said, suddenly much keener to get out there and join the party. "The energy signatures. The … I've always known Mum and Steph. I guess that tingle was my fluence communicating with theirs, but because I wasn't connected with mine, I didn't get it. I know yours now, obviously, and I'm getting used to Georgia and Nicholas. There were times … before … I'd be walking through a crowded street and I'd get the strangest feeling … like …

like I'd just brushed past someone I knew, only there was no one I knew in sight … like … like déjà vu."

"That's it: déjà vu. You'll be able to sense them all. Over time, you'll learn hundreds of different signatures, just like you recognise thousands of faces. You'll even be able to get a bit of a read of some characters without having to … you know … get to know them."

Sometimes the depth of this hitherto unimagined world was still baffling to me, but I was becoming more and more eager to dive in. "Come on, then," I said. "What are we waiting for?" And with one lingering kiss, I opened the door and stepped out onto the lawn.

There was a delightful atmosphere at the party. It was a warm, sunny day and everyone was relaxed and here to have fun. Old friends greeted each other and talked animatedly, strangers mingled, and the staff kept everybody seamlessly supplied with food and drink. Scott and I meandered slowly through the crowd, and I was fascinated to feel how my fluence responded to others. I caught myself stopping and staring rudely on a number of occasions at the particular strength I sensed in a person or at a particular person whom I recognised as a well-known political figure or other celebrity. My little noises of surprise and excitement kept Scott highly entertained.

I found that I could already easily pick the fluencers from the ordinaries, and if I stopped and closed my eyes, I could even sense their presence and positions across the grounds like little pinpricks of light of varying shapes and colours. Each fluence had its own slightly different characteristics, and yet they all presented to my mind in the same sort of way. It was enlightening, and I was amazed at how easy it was, as if the information had been locked away just behind a closed door, and now that I had been given the key to unlock that door, the skills and the power were quickly being unleashed.

Scott and I continued to stroll amongst the guests,

ordinaries and fluencers alike, and I thoroughly enjoyed the opportunity to practise skills that I had been building over the last few months. I utilised all of my senses to examine people, beginning to understand that combining my fluence with my ordinary senses gave me a more thorough picture and understanding of a person. I looked at their clothes and watched their body language. I listened to their voices and read their emotions. I felt strong and in control. It was a wonderful feeling that had been missing from my life. I was becoming who I was meant to be.

A man in his early thirties came rushing over to us, a huge smile on his face, and I knew immediately that he was a fluencer. As well as the telltale tingle in the back of my mind and the spark of recognition that flashed between our fluences, he had a quality about him that caught my senses. It was a feeling, an extension of being that he carried about his person. When I had first encountered Daniel, I had noticed an absence. When I had met Scott, the impact of our bond had overshadowed anything else. I had known what Georgia and Nicholas were when I first walked into their kitchen, but since learning of their existence, this was the first time that I had been approached by a fluencer in this way, and I was surprised at how natural it was to detect. I nodded towards the man and squeezed Scott's arm.

"The man coming towards us now: dark hair, dark suit," I whispered.

Scott nodded. "Easy, see? And you wanted to meet my friends. This is one of the best of them."

The man reached us. "Scott," he said enthusiastically with his right hand outstretched.

Scott took it and pulled him in close, clapping his left hand on the man's back. The other man followed suit. They straightened up and smiled fondly at each other.

"Mark," Scott declared happily, "it's good to see you. How long's it been?"

But Mark wasn't paying attention to Scott anymore. He

appeared to be totally captivated by me.

"Hello, there," he said, this time holding his hand out to me, which I took to shake. "I don't believe we've met. I'm Mark, Scott's friend, confidante, partner in crime. You must be … well, I have no idea who you must be, but … well, you're lovely."

I blushed deeply, and Scott draped an arm protectively around my shoulder. Mark's words and manner were a little over familiar. He kept hold of my hand for longer than was polite, and I could feel his fluence probing my mind. I didn't like the sensation. It was invasive, and I had never met the man before. I used all of my energy to force him back out again, simultaneously snatching my hand away.

"Isabel," I told him tersely.

"Oh, I'm sorry, Isabel," Mark said, looking confused and staggering backwards a step from the force of my expulsion. "Have I caused offence? I didn't mean to … really, I …" Mark's apology was genuine. His remorse emanated from his mind, and I softened towards him. Perhaps I was being overly sensitive. I wasn't used to this. Scott came to my rescue.

"Mark, this is Isabel. She's my …"

Mark was glancing between us, a look of joy spreading across his face. He took in Scott's arm and the spark between us, and before Scott could go on, he exclaimed, "Oh, Scott, mate, I can feel it. Of course she is. About bloody time too. Congratulations, man, this is wonderful. And Isabel, so sorry again. I forgot my manners. You were just so … and I just …" He turned back to Scott. "And where did you find this beauty? And when? And why is this the first I've heard about it?"

Scott steered us to a quiet table and sat us down. "It's a long story," he began. He looked to me for my permission to tell it and I nodded. "Well, we met here when Mum and Dad moved to town."

"Whoa, hang on a minute, mate, that's bloody months

ago. Why didn't you mention …? Why didn't you call me?" Mark exclaimed.

"It's complicated," Scott assured him. "But first, let me introduce the two of you properly. Isabel Bliss, this is Mark Carpenter. Me and Mark grew up together. We went to school together. Well, almost. Mark was in Daniel's class at school, but they didn't really … well, they didn't see eye to eye."

Mark spluttered. "That's one way to put it," he said. "Where is the bastard anyway? Is he here?"

"I think so," said Scott. "I haven't seen him, but he should be around."

Mark pulled a sour face that made me laugh. I immediately forgave his earlier indiscretion.

"I apologise on Mark's behalf," Scott said to me. "And on mine. I should have warned you. This here's a good man. I'd trust him with my life, but he's got no manners. He uses the fluence like it's his personal information service. He doesn't think about how his invasion might bother people."

"Invasion? Bother people?" Mark choked. "I was only saying hello, getting to know her a bit. I never thought … I didn't know …"

"Isabel isn't used to that kind of introduction," Scott explained sensitively. "It's not … she's not … she's only recently discovered the fluence. It's all a bit new."

Mark's eyes almost popped out of his head. "Holy … what the …? How? I'm so sorry, love. If I'd had any idea, I would never've. Why didn't you warn me?" he snarled at Scott.

"Don't worry about it," I said. "It is all new, but I'm getting there. No, I'm not used to people saying hello by letting themselves into my mind. It sort of feels … well, kind of strangely intimate … weird."

"Intimate, eh?" He winked at Scott. "Hear that, mate? Intimate with your girl."

I blushed again and Scott laughed, coming to my rescue

once more. "It's hard for us to understand how it feels for you," he said, looking at me. "We've been around it all our lives. It's actually normal for fluencers to suss other fluencers out that way when they first meet, but for you it's a whole new experience. For you, your mind is kind of a personal space." He and Mark both laughed.

I joined in. "And you think I'm the weird one," I pointed out sarcastically.

At that moment, Georgia glided over to our table, looking gorgeous as always in a light chocolate ruched dress with white lace trimmings and an almost obscenely high split on her right thigh. Her hair was parted at the side and tumbling charmingly over her shoulders.

"Mark," she purred. "How good to see you. I'm so glad you could make it. He's missed you." She cocked her thumb towards Scott. "Isabel, how about we leave the boys to catch up and you and me do a bit of mingling?"

As always, Georgia's ability to make me feel like I was the most important person at the party was alluring. She made me want to be with her, and I was flattered that she would take time out from her distinguished guests to spend with me. I looked at Scott nervously.

He laughed. "Go on. Go and have some girl time."

I nodded, stood and let Georgia escort me away from the table.

"Sorry if you were enjoying yourself," Georgia said. "I thought it would do the boys good to catch up, and to be honest, I needed a break myself."

I looked at her suspiciously, unconvinced that Georgia would need to take a break from party mingling.

Georgia giggled at my look. "Scott's so right about you. You're too easy to read; even your eyes give you away. Every thought's written plainly across your face."

I blushed again, and she went on, "Honestly, it's true. I love these dos. I love seeing everyone and showing off a bit, but these people can get tiresome. Everyone's so interested in impressing everyone else, you never really get any proper conversation, and plus, I've been dying to put your lessons to the test all day. I want to see you use it. I want to see how much you've taken in, how much stronger you are. Come on, let's see, shall we?"

We spent the next half an hour wandering around the lawn amongst the merry guests, and Georgia put me through my paces. She challenged me to read and interpret people's emotions without letting them impinge on my own mood. She also challenged me to modify people's feelings. We went from one ordinary to the next in quick succession, giving my fluence and senses a workout that left me feeling drained but satisfied with my performance.

"The improvement is incredible," Georgia said excitedly. "To go from having not connected with your fluence at all just weeks ago to this much control. I mean, honestly, I'm impressed."

I could sense her genuine delight and was proud at how far I had come. I really did feel so much stronger. My connection with the fluence had made everything easier, more natural. I felt like soon I would be able to do anything.

"OK, here's a test for you," Georgia declared. "The two middle-aged, portly gents over here." She pointed. "They seem to be having quite a heated disagreement, which is ruining the ambience of my party. It doesn't matter what it's about. What matters is whether you can manipulate their emotions enough for them to call a truce and get back to enjoying themselves. I do so hate to see anyone not entering into the spirit of my little gatherings."

I looked at the men. They were ordinaries, clearly under the influence of too much champagne. Their faces were red, their voices were raised, and their emotions were high as they argued with one another. As I got closer, I could feel their anger in the air. Even that change in my perception was noteworthy. Up until a few months ago, the anger would have barrelled into me without warning. I would not have known that it was coming until it was too late, and I would not have stood a chance against it. It would have infected my mind and caused me to feel the same anger that was driving the men to quarrel. Today, I could stand in the vicinity of this heightened emotion and sense it, read it dispassionately, without being overcome by it. I smiled to myself and embraced my strength and power, calling the fluence to me.

I concentrated on the men, focused on their position and generated a seed of calm good humour, which I expanded like a balloon in the recess of my mind. I maintained my focus and transmitted the emotion to them, concentrating on enveloping their anger with my contentment. There was no immediate perceivable change in the demeanour of the men, but I continued to concentrate, willing my emotional energy to supplant their own, and gradually, it began to work. The men's aggressive body language started to dissipate, their voices took on more convivial tones, and steadily, they relaxed. I kept my focus sharp, and within a few minutes, the argument had ceased completely and the men were sipping their champagne happily once more.

I relaxed and breathed a sigh of relief.

Georgia was practically jumping for joy beside me. "Isabel, that was wonderful," she exclaimed. "I mean it, wonderful. I don't even think … wow, Isabel, you are so strong. You'll be manipulating me before you know it." She tittered at her own joke.

I was pleased with myself and glowed under her praise. "I just hope no one was watching," I said. "I'm not exactly subtle. I was staring right at them. I had to. My tongue was probably sticking out between my teeth."

Georgia laughed. "Subtlety comes with practice, but it doesn't matter at the moment. Nobody noticed, and it's not like they'd know what was going on even if they saw you staring. People love a good argument, especially between grown men who should know better. They'd just assume you were nosy. It's not like the ordinaries are going to guess you were performing emotional energy control. They'd believe in flying pigs before the truth. They don't have the capacity for the truth."

I was a little offended on behalf of all of the intelligent, normal people in the world. I had lived amongst them, believing myself to be one of them, and Georgia's all-encompassing presumption seemed rather condescending, but there was gentle laughter in her eyes. I smiled with her.

"And," she went on. "If they did, they'd be the ones branded insane, not you." She smiled her beautiful, dimpled smile and lowered her voice. "Can I let you into a secret?" she asked furtively

"Of course," I replied, intrigued.

"It's so lovely having another girl around the place. I've been one woman amongst three men for so long, and female company is refreshing. I mean, I've got friends. I'm not suggesting that I live a sad and lonely life, but going out with girlfriends isn't the same as having a girl around the house, you know … like … family."

I felt myself blush at the ever-increasing affection from this consummate woman. I considered myself to be incredibly lucky to be in her inner circle. It was wonderful to be so wholeheartedly accepted and accepted for my true self around others. She lowered her voice even more to a conspiratorial whisper. "I always wanted a daughter."

I was lost for words. It felt as if my heart would burst with the kindness and tenderness flowing between us. The way that the Callahans had welcomed me into their family was humbling, and it had come exactly when I needed it the most. They were there for me now, no questions asked, no judgement or condemnation, no suggestion that I hide any part of myself. I had embraced their love and thrown myself into my lessons and exercises in a fervent desire to impress them with my progress. For it to be recognised and praised in such a way was exhilarating and a little overwhelming. I said nothing because I could not speak, and Georgia went on.

"You're such a bright, strong, beautiful woman, Isabel. I've no doubt you're going to go from strength to strength. I only wish I could've known you sooner, that I could have been a part of your childhood or made the transition easier for you. I see young fluencers growing up, confident and secure with their senses. You're already stronger than many who've lived with it their whole lives. I'm so proud of you.

"I hate what your mum ... well, you know, I hate that you've struggled without understanding for so long and you've found yourself so late. It isn't right, but I'm so happy to be part of your life now. I hope you've started to see me, us, as family now, Isabel. I hope I can be like a second ... well, you know. You don't need people in your life who are bad for you, who don't support you. I just want to be here for you. Scott ... he loves you so much. You're one of us now. Family. We'll always be here for you."

As Georgia spoke, I looked into her eyes and saw tears shining there. I felt myself welling up in response. She made me feel so cared for, and I was filled with a surprising depth of gratitude and love. I nodded, still unsure if I could trust myself to speak but happy to know that it wasn't necessary because Georgia already knew exactly how I felt, and that was enough. She pulled me into a brief, tight hug and then released me.

"Oh, talking of family, we're going to London for a few days in May," she said. "All of us. Nicholas's got a big trial, and we thought we'd make a holiday of it. It happens to fall in the half term holidays, so you can come along. You must come. Say you'll come."

I just nodded wordlessly.

"Right. That's settled, and enough silliness. I don't usually let my emotions run away with me like this. I think maybe I've had one or two too many champagnes myself." She smiled. "I bet I've worn you out. You've worked hard. Go, sit back down with Scott and enjoy the rest of the party."

I nodded again. "I do feel like I could do with a rest," I

managed. "Thank you, Georgia. You don't know how … you can't … you're the best. Thank you so much."

"Of course. Go and treat yourself to a glass of champagne," Georgia suggested.

I returned to Scott and Mark, who were chatting together happily. Scott's face lit up and the flames in his eyes ignited when I arrived. I smiled at him, and our eyes locked together in a private moment until Mark severed the connection with a deliberate cough.

"Sorry to interrupt." He laughed. "Hi. Remember me? Boy, you two've got it bad."

Scott just nodded. He didn't look away. "You'd better believe it," he said.

The remainder of the party was a blur of happiness. I spent the early afternoon sitting in the sunshine with Scott, marvelling at how many fluencers there were and the effect that their proximity had on me while he introduced me to more of his friends. Each one of them seemed genuinely happy to meet me and thrilled that Scott had found his bond. Every one of them expressed sympathy for my situation, joy for my liberation and accepted me absolutely. I was welcomed for who and what I was, and I felt part of a community for the first time in my life. They talked about getting together again in order for me to really get to know them, and I felt overwhelmed, like they really could become my friends too. It was a wonderful feeling. I had a partner, a family and allies all around me.

I only saw Daniel once, briefly, at the party. He looked smart in a light suit but was situated slightly apart from the rest of the guests. He was sitting at a table on the edge of the lawn with a man who was tall and thin with receding mousey brown hair and an air of dishevelment about him, a rough edge. He was a fluencer. I felt the faint tingle of recognition between my fluence and his, and I could sense his energy, which felt disagreeable to me. Even from a distance, I could see that his skin was in bad condition, with sunken eyes and blotchy cheeks, and his teeth didn't seem to fit inside his mouth properly. He was strangely familiar, although I couldn't quite place him. He didn't seem to fit in with the other guests, but neither did Daniel. It wasn't really much of a surprise that he would be in the company of another misfit.

It seemed that Daniel had done his utmost to avoid the other fluencers, and in fact, pretty much everyone else at the party, consistent with his modus operandi. I was relieved that I hadn't had to spend any time with him and pleased to discover that not a single person that I had met today had anything nice to say about him. His conversation with the unappealing man appeared to be hushed and intense, and as I watched, Daniel sat back in his chair with a satisfied smile. The two men shook hands, and the familiar stranger stood up and walked away.

After the majority of the guests had left, the van reappeared and the staff began to pack everything away, leaving the Callahan's lawn unblemished once more. I was amazed by how easy it had all been. Scott suggested that we retire to the solarium. There was a chill in the air, and I was happy to agree.

I floated around the solarium in my own little bubble of happiness. I skimmed my hand through the fresh water of the fountain and gently caressed the giant leaves of the ferns and tropical plants. I always felt at peace in this room and had an even deeper sense of contentment and belonging after meeting so many wonderful people that I had something so incredible in common with. Scott had turned out to be my gateway into a world of wonders, and I was filled with gladness to find that I belonged.

My life wasn't perfect. I had relationships that needed repairing and some big questions to answer. There were going to be challenges ahead, but I knew that with Scott and the Callahans on my side and this community of brilliant, gifted people to embrace, nothing was impossible.

Scott was sitting in our favourite chair, watching me with

a satisfied smile on his face. He could feel my contentment and was clearly feeling rather smug. If he hadn't moved to town, if I hadn't fallen at his brother's feet, we may have never met. He might have spent his whole life searching for something that he knew was missing, and I might have spent my whole life not knowing who I was, what I could be and not even knowing that I was missing the other half of me, the missing piece of my soul.

I looked right back at him and smiled. He had earned that smug grin. He had convinced me to let his mum throw this party, and he had convinced me to give these people a chance. He had been right.

I approached him, not letting my eyes waver from his for a second. I wanted him to feel my emotions. I wanted him to know how happy I was, how grateful I was to him and how much he affected every part of my life. I didn't need words. We knew each other too well and sensed the joy in each other, but I wanted him to hear it too. There's something about actually saying the words that makes the concept somehow more solid.

"I love you, Scott Callhan," I told him. "You've changed my life. You've made me complete, and I want the whole world to know it," He simply nodded, and I continued. "Thank you for today. Thank you for making me see that what we have is worth celebrating and sharing with our friends. Thank you for sharing your friends with me. Thank you for … thank you for just … for being you … for being what I need … for being mine."

I had reached him now, and I climbed onto his knee, straddling him. There were scant inches between our faces. His eyes burst into flames, and I knew that he could see the answering waves crashing in mine.

"Belle," he replied. "You honour me with your gratitude, but it's not needed … I don't need it. Finding you was inevitable for me. I would have searched the globe for you, but some invisible force drew me here and guided me to you.

It is me who should be thanking you for trusting me, for trusting what your heart … what your mind found when we met. You woke a dormant part of my soul that had been bound … confined … frustrated to live a half life without you. You threw away so much for me. You risked so much, and I'm so glad I asked it of you and that you were brave enough to open yourself up to possibilities you had never dreamed of.

"I love you too, Belle. Everything about you is perfect for me, and I'll spend the rest of my life making sure I'm perfect for you. Your eyes are alight with love, with passion, with the fervour of the whole world's oceans, and I will drown in them forever. My own eyes are alight with the fire to quell those waves. We were made for each other.

"Kiss me, Belle. Kiss me now. Kiss me today. Kiss me every day for the rest of our lives. I am yours. I am here and I am yours. Just kiss me."

It was time to let go of the past. It was time to let it all go and it was time for the rest of our lives to begin. How could I refuse?

I kissed him.

Chapter 33

"Hey, sleepyhead. It's getting chilly and you're dribbling on my good shirt. Shall we go to bed?" Scott murmured, caressing my arm softly and waking me from my slumber.

I stretched and yawned. "Of course. I didn't mean to fall asleep, but the sun ... the sound of the fountain ... your arms ... and ... hey, I wasn't dribbling."

"Whatever you say, sweetheart."

I laughed. "You go on up. I'm just going to grab a glass of water. Do you want one?"

"No, thanks. I'll see you upstairs in a minute."

He kissed me softly and stood to leave. I wrapped my arms around his waist and held him still for a moment longer before letting him go.

"See you in a minute, my love. I won't be long. I love you."

"I love you too."

I padded drowsily into the kitchen and filled a glass of ice-cold water from the fridge. As I headed towards the stairs, I noticed that the door to Nicholas's office had been left slightly ajar, which was highly unusual. Nicholas was fastidious about keeping his workspace private, rarely inviting even Georgia into his inner sanctum. However, it was not this omission that stopped me in my tracks. As I crept past the open door, not wanting to interrupt the occupants, an intense flare of violent temper imbued with Nicholas's emotional signature caused me to hesitate at the foot of the stairs.

It was the first time that I had ever felt any loss of control from Nicholas, and it was staggeringly different to his usual calm, measured feelings. This effluence was menacing, full of rage and intimidation, and even from my safe distance, it frightened me. It also intrigued me, and I was curious enough to pause on the stairs, behind a pillar and out of sight of the office door, to eavesdrop on the conversation. I put my lessons to good use and reined in my own emotional signature, effectively making my energy invisible to the people in the room.

"He shouldn't have been here today," Nicholas growled. "Today of all days. What were you thinking? What if someone had recognised him? You don't think, boy. You don't think!"

"No one saw him," Daniel replied dismissively. "No one cares. All those tossers care about is how much the champagne cost and who spent most on their frightful dress. We need him, and we're in danger of losing his loyalty."

Nicholas laughed. It was an intimidating sound, nothing like the gentle chuckle that I had become used to.

"We own him," he spat. "I own him, and he won't forget that in a hurry. She's stronger than you think, and you could have jeopardised everything. Don't forget what all this is for. Don't underestimate her, boy. It's her that we need."

My heart was in my mouth and my blood had turned to ice. There was something about the way that Nicholas spoke that made him sound dangerous, and there was something about his words that made me think that he was talking about me. I had never seen this side of him before. I was rooted to the spot, with my heart hammering in my ears.

"Well, I've got that covered too, haven't I?" Daniel replied angrily. "You gave me a job to do and I'm doing it. I always do. You think I want to hang around that vapid, try-hard ... *ordinary?* She's so weak ... so easy to manipulate ... putty in my hands ... an insult to my ... intellect. But I'm doing it ... for you ... for the family. I'll play my part. You'll have what you want. I'm just waiting for the opportunity to twist the knife a little deeper before I discard Donna Carpenter altogether."

The arrogance and contempt in Daniel's voice made the hairs on the back of my neck stand on end, but when I heard my best friend's name cross his lips, I think my heart actually stopped beating for a moment. I couldn't process what he said.

"Just don't forget why we're here," Nicholas reminded him. "No more moves like today. No more risks."

"Whatever," Daniel replied flippantly.

There was a moment of absolute stillness and then an eruption of fury so powerful that the energy burst from the room and shocked my heart back into rhythm. Nicholas's voice followed it eerily quietly, but it carried as clear as a bell.

"No more insolence from you. Do not forget who you are talking to. Do not forget who I am."

Daniel's arrogance was gone in an instant.

"Sorry, father," he replied shakily.

Nicholas seemed to collect himself.

"And how was she today?" he asked, and this time it was Georgia who replied.

"She's fun," she said. "So much fun. You were right, her power's strong. She'll give us what we need. Beth played right into our hands, lying and hiding for all these years. She's desperate to be loved … desperate for understanding … for a *proper* mother. Someone to teach her all the things she missed out on growing up with that pitiful excuse of a fluencer. I'm happy to fill that void and she's lapping it up. She's so desperate, it's almost too easy. We're right on track."

She laughed, and it was another harsh, ugly sound. Nicholas and Daniel joined in, and I couldn't think straight. I didn't want to hear it. I didn't want to hear any more of it, but I couldn't move.

"Weeks," Nicholas said. "Just a matter of weeks to go. It's all coming together. It's right around the corner. I can almost taste it. We need her to realise her potential. We need her to be strong. We need the bond to hold, to bind her to our family. We need her on our side … willingly, if possible, but with everything in place, she won't have a choice. Beth, Max, Scott, Donna … and Mr Nelson … we couldn't have planned it better.

"Have you seen these papers? Look at this file. Let's see ...."

I heard papers being shuffled around, and then Nicholas's voice continued.

"Blah blah blah, domestic abuse, controlling or coercive behaviour, assault, grievous bodily harm, causing unnecessary suffering to a protected animal ... it's juicy." There was that awful laugh again. "Oh, they've sent some photos with the file. Look at these, love. Ouch, hmm. Ooh, Mrs Nelson, that looks sore. Mr Nelson ... you naughty man. What a stroke of luck. Right. We all know what we've got to do. Love, keep her close ... keep her happy. Daniel, keep out of her way ... don't rouse her suspicions. We're so close. We're so close."

The anger was totally gone and had been replaced by an even more chilling sense of maniacal exhilaration.

Daniel and Georgia replied simultaneously, like trained automatons.

"Yes, father."

"Yes, dear."

The office door opened wide and Daniel left the room, not bothering to close it after him. I didn't have time to move. I didn't have time to hide. I remained motionless, not even daring to breathe and keeping my emotions locked behind my shield with a force of will I had only just discovered. I swallowed a sigh of relief when he turned right and headed towards the back of the house.

I peeked around the side of the bannister pillar and got my first glimpse inside Nicholas's office. He and Georgia were standing behind his desk, with photographs of Mrs Nelson spread out in front of them. I could barely make out Cathy, lying on that bed, her face contorted, covered in red and purple bruising and congealing blood, but I didn't need to see the pictures to recall the scene. For an awful moment it was as if I were back in that room: the fear, the horror, the adrenalin. I could hear the awful sucking, panting noise that had taken the place of Cathy's breathing, and my heart began to race like it had done that day seven months ago.

I struggled to make sense of what I had just seen and heard. They were planning on using everyone that I loved to ensure that I did whatever it was that they wanted me to do: my family, Donna, even Cathy and Josh Nelson. What it was that they wanted of me, I didn't know, but Mum had been right all along. The Nelsons were dangerous. They didn't love me. I hadn't been welcomed into their family. They were using me, manipulating me, and had been doing so from the start, exploiting my weaknesses — the fragility of my relationship with Mum, my love for Scott — and I had inadvertently bound myself to this family irrevocably through that love.

Scott. The bond. He couldn't be a part of this. He couldn't be. What we had was real. It had to be real. It had to be. It just had to be, and as that thought and the crippling fear ran through my head over and over again, the roar set up in my ears and I thought that I might black out. I couldn't afford to let them find me passed out at the bottom of the stairs. I couldn't allow Scott to sense my distress through the bond and come rushing down and cause a scene, so I took a deep breath in and out and looked once more into the office, where the photographs were spread out on the desk. This time I noticed something else.

Above the couple that I had grown to love, the people that had come to mean so much to me, above and behind them, mounted on the office wall, was a huge portrait, the most hideous portrait that I had ever seen. The subject had the same piercing stare, the same gleam in his eye that Nicholas was wearing at that very moment. They shared an arrogance, an absolute belief in their version of reality, and it was chilling to recognise the resemblance, to realise what that sort of arrogance could do.

Adolf Hitler stared right at me, his beady eyes boring into

my soul, and underneath his upright pose was a sickening quote from Mein Kampf:

If nature does not wish that weaker individuals should mate with the stronger, she wishes even less that a superior race should intermingle with an inferior one, because in such a case, all her efforts, throughout hundreds of thousands of years, to establish an evolutionary higher stage of being, may thus be rendered futile.

Adolf Hitler. One of the most despised figures in human history. Dictator, murderer, racist, zealot, supremacist, madman. *Fluencer*? Just a few hours earlier, I had believed that I had found my place in the world, that I was surrounded by love and happiness, but it had all come crashing down in an instant. It was all a lie. All of it. I had been duped, conned, played for a fool. I had been lured into the lion's den, into a pit of vipers, and I was teetering on the edge, peering into a shadowy darkness beyond which lay *The Essence of Insanity.*

Acknowledgements

Thank you to my husband, Dean. Your love and belief in me is what got us here. Life can easily get in the way, and this has been a long process. I would have given up many times if you hadn't been certain that I had what it takes. Thank you for reading my book, even though there was not an alien, zombie or battlefield in sight. Thank you for your notes, thank you for your love, and thank you for forcing me to carry on when it got hard.

Thank you to my children, all of you. Rose, Amelia, Hattie, Tilly and Arthur. Life has not always been easy for you guys and you all have your own challenges to face, but you are incredible and I am bursting with pride for each of you. Thank you for picking up the slack when I was writing and giving me space to get it done.

Michelle, your willingness to give me so much of your time was incredibly generous. Your notes were fair, and the fact that you actually seemed to enjoy the story was exactly the encouragement that I needed. When I knew that you were waiting for the next chapter, I could hardly not write it, now, could I? I owe you so much, my beautiful friend. Thank you.

To my other readers, Deb and Dave, thank you for your time and your thoughts, and thank you, Sarah, for being my technical advisor. I couldn't have done it without each and every one of you.

A final note to my canine writing companions. To Bobby, may he rest in peace, and his successor, Bonnie. For your unconditional love, patience and endless desire to sit by my side. Thank you.

About The Author

Emily Astillberry is an author and RSPCA Inspector from Norfolk. She has a degree in English Literature and Linguistics from York University and has been investigating animal cruelty, neglect and rescuing sick and injured animals for almost 20 years. In her day job, Emily deals with very difficult and often emotional situations. She meets all sorts of people from all kinds of backgrounds. Her career provides a lot of the inspiration for themes and characters that can be found in her fictional work.

At home, in an old cottage in the country, Emily lives with her husband, 5 children, 3 dogs, 2 cats, 2 giant African land snails and a varying number of free-range hens – all rescued of course! Finding time to write can be a challenge! She is happiest outdoors, growing fruit and vegetables in the garden, walking the dogs and family holidays usually involve walking up mountains in summer, skiing down them in winter and sleeping in a tent whenever possible.

Emily loves spending time with her large, noisy, chaotic family, cooking meals for friends and playing board games. She always has at least one book on the go and has always dreamed of writing a novel. 'The Essence of Bliss' is Emily's first published novel.

www.facebook.com/profile.php?id=61567176741752Author

www.instagram.com/emily.astillberry

www.blossomspringpublishing.com

Printed in Dunstable, United Kingdom